The Christmas Rabbit

GILMAN JEFFERS

Copyright © 2022 Gilman Jeffers
All rights reserved
First Edition

NEWMAN SPRINGS PUBLISHING
320 Broad Street
Red Bank, NJ 07701

First originally published by Newman Springs Publishing 2022

ISBN 978-1-68498-665-1 (Paperback)
ISBN 978-1-68498-666-8 (Hardcover)
ISBN 978-1-68498-667-5 (Digital)

Printed in the United States of America

ACKNOWLEDGMENTS

No one writes a novel on their own—even one such as this which occurs wholly within the author's imagination. Why, even the writers of the greatest story ever told had help! And with that in mind, I'd like to thank the following people for their support in making this work possible:

Rick and Jim McGinnis—for always being there whenever I had to impose upon them.

Joan and Carl Sorenson Sr. for taking care of a young kid and his father when there was no one else to do it.

Al and Nancy Amorello and Daniel and Particia Gover—for supporting and feeding a young college kid as he ventured into the world and went about the slow business (for him anyway) of finding his voice.

Melissa Salyer—for saving my life thirty years ago. She'll deny it, of course—but I know where my head was at.

Charles Wardell—for constantly coming to my rescue in terms of home repair done for free, allowing me to focus my energies where my talents lie.

Paula Campbell—for always keeping me honest and straight and for never letting me get away with a damned thing!

Virginia and Danapel deVeer—for just being who they are!

Michael Rotondo and Sherryl Schrader—for their twenty-five-year friendship, for their constant support, both in encouragement and financial help, which allowed a working-class dude the luxury of time needed to complete this work while living on the crazy island of Martha's Vineyard. For those of you who think that everyone living here are as well-off as Mike and Sherryl, I assure you, we are not. For most of us, it's a struggle to eke out a living and keep our heads above water. What makes them special is their generosity and devotion to their friends.

Audrey Jeffers—for a lifetime of patience. I know, kid—it ain't been easy being my sister!

My special thanks go out to everyone at Newman Springs for their hard work and patience as they guided and led an inexperienced writer to produce this work. A mediocre talent at best, I could not have achieved this with your patience and expertise. To all of you, my profound thanks!

And finally, there's George, Jeananne, and Ronny—to whom this work is dedicated. In this crazy day and whacky age, a child can count themselves fortunate if they've had one good and responsible parent—God bless me, I've had three!

I love and thank you all.

PROLOGUE

The rabbit, caught in a snare, lay dying. Its right hind leg entangled in wire, raw from abrasion, and encrusted in dried blood. The cold and unforgiving metal wore away fur and bared flesh, biting cruelly into the exposed bone and muscle. The rabbit had been practicing a series of contortions, rolling violently and tugging on the wire, all the while tightening the noose around its hindquarter as it tried in a final act of desperation to reach around and bite off its own foot—a last-ditch attempt at freedom and, more importantly, purpose. That the rabbit had only partially succeeded was certainly not due to any lack of effort. Such sacrifice from soldiers and heroes was often called for. It had, after all, a duty of some consequence to perform, a task of some importance to accomplish.

That it probably wouldn't live to see the job through no longer mattered. If it had to die, at least it would die trying, and if it did die, then better off dead than alive with the humiliation of the entire world knowing you'd failed your sacred trust. So between short pauses for breath, fleeting daydreams about cool sips of water, and the lagomorphic longing for a single piece of lettuce upon which to find sustenance enough to continue the fight, it practiced its contortions, bringing sharp little teeth for seconds at a time into contact with its ensnared hind leg as it rolled around in a panic.

Time and again, pitted against the wire, it tried to free itself, but the snare seemed inescapable. That was the snare's purpose, of course, and had it been around its neck, the rabbit would've been dead already, and little leporide knew it—even though this was its first encounter with the dreaded wire for which it trained so hard. In fact, preparation for this mission demanded it be well disciplined in things like snares, pit traps, and other such challenges that might put themselves between it and its duty. For this rabbit, our rabbit, was on a quest long prepared for and its undertaking the fulfillment of much training and sacrifice.

Knowledge and lore concerning dogs and cats and other such predators and their habits had been included in our rabbit's curriculum, as well as general information about snares and pit traps. These lessons were drilled into our rabbit. It had been weaned and nurtured on such wisdom. It cut its teeth on the various theories and assorted tactics to be learned in the art of "rabbit survival." Our rabbit, after all, came from a long line of rabbits, all of whom kept up the tradition of strict training and discipline needed for this once-in-a-lifetime adventure. In truth, any rabbit unfortunate enough to be chosen for the ordeal, and moreover lucky enough to live through it, agreed that once in a lifetime was more than enough. Those few who returned successfully did so profoundly changed. It was said they could see things ordinary rabbits couldn't, and although there was no proof, it was a story believed by all as these returnees were observed by others to be rather detached from their surroundings and their fellows, often painfully reliving some hellish experience from their nightmare trek on the road. They vacantly stared off into space while conversing with those who seemed to be absent. Their eyes glazed over in the middle of the day, and their hind legs often thumped out a tattoo of warnings for dangers which didn't exist. Other rabbits took such peculiarities in stride. Odd behavior was expected of those who'd endured so much—in fact it was sort of looked forward to…

Be that as it may, the strange behavior of the returnees and the eager acceptance by those they returned to, not only of themselves but of their acquired oddities, only served to encourage the notion that they were visionaries. Anyone could see it for themselves if they wanted to, and most did. Therefore most believed. Certainly, our rabbit, caught in a trap and slowly dying, believed. Our rabbit knew those returnees had visions. By now it had seen a few things itself and hoped never to see anything like them ever again. It just wanted to go home. It was tired and wanted this ordeal to be over. After all the years of training and preparation, to fail now when so near the end of the trail was more than one poor rabbit should have to endure. It was a rabbit tragedy—or as rabbits would say, "a trabitty." Those seasons of anguishing tutelage under the instruction of "those who'd been there"—sifting through their mad chatter in search of clues describing the proper trail to follow—after all that…only to fail now. "One trail's as good as another." Those who'd been there were fond of saying, or "The world is wide, and the paths are many." They had a slew of such sayings as they were stuffed with adages like cabbages. Some adages were deep, but most seemed pointless, and since the returnees were apt to be so deep that they themselves seemed pointless, their trainees, it seemed, could find very little point in delving too deeply for knowledge and instruction. Therefore clues and insights regarding the quest went largely unearthed.

Now caught in a trap and dying, our rabbit came to the realization those returnees were worth damn little and their tutelage even less. Sure, they knew about the wide world—what was out there and what should be avoided, but they were as mad as hatters in their explanations, and the poor trainees had no common frame of referent upon which to anchor such enigmatic references. Rabbits, in fact, do not get around much, preferring a life closer to home and as a rule are not known to be world-class travelers. The world *was* wide, and trying to explain it to someone who'd never been out there could be painfully futile. Like describing sight to the sightless—it was an arduous task, although not impossible if the instructor was on the ball. However, it was the considered opinion of everyone that the Mad Rabbits had fallen off the ball a long time ago and those in the know despaired of them ever climbing back on. As a consequence, most training for the quest was left in the paws of "might-have-been's"—those earlier trainees who for one reason or another had been passed over in favor of another rabbit of hardier stock who was deemed more qualified by the Council to conquer the road and get the job done.

The Council consisted of those Mad Rabbits who'd returned, gathered together in a hole and relieved for the moment, as if by miracle, of their deranged and disoriented babble and their spastic thumping of false alarms for dangers which didn't exist. But they did exist. They were everywhere, and it was that fact—that one fact and that one fact only—which the returnees futilely endeavored to communicate to their patrons—that, of course, and the notion that the whole idea of the quest and its undertaking be revisited. That it be picked apart and reexamined on the basis it was pure foolishness and a trabbity of the worst order that any rabbit should have to endure so much. They were never listened to. Who, after all, could understand their disoriented chatter? So reluctantly, when the season came, the Mad Rabbits would then give their permission for the next bold adventurer to continue the tradition of its predecessors by simply pointing him or her out to the others and then banishing them, never to return until they got the job done. Most seasonal sojourners never came back. Those few who did returned mad as said before, often coming home long after their expected due dates but before the anticipated return of their successors, implying skipped generations of failure, and thus often came home to a warren of strangers as these adventurers were apt to be gone as long as one year—sometimes as many as *five*, and the rare returnee who made it back to claim its seat on the council and join forever the ranks of the mad, came home to find most friends gone on the long run and returned to the dust from which they'd sprung.

Because the bulk of the training was handled by second-stringers, it seemed preordained it would therefore be substandard. To someone looking in, it would have been obvious in its deficiencies. But because rabbits don't get out much they rarely get the chance to look at things from such a perspective. Therefore inadequacies in the training program went largely unnoticed and unannounced. If a young coney were apt to spot something suspect in its curriculum and question its elders regarding the matter, it quickly learned such inquiries were severely discouraged because, of course, no one had the answers to such inquiries and because deep down in the hearts of rabbits, in that place within them they rarely showed others or even acknowledged to themselves, lay the knowledge that free thinking was dangerous. Especially free thinking about the quest. The quest embodied their entire purpose. It was holy—both in its nature and execution. It was their reason to live. It also went contrary to everything a good rabbit was supposed to be although by now these rabbits had forgotten that. Still, they balked at such questions because deep down they knew...they knew. Such questions brought cuffs to the ears or nips to the hindquarters proving once again that the truth does indeed hurt. Those brave enough to persist in their inquiries regarding forbidden subjects were weeded out of training and not allowed contact or conversation with their peers. These castaways became social pariahs, avoided and shunned by all with the exception of the returnees, but as has been pointed out before—the Mad Rabbits weren't saying much.

    Yes, the training was inferior. Having never been there themselves, these "might-have-been's" based all their lessons on rumor and innuendo, which as, anyone knows, are among the most highly suspect and volatile of all substances. Because they stayed close to home, the enforced marches conducted under the supervision of the might-have-been's and designed to toughen up youngsters by whipping 'em into shape, amounted to not much more than mere traipses through the garden. Hardly the curriculum needed to prepare oneself for the contingencies of this day, as our rabbit who lay trapped and dying was finding out.

    When it started on its adventure, almost three and a half years ago, our rabbit had been a spry young coney, full of salt and vinegar, sleek and fast with shiny gray fur which glistened in the morning dew. It held its ears in a constant state of attention, and its nose was forever wriggling and twitching as it sought out sounds and smells and other sensations while reveling in the newness and wonder of the open road. Now, however, the effects of the open road and the subsequent wear and tear were self-evident. Our rabbit had seen five summers—three of them on the quest. In those three years, it had been assaulted by more sounds, smells, and sensations than any sensible rabbit would strive to seek out. Yet seek them out it did—and those it didn't seek out, sought it. In truth, it had been a long and weary three years. Not any longer. Not now. Now there was little sensation to be felt and very little memory left to employ in order to relive it. Fading from memory were the sensations, sounds, and smells that made up the entirety of its experience. The croaking of night lizards near the small pool of water down yonder, which our rabbit heard and which led it in this fatal direction, was now barely audible.

Our rabbit had been lost for days now in this hellish place, very little water, no food, and the sun day after day pounding down upon it as the heavenly torch assaulted the arid and empty landscape. Our rabbit had gone without water for a day and a half—not even the merest trace of morning dew on the rare desert flower. When it finally stumbled upon moisture's sweet scent, our rabbit threw caution to the wind. Soon the hot desert winds would have it. The sun was coming up, our rabbit had no way to shelter, and today it would surely die. As to the water itself, our rabbit could no longer be certain in which direction it lay—even though the ability to find water is one of the strongest instincts animals have. It was that tired, that weary.

Slowly receding were its memories of happier times, of its life in the warren when despite all the training, the only thing a coney on the prowl had to watch out for was vexing Mad Rabbits. It was often and unknowingly done—just about anything was apt to set them off, and when it happened, they were best avoided. Our rabbit now suspected all the to-do over Mad Rabbits and their vexing didn't matter much, although the process of slowly forgetting interested it, at least on an academic level.

It is said by some that when you're dying, your whole life flashes before you. Perhaps it's true in most cases, but when you're as bad off as our rabbit, nothing seems to go quickly. There are no flashes whatsoever, and what little is left of the hope, life, and love still residing within seems to slowly leak out. Bit by bit you feel yourself bleaching away like a colored sock that gets washed with the whites. Our rabbit was this sock, and oncoming death the bleach slowly robbing its memory of color. But that was okay. At this point anything was okay. It was about to begin a journey even longer than the one it was finishing up and if the onset of said journey freed it from the snare it certainly wasn't going to complain about the one-way ticket.

Beside him in the sand, lying cracked and broken from his thrashing, lay a multicolored egg. Our rabbit, of course, had been carrying it. That was its mission. That was its quest. To deliver these lively and festive ova to deserving children everywhere. For this rabbit, our rabbit, was the Easter Bunny, and as you can see, he was in trouble.

The Easter Bunny was technically neither. First off, the quest came into being long before Easter, and second, he was not a bunny or really even a rabbit but a hare. When one is looking for the perfect sort of rabbit for this type of undertaking, one naturally looks to the hare or jackrabbit. It is larger, faster, and stronger than the garden-variety rabbit, which make it the best choice possible in an Easter Bunny. It has larger ears than most rabbits, which allow it to hear predators from further off. Its instincts are keener; it is an excellent sneak and consummate thief—both important to the trade as will be seen later. But what made the hare good, what made it the absolute best choice for the quest among all rabbits anywhere, was its blind trust in its fellows—who, of course, ultimately betrayed it because whenever the pellets hit the wind and a crowd needs a scapegoat, rest assured it will find one. This holds true for rabbits just as it does for people, perhaps more so.

No doubt you're getting a clearer picture of our rabbit and those he came from. No doubt you're beginning to understand that all the rabbits in this warren, not just the returnees, were mad—it was just a question of degree. How did they get this way? Who knows? Did decades in pursuit of the quest and the generations which occupied them cause this hysteria, or was the quest itself an outgrowth of such insanity? The answers to these questions lie so far back in time and legend no one knows for sure. Nevertheless, I will attempt to relate them.

BOOK 1
Olden Days

A long, long, time ago, way back in Olden Days, before you and I, our parents and grandparents, or even our great-grandparents were born, when the seas were bluer and the grass greener, when the lands about the earth lay differently than they do now and the stars splayed across the heavens were hung in different positions than those which they currently occupy—when in fact, The Powers That Be had more influence in the world than they do at present, they decided rabbits should be about the business of giving gifts to small children on an annual basis. The jackrabbits were tricked and pressed into this service by their cousins—those cottontails, snowshoes, lops, and swamps—all of whom wanted no truck with mixing it up with human youngsters. These cousins were the true visionaries in the lagomorphic ancestral chain, having foreseen the day when world opinion would not smile favorably upon strangers who gave treats to young kiddies. Envisioning an age when such persons would be the subject of trashy and cheap docudramas or become the unwilling participants in a grueling hour of cross examination at the hands of hostile strangers—the audience animal that forever haunts the watering holes of the afternoon talk shows—and knowing the tons of hate mail they would inevitably receive for trying to do a good deed, these early rabbits sidestepped the whole issue by hopping right over it and leaving the jackrabbit alone by itself, to answer to The Powers That Be for crimes committed by the entire species.

Rabbits are universally known for being excellent sneaks and consummate thieves. This is true of all breeds, as well as being as true today as it was in Olden Days. It's the one thing all rabbits have in common—the glue which binds them together and which makes them insufferable to the rest of us. And though this held true in Olden Days, such sneaking and thieving were nevertheless much harder to get away with as the world was smaller and these types of indiscretions more easily noticed. Back in Olden Days, there weren't many animals around and even fewer people—you had to look hard to find either. Society was just getting its collective hoof off the ground. There were a few men, a few animals, and The Powers That Be.

One of the few two-legged around back then was a farmer named Santos. Santos was a bear of a man yet in most instances had the disposition of a lamb—as well as its intelligence too. He would have come to be known as the Gentle Ben of his times had he not already been regarded as a fool and an idiot twice over. He loved his neighbors, the few there were, as he loved himself; but since he really didn't hold himself in high regard, I guess this doesn't say much. He hated farming, could barely tolerate his wife, and could not control his children. His hair was thick and black and felt like wool. His beard felt likewise, and he grew it to cover a birthmark on his chin, shaped like an eagle's talon. His father had the birthmark, as did his father before him, and for generations the Santos clan had been teased about it. In later years, both the hair on his head and the beard on his face would grow into a lustrous satiny white blanket which would make him world-famous. His eyes were a fiery blue, and his face was seamless, although again, in later years life in a harsher and colder environment would etch lines into that once-unsullied visage. Wind, ice, and the good booze to go with them would carve that ageless profile, rendering unto it a look of wisdom and patience. But it would be a look only and skin-deep at that. People of a later age would mistake those wrinkles for good humor lines—the kind you once saw on such faces as Milton Berle and George Burns. The kind which seemed to say, "I've lived long, I've suffered much, and I still have the good grace to laugh about it!" And perhaps a few of the lines and etchings on Santos's countenance would be the result of laughter and good humor, but most would be put there by good scotch blended with an indifferent rye. However, back in Olden Days, Santos's hair was still glossy and black. He only drank socially—which being a social outcast meant he only drank rarely. His life was simple, and

THE CHRISTMAS RABBIT

looking at it, you and I would think with the exceptions of an indifferent wife, wayward children, and the contempt of his neighbors, that he led a carefree and simple existence—and so he did, with one exception. One thing preyed upon his mind. Life was simple. He was simple. And the rabbits were simply robbing him blind by sneaking into his garden and stealing his vegetables. Gone were his prize-winning lettuces and his blue-ribbon carrots—the little thieves made off with darn near every last one as well as stealing most of the taters and the rutabagas too. It was insufferable. Humiliating in the extreme. And had been ongoing, in fact for quite a while. For seasons past, considering himself a patient sort, Santos saw fit to endure it—all in the spirit of good fellowship. Rabbits, however, breed like cattle; along with sneaking and thieving, it's the only thing they do well, and as their numbers increased the attacks and raids on the farmer's garden grew in proportion. The farmer reasoned that *being the farmer*, the vegetables belonged to him and although the attacks did very little damage to his food supplies and his family did not suffer from them as a consequence (in fact, like Santos himself, most of his family were rather portly—a sign of good living), the vegetables were still *his*, and the rabbits, he felt, could have asked. And had they asked and had he turned them down, still thought Santos, the rabbits could've offered a trade! Finally, after many progressive attacks which grew both in frequency and proportion, the farmer, feeling he'd been pushed to his limits, decided to capture all the rabbits. As to what he would do with the lot once he had them under his thumb, he hadn't a clue. Hadn't thought that far ahead. He had all he could do to think in the present. Thinking was new to him as were farming and hunting and just about everything else. He hadn't mastered any of it yet. In truth, Santos was pretty naive about life in general and therefore winging it. How he would go about the business of settling up with them if and when they were caught, he hadn't worked out, but he set himself the goal of accomplishing their capture nevertheless. That he was even more inadequately prepared for his task than *"our rabbit of later days"* was obvious. As a result, he would fail for the very same reasons, and had he known he would have so much in common with the descendants of his enemies, he no doubt would've committed suicide, ending his misery as well as this tale; but didn't see this similarity in himself until thankfully, much, much later. Back then he was just interested in the practicalities of resolving the problem and to that end set himself a goal to accomplish.

For the next few months, Farmer Santos became the terror of the woods and forest, or so he liked to think. Dressed in chartreuse from head to toe, a color he preferred because it reminded him of vegetables green and growing, he took great care to blend in with the arboreal background, hiding his ample bulk in order to harass his quarry and attack from ambush. He haunted the waterholes and frequented those places which rabbits preferred, attempting to pounce upon them from cover. But rabbits cover their tracks with the best of 'em and invariably saw through his weak attempts at camouflage. More often than not, while Santos was tramping through the woods, they would pounce upon him from cover of their own. One rabbit is not a threat. Twenty or thirty rabbits bounding up out of nowhere with fur flying and eyes blazing, all trying to smother you and nip you with their wicked little teeth is perhaps not fatal either. It all happens so quickly however that when it does occur, it is certainly startling and inconvenient to say the least. When it happened to Santos—and it happened often—most rabbits did little damage, but a few invariably broke skin and one or two always drew blood.

To be fair, the rabbits were as desperate as Santos was angry. They, too, had children of their own to feed and a lot more of them. Whereas Santos had two, the rabbits had hundreds, and so from their point of view were more than entitled to their share of the garden's bounty. It was, after all, survival. So the feud escalated into a small war and there were bad feelings, perhaps legitimately, on both sides. Still the rabbits caused Santos very little trouble, and if that was true, then the reverse even more so.

Although he fancied himself a green thumb, Santos was a lousy farmer and even worse hunter—especially a hunter of rabbits. He hadn't found his niche yet. That would come later. Back then, he was merely known as an indifferent farmer, certainly no maggot despite his efforts (even those who'd sampled his prize-winning lettuces, his blue-ribbon carrots, his taters and rutabagas too, attributed the

THE CHRISTMAS RABBIT

quality of such specimens to the result of good soil more than anything else), and the worst hunter of rabbits anywhere. He was slow in his plan and even slower in execution. He tried clubbing them but invariably struck bare earth. The rabbits were too quick. He tried throwing rocks at them, but by the time he bent over and picked one up, the rabbits would scatter while hurling insults at him—verbal rocks of their own, as they laughingly scampered and fled.

"Hey, Slomoe," they would taunt, or "Yo! Pithecanthropus Wideus," or as rabbits put it, "Pithecanthropus Wideass!" But far and away, their favorite adjective to hurl at him was "The Tortoise," uttered no doubt because it made fun of the fact he was always dressed in green, was bulky beyond belief, and slower than cold molasses.

In utter despair, Santos tried hiding in trees and falling upon them as they happened to pass beneath. The only things injured were Santos's pride and his rear end. On the few occasions when it appeared he might actually gain the upper hand and the rabbits stumble upon him unaware, his excitement inevitably betrayed him. He would start to tremble and twitch, the ardor of the hunt fully upon him. Sweating and nervous, he would nevertheless endeavor to remain steady and calm, to become one with the forest, as the rabbits approached. It was at this point his excitement would inevitably lead him into a self-afflicted double-cross. The rabbits would approach. Hopping a few steps, some would pause, perhaps to nibble an occasional blade of grass or an early dandelion rare and not yet in season. Or perhaps not. In truth, such foraging held very little interest for them—the pickings after all were far better down to Farmer Santos's. Others paused just to sniff the air, both to relish the smells of the forest and to alert themselves to its dangers. As it was, the rabbits happened to be upwind of Santos who knew nothing of winds, either their ups or downs and who only knew they could be cold in winter, requiring more blankets. As to just how cold winter winds could blow Santos had as yet merely the barest glimmer of understanding. He lived at this point in a moderate climate. He knew winter, and he knew summer too, while giving little thought to the seasons in between. Someday winter would be all he knew. He and winter would grow real close, caressing each other like long-lost lovers. Winter would be almost all he was left with after the rabbits and The Powers That Be got done with him, but thankfully he knew nothing of these matters as of yet, and one wonders how he would've managed if he had. That would come later. For now it was just Santos and the rabbits, the rabbits and Santos. Closer and closer they approached until Santos, bursting with excitement, acted the part of the young and inexperienced hunter who upon aligning his target in his sights, lets out a, "Ho!"…causing the prey to scatter, which was just what the rabbits did. A "Ho!" from Santos was not merely a "Ho!" but a "Ho!" It impelled the rabbits to disband and disperse, leaving only cruel laughter in their wake. Santos would take off after two or three heading in the same direction. Throwing rocks and swinging his club, he would be constantly, "Ho-Ho-Hoing" with frustrated excitement. He rarely hit a rabbit with his rocks, and as far as I know, the only target his club ever encountered was his own foot on the downswing. He was forever whacking himself with it and you would think he would've given up; but Santos was too stubborn and it was his first club. How was he to know it was actually too large and way out of balance?

Along with being their chief provider, Santos became the rabbit's sole source of entertainment. They continually roamed the forest seeking after his presence. When they met, the rabbits would feign fright and flee, returning secretly to pounce and bite, nip and tear, laughing wildly all the time because, of course, they were having immense fun—and while they were busy frolicking and having at Santos, their confederates were busy having at his vegetables as he was not around to protect them, having been detained elsewhere.

Word of the feud between the farmer and the rabbits spread through the few hamlets there were and throughout the forest. There were at this time no cities to which the word could be spread. In Olden Days, they had no use for such things—there not being nearly enough people to fill 'em. At this time, if every person that ever was—with the exception of one family which we'll get to later, were all gathered together—they might, just might, make up a sizable township, but only if they counted the women twice and gave them the right to vote.

THE CHRISTMAS RABBIT

When there are so few people with so little on their minds, it's not hard for something even as mundane as the events described to grab hold of their collective attentions. Rumors about the wild man and his incredible battles with the fierce denizens of the forest grew quickly into legend. And by this, I mean, not only did they spread rapidly, but through design or accident, became embellished to the point where the rabbits were described as being ten feet tall and not even rabbits at all but rabid bears. Rabid bears whose parents had abused and abandoned them. Bad bears with an attitude. Men and animals alike came from miles around to witness the titanic struggle. When they arrived and saw what the to-do was all about, most went away with frowns on their faces, feeling both disappointed and cheated. The animals took umbrage over the notion that one of their own should be harassed in its own forest for doing what came naturally. In rabbits, the rest of the animal kingdom found a cause to rally around, for they could all sense the threat. Men, on the other hand, felt it was damned foolish to be engaged in a war with something so small and helpless, and to do so spoke ill of them as a species. They would not always think like this. In later years, that would become one of their requirements for wars—small and helpless victims to pick on; but for now picking fights with smaller opponents was frowned upon. Losing them was to be even more despised. Men were angry and embarrassed. The animal kingdom felt threatened and was therefore restless. Santos was on edge to the point of falling off the deep end. And the rabbits? Doing just fine. They had food, entertainment, and were fast becoming celebrities!

Rabbits have no business being in the limelight where they can stand out for all to see. Nature has designed them to blend in with their background as an escape mechanism since they're so low on the food chain. To have them strutting their stuff with smug smiles on their teeny faces while boldly showing off in such a manner upsets the balance of things. Rabbits bragging about themselves are just too disconcerting for those of us around them to endure for too long. The rabbits, too, began to gang up on others besides Santos, just to prove to themselves and to the world at large they could do it. For a while no one was safe—either two- or four-legged, as rabbits of all kinds gathered in mixed groups in the depths of the forest and other such shadowed and quiet spaces to plan strategies and prepare hunts. They became big-game hunters, and the world at large became their preserve. They tackled tigers and beat up on those very same bad and abandoned bears they'd been accused of being. The first species to ever try pack-hunting, the rabbits became drunk in their new abilities. With mighty paws and the power of group dynamics, they tore asunder the links in the food chain which heretofore bound them helpless. Trees toppled and elephants rolled as the rabbits flexed their muscle. In the fight for survival, the best defense became a good offense.

Suffering from a crisis in confidence and having to endure not only the unwanted attentions of the rabbits but the dispersions cast his way by his neighbors too, Santos was more often than not quarrelsome and at the slightest provocation or insult to his manhood could be counted upon to challenge his tormentor to a duel of honor. These duels amounted to no more than fisticuffs or what passed for fisticuffs back then, and very little damage was done to anyone, including Santos, who invariably got worse than he gave. No challenge to rabbits, he presented very little threat to anyone else either. His family also suffered. His wife was gossiped about and expelled from her quilting bee. His children got teased at school, picked upon, and invariably beaten up. Santos got a double dose one day while rushing out to defend his children from their adolescent persecutors. The teens turned their attention on him instead and adopting the tactics of the rabbits, attacked en masse. There was tension and confusion everywhere, and everyone and everything began to question their place in the scheme of things. Something had to be done and done quickly, and that's when The Powers That Be got involved.

Even back in Olden Days, The Powers That Be had been around longer than just about anyone else. Although they didn't create the heavens and earth, they'd been around long enough to write about it and gobble up the glory. But because their speculations and theories about how the whole ball of wax got started were in no way substantiated by any facts whatsoever, and moreover because the descriptions of their own roles in bringing about the "Big Bang" were more spectacular than most folk, two- or four-legged, felt they deserved credit for, their accounts went largely unread and these days can only be found in out-of-print bookstores. Not really gods, slightly less than fallen angels, they were more like busybodies, and it was said they were three spiteful witches whose husbands left them early on in their respective marriages when their incessant harping and gossiping caused problems at home. That didn't stop their gossiping, however, or their need to interfere in the lives of others, no matter how badly they were screwing up their own. Nor did they consider such interference duty but rather regarded it as delight.

Gone for eons now—and good riddance, thought the trio—were their no-good husbands. Unemployed for ages, those freeloaders had been lost to the vagaries of time, loose women, strong drink, and the irresponsible cronies who went with them. Simply stated, after putting in a hard day at the universe and having to come home to them, their menfolk simply bugged out. Antares was the Powers' best guess as to where their menfolk ended up, and they could stay there and choke was the collective opinion of The Powers That Be. But without men around to harp upon and because their children had grown up and left for their own reasons—also never to return—the Powers felt adrift in the universe at large, and it didn't help their dispositions that because they were so shrewish and bad-tempered, someone more powerful than they whose existence they chose nevertheless to deny had confined them to this ball of dirt and told them to make the best of it. Yeah right. Corporeal life, which they mimicked in order to blend in and get by, was inane—not only in its variety but in its seemingly universal desire to go its own way, refusing the direction and guidance of its betters. Such resistance made for extended hours and long days at the office. The extra hours, of which there seemed to be more and more lately, only added to the oppressive emptiness which could be felt throughout their home were you one of the unfortunate few unlucky enough to have visited it. The trio were striving for purpose in a place which seemed at least to them, to have none, as well as desperately trying to legitimize their own worth—all the while secretly resenting the lack of respect and appreciation they felt was due them for having matroned families of their own, raised children, and put up with the buffaloes they called husbands. More stubborn than the Mexican mule, it was the opinion of The Powers That Be that husbands were the dumbest asses in creation. It's not surprising then to find they had chips on their shoulders the size of Mount Everest and these chips and the bitterness upon which they were buttressed would cause cracks in the foundations they tried to lay for others. But their hearts, supposedly, were in the right place—somewhere left of their elbows. They were the cosmic Stepford wives were these witches who would later become known as The Powers That Be and who in the fullness of time, would come to call each other "sister." It was rumored even back in Olden Days that each of the trio had once been beautiful, but even in Olden Days, that was a long time ago. Ages of common experience and shared bitterness as well as similarities of attitude and aggressive posture, along with a comparative amount of cheap makeup copiously applied with carefree abandon, robbed their collective skin tone of any color whatsoever, making their faces appear like pasty-white, dried-up old prunes. This, along with eons of consuming fatty foods and chocolate-covered cherries, both enjoyed while gossiping among themselves and handing out reams of advice to those who would've rather remained ignorant and in the dark, snatched from them whatever attractiveness with which they might once have been endowed. It was therefore the consensus of everyone everywhere—whether two-legged, four-legged, or no-legged at all—that The Powers That Be, despite what they claimed were their own good intensions, were nevertheless a sore trial for anyone having the misfortune to have dealings with them, and rumor of their impending arrival could cause stampedes in the herds of grazers and feeders which were said to roam the plains back in Olden Days. But because their numbers were so few those herds more closely resembled encounter groups. Still, any local populace, no matter how big or small and whether they had legs or not and notwithstanding how secure within their own little niche they felt themselves to be, were apt to dread the announcement of the imminent arrival of those three unwanted guests. Because guests were how they always saw themselves—and paying guests at that, although no one had ever seen them fork over so much as a copper sou—who made unreasonable demands upon those whom they visited and who were a constant disturbance to the neighbors around them. No one upon whom they descended, of course, would dare to throw them out for despite their overall unpleasantness and their general need to meddle in the lives of others who, had they been asked, would have stated that they much preferred to be left alone, and notwithstanding the airs the trio would most certainly put on while engaged in such bitching and meddling, the ladies were not without a certain inherent power—which they were quick to use or hold above you if you crossed 'em. They were like rich aunts with no children and huge wills...and they could be plain misery.

It's no wonder then that when word got out they were coming with the intention of settling the dispute and restoring order, everyone panicked...everyone that is, except Santos and the rabbits. Santos was too stupid and moreover too stubborn to get out of the way of a speeding bus had such things been around back then. Whether or not The Powers That Be were coming, the rabbits were still raiding his garden, and therefore his efforts at vigilance would not cease. The rabbits, on the other hand, being the sneaks and thieves they were, also made excellent spies and had a very efficient interforest underground information network consisting of interwoven tunnels and secret runs, all coming up in hidden holes and dead logs throughout the forest. These made excellent sentry stations from which to search out the land and spy on its inhabitants. Very little escaped them, or so they thought. They were well aware of the impending arrival of The Powers That Be, and hiding along the way, the rabbits listened to the trio as they hatched their plans whilst journeying through the wood. In this way, the rabbits were appraised of the ladies designs and so took measure and made counterplans of their own. It was learned by the rabbits that The Powers That Be intended to hide in the garden of Farmer Santos that they might catch the perpetrators both firsthand and red-handed and with both paws in the cookie jar, whereupon said perpetrators would be sent up the proverbial creek sans paddle.

In truth, the rabbits were a bit apprehensive about the whole business and feeling as if they'd bitten off a mite more than they could chew. It was one thing to prowl the countryside, harassing dumb farmers and having fun. It was also one thing to pretend indifference and feign nonchalance when confronted by others about the impending arrival of the "You-Know-Who's" (this close to home, they weren't even mentioned by name—as if doing so could somehow conjure them up). But it was another thing entirely to face them off in direct confrontation. It was believed back in days of yore that these three matrons had invented PMS, and it was said the affliction suited them so well that instead of lasting a week it hung around all month. The rabbits, therefore, were terrified and without a clue as to what to do, so when I say they took measures and plans, I need to point out that like most good discoveries and useful applications which are unearthed and therefore discovered by anyone anywhere, the rabbits, through blind luck, providence, and the ability to recognize a sucker when they saw one, stumbled into their solution.

It was about this time as the situation was coming to a head that a certain hare, or jackrabbit, was returning from vacation. Like all rabbits—Lops, Swamps, and everyone else—he'd put in his time harassing the farmer and raiding his garden and was deserving of his two weeks off and therefore took them. He spent them in a whirlwind tour of New York City, seeing the bright lights and frequenting the singles bars—there not being an actual city however; the bright lights were merely stars. Beautiful enough, he supposed, but the meat markets were bare watering holes and no more sophisticated than the local dive back home. Not at all what one expected in a trip to the Big Apple, but being adventurous and having plenty to spend, he made friends easily enough and made out adequately too. He was away when word got out about the coming of The Powers That Be and so had no news of their impending arrival upon his return.

He was still a good way from home and about a mile from the forest when he first received word. It was dusk of an early spring evening; a rosy glow splashed the western skies while overhead a few early stars had come out to twinkle and fascinate. That this jackrabbit's name translated to what in our language is the equivalent of "Jack" (although perhaps "Jacque" was indeed a closer rendition) was the merest of coincidences, and the fact *"our rabbit"* of later days was

THE CHRISTMAS RABBIT

likewise handled, even more so. No doubt it is just another example of the great karmic wheel rolling on and on and coming full circle. Be that as it may, the first Jack was basking in the evening airs and leisurely strolling toward home, enjoying the cool of the forest and traveling slowly as he was a bit early yet, close to home, and therefore had time on his paws. He came to a sudden halt when he happened upon a darling little doe whom he recognized, a ways off to his right, waving frantically and calling him to her.

This young doe's name was Nutmeg, and she was so called because her rich, brown-red fur, which all the bucks found so irresistible and which was the cause of much scuffling among the older males who were always eager and ready for mating, had the same burnt-orange coloring as the spice which all rabbits loved so well and used as an aphrodisiac—although they used damned little when they did as it was strong stuff and rabbits have never needed much in the way of love potions to encourage them anyway. Still, Nutmeg was considered attractive and encouraging to all who met her. Jack, however, had never been much impressed. His nose forever twitching whilst dreaming of places like New York City and the sights to be seen and smelt there, dreamt different dreams altogether, and if Nutmeg occasionally wandered into them, Jack was damned sure she wandered into everybody else's as well—if not their holes too. She was the ultimate lottery prize in a sweepstakes where everybody had a winning number, and everybody hoped their number would be up. Jack, who felt he had better things to do with his time—she wasn't after all the only breeder on the block—and who furthermore felt less than encouraged by his chances when pitted against such incredible odds, sought encouragement elsewhere. Now after his adventure in the Big Apple—of which he could find none during his entire two week stay—felt more than encouraged by the sight of her and being that they were alone and just outside of the forest reasoned that the odds were finally stacked in his favor. He felt engorged, larger than life, and knew he need look no further to find a satisfactory conclusion to his holiday. A growing homesickness and the relief of knowing his journey was almost over (even now the familiarity of sights and smells recognized and known intimately were filling him slowly but comfortably with a warm fuzzy feeling from his toes up as he basked in the glow of accepted surroundings, of being home), coupled with the unrivalled beauty of Nutmeg herself served to undo him.

She seemed to be signaling her eagerness, and Jack, eager himself, was ready to make camp on the spot. Nutmeg however had other plans. Earlier she'd been approached by others—Rabbits of Influence and standing from various warrens, who explained the situation and its implications to her, both for rabbits as a species and her in particular if she didn't cooperate. They further went on to describe the rich rewards which were hers for the asking if she went along with their plans and played ball in their court, describing the influence and consideration she could earn for herself simply for being a patriot. She saw it their way, and their way was to hand Jack over to The Powers That Be on a platter. Knowing they couldn't win, the Rabbits of Influence decided not to lose instead and therefore deemed it best for all—especially themselves since they'd organized most of the raiding down to Farmer Santos's and were responsible for a good deal of the trouble after—if just one rabbit could be made to suffer for the crimes of the group, and to this end a lottery of a very different sort was organized. But when one of these very same influential rabbits was chosen, the whole process was deemed hogwash and judged to be very discriminating and extremely unfair to the poor fellow who'd had the misfortune of being selected. There was some thought given to going two out of three, but in the end, it was simply decided to choose someone else. This in itself presented an entirely different problem as they could not choose just anybody. This anybody had to be a nobody or at least a somebody nobody else much cared for. It would not due to make martyrs. In the end, having few bodies that fit the bill, they opted for the antibody in the body of Jack Rabbit who, others agreed, was just about anti-everything which had anything to do with being a rabbit and who with his faraway dreams and big plans was not well thought of by those who had to suffer him. "Let the Witches have him," they reasoned. "Who needs him anyway?" Jack also had the added misfortune of not being there to defend himself when the Rabbits of Influence appointed him as their sacrifice, and maybe had he been, things might have worked out differently...but one doubts it.

It was decided Nutmeg would seduce Jack and lead him to Farmer Santos's, where she would get him to steal her something. No doubt he would be caught red-handed in the act by the terrible trio. The Witches were hiding by now behind the beanpoles and in the corn, filled with self-righteous justification, a point to be proven, and the unwholesome need to pounce upon the recipient of their instruction. Jack was Welsh rabbit already and didn't even know it.

Nutmeg positioned herself upon the path not far from the forest and was ready for Jack when he came traipsing along. When she sang out, it was with a song that pierced him from his heart to his groin like an arrow shot from cupid's bow.

Rabbits do not sing nor speak in quite the same manner as you and I. And although there is some vocalization—indeed, it would be a terrible trabbity if there weren't—they having such ears for it and all, most communication occurs at what we would regard a subliminal level, consisting of movements and nods, the twist of an ear or the shake of a tail. Rabbits also use pheromones the way you and I employ adjectives and adverbs to convey feeling and communicate mood, all done very quietly, of course, and almost unconsciously—except when they were communicating with Santos. Then the rabbits were conscious of everything and put forth the extra effort. Pheromones, curse words, and whatever they could lay paws to, the rabbits employed in their ongoing and escalating campaign of belligerence and embarrassment. Knowing Santos for the cheapskate he was, the rabbits felt such tactics no more than the fat farmer deserved. No gesture or epithet became too vulgar, and it was rabbits, not men, who invented the middle finger, or at least attached to it, its unwholesome significance.

But as with so many sayings, both of rabbits and of men, it's not so much what you say but how you say it, and Nutmeg seemed to be saying plenty. So much that in his excitement, Jack hopped over on five feet. "Jacque," Nutmeg said as he approached, rendering his name in the classic French which everyone knows drives rabbits to distraction while igniting their passions like the full moon lights up the night-time sky, "I've eagerly awaited your return, my prince." She batted an eyelash as she slowly licked her paw and ran it seductively back along her ears.

Fully excited, envying her tongue, wanting to lick her too and not necessarily behind the ears—although that would do for a start— Jack was nevertheless not entirely taken unawares. *Prince? Not me,* thought he. He had no claims to royalty. Ambitions, yes; bloodlines, no. In fact, the jackrabbit is just about the most common and plain looking of all rabbits if you disregard its size. Not a looker among them, they are hardly the Prince Charming's of rabbitry. This holds true for all jackrabbits and was especially so of Jack, whose looks and whose lines left few females enthralled. Jack knew this to be true just as he knew the main reason he'd done so well in New York City was due not to his look and his line but rather the copious amounts of cash he'd carried in his wallet, which he'd lavished with wild abandon upon those who'd lavished wildly upon him. So he was just the slightest bit suspicious with his guard halfway up—although he would've done better for himself had he been consciously concerned with his armor fully girded. But alas, back then, rabbits did very little consciously—except of course where Santos was concerned, and it would not do at all, Jack felt, to be stamping out warnings and red alerts like some frightened coney on the run with such a charming seductress so near at hand.

Nutmeg's experiences with insecure males were many. She was reading Jack as if she'd mastered Evelyn Wood's course. She sensed his anxiety and made move to put an end to it. This entire plan, silly as it was, depended upon Jack feeling anything but insecure. If he were the slightest bit leery, he would certainly sense those hawks in the cornfield and all her careful planning would come to naught. Her soon-to-be won and newly acquired standing within her community would be flushed down the toilet as well, and Nutmeg was having none of that! A lifetime on your back, as anyone knows who's done it, is not an easy job. You put up with a lot and get very little in return except those things for which you did not bargain—those you get plenty of, and Nutmeg had experienced more than her share. This was her chance to rise above it all, to get ahead of the game! If

THE CHRISTMAS RABBIT

she succeeded, she'd be canonized. Should she fail, she would merely become cannon fodder and in a worse position, no doubt, than Jack. Given the choices between the two extremes, one cannot, I suppose, blame Nutmeg for her actions even if one does not necessarily approve of them. Even in Olden Days, it could be a dirty rotten world, just as it often is today—a world wherein it seemed appropriate and even looked upon with favor to be your brother's betrayer. Brother's keepers more often than not fell victim to their own generosity and silly desire to "do unto others." Their self-sacrifice and goodwill invariably kept them one step behind everyone else until they wound up merely recording tabs and taking notes on those who got ahead in life, whereas betrayers if they betrayed the right person to the proper people at the appropriate time could make out quite handily. In fact, betrayal has always paid off well in the short run. It's in the long run that betrayal gets sticky. But since neither rabbits nor people have ever been very adept at putting much thought into the long run, "long run" itself ceased being a term rabbits put stock in, dropping its usage from their vocabularies until it held little meaning. Immediate and short-term self-gratification had been, and always would be, the ticket. Even if wrong and even if entropic in its nature and manifested results. But screw it—who lives forever, right?

"Jacque," Nutmeg whispered, "don't you want me?" Jack, who wanted her plenty, could barely answer. He nodded but whether in the affirmative or negative, Nutmeg could not be sure. His head did not go up and down indicating yes, nor did it go side to side symbolizing no. It moved in a forty-five-degree angle as if in spasm, which was indeed the truth as Jack lost complete control of himself. He would go on to ejaculate prematurely—something which until then had been completely unknown among rabbits. His seed, when it came bursting forth, spewed all over Nutmeg's coppery fur, causing at first fright and then anger as she thought of her coat nearly ruined. It would cost a small fortune to have laundered and repaired, for as everyone knows, delicates like rabbit fur cannot be washed. They must be dry-cleaned.

Jack felt miserable to be the cause of such a mess and offered to do anything in order to make it up to her. "What can you do?" she asked shortly. "What can anyone do?"

In truth, she was mortified. Jack's spunk, now drying on her toosh, was causing her fur to clump in little balls which pulled irritatingly on the skin of her fanny. Worse though, until she got herself cleaned, his mark would be visible to everyone and so proclaim to all who could see, her habits. And although everyone, including Jack, knew all there was to know about Nutmeg and her habits, she still felt there was such a thing as propriety and the sake of a good appearance—even if adorned only for its own sake. "Jack," she continued half in tears, "how could you miss? Rabbits never miss. Never!" Jack, who before his trip to New York had never even taken aim and who therefore knew little about missing the target and even less about hitting it, now found he had little to offer in the way of explanation and instead mumbled an embarrassed apology. Bowing his head in shame, he slowly turned away and began his dispirited shuffle toward home. But of course, that wouldn't do.

"Wait..." the word, whispered pheromonally and laced with all the seductive wile Nutmeg could bring to bear, seemed to suspend itself in the air behind Jack, syrupy and sweet, like wood smoke in autumn. Hanging there thick, it conveyed to the listener much more than the simple meaning of the word itself. It spoke of desire and comfort, anticipation and release. It evoked warmth and good cheer like yule logs burning in the fireplace and suspended on the edge of forever like warm wet fog blown upon a south sea wind, enveloped him totally, surrounding him on all sides and robbing him of what little sense he had left until he stood disoriented and helpless, feeling as if he were drowning—which, of course, he was.

Those Rabbits of Influence certainly knew their business, and in choosing her, it was their combined experience bespeaking volumes because there *were, in fact,* other breeders on the block; but as all the influential rabbits knew, there was only *one* Nutmeg. So even though Jack was submerged in desire and not water, drowning—he came to realize—was indeed one of the more pleasant ways to go, and he found himself wishing he might somehow survive the ordeal in

THE CHRISTMAS RABBIT

order to offer up a testimonial. Nutmeg however had no intentions of letting Jack depart this earth, at least not yet; he still had a job to do, and so did she, although she was screwing hers up and knew it.

"Wait…"

Again the word was uttered only to linger in the air like a note from silvery bells rung at high noon. It was high noon even though it was early evening, and Jack was the Gary Cooper for whom the bells tolled. He was locked in mortal combat with a deadly enemy who wore the mask of friendship. Completely out of his depth, he heard wedding marches while the band played a funeral dirge. Slowly he turned back, and succumbing to the deep-blue irises of Nutmeg's eyes as she smiled sweetly at him, felt the last of his resistance become so much chaff to be blown away by the gentle breeze. He fell to his knees, whispering to her of his newfound love and his unworthiness to even chew her pellets. Would she dig a hole with him, build a nest, and raise a family? Poor young buck. She had him right where she wanted him and so sent him on his blind and stupid way.

"Maybe," she replied to his ardent confession, "if you get me a carrot."

Carrots grew wild in the forest as they did in the fields and valleys surrounding it although they were not always easy to find—especially this early in the season. One might search for days and come up empty, and God only knew whom Nutmeg would be interested in by then. It was nice enough to dream about their future together, but Jack, who knew Nutmeg and her habits well, realized it probably wouldn't last more than a fortnight, and if he were to capitalize on his good fortune—especially after the debacle of a few moments ago—he needed to act and act quickly. The only place one could be assured of finding a carrot this early in spring was, of course, down to farmer Santos's, and so like a well-aimed arrow, he sped off in that direction.

Nutmeg was employing the first example of what would later be known as "the carrot and the stick" method of persuasion. Farmers much more knowledgeable than Santos would eventually use a version of this method to get their stupid and stubborn mules to plow their respective north forties though at this time north forties did not exist and Nutmeg was actually the carrot. Therefore, the carrot became the stick, and the only mule involved was a dumb horse's ass named Jack who should've seen it coming and who should've known better. Still, so many so much wiser have made mistakes so similar that we can hardly blame him.

Racing like the wind and feeling like a knight of old—although in truth knights of old had not been invented yet—on a quest dedicated to his lady fair, Jack approached the farm with all speed, throwing caution to the wind. On his worst day, he could run circles around Old Slomoe and the Tortoise was probably abed anyway. Farmers are dull, and Santos, the dullest of the lot, rarely went out for the nightlife and could be counted upon to be asleep by seven o'clock. It was five minutes till eight when Jack broke the cover of the woods and bounded up the rutted dirt lane which led to the farmer's gate. The sun had set entirely some twenty minutes ago, and the early evening was dark and quiet. No night birds flew, no pinkletinks tinked. The full moon rode high in the night sky, although hanging there suspended, she was veiled by a thin cover of clouds which since dusk had been ponderously sailing in from the west. They diffused her light as they soared secretly by, casting an opaqueness about her edges and partially robbing her of her fulsome figure. Therefore she had no rays or beams that evening with which to illuminate our poor traveler and help guide him on his way. He'd have to rely on instinct and brains. So it was a trabbity of his own making that his instincts were so screwed up, his head was in his butt, and his nads were doing his thinking for him. A typical problem for males back then and a common ailment which still assails us now. So quiet was this hush and so unnatural that Jack felt as if the night were a shroud enveloping him, but attributed this uneasiness to his burning desire for Nutmeg. The very air seemed clouded with anticipation, and the world itself seemed poised on the brink of impending and momentous events whose influences and implications would affect not only himself but hosts of others too. It was powerful and addictive this feeling which tasted of Karma and Destiny, Fate and Kismet. Jack drank it up like fine wine, and doing so made him feel ten feet tall. Fortunately, even standing on his hind legs, he barely measured two feet, and so coming up to the gate, he continued to where it joined the fence, quietly slipping under its lower rung and into the garden whereupon he made straight for the tomatoes. Rabbits do not like tomatoes, and until merely a few lifetimes ago, thought they were poisonous. They aren't, of course. The first rabbit to sample the fruit probably got a bad one and as it was a new experience, was ignorant of the fact. But fear and mistrust spread so easily, needing so little nurturing that the rabbit in question spread the word to all who would listen. Those it told heeded the warning needlessly and in turn spread the word themselves until all rabbits believed the tale. Even now Jack didn't get too close—just near enough for their leafy stems to provide him cover while he gave the layout a quick scanning. All seemed to be in order. There were no candles blowing in Santos's windows and thus no light coming from the house. Good. The farmer, his wife, and their two little snotlings were settled down for the evening. Slowly he made his way past the turnips, bypassing the rutabagas which gave him heartburn, and foregoing the lettuce—which, although a personal favorite, held little interest for Nutmeg who was partial to big, stiff carrots.

Arriving at the sight of his buried treasures, Jack began to examine each individual carrot as it grew in its row, smelling their tops and partially uncovering their nether regions that he might better judge appearance and texture, firmness and taste. He was more than critical in his selection as this was food for Nutmeg, and if she found it worthy, she just might make a meal out of him. So he took more than what most of us would judge to be enough time to select just the right carrot, and perhaps that was his downfall. Had he gotten in and gotten out, then maybe he would've gotten away with it, but he got in and stayed there, farting around and judging carrots as if any two were so dissimilar that the choice of one over the next might really make a difference one way or the other. Farting and judging, they jumped him.

Jack sat among the roots essaying and evaluating when... "Ho! Ho! Ho!" A cry sprang up throughout the garden while bright lights suddenly lit up the nighttime shadows. And such lights! They blinded him! Jack who knew only candles, and who didn't know much about them had never seen lights like these. They were as bright as stars descended from heaven. Blazing and humming they emitted their harsh and revealing rays, slicing through the night like sharp knives through warm wax and painting the evening gloom in a sickly sterile glare which when viewed directly caused the eyes to water.

Out of nowhere it seemed, and still "Ho-Ho-Hoing," Santos charged forth in his slow, ponderous way only to trip over a potato vine and go crashing into the dirt at Jack's feet. The violence of his tumble bowled the rabbit over, and he lay flat on his back with the breath knocked out of him and staring up at the unearthly lights.

As he lay there regaining his wind, Jack's eyes began to adjust to the increase in incandescence, and he took note of the fact that the lights seemed to be the fruit of strange shiny trees which had seemingly sprung up out of nowhere at key points around the garden, growing to maturity instantly. Certainly, Jack, who'd made many trips to the garden in the past, had not taken note of them, and lying there, he doubted he would've forgotten such strange timber had he chanced to pass its way before. Santos, it seemed, despite being as clumsy as ever, really cooked up a dilly here, and Jack had to give him credit for it, all the while wondering if he and his fellow confederates hadn't underestimated the old Tortoise. Even now with his eyes fully recovered, the lights were so bright they hid in shadow everything behind them until Jack, disoriented and confused, could no longer tell which direction was which or in what way lay the best means of escape.

The fruit lights got brighter still and began to hum even louder when all of a sudden, Santos stopped "Ho-Ho-Hoing" and started screaming instead. Jack came to realize Santos knew no more about these strange stars than he did and now found he had to attribute them to someone or something else. He thought back to conversations he'd had with others and how the subject of those conversations would sometimes drift over to the topic of the stars and just what might be out there in the great beyond and whether or not circling those stars there might be planets like ours, and if so, who might live upon them if there were. Jack came to the conclusion he and Santos were witnessing what could only be an alien invasion. Extraterrestrials with unknown powers and strange glowing lights.

THE CHRISTMAS RABBIT

Martians and Venusians. Plutonians with a hair across their ass and hell-bent on conquest.

Not caring he was blind as a bat, Jack screwed himself up to bolt when three cries issued forth from the darkness beyond and broke through the incessant hum of the strange fruit lights. They pierced the night like the howls of banshees, and each was slightly different although somehow similar. They rang out from three different positions as if they were the focal points on a triangle, and as they grew louder, sounded as though they were moving closer.

"Idiot!" cried one.

"Fool!" cried another.

"Yah!" sounded the third.

Not sure if the insults were directed at himself or the farmer, Jack tried raising his head in an effort to determine the identity of the howlers. He could see three forms approaching him from three different sides, all dressed in black. As they neared, he finally recognized them and in so doing mumbled a quiet and disheartening, "Oh, no…"

Although Jack was unaware of their arrival, he nonetheless knew of their reputations, and ten fleets of Martians with a couple of platoons of Venusians thrown in for good measure were less to be feared than those who approached him now. It was the three witches from hell: Helgayarn, Brunnhilde, and Betty—The Powers That Be—and although two of them had names which bespoke a Norse heritage, only Betty was Norwegian. God only knew where the other two came from. Being a foreigner and not understanding the local lingo too well, the only contributions Betty made to a conversation were apt to be "Yah" and "Oh, yah." Betty was the silent partner of this trio and could be counted upon to go along with whatever the other two decided. The other two said enough anyway. Helgayarn, Brunnhilde, and Betty. They sounded like an astral law firm—and they were. They were bullies enough to enforce their own brand of law, and they were firm in applying it, however narrow-mindedly they laid it down. Helgayarn was the brunette, Brunnhilde was the darker of the trio, and Betty, of course, the blonde—although as has been said before, they'd grown so similar, so old and prudish, their respective manes lost color, progressed through gray, and were now snow-white. Or would've been if not for the powder-blue tint which their hairdressers took such careful pains to apply on their weekly appointments at the beauty parlor, though given the extremes their stylists took to maintain even this level of morbid appearance, perhaps *beauty parlor* is too unfitting an adjective. Perhaps "Little Shop of Miracles" described it best, but white hair or blue, the trio were not above splitting a hair or a hare for that matter, in order to make a point. Thus Jack knew the tide was coming in fast and that the pellets were about to hit the wind.

Noticing their approach and thinking they were on his side, Santos grabbed ahold of Jack when he wasn't looking and through sheer mass and weight held him down captive until the witches could arrive full-fledged upon the scene. When they did, the farmer held the rabbit up, displaying him as if he were a trophy.

"Look!" cried Santos. "Didn't I say it? Caught red-handed and stealing my vegetables…and now soon for the pot!" The farmer raised himself from the ground and, carrying Jack, started back toward his house as if to make good on his threat.

"Not so fast, fat boy," said Brunnhilde, tripping him and causing him to fall once again and taste the loamy soil.

"Hey, we agreed!" cried Santos. "You ladies said if we caught one of these scoundrels pilfering my vegetables, it was mine—that it was dinner!"

It was true. The Powers That Be agreed earlier in the day when they'd first approached Santos and made him aware of their intentions. Even Betty contributed an enthusiastic "Yah!" to the bargain. Santos was feeling injured, abused, and in short—used. Things were happening he'd not been made aware of. The vegetables were still his, and bargains agreed to, he reasoned, should be honored. Those lights now…they weren't part of the plan at all, or if they were, they weren't part of the plan The Powers That Be saw fit to let him be party to. In Santos's opinion, this was fast becoming one sorry party, and he was beginning to wish its participants would just part company. Apart from that, things were okay. His vegetables were safe, and that's what mattered.

THE CHRISTMAS RABBIT

"Say, just what in the good earth is going on here," he asked, "and what the heck are those shiny things on poles?"

"They're lights, you idiot!" screamed Helgayarn, turning savagely upon him. "You fool—you were supposed to stay out of it! Now you've ruined everything—I should call up a drought and strike down your vegetables to the last parsnip! I should turn your family into cattle! At least then there would be someone around here with whom you could stand on equal footing!" Helgayarn was the boss witch of the three and did not put up with being balked or thwarted—not by the other two and certainly not by dumb farmers. Farm boys who thought they knew so much and who were forever jumping the gun and fouling up their own plans as well as the plans of others were a constant irritation to Helgayarn, whose ex-husband had been a dumb farmer himself. Eons ago, Helgayarn harbored dreams of becoming a Ziegfeld girl. Her dumb farmer husband, with ideas of his own, put the quash on that. Every day he had her up with the sun, milking cows, feeding chickens, and doing hundreds of other things poor dumb farmer's wives have been condemned to do since farming began. And all before breakfast! Then came the noontime chores and the dinner-hour projects! With so much to do, no farmer's wife could possibly find time enough to put in the practice necessary to become a Ziegfeld girl. There were, after all, only so many hours in a millennium. When Helgayarn finally got her chance at an audition, having had her mind for so long on things like domesticating livestock and soil rotation, it was no wonder she failed miserably. She sang off-key, danced out of step, and after having her dream crushed so completely by the selfish desires of one dumb farmer, is it any wonder she became such a witch? Most folk, two- or four-legged, don't think so. And now to be saddled with another dumb farmer… it was almost more than she could take. Dumb farmers, like bad pennies, had a way of continually turning up. She pierced Santos with a glare, causing him to thrash on the ground in fright. "Stand up!" she yelled. And he did. "Put down that rabbit!" He did that too. "Do you have any idea what you've done?" Helgayarn asked. "Do you see the confusion you've caused and the embarrassing situation you've put us all in?" As confused as ever, Santos did not see and begged to point it out. "My ladies," he cried, "surely, you're wrong." Picking up Jack again, the farmer continued, "Look! Here he is—a proven thief, and we've...I mean, *you've* caught him red-handed!"

"Caught who? Caught what?" Brunnhilde interjected shrewishly. "Where are the stolen vegetables?"

Santos looked around, inspecting his garden and accounting for all its produce. It was true. Based upon the tally taken when the Witches first arrived, there was nothing missing. Everything was in its place—each tater, each rutabaga, and every head of lettuce. Jack, it seemed, hadn't stolen anything. Yet.

Helgayarn found reading little minds like the one which resided in Santos to be impossibly easy and therefore knowing what he was thinking decided to make him squirm a little. "Well..."

"Well, what?"

"Well, what do you have to say for yourself, fool?" Santos however did not have much in the way of spare verbiage to put to use in situations such as this. The trio confronting him had all the combined patience and humor of a Supreme Court Justice writing a minority opinion and were not to be crossed, no matter how innocent and unknowing the crossing or crosser. Santos was about to be buried in fertilizer up to his ears and was just beginning to realize it.

Thinking the attentions of The Powers That Be were diverted elsewhere, Jack chose that particular moment to escape. Focusing all his energy by taking the three deep breaths that channeled power, he directed that energy through his body and into his teeth. His teeth became him, and he became them. While on his trip to the Big Apple, Jack perchance had wandered into Central Park, where he met a tired old hippie reliving a flashback, who gave him a tome titled *Zen and the Art of Primitive Tool Repair*. Jack read the book on the journey home but, being a rabbit, had no concept of primitive tools. He did, however, find Zen philosophy fascinating and took to it immediately. As a rabbit who was part of a troop known for its ongoing war with a certain farmer, Jack found the martial admonitions which Zen incorporated admirably suited to him, and so began practicing its exercises while still on the road. Now he cast his mind into the void, and in so doing his mind became no mind at all. He

THE CHRISTMAS RABBIT

thought of biting down on Santos's hand just for the sake of doing it and did just that, catching him in the web of flesh which separates the thumb and forefinger. Jack sliced through it like a hot knife through butter. Blood splattered everywhere, and Santos, letting out the Ho of Ho's, bounded about wildly. In the confusion, the farmer dropped the rabbit, who hit the ground running but who did not, after all, get very far. Betty, tied of tongue but fleet of foot, scrambled after him and, picking him up just as he was about to reach cover, returned him to the group. In the meantime, Brunnhilde managed to apply a temporary dressing to the injured hand of the distraught farmer who stood there weeping over his wounded appendage while thinking things couldn't possibly get worse. Poor old sod. *Things* hadn't even started yet.

Helgayarn became furious at this unlikely turn of events. The situation was out of control and going into a tailspin. Never before had she allowed such a thing to happen. Always in the past she and the other two maintained a firm hand when settling such disputes, thus confirming their own authority within bounds they themselves set. They had many responsibilities, did the trio, and much to do. This was to be a quiet affair and quickly settled, for they had more important business elsewhere. There was a whole wide world which needed running. Not only did they find themselves pressed for time, but for years now The Powers That Be found they were hard-pressed to maintain their reputations. Too much talk and too much idle time on the hands of the masses, she supposed. But the truth was, most folk—regardless of the number of legs used to support themselves—who had dealings with the trio were unhappy with their pronouncements, and because most of those whose lives the ladies interfered with felt the cure was far worse than the disease, there had been for some years talk of throwing them over in favor of someone or something else. A golden calf perhaps. And would it matter what replaced them if indeed they were defrocked? Helgayarn reasoned it wouldn't, given whoever or whatever stood for substitution would see to it they were buried up to their ears in cattle craps. Helgayarn liked having both feet planted firmly on the ground, not in it, and knew if word got out about this bungled affair, it would only add fuel to the flames which ever sought to burn away their authority in the holy fires of self-righteous criticism. It was time, therefore, to extinguish these dangerous fires by breaking out the water cannons! Turning toward Betty, she grabbed Jack and began interrogating him. "Hare," she asked, "what are you doing here?" Jack could lie as well as steal and so replied, "I was out for a walk and stopped to smell the roses." But Helgayarn wasn't buying and furthermore detested being mocked by smart-assed leporides. In rising fury, she began squeezing him. Jack's eyes bulged out of their sockets as the witch cut off his wind. He squirmed violently in her hands, trying to make good his escape, but to no avail. Her grip was like iron. Once again he focused his energy, cast his mind into the void, and bit down deeply, but as he was new to Zen, discovered he hadn't nearly the control or power necessary to pierce that tough old hide. Helgayarn merely laughed while poor Jack chipped a tooth. Easing her choke hold somewhat, she allowed him a futile breath. "Cattle craps," said she, "there are no roses here."

Having recovered but feeling he was soon for the spit anyway, Jack decided to keep up the bravado and play smooth till the end. "Yes, now you're holding me up," he replied, "I can see that! May I go?"

Helgayarn shrieked and threw him to the ground. "You were after the vegetables!" she screamed. "Don't try to deny it!"

"Prove it, witch."

Helgayarn screamed again, getting ready to crush Jack's head with the heel of her boot, but Brunnhilde, who'd always been the most even-tempered and levelheaded of the three, jumped in and physically restrained her. "No, Helly," she whispered, "not that way. Even though this little leporide deserves it and the idiot farmer doubly so for letting this matter get so out of hand, still, who knows who could be watching and misconstrue this justified response as just another obvious abuse of authority? You know how jealous they all are and how they covet our position—think! This must be done properly and moreover must set a precedent."

Brunnhilde managed to calm Helgayarn down just enough to do that—think. And as she thought, a wicked smile spread slowly across her face. She tenderly picked Jack up with one hand and wrapped the other like an old comrade around the shoulder of Farmer Santos, and whilst giving voice to a sigh of contentment, an idea slowly formed in what passed for her heart. Brunnhilde was right, she reasoned. Matters would have to take their proper course. There could be no quick fixes now, and although it would be time-consuming, perhaps such courses, when the need to traverse them arose, were for the best. Make it public, and do it in the open for all to see. It would help to reaffirm the law and reaffirm them too, for once judgment was passed and punishment handed out, there would be little talk of rebellion anymore and no mention of golden calves whatsoever—of that she was sure! She handed Santos over to her *sisters*, instructing them to detain him.

Turning her full attention to Jack, she said, "So it's proof you demand, is it? Very well. I call into assembly a duly convened session of the Constitutional Cosmic Court, which will gather and hear testimony regarding this incident and those preceding it, one week from today. This should give our two defendants more than ample time to retain council and subpoena witnesses."

Such a pronouncement surprised Brunnhilde and Betty, catching them off guard. Although not entirely unknown, Constitutional Cosmic Courts were rare in their occurrence. Indeed, throughout all history, from on back to the Garden right up till these "Olden Days," The Powers That Be saw fit to convene only three of 'em. Such courts when constituted were considered by all involved to be the last step in the arbitration process simply because the notion of arbitration itself was thrown on the trash heap by the Witches who would make a show of carefully considering presented evidence and pronouncing judgment, which, however ill-considered, was nevertheless legally binding upon all participants and most bystanders too. Such Courts were not to be taken lightly, not even by the witch who convened them.

If Brunnhilde and Betty were surprised by Helgayarn's pronouncement, Jack and Santos were terrified. A Constitutional Cosmic Court was in fact a kangaroo court which merely gave license to The Powers That Be to act like the tyrants and despots everyone knew them for—which the trio did on a day-to-day basis anyway albeit in a somewhat limited fashion. But with the symbolism of the law to back them, they could practice such tyrannies, engaging in despotism to its fullest.

"And you, hare," said Helgayarn, "by coming here to steal, you've gotten in my hair, and when proof is presented of your perfidy, you and all your heirs will be called upon to pay the penalty. Do you hear that?"

"I hear," said the hare, "and, in truth, couldn't care."

It was a lie and too obviously poor poetry, but one expects lies in something so small when confronted by someone so large. Desperation is the true mother of invention, and when you're engaged against a superior opponent and therefore have no hope of winning, when all there is to be gained or lost is your life—bluff! Whatever you have to lose you'll most likely give up anyway so what harm is actually done? And as for poor poetry—anyone who can work up spit enough to offer sass when in the throes of a mess like the one just described deserves credit for having testes the size of temples—even if such attributes get you killed!

Jack however did not have such gargantuan genitalia, which of course would have looked damned silly on a rabbit his size. What he did have was a thorough working knowledge of the bluff and its practical applications when put to good use. Yet what he lacked entirely was any experience with the game of poker whatsoever. Never heard of it—and so despite his bravado and his false presentation of pseudo bravery, did not realize bluffs are useless when your opponent holds a full house...and in this hand, the ladies were aces high. "Lock the little one up," ordered Helgayarn, "and put the fat boy under 'house arrest.' No visitors for either—except for counsel—and even then only by permission."

This was just another in a long list of examples of lousy decision-making on the part of The Powers That Be for which they were world famous and universally reviled. An earlier case in point was their decision to divide the year into seasons, which went on to become one of their most famous solutions while at the same time being referred to as one of their biggest screwups. You see, some of us like a warm climate, while some of us prefer it a bit cooler, and still others prefer it just right. When the world was first getting settled, those with different preferences in environment and climate gathered themselves into individual factions and interest groups in order to better petition The Powers That Be for separate living accommodations which catered to their specific needs and predispositions. Taken as a whole, the Witches thought it a capital idea. Everything and everyone in their place would make the whole ball of wax much easier to control and simpler to give orders to. There would be no "misunderstandings" in a situation like that, no well-reasoned pleas concerning the misinterpretation of orders and directives. Plants would grow where they were told to. Wild cattle, be they in groups or herds, would graze only those hills and valleys which abutted their individual boundaries. There would be no more stampeding across the plains—prairie fires or not—and damn it, there'd finally be some order around here! Rabbits and men, both enemies of long-standing, could finally be kept apart, and that in itself made the whole idea worthwhile. Helgayarn, Brunnhilde, and Betty berated each other for not having thought it up themselves and then promptly set to turning someone else's insight into action. Segregating and assigning, the trio gathered the forces. Laid the magic spells. Danced the dances and incited the incantations. They put their hands upon the wheel of earth, known formally back then as Mungo, and made *the adjustment*, and all the adjustment accomplished was to send the world spinning crazily on its axis and in its orbit. Now almost anywhere could have warm climates, cool ones, or weather which was just right whether you wanted it or not; it was just a question of the time of the year. Now everybody had everything they wanted some of the time, but nobody felt they had enough of what they wanted more often than not. Freezing in winter, they dreamt of spring and her warm gentle breezes bathing the brow of a tired and tortured landscape stripped barren and laid bare by the previous season's frosts. Or toiling in the stifling heat of high summer longed only for the cool of autumn and for the day she would finally fall from the sky, breaking the back of August and in so doing provide some measure of relief from that bitter yellow bastard who so mercilessly ruled the heavens from mid-June through September. Moreover most folk, having finally got what they wanted for at least some of the time, resented that they would soon lose it nevertheless through no fault of their own but rather as a matter of mere circumstance in a world gone crazy and spinning out of control. Thus "seasons" came into existence, and all of us to one degree or another—with the exception of The Powers That Be who, it seemed, could exist anywhere and actually thrived on inclement weather—became their slaves. For most of us, such slavery became mere annoyance, but for some the seasons became life-threatening and still are today, forcing many into migrations which take them far to the south, only to retake the trip in reverse after the briefest of rests, then turn around and do it all over again. And that said nothing about the lateral cross-travelers who were out there then, are out there still, and who with their own seasonal issues have become migraines too. In truth, seasons were not among their more popular pronouncements, and it was upon decisions like these that Helgayarn, Brunnhilde, and Betty built their questionable reputations.

So it comes as no surprise that with a history of blunders, bungles, and miscues the trio should err further still, which is just what they did when they confined Santos to his house without any visitors because given that decree his wife and family with no visible means of support were by necessity forced from their home to seek temporary lodging elsewhere. Being so closely associated with Santos (you can't, alas, choose your family), as has been pointed out earlier, did not exactly endear them to the population at large, and so they were shunned by nearly everyone. They became the neglected neighbors nobody wanted to live next to, let alone nurture, in their hour of need. The Salvation Army sent them away. Beggars turned them out of their holes while the Lions' Club roared at them with an admonishment to look elsewhere. Even the innkeeper told them all the rooms were taken, and when they inquired as to the barn, were informed that the manger was booked too. In the end, with no place to go and at the mercy of the elements, Mrs. Santos and her two children went begging alms of The Powers That Be who were comfortably settled in for their stay in a pasture away east, ensconced in a fully loaded, custom-designed, Winnebago covered wagon which they'd bought

THE CHRISTMAS RABBIT

for a song and now traveled in exclusively. It slept eight, had AC hookups—which would come in right handy when someone finally invented AC, and a full kitchen complete with microwave and wet bar. For get up and go, it got up and went, coming fully rigged with a fuel efficient straight six (Clydesdales harnessed two-by-two and stacked three deep). The reins were light to the touch, and it had antilock brakes and a passenger side airbag. It was state of the art in travel back in Olden Days, and the Witches had four payments left before they could claim it as their very own. Being it was state of the art and not fully paid for and given the fact it was custom-designed and therefore a one-of-a-kind issue (in truth, no one at that time but The Powers That Be could afford such a blatantly excessive display of luxury and material ease), although there was within its confines room to spare, the trio were reluctant to share such excess with anyone—let alone the three waifs who now came knocking at the door begging for charity. "Cattle craps!" exclaimed Helgayarn who saw them coming, knew exactly what they were about, and who was determined to throw them off the very dooryard before they even knocked.

"Yah!" exclaimed Betty in eager agreement. "Oh yah!"

Once again, it was Brunnhilde the levelheaded who saw through to the heart of the matter and who, in seeing, temporarily at least, averted scandal and disaster. "No, no, dears," she said. "We can't do that. In fact, that's the last thing we can do! We must welcome them. We must help them."

Helgayarn, who helped no one unless they helped her first and who could be very rarely counted upon to return a favor, thought herself too busy with the upcoming trial and its attendant preparations to devote what little time she had left to entertaining street urchins who wanted a taste of the easy life. Life was hard, and Helgayarn was here to say so and say it loudly. Let the street people stay in the street until they accepted some responsibility for themselves and started dealing with the messes in their lives. She would not help them. She was too concerned with the big picture to allow herself to get bogged down with individual details and problems of others. She was wrapped up in the whole ball of wax and in keeping it rolling. If it rolled less smoothly at times than it should have—at least it kept turning! It never stopped and, in Helgayarn's opinion, could not slow down now to take on passengers. "Bunny," she said affectionately, "we just won't answer the door. They'll grow tired and hungrier still, then leave to look elsewhere. Dirty little scavengers—let them blow!"

"Listen to me, darling," replied Brunnhilde, "folk are watching! And they're looking for excuses to complain!" She wrung her hands nervously while pacing back and forth across the kitchen floor. It irritated Brunnhilde when Helgayarn called her Bunny, for if the truth be known, Bunnies had always been a plague to The Powers That Be who formulated any number of plans to rid the world of the vermin, but who in the end lacked the necessary gumption to carry any of them out. Although they liked to show off and go on as if they were the "Lords of Creation," The Powers That Be knew they weren't and were not too sure of just who was. It had after all been a long time ago—who remembers that far back? But they were sure it was someone, and there was no percentage, they reasoned, in pissing that someone off by destroying an entire species. Said someone was sure to take it personally and The Powers That Be who felt unappreciated already for efforts that went largely unnoticed and undervalued saw no percentage whatsoever in proving that point. *Bunny was such a common name*, thought Brunnhilde. Too plain a handle for a Power That Be. It was hard to get respect when tagged with such a moniker, and Brunnhilde was forever overachieving in a useless effort to try and compensate for it. It was a name which could doom you to a life of unending anonymity if you weren't careful and blend you so far into the background you might never again find your way into the rich thickness of the warm center, which is, of course, your rightful place if you're a Power That Be. Bunny was not a name folk put a lot of confidence in. It sounded too whimsical. Anyone named Bunny was having too much fun to be taken too seriously. Even now as I relate this tale, think you back to all the famous women in the world that ever were, and not one of them is named Bunny. There are no Florence Nightenbunnies or any Congresswomen named Bunny. There are no Queen Bunnies. Queen Bees, yes. Queen Bunnies, no. And it is doubtful that Helen's face would've launched a thousand ships had she been the Bunny of Troy. Even rabbits, to give them their due, who have always had strong females throughout their history that have led their respective warrens through any number of near disasters and cataclysms, have *never* had a queen named Bunny. It was felt by the mothers who named them that such queens so saddled would be forever underachieving, and so as an identifier of royalty was a name invariably passed over. Brunnhilde, knowing even rabbits thought the name foolish, could not help but feel embarrassed when Helly referred to her that way. She felt so now. Helgayarn, Brunnhilde supposed, often used the name just to arouse this ugly embarrassment lurking deep within, for doing so, Brunnhilde realized, always allowed Helly to gain the upper hand in conversation and most often get her way.

But not this time, determined Brunnhilde. This time the situation was a little too dicey to allow her sister the convenience of winning an easy argument. The very fact that this issue should have been settled quickly and quietly only served to exacerbate the matter at hand and in so doing serve to wear away their credibility with the community at large. Brunnhilde felt they were standing on eggshells whilst walking upon the edge of a knife. *Not good*, she reasoned, *not good at all*. "No, and no again!" she said and stopping her pacing, turned to confront Helgayarn with the unpleasant facts her sister seemed determine to ignore. "Folk," she went on to say, "both two- and four-legged, are saying we're responsible for this mess. That we should've seen it coming and moreover, not only are we responsible for the situation in general, but for those three waifs in particular who through no fault of their own other than close association and family ties have been caught up in this. A plague on that damned farmer and those rabbits! May they be a toil and irritation to each other on down through the ages for all the trouble they've caused!" She paused to pick a cuticle and gather her thoughts before continuing. "Listen to me," she said, "it doesn't matter if we're to blame or not—what matters is what others think! We exist as who we are by keeping the rabble buffaloed with our parlor tricks." Helgayarn bridled and made as if to disagree, but Brunnhilde cut her off. "It's true! We have 'em snowballed! Sure, we have the power, and we can lay down the charms and spells, but we don't really know what we're doing, do we? At best, we're apprentice magicians busy in the effort of trying to distract our marks with our sleight of hand. It's a shame our sleight of hand always seems to go slightly out of control. We do things and cause events which we did not intend. Remember seasons. And tides!" Her sisters winced.

"Remember how much bluffing and covering up we had to do in the wake of those fiascos! Too much hush money and too many folk knowing we're not infallible. It's dangerous. Worse—it's bad for business! We need to nip this thing in the bud and do so quickly. We need a small magic—something that won't get out of control but which will nevertheless leave a lasting impression! While we're searching for it, for appearance's sake, let us pretend charity and take the waifs in. It can do no harm." A self-centered smile, which bespoke of a plan slowly forming, spread unevenly across Brunnhilde's face.

Helgayarn, who recognized the smile and who knew well the feeling, could barely contain her excitement. "Do go on, dear," she said gleefully, "and tell us!"

"Yah!" shouted an excited Betty.

"Well then," continued Brunnhilde, "it may be such generosity on our parts does us a world of good. Think about it, dears! How can we help but look like three charitable matrons of old—which we in fact are if you overlook charitable—who with a distasteful duty before them nevertheless give of themselves for a family in need. That this strumpet is a mere commoner, quite dull, and with an unruly brood in tow, only helps serve to 'blow our trumpets' for whom but the most charitable of souls, regardless of how powerful they might be, would play hostesses to such a feral mob? Who but guardian angels and fairy godmothers are so giving of themselves? We have here a public relations coup we can't afford to miss! Even if we screw up the big show, which between the three of us we probably will, so long as we provide for the cow and her calves, we should be able to keep the rest of the herd from stampeding.

Betty offered up her agreement with a hearty, "Yah!" as she carefully considered the plan.

THE CHRISTMAS RABBIT

Although she found herself uncomfortable with Brunnhilde's assertion that they would no doubt screw up and therefore caught herself wincing yet again, Helgayarn nevertheless found such deliciousness painted upon her own countenance and went on to add that while lodging with them the human livestock could be made to do chores and wait upon their individual persons. "They shall serve us high tea!" she laughingly said.

In truth, because they were so frazzled and frantic and because each thought such domestic chores beneath them, the Witches made lousy housekeepers and were forever hiring for themselves domestic engineers which even back then cost a small fortune. Due to unions, the title "engineer" was a distinction which could apply to anyone with cheek enough to claim it. Garbage men were sanitation engineers, crossing guards were traffic engineers—even those who drove the newfangled trains were calling themselves engineers, and none of 'em came cheap. It seemed even in Olden Days, the title of "engineer" gave one license to mark up one's bill by a minimum 25 percent. Now the trio found themselves gloating at each other because not only were they about to "engineer" a public relations coup but they were also assured of acquiring for themselves a domestic engineer with years of experience and expertise—all for the price of an indentured servant! All they had to do was feed and shelter the family and treat them kindly—and then only when they were sure others were watching. The rest of the time, the woman and her children could be made to work like dogs. Moreover, felt the Powers, their three charges should end their experience grateful in their good fortune for despite the unusual circumstances in which they would find themselves and notwithstanding the long days of hard work they'd be made to endure, it was not just anyone who got to be a servant to The Powers That Be. The family's memoirs of their moments while midst the magnificence of such venerated personages would be much sought after by vapid and ignorant peasants, as for example, the members of Mrs. Santos's quilting bee who gossiped continually and who lusted after tales about lordly folk. The telling and retelling would earn the farmer's wife her membership back and perhaps the chairmanship of the bee as well while their experiences put down on paper would provide for her children the stuff of successful résumés as they grew up and made their way in the world.

The Witches were congratulating each other on their wit and good planning, glad-handing and feeling smug, when the waifs knocked upon the door and begged admittance. The family was let in while a small crowd gathered upon the fringes of the forest looked on in wonder to witness such an event.

From the onset of the family's arrival, it was clear to The Powers That Be they'd made a dreadful mistake. The woman's reputation, it seemed, was not entirely undeserved. As a domestic engineer, she was about as trustworthy and reliable as a mad scientist. Indeed, the one meal with its subsequent courses, which she'd prepared for them during her stay, tasted as if it had been boiled in a beaker deep in some underground laboratory. Things swam in her soups, and they bit back if you weren't careful. Her braised leg of lamb brought tears to one's taste buds, and her fish baked in foil had far too much oil. Her lunches and brunches were littered with leftovers of dinners long gone and all as equally unappealing as the recipes just mentioned. Her high tea was so low snails couldn't pass under it without ducking their heads, and the Witches knew the pellets were about to hit the wind that evening when they all sat down to dinner.

The children, Junior and Laddie, had instincts for recognizing and avoiding trouble which were much sharper than either of their parents; and since their arrival had been sitting meekly and quietly upon a couch while preparing themselves for the worst. They were two boys, two years apart, who'd seen far too much trouble in too short a span to take anything too casually. Saddled with such parents, they were self-trained to be sensitive to the unstable and neurotic. Forced to condition themselves as a survival trait, they'd learned to gauge both mood and wind as they navigated the dangerous waters of their parents' emotional instabilities, and when either started to blow, the lads sure enough shortened sail and made for the lee side. The fact they'd become town targets for trouble in a time when towns barely existed only served to sharpen their senses. They became adept at reading other folk like the weather, which is to say despite all the practice, they were more often wrong than not. Still they avoided more trouble than they found, and that's exactly what they were striving for now. Each had been reading Helgayarn, Brunnhilde, and Betty since their arrival, trying to decipher subtle cues in posture and position, attention and attitude. They didn't quite understand the language the Witches employed despite the trio's use of the "common tongue," but in any dialect, the boys knew misery and trouble when they heard it and therefore determined the safety of the couch where they were out of the way and hopefully unobtrusive as their mother sucked up to the trio while answering their interrogations offered the best opportunity of extracting themselves from the dangerous morass into which they were sinking. They just wanted the ordeal between their father and the rabbits to be over, and neither no longer gave a damn one way or the other who won or who lost. They just wanted their normalcy back which they could now barely remember and saw only as a fleeting vision of better days and bygone times, lost in the first salvo of the ever escalating conflict between their father and the lapins. Now they found themselves at the mercy of three crazies and awaiting their fate—for surely whatever befell the old man would descend upon them too. Yet despite this, their mother was glad to be here! So they sat on the couch, out of sight, and hopefully out of mind, resolved for their own sake to be on their best behavior. Until dinner.

When Mrs. Santos rang the dinner bell, Helgayarn, Brunnhilde, and Betty were already seated at the dining room table armed with their criticisms and waiting to be served. The children arose from the couch and promptly asked to be excused. "Aren't you eating?" asked Helgayarn, who never before encountered children who weren't hungry. The older boy looked at the younger, who in turn gazed back at him embarrassed that the only suggestion he had offered his brother regarding the dilemma they now faced was the silent witness of his moral support. Sighing, the older boy turned to the Witches, saying simply, "Yes."

"Well then, sit down," urged Helgayarn, pulling out a chair as if to demonstrate. "We don't bite—at least not very hard!" The trio broke out in peals of girlish laughter. Such handsome men as yourselves," said Brunnhilde, "must eat if they're to grow up big and strong."

"Nope, not that," the older of the two brothers replied as he pointed to his mother in the kitchen and to the serving platters she was gathering up. *Good thing they're covered*, thought the older brother, *we still have a chance to get out of this.* "Mom and Dad are partial to polecat stews. My brother and I, being vegetarians, always eat separately." The older brother, named Junior, was lying. His father let himself be pushed around by a gang of rambunctious rabbits—it's for certain he was no match for polecats or for making stew out of those who made it their business to make misery for intruders who dared cross 'em. Still all of Mrs. Santos's recipes tasted like stewed polecat and were to be avoided. Always. Thus the children made a habit of wandering into the garden where they took their meals separately. The farmer and his wife, too tired to argue, let them have their way.

"May we be excused now?" the older brother asked again.

Clearly at a loss, Helgayarn was more than a little perturbed. Once the decision had been reached to take the family in, it had been her intention to have the waifs break bread with them daily. It was both humble and generous in appearance. Such outward displays of charity regardless of the inward motives which drove them could only serve to bolster their standing with the public and so provide the trio a more firmer footing when dealing with those grumblers and whiners who felt they flaunted their powers flagrantly in the faces of others, while the mileage Mrs. Santos could get out of the current circumstance was limited only by her own wit and her ability to cash in on a winning ticket when she finally had one. But now the children weren't eating, and it cast a decidedly different flavor upon the whole affair which itself was beginning to smell like polecat stew. There were those who would wonder why the boys weren't eating. Some would infer they weren't being allowed to eat and were instead being starved in order to better punish the parents. Others would say that the children were on a hunger strike and would spread rumor and innuendo implying the children were starving themselves as a means of protest and as a way of avoiding poisoning and death at the hands of The Powers That Be who were subtly slipping those poisons into the food with the intent of killing the entire family. The fact Mrs. Santos ate cheerfully alongside the trio would itself engender no question marks. Many of those watching had the misfortune of sampling some of her more disastrous displays of culinary culpability in times gone by and knew therefore that if the farmer's wife could survive her own cooking, the poisons of The Powers That Be, no matter how powerful or how often applied, would be impotent in their attempts to assassinate her. Lucky for her, because the trio did try to poison her—but only after eating her food. Then the ladies got to feeling threatened too. But for now the children were simply refusing to eat, and Helgayarn was perplexed. She and her sisters would have to think this through very carefully. In the meantime, there would be other meals for the children to attend and partake of, and so they would—but for the present they could just go to their rooms!

"We don't have any rooms," said the older brother. "We have a couch."

"That's right!" the younger brother chimed in agreement. "We have a couch! We have rooms too." The smile fell slowly from his face, and he sadly looked away. "Only they're back home with Da." He spoke as if he and his father were separated by leagues uncounted when in fact they were barely a half mile apart. It wasn't the distance but the simple fact of separation itself which seemed to prey upon the boy's mind. He was used to having things a certain way and in having a family who, however odd in its personalities and players, was nonetheless nuclear in its makeup. This cohesion midst the confusion and near anarchy which seemed to constitute most of his life was the singular anchor in the young lad's heart and mind, holding him fast in a turbulent sea boiling with strife and hard feelings. It was his only grip on reality and fast slipping away. With his world turned upside down, such a tenuous connection was in danger of breaking entirely, and no matter how things turned out, Helgayarn felt sure this one faced the hazard of emotional scarring which would stay with him always. Public opinion would find the trio guilty of inflicting those stripes, she knew, and there would be trouble. She therefore sought to forestall it before it could get started and so told them, not unkindly, there were rooms in the wagon to spare and that they should choose one of those. "Sleep now, children," she said. "Rest easy in our house, for your troubles have been many and our succor bountiful." Her tone bespoke kindness and concern, but her eyes pierced the boys like arrows, as though she were looking through their chests and out their backs to a place only she could see.

Junior felt like Jonathan Harker upon being greeted by Dracula at the castle's front door. "Thank you, most noble," he replied, bowing his head and sucking up a little himself. "Your grace and kindness are too rich a reward for one so young and unworthy as I." He laid it on thick like the prodigy he was, and it was this skill when he chose to employ it, which lay at the heart of his individual tribulations. Being his father's son, he would have done much better for himself to lay low and keep quiet, and yet because he was his father's son, he felt it incumbent upon himself to defend Santos from his dozens of detractors. But ironically, it was the fact he was his mother's son at heart (although nobody at the time knew this—not even Mrs. Santos) and had inherited her practical approach to problem-solving which led to all his troubles. Knowing he couldn't lick all his father's detractors in an outright fight, he decided to make fools of them instead. To this end, he assiduously applied himself to the gathering and absorption of everything pertaining to anything. He read voraciously, and with avid interest, tome after tome, regardless of topic, until in conversation at least, he seemed to know a good deal about whatever subject was being discussed and took delight in pointing it out to you, often at your own expense. He paid special attention to language and self-help books written to enhance one's ability to communicate and polish one's skills in the art of oration (although he stayed away from and refused to peruse The Powers That Be's instructional on this subject—like their history of the world it was considered self-promotional trash) because he enjoyed arguments and debates for the opportunity they afforded him to hurl back insults at those who took after his father so.

Such limberness with language seemed snotty coming from an adult. From a child, it was downright impudent. Nobody likes a smart-ass—especially when he barely stands above your middle. This one had way too much fun applying his army of adjectives and

THE CHRISTMAS RABBIT

adverbs to his own advantage as he flayed you open with his tongue, using it to lick you seductively, making you wet with compliments and sweet-sounding platitudes, only to lay the groundwork for the inevitable insult that was sure to follow. He employed the one to set up the other. His favorite targets were the folk who took after his father. He did not see they might have legitimate or at least arguable reasons for their actions and probably would not have cared if he did. Battle lines, it seems, had been drawn, and he knew upon which side his bread was buttered, rancid or not. Those who continually lost a verbal battle of wits with the young lad and who felt the scorn of insults and bad jokes hurled back at them not only from the boy but from those who laughingly looked on could not, of course, punish the young man by spanking him or even better fattening his lip as he surely deserved. First off, a lifetime of dodging similar situations and not always succeeding taught him to be quicker than most folk he contended with and therefore nine times out of ten could avoid serious reprisals simply by outrunning 'em. Adults thought him to be a smart-mouthed little bastard, and although they would have loved the chance to contend with him in a different sort of arena entirely, in Olden Days hitting someone else's children was regarded with distaste. Even getting their own children to do it, any of whom were capable and all of whom were eager for the chance as they had their own reasons for despising him, would not have been considered proper. It seemed as well as being a smart-ass, the kid really was pretty bright—an evolutionary leap when you considered the parents. In school he knew all the answers often before the questions were asked and was damned proud of the fact. He shouted those answers out continually, always interrupting the teacher and never giving anyone else in class a chance to display their acumen. Even without parents like his, anyone anywhere who's ever been a kid that attended public school knows what happens to show-offs like that. They're hounded and pounded until such hounding and pounding becomes an integral part of their daily lives. They come to expect it—perhaps even look forward to it, sensing nothing but emptiness within when not on the lookout.

Be that as it may, this skill or curse if you choose to see such things that way, served the young lad well in this particular instance. Having been sucked up to for so long, the Witches considered such suction and the compliments which came with it, whether heartfelt or not, no more than they merited. They were so full of impudence they exuded it with each exhaled breath until it surrounded them like misty fog and followed them everywhere. They'd been rebreathing this fog like you would your own breath if your head were in a paper bag and had been doing so for so long they could no longer taste its sourness and were completely unaware of its presence. Therefore, thinking they had the boy in the palms of their talons allowed themselves to puff up with pride as they drank in his approval and fanned themselves on his flattery.

"Which room, oh, Visions of Venus, would you have us take?"

Temporarily silenced by the sweet-sounding platitudes ushering from the boy's quick-silvered tongue, Helgayarn sat soaking them up like steam from a sauna as did Brunnhilde and Betty. The boy simply had them entranced. Had them entranced and knew it.

Good, thought he, *we just might get out of this!*

"Take any room in the back," Helgayarn replied, pointing languidly to the rear of the Winnebago where stood three silent doorways, cold and quiet, like sentinels forever on watch. They were intricate in their carving and purposefully so—the better to intimidate and cause unease. But the boy had no further cards to play. It was time to check, bet, or bluff, and since they were helpless anyway and at the mercy of their hostesses, he boldly marched to a door and opened it. To his relief upon the other side lay an ordinary bedroom with twin beds to occupy it. Acting as if he were about to retire for the evening, the older boy called his younger brother to him, and together they entered the bedroom, pulling the door closed behind them. Junior had no intention of staying, but knowing for himself how these things must invariably play out, climbed into bed anyway and made his brother do likewise. A short time later, Mrs. Santos came in to kiss them good night and finding both asleep, left the room quietly, and shut the door. It was the signal the elder of the two brothers had been waiting for. Mother could always be counted on to come in and kiss them good night just as it could likewise be depended upon that having done so she'd leave them alone, ignoring them in all but an outright emergency until the sun rose the next day. If they awoke in the middle of the night whining and wanting a cool drink of water, she reasoned it was Santos's job to put things right. He was the farmer after all, the one who thrived on long and unusual hours. But since his father was not there, Junior reasoned they were relatively safe until morning, and so slipping quietly out the bedroom window, he gathered up his brother and made his way to the garden where the vegetables were fresh and where dinner, if always served raw, was at least edible. Dinner of another sort was about to be served in the Winnebago back yonder, and the lad wanted to put as much distance between *that* and himself as possible.

Having made their way back to the farm, the boys proceeded on home that they might get a glimpse of father and, if they were lucky, a word with him too. Things were looking grim as far as the older brother was concerned, and although even in Olden Days advice was known to be a dangerous gift (especially if you considered the source the boy was contemplating), he knew himself to be playing far out of his league and so was desperate for it, whatever the wellspring; and because back in Olden Days, there were no newspapers and therefore no syndicated advice columnists to fill the pages of such publications with their inane chatter and vapid dribble, the older boy being who he was, was left with a single source from which to obtain council. To that end, he approached the house—not that he wasn't without certain misgivings. This was, after all, his father he was thinking of enlisting. And though he knew himself to be his father's superior in mental acumen—he'd proven it last year at the country fair. (That's *country fair*, not *county fair*, and so called because there were no counties back then. There was country galore, however, plenty of it—virgin-ripe and ready for picking. Back in Olden Days, it was a chore to step outside your door and not be in the country. It assaulted you from all sides. Therefore, the country fair was held wherever the hawkers decided to pitch their tents.) He'd proven it by thinking rings around the old man and everyone else in the Circular Thinking Contest. In fact, having defeated all other contestants, Junior was designated "Fair Champion." But because he was anything other than fair in his treatment to those who lost to him while acting smarmy and offering up off-color comments about the entire affair anyway, his designation was deleted, and they took back his blue ribbon. Still there was no denying—unless of course you were The Powers That Be—that young Junior was just about the sharpest tack walking around on two legs or four and, yet for all that, with what he now faced, still felt a desperate need for a different perspective. Father, whose perspective was uniquely singular, certainly fit that bill, thought the boy, although no doubt his recommendations would be replete with useless adages and metaphors culled from his own life experience. "Walk softly," he might say, "and carry a big stick," while producing that silly club of his as if to prove a point. It was a theme his father expounded upon ceaselessly when hunting rabbits and the boy had grown tired of hearing it. But who else was there to turn to?

Hand in hand and with the utmost quiet, the two brothers crept within twenty yards of the house only to find they could go no further. The evening was full, the stars were out, and the moon was pregnant with light. In those watch fires of the night, the two boys took note of three large wolfhounds in the dooryard who had no doubt been placed there by The Powers That Be to guard father and further ensure he kept to himself.

The hounds performed their duties well for although they were dogs which is to say their vision was lousy, their sensitive smellers sampling the nighttime breezes sensed the scintillating scent of the boys. These three canines had been individually trained by The Powers That Be, who stole them from their litters when they were young—barely six weeks, and who put emphasis on enhancing those abilities for which that particular breed of hound was so well-known. They could hear a rabbit in a hole from a hundred yards away. As chasers, they could give that same rabbit a five-minute head start and still run it to ground. Their smellers were so sharp it was rumored their noses could cut. These were three canny canines whose orders had been issued, and no one was to be granted admission into the farmer's hut except for The Powers That Be and the farmer's attorney,

THE CHRISTMAS RABBIT

who, being a lawyer, would of course be recognizable by his smell. The larger of the three wolfhounds was the leader and as such while taking note of the boys' scent on the wind began to utter a low ominous growl which issued deep from somewhere in its chest, rumbling darkly, as if revving up and storing energy before it's inevitable release as a full-fledged bark. The leader was mean and dangerous enough to stand alone and indomitable. It required no assistance when it came to scaring off intruders or intimidating helpless prey. Its growl froze the children with fear and they stood like statues, their feet bolted to the ground, unable to proceed further or return from whence they came. But twenty yards out seemed to be a safety buffer of sorts for although the other two hounds joined their leader by voicing intimidating growls of their own, none of the three seemed inclined to leave the dooryard unattended, fearing no doubt, the escape of their prisoner. Clearly they were there to keep Santos inside and to prevent ingress from without, no matter how sustained the attack or determined the effort.

Their growling brought Santos to the screen door. Something was happening just past the dooryard, and he wanted to know what. *Probably those damned rabbits*, thought he, *and up to one of their tricks!* They'd not be above trying to make off with all his produce now that they knew him to be helpless and locked up. One of the dogs, hearing Santos approach the screen door, spun quickly around like an evil roulette wheel as if to say, "Take your chances, bub." It prominently displayed its sharp white teeth. Foamy goo, *saliva*, Santos supposed, ran whitely over its lips and down its muscular jaw. He could go no further and relished the thought of rabbits under the care of such tender ministrations if he could but entice them a little closer. "Come," he yelled eagerly into the night. "Come—there are carrots for all and taters too!"

"Is it safe?" asked a returning voice.

"Of course," Santos replied slyly, and he creaked the door open a bare inch as if to prove his point. He recognized that voice; he was sure. No doubt disguised somehow in order to throw him off. *Those rabbits*, he thought, *must think him pretty stupid to fall for so obvious a trick.* "Don't worry about the dogs," he said with a chuckle, "their bark is worse than their bite. I know—I've tested it!" He was lying but those pesky rabbits had no way of knowing that!

"Okay, Da," came the reply. "We're coming in." Two shapes just slightly over two feet tall began to approach the cottage. "Do you think it's safe?" asked one of them. "After all, these dogs belong to the You-Know-Who's." Junior was talking quietly and moving slowly. Thankfully, this time Santos realized his mistake. "Go back!" he yelled. "Go back!"

"But you said—"

"Never mind what I said! Since when have I ever said anything worth listening to?" A truer statement had never been spoken and up until now Junior could not think of a single sentence uttered by his father that proved otherwise. Such thoughts made the young lad feel bad. It made him feel even worse, realizing his father knew he felt that way. Had always known it seemed but who nevertheless made an honest attempt to do right by those he loved, no matter how futile the endeavor or how under appreciated the effort. Junior looked around at his immediate surroundings. He saw the shadow of the house with his father framed inside while he and Laddie remained mercifully hidden within the gloom. Yonder he could make out the gray shadings of the garden as it basked in the moonlight. It was as though he were viewing it for the first time. And though it seemed to him ironic that it took standing in the dark to make him see things in a new light, such was the case and that irony brought with it the guilt which seemed to lay in the line of sight of his new found vision.

Except for where his father stood, the house itself had grown dark with the emptiness which seemed to occupy it. For it was just a house—albeit a small one with a few leaks and bad plumbing. And it stood on a farm renowned for its produce, whatever the reason. A well-defined fence, or rather a selection of fences of all kinds and sizes joined end-to-end, circled the property, although repairs were needed and in more than one place. Santos, it seemed, caught up in his crusade, was involved in critical experimentation in order to determine which sort of fence was best suited as a bulwark against rabbits and thus joined chain links to board fence, and brick wall to barbed wire. Nothing was left untried in this circular perimeter he attempted to

THE CHRISTMAS RABBIT

define around his property. In one section, he had redoubts and ramparts and a retaining wall which ran wild. In another he'd grown hedges a hundred feet high—though like his prize-winning vegetables, he hadn't a clue as to how he'd managed it—until he built for his family a veritable fortress. Impervious to all. To all, that is, except the rabbits who were forever finding their way under, over, and around it and The Powers That Be, whose own impudence was more than equal to the imperviousness of mere walls no matter what they were made of or how highly constructed. Still, thought the boy, he'd always felt protected here despite the inept arms which held him, and it wasn't until he left the dubious safety of his father's succor that he suddenly realized he'd ever encountered any trouble. And for what? What did his father do, after all, but dare to be different? Those who came to laugh and make fun also came to trade, for despite his father's perceived eccentricities people knew good food when they tasted it—which was why Farmer Santos's roadside produce stand did thriving commerce; his restaurant, however, called the Country Kitchen, and run by Mrs. Santos, fared horribly, the fare itself being horrible, and thus had one foot perpetually into foreclosure—but his vegetables always brought a high price being traded for meats and skins, salt and other necessary items, along with the bad jokes and ill humor which inevitably came with them. "Let them laugh!" his father said. Now the boy had to wonder whether or not his father had been right all along and laughing loudest as he made his way merrily to the bank. The boy felt the cold hand of guilt settle uncomfortably upon him as he thought back to those times when right or wrong, silly or not, his father defended his own right to be while his eldest son hung his head in shame, slinking quietly away, embarrassed at having a sire who carried on so. Now those arms seemed not so inept after all. Now they seemed unique and deserving of the respect and admiration entitled to them for providing all they did and so abundantly. Despite their own reputations, there were others out there, the young lad knew, who didn't eat half as heartily. In fact, when taken as a whole, he had to admit his family was doing comparatively well, and he had his father, however odd, to thank for that.

"Da—"

"It's okay, son," Santos replied. "I understand."

"Da, what about the dogs?" the boy asked. "I can't quite see 'em! Should I walk quiet and get my stick?"

"No," came the farmer's sudden reply. "Stay where you are! Just what are you doing out there anyway?" Santos pushed on the screen door, his face pressed anxiously against the wire mesh as he sought a clearer view of his children and the certainty they were safe. "Go home to Ma!"

Regardless of his recent revelation, Junior found that his eyes rolled tiredly, exhausted by the inanity parading itself at the front door. Kids, he knew, weren't supposed to go through these kinds of cattle craps. At least not until they had their own kids. "Da...we are home. We just can't come in, remember?" Junior looked down at the ground and slowly shuffled his feet while his brother quietly stood by, doing the same. In the elder's case, such scuttling was merely a display of impatience brought about no doubt, by having to support an unfair portion of the world's weight at too early an age, whereas the younger of the two was trying in vain to deal with a compelling urge to pee. Even though bathrooms as we know them did not exist in Olden Days and outhouses were the up-and-coming thing, the compulsion was there nevertheless and growing minute by minute in this little boy who'd been forced by circumstance to sit on an uncomfortable couch for the entire day and then smartly whisked off to bed.

Santos looked around as if suddenly realizing where he was. "Quite," he replied contritely. "Where in Hades is your ma?"

"With them." Santos understood *them* to mean the rabbits who'd obviously used this unique opportunity and the chance it presented to capture and kidnap his wife. God, the children were lucky to be alive! He pictured with dread, the tortures they were inflicting upon the Mrs. in some secret burrow or hidden away hole while awaiting ransom.

"Where's my club?" he screamed, spinning wildly around in circles in a vain attempt to locate, and put his hands upon it. "The conniving little furs—this time they've gone too far!"

THE CHRISTMAS RABBIT

Seeing his father in a frenzy, Junior realized his mistake. "No, Da," he yelled back. "Ma's not with the rabbits—she's with the You-Know-Who's."

The farmer's ravings came to an abrupt halt as Santos quietly settled in at the screen door. "Them?" he asked timidly.

"Yes, them," the boy replied.

Santos ran his hands through his hair as if sifting it for clues to the riddles which perplexed him. "Junior, why would she go there? And having gone, why on earth would they take her in?"

Junior hesitated before replying. "Da," he said, "you know how we're regarded around here. Where else was there to go? And as for the You-Know-Who's, who knows why they do anything? They didn't seem put out by our arrival but instead greeted us with enthusiasm. Or pretended to anyway. It worries me, Da. I'm scared."

"Don't be," replied Santos. "Your Ma's a big girl. She'll be all right if she keeps her head."

"Da...she's cooking them dinner." A pitiful moan rang out in the darkness beyond. It was Jack Rabbit, alone and locked in his cage, who with his big ears listened in on their entire conversation and whimpered in terror. Jack knew that after one taste of the infamous Santos stew, The Powers That Be might be prompted into any number of unusual and terrifying retributions. Floods, droughts, random hangings—anything. "What's that noise?" cried Santos jumping back from the screen door, causing his ample bulk to shake roly-poly, which in turn led him to overbalance and go crashing to the floor like a bowl of tipped-over Jell-O.

"It's just the rabbit."

On his back and staring at the kitchen ceiling, Santos considered that he just might be going mad. Here he was a prisoner in his own house guarded by three hellish hounds while somewhere out there lurked an enemy out to steal vegetables which didn't belong to him. The wind was knocked out of the poor farmer. He'd taken a hard fall as he always did when he fell, and he fell often. "Where is he?" Santos managed to croak while gasping for breath. His hands grasped hold of the doorjamb like a pair of well-oiled vice grips. Just the thought of his precious vegetables in the paws of that dirty little beast was enough to drive him crazy. Although flat on his back, he sprang up like a cat. A cat with a head injury. A cat with a head injury caught in a herd of stampeding buffaloes who after they pass, if it lives, slowly gets to its feet and shakes itself off while preening its mane with feigned indifference as if this sort of falling around and being trampled upon were a normal occurrence and therefore something grown used to, which in this case was not too far from the truth. The screen door shook in its frame as Santos trembled with rage. The three wolfhounds began growling once again, all fangs and menace, convinced he was trying to escape.

"It's okay, Da," Junior cried out. "The rabbit's in the garden."

"The garden? Boy, chase him outta there!"

Junior offered up a tired sigh. "He's locked in a cage, remember? Those witches did it."

"Don't call 'em that, son," his father admonished, "because they are and they just might hear you!"

"'The You-Know-Who's then."

"Well, okay," the farmer replied, reluctantly giving in, "maybe just this once." He could think of no more descriptive epithet himself and for now was only concerned about that damned rabbit! "Listen, boy," he said, "you gotta kill him. He's only one rabbit—you won't even need a big stick. A small branch should do it!"

Junior was skeptical, knowing it was the last thing he dared do. Not that he was afraid—although truth be told, having watched the rabbits tear into his father time after time, the young lad was justifiably cautious. But it was the You-Know-Whos who'd caged the poor animal, and the boy thought it more misery than he could afford to interfere with their plans. "Da," he replied, "I can't."

"I suppose not," Santos replied in half-hearted agreement, smiling wistfully as a person sometimes will when they're denied through fate or circumstance a thing long desired. He took a moment to indulge himself in a small daydream wherein he captured for himself, just once, a rabbit—even if it was a small one and even if it was a cripple and subsequently escaped. But oh, to be able to say he'd done it! It was a pleasant dream, and it cried out to him to stay there dreaming and so remain untouched by the cataclysmic events which he could feel forming around his person making the air about him muggy and wet, as if dripping with uneasy anticipation. Forming yes, informative, no. This current situation and its subsequent mugginess defied his poor attempts at definition. But he didn't need a dictionary or a road map to understand cattle craps or to realize when he was standing in 'em. Even he wasn't that stupid. For the life of him though, he could not understand why this had all come about or how deep "deep" really was. Given this, it's surprising then to find him giving wise council and yet even that sometimes happens when you're winging it. Because when you wing it, life is a crapshoot, which means even if you're unlucky, you'll occasionally roll a seven. It's what keeps suckers coming back to the table and though the farmer found the situation inconceivable, still through some latent omniscience which like his common sense lay dormant and unused for far too long, suddenly awoke and paraded before him possible fates worse than death. Or maybe it was just dumb luck. Either way, a fount of wisdom spewed from his lips, and it is my belief this happened because it's an unwritten law that all tales must have happy endings, which this one would not have had this not occurred, and it's comforting to know that even for poor souls like Jack and Santos—and despite the many disagreeable influences in the world such as The Powers That Be—things have a way of finally working out—even if it takes forever, and even if you don't live to see it. The advice Santos offered was direct and simple.

"Junior, go take Laddie for a walk."

Of course, this wasn't his counsel—even Santos could do better but it was obvious that his youngest, waiting in the dusk of evening, had to go and standing there beside his brother, barely discernable in the dark, doing the compulsion fidget and casting eerily moving shadows in the gloom of the dooryard, Laddie was attracting the attention of the three wolfhounds who did not like fidgeters. Fidgeters made the hounds nervous for they'd been trained to assume fidgeters were often plotters, planners, and hatchers of secret little schemes designed to bestow upon their persons what each felt was their own share of Manifest Destiny. The Powers That Be wanted no truck with intrigue of this sort, preferring to keeping all the Manifest

Destiny to themselves. It was a powerful thing, Manifest Destiny, and not to be played with by amateurs. Thus the trio were ever alert for pretenders and posturers and persons of small-minded ambition. Such pretenders to power often fidgeted under the compulsion to show others they were the equals of their betters. The Powers That Be trained their dogs to be sensitive to such behavior and to report back upon it later. That's why the wolfhounds were such good hunters of rabbits. Rabbits are always fidgeting, twitching, and generally up to no good. Plotters and planners all, they bore careful watching. The Witches knew this and, to attenuate their dogs to such, had them begin training when pups by stalking rabbits. That an individual might fidget and twitch in response to a different set of stimuli altogether had not occurred to the hounds. They were after all, no matter how clever and well trained, just dogs and therefore not too swift upon their mental feet. Being canines, if they had to go no matter where or when, they went proudly. The concept of "holding it in" went way beyond them and was altogether too alien a notion to be considered, let alone given credence to. That someone or something else suffering a compulsion attack but constrained nevertheless by etiquette, might "hold it in" and in doing so twitch and fidget for reasons altogether unrelated to plotting and planning, went by the hounds entirely disregarded. The Powers That Be regarded it…but then dismissed the idea anyway. They were taking no chances and it was better to be safe than sorry. As for Helgayarn, Brunnhilde, and Betty, they suffered under no such compulsion. Somehow they held their own, keeping it all in, and maybe it's why they were so sour. Perhaps they were afflicted with the world's worst case of constipation. Who wouldn't be contrary under such conditions? They gave true meaning to the phrase, "full of crap," and in fact, such phrase had been coined behind their backs in order to more accurately paint their portraits.

    Santos knew nothing of these matters except the general idea of "going" and the proper where's and when's of going when one got down to it. Had he known anything else then perhaps he would've gotten himself a good hound too and none of this tale would need telling. He had, however, gotten himself a bad hound. Not a bad hound as hounds go whether they're going or not, just not a very good hound for going in general as it was forever resistant to house breaking and a bad hound indeed for going after rabbits. Where the farmer should've gotten a wolfhound or even a Shepherd or Rottweiler, young and fast and in its prime, he instead purchased for the family an old Chihuahua, forlorn, tired, and neurotic with nerves, that sadly it seemed, would soon need putting down at the pound. It did its best, but when it tried to make trouble, the rabbits simply pushed it out of the way. Santos didn't understand any of this and moreover, didn't want to. The complexities of just about everything always seemed to elude him. But there was no need to read the fine print in this. They were in trouble, and he'd best do something it and do it quickly.

"Junior," he repeated, "take your brother for a walk out by the garden and let him go. When he's done, leave him where he'll be safe and come back to me."

The young man did as he was told and, having deposited Laddie safely in the garden next to Jack, dug up two carrots and offered one to each. Not realizing how hungry he'd been until he'd had the chance to relieve himself, Laddie quickly accepted his dinner. Not being partial to carrots and feeling as if they'd gotten him into enough trouble already, Jack refused. Junior gave Laddie the second carrot and returned to his father.

He approached to within a safe twenty yards, the hounds ever alert to his presence. The wind shifted. It now blew from behind, coming from down yonder, past the garden and from the general direction of the Witches' temporary campsite. As it changed direction, the wind rustled leaves on the trees, causing them to engage in their ceaseless whispering. The wolfhounds did not like whisperers who could also be counted upon to be plotters and so increased their vigilance. The fact that each wind blowing brings about its own change did not sit comfortably with them either. No one, the hounds knew, was ever allowed to have "change" in their pockets except The Powers That Be who kept all Manifest Destiny and the subsequent change it brought about in their own pockets and on their own persons. Therefore the hounds could not help but wonder just what the wind and leaves were whispering about in the depths of the wood and whether or not they were in league with the boy lurking in the shadows, here to hatch plots with his father. The boy spoke, continuing his plotting. "Da, I'm back." He could see his father still standing in the doorway, face pressed anxiously against the screen door, causing little tufts of his luxurious beard to protrude through the wire mesh like black spaghetti in a colander.

"Junior, is that you?" Junior wondered just who besides himself his father thought it could be and tiredly replied in the negative. "No, it's the rabbit."

"You son of a bitch!" Santos screamed. "What did you do with my boys?' He made as if to throw open the door, but the hounds, chomping at their own collars, spun about instantly and leapt upon the porch to resume their sentry duty in front of the screen door. One hound rearing up on its hind legs threw itself at the door, its maw an open grave filled with foamy saliva and sharp white teeth. The saliva ran in vicious gobs out its mouth and over its lips, which were pulled back in a fearsome snarl. It continually rammed the door seeking ingress, its snout pressed wickedly against the screen as it tried to eat its way through the wire mesh. Santos likewise pressed against the opposite side was beyond concern. His children were out there and at the mercy of terrorists! As he pushed to open, the wolfhound on the other side pushed to close. In their mutual savagery, they were well matched, and it made for a good contest. The door would not budge. Perhaps it was because the combatants were equally pitted, one against the other. However, it was more likely the door remained stationary because Santos in his haste, forgot to unhook the eyebolt and so it remained closed despite the jarring. Santos and the hound were in each other's faces separated only by the wire mesh, pushing and clawing and exchanging fierce growls. The door was made of solid oak and the mesh a heavy gauge. Although the hook threatened once or twice to pop out of the eye, the occurrence never happened and a result the best either antagonist could do was to rumble rudely at one another while trading vicious licks through the screen door.

Junior looked upon the scene with exasperation. Father could be so trying at times! "Da!" he said again. "It's me. I'm all right!"

THE CHRISTMAS RABBIT

He pranced about, waving his arms while jumping up and down to prove the point.

Hearing his voice, the hounds wheeled about and once again leapt off the porch, all teeth and full of further rumblings, to retake their positions in the dooryard. Snarling, their lips were pulled tightly back from their fangs as their eyes tried to pierce the deep gloom of night. They were beyond merely irritated. They were at the uttermost edges of patience and at the limits of their restraint. Despite the depth of their training, these dogs were getting doggone fidgety in and of themselves and were apt to break at any moment. The ensuing melee would no doubt be bloody—even Santos could see that—as the hounds strung tighter than high-tension wire, dashed madly throughout the yard with foam on their lips, ripping and tearing anything into which they could sink their teeth. Little boys, rabbits—even vegetables weren't safe. Being out of reach the canines would doubtless leave the whispering leaves to themselves while allowing the wind to pass by unchallenged…but everything else would be dog food.

"Boy—you escaped!" Santos cried with relief.

"Da, I was only pulling your leg…you know, a joke."

The farmer pounded the door in frustration. He loved his son and was secretly proud of the fact that the boy far surpassed him in native wit and intelligence (although truth to tell there were earthworms in the garden that could challenge him there) and therefore took most of the boy's jokes at his expense with a grain of salt and fatherly patience; however, now was not the time to display such leniency. "Quit that screwing around," he said, "and save the jokes for Jack. We're in it up to our ears, boy!"

There was a certain comfort, Junior felt, knowing one's father was the master of the understatement, an authority on the obvious—although these more often than not avoided Santos too. Still such attributes on his father's part gave Junior an advantage when it came to dealing with his parents most children never realized. In terms of who was really the boss around here this perceived advantage left the boy two steps ahead and never having to look back, with his father constantly trying, in between his pursuit of the rabbits, to catch up.

Therefore, Junior most often got his own way, being allowed to steer his own course and make his own choices. It was an arrangement with which up until now he felt generally at ease. But now he sensed keenly what he'd been apparently lacking all the time and therefore unaware of—direction. Being smarter than everybody else the young lad never needed it. To him, one path *had* always been as good as the other, and heretofore he'd no problem in choosing between them or in finding his way back after having thoroughly explored his choice. Now he felt like a lost traveler without a road map and stranded at an unmarked intersection of life's highway—for the only one within miles he could turn to was another confused traveler who was more bewildered than himself as to the nature of the particular maze in which they were lost or the proper course to follow which would allow them to most readily navigate its labyrinth. "Da," he cried anxiously, "what are we going to do?"

Santos had no advice to give and always secretly dreaded the day when his son would ask for it. And although it is true that in this instance he for once got it right it did nothing to assuage his unease, for he had no idea he was getting it at all, one way or the other. He was "winging" again, but it would do no good to let the boy see that. "Easy, lad," he replied, trying to soothe the young man, "no doubt events will fall into place." The farmer tried to sound bold as he said it, lacing each syllable with all the braggadocio and invective his trembling vocal chords could muster but secretly harbored fears that with the Witches involved falling in their places could well mean falling dead on their faces. These worries prompted him to give thought to his youngest who now lay hidden and out of sight. "Junior," he asked, "where's Laddie?"

"Jiminy Cricket," Junior replied. "He's in the garden, remember? Where you told me to leave him!"

"Oh, quite… What's he doing there?"

"For Pete's sake! I don't know—sitting with the rabbit, I guess, and eating a carrot!"

Alarmed, Santos stared out at the garden. The inky blackness wrapped it in shadow while hiding those who lay concealed within. The bean poles swaying in the darkness and ripe with fruit, looked

THE CHRISTMAS RABBIT

like shaggy old monsters as they undulated slowly in the nighttime breeze while the tomato vines resembled eerily, the "Petunia Person" from the Bugs Bunny cartoons, with the flowers growing out of its head. Santos could not know this, of course—Bugs Bunny hadn't been drawn yet and a good thing too. Santos had more than his helping of trouble with the rabbits he had, serving the supper. He didn't need another in addition to those—especially one who would transcend the norm by taking such table service to incredible new heights and making it an art form. There was misery enough here already, and the farmer knew whatever his vegetables resembled as they swayed there whispering secrets in the nighttime breezes, he'd feel much better about them if they practiced their mimicry someplace else and away from his little boy. Strange, thought he, how leeks, lettuces, and the like never seemed before to be so secretly sly and queer. Colorful and bright in the sunlight with their greens almost glowing while their reds and yellows splashed the farm in an orgy of hue and tint, their demeanor changed with the setting of the sun. Now they stood silently, their colors hidden, as if the joy of living had been sucked out of them by the coming night so that they remained coldly calculating and acting like sentinels as they guarded his son. "Junior," he queried, "you didn't, you know, put Laddie in the cage with the rabbit, did you?"

"Da!"

"Well, I can't see him!"

Junior looked around in disbelief. "It's dark out."

"True," Santos said with pride, "but he's such a radiant young lad—I thought he'd stand out!"

"Da, standing out is what got us in trouble!" The young lad kicked the ground in frustration, digging up little clods of earth and scattering them randomly. It felt good to kick something! He decided he didn't like being the adult in the family. As much as he got his own way, and as often as he got to get it, still he felt in times like these that DNA had done him dirty by making him the singular dominant in an otherwise recessive gene pool. Held back and bound by the double helical chain of his parentage, he felt robbed of the wisdom and parental protection that was every child's rightful expectation. It was a rightful expectation, and he had been robbed, but DNA didn't do him dirty even though his parents ended up rubbing him in dung.

    Shortly after his birth, having learned from their doctor their newborn son suffered from some obscure disease hardly mentionable and barely pronounceable anyway, convinced it was terminal, and after having tried for years to have children of their own only to fail despite an overabundance of attention and effort, we can perhaps see what might have lead Juniors *real* parents, the Dawes, to sneak into the maternity ward late one night and switch their ailing son for the healthy son of Mrs. Santos—even if we can't understand it. Nevertheless, it happened. It was a terrible thing to do no matter what the circumstances, and their stomachs soured as they did it. But fate pays you back. It always does, and this couple should've known that even if they knew nothing else, just as they should've known not to mess with the Family Santos—which even back then enjoyed, some would say suffered, a reputation for oddity. It was, after all, plain to see that the Santoses were doing quite well despite the nearly insurmountable odds stacked against them. Any other family would have buckled by now, and yet somehow the Santoses seemed to bear up under it—if only just barely. You would think any fool looking could see for himself that these were people whom fate and coincidence stood guard over as if saving them for something important. How else could you explain such unwarranted success? How else account for the unaccountable? There are people in this life who seem to sail through it, the wind off their quarters and their sheets full of hot air despite the fact you and I both know their riggings are all tangled and in knots. Yet on they sail, calm seas and no storms. Life is easy for such as they, and we know someone somewhere must be watching out for them. At times we may even get a little jealous. It's okay. It's normal, and we can admit it. No one's going to tell. Yet no matter how green we become, the one thing we never do if we're smart is to get in their way. It's not that we're particularly afraid of them or feel out of our league—in fact, the exact opposite is true, and we know ourselves to be their superiors in every way. But things just have a way of working out for them. For some unknown reason, they have karma at their helm, and she steers them a bold course and does so for motives of her own. Common sense tells us to have nothing to do with such people for the fates smile kindly upon them. These folks are caught up in the middle of great forces they can barely sense let alone understand, and they're bad juju for people like us. They have a way of turning our worlds upside down by mere association while they alone walk right side up. They're not good for us, and we have as little to do with them as possible, sensing perhaps, the bad ends most of them will inevitably lead us to while avoiding such calamity themselves.

    The farmer and his wife were nothing like those just mentioned. It was never smooth sailing upon the good ship Santos, which was forever off course and rudderless, adrift upon seas of confusion, and caught in a gray and unyielding trough as said seas strove unceasingly to suck them under. Somehow, against all odds, they invariably made headway. It was more than uncanny. It was terrifying when contemplated too closely. It proved the world and everything in it was capricious at best, and spinning for reasons of its own while everyone held on helplessly and went along for the ride. The family Santos in all its generations, each wrapped in tall tale, rumor, and eccentricity, and displaying such devices with pride as if they were part of the family crest, stood there with all their ancestors that ever were and all their descendants yet-to-be, as an apparent warning to us we are never in control of anything, that we succeed or fail for reasons beyond our understanding as if we were a chorus of puppets all having our strings pulled. Clan Santos, in their very existence, embodied the idea that any action taken as a matter of free will was, in fact, merely an act of conceit—that all affairs were preordained and taken into account by someone or something who was going to have their own way in the matter despite what you or I or anyone else have to say about it. How else could one explain this family and all the weird history which wrapped itself about them? For the farmer was not the first scion of the clan to be taken note of. His family tree and the progenitors who made up its roots and branches had long since become the stuff of legend for their many eccentricities and oddities by folk throughout the land who of an evening sat quietly by the fire listening to tales and stories told by their elders of that mad family from across the way and the wacky deeds of its various members. It seemed that in their eccentricity, Clan Santos provided the best bad example for miles around, and parents passed on legends of this family to their children as if each legend were a lesson. Most of it was made up, of course, and most folk suspected it was so, for how could any one person never mind an entire clan, survive let alone thrive, in the face of such seemingly odd and bizarre circumstances? Just as most folk knew not every member of the Santos family had been thus afflicted. Not even half so the stories told, and barely a third at that. Still a third of the pie was quite a big slice and one funny apple could spoil a whole barrel. Just because an ancient progenitor of House Santos might prove him or herself to be improbably normal did not mean he or she or those around them would not be affected and influenced by a third cousin, twice removed, who wasn't. But the bulk of karma, it seemed, was passed on in some indirect sort of way from father to son and occasionally daughter, until it culminated in the person of Farmer Santos. It did not manifest itself with each and every generation, oh no. Even fate feared to tamper too much or too directly one way or the other with that particular family, afraid perhaps that even it had bitten off more than it could chew. So it paused, often for a generation or two and sometimes more, to give karma and kismet a rest (and lord knows they needed it), usually when circumstances got flakiest, as they seemed to be now. One could never be sure where, when, or on what branch of the tree this influence might crop up like a blight, infecting what would otherwise have been fine timber. The family knew only two things—first, however fate chose its players within this family, and for whatever the reason, its influence could be felt most acutely on those family members who could claim to be direct descendants of Elizias Santos, the ancient patriarch of Clan Santos and the personage with whom all the trouble and weirdness seems to have begun. Second, those directly under the influence to whatever degree manifested a strange strawberry-colored birthmark which bore the likeness of an eagle's talon on their persons, much the same as the one Farmer Santos hid discreetly under his luxurious black beard. This mark was never in the same place and not always on a body part which could be hidden, and the family came to regard it as karma's calling card. It was as good an explanation as any, and it seemed to hold true for like it or not every member thus tattooed, from grand old Elizias on down, dueled defiantly with destiny. It was Elizias himself, the patriarch of the clan, who at the ripe old age of sixty-five, after siring five children—all of whom had the birthmark, set out on a sea voyage to prove the earth was flat. We, of course, know it ain't so. However, that didn't stop old Elizias. With his two eldest sons and a crew of twenty, he set sail to make his point. And despite the fact our planet is round Elizias managed to find the edge anyway, sailing right off its precipice and into oblivion, taking his two sons with him and nineteen of the crew. It was a lone survivor that somehow managed to find his way back to well-traveled shipping lanes who returned with the tale of disaster. He described a sea where the ocean was solid and the air was liquefied, where the sun rose in the west and set in the east, where the moon shone continually with the color of blood and where the stars fell from the sky at night, spitting brimstone and sulfur. "The Great Sea of Despair" was the name this survivor gave to that vast part of the ocean and not a soul who heard his tale doubted his account for no one had been born yet who could lie so convincingly. Yet when an attempt was made to retrace the route and perhaps locate Elizias and the great crack in the earth, not a clue regarding either could be found—despite the fact the sole survivor of the previous voyage was pressed into service and therefore made to be an unwilling participant of the recovery effort. Chained to the mast so he could not escape, he was fed short rations with little water to ensure his passivity and cooperation. Still, the Great Sea of Despair was not to be located. Some began to doubt his tale and scoff at the mariner—until the third eldest son, having fathered a son and a daughter himself who thankfully were free of the mark, set sail with another crew of twenty…never to be seen nor heard from again.

Fate took a rest in the third son's children, but not for long. Their children each had the birthmark, as did their children's children. And so it went, although no other Santos ever again took to sea. They didn't need to journey abroad to find the eccentric and unusual. Weirdness and eccentricity were awaiting them right at home. There was old Rhymin' Santos, who always talked backward and always in verse despite his best efforts to talk straight. There was Sandy Santos, the man who wouldn't die—he lived to the ripe old age of 210 despite being knifed five times and gut-shot twice as well as having endured three bouts of malaria, a case of whooping cough, and the first documented incidence of the Clap. There was Elva Santos, matron of old, who it was said could talk to all the animals although her favorite conversationalists were cats—and of course, she despised rabbits. And Wrongway Santos, who forever walked backward yet made forward progress nevertheless. Ebenezer Santos, a miserly misanthrope, affectionately known as "The Scrooge" who, when he died, became the only person in recorded history to discover a way to "take it all with him" only to find once he got to where he was going that there was nowhere to spend it. And hosts of others on and on and down through the ages until the epitome of eccentricity was reached in Farmer Santos himself. And I must reiterate—all these personages were well-known and referred to back in Olden Days, so Junior's parents, the Dawes, should've realized the trouble they were buying into, and perhaps they did but decided to go ahead with their nefarious scheme anyway. Here's how it happened:

Having been told by their quack doctor that their baby was a terminal case, his parents snuck in to the maternity ward late one night and switched him for the sickly child of Mrs. Santos. Their doctor, who was also the Santos's physician as well, was the quack of quacks, and it was Mrs. Santos's child who actually had the terminal illness. The confusion occurred when the doctor mixed up the medical charts, allowing the mistake to go unnoticed—the hospital being severely understaffed and the nurses spread far too thin to take note. The one person who did catch on was quickly and quietly bought off and for a pitiful sum at that. Santos had been waylaid by rabbits en route to the hospital and was unable to protect his offspring while Mrs. Santos, having given birth to a sickly son who was born malformed and twisted almost beyond description, suffered through thirty-eight hours of backbreaking, soul-wrenching labor, and was thus drugged beyond belief during the birth and afterward too and therefore blissfully unaware she'd even brought forth a son.

THE CHRISTMAS RABBIT

The chart-mixing quack presided over both deliveries while single-handedly trying to run the infirmary and the emergency room as well. As said, the hospital was short-staffed and he was the only doctor in that neck of the woods. Pushed beyond his limits and strung out on coffee and the acrid scent of rubbing alcohol, it is perhaps understandable to see how he could've made such a colossal blunder. Be that as it may, when he found a free moment, he went, mixed-up medical chart in hand, to console the unfortunate Dawes.

Junior's parents were practical people from a faraway place who spoke in a funny accent and who gave little thought to the consequences of their actions. Not great people but not bad ones either as people go—just simply not up to the tests in human kindness and fair play with which they were now confronted. They listened carefully as the doctor deciphered the medicalese and hospital jargon contained on the mixed-up chart, all the time doing his best to make less of the worst of it. The Dawes were not fooled though. They kept pressing him with their questions and backing him into corners from which he found it increasingly difficult to escape, until he did what all doctors do when in similar situations—he fell back on the same medical jargon and technical crap he'd been called upon to explain in the first place. Finally, not having the answers to those difficult questions as is so often the case, the quack resorted to simple bull. "Cattle craps!" exclaimed Mrs. Dawe, angry, heartbroken, and frustrated. "This can nae be right. Our wee bairn looks as healthy as a horse and as sweet as an angel." Her husband held her comfortingly and tried to soothe her while the doctor, unaware of the mix-up and his own mistake, looked on with heartfelt pity. This poor woman had enough misery coming her way. If seeing her child as a little cherub helped her to deal with and make sense of this terrible tragedy, then far be it for him to convince her otherwise by pointing out that what she gave birth to appeared angelic in no way whatsoever and in fact had exited her womb looking more like a wounded water buffalo. In the end, lost in a sea of seemingly endless and inexplicable symptoms and tired of trying to fathom a tidal wave of unintelligible answers to questions they weren't even aware they were asking, the Dawes, in their heart-wrenching sadness, finally gave up trying to understand the hows and whys of the tragedy and concentrated instead on finding a solution. They could not, of course, unmake the baby. Even if it were possible—if doing so meant reliving the whole ordeal in reverse then Mrs. Dawe preferred a different resolution. Simple abandonment, they knew, would be looked upon with utter contempt and was therefore not an option and murder was too new of an idea for either of them to be familiar with. There was, however, just down the hall, the dumb farmer's wife fresh from a delivery of her own and out cold. The farmer and his wife's reputations preceded them, of course, and therefore weren't unknown to the couple contemplating the switch, who rationalized to themselves that given the identity and reputation of the two parents, exchanging the Santos child for their own would in fact be doing it a favor. And they would have been right had they been correct with their assumptions but since they were wrong through no fault of their own, ended up being boneheaded kidnappers and entirely at fault. The sadness and misery they heaped upon themselves was certainly no more than they merited although the unhappiness poor Junior inherited for having been an innocent victim who just happened to be in the right place but in the wrong hands was surely more than he deserved—even if he did turn out to be such a tiresome and overbearing little snot!

"Maybe," Junior now said, "blending into the background and behaving like normal people is exactly what's called for here." He paused for a few seconds to let that sink into the Old Man's head and then continued. "Give up a few carrots, why don't ya—and let the whole thing blow over! Whaddya say?"

"Give up?" Santos asked incredulously. "There's such a thing as principle, son. Those vegetables are mine! Do you hear me? Mine! No gang of four-footed ruffians or tribunal of menopausal matrons will make me hand them over!" It was true; there was such a thing as principle. It was alive and doing well, even back in Olden Days. It was standing up for it however that often caused trouble—just as it still does today. Principles often become the gallows we build upon which we hang ourselves. Or we carefully shape and mold them into tall narrow pedestals so we can precariously balance atop of them. When the inevitable fall comes, as it usually does, we end up busting

THE CHRISTMAS RABBIT

our butts or quite possibly breaking our necks. Principally speaking, as a paying investment, principles are often a high-risk venture netting a very low yield and hardly worth the principal themselves let alone any interest one might have to pay for having held them in the first place. Junior understood this. Santos didn't. Instead, he chose to keep his principles in a revolving account while letting them grow and compound until he became buried under their weight. When his stock split—and it split often—it created dangerous cracks in his portfolio, causing his market to crash and his principles to flounder, which, of course, led to a depression for him and his entire family. Ironically, it was his conflict with the rabbits which led to his partial salvation, for as everyone knows, there's nothing like a good war to get you out of a deep depression. "Not the merest turnip," he continued, "will I turn over to thieves and ruffians—"

"But, Da," Junior replied with a shake of his head, "look around you—we have rows upon rows of em'!" It was true. In terms of both quality and quantity, they were rowing right along.

"So?" asked Santos offhandedly, as if such a fact mattered one way or the other. "Am I to give them away to any beggar or thief who just happens to hop by, is that it?"

"Well," the boy countered, "there is the idea of charity. After all, could it hurt?"

"Well, it certainly couldn't help! And besides, charity begins at home. How many times have I told you that?"

Junior looked around forlornly in the dark, despairing entirely of the notion he would ever get his father to see the point—that although charity did indeed begin at home, the word *begin* implied it had a journey upon which to embark, that it left the house, got out for a while, and saw a bit of the world while making a few friends and leaving a few memories. To do less, especially when gifted with so much and in the face of such dire consequences, was not only uncharitable but not very good strategy either, thought Junior, who deemed a few vegetables handpicked by Da himself and offered to all and sundry with particular emphasis placed upon rabbits would do much to diffuse the situation.

Santos, however, didn't see it that way. "And besides," he continued, "there's talk roundabout, regarding another possible Ice Age, whatever that is. Therefore we need to stock up and hoard for ourselves!" Junior could have explained in a minute the notion of Ice Age, and just what said notion might imply, however explaining it in terms simple enough for his father to comprehend could take hours. With dinner being served at any moment, he felt that neither he nor his father had the luxury of indulging themselves in such trivia. And besides, what bearing could it have upon their current situation? Junior could see none, but neither could he see the value in wasting precious moments arguing with his father by pointing that out. What he didn't realize and therefore couldn't relate to was that in this instance Santos was probably right.

Back when they first stumbled upon the idea of seasons and the delicious notion of climate control such seasons would engender along with the subsequent boundaries they would therefore erect, and knowing those boundaries would no doubt add leverage to their already fulsomely fulcrumed positions as they strove to push the world at large in a direction it preferred not going, The Powers That Be attacked the problem with unbridled passion and blind ambition. It's a pity for us all they didn't take better care to see exactly where they were stepping because they ended up pushing all of us, then and now, into the biggest pile of cattle craps that has ever been anywhere anytime, and from which ultimately, there appears to be no escape. In their haste to get the ball rolling, the trio turned in a package of exotic elixirs and potions, poorly conceived and inadequately mixed, based upon formulas ill formed and improperly stirred and all deriving from erroneous equations—the effort and expenditure of The Powers That Be as they put all of their meager skills into the problem's resolution. The rub, they felt, came not in doing the job itself. That, they knew, was easy. The mechanics and the math of it were child's play and therefore obvious. It was in laying the proper foundation which would allow the experiment to take root and grow that they were rubbing up against problems. To effect the changes they desired, they took elements of climate from one part of the planet and shifted them to another where they were wanted and needed. Wind and water, cold and heat, dampness and aridity—it was an enormous undertaking and one beyond the scope of anything they'd heretofore attempted. What they needed was a catalyst. What they came up with was a catastrophe. Knowing opposites such as heat and cold, fire and ice, are first attracted to each other before they're mutually repelled and needing an instrument that would gather those opposites up and then ultimately scatter them until each landed in its respective place, they invented the glacier—which as everyone knows who's seen one before, plays hell with the weather and can change an environment faster than a mother of five can change a diaper. The problem with their crazy concoction was a twisted mixture of snowballs and silly putty, which constitutes the major ingredient of what would much later come to be known as the "superball." It was a dangerous decoction, highly unstable, and a bear to formulate, so when the Witches first let go their glacier they, in fact, let loose a gusher that became the first Ice Age, and just like those superballs we all remember from the psychedelic sixties; once it was let go, it seemed it could do nothing but gather continued momentum. Onward and outward it went, gathering speed and gobbling up territory until it covered nearly two thirds of the planet. Weather patterns shifted as well as the continents they blew over while oceans froze solid and tropical jungles grew arid and desertlike. The howling winds scattered loess and fine soil in a frenzy that created a thick dusty cloud which hovered close to the earth, choking those unfortunate few left who were around back then but who weren't lucky enough to be wiped out in the initial disaster. Eventually, after many seasons of continued suffering, the glacier drew back and over time things returned to normal—except, of course, now the few who were left were stuck with those damned seasons, which none of them wanted in the first place.

    It would not go away forever though would this huge hungry beast that came to be known as Ice Age. Because of its basic matrix, even in retreat, it bounced continuously, never stopping its agitated movement; and like the superball, just when you thought you were rid of it, came hurtling back at an entirely unexpected time and from a completely unanticipated direction. So it retreated but did so with the intention of coming back even stronger—which it did as the

Second Ice Age, remembered by elder folk in Olden days as a time best forgotten. Thus, when they spoke of a coming Third Ice Age, they spoke from experience, and there could be no doubt what they spoke was the truth in its simplicity and therefore treated like gospel. None of this impressed Junior, however, who felt its immediacy was a question of perspective. Imminent in glacial terms, he knew, could mean as much as five thousand years or perhaps even twenty. It was therefore not a concern he felt needed to be on the front burner. "So what?" he asked his father despairingly, "are we supposed to do with the vegetables, blanch 'em?"

Santos thought it a capital idea and began to envision an Eden wherein all his produce, including the rutabagas, were parboiled and safely tucked away in mason jars with rabbit-proof lids equipped with Yale padlocks and security card accesses when the whispering wind, blowing down from the Winnebago, brought to his nostrils the most noxious odor any nose has ever had the misfortune of "nosing" anywhere. Sweet and sour like rotting rhubarb, it was thoroughly corrupt. The wind which carried it blew on by, but somehow the stench lingered pungent and thick. In the garden the lettuce leaves wilted and the tomato vines drooped. The three wolfhounds, having the most sensitive smellers, began rolling around on the ground and howling with their tails tucked between their legs. Their ears drooped in defeat until finally the virulence of the olfactory assault simply overloaded their senses, causing them to roll over as if dead. Santos breathed a sigh of contentment as he recognized the familiar scent of his wife's home cooking. Judging by his smeller, the farmer determined his wife had far outdone herself. True, it smelled pretty sour and therefore probably tasted worse than a cattle crap creamsicle, but Santos had never known better and, being a cheapskate, rarely afforded his family the opportunity to eat out. Suddenly he remembered just whom it was that was being served this dubious repast and therefore knew the time had come for him to take control. "Junior!" he commanded. "You have to take Laddie and go!"

"Go? Da, I just took Laddie and went! Will you please focus?" Junior, who perhaps didn't understand and who was therefore not as smart as he liked to make out, was beyond frustrated and well on the way to being out-and-out terrified. But the farmer didn't hold it against him. Impotent fear in the face of a seemingly insurmountable obstacle could do that to a person—it was something Santos himself had a measure of expertise in and which he could relate to and sympathize with. "Boy," he said gently, "I don't mean go, I mean leave."

Junior looked up at the stars as if seeking guidance. Turning back to his Da, he asked, "What good will whispering like leaves do?"

"No, no, no!" Santos screamed in reply, only to pause for the briefest of moments to consider just how silly *that* sounded. "I don't mean be like leaves and whisper—I mean, be like leaves and leave! Scram, scat, vamoose. Hit the road!"

Junior's face fell as he misjudged both his father's meaning and intent. Da, it seemed, didn't love him anymore and perhaps even considered him at least partially responsible for the mess they were in. *No doubt he's right,* Junior thought. The self-loathing and guilt which merely harried him earlier now came back with full force to assail him like a charging rhino, and he could feel it pressing painfully inward, squeezing him like an overripe peach. His stomach, suddenly sour, felt as though it dropped through his groin and down to the bottom of his feet only to lie there uncomfortably in an ungainly purplish lump, churning sourly and excreting bile. A high-pitched buzzing began its assault on his ears while his temples pounded like bass drums, sending echoes and reverberations crawling down his neck to entwine themselves like serpents around the vertebrae of his spine and squeezing like pythons, applied their pressures in an almost offhanded and detached sort of way—like snakes choking squirrels. Slowly the boy came forward—not out of fear of the dogs who were beyond anyone's help and too caught up in the throes of the malignant miasma which surrounded them to do too much or care one way or the other about who or what might be invading the space they'd been designated to defend, but rather the onerous weight of guilt which now rested squarely upon him served to leaden his footsteps, causing his feet to sink deeply into the soft loamy soil with every step he took. He passed the dogs without incident, having only to take care he was not bowled over as they rolled around fitfully in their semicoma. With head bowed, he came up to the porch but then stopped at the foot of the steps, unsure of himself and his position. Slowly he looked up and confronting the tender look of affection he saw displayed in his Da's eyes, felt confused and lost at sea. "Da," he meekly asked, "what did I do?"

For in truth, although Junior did, in fact, feel as if the responsibility for this current disaster could be laid squarely at his feet he could not, for the life of him, understand why.

More confused than normal, Santos replied, "Do? Why you didn't do anything, boy! It was those damned rabbits who started all this—but I'll finish it!" He shook the screen door as if to display his determination.

"Then why are you sending Laddie and I away?" Junior asked. "If we didn't do anything, then why do we have to go?" Junior's eyes began to slowly water, filling with tears and causing his Da to become an indistinct blur in the evening gloom, a fuzzy silhouette casting inky shadows in the weak and wavering beams issuing from the kitchen's singular candle which sputtered a tired and sickly flame from somewhere deep within the room. He did not want to go away and was sure Laddie would not take well to the idea either.

Looking down at the boy, Santos felt that his heart must surely break. But there could be no help for it. They were in cattle craps up to their ears, and it was his responsibility to shovel them out in any manner he could. He had to be firm now and not give in to misguided emotion—especially when there was such temptation to do so. Either way, Santos knew, there was bound to be trouble and lots of it. The boy would need every ounce of skill, cunning, and dumb luck he could lay hold of if he were to save himself and his brother from the unseemly fate which Santos could sense weaving itself around them. His original intent had been for the boys to gather up their mother before leaving but since learning of the dinner plans and subsequently smelling them too, now harbored doubts about whether or not the Witches would let his wife go free and instead determined they were more likely to detain and punish her too—if that is, the trio were still standing by the time they partook of dessert. "Boy," he said kindly, "there's no guilt for you here, so don't go taking any with you when you leave, but you can see the situation we're in, can't you?" He pointed off in the general direction of the trio's campsite. "You know how crazy those three are, don't you?"

"Yes," Junior replied. "That's why you need me here with you! I can help. I—"

"That," interrupted the farmer, "is exactly what I don't need. And the best way you can help me is by helping you and your brother to get out of here!" The farmer knew he was getting overly excited and saw his agitation mirrored in the young lad's countenance. Santos took the fist of his right hand and enclosed it within the palm of his left while bringing both thoughtfully up to rest under his chin as if to support his brain while it puzzled this ponderous problem through. "Look," he said, "I know you're pretty bright and all that—I mean, you ain't much to look at, boy—Laddie's the looker, but you've got my brains (which thankfully he did not)—and yet the best either of us can admit to is we don't know what the heck is gonna happen here." Santos paused to let the grim reality of that fact settle in. "I want you and Laddie away from here when the pellets hit the wind."

"But what about you and Ma?"

"Don't worry about us," Santos replied, "we'll be okay."

Junior looking up at his Da, offering him a puzzled frown. "If you're going to be all right," he asked, "then why do we have to leave?"

Santos was at a loss. The boy had him there. Just another example, he supposed, of his son's greater mastery of the art of circular thinking. "Okay," he replied, both anxious and frustrated, "we're not going to be okay—we're in mortal danger—which is why I want you to take your brother and go. Quickly. Okay?"

"Okay."

Too many more bouts of these verbal fisticuffs, traded under the pressure of such oncoming dread and exchanged with his son in a contest in which he knew Junior held the advantage, and Santos felt sure that rather than be okay, he'd be k'od, and so prompted the young lad to get moving.

"Well, what are you waiting for?" asked he. "Roll on out!"

"But, Da," Junior asked while looking about uncertainly, unsure of where to flee, "where do we go, and more importantly, when can we come back?"

"Where and when," replied Santos, "are not as important as *how far*. You just keep running, boy, and don't stop. As to coming home, when it's safe to come back, I'll come get you myself."

"How?"

"Whaddya mean *how*?"

"I mean *how*," Junior replied, kicking the ground. "We're going and you're staying, so how are you going to find us? You want we should leave a trail of breadcrumbs?"

"No, of course not," Santos replied, ignoring his son's sarcasm. "Breadcrumbs won't do at all—the rabbits will eat 'em! Use radishes instead. Everybody knows rabbits hate radishes—you should be safe!"

"Da!" Junior replied. "If the rabbits hate them so much, why not just grow radishes? Then wouldn't they just bother someone else? Our problems would be solved!"

"Perhaps, boy," Santos answered in wistful reply, "but I'm not overly fond of the little garnish myself, and besides you've seen what your Ma can do with a pound of taters. Can you imagine the trouble she'd cause with a ration of radishes? There'd be no end to it. It's too frightening to imagine!" He let his hands fall to his sides, weary and tired. "Best be going now."

Still Junior held out. "But, Da, radishes won't work. Even if they're not your particular favorite or held in much regard by rabbits either—that's not going to hold true for everyone. Someone or something is bound to come along and eat 'em." Santos scratched his head. "Can't for the life of me see why," he replied.

"Trust me, Da, this one's a no-brainer. Radishes won't work, and besides, since you hate 'em so, we didn't plant any this year, remember?"

"Oh right!" Santos chuckled, laughing off that serious lapse. "Rocks then," he said. "Leave a trail of rocks."

Junior stared at his father in amazed disbelief. *No one*, he thought, *could possibly be so naive*. "Rocks? Da, there isn't a sack big enough to carry all the rocks we'll need."

"Well, use two then. Laddie can help."

"Da!"

"Besides, they make good weapons."

THE CHRISTMAS RABBIT

"Oh yeah?" Junior replied, and he bent down to gather one up as if to test his Da's last statement. Choosing a specimen about the size of an egg, he began to playfully toss it back and forth from hand to hand, measuring its weight and balance. It felt cold in his palm. Its coarse grain and rough edges, chaffing his skin as it was tossed from hand to hand, caused him to break out in a sweat as he stood there contemplating it. In his gut, Junior knew this was a mistake. Rocks, and the reasons for throwing them, were what landed them in this predicament in the first place. He, therefore, had little faith in their utility, however applied, as a means of extracting them from the situation in which they found themselves. Suddenly the rock and all it stood for felt dirty and corrupt in his palm, and he threw it down with disgust. As he did so an idea came to him, and it was brilliant! "Da!" he shouted gleefully. "Let me be your attorney! Who's got the biggest mouth? Me! Who can lay it on as thick as buffalo hides? Me again! Who can charm the birds out of their trees while at the same time baffle 'em with bull and confuse 'em with cattle craps? Me—that's who!" Junior danced about, barely able to contain his excitement as his plan took shape. "Oh, Da, *pulease* say I can do it!"

Santos looked at his boy with admiration. No doubt everything the young lad said was true, and Santos found himself in awe as he contemplated his son and just what he might become when, and if, he finally came into his own. He'd be unstoppable. A worthy ally and a wicked enemy. Santos wondered if and when this were all over and done, and if they each respectively lived through it, whether or not it would be time to take the young lad with him when he went out hunting rabbits. Together, he knew, they could easily end the dispute in a fortnight. He felt sure of it. But the problem with his son's plan was it just might work—too well, in fact, and the Witches, having been outdone, outargued, and embarrassed by a youngster would surely pull out all the stops in an effort to get even. Santos shuddered at the implied consequences of such unbridled revenge. "No, son," he admonished, "I don't want you in this. No way, no how. It's time to take Laddie and get going."

Just as these last words were uttered, three dreadful shrieks pierced the gloom. Tearing through the night air their pitch started off high and whiny like the howl of banshees or the sound of fingernails scraping across blackboards, and then on an uneven scale each descended in note, both deep and loud, until they sounded like the very ground itself suffering through the throes of a major quake, as it groaned in agony and wailed in the torment of being twisted. The unearthly din woke the wolfhounds who, ignoring Junior even though he was in the dooryard, took off as if an alarm had been rung. "They've tasted Ma's cooking," Santos cried out in dismay, "now run for your lives!"

"But how—"

"There's no time left to argue! I'll find you even if I have to search for a hundred lifetimes to do it. Now go!" And so, with his head bowed and his spirits low, Junior started back toward the garden, to Laddie, and to his uncertain future.

"Wait!" Santos cried out to his receding form, "make me a promise, boy, before you go." Junior turned around. He couldn't believe it. The dogs were gone, all hell was about to break loose, and his father still remained in the house. "Why don't you just come with us?" he asked. "The dogs have left. We can make good our escape and in the confusion, gather up Ma!"

"Can't do," his Da replied. "Oh, I know, given your Ma's cooking, there's a better-than-even chance that the Witches may have eaten their last meal, but then again, they may not."

"Do you really think so?"

"I don't know what to think, son—but it's possible. If anything could lay 'em out, it would be your Ma's cooking! But perhaps they're even tough enough to withstand that—in which case either they or their stupid dogs are bound to come back, and none of them will be at all happy with me if upon their return they've found I've absconded. Besides, someone has to stay behind and protect mother. So what about that promise?"

"What promise?" Junior asked.

"The one you were just about to make," replied Santos,

"Da, I can't make a promise if I don't know what it is—not even to you."

"Consider it a condemned man's last wish."

THE CHRISTMAS RABBIT

"All right," Junior replied ambivalently, "I'll consider it. Now what the heck is it?"

"Junior!"

"Okay. What is it"?

"The rabbit son, before you leave, why don't you put him out of his misery?"

"Da," Junior replied uncertainly, "I don't know. At the very least, it sounds time-consuming. Can we afford to waste such precious moments when the ladies, if they live, are most likely to do it for you?"

"I think the trio are in league with those four-footed ruffians," Santos replied, "and therefore nothing can be relied upon. Nothing. So promise me—out of his misery, once and for all, before you take off!" Santos brought all his skills in parental persuasion to bear upon his young son in order to ensure himself his last request would be fulfilled.

Of course, his skills were negligible and, when taken as a whole, amounted to very little. However, as in all cases like this, wherein misguided parents seek to control both the destiny and direction of their children's lives, little skill in constructive persuasion is actually needed. Whatever abilities in inducement parents lack can be more than compensated for by the amount of implied guilt they bring to bear instead. Even back in Olden Days, parents had been doing this for years and Santos was no exception. Finally, feeling as though he'd been unwillingly backed into an uncomfortable corner from which he could not escape, Junior reluctantly agreed.

Walking back to the garden to gather up Laddie, Junior pondered his vow while wondering if there was some way for him to do it and yet still be able to live with himself after fulfilling his promise. It was an unfair situation, although Junior knew there was no use in crying about it. Parents had been putting their children in unfair situations for ages and he saw no hope of them ever letting up. Perhaps, thought the young lad, if parents were merely self-centered, then there might be some chance of cessation. But because most parents tried to do well and honestly had their children's best interests at heart and yet were nevertheless preoccupied with their own dislikes and prejudices, Junior felt such unfairness would perpetuate and continue, unchecked and unabated. It was the way of the world, and Junior saw no hope of derailing it. It didn't mean, however, that something creative couldn't be done in this particular case. Thus, Junior gave himself over to contemplation and by the time he reached the garden, had his answer.

One of his Da's problems, Junior knew, was that he was not always as exact with his wording as he should've been. This left much of what he said open to scrutiny and therefore misinterpretation. In fact, Junior learned early on that taking anything his Da said at face value was an unwarranted gamble and inherently risky. Da said, "Put the rabbit out of its misery," and that's just what Junior figured to do but not however in the way his father figured he'd do it. Putting something out of its misery could be accomplished by any number of given methods. Junior chose the one that would least likely add fuel to the already dangerous fire which even now threatened to flare up out of control and consume them. Junior sought to put out such a dangerous conflagration and by doing so, secure an ally. He walked up to Jack's cage. "I've come," he said, "as my Da requested, to put you out of your misery."

"Are you man enough?" Jack replied, baring his wicked little teeth. "Just ask your father—I cut him to ribbons!"

"Oh, do tell!" Junior exclaimed. "I saw the cut for myself, and you barely broke skin! I think he'll live."

Jack affected an air of indifference. "Oh really?" he replied. "Just you let me outta here, sonny, and the two of us will have another go at it! What do you think about that?" Jack scratched at his cage while hissing at his confinement, displaying, he felt, his unbridled ferocity.

Junior laughed…and then laughed some more. My, but it felt good to let loose with a hearty chuckle! Jack was after all, just one rabbit and not really a threat to anybody with the exception perhaps of Da. Still, Junior had a job to do and very little time in which to do it. "I'm not going to bandy words with you," he replied and with that opened the door to the cage and let it fall. "There," he said, "the cage is open. You're free and out of your misery."

THE CHRISTMAS RABBIT

Jack scrunched down upon the floor of the cage prepared for an attack, scenting the air furiously and seeking out hidden menace. "What gives?" he asked. Why are you letting me go?"

"Does it matter?" Junior replied. "You're free."

Jack felt the fur on the nape of his neck bristling. "Does it matter? It damned well matters to me! Jack scrutinized the immediate area carefully to assure himself there were no hidden traps. You belong to that nut back there in the house—why should I trust you?"

"I'm his son…"

"Exactly," Jack interrupted. "Just another next-generation farm boy out to deprive an honest rabbit of a hard-earned carrot!"

Junior couldn't believe his ears. Of all the cheek! He wondered if perhaps he'd made a mistake and erred in his plans. *Well, too late,* he thought. *The little rascal will bound out of the cage before I can get the door closed.* "Hard-earned?" he asked, his voice laced with sarcasm. "You steal our carrots and anything else you and your kind can get your dirty little paws on. You're thieves—and you deserve what you get!"

"Of course, we're thieves," Jack replied, taking a tentative hop out of the cage in case the young lad was having second thoughts. "But," he continued, "if that's the way you see things, then we're all thieves—you, me, that nut in the house—"

"I told you," Junior said dangerously, "that's my Da!"

"All right," Jack replied to placate him. "All right. But you can't deny the truth of the matter. You're just as guilty as I."

Junior squinted with skepticism, wondering what sort of cattle craps he was being asked to consume. "Oh," he replied, "and why is that?"

Jack shook his head, laughing softly to himself as one does when one is trying to get another to see a point which up until then has remained hidden. He paused to flick a speck of dirt from off his paw. "They say you're the smart one in the family—that your brain works fast and your tongue even faster. All that true?"

"Well," Junior replied shyly, "I hate to brag."

"Then why can't you see it?"

"See what?"

"That we're all thieves."

"How so?" Junior asked.

Jack scrutinized the young lad carefully for a second or two as he tried to make the little twit see his point. "Look around you," he said, "and tell me what you see."

Junior did as he was told, casting his eyes this way and that, his orbs trying to pierce the gloom. Frustrated, he replied, "I can't see anything. It's dark out and the beanpoles are blocking my view."

"No kidding," the rabbit replied acidly. "But you know what's out there anyway. Describe it to me."

"Well," Junior replied, uncertain as to how to begin, "there's the house, of course, right over there, and the garden we're standing in."

"Right," Jack agreed. "And how did they get here?"

"Come again?"

Jack looked around and laughed some more. "I mean," said he, "just how in hell did they get here? Did they just spring up like weeds overnight, or is there another answer?"

Junior bowed his head while shuffling his feet nervously. He was an exceptionally bright boy, more so than Jack Rabbit gave him credit for. He rarely lost an argument but sensed nevertheless he might be about to lose one now for he could see where this rascally rabbit's chain of logic was heading and knew from a certain point of view, the rabbit's anyway, that the hare was right. "Well, no," he reluctantly replied. "Da and I cleared the land."

"And then some," Jack said. "You cleared it all right. And knocked down quite a number of good trees to do it. Why, I'm told there was an ancient willow back in my great-grandfather's time, which stood right where your house stands now. This land belonged to that tree long before it belonged to you. That tree fed off this land and nourished itself on the soil in which it was planted. You stole from that old tree. And not just the tree. There were birds living in old man willow. Birds of a feather all flocking together—and squirrels and chipmunks too. When you knocked down that tree, you stole their home—and as if that wasn't enough, you added insult to injury by carving up their home to make a house for yourselves." Jack stamped his hind legs. He was normally a pretty easygoing fellow.

THE CHRISTMAS RABBIT

Easygoing, that is, until he mounted his soapbox and got to preaching. "So whaddya say to that?"

"I'd say despite all the 'raping and pillaging,' you're charging us with you rabbits have come out of it pretty handily, and now have all the taters, carrots, and rutabagas any warren could ever walk away with and therefore are in no position to criticize!"

"Don't go clouding up the issue with facts," the rabbit replied snidely. "This isn't about facts. It's about consequences—try again!"

"How about 'I'm sorry'?" Junior offered up contritely.

"Not good enough!" Jack stamped his hind legs again. "You know, there was a wise old owl who lived in that tree. A good friend of my Grandpap's. Anyway, after Santos got done the wise old owl, the birds of a feather, the squirrels, the chipmunks, and everyone else that called Old Man Willow home were forced to relocate and are now making out as best as they can in that confounded high rise development on the other side of the forest." He paused momentarily to hop over to a head of lettuce and rip off a leaf, all the while keeping a baleful eye cast upon Junior, making it plain to him he considered the lettuce leaf rightfully earned and worth contending for. Junior took the point and not the lettuce as he'd first intended. Meanwhile Jack, between munches, resumed his lecture. "That high-rise, sonny—you ever been there?"

"No!" Junior replied shortly, his voice harsh with anger. To him it wasn't so much that the rabbit might be right. It very well could be. Junior didn't care. He'd many arguments and debates in the past, although none with his Da, wherein he felt his opponent was indeed on the correct side of the issue. That never stopped Junior from arguing and in fact only made his inevitable conquest in verbal fisticuffs that much sweeter. Inevitable, that is, until now. Now he was losing, and to a rabbit at that. Junior felt a momentary chill as he realized the bitter truth which lay hidden in a silly adage which he'd heard just the other day. "Like father, like son." Yesterday such a silly saying brought tears of laughter to his eyes. Now it petrified him more than he could say. Mistaking such fright for fear of him, Jack pressed his point home. "It's a terrible place," he said, meaning the high rise. "It's old. It was old even back when it was new. Older than the hills and then some. It's called Sequoia Estates, and I'm told it was quite the place when it first finished growing and opened up. All the apartments and each of the suites on every branch were spotless. All and sundry shared magnificent views of the forest and the ocean beyond. Because rents were reasonable there were immediate inquiries as to occupancy and vacancy. It was touted as being 'modern' and noted for having everything under one roof, and that was true enough, I suppose. I mean, the place is just so big! Each unit is practically a forest in and of itself!" He paused for a moment to munch a little more leaf and to let the boy catch up with his train of thought.

"It sounds," Junior replied, "as though my Da did them a favor."

Jack uttered a derisive laugh by way of reply. "Hardly! What I just described to you was Sequoia Estates, when it was brand-spanking-new and just opened for occupancy—but that was ages ago. Let me tell you about it now. I just came back from a trip to New York. I even took the train. From it you can see Sequoia Estates as you're leaving the forest or entering it for that matter depending upon which side of the train you happen to be seated and which direction it is moving when you take your seat, and let me assure you, it has seen better days. And those better days were so long ago the only thing remaining of them are the brochures the bellhops hand you when you first check in. Now it's old and lichen-ridden from top to bottom, and very little light gets into the basement apartments. What were once sunny single-family dwellings, all cheery and well lit, have become with the passage of time, damp dismal dungeons filled with shade and shadow. The plumbing leaks, the water drips constantly, and all that lichen hanging there taking up space blocks the breeze so the air-conditioning runs poorly and hardly even works! Its roots are deep as any foundation should be, but time and weather have hollowed parts of the bole and rotted it away. There are certain wings where the entire branch and all of the flats and apartments it compromises are rotten to the core and in danger of falling off. And of course, it's much too tall. Always was, ever since they opened it, and no elevators. Can you imagine that? You'd think the designers would have planned and accounted for such an obvious need. But alas, no—such a convenience, it seems, was never considered.

THE CHRISTMAS RABBIT

Anyway, as old and rundown as it has become, it nevertheless maintains a steady occupancy and did so when your old man chopped down the willow. As a result, when they moved in, all those who'd been evicted by your Da were forced to take a loft apartment as those were all that were left. No problem for the birds of a feather, but it's a hell of a long truck, both in the coming and the going, for such as the poor squirrels—especially when they're carrying a week's worth of groceries. The wise old owl had to take a loft too and although he can fly he's no spring chicken anymore!"

"What," replied Junior with a tired sigh, "has any of this to do with me?"

Jack stared at him incredulously as if his ears, big as they were, misunderstood what they'd just heard. "Don't you see?" he asked. "You helped clear this land and in doing so aided your Da in driving out those who were here first. You stole from them, and that makes you responsible."

"Now, wait a minute," Junior replied in his own defense. "I was only doing what I was told. And besides, I was only five at the time! I did more getting in the way than anything else—"

"Relax," Jack said soothingly. "I'm not here to find fault, and I don't blame you."

"But—"

"I just say all this, sonny, to prove my point."

"And what's that?"

"That the world is a tough old whore, and she's set up so we all have to feed off each other in order to survive. That's all your Da was doing back then, and when we claim a carrot or rip off a rutabaga, it's all we're doing now."

"If this is about eating," Junior countered in his best smart-assed manner, "why don't you just change your diet or go someplace else and leave us alone?"

"Ain't no place else," Jack replied.

"What do you mean?" Junior asked. "The forest is full of food." Overhead a bat flew by flapping its wings in the erratic and spastic way bats do, whirling, looping, and seemingly out of control as it flitted here and there, startling all three of them, including Laddie, who, up until that moment, had chosen to remain silent. "Junior," he now said—and he shook as he said it for he was both frightened and cold and it was long past his bedtime—"I want to go home. Please!" With that, he started to cry, afraid for his parents and afraid for himself.

"Easy, pal," Junior softly replied as he rubbed his young brother's head affectionately, gently tousling his hair. "We'll be leaving soon." Turning back to Jack, he pressed his question. "Well, are you going to answer me? What about the forest—surely there's food there?"

"Too much like work," Jack said offhandedly as he occupied himself with smoothing out his ruffled coat, which got slightly disheveled when they were startled by the bat. "Don't get me wrong," he continued, "there's food out there, I suppose, but you'd have to dig day and night to lay up enough grub to see you through the week. Screw that! Unlike farmers who enjoy working around the clock, we rabbits have a social life. There's fun to be had!" He paused for a quick second as he thought back on yesterday and his encounter with Nutmeg. "Boy, is there ever fun to be had!"

"Too much fun perhaps?' asked the boy, catching sight of a wistful longing, no doubt unfulfilled, which he could see reflected in the gleam of the rabbit's eyes.

"Perhaps," Jack said. "But if so, that's my lookout, get it?"

"Okay," Junior grudgingly replied. "But what about another farm?"

"Ain't none."

Junior's face screwed up with sour disagreement. "Cattle craps!" said he. "I can think of at least ten different farms around here. You and your friends could raid any one of them."

"Who?" Jack asked. "Where?"

"Well," Junior replied, considering the problem, "there's old man Sod down by the river. You could go there."

"Yeah?" Jack countered sarcastically. "And do what? He's a dairy farmer. What use has a rabbit got for milk and cheese?"

"All right," Junior replied, conceding the point. "What about young Billy Ocean then, who lives down by the sea?"

Jack laughed and laughed loudly. "He's a freaking kelp farmer. Oh, the stuff is edible enough, I suppose, but seafood?"

Junior, who didn't much care for seafood either, found that once again, he was forced to agree. "Well, what about Lucas Lardlock?"

"Same problem as old man Sod," Jack replied, "except he's a pig farmer—you want us rabbits to be eating pork chops for the rest of our lives? I know pork is the 'other white meat,' but rabbits don't eat meat—unless, of course, we're taking a bite out of your old man! Get serious and try again."

"Fannie Farmer?"

"Nope, grows chocolate."

"Tom Oakley then."

"Sorry—tree farmer—and although the bark's great for flossing your teeth, it plays havoc on the colon when you're digesting it."

"Sam Sergeant?" Junior asked.

"In the name of the Witches, no!" Jack cried anxiously. "He's an ant farmer and raises army ants at that! He's teaching them all our tricks—drilling them company by company and forming them up in platoons. Soon they'll be ready to kick the cattle craps outta somebody, and, sonny, let me tell ya—you don't want to be anywhere around here when they do. Crimeny! I hear they call him Sergeant Sergeant! Besides your father isn't he the most paranoid and obsessive person you've ever heard tell of?"

"It does seem a bit over the top." Junior had to admit it sounded pretty strange and moreover gave his father's deeds a close run for their money. But that still didn't resolve the problem of an alternate farm, so he continued. "What about Ma and Pa Kettle down in the valley? Certainly, they're not a threat to anybody."

"Goodness no!" Jack replied. "They're harmless old hippies and too stoned to do anyone any harm. But they're pot farmers! Rabbits and reefer don't mix. It gives us the munchies while doing strange things to our heads and making us silly. We prefer to just say no."

Exasperated, Junior asked, "What about Dr. Cy Cohen?"

"Him?" Jack asked incredulously. "The nutty Jew with the net?"

"Well, he's got a PhD," Junior replied. "He is, after all, a doctor. This way, if there's any drugs involved, at least you'd have a prescription."

"Yeah," Jack said acidly, "For Thorazine. The guy's a funny farmer. You want I should have to spend the rest of my life locked up in a padded cage and eating strained gruel from a rubber dish? Thank you, no! I'd much rather cling to my neuroses if you don't mind."

Junior plowed through every farmer he could think of. No doubt there were more than listed here, but not being a member of the Grange (his Da had been kicked out a few years back), he didn't have access to the mailing list. Filled with the frustration that came from having lost his first verbal battle, Junior succumbed to the temptation to carry on in an unsportsmanlike fashion. Seeing but one way to get the last word in and thus declare himself the winner, whether he won or not, Junior attacked from an entirely different and seemingly irrelevant direction. In the best traditions of unsportsmanlike conduct, he struck with force and below the belt. "You think you're pretty smart, don't cha?"

"Yep," Jack replied confidently.

"Think you got all the answers, don't cha?"

"More 'n' you, squirt."

Junior offered the rabbit a shark's sly smile and then laid down his trap. "So why are you here?"

"I just told you," Jack replied, "it's the way of things to feed off—"

"Oh no," Junior interrupted. "Don't hand me that wheelbarrow full of cattle craps! Why, specifically, are you here, and if you're so smart, how did you come to get caught?"

"Specifically," Jack replied, "is none of your damned business! However, as to getting caught, it was just a matter of bad luck and poor timing."

Junior howled with glee. He had him. Chortling, he clutched his sides. Pointing a shaking finger, palsied with laughter, he told Jack between chuckles that it hadn't been a matter of bad luck and poor timing at all but rather bad friends and poor judgment.

"What do you mean?" Jack asked nervously. The brat was far more confident than any little snot nose had a right to be when handed a defeat like the one he'd just been served. It made the rabbit wary.

"What I mean," Junior relished, "is you got used! Taken advantage of by some doe for some dough—or at least that's the forest scuttlebutt. You came here looking to get screwed, and oh boy! That's just what you got!"

Jack stood there trembling, overcome with a profound sense of loss so deep it could be felt as a physical manifestation weighing heavily upon his heart. For of course, the little cattle crapper was right. He could see that now. Now that it was too late. Nutmeg, who beforehand had never shown him even the slightest bit of interest and who had a line of suitors stretching back through the forest and practically to the sea, had better things to do with her time than wait upon him to come traipsing back from wherever. He wondered bitterly as to the exact nature of the deal, who it was that bribed her, and just what they'd promised in return for his hide. Just how much did Nutmeg consider him worth? Jack was determined to find out. "Listen, sport," he said to Junior, "What you just said has done me a world of good. It's cleared my head and allowed me to see straight. So let's let bygones be bygones. Now give me your paw, whaddya say?"

Touched, Junior accepted the extended paw and the genuine offer of friendship. He'd never been too sanguine about his Da's war with the rabbits anyway, and not being too popular himself, had few chances to wear this comfortable cloak of camaraderie in which he now found himself enveloped. As it warmed and comforted him while easing his worries, he paused to reflect on the irony. That he could somehow make friends with the enemy. But hadn't that been just what he was about when he first offered Jack the carrot? And furthermore, wasn't the act of freeing Jack a manifestation of such friendship too? Junior wasn't sure. Those actions were noble in and of themselves, but were they friendly? Certainly, they did not stir the embers of his soul with the same fires as that simple handshake and exchange of confidences. Had he known beforehand it was this easy to make friends, he might have lost an argument or two on purpose. Such victories had always left him feeling empty. Now he felt full!

"Listen, lad," Jack continued, "you know we rabbits and your father don't often see eye to eye, but I overheard your conversation with him and he's right, boy. Take your brother and scatter. If the

Witches ain't dead yet then they're certainly gonna want a piece of you kids too when they recover."

Junior shook his head violently. "I can't," he replied. "Ma's all alone. Someone has to rescue her."

"Boy, there's nothing you can do." The rabbit said. "And besides, so long as your mother has got something cooking in the oven she can more than take care of herself. The Witches, if they haven't expired already, will be wary of approaching too close."

"But—"

"No buts," Jack said. "Besides the fact we're all pretty much helpless here, have you considered the tactical advantage your running away gives to both your father and me?" In truth, the boy didn't see it and said so. Jack chuckled softly, the kindly tutor helping his pet student through a difficult problem. "You're sharp, kiddo," he said. "There's no doubt about that—but you need to walk around the block a few more times before you start calling yourself street-smart. You're the material witness both your father, and I will want to call upon to testify and you'll be missing. If we're lucky there might even be a mistrial—although who knows what would happen then! You gotta flee, boy. You gotta!"

"I'll think about it," Junior replied, but he couldn't shake off his ambivalence regarding the plan. Running, he knew, never solved anything no matter how big the problem or how bad the odds. He himself had much experience in fleeing from overwhelming foes, and although he usually got away, he would nevertheless at some point encounter them again, and there never seemed to be a lack of them.

"You do that," Jack said earnestly, "and act upon it!" The moon suddenly broke through the clouds and cast its luminescence upon them. Jack took it as a sign to depart. "Time to go," he said, "and if you'll take my advice, you'll get going too and get out of here!" He made as if to hop off when Junior stopped him. "Wait!" said the boy. "Where should we go?"

Jack uttered a frustrated sigh. It was time to be moving, and he wanted to go. There were limits to friendships—especially new ones, and the boy with his questions, was straining them. Still, he couldn't leave the two young lads without guidance, could he? If he did, they'd be forced to turn to their father, and he'd forever have to bear the guilt of that. He turned around, scrutinizing Junior as if measuring his mettle. The boy was smart despite being too cocky for his own well-being. But that trait just might serve him in good stead given what Jack had in mind—dangerous, no doubt, but Jack deemed it a cakewalk compared to hanging around and waiting for trouble. "New York, kiddo. Go to New York."

"New York?" Junior was startled. "I don't know anyone in New York!"

"Exactly," replied the rabbit. "And nobody knows you either. You can disappear without a trace. Get lost in the cracks!"

"Yeah," Junior said, "and never get found again. I've heard about New York. Kids like us go there as runaways, and the ground sucks us up. We're never heard from again." And it was true, even back then, even in Olden Days, New York, with its Big Apple, was a monster which fed continuously on lost and abandoned children. They fled there, hearts full of dreams, their heads in the clouds and running away from problems at home and other bad business. Fleeing for most of them was both a last and desperate resort. They arrived empty-handed and penniless. Innocent and broke, hungry more often than not, they made perfect marks for the gangs of grifters, whores, pimps, and hosts of other sly foxes that inhabited New York even back then. The scum thrived there. Even had the Witches succeeded in their attempts to partition and segregate each according to their own kind, still the lowlifes inhabiting the Apple could not have asked for a more natural or conducive environment.

"It's the wilderness, that's true," replied Jack, "and fraught with danger—but I think you can handle it." He reached into his pouch and removed a book (back in Olden Days, jackrabbits, like kangaroos, had pouches. They would not lose them until The Powers That Be, as part of the sentence they would hand down, stripped them of their pockets in an effort to make their labor more difficult). Opening the front cover, he handed it to the boy with the title page visible. Junior took it and read. The name of the tome, it seemed, was *Zen and the Art of Primitive Tool Repair*. He looked at Jack curiously, for despite being an avid reader, had never run across this particular volume. "What's it about?" he asked.

"Never mind," replied the rabbit. "You can find out for yourself as you read it on your journey. For now, just read the title page." Junior did as he was told, his eyes poring over the type set there. An inscription was handwritten on the bottom. It read, "To Jack, may your pad have plenty and may your fur grow with fervor. Keep the peace, hare—as I keep it here, hear? Good karma, Thor Rowe." Junior looked up incredulously. "Thor Rowe?" he asked. "Really, Jack, who is this guy?"

"Don't know much about him," Jack replied, "other than the fact he's the author of that book."

Junior flipped through its pages, his curiosity aroused. "Is it any good?" he asked.

Jack cocked his head to one side, considering the question. "Well," he said hesitantly, "it is and it isn't, I suppose—and it's not that it isn't well written because it is…it's just deep, is all. I only understood about half of it."

"Half?"

"Yeah, half," replied the rabbit. "Its philosophical points are well argued and hammered home, while the martial intuitions, although merely implied by choice of grammar and syntax, are easily understood and with a little effort, can be practically applied. Thor often cites and gives credit to some far eastern mystic named Harehito Rabbakami as his informed source—boy, would I like to meet that guy! Tools though—I just don't get it! What the hell are hammers anyway?"

"They're tools," Junior replied.

"I figured that out for myself," Jack replied caustically. "But what are tools?"

Junior looked about the garden, searching for a hoe or a spade—anything with which he might demonstrate the concept. There were, however, none to be found, and Junior should've known better. Ever afraid for his vegetables and distressed at the amount of pilfering done by those furry little thieves, Santos made careful work at the end of each day to ensure every rake and shovel used in the garden

THE CHRISTMAS RABBIT

was systematically accounted for and locked away in the tool shed. He left nothing lying around unattended which might aid the rabbits in their efforts. The rabbits, no doubt, thought him a fool as they wormed their way under his walls and through his fences. They took more than too much already was the opinion of Farmer Santos, and fool or not, he'd be damned if he'd give them a hand by lending them his hardware. Let them grub in the dirt like the nasty little beasts they were! Realizing there were no tools to be had, Junior gave consideration to the best way to explain the concept to Jack without an apparent example. "Tools," he said, "are instruments you use in order to accomplish a specific task or purpose—like the big stick my Da carries when he's out in the woods."

"Ah," Jack replied with sudden insight. "They're weapons! Of course—I should've realized, given the book's implied martial concepts—"

"Forget it," Junior said. "Why are you giving me this anyway?" he asked, suddenly suspicious of the rabbit and his newfound friendship.

"Relax," Jack said soothingly. "It's just when you get there—New York, I mean—go to Greenwich Village, and ask for Thor. If you can't find him there then go to Central Park and do likewise—but make sure you go in broad daylight! When you find him, show him the book as proof you know me, and he'll tighten ya up."

"Tighten me up?"

"You know," answered Jack, "take care of you. "Tightening you up is Big Apple speak for settling you in, and you'll learn all about it once you get there."

"But who is this guy?" Junior asked. "Is he safe? Is he normal?"

"As normal, I suppose, as anyone from New York can be. Look, what difference does it make? Normal or not—you just mention my name, and you'll be well taken care of."

Junior breathed an ambivalent sigh. He was not at all thrilled with the idea of leaving home and striking out for new places. Exotic locales such as New York and Passaic were much more interesting, he deemed, when viewed from the controlled safety of a good book. At least then, when you tired of such places, you could wander off to someplace else.

"Better get going, boy," said the rabbit.

"But I don't know the way to New York. How do we get there?"

"Take the train, son," said Jack. "Just keep your nose clean and outta the Bar Car, and you should do all right."

"And what about you," Junior asked as he grabbed Laddie's hand to lead him out of the garden, "where are you going?"

"Back to the warren," Jack replied vehemently. "I've some scores to settle!"

"Are you crazy?" the incredulous young lad asked. "Why don't you come to New York with us, seeing as how you know the way? If you go back to the warren they'll carve you up."

Jack offered the young lad a puzzled frown. "It's just Nutmeg," he said, "I can handle her."

"And the others?" asked Junior.

"What others?"

"The ones who put her up to it," the boy responded. "You don't think she was in this alone, do you? Somebody was paying her off!"

"Well," Jack replied stiffly, unwilling to admit what had already been pointed out, "I suppose that makes the most sense...but I'm going back anyway."

"Why put your head in the noose?" Junior asked. "Surely those who hired her will be lying in wait for you. Maybe even The Powers That Be! What will you accomplish then?"

"Lad," Jack replied tiredly, "someday you're gonna understand just what it is that binds male to female, and when you do, you'll probably end up in as sorry a state as me. Having failed, whoever hired her is going to come gunning for Nutmeg, and the truth is, I love her. I have to be there to save her when they do."

"But—" Junior broke off abruptly as he was delivering his response to the backside of a retreating rabbit who bounded off into the forest, never to be seen by either of the boys again. Alone in the garden, the brothers hunkered down as they discussed between them what was best done. Laddie was of the opinion since both the rabbit and Da agreed on a specific course of action, they, as its executioners, would do well follow it through. Junior, however, remained unconvinced, knowing Laddie was too young yet to make such judgments and too inexperienced to have learned two wrongs do not necessarily make a right—whatever the context, moral or practical. In that, thought Junior, Laddie was a chip off the old block.

So taking Laddie's hand, Junior slowly made his way back to the Winnebago. His Ma was still trapped inside, and despite the counsel of Da and Jack, he was determined not to flee until he exhausted all possible resources in an attempt to rescue her. Slow and quiet, like snails slinking along in the moonlight, they made their way through the tall grass and bushes as they retraced their route to the witches' campsite. They were taking more than extra care in their step because somewhere out there were the three wolfhounds who, when they took off from the dooryard, did not look happy. Junior thought it in their best interest to avoid them.

The Winnebago covered wagon rested in the middle of a field on the edge of the wood about a half mile from the farmhouse, and going to was a lot slower than coming from. Coming from, they'd been almost carefree, just happy to have snuck out and gotten away. Now returning weighed down by worry in the watches of the night and made heavy by the yolk of fear which lay uncomfortably upon them, the boys—ever alert for screaming witches and mad dogs—were about to attempt something even more insane than sneaking out—sneaking back in. Those hounds didn't go bounding off for no reason. They'd been called and that could only mean trouble. Hand in hand, Junior led Laddie back to the wagon, taking extra care to stay hidden and unobserved. The night breeze seemed to whisper slyly as if alerting unseen watchers to their passage. The two boys started at the slightest noise. Their journey was accomplished by means of fits and starts as they paused often, taking adequate care to survey their surroundings and gain for themselves reliable intelligence regarding enemy positions.

It was in this way, while still some distance from the Winnebago, that Junior happened to spy The Powers That Be gathered together in a circle with their dogs waiting upon them. Junior and Laddie were hidden in a patch of blueberry bushes, which grew like weeds upon the fringes of the forest. It was his ears more than his eyes that alerted the older brother to their presence. The trio were about three hundred feet off to their left, he guessed, and he could hear them moaning in between violent regurgitations. A pale, sickly green aura seemed to emanate from their persons as they clung to each other, sick. The putrid green hovering about them like cold, wet mist was punctuated with frenzied streaks of fluorescent yellow that burst forth and which seemed to coincide with each individual upchuck. Up would come a chuck hurtled violently from the stomach of Helgayarn, Brunnhilde, or Betty—to be followed by the fluorescent yellow flare as it shot through the pale green aura from which it had sprung.

It seemed to Junior lying undetected in the bushes that amid their pitiful moans and groans and during their short pauses between purges, the Witches were half-heartedly attempting to carry on a conversation and arrive at some consensus. He could not make out specific words from such a distance but could tell from the tenor of the voices being carried on the evening's breeze that the conversation was chock-full of accusation, blame, and bad feelings. So it was plain to Junior that the trio were up to something and not just chucking. Junior knew that forewarned is forearmed and subsequently decided it was worth the risk to try and close in and discover what he could. "Look, Laddie," he whispered, "I'm gonna move in and see if I can find out what's going on. You wait here."

Laddie shook his head. He'd been waiting at the heels of others all night and was getting tired of it. He wanted a bed for the night—even if it was somewhere out in the middle of the forest—and he wanted it now. He could neither understand all this intrigue nor the reasons behind it. "I want to go with you," he replied.

"You can't," said Junior. "It's too dangerous. And besides, I'm going to have to sneak over there and you're too noisy."

It was true. Laddie, unlike his brother, came by his name honestly and could be counted upon to be every bit as clumsy as the old man, perhaps more so. Junior knew they couldn't take the chance. Shouldn't take it—even with himself going alone but, because of his mother, knew they couldn't afford to not take it either. He felt

THE CHRISTMAS RABBIT

damned if he did and damned if he didn't, but he'd be damned, he thought, if he'd damn Laddie along with himself just to make a point.

"Damn it, Laddie!" he hissed. "You just mind your elders, and do what you're told. Ma could be in trouble, and it'll only get worse if you screw it up!"

"Okay," Laddie replied, "okay. I'll do it. But hurry up, will you? I want to get out of here."

Junior gave him an affectionate pat on the head. "All right," he replied. "I'll try to hurry. But you listen now—if I get caught or even if I'm spotted, you just turn your back and run, understand?"

Laddie, shaking with fright, replied, "I can't! I don't know where to go or what to do." His voice, squeaky with panic, started to rise as they lay hidden in the blueberry bush. "I'll get caught," he went on, "I'll—"

"Enough," Junior replied, interrupting his brother and cutting him off by placing a judicious hand over the young lad's mouth, "I won't get caught, okay?" Laddie looked up at him, eyes filled with doubt. "You better not," he said.

"I won't, I promise," Junior stated with false confidence.

"Okay."

Laddie didn't like it, and Junior knew it, but what else was there to be done? He reached over and gave his brother a comradely hug. "Back in a minute, chum," he said. Laddie, fearing he'd never see his brother again, returned the hug fiercely. "Junior," he tearfully whispered, "I love you. Please be careful." Junior felt his entire being infused with warmth. Despite being a little squirt and a pain in the duff, his brother often said just the right thing. Junior returned his brother's affection with equal fervor and then breaking away, crept slowly off toward The Powers That Be.

*****

Mrs. Santos waited until she was sure the boys were well asleep before she served the dinner's first course. This was an important opportunity, she knew, and she didn't want the boys, who'd already cast a dark cloud over the affair by refusing to eat, screwing it up. So during the fifteen minutes she judged the boys would need to settle down and fall away into slumber, she tried to engage the ladies with various attempts at "small talk." Her misguided and subsequently useless efforts were endeavors on her part to draw them out but also gambits played to hide her own nervousness. From calorie-counting to shopping on a budget, she tried to engage them with any subject upon which her little mind seized. Many of the topics were quilting bee standards and were reliable as conversation starters. Now these themes, having been brought forward, fell flat on the floor as Helgayarn, Brunnhilde, and Betty looked on with disdainful silence, their eyebrows arching in derision, and not uttering a word one way or the other. They were in their critique mode, ready to judge, evaluate, and record for posterity. Neutrality was their watchword and not by speech or gesture would the three of them give any indication of their appraisal. Let the food speak for itself and no fraternization allowed!

The first course was, of course, the soup. Mrs. Santos brought it to the table in a steaming white crock with a pressure-sensitive lid. She popped the top and the steam came hissing out as if screaming. The Witches, caught by surprise, took a cautionary step backward.

"Dear me," uttered Brunnhilde. "What on earth is that?"

"Yah," agreed Betty with a marked lack of enthusiasm.

Mrs. Santos didn't have the nerve to look miffed or insulted. From aside, she noticed Helgayarn eyeing both her and the soup dangerously. The big witch poked at the crock with her spoon but didn't dare touch it. Gray and greasy, the crock's contents looked like a small oil slick lying in a pot. It bubbled and swirled and for a fleeting moment Helgayarn had to wonder just who was the more powerful magician here and who was not. "So answer her," she said. "Just what on earth is this?"

"It's shark fin soup," Mrs. Santos replied, trying hard not to display her indignation. "I got the recipe from young Billy Ocean who lives down by the sea."

"Yes," said Brunnhilde. "We know him and have sampled his soups, but my word—they never looked or smelled quite like this!"

THE CHRISTMAS RABBIT

"Of course not," Mrs. Santos said testily, bridling under the insult. Grabbing ahold of a ladle, the farmer's wife commenced to stir the contents of the pot. "Like any good chef—I've added my own personal touch. It's one of my husband's favorites! I do hope you like it." She ladled a serving into each of their bowls. "Hurry now," she said. "You've got to eat it while it's hot!"

Eyeing her with silent trepidation, Betty stuck her spoon tentatively in her bowl. Something under the surface grabbed ahold of the utensil violently and pulled it to the bottom of the crock. The soup boiled furiously, its contents swirling in ferment. "Say," said Brunnhilde looking on, "what the—"

"I told you," Mrs. Santos replied quickly. "It's shark fin soup. What did you expect?"

Again, eyeing the farmer's wife darkly, Helgayarn handed Betty another spoon. "Well, I don't rightly know," she replied, completely at a loss. "But please, go on."

"Actually," Mrs. Santos said with a nervous chuckle, "it's baby shark fin soup. They're always getting tangled up and caught in Billy Ocean's kelp crop. They're a pain in his butt, and so he'll practically give 'em away just to be rid of the darned things. I got a good deal! They're baby great whites, you know. Great whites make great soup, don't you think?"

Looking down at her bowl, Helgayarn spied a dorsal fin as it broke the surface, cut across to the other side of her serving dish, and then submerged. "But they're alive," she said, repulsed.

"Of course they're alive—I like a meal that fights back, don't you?" asked Mrs. Santos. "That way, you truly earn your bread and butter—come now, eat!"

Brunnhilde shot Helgayarn a nervous glance. "I don't know about this," she said, voice edgy with trepidation and eyes flashing. Helgayarn returned her sister's glance with one of her own. "Tough," she replied. "You got us into this by letting her through the door. So eat!" Brunnhilde acquiesced, and the three of them each took a nervous taste. Like sour grapes long fallen off the vine and lying dank and rotting upon the ground, the soup had a pungency which assaulted their taste buds and attacked their sinuses only to pull them out through the cavities of their nostrils. Their faces screwed up, and their throats fought back as the Witches, in an effort to prove they weren't afraid of anything, swallowed their soup. Through watery eyes, Helgayarn could see that Betty was having an extremely nasty piece of bad luck. Owing to her Norse attributes, she was taller and broader than the other two, and she wore larger clothes and bigger shoes. Because there was more of her to sustain, her portions at mealtimes were subsequently larger, requiring, of course, bigger eating utensils to shovel her servings in. Her spoon, therefore, was a small ladle in and of itself. The baby shark she'd captured when she first dug in lay at the bottom of the spoon covered in broth, silent and unnoticed. Biding its time, it waited for Betty to take her first tentative taste and then struck with a fury. As she raised the spoon, it breached up from the bottom of the utensil and bit deeply into her lower lip. Piercing skin and mangling flesh, it drew forth her rich, blue blood. In a panic, she let go a terrified, "Yah!" as she tried in vain to get the little monster to disengage. The shark though was having none of it and only bit down harder. With such teeth as its, it needed no Zen, yoga, or any of the other hundreds of methods used to channel power in order to pierce hides, soft or tough. Ripping, tearing, and piercing were its life's work, and from its point of view, it had damned little life left with which to practice its occupation and was therefore determined to use what meager amount remained to pay someone back for its capture. Back and forth it thrashed, its teeth like razors, as it shredded Betty's lower lip. Her scream galvanized Helgayarn into action. Leaping from the table, Helly took hold of her steak knife, and coming alongside Betty, with a quick flick of her wrist severed the baby shark, separating its head from its body. The torso fell to the floor in a disgusting lump, but the head hung on. Sharks do not give up the ghost easily. Never ones to meekly roll over and play dead they are extremely hard to kill—even for The Powers That Be. Losing its body only strengthened its resolve, and it bit that much deeper. As Betty screamed a bloody murder of "Yah's," Helgayarn was forced to take up the knife again and pry the beast from her sister's mangled mouth. Its head fell to the floor whereupon it attacked its own body. In its last throes, it apparently didn't care who got hurt. "Good gravy!" exclaimed Helgayarn, fighting off a wave of nausea and disgust. She reached out with her foot and stamping down, crushed the shark's head, which crunched sickeningly under her heel as the cartilage split and snapped. Looking on, Betty felt her stomach roll.

Brunnhilde retrieved her sewing kit and busied herself stitching up Betty's lower lip. Sensing impending disaster, Mrs. Santos quickly cleared the table of any traces of the appetizer. "Soup not to your liking?" she innocently asked. "Perhaps we're ready for the salad then, yes?"

Helgayarn shot her a vile look but resumed her place at the head of the table. They were deep in cattle craps now, Helly knew, yet nothing remained for them but to tough it out, and the sooner done, the better.

"Maybe," Mrs. Santos asked timidly as she pointed to Betty, "the lady wishes to retire for the evening?"

"Yrr," Betty replied languidly as she looked appealingly toward Helly, forlorn and with lip torn, unable to engage her singular adverb. Brunnhilde held her comfortingly while flashing Helgayarn a clandestine gesture. "Kill her," the gesture said. "Kill her quickly, and kill her quietly if you can—but don't be afraid to make a whole lot of noise if you have to!"

"No," said Helgayarn with finality, to Mrs. Santos's question, Brunnhilde's gesture, and Betty's silent appeal. They were The Powers That Be, and she'd be damned if they were going to be gotten the better of by some goombah who, despite appearances, was more than she seemed. "We're staying right here and eating dinner!"

"But, Helly," exclaimed a fearful Brunnhilde, "you can't be serious! Poor Betty's been wounded and who knows what—"

"Listen, Bunny," demanded Helgayarn, lacing her nickname with all the taunting sarcasm she could bring to bear and interrupting her, "this was your idea." She shot a hard glance at Betty. "And you agreed!"

"Well so did you," Brunnhilde replied in their defense.

"Yrr," Betty added weakly.

Helgayarn gave both a baleful eye then turned to cast it upon the frightened personage of Mrs. Santos who stood tearfully in the kitchen tossing the salad. The farmer's wife was in mortal terror for her life; moreover, she was feeling deeply insulted by the dispersions cast at her and her cooking. For a tempting moment, Helgayarn coldly considered doing the farmer's wife once and for all but then thought better of it. Returning her attentions back to Brunnhilde and Betty, she said, "Yes, I agreed, and I'm still here. Now. Sit. Down!"

Under protest, Brunnhilde reluctantly consented to resume her seat, as did Betty, who offered up a resigned "Yrr" in affirmation. "We'll sit," Brunnhilde said sourly, "Hell, Helly—we'll even eat if that's what you want. But you first. Do you hear me? You first!"

"So be it," replied Helgayarn, her voice cold as the North Wind. "Me first, but you two immediately after." Her manner left little room for anything other than compliance. Mrs. Santos, who up until now held out hope regarding the outcome of this affair, found herself facing a change of opinion. She did not want to be held responsible for someone else's lack of culinary adventurism. "See here," she tentatively inquired, "maybe we should cancel the rest of dinner and call it a day?" The trio eyed her darkly and in absolute silence. "I know!" she continued, "Let's all get some sleep, and tomorrow morning I'll rustle us up some breakfast!"

"You just get to rustling up those plates, woman," Helgayarn replied harshly, "and serve that damned salad!"

"But," the farmer's wife interjected, "you're all looking so pale and peaked…"

A thundercloud formed on Helgayarn's brow. Her eyes flashed lightning, and Mrs. Santos realized her last observation wasn't perhaps the right thing to bring up to three such as they, who no doubt wished to think themselves more than equal to anything she could dish out.

"Just serve it," Helgayarn coldly replied, "and serve it in silence." Santos would've endeavored one more time to make his point and therefore would've died instantly. His wife, dumb but not that dumb, found a pearl of wisdom and smartly shut up.

THE CHRISTMAS RABBIT

The vegetables, down to the last lettuce leaf, were succulent beyond compare and all of blue-ribbon quality. They had after all come from the farmer's garden and thus rightly deserved such unearned accolades—even the Witches had to concede that—although they did so in silence, stonily refusing a vocal admission. Lying in their bowls, they looked like ambrosia, their colors and shapes appearing bright and clean. Carrots and onions—they all sang a song of freshness and good eatin', and they made the trio's mouths water. "This is more like it!" Helgayarn said gleefully. But then she took note of the dressing.

The salad dressing, a recipe of Mrs. Santos's own devising, was black and sooty and looked as though it had been scooped from the scum which floated atop the La Brea Tar Pits. When Helgayarn poured it on the produce, it immediately wilted the lettuce and shriveled the leeks. As to what it was doing to the onions and the rutabagas, Helgayarn couldn't even begin to guess. *Dear me*, she thought, *will this meal never end?*

"I told you," said Brunnhilde, eyeing her elder sister caustically, her voice ringing with indignant and bitter satisfaction. "I told you, and now you have to eat it!"

"Yrr!" Betty added fiercely.

Helgayarn took solace in the fact that so would they. She sent her eyebrow clouds thundering across the table, causing Brunnhilde and Betty to wisely stifle themselves. The boss witch speared a forkful of salad, which sizzled as the tines pierced their targets. Saying a silent prayer to herself, she raised the fork to her lips and placed its contents in her mouth. Her eyes immediately began to water, and her nasal passages collapsed in agony. Worse than wasabi, the salad dressing burned holes in her tongue and the roof of her mouth. More powerful than napalm, which The Powers That Be hadn't even invented yet, it blackened and burned the enamel of her teeth until she thought they must surely fall out. But she wasn't going to go through this alone, so being careful to keep her lips shut, put on a brave smile while indicating to the others that they should join her. Not wanting to but knowing they had no choice, Brunnhilde and Betty reluctantly followed suit and with Helgayarn leading them, the trio somehow made it through the salad, bite by bitter bite. After the first mouthful, the trio begged Mrs. Santos for water—copious amounts of water in an effort to wash the dressing down and relieve somewhat the infernos occurring within their inflamed intestines. The salad dressing brought about the first known case of ulcers anywhere at anytime, with so much water required to relieve the burning Mrs. Santos was hard put to keep their glasses full, and between the three of them, Helgayarn, Brunnhilde, and Betty drank a small lake of it. There was, however, one positive aspect to this course. The dressing, being extremely caustic, seared the flesh it touched, cauterizing Betty's lower lip so even though it burned away Brunnhilde's stitches, it stopped the bleeding nevertheless. She was grateful enough for that even though it left a scar, which she bears even to this day. Having endured as much of the second course as was possible for her to withstand, Betty left one tomato, quivering and covered in gray gook, at the bottom of her dish while defiantly looking at Helgayarn and daring her to do something about it. Uncharacteristically, the boss witch overlooked it and pretended not to notice.

Mrs. Santos cleared away the dishes yet again and served the main course. She brought it from the kitchen to the dining room on a great golden platter topped with a silver lid. Carrying it high above her head, she brought it to the table and proudly placed it down—after all, considering the soup, the salad seemed to go okay… marginally at least. *Perhaps*, thought she, *I can redeem myself with my famous "eye of round roast"!* Pausing briefly for effect, she then, with flourish, uncovered the lid.

There on the platter, its image reflected over and over by the serving dish's gold plating, lay a huge and gelatinous eye, parboiled and resting uncomfortably in its lid, which was parboiled to a sizzling golden brown. Fully a foot across it was shot through with thick red veins that had gone purple, being thoroughly cooked. Its lashes, having been singed from the heat, melted away to mere stubble.

Brunnhilde felt her stomach flip. "What on earth is that?" she cried painfully, trying hard not to wretch.

The Farmer's wife was genuinely surprised. Couldn't they tell? "Why, it's Eye of Round Roast," she replied. "Surely anyone can see that! Of course, for you, ladies, I've gone the extra yard in your honor and used genuine ogre eye." She paused a moment for what she thought would be a forthcoming compliment. When it became obvious none would be uttered she swallowed her pride and continued, pointing out to the trio that ogre eye was awfully difficult to come by, especially this late in the season, thereby implying the Witches should be grateful for whatever they got. "It cost me plenty," Mrs. Santos said in order to prove her point. "I had to trade a cartload of my husband's vegetables for it with that lad, the Giant Killer, who by the way told me to tell you your magic beans were a gyp and he wants his cow back! Two bushels of taters it cost me and a peck of carrots!" She was nearly shrieking in anger, unmindful or perhaps uncaring of the fact that such a lack of protocol on her part and subsequent display of bad manners had ended the lives of many a chef who dared defend both themselves and their questionable cooking.

Ungrateful high and mighties, she thought to herself! *Invite me in and then make me slave away all day in front of a hot stove while ordering me around as if I were some common serving wench!* "Surely," she asked, "one of you can say something?"

The trio were remarkably silent while looking down with horror at the main course when suddenly it winked back. That scared the cattle craps out of the trio and Mrs. Santos too. All four of them jumped back from the table.

"Not quite done yet," the farmer's wife said, laughing nervously. Suddenly she pointed beyond them and back toward the table, her finger shaking and her eyes wide with fright. The trio, fearing an attack from behind, spun about to confront again the eye, which lay on the platter blinking over and over. Blood tears formed in its ducts and when they accumulated to a sufficient degree, ran wetly over the lid to coagulate in cold, hard lumps on the serving dish. This was the last straw for both Brunnhilde and Betty, whose stomachs were beyond flip-flops and well into somersaults and triple gainers. "Yrr," they cried simultaneously, and holding back wretches while clutching their tummies, they broke for the front door and headed out into the field where they could be sick in privacy. Swaying on her feet and almost out on them too, Helgayarn nevertheless remained behind, eyeing the chef balefully. "Wait!" she finally cried to others who were well on their way to retreat. "Wait!" Her own intestines uttered a terrific rumble. A tearing groan shook her spleen and reverberated in her kidneys. It tied her intestines in knots as it seemingly melted her insides from the inside, out. To Helgayarn, it felt as if her organs were hot tallow running slowly down the meridian of her spine, only to gather thickly on either side of her pelvis and thus pour into the hollow vessels which were her wooden legs. "I mean," she gasped, "wait for me!" Like a thunder squall, she tore out of the Winnebago, blowing the door of covered wagon completely off its hinges. The violence of her passage stampeded the Clydesdales who'd been peacefully munching their oats in a corner and minding their own business.

Wheeling and spinning like dervishes, The Powers That Be clutched at their sides as they sped away in a fury, tearing up the ground behind them and leaving small dust clouds in their wake. Tumbling and rolling, they finally came to a furious halt, only to end up in an ungainly heap with one piled atop of the other. Slowly, heads still spinning and stomachs still rolling, nauseated and unwell, they picked themselves up from out of the mud. Leaning upon each other, more for moral support than anything else, they rose from the morass in an uneven triangle, clinging one to the other, loamy and wet. "Cattle craps," said Helgayarn weakly as she looked down at her feet only to notice she'd stepped in some.

"Oh my," Brunnhilde uttered desperately. Doubling over in nausea and pain, she upped a chuck. "Oh, sisters," she cried between regurgitations, "I've got snakes in my stomach!"

"Screw that!" Helgayarn replied angrily. "I've got dung on my desert boots!" And with that, the trio started upping and chucking and hurling by the heapload as Mrs. Santos's meal attacked them on dual fronts. Inside their digestive tracts, it assaulted their bodies with a virulence unmatched by any enemy they had heretofore faced. It ate at the linings of their stomachs as it tied their intestines in half hitches, while in their heads each sickening course with all of its ugly grotesqueness remembered replayed itself over and over in their minds only to climax in a horrible half-cooked eye which

THE CHRISTMAS RABBIT

blinked savagely, turning recent memory into nightmare. Finally, blind to all else but their sickness, they called to their dogs—which came running.

It was in this condition that Junior and Laddie nearly stumbled upon them and took note. As Junior crept toward them, their rumblings began to slowly subside. Not that they were feeling any better. In fact, they were feeling worse. They'd purged everything from within themselves and were now dry-heaving. Infinitely more painful, Junior knew, making them subsequently more dangerous—and Junior knew that too. But at least their long pauses between periods of gastrointestinal violence afforded him some quiet opportunity in which he could hear an intelligible conversation and so make some assessment of the situation.

Creeping closer, Junior began to distinguish between individual voices, picking up a word or two as he inched forward. Finally, he reached a place of concealment where he could eavesdrop on the entire conversation and judged himself to be close enough. In the gathering gloom, he couldn't be sure who was who, but he didn't think such particulars mattered. What was paramount was not getting caught by those three because what really mattered, Junior knew, when dealing with such a trio in a situation like this was that three, dividing up one, would equal nine—which was the number of pieces they'd carve him into if they found him; yet to take the safe road and leave, perhaps missing some vital clue in their disjointed conversation which took place between dry heaves, seemed to him to be the poorer choice of the two, although he would no doubt agree with both you and I that six of one or half a dozen of the other—it was a sour choice no matter how you sliced it.

"Listen," he could hear Helgayarn saying between stomach rumbles, "the trial is at least a week away. That's twenty-one meals between now and then. Twenty-one chances to finish the job she's started—not even counting in between meal snacks! We've simply got to kill her."

"Helly!" Junior heard another voice say, "That's murder!"

"No, it's not," came the reply. "It's strictly self-defense. It's her or us—and I'll tell you something else, I saw that look on both of your faces earlier and I agree. There's more to this woman than meets the eye! Do you concur, Betty, my dear?" Betty uttered an affirmative, "Yah!" which still sounded like "Yrr!" despite her lack of stitches.

"Where, I wonder," Helgayarn continued, "did she acquire such skills with poisons and alkalis? She's obviously been very well trained and that smacks of a far-reaching plot, full of subterfuge and deceit! Kill them all, I say—the rabbit, the farmer, the wife, the kids, and anybody else who seems to be even remotely suspicious!" She swayed on her feet as she fell into another round of violent dry-heaving while Brunnhilde, vainly trying catch her own breath, offered up a weak reply. "But, dear," she said gamely between gulping gasps, "even if you're right—and after all we've just been through, I grant that you indeed are—can we afford to simply kill them? Remember, the whole world is watching!"

"Can we afford not to?"

Brunnhilde grimly conceded *that* point as well, spitting out an affirmative along with the last of her bile. "Well," she said tiredly, "we can't do anything about it tonight, do you agree?"

"Of course not," Helgayarn replied languidly, still in the throes of retching.

"Yrr," came Betty's weak reply. Helgayarn looked the two of them over and then took stock of herself. They were a sorry lot, to be sure. Covered in mud, spattered with disgorge, and stinking of cattle craps, they were in no shape to go another round with the redoubtable Mrs. Santos. "And certainly," Helgayarn said, "we're all agreed we're not going back to the wagon tonight, aren't we?" She added this last hopefully, almost as if it were a plea.

"Oh heavens no!" replied Brunnhilde, spooked and shaken to her very core by just the thought of it. She looked at the other two in fright, lips trembling and eyes wild. "She was going to serve a Chocolate Mousse for desert, and I just don't think we dare, do you?"

Contemplating the prospect, Helgayarn's stomach threatened to roll yet again as she tried to imagine for herself just what it might be that would pass for chocolate mousse in Mrs. Santos's recipe book. The big witch did not do this willingly but felt herself pulled toward the notion nevertheless, compelled as if she were an iron filling being

THE CHRISTMAS RABBIT

uneasily drawn toward a repulsive magnet. Flirting with death—it was a new experience for Helgayarn and it scared her. She sensed an unlimited source of power buried within those recipes and knew if she and her sisters could come to control them and thus their chef, they'd be unstoppable. They had their detractors—those persons of small-minded ambition who were forever waiting in the wings for their chance to grab a slice of Manifest Destiny, and she knew having the threat hanging over their heads of being force-fed Mrs. Santos's shark fin soup would go a long way to silencing the lot of 'em. But did they dare pursue such a dangerous course? And were they powerful enough to defend themselves if such a plan backfired? Helgayarn didn't think so. To let the woman live while trying to control both her and her recipes would allow rumor of their near demise to spread and to spread quickly. Folk would flock from the world over to take cooking lessons from the wench, learning her recipes and perhaps adding minor mischiefs over their own until it became unsafe for the trio to ever pick up their forks again, thus being forced into semiseclusion and subsequent starvation for fear of gastrointestinal attack. Life for them, Helgayarn knew, would become pure misery, and since misery loves company, there'd be no end to the number of homicidal chefs who'd try to braise, broil, and barbeque The Powers That Be out of existence. No, Brunnhilde's ambivalence about murder aside, right or wrong, good or bad, and no matter how the chips fell when they landed, the woman had to die—and they'd kill the family too, along with that pesky rabbit, just to ensure the point was driven home. "Come, dears," she said, still weak and out of sorts, "let us quit this place before that witch decides to deliver the desert personally." Arm in arm, leaning one upon the other for support, and led by their wolfhounds, the Witches stumbled off into the depths of the forest to recover and lay strategy and were not seen again till noon next day. They passed within three feet of Junior lying like stone in the tall grass and within two feet of Laddie waiting patiently in the blueberry bushes. In each case, the wolfhounds growled and gave warning, but still in the throes of Mrs. Santos's culinary culpability, The Powers That Be were too ill to take note.

When they faded from sight, Junior judged it safe enough to attempt ingress into the wagon and gathering up Laddie, returned to the Winnebago. The window from which they'd accomplished their escape remained partially open. He boosted his brother through and then entering himself, admonished Laddie to silence and climbed uneasily into bed to try and get some rest. Tomorrow was going to be a busy day.

Sleep seemed as if it would never come. Junior lay tossing and turning, replaying in his mind the overheard conversation of The Powers That Be. He knew the game in which he'd become a reluctant player was one of high stakes, and that they were all marked for death. He worried and fretted about what was to be done. He certainly couldn't argue his way out of this, yet he could not leave his mother alone and helpless. That would never do, but he was clueless as to how to accomplish her rescue. Exhausted with fear, he finally fell into a fitful sleep and did not awake until his mother roused them the next day to help wash the dishes and aid in chores.

All next morning and well into the afternoon, the farmer's wife ran amok about the wagon with a passionate fury for cleaning. Having the situation explained to her even as she'd first crossed the threshold the day before and having further been told exactly what would be expected of her for partaking of the largess offered by the trio in her hour of need, she resolved then and there to suck up to the Witches as best she could. To that end, she'd cooked the meal of her life the evening before—a crowning achievement in a lifetime of culinary confusion, which ultimately ended in catastrophe. It wasn't her fault the trio couldn't appreciate a good feed when it was set before them. Still she knew she'd have to make up for it somehow, if only for her own sake and ambition. In one thing, these great ladies were right, she reasoned. Opportunities like this did only come along once in a lifetime, and most folk didn't even get those kinds of odds. She also knew the trio's failure to appreciate last night's meal had all but blown her chances.

She considered all those gathered at the edge of the clearing the day before, watching as she and her children entered into the dwelling of The Powers That Be. Those horrible people, some neighbors, some strangers from far away, all of whom had gone to great trouble to give her and hers such grief in such copious amounts—and all because she and her children had the misfortune of being the dumb farmer's family. Life wasn't fair, and the farmer's wife knew it—she didn't need Helgayarn shouting out such facts at the limit of her lungs to be cognizant of that. But she also knew events had a strange way of going topsy-turvy, and they could be counted upon from time to time to completely reverse their supposedly preordained courses. Events swam smoothly in a seemingly endless manner until they suddenly started sinking or such events having led you to the brink of despair would suddenly thrust you upon the summit of ecstasy. To coin a phrase, "shit happened"—although not often and certainly not to everybody. You had to be fortunate in two things. First, you had to be lucky enough or unlucky enough, depending upon your situation and your perspective toward it, to be in the right place at the right time. Second, you had to be smart enough to recognize being there when you were. She felt she'd reached such a watershed moment now. Everything hinged upon her ability to salvage some good out of last evening's wreckage. If she could accomplish that, then she was sure she could win for herself a new life and better social standing. Whether or not her husband got out this with his skin intact remained to be seen but she was sure she could gain for herself a higher rung on life's ladder of social strata. Folk would come from miles around to seek her out, forever curious about her intimate relations with The Powers That Be. She'd do the talk show circuit and perhaps a lecture tour too. Folk, both two- and four-legged, would come to see her as an impassioned intermediary in their perpetual plea bargaining with the terrible trio.

The Powers…and Martha! She liked the sound of that! And although her name wasn't Martha, Mrs. Santos was willing to change it if doing so meant getting the recognition she thought she so rightly deserved. But even more than her reputation or the prospect of semi-divine status she felt she could secure for herself if she were successful in her endeavors, Mrs. Santos found herself relishing the revenge she could taste. Such success would provide the opportunity to inflict payback upon those who in the past abused her so. Nothing serious or life-threatening, she thought to herself (unless, of course, they deserved it), just the chance to return in good measure each little antagonism she and her children had been made to endure. What a pain in the ass she'd become! What an obnoxious boor! She'd meddle and interfere in the lives of others with ardent glee and reckless abandon. She'd become the physical embodiment of the terrible trio and, in effect, become "The Power Made Flesh"! Folk would forever seek her out and then rue the day they found her. Her opinion, perpetually sought after, would be respected in public while being reviled in private—which was fine with her for who, out in the open, would have the nerve to gainsay? No one would dare to give her lip with friends so powerful. If her silent detractors should suddenly display such temerity she'd see to it their heads were stepped upon and crushed!

Drunk on wine she hadn't even sampled yet Mrs. Santos attacked her mission with a fervor she'd never displayed for past endeavors. Intent on making the Witches a lunch they'd never forget, she decided also to try and straighten up the wagon and make order out of the clutter which filled it. But if her cooking was like a schizoid's bad dream, then her attempts at cleaning and rearranging were like a psychotic's worst nightmare. Her method of straightening up a mess was to simply move it from one spot to another. Corners became storage areas for piles of dust and debris and she continually lost or misplaced personal items belonging to the trio.

Like the farmer's wife, The Powers That Be fancied themselves chefs of the highest order although they rarely prepared for themselves a meal and ate only when they had company, which is to say when they had someone else to both cook for them and clean up afterward and thus ate only to show off and critique other chefs; for being world-class travelers, they ate everywhere. And recognizing the potential marketability of that simple indulgence published annually a well-known and often-cited travelers handbook entitled '*Miserable Meals And The Sloppy Chefs Who Serve Them—An Adventure In World-Class Dining By The Powers That Be.*' The annual publication was an exercise in faultfinding pure and simple—why shouldn't it be? The trio didn't really need to partake of food as

THE CHRISTMAS RABBIT

you and I know it, but when they wanted it, there was plenty to be had; for although folk at this time were in short supply, chefs were in abundance, and there were questionable cooks aplenty to stir a soup or rack a roast, all of whom anticipated with dread the coming of that hellish trio to their respective eateries and dining establishments. Armed with their handbook alone, the trio descended like vultures upon such dens of food consumption, often without warning while demanding tables without reservations and during the dinner hour at that. They requested changes in the menu and often ordered items not listed on the carte. They would drive poor waiters and waitresses to distraction by demanding the impossible, such as pizza in a Chinese restaurant and making other such outrageous requests. Finally, they ate from the salad bar whether it was included with the meal or not and then, without paying the bill, would leave with a small frown on their brows and even smaller tip on the table. As vigilant as watchdogs and as detail-oriented as Lewis and Clark, they were forever mapping out a series of culinary catastrophes and adding them to their growing catalogue of dietary disasters, which with each subsequent edition, was fast-approaching encyclopedic proportions even back then, even in Olden Days and was therefore regarded as *The Authority* to fine dining anywhere by everyone everywhere. That all these everybodies were nobodies living out in the middle of nowhere and at the mercy of horizons severely limited did not hurt the publication's popularity. That most of the publication's readers would never get to see places like Passaic, New Jersey, let alone dine there or in any of the other exotic locales referenced in the tome did not stop it from selling off the shelf upon its arrival at the bookstore, for you see, back in Olden Days, life was hard and full of drudgery as each day, one after the other, plodded slowly by. There were no horizons—oh, they were out there to be sure, but with very few ways to get to them, it seemed like an incredibly long distance to travel just for lunch and hardly worth the effort if you did. There was the newfangled train, of course, which could take you further and get you there faster than had ever before been possible, but it was too confounded and modern for most folk, too full of wheels and gears and other barely understood contraptions few back then had very little experience with or trust in for that matter. Indeed, Jack Rabbit on his trip to New York had been the first and only passenger on the train's maiden run. Since then it delivered only mail. Thus, reading about the experiences of those whose lives were so obviously richer and fuller than your own became one of the few ways to entertain oneself and pass the time.

Still, when the compulsion to cook fell upon them, the trio could whip up a meal and a half though, again, food as you and I know it was not what they served up. Their recipes were the meals which fed the planet, and like the mothers they were, the trio strove to ensure the planet ate a well-rounded and balanced diet.

Brewing in pots and boiling in beakers throughout the kitchen and the rest of the Winnebago too were the half-baked spells and charms of making which were the tools of the trio's trade. In one pot, there lay a scintillating decoction of *Tidal Wave Tea*, which they planned to throw into the Pacific Ocean after it thoroughly steeped, and so rearrange the West Coast. In another—inky, black, and pregnant with waiting—were the ingredients for a major hurricane. The Witches brewed it last winter and now it lay sealed off in a mason jar, fermenting. They planned to unleash it upon the Atlantic Seaboard that summer. There was *Snowstorm Soup* which went well with *Ice Cream*; *Fillet of Drought* in a rich lemon sauce, and of course, the ever handy and always popular *Quaker Oats*—plus a host of others too numerous to mention or adequately describe. The planet, always hungry, ate well.

The trio had so many recipes brewing they were in danger of simply running out of room for lack of organization and space. Mrs. Santos, who didn't know cattle craps about effective organization, in an attempt to save her own skin and win her dreamt-of status, decided to try and help them anyway by tidying up. What was needed here was a plan. She'd just have to come up with one. In fact, she came up with five but disregarded the first two immediately as the logistical nightmares they were. The third, she threw out for lack of material. The fourth, she decided against when she contemplated The Powers That Be, their response to the plan itself, and what they might do to her as a result if she carried it through. Thus she settled

THE CHRISTMAS RABBIT

on plan 5. Plan 5 was a last-ditch attempt on her part to salvage whatever good graces The Powers That Be had left as they feebly tried to nurse themselves through the lingering agony and vomitous wreckage of the hurled aftermath of last night's dinner—which even Mrs. Santos, had she been pushed into a corner, would have to admit had been less than a success. She grabbed her own battered and dog-eared copy of *Sloppy Chefs* and, referencing those chapters on meals, mannerisms, and methods, offered up so self-righteously within the tome's dusty pages, weighed her own actions against the trio's subsequent behavior in an effort to make sense out of last night's fiasco and so determine for herself where, and more importantly how, she might have erred. She could find no fault with either her presentation or the meal itself but knew nevertheless such setbacks were often one's lot in life and thus both inevitable and unavoidable. She therefore determined to herself to attribute these particular dashed hopes and discomfitures to the convergence and combination of bad luck, rambunctious children, and the too obviously uppity airs of three swells who thought themselves better than her and who had the bad grace to be unwell after dinner. They were better than her, or at least bigger, and Mrs. Santos, no lightweight herself, longed for that kind of muscle to throw around. Poor dear. In truth, Mrs. Santos was terrified of the trio and in her terror was striving desperately to please. Yes, she was a kiss ass, and it's true she was small-minded in her need to exact petty revenge upon those onlookers who'd so taken after her in the past, and no one would argue the point that when it came to brains or a lack thereof, she was only exceeded and thus underachieved, by her inestimable husband, who of course felt proud to claim first place in anything even if it meant being declared the winner in contest of losers. But should we blame her for these traits? She was who she was, and if who she was was less than who she should be—for whatever the reason—at least she was still there! Toughing it out with a no-good husband in a dead-end marriage and desperate enough to get away at any cost, if only for the sake of the children—and eager enough to leave them too were an offer to be tendered from the right quarter. *The Powers...and Martha. The Powers...and Martha.* It was a siren song singing to her about a sweeter life on the other side of the rainbow. A life where there weren't any men or if there were they were all to a man, capable and ambitious, as well as thoughtful and attentive (handsome wouldn't hurt either), as they lovingly hoisted you onto the backs of their brilliant white chargers and rode you off into the sunrise of a new tomorrow. It was a silly dream, of course, but one which she succumbed to daily as most women will when the men in their lives are less than they should be more often than is called for. For of course, no one can be all they should be all of the time, and who would want to anyway? The Powers That Be, that's who. They were all they could be more often than not and more than was called for the rest of the time. Those three witches were dogs whose bite tore the bark right off you, and so, plan 5.

To comprehend just how scatterbrained and ill-conceived was plan 5, you first need to understand plan 5 was actually plan 7—plans 5 and 6 having been scrapped like the others. Mrs. Santos, not having made it through grade school, could not count past five and used the fingers of her right hand when numbering anything. If there were more objects than fingers, Mrs. Santos always took that unknown number to be 5. Five was the number of the stars in the sky (actually in Olden Days and at that stage in creation, there were only twenty-two) and trees in the forest. One supposes she could've at least figured out ten by making use of her other hand, but those digits were busy, having been designated A-E-I-O-U, the five vowels.

The final plan 5, to put it simply, was, "The more hands the better," and since The Powers That Be were apparently absent for the day, still unwell and unlikely to help anyway, then presumably that left things in the hands of her and children who had the only hands handy other than her own. It was dicey, she knew, having little hands handle such hazardous materials, but what could she do? There was simply too much that needed to be done for one person to accomplish before the terrible trio returned.

Mrs. Santos remembered a time before the children were born when she and her husband traveled to the other side of the forest to trade his vegetables on the open market. Halfway through their journey, they came upon a little clearing in the depths of the wood, and there they'd met the Old Woman Who Lived in a Shoe. This woman being nearly as famous as her husband and herself was well-known to Mrs. Santos, and it seemed that the rumors the farmer's wife heard about her were true. The woman, it appeared, bred like a herd of horny cattle and seemed to have an avalanche of children, no two of which bore any resemblance to the other, suggesting different fathers for each. *An obvious slut*, thought Mrs. Santos, but one whose reputation it seemed, was not entirely deserved, for despite living in a shoe and having children who seemed to number in the hundreds, rather than not knowing what to do with them appeared instead to have a firm grip upon the situation and to have all the little brats well in hand, putting them to work and doing chores. The shoe itself was located in the middle of the clearing and was the size of a small mansion. It once belonged to a giant of old who, it was rumored, died in his sleep. The rumor got started when he was found expired in bed. The truth was, he was screwed to death by the Shoe Lady, who coveted his footwear and used sex like an avenging sword to obtain what she wanted. The ogre died with his boots on and a smile. Having been turned down for a building loan because of her questionable character and unsavory means of employment and having been denied the loan by the giant himself who was a colossus in the banking industry as well as an all-around ogre to boot, she disposed of the gargantuan with the only tool she had handy and took up residence in his shoe. Being well organized and having over the course of years given birth to heaps of helping hands, the Shoe Lady took much care and went to great lengths to ensure said shoe was properly maintained and well cared for. Such diligence not only increased the property value but, more importantly, was good for business.

    The shoe itself was really a boot and fashioned from elephant hide and chain mail. On the day Mr. and Mrs. Santos came upon it, children by the score could be seen clinging to ropes and ladders suspended from its sides, furiously applying saddle soap and WD-40 in an ongoing effort to keep it supple and looking new—as no one, even in Olden Days, wanted to take their commerce to a seedy-looking and rundown old whorehouse. Displayed out in the front yard was this sign, hand-lettered in Day-Glo paint:

"THE BIG BOOTIE"
AN ADVENTURE IN SEXUAL ESCAPADE & EXTRAVAGANZA!
BY
THE SHOE LADY—HOOKER FOR HIRE!
DIRTY PICTURES, POST-IT NOTES, & PLAYING CARDS!
FRENCH TICKLERS!
SEXY LINGERIE—FOR SALE OR RENT!
KARMA SUTRAS!
SLOPPY JOES!
MESOPOTAMIAN MEDICAL ASSOCIATION APPROVED!
CLEAN, SAFE, AND DISCREET!
FRESH CRABS CAUGHT DAILY!
WEEKLY SPECIALS!
VIRGINS WELCOME!
THREESOMES AVAILABLE UPON REQUEST!
"YOU'VE SAMPLED YOUR WIFE—NOW TASTE THE HIGH LIFE!!!"

One entered the shoe by first taking a number and then getting in a line which started at the top of the boot, ran down the tongue, over the toe, and into the forest. The line was made up chiefly of men which were the Shoe Lady's main source of commerce, although scattered among them were a handful of women whom the Shoe Lady was not averse to doing either if the price was right.

Having arrived just after sunup, the Santoses found the line to be relatively small—just barely one hundred yards from the shoe and into the wood. And being themselves country bumpkins, naive, and with very little knowledge of the world beyond the borders of their farm, decided to take a number, get in line, and see what the to-do was all about. But even this early, business was nevertheless brisk, and the number they drew was 845, which of course meant nothing to the Mrs.

It was well into the afternoon before the couple approached the shoe itself and began their slow ascent up the tongue by climbing the shoelaces. During their lengthy stay in line, they said nothing to anyone, either before or behind them, as they did not want to give the impression they were regular customers. Finally their num-

THE CHRISTMAS RABBIT

ber came up and they descended into the very sole of the shoe by climbing over the instep and down the ladder. It was a slow descent, made one rung at a time and with lengthy pauses between rundles as the line advanced. This prolonged descent afforded the Santos's the opportunity to get a good glimpse of the interior of the boot, which provided them with rare insight into a lifestyle so totally beyond their ken that they were reduced to sinking in silence, mouths agape, while wondering about the length of the line and where they were going—for although they'd seen hundreds of others entering the shoe they'd as yet seen no one come out. But it had to have an exit, for as big as it was, even Santos could see there wasn't nearly enough room to accommodate the throngs of patrons who'd entered previously.

The interior walls of the boot were papered in a garish maroon, crushed velvet overlay, soft to the touch and satiny as sheets, meant to convey an air of luxury and opulence. Mrs. Santos, however, viewed such trimmings as mere tack, rising barely to the level of what she deemed "cheap and seedy" despite the obvious amount of indolent wealth on display. She conceded that the Shoe Lady was certainly doing well—no *butts* about it—the bling, baubles, knickknacks and whim-whams on display and for sale attested to that. But was this any way to make a living? The lamps, which cast a warm glow throughout the heart of the boot, were blown from the finest crystal, set upon stands of pure gold, and inlaid with the rarest of jewels. These stones resting in their settings, captured the rays of the lamps in which they were set, refracting and reflecting over and over, thus casting everyone and everything throughout within in a gossamer shimmer. Matching the walls, the plush carpets were maroon as were the sofas and divans, also covered in crushed velvet. The end and coffee tables were fashioned from mahogany and redwood, as close to maroon, Mrs. Santos supposed, as the Shoe Lady could get. Each table was stocked with pleasurable dainties and foodstuffs by attendants who stood behind them serving patrons as they passed. Santos, by virtue of years of habit, developed a fondness for his wife's cooking, and having sampled the fare offered, found it bland and unappealing. Yet despite her reservations regarding both the Shoe Lady and her chosen occupation, Mrs. Santos gorged. After all, it wasn't often back in Olden Days that you got a free feed. When the rare one came, you did your best to overlook the source. The farmer however did accept a drink as they made their way past the bar pausing both to enjoy the offered beverage and in appreciation of the nude canvas displayed with prominence behind the barmaid. Mrs. Santos merely "humphed" through her cheese and crackers.

They came at last to a final table upon which were displayed various novelty items designed to commemorate their visit and obviously for sale. There were small statues, naked images no doubt, of the Shoe Lady in all her wanton luster. Elbows bent with hands at her sides, her face carved in sexual tension, she looked as though she were readying for a gunfight. The inscriptions on the bases of the statues read, "I Slapped Leather with the Shoe Lady and Lived to Brag about It!" There were feathered writing quills with an image of the Shoe Lady clothed in a bikini cast upon the feathers. When you turned the quill upside down, the bikini disappeared to reveal the Shoe Lady in glorious nude. There were bumper stickers—although no one at that time had bumpers for them—still such lack did not inhibit their sale—which read, "No Flies on Me—I Sleep with the Shoe Lady" and "Streetwalk Don't Jaywalk." There were buttons which read "Easy Virtue," "Comin' Home While Steppin' Out," "Who needs Viagra—I've Got the Shoe Lady!" and hosts of others. Plus pin-up calendars, centerfolds, and mass-produced posters. Business, it seemed, was booming, and despite a frosty glare from his wife, the farmer bought one of everything.

As they passed over the shoe's arch and beyond the last table, they came to a door which gave ingress to the boot's toe. Above the door there were two lamps, one red and one green. Observing both and the few patrons ahead of them, Santos noticed the red light would go on when someone passed through the door and closed it behind them. The red lamp would remain lit for an indeterminate amount of time and then suddenly go out, to be replaced with its green counterpart, which seemed to be the signal for the next customer to advance. This happened again and again until the couple were next in line at the door. The green lamp emitted its tinted glow. Santos turned the knob and giving a tentative push, peered cautiously

THE CHRISTMAS RABBIT

inside. Both he and the Mrs. took note of the tall redheaded woman whose back was toward them and giving orders to two attendants who were busily making her bed with clean sheets. Over in a corner stood a large hamper overstuffed with soiled linens—a testament, one supposes, to the general care and cleanliness with which the Shoe Lady approached her profession.

As she turned to look at them, the couple were surprised to find a radiant beauty rather than the old hag they'd come to expect. Obviously, all the doodads on display were more than mere propaganda. Fulsomely figured but not fat at all, the Shoe Lady stood there, the first paid, and fully functioning fulcrum, of sexual vitality, exerting her leverage on either end of the sexual seesaw and gazing at them out of the most beautiful pair of violet eyes either had ever seen or heard tell of. She wore a shimmering blue negligee that was nearly translucent, accenting certain glories while concealing others.

"Well," their hostess said with surprise, her voice soft and cultured, "what do we have here? It's not often I get called upon to do a *ménage à trois!* Most wives shoot their husbands if they find them here. Not many dare to come along for the ride!" She stretched seductively, arms over her head with breasts pointing like beacons. "My compliments," she continued, speaking to the woman who stood there shivering. All sinew and muscle and purring enticingly, the Shoe Lady was scaring the hell out of Mrs. Santos, who noticed her husband, filled with desire, eyeing the woman greedily. "You don't understand," the farmer's wife stammered. "This isn't what it seems! We're...we're just tourists!"

"Tourists?" the Shoe Lady asked incredulously. "This is Olden Days, darling. Nobody has the time or the luxury to be tourists!" She eyed them carefully, full of suspicion, and asked if they were brother and sister. "Because let's just understand something now!" she exclaimed. "Although I'm the queen of kinky, there are some things that even *I* won't do!"

"Quite right," the farmer replied with wholehearted agreement. "Honey, why don't you wait outside?"

"Outside? This is our honeymoon!" They were due to go to Viagra Falls later, but for now Mrs. Santos was mortified. Never in her life had she been so embarrassed—and that was saying much. Damned men! "Now you just listen here, mister," she said, her voice near screeching as she looked at the Shoe Lady wickedly. "We said we we're coming in to sell vegetables, not buy meat off the hoof!" Poor Santos, like most men back then and now, when he thought at all, did so using the brain dangling between his legs and not the one planted atop of his neck, and to be fair to the poor fellow the subject of what would actually transpire once they gained ingress to the famed and fabled shoe had never, in fact, been brought up. Mrs. Santos however felt she was more than justified in believing the subject of "just selling vegetables" while having a quick peek for themselves should've been inferred regardless of whether or not it had actually been voiced.

The Shoe Lady let loose a raucous laugh, suddenly realizing who they were, for of course there was only one person for miles around stupid enough to bring his wife into a place like this and on the eve of their nuptials at that!

"You're that silly farmer who hunts rabbits, aren't you?" she asked. "And you're his equally infamous wife, 'Le Chef Of Death'!"

"No!" replied Santos shortly, his voice sour with injury. "Well, that is to say, I mean yes—but I'm not silly! What I do is serious business." He looked to his wife for support, but she rightly denied him even the merest of affirmations. "Consider yourself lucky," he continued, "that you never have to leave the house!"

The Shoe Lady lay slowly across her bed and then languidly rose on all fours as if getting ready to pounce… "But of course," she said in a voice smooth as silk while offering them a shark's smile as she said it. "We don't often get celebrities here at the boot—after all, this isn't Martha's Vineyard!" She rose momentarily to her knees, crossing her arms erotically over her ample breasts, and then slid back into a crouch. "So…you came here to sell vegetables, did you? Interesting. And poor me—with only my body to barter! Tell me, if you would, just how much is a sack of potatoes going for these days?"

"Taters?" Santos replied eagerly. "How about we trade even—tit for tat?" The missus kicked him viciously in the shins.

"Relax, Mum," said the Shoe Lady, enjoying her tease. "It's only normal, you know."

THE CHRISTMAS RABBIT

Mrs. Santos's eyes pierced the harlot like rotating drill bits. "Normal," said she, her voice dripping venom, "and just how's that?"

"Well," the Shoe Lady mockingly replied, "screwing your spouse is a lot like going to the 7-Eleven, isn't it?"

"Whaddya mean?"

"Even if it is the only place open at three in the morning it's the same old thing and the coffee's cold more often than not—if you get my drift…" She offered the farmer's wife a sly wink. "Live a little, sister! Variety's the spice of life, and I say yours needs seasoning—what say we all get salty and wet?" The Shoe Lady slid graciously from the bed and extending a hand to each, invited them to her. Santos, under her spell, came willingly. Mrs. Santos, with a yell, did not, and grabbing her husband, pulled him toward her, hands grasping like pliers and gripping like a vice. "Don't you touch him, harpy!" she screamed. "We're decent folk and don't need to be mixing it up with the likes of you!"

The Shoe Lady was losing patience. She could take the slurs and insults along with the pretended mortification, for as a matter of course, she'd heard it all before and more often than not until now such dispersions rolled off her like rainwater. What she couldn't stand and therefore would absolutely not put up with was the loss of valuable time doing nothing and beating around her bush while the line on the other side of the door backed up and grew ever longer. "C'mon, dearie," she said, giving voice to her exasperation, "the clock is running and we ain't got all day. I've got mouths to feed!"

"This way?" Mrs. Santos asked.

"Any way," came the reply, "any way I can."

"But what do the children think of all this?"

"What are they supposed to think?" the Shoe Lady sharply retorted. "They love their mother!" Insulted, the Shoe Lady wanted nothing more to do with these two other than to put them in their place—especially the woman who too obviously felt everything here was beneath her. How dare that one, who lived with whom she did the way she did, be incredulous and disdaining of anyone else, no matter how they lived? Married to the farmer, the woman all but stated boldly to anyone who'd listen that you did what you had to in order to get by. "Who are you to be questioning anyone else's lifestyles anyway, Ms.

Prim and Proper? You—who with your sodling here are the laughing stock of half the forest and well beyond! How dare you take after me? At least I have friends. Where are yours? Oh, that's right—you lost 'em all when they kicked you out of the quilting bee! Shunned by your betters and despised by your neighbors! What will you do when your children are born? I may be looked down upon for the size of my family, but all of my children will be sittin' pretty! My banking giant, bless him, before he died he invested my earnings in various stocks, bonds, and sheltered annuities. All of them did well until now I don't know how much I'm worth. Couldn't count it if I tried." Mrs. Santos, limited in her counting to five, could well believe that. "And all of it," continued the Shoe Lady, "goes to the kids. There's enough there to see the whole lot through college and then some."

Despite her general misgivings and personal dislike, and feeling no less threatened regardless of their hostess's justifications, Mrs. Santos couldn't help but be somewhat impressed with the harlot's accomplishments. It had to take a lot of careful thought, intricate planning, and diligent effort to provide so much for so many. Because even back then, even in Olden Days, higher education didn't come cheap. It broke many a family, sending them into indentured servitude. Yet forced to grudgingly acknowledge the Shoe Lady's accomplishments, Mrs. Santos still couldn't let go of her prejudices and derision. They rubbed her raw like an open wound for at their heart was a morbid curiosity to find out why such a wench, no matter how good-looking, could attract her husband who, standing there slack-jawed, was obviously smitten with her charms. "But the children," she asked again, "what do they say when they see what goes on here?"

The Shoe Lady tapped her foot on the floor while rapping her fingers against the wall as she slowly tried to gather her patience. *"Holier Than Thou"* was assuming again—as if she alone knew so much! "What kind of mother do you think I am?" she asked snootily. "The children never come in here during office hours! I'd never let them see this. They're just kids, for Pete's sake!"

Overall Mrs. Santos remained indeterminately unconvinced yet allowed that perhaps some things were best left to themselves, and to heck with trying to figure out her husband's strange attractions. It was time to go and go quickly…but she saw no exit. "We're leaving!" said she, although unsure of how.

"But, dear," interjected her husband, "to leave now would be rude." He eyed the Shoe Lady greedily. "Besides, we still have vegetables to barter with. Let us take them out in trade!"

Mrs. Santos's answer was to grab him firmly by the earlobe and twist. "Listen, mister," she said as she squeezed, "no husband of mine is going to go mixing it up and making mookie with some slick-talking strumpet!" She flashed the Shoe Lady a glare that would wilt flowers. "She's nothing but a little home-wrecker. Well, before I let her wreck ours, we're getting out of here! Do you hear me?"

Santos reluctantly nodded even though he barely heard her admonishment as only one ear out of two was working. The other, beet-red and thick as cauliflower, lay twisted and pinched in the vise-like grip of his loving wife. For an instant, he wanted to raise his hand and whack her—if only in self-defense, but didn't. It could be, he thought, that she was justified in her emotional outburst. Perhaps she had a legitimate reason for carrying on so. Or perhaps not. Either way, right or wrong, Santos at least knew enough to realize that love often hurt, and when it did, stoicism and the ability to take your licks were the only attributes that got you through and out to the other side. But darn it—sometimes he wished she would lighten up a bit and get into the spirit of things! If only she'd let her hair down and do the Samba! Here they were, in one of the tourist meccas of the forest and considered by many to be one of the four wonders of the world (back in Olden Days, there were only four as the Pyramids, Stonehenge, and the Great Wall of China hadn't been built yet; there were The Powers That Be, Helgayarn, Brunnhilde, and Betty, who knew they were wonderful even if nobody else shared that opinion, and the Shoe Lady who, though not always respected, was nevertheless deemed a wonder by all with whom she conducted commerce), and his wife refused to loosen up a little and in so doing appreciate the spectacle who paraded herself before them.

Oh well, thought he, *such is wife*. Resigned to the inevitable, Santos offered up a tired, shuffling sigh while reluctantly agreeing that yes, they should go, and then using a handy pry bar whose true purpose he dared not even guess, unclasped his wife's hand from his ear, turned her about, and led her back toward the door from which they'd entered.

"Stop!" said the Shoe Lady in horrified embarrassment while running between them and throwing her back against the door, using her body as a blockade. Santos took note, studying her moves while memorizing her every step for future reference in his ongoing war with the rabbits. There were formidable defensive postures inherent in those blocks. Positions which would allow him to repel an aggressor while at the same time launch a vicious counterattack! So he examined each maneuver from every angle, intending to put them to use against his enemies when he returned home. "You can't go out that way," said the Shoe Lady. "No one ever goes out that way! What would people think?"

The farmer and his wife were puzzled. What would people think? Why, the same things, they reasoned, people thought when standing in line and waiting to get in! As a means of reply, they offered the Shoe Lady a mutual shrug.

"You go out the secret door like everybody else!"

"What secret door?" the couple asked.

The Shoe Lady offered the pair a sour look as if they'd jointly farted in public or committed some other serious breach of etiquette. Trust dumb farmers, she thought, and the women who put up with them, to have no sense whatsoever when it came to social graces or the means of preserving them. Highly independent, the Shoe Lady was certainly no champion of The Powers That Be, resenting their meddlesome interference. But when it came to farmers, she had a hard time finding fault with their opinions. "The door that's hidden!" she replied. "It wouldn't be much of a secret door if it stood there out in the open now, would it?"

In their confusion, the befuddled couple allowed as how that could only be true. "But why keep it hidden?" asked Mrs. Santos. "I mean, you wait in line all day just to get in so that everybody knows you're out there—what's the point?"

"Would you be surprised," the Shoe Lady asked with a chuckle, "to learn that most of my customers are embarrassed by their patronage?"

THE CHRISTMAS RABBIT

"Certainly not!" miffed Mrs. Santos. "What I'm surprised by is the fact they'd wait in line all day in the first place, risking observation and exposure only to duck and hide after the fact like guilty children caught with their hands in the cookie jar!"

"Well then," said the Shoe Lady with a self-assured reply, "you don't know much about men, do you? The male thought process is centered in the lower half of their bodies."

Mistaking her meaning, Mrs. Santos took the Shoe Lady's observation to mean that men's heads were in their asses. With her own husband as an example, she could only agree. "How true!" she exclaimed while slapping her husband's ample rump in acknowledgment. "They're all looking up the Hershey Highway and not very bright, are they?"

"That may be," replied the Shoe Lady, running a hand through her hair, "but I wasn't referring to that particular part of their anatomy. I meant men are led around by their penises. Their phalluses are like divining rods, pointing them in a specific direction, and off they go not giving a moment's thought to the consequences of their journey until after they've arrived." Considering this remark, Mrs. Santos found it filled her with mild trepidation. She didn't like what she'd just heard, fearing its implications while marveling to herself at the fact that a mere matter of anatomical inches one way or the other was causing her such an inordinate amount of unease.

The Shoe Lady recognized the woman's panic for what it was. She'd been the cause many similar attacks in a variety of other females whose husbands paid her visits. The fear was common to women, she knew, who, after willingly allowing prideful brutish men to suck their lives dry with their incessant demands and childlike needs, thought they deserved the hard earned reward of faithfulness and ongoing fidelity for having put up with so much in such an uncomplaining manner. To find out such devotion and sacrifice of self could be so easily negated by the egotistical and self-centered desires of uncaring and unappreciative spouses was often more than most wives could take. Like this one, they lost their composure. Well, let them, thought the Shoe Lady. It was their own fault for listening to old wives tales regarding the joy and bliss of marriage and not using the common sense they were born with. Still, teasing them could be so much fun! Therefore the Shoe Lady decided to play on a little more. "They give way to passion," said she, referring to men, "and then worry about the repercussions and the fruits of their harvests only after they've sown their seed. We can either put up with them or fight back."

"Fight back?" asked Mrs. Santos. "How do we fight back?"

"By going them one better!" answered the Shoe Lady. "By doing them all and charging them double for the pleasure! Whaddya say—there's a helluva line out there, all hot and eager! Wanna be my partner?"

Santos looked on nervously, watching as his wife considered the offer. It was tempting, thought Mrs. Santos, envisioning the long line of lusty males, all of them libidinous and ready to pay cold hard cash for the privilege. But in the final analysis, she lacked the courage of the Shoe Lady's convictions. "There must be some other way," she timidly responded.

"Nope," replied the Shoe Lady. "It's either fight them on their own ground or meekly play the game by their rules while never trusting any of them when they're out of our sight!"

"All of them?" asked the farmer's wife, afraid of the answer.

"All of them," assured the Shoe Lady. "It started with Adam, and it's what got him into trouble in the first place. He—"

"Adam who?" asked Santos, cutting the Shoe Lady off. Not comfortable with the dispersions being cast his way by this woman for fear they were probably true, he felt the need to say something—anything in his own sex's defense. Even if anything were nothing more than a question who's only purpose was to break her concentration while derailing her criticisms.

"Adam and Eve, that's who!"

Even in Olden Days, Adam and Eve's times were so far gone and in the past as to be considered "Olden Days" themselves, causing their histories to be viewed more as legends than as actual fact. "How could you possibly know that?" Mrs. Santos asked incredulously in an attempt to reassert herself. It was the opinion of Mrs. Santos that this lady was far too cocky—in both her opinions and pronouncements, and it was high time someone took her down a couple of pegs.

THE CHRISTMAS RABBIT

The Shoe Lady looked at the farmer's wife condescendingly and with simple self-assurance replied, "Eve was my mother."

Mrs. Santos didn't believe her. That was ages ago and simply not possible. Feeling smug and confident, she made a point of telling the harpy so.

"I knew you wouldn't believe me," the Shoe Lady tiredly replied with an air of having gone through this same conversation many times in the past. Going to the oaken chest at the foot of her bed, the Shoe Lady knelt down and opened it. Reaching inside, she removed a small jewel box, intricately carved and inlaid with gold and silver. In it resided her most prized possession. Opening the box, she took it out, all neat and folded, and walking back to Mrs. Santos, put it gently in her hand.

"What's this?" asked Mrs. Santos as she examined the parchment handed to her. The document felt old and corrupted and lay uneasily in her palm.

"It's my birth certificate," said the Shoe Lady. "Open it and see for yourself."

Mrs. Santos did as she was told, gently peeling back the tender folds as her husband looked on. The document itself was yellow and parched c it read:

Χερτιφιχατε Οφ Συχχεσσφυλ Χενχεπτιον
(Certificate of Successful Conception)

Νανε: Σγοε Λαδε   Γενγερ: Φεμαλε
(Name: Shoe Lady)   (Gender: Female)

Μοτηερ: Εϖε   Φατηερ: Αδαμ
(Mother: Eve)   (Father: Adam)

Πλαχε οφ Βιρτη: Μεσοποταμια Μεμοριαλ Ηοσπιταλ
(Place of Birth: Mesopotamia Memorial Hospital)

Τιμε Οφ Βιρτη: 6:55 α.μ.Τυεσδαψ, ϑανυαρψ 23, 0105
(Time of Birth: 6:55 a.m. Tuesday, January 23, 0105)

Σεξ: Ωιλλνγ   Ωιτνεσσ: ***Αρκιε***
(Sex: Willing)   Witness: ***Arkie***

The farmer and his wife were stunned. The proof was right there before them, official-looking and witnessed in red ink. *"You really are the Old Woman Who Lives in a Shoe!"* said the incredulous Mrs. Santos. "But how can one so old look so young?"

"Sex, sex, and more sex!" the harlot replied. "If you keep running without slowing down, then old age never has a chance to catch you up!"

"But who's Arkie?" asked the farmer.

"Arkie," said the Shoe Lady, "became my mother's lover shortly after Adam fell from grace. Adam's sins made him sour. He was constantly holding Eve accountable for his troubles when he should've been blaming himself—after all, no one forced him to eat the apple! He grew irritable toward her, cold and distant. When at last he went looking for it somewhere else, my mother in turn sought solace in the arms of another, my father, Arkie."

Santos considered his wife and tried to imagine her wrapped in the loving embrace of another. Just the thought of her cheating on him made his blood run cold and his jealousy boil over. It was one thing for a male to want to sleep around—it was the way of nature. The stallion had his herd, the wolf had his pack, and mighty lion, puffed up with power and sexual prowess, had his pride. So why not men? But women? It was too unseemly. "Didn't Adam object?" he cried.

"He didn't know," answered the Shoe Lady. "Arkie was my mother's clandestine lover. Clandestine, that is, until she caught preggers. Then the truth came out. It was a nasty piece of business, resulting in a bitter divorce, but by then what could Adam do? It was already too late."

"Oh, screw this!" said Mrs. Santos. "Even if it's all true, it happened so long ago it can't possibly have any bearing upon us today. It fills me with rage to see my husband take after you so. What I want to know is, why do other wives put up with it?"

The Shoe Lady cracked her knuckles while looking the pair over with uncertainty, as if afraid of saying too much, thus exposing secrets and leaving herself open to the ridicule of others should the pair engage in blabber and divulge such confidences as she contemplated revealing to them. But this was the dumb farmer and his wife, and no one would deign to listen to them even if they chose to pass her secrets on. And in truth, she took a certain satisfaction for herself when confiding such hermeticisms to someone else—especially when such arcanum, cabala, and esoterica were bound to provide shocks to the listener's spirits! "Sometimes," she continued, "it's easier to believe a lie than to seek too diligently after the truth."

"Come again?" asked a puzzled Mrs. Santos.

"What I mean to say," replied the Shoe Lady, standing both tall and proud in her confession, "is that I'm the grandmother all men go to see—thus the 'Old Woman' part of my title."

"You?" said Mrs. Santos, feeling scandalized. "You're the infamous grandmother? That's disgusting!"

"Well, don't blame me," the Shoe Lady retorted defensively. "I don't say it—the men do. I'm proud of my profession and the living it provides. It's the men who feel guilty afterward and thus end up thinking they have something to hide. It's a trick they learned long ago from my sister, and they've been putting it to good use ever since."

Mrs. Santos viewed the Shoe Lady's last remark with skepticism while wondering just what kind of cattle craps she was being asked to swallow. She knew of no sister and made a point of saying so. "Well," replied the Shoe Lady, "she had nowhere near my lust for life!" Her enthusiasm evaporated quickly as if a winter draft were blowing away the last tattered remnants of warmth and sunshine from an unseasonably mild autumn while being left out to dry like old laundry on a clothesline and whipping in the wind. Filling the empty space as it rode on those wintry gusts the cold melancholy of despair descended upon the Shoe Lady as she thought about her sister, whom she hadn't seen for ages. "My sister's passed," she sadly replied, and a single tear ran forlornly down her cheek.

"Away?" asked Mrs. Santos, uncertain of what the old whore meant and unnerved and shaken by the sight of that lone teardrop. Feeling threatened by the Shoe Lady's insinuations, Mrs. Santos viewed her as an enemy, and one didn't, she knew, take pity upon one's enemies. Discovering their faults and weaknesses, one pounced upon one's enemies in an effort to exploit those character deficiencies before their enemies could do likewise, and such pouncing left little room for charity. Now, to discover pity within herself—and for a harlot at that—the farmer's wife viewed the solitary droplet with acute discomfort as it made its lonely journey down the side of the Shoe Lady's visage. Mrs. Santos found herself torn between the desire to reach out and the urge to mock and pull away, afraid of the woman both on principle and for the uncertainties she'd brought to light regarding her own standing with her husband.

"Both away and into legend," came the Shoe Lady's wistful reply.

"Legend?"

"Of course," said the Shoe Lady. "Surely you've heard of her?" In fact, both the farmer and his wife had heard of her—they just hadn't made the connection yet. "My sister," said the Shoe Lady, "was Little Red Riding Hood, and it was she who first used the line about going to see Grandmother when in fact who she really ran off to be with was the big bad wolf in sheep's clothing. A frigging man, if you can believe it! Phallus that he was he stole her heart while robbing her of her virginity and absconding with her excuse, only to share it with his no-good buddies who in turn passed it on to all their friends. Now they all use it. Having lost both her maidenhead and her alibi to a bastard who used and then discarded her and having subsequently become the laughingstock of the Old Forest, she committed suicide. Selfish men! They stole from her, and if I could just for once contract the clap, I'd pay them all back, I surely would!"

This last tirade of the Shoe Lady's exceeded the bounds of Mrs. Santos's emotional endurance. Her nerves were shot, perhaps beyond recovery. Whether true or not, the Shoe Lady's tales were twisting and warping the fabric of her reality, and it was definitely time to leave. "Please," she cried to her husband, "please let us take our leave of this awful woman and be on our way!" As she pleaded with her husband, a sudden burst of tears ran down her cheeks like rainwater only to collect in the folds of her doubled and tripled chin. And it may be true what The Shoe Lady said earlier—that men are led around by their dingles. But such a guide only takes them so far.

THE CHRISTMAS RABBIT

In the end, whether good or evil, smart or stupid, and for reasons only they can understand, it is their hearts that men look to for final direction. Santos now looked to his and moved by pity, considered his wife and demanded of the Shoe Lady the knowledge and whereabouts of the secret door.

"It's under the bed."

"Under the bed?"

"Yes, that's what I said! There's a trapdoor. It leads through the toe and down into a tunnel which empties out in the middle of the forest. From there you can make your own way to wherever, unobserved and unnoticed by any passersby. But wherever you go, just make sure it's away from here! Now, vamoose—get a move on! Time's a-wastin', and I've got me a line of customers who need servicing!"

The couple quickly scurried under the bed—although for each of them it was a tight fit—and down the hole. But not before Santos, who being a man and thus subject to the master between his legs, turned around for one last wistful look at the Shoe Lady while indulging himself in a tiny daydream of what would unfortunately never be.

Now standing in the clutter which filled the Winnebago, Mrs. Santos found a new appreciation for the Shoe Lady and the affairs she managed. The Shoe Lady kept a clean house in a dirty business, and that said a lot. How Mrs. Santos wished for even half of the old harlot's children. With even a quarter of them all turning to and busy as bees, she just might get this cleaning job done and still leave herself enough time to prepare lunch. But she only had two extra sets of hands in Junior and Laddie, and they would just have to do.

She went into their bedroom expecting she would have to rouse them from sleep even though it was past noon. She was surprised to find both wide awake and dressed. "Well," she said with delight, "making a day of it, are we? Good. There's plenty of work to be done so just hustle yourselves on out into the living room and get busy doing it!"

Junior looked at Laddie and Laddie looked back. "Ma," Junior said, "we need to talk."

"Work first, talk later," their mother replied. Of course, there was no mention made of breakfast. Like lunch and dinner, when prepared by their mother, it was a meal the boys avoided religiously. "But, Ma, we really need to—"

Junior was suddenly cut off by the onset of a gale wind as it blew through the entrance to the wagon, which having suffered from the violence of the evening before, was still missing its door. The gale raged through the doorway, tearing at the curtains and whipsawing everyone's hair as it expended its turgid breath. Riding on the wings of that squall was a small thundercloud which passed through the entrance, filling the wagon and enveloping it. Lightning flashed as it filled the room. It felt dank and wet as it wrapped itself around the farmer's wife and her children. Growing in violence, it shook the walls of the Winnebago, first spitting out rain, deadly cold and freezing to the touch, and culminating in a fiery hail that scorched whatever it fell upon. The family knelt down in the middle of the living room, huddled around each other to protect themselves from the storm's fury. It reached a crescendo and then with a violent boom of thunder, suddenly ceased, disappearing as quickly as it came. With his arms wrapped about his mother and brother, Junior had the sensation that the three of them passed abruptly into the eye of a hurricane. Looking up, he saw that the air inside the trailer had magically cleared. Within this sudden lull stood The Powers That Be, their eyes glowing red, blazing with fury as they stood there reeking of vomit, stale corruption, and cow manure but nevertheless smiling like the great white sharks they'd been made to consume for dinner the evening before. Their pale hands shook with rage while their bodies, twitching with spite and residual illness, remained in the throes of the nausea brought about by last night's meal. Their eyes fell upon the kneeling trio and pierced them like swords. "Oh, madam," said they, "do rise and come forward, dear. We've a present for you!" And they did. Concealed within the palms of their left hands, the Witches each held a tiny dart dipped in a most vile and toxic poison. It was by far one of the most lethal tricks in their repertoire, having been distilled from the blood of pregnant black widow spiders. Yet for all its toxicity, it wasn't nearly as corrosive as the meal they'd been made to sit through the evening before. "Come, dear," they said. "Come and take your medicine."

Mistaking their meaning, Mrs. Santos was eager to advance. Now was the beginning of a whole new life, and her labors of yesterday were about to bear rich fruit! It was no more, she felt, than she deserved. She was right, of course, while being wrong at the same time.

Having spied upon the trio the previous night Junior knew exactly what his mother could expect even if she did not, and having sampled for himself his mother's cooking, knew as well that their dark gift was indeed no more than his mother deserved—and perhaps less. But she was, after all, to the best of his knowledge, his mother. He couldn't let her suffer such a fate as the one which now awaited her. So whether she deserved it or not, Junior, being the dutiful son he thought himself to be, would just have to find a way to rescue her. But how?

He was smart enough to realize if it came down to a simple fight that he was far outmatched while conceding to himself that there wasn't time for a verbal battle of wits whether he could win the day or not. What then to do? Was it possible to turn their own power against them?

Pressed for a solution, needing it quickly, and outmatched in a contest he couldn't win fairly, in desperation Junior did the only thing possible which presented to him any hope of saving his mother. Running into the kitchen, he reached up quickly to the counter and, grabbing ahold of it, knocked over the box of Quaker Oats...and had that been all that happened, then perhaps events might have come out differently, but of course, such events aren't so simple. They never are. Things have a way of getting out of control and beyond you, and this was as true in Olden Days as it is today and doubly so at that.

When the oats spilled, they came out with a terrific rumble and crash. The ground shook, trees fell, and the entire landscape for miles around groaned in agony. All this happened in the space of about three or four seconds, and the damage was just getting started. The terrific shaking spilled the Tidal Wave Tea, the Snowstorm Soup, the

Ice Cream, the Hurricane in a Jar, and all the other foodstuffs the trio had been preparing in order to feed a hungry planet. To call it a disaster was to understate a catastrophe.

This catastrophe produced both droughts and floods, which occurred alongside each other. Blizzards of snow and hail fought with squalls of rain for the same airspace. Dense fog—cold, damp, and wet as it came rolling in—competed and vied with high winds that were hot, arid, and bitter. The violence of their mixing produced tornadoes and twisters of terrific proportions that went ripping up and down the length of the forest and all the way to the sea, uprooting trees and houses and those who dwell in both, while the Tidal Wave Tea caused a curler so convulsive that it nearly covered the forest and washed it away.

When Helgayarn saw the oats go, she knew then and there that they were all in for the most serious helping of cattle craps that has ever been served up—but what could she do? Even for a Power That Be it was already too late. Her one coherent thought was that she would have to get that little truant who caused this disaster, and yet before she could complete the notion, was swept away by the floodwaters. Churning and turning, gurgling and gasping, she was borne aloft on the crest of rising tides and carried clear down to the other end of the valley, some hundreds of miles away. Brunnhilde was right behind her, screaming and choking on the mud and grit that the torrent produced. Betty was soon to follow and, "Yah!" was about all she had to say.

Such great forces released all at once and all in one place at that were too much for the poor landscape to take. With a groan that could be heard around the world the land split into separate pieces becoming what people would later refer to as the seven continents—eight if you counted Greenland. The few folk that survived the disaster were months digging out and cleaning up, and the trial, of course, had to be postponed as it took a whole month for The Powers That Be to make their treacherous way back through the wreckage.

And what of the Santos's and the rabbits? Well, as has been pointed out before, rabbits have their own ways of finding things out and as a result had been spying on Junior even as he had been eavesdropping on the Witches. They therefore had a pretty good idea of what occurred immediately after dinner and subsequently what might occur once the Witches had been afforded the opportunity to partially recover. Expecting the worst, they sent out the alarm to all of their brethren and then dug in deep and simply rode out the williwaw while holding on for dear life. They even included Jack in their efforts, although at first they were disinclined. But a Rabbit of Influence pointed out that they would need all the paws they could get if they were to complete the digging before sunrise and so be ready to meet the contingencies of the day. Accepting this necessity, the group acquiesced; however upon completion of the work and notwithstanding Jack's own individual efforts to see the endeavor accomplished, the rabbit s made ready to throw the poor bastard out anyway, but alas, there simply wasn't time…the storm had broken.

No one knew how the farmer and his wife survived, but they did. Suffice it to say that if her questionable cooking couldn't kill them, then nothing short of the end of the universe was going to be able to do 'em in either.

Junior and Laddie cheated death by grabbing ahold of an abandoned loveseat—part of the wreckage and flotsam of the washed-away Winnebago, and flipping it over, used it as a life raft to ride out the high winds and waves. During the more heightened periods of violence, they were threatened with loss of handholds but somehow maintained their grips. It seems that even in Olden Days, someone was watching out for drunks and small children. When the environment finally quieted and the storm subsided, the brothers found themselves hundreds of miles away from their home and washed up by the railroad tracks, which now bent and twisted like sourdough pretzels, made useless conveyances for the newfangled trains that rode upon them. So following their uneven course, the brothers started walking and made their protracted way to New York, having many adventures en route. When they arrived, they were found and adopted by Junior's real parents, the Dawes, to whom they gave misery and grief till the end of their days and so, for the most part, pass out of this tale.

The trial finally came about despite the lengthy postponement. Santos's house was thoroughly destroyed along with just about everything else, and he could no longer be quartered there while waiting upon his day in court. Instead the Witches gathered the forces, chanted the incantations, spoke the spells, and did the Watusi—all of which served to smelt some iron with which to fashion for the farmer some bars and a cage and it was in these that he awaited his court date. In the wake of the upheaval, the surrounding lands were twisted and broken, and raw ore of all types lay exposed for the taking. It was simply a matter of knowing what to do with it. The Witches therefore fashioned *two cages*, and into the larger of the two, they threw both farmer and wife—although Helgayarn, being the boss witch, was of a mind that they should just simply kill her. Once again it was Brunnhilde the Levelheaded, champion of restraint and advocate of the good appearance—if only for appearance's sake—who came to Mrs. Santos's temporary rescue. Like Helgayarn, Brunnhilde too wanted to kill that dame after nearly dying from her disastrous dinner. However, in the wake of the cataclysm, which came to be known the world over as *Hurricane Junior*, and their subsequent return from the other end of the valley—which was chock-full of misadventures and was a story in and of itself, Brunnhilde had much time to interview the surviving few whom they met upon their way. Between their digging, rearranging, and general straightening out, those survivors, both two- and four-legged, let her know both singly and as a group that they were not at all happy with the way things turned out. In fact, they were pretty upset regarding the whole ordeal and blaming The Powers That Be for their sad state of affairs. They knew, of course, that Santos's feud with the rabbits lay at the heart of their troubles and that his wife's subsequent dinner and his son's attempt to save her after serving it were all contributing factors and therefore had to be taken into account. But they reasoned that no matter how they counted it or factored in the participatory players, the answer one continually came up with and therefore the personages most responsible for blame were The Powers That Be who, if they really had the power, wisdom, and authority they were forever bragging about, should've seen this coming and taken appropriate steps to prevent it.

THE CHRISTMAS RABBIT

Given the collective mood of the refugees and their overall opinion of who was mostly responsible, Brunnhilde knew that a simple killing would not satisfy their craving for retribution and revenge; moreover, such an act would do nothing to restore to either her or her sisters, their prestige and position which they so ardently coveted and which they'd lost much of in the disaster's aftermath. With the loss of such prestige and position went also the authority to meddle, and without it, Brunnhilde knew, their existence counted for very little. The refugees wanted a grand compensation. She knew that a gaudy trial with all the trimmings and all the symbolism the trio could muster was only thing that would serve when it came time to pronounce sentence, mete out judgment, and restore their community standing. So using all her powers of persuasion and with Betty continually "yahing" in agreement, Bunny convinced Helly to simply lock the woman up. They could always kill her after the trial, Brunnhilde reasoned, since being the proceeding's judges, they were assured that the farmer and his wife would be found guilty of whatever charges they saw fit to cite them with. Certainly, one or two of those charges would carry the death penalty.

After the floodwaters receded and the Witches returned, Jack was handily turned over to The Powers That Be by the Rabbits of Influence who, in the wake of the disaster, unsure of how things would turn out or where blame would be laid, were taking no chances and handed over Nutmeg too, claiming that she'd been the lone conspirator in the nefarious scheme to rob Santos of his produce. It goes without saying that she denied the charges and pointed to a larger conspiracy—just as the Rabbits of Influence knew she would—but they rightly guessed that given her reputation and her loose way of living, nothing she claimed would be taken too seriously.

The date of the trial was set to coincide with the winter solstice, the shortest day of the year. Helgayarn, the head of the tribunal, wanted the four defendants dead and in the ground no later than one minute after sundown. Then she could turn her attention to finding that snot-nosed little brat who both caused the recent upheaval and who somehow slipped away in the confusion. She didn't for a moment count him as having died by his own actions. Even a Power That Be, she knew, was never that lucky.

The entire legalistic affair was nothing short of chicanery. To begin with, not a soul could be found in the immediate area, neither man nor animal, who did not enter the courtroom with some preconceived notion as to guilt and responsibility and what should therefore be done about it. That they'd already formed opinions and that most of those opinions bore out the verdict that the four on trial were guilty would have, under normal circumstances, pleased The Powers That Be. However, secret whispering intercepted by spies and related back to the trio indicated that most folk, both men and beasts, still held that the Witches were themselves largely responsible. And although no one around back then had gumption enough to do much about it other than grumble, the Witches knew that this consensus, were it brought forward in court, would cause them heap loads of cattle craps and concurrent troubles.

Given that locals always talk, and believing that anyone was apt to say *anything* while under oath, the trio therefore ruled that the surviving few were too prejudiced by ill will and bad feeling to be in command of the necessary temperament and impartiality needed to be sworn in, either as credible witnesses or dispassionate jurors. Objectivity, declared the trio, was forever behind them. The survivors would have plenty of time, the trio knew, in which to lay blame, pick scapegoats, and assign grudges—although in truth, such things have never required much effort, either then or now, and are easily realized. Laying blame is simple. It goes down quicker than new linoleum and scapegoats are always easy to find so along as we all have each other to turn to, and once we've found and fixed ourselves upon our chosen scapegoat then assigning it a grudge merely becomes a matter of choosing which one.

Be that as it may, the trio felt that the present sentiment only served to aggravate such possibilities. All the signs were there. Everyone, it seemed, had their own lawyer with whom they filed concurrent petitions and class actions suits as addendums to the actual trial itself—and none of us should be surprised at this because even back then, even in Olden Days, lawyers were a plague unleashed

THE CHRISTMAS RABBIT

upon the rest of us. They bred like flies, thrived on misery and, like mold in a Petri dish, kept increasing in both size and virulence until they spilt out of their confines and fell to the floor, infecting all around them. Their worst idea ever, lawyers were just another in the long list of ill-conceived solutions first propounded and then put forward by The Powers That Be.

Early on in their ascensions, the authority of The Powers That Be to both rule over and meddle in the affairs of others was offered a serious challenge by a powerful and well-organized special interest. This special interest, the MMA (Mesopotamian Medical Association), was not even known as such back then. They were simply referred to as the HMO, but however they were designated, and regardless of who did the name-calling, the HMO were good at throwing their weight around, and the trio knew it. Those *Homos*, as the Witches liked to refer to them, cast their own bones and feathers. They prescribed their potions and pedaled their aspirin. They, too, thrived on misery, and their services were much sought after when it befell. They took to making house calls and charging for them and since the misery that they most often addressed and the ailments prescribed for followed upon the heels of some prior action propounded, perpetuated, or provoked by the trio, the Homos came to be regarded as the treatment for, although not necessarily the cure to The Powers That Be. It was intolerable. As if they could be cured! The Powers That Be grew jealous of the Homos' growing influence. Determined to discredit them and so undermine their good standing and position within the community, the Powers sought after some means to offer up a challenge to them. The hacks carefully studied the quacks in an effort to discover an exploitable weakness which they could turn to their advantage. Yet despite intense scrutiny and meticulous examination, having turned the quacks both upside down and inside out, Helgayarn, Brunnhilde, and Betty were frustrated by their inability to unearth such a tool or grasp ahold of its handle. The trio, caught in the turmoil of growing criticism regarding their endeavors and confronted with a legitimate challenge to their authority, found that before the Homos, they felt impotent and helpless. Until they took note of one of the Homos' prescribed procedures, often employed and universally applied. It seemed to the trio that what most often the quacks and pill pushers prescribed for their patients when in the throes of various miseries and sufferings, was a good bleeding. Bleeding, felt the Homos, let the bad air out and the good air in, and so they made use of various leeches in numerous sizes, pasting them all over their patients' bodies in a futile though nevertheless valiant attempt to treat a disease for which the parasites were not specifically the cure. Bloodsucking leeches draining the life out of a person! Needless to say, The Powers That Be were suitably impressed although they kept such admiration to themselves, always careful to maintain their normal demeanor when questioned about this unusual treatment method—dour, aloof, and unimpressed. Secretly, however, they were agog at the procedure and the method of administration used to employ it and whispered gleefully to each other about the idea itself and the methods one might use to improve and develop it until finally the trio held that the Homos weren't so special after all and that to go them one better would be a matter of minimal effort. Therefore, in an attempt to improve upon the leach the trio gathered unto themselves a select assortment of the species, chosen both for size and vigor, and employing high growth foods, selective breeding, gene manipulation, and steroids, went about the task of fortifying them by making them larger, more virulent, and less susceptible to penicillin, until at last they turned out the lawyer—the most insidious parasite and prolific bloodsucker ever to come down the pike. Lawyers made all their other solutions, including *Tides*, *Tidal Waves*, and *Ice Ages* seem like a surprise visit from Publisher's Clearinghouse—and like the farmer and his wife, nothing short of the end of the universe was ever going to be able to eradicate them.

In the wake of *Hurricane Junior* this glut of shysters and pettifoggers had clients galore, each looking to sue somebody and all knowing that the only bodies worth the effort were the trio themselves. Therefore the ladies rendered a unanimous decision in favor of a venue change but soon found that enacting it was a different matter altogether. Everywhere they looked they took note that bias and bad feelings were rearing their ugly heads while the lawyers and the clients they fed off were to be found by the boatload, each armed with countersuits and depositions and waiting to pounce upon the three hags. All they would require, the trio knew, was one small-minded attorney with the courage enough to file first…then the rest would follow suit like an avalanche. It seemed a foregone conclusion then that finding a suitable venue, one free of preconceived notions regarding guilt and responsibility and so, by inference, risk-free to The Powers That Be, was beyond even the trio and therefore impossible. Then Brunnhilde suggested Australia.

"Australia," inquired an incredulous Helgayarn, "but that's a bit far afield, isn't it?" Brunnhilde reluctantly agreed that this was so but stated her case anyway. "It's one of the few places far enough out," she replied, "to be isolated from public opinion."

Betty gave to her sister her sterling endorsement. "Yah!"

"I don't know," Helgayarn replied. "It seems awfully dicey to me and a tiresome chore, to say the least, to ship all the lawyers, litigants, deposers, and witnesses from here to there. We'll be a month of Sundays doing it—even if we use Federal Express!" It was true. The logistics of such an undertaking were a nightmare. In the end, rather than shipping the whole shebang to the Land Down Under, the trio instead decided to impanel an Australian jury and bring 'em to the forest. It was a journey of some length, although perhaps not as long as some of you might imagine since the continental breakaway only recently occurred and Australia, along with everything else, had only drifted a couple of hundred feet. Still, it was an arduous undertaking nevertheless to get a jury from the Land Down Under (which hadn't really gone under yet—more like sideways) to the forest and beyond the capabilities of anyone—except, of course, The Powers That Be, who being the big blowhards that they were, whipped up a terrific wind, bringing the catamaran and the jurors who sailed upon it, from Australia to the Forest by the Sea, in record time.

The jury itself was aptly chosen for the affair, having been made up of twelve wallabies and a koala bear to serve as alternate—making it a true kangaroo court, both in appearance and function.

The two attorneys for the defense and the prosecutor as well were three wise old birds from the venerable firm of Owl, Owl, & Peacock. That two hacks from the same house should be representing opposing clients in a litigation and, further, should a third hack from that very same firm represent the state in the same case, might appear to you and I to be a conflict of interest. But believe you me, there were no conflicting interests here—these shysters had one interest and one interest only, and that was to suck up to the Witches just as far as their little brown beaks would let them.

Because Jack spent all his savings in New York and because Santos had impounded from him anything of value that was salvageable after the disaster, each was declared to be indigent and therefore had their mouthpieces appointed for them. Bad for them. Good for The Powers That Be, who could then pick and choose from a whole slew of ambulance chasers in order to find just the very three they needed who could be molded, folded, and shaped into perfectly functioning, court-appointed puppets, the strings of whom could be easily pulled without anyone else even noticing they were there; and yet finding these three was not as easy as you or I might suppose. Because even in Olden Days and especially in the wake of the disaster, although animals were rare and people even rarer still, pettifoggers, as has been stated before, were thriving, and there were far too many of them, even back then, than was good for folk. Such numbers in such variety made picking and choosing while culling through the cartloads of cattle crappers both onerous and time-consuming. However, where there's a will there's a way, and eventually through sifting the slime and whatnot, the trio narrowed it down to the three previously mentioned.

Court was convened in a hollowed-out bole of an ancient redwood that stood almost adjacent to what was left of Sequoia Estates and was so chosen in order to accommodate the large crowds that were to be expected. The trio wanted plenty of witnesses—both to their power and their willingness to use it upon those they deemed troublemakers.

Led into court with his wife at his side and with Brunnhilde as guard, Santos was met by the roar of the crowd. It sounded like an arena full of Romans greeting the sacrificial Christian. But since neither existed yet, either Romans or sacrificial Christians, Santos mistook the crowd's bellow as an indication of his personal approval

THE CHRISTMAS RABBIT

rating. With hands clasped over his head and arms waving to and fro, he returned their roar with one of his own, a good and hearty "Ho!" He no doubt thought that victory was in the bag. It wasn't; he was.

Immediately after the farmer and his wife, Jack, along with Nutmeg, was led in by Betty, and upon hearing the derisive roar that was fostered upon Santos and seeing him return it with one of his own could not help but think, *What an idiot!* On his worst day, Jack could run circles around the Tortoise—both physically and mentally; and to give Jack credit, he knew that this was no big feat and therefore nothing to brag about. But even Santos, he thought, should be able to recognize the roar of hungry lions when he was about to be thrown to them! He looked up at Betty as they walked down the center aisle. "Well, this is it, isn't it?" he asked.

"Yah," Betty replied.

"It would be foolish to try and run, wouldn't it?"

"Yah."

In his nervousness, Jack tripped and fell over a tree root, dragging Nutmeg down with him. Betty stooped over and, gently picking them up, placed each upon their feet.

"Thank you," Jack said.

"Yah," replied Betty.

Nutmeg said nothing.

Jack paused for a minute to scratch his nose and gather his wits. There had to be a way out of this. There had to be. Overhead a loon, serving as court crier, sang out the minutes in order to warn those not already seated within the bole of the massive sequoia that the appointed hour was fast approaching and that stragglers should make all effort to find and then take their respective places in the gallery.

Not really expecting an answer, Jack asked his captor a question anyway, "Isn't there anything we can do to escape?"

Betty gave the question considerable thought. "Yah," she said.

"That's it?" Jack asked with mounting fury. "Yah?"

"Yah."

"I suppose then," said the rabbit, "that we're to just kill ourselves and end it quickly, right?"

"Yah."

"Well, I won't go quickly. And I certainly won't go quietly!"

"Yah!"

"Tell me," asked the rabbit sourly, his pheromones made flinty and bitter by mounting fear of the inevitable, "do the three of you enjoy doing this to those who can't fight back?" It was a dangerous question—both in the asking and the answering, and Betty knew it. But she also knew that these two, along with the other couple, were not likely to survive the day and therefore live long enough to tell anyone her reply. Thus she did not hesitate when giving her answer.

"Yah."

Jack gave her a look that would quiver lettuce. Unfortunately for him, Betty wasn't lettuce. She hardly even shivered, and the spasms she did display were not out of fear but from a small chuckle uttered in response to the growing sense of humor residing deep within her. Betty found this whole ordeal—minus that dreadful meal, of course—to be extremely funny unlike her sisters, who, being perpetual paranoids, were blind to its humorous aspects and who only viewed the scenario as it played out to be an attempt to grab power—if not by those directly involved than by others who were watching and waiting in the wings. Helgayarn and Brunnhilde had little sense of humor—especially in moments like this. Betty, on the other hand, thought it to be the height of hilarity and lived for just such eventualities. When you don't talk much, when all you do is listen to what's going on around you and to what others say, then occurrences such as these become times to be savored for the words spoken within them. Unknown to the other two who would not have liked it one darned bit, Betty, not being much of a talker, was a terrific listener and even better stenographer. In her silence, she secretly kept a journal and intended on some day publishing her memoirs—with or without the approval of the other two. She even had a working title, *In My Own Words—Confessions of a Witch by Betty, Power That Be*. Granted, the title was a little wordy and would no doubt need some reworking—but the book, she was sure, would be a smash. It would not be kind to anyone but her. It would ream Helgayarn and Brunnhilde for being the bullies they were and would make Betty a fortune if she could only finish it. Then she'd shake the dust of those two from

THE CHRISTMAS RABBIT

her feet—of that you could be sure! It was Betty's opinion that in moments like this, when folk reached a stage of crisis wherein everything they clung to hung in precarious balance and threatened to teeter, those folk often said and did the most outlandish things! In this Betty was usually right, and so she hung on Jack and on every word he uttered, waiting for both the profound and hilarious. Oftentimes, she knew, it was hard to separate the one from the other. Thus she recorded everything in order to quietly reflect upon her observations later. For now, however, she was here with Jack and would therefore make every effort to see that the rabbit's last words were jotted down for posterity.

Betty observed that the female did not have much to say. Although not surprised, Betty pondered this nevertheless. Females, no matter who they are or what they are, love to talk. It's in their genes, and Betty had only to consider her sisters to be assured of that. My—but how those two loved to blow their own trumpets! Still, Nutmeg said nothing. She just half-heartedly hopped along with her head bowed and her tail between her legs. Betty did not find her silence unusual as she knew all about Nutmeg and realized that although the doe was great at oral, words were never going to be her forte—even if by some unforeseen miracle she later found the time to practice them. No, deeds were Nutmeg's meat! Always had been. For Nutmeg, actions always spoke louder than words. And what action! Betty knew that rabbits down through the ages would praise Nutmeg and her talents, thus ruing the day that the Witches robbed them of her prowess!

Oh well, thought Betty, too bad. They shouldn't have handed her over so readily.

Feeling as if he had nothing to lose, which he didn't, Jack asked Betty if she liked being a witch.

"Yah."

"Do you ever say anything besides yah?"

"Yah."

"Wonderful," Jack replied. It would be his luck, he knew, to finish up his days by having a conversation with someone who had a one-word vocabulary and who spoke in monotone at that. Well, he supposed, one word was better than none at all. "My lawyer," he ventured, "seems like a pretty sharp bird."

"Yah," came the expected reply.

"Taking into consideration the fact he's so crafty, shouldn't I think it rather strange that you three are allowing him to represent me?" Jack looked up into Betty's eyes, trying to discover for himself a hint of guile or deceit. "I should think that you three would want a second-string public defender," he continued, "with an overbooked caseload and fresh out of law school."

"Yah."

"Then why the bird?" Jack asked. "And I've heard that the fat boy's mouthpiece is from the same law firm. Shouldn't I be worried about conflicting interests and fair representation?"

Betty paused before answering to pick her nose and flick a booger. "Yah," she said after completing her drilling.

Someone in the gallery threw a rock, which connected squarely with Jack's head. Stunned and bloody, the rabbit fell to the ground. "That'll teach you!" the rock thrower cried. "I lost my home in the flood because of you! And all my cattle are dead!" A chorus of yays shouted out by an angry crowd, followed upon the heels of the stone thrower's last remark, and then someone else shouted, "Draw and quarter the ratty little beast! A death done quick is too good for him—and twice for the farmer!" Folk, both two- and four-legged, were not happy with their lot, the loss of their homes and property, and the realization that they were powerless to avenge themselves upon those truly responsible for their suffering only fed the appetite of their runaway emotions. They only knew that through no fault of their own, most of them were in for some really tough times. Since the true perpetrators of their suffering were unassailable and therefore untouchable, someone else, they reasoned, should be held accountable and made to pay for their hard luck and sorrows. The farmer and the rabbit, who started all this mess with that silly feud of theirs, looked as though they were likely enough candidates, so why the heck not?

Betty gently picked Jack up, wiping the blood off his head and smoothing out the fur between his ears and on the bridge of his nose.

THE CHRISTMAS RABBIT

"Good grief," Jack weakly managed, "they're blaming me for earthquakes and floods? But I wasn't even there!"

"Yah!" Betty replied with a chuckle. The situation was getting funnier by the moment. Pretty soon, she knew, her sides would be splitting. Maybe, thought she, if they split wide enough then all the noxious gases and poisons trapped within would leak out and cause the thousands here to get sick and vomit. Wouldn't that be delicious!

"I shouldn't be taking the heat for those things," Jack said, his anger steeping. "For that matter, neither should Farm Boy. If anyone's to blame, it's you three witches! You're the ones that were cooking up those infernal concoctions! *Snowstorm Soup*, *Tidal Wave Tea*, and the rest of the bloody lot! You're to blame—you!"

"Yah!"

"Oh, lick my furry—" But he stopped, sensing that there was only so much Betty would be willing to take, even in such circumstances as these. True, it didn't matter, he supposed, since he was about to die anyway. But when death awaits you right around the corner, then those few remaining moments it leaves you with become precious and you begrudge giving up even one of them. Then again, there was always the chance, however slim, that he might burrow his way out of this mess. If that were ever going to happen, then he knew that he needed to watch his tongue and keep his wits. "I'm sorry," he said. "Will you accept my apology for losing my temper?"

"Yah."

"I'm forgiven, I'm sure."

"Yah."

From out of the crowd a scalper who'd bought up all the front row tickets in the gallery approached Jack with the intention of making a profit. Weaving a path in between bodies packed tighter than sardines in a can, he pushed and jostled his way through the throng, using a judiciously placed elbow from time to time in order to open up space and make way. He finally reached his target.

"Hey, boy!" he said, "I got me two front row seats left! Great for seeing the show! Got you your tickets yet?"

"You banana head," Jack replied. "I am the show!"

The ticket scalper eyed him suspiciously then recognizing who he was, merely frowned. "I should have seen right away," he replied as his eyes fell away from Jack and turned to regard Nutmeg instead. "How about one for the missus?" he asked.

"She's not the missus," Jack said, "and she's part of the show too!"

Not one to give up on a sale, the scalper spun about to confront Jack once more. "Well, how about buying a couple anyway?" he asked. "After all, it's a bet that you're not going to need moolah where you're going! And I, my good beast, still have a family to feed." He paused for a moment and, reaching into his pocket, retrieved his wallet, which he opened to reveal photos. "And it's not going to be easy," he continued, shoving the picture in Jack's face, "in the wake of all this ruckus you've started."

"I didn't start it!" Jack vehemently replied. "And besides, I don't have any money. I'm a rabbit, you idiot! We don't use money. Our currency's acorns, and frankly my tree's a little bare at the moment. Attorney's fees and all that."

"Your attorney's court-appointed," countered the scalper. "Everybody knows that! C'mon, give a hardworkin' fella a break, why don't ya? You and the farmer may not need tickets to get in, but that didn't stop *him* from buying six! So c'mon, whaddya say?"

"Piss off!" yelled Jack.

The scalper offered the rabbit a sour appraisal, still not entirely convinced that Jack was as broke as he claimed. No doubt, this one, thought the scalper, is trying to follow in the footsteps of the farmer's wacky ancestor, Ebenezer, and take it all with him. There was no commission here, he realized, and so turning toward Betty, put on his best salesman's face.

"How about you, ma'am? I've still got two prime seats left!"

"You idiot!" Jack repeated. "She's a witch, and witches get in for free!"

"Yah," Betty replied with darkly shaded undertones. The scalper hung his head, gave up, and drifted off into the crowd.

"Asshole!" Jack whispered viciously to the scalper's retreating back.

"Yah," Betty said solemnly, agreeing with his quiet epithet. She stared intently at the dwindling form of the scalper as the crowd swallowed him up, her eyes burning his countenance into her memory and photographing his receding image onto the blank pages of her soul. She'd remember this one—of that you could be sure.

It was easy for the rabbit to read, both from the look in her eyes and the clouds on her brow, that Betty was not pleased with the fact that she'd not been immediately recognizable to the ticket seller, who instead had to be prompted into recognition. She paused for a couple of moments to wonder if Helgayarn was trying to steal somehow her allotted portion of Manifest Destiny and the subsequent change it brought about, thus making her less noteworthy and memorable to the mere mortals who served her while Helgayarn grew more so instead. Perhaps it was a conspiracy. Perhaps right now, even as she was tied up with this rabbit, both Helgayarn and Brunnhilde were secretly discussing amongst themselves the best means of bringing to fulfillment their joint endeavor to rob her of all manifest destiny and subsequent change, making her a pauper and depriving her completely of the recognition which she rightly deserved and which, like Helgayarn and Brunnhilde, guarded jealously. With recognition went the authority to get things done for being imperfect; although never admitting to it, the Witches derived a large portion of their authority to act from the belief of those few mortals who through self-deception or misguided faith dared hold out hope that the trio could accomplish anything worthwhile or noteworthy in the first place. It therefore angered Betty to think that Helgayarn and Brunnhilde might be secretly robbing her of her deserved portion of recognition and limelight. This limelight, after all, was such a lovely shade of green, and she thoroughly enjoyed having all her doings and affairs tainted and stained in its colorful hue and tint. It was the only reason for getting into this "Power That Be" business in the first place. Oh, there was the power, of course, and the uneasy license the trio had with which to dispense it. But having the power in and of itself was poor compensation for the long hours which by necessity had to be put in while dispensing it. It was the fame and recognition that really made the tedious business worthwhile; for being a Power That

Be was a helluva lot of work—even for three such talented dames as they. The reward for such a busy day came in the instant recognition you received in any place to which you might venture. Such recognition manifested itself in various ways, such as having tables at restaurants and the diners who supped at them, instantly cleared away upon word of your impending arrival. It was always being asked to the front of the line. It was having your opinion sought after constantly—often on subjects that you knew nothing about while having at your disposal the experience of years of parlor talk and attendance at chic art openings which endowed you with the savvy and ability to make any outrageous criticism sound both conversant and relevant. It was celebrity status and once tasted, no other fruit could ever be quite so sweet.

It both angered and frightened Betty to think that she might be losing her Manifest Destiny, its subsequent change (which even at this moment she was jingling in her pockets), and her celebrity status all in one fell swoop. Such was the way of carefully constructed conspiracies. Let the other two have their day, thought she. Someday my book will tell all and then they'll get theirs! And maybe somewhere, hidden between its lines, I'll write a very special little magic for that snot-nosed little ticket scalper. And maybe, just maybe when he reads it, he'll shrivel up like a ripe and rancid old toadstool and then somebody else, crying out in disgust at his deteriorating visage, will step on and squash him! It would serve him right, she thought, for being so damned cheeky as to not recognize me in the first place!

Jack, who stood looking at Betty and who wasn't half dumb for a rabbit—although no one was going to confess it—sensed some of what was going on in her thoughts as she stood there staring intently after the disappearing form of the hawker. There might be an opening here, he thought, but could he exploit it? He'd have to be careful—but how could one err on the side of caution when despite the need for such discretion necessity demanded that he hurry his play up? They were already two thirds of the way down the aisle and fast approaching the hole into hell. The ancient sequoia in which they stood, jam-packed and crowded to the rafters, seemed to coalesce around him, all musty and dusty as though it expected to be fed,

THE CHRISTMAS RABBIT

while from every tier, from trunk to uppermost branch, the roar of hungry lions reverberated and echoed until his ears rang and his nose bled. "Jiminy Cricket!" said he, having to yell in order to be heard over the crowd. "That guy! He's the one who should be making this walk. Imagine—the nerve of him, selling tickets to a show and not even knowing who's on the playbill. Damned poor form, I'd say!"

"Yah," came Betty's reply.

"And of course it goes without saying," although Jack said it anyway, "that you should've been distinguishable instantly—after all, one such as yourself naturally stands out in a crowd. Piss poor form!"

"Yah."

Using his weather eye, Jack attempted to gauge the ill winds in those thunderclouds forming on Betty's eyebrows. "I wonder," he asked, "if the other two were approached about tickets? As if they, like you, even needed tickets! But I suppose not. They're already up on the stand and behind the judge's bench. It's plain enough to see who they are." Jack paused momentarily to let his words do their work for him. *Let her chew on that for a bit*, thought he, *maybe she'll choke!* When a minute or so passed, he continued, "Say, how come you're down here with me anyway? Isn't this a job for the bailiff?

"Yah!" Betty replied, spitting out the word.

"Well," said Jack in his most reasonable and conciliatory manner, "I should think you know your own business, and I'm sure that you do—but it does beg the question, what are you doing down here? Surely you belong up there, with them! No bailiff after, all, ever gets mentioned in any of the histories and storybooks! Are the other two stealing your best lines?"

"Yah!"

"That's rather mean-spirited of them and unfair, I should think."

"Yah!"

Jack strove earnestly to keep his poker face. Sometime between his initial capture and now, he'd picked up the game and learned its nuances and so knew that it was time to raise the stakes or fold. "How about you just let me go?" he asked. "It'll serve the other two right! Then together you and I will take on the lot of them—and maybe throw the Tortoise into the bargain too?"

Betty merely looked at him.

"C'mon," Jack urged. "Do it! Together we can make our joint escape and lay low somewhere deep in the forest. I know plenty of places! And then, when the time's right, we can come back with fists and fur flying and kick all of their behinds! Whaddya say?"

Betty, laughing like a lunatic at the hilarity of the notion, pushed him through the gate and into the defendant's box. *"Not a chance,"* she replied.

As Jack tumbled into the box, Helgayarn banged her gavel, officially calling the court into session. Betty left Jack at the table for the defense and in the not-too-reliable talons of his attorney. Then she quietly made her way to the judge's bench to stand alongside Helgayarn and Bunny.

Helgayarn gave the command for all to rise.

Over at the defense table, Jack's mouthpiece was having a hard time of it and could not get Jack, who now accepted defeat but who was nonetheless going to stick to his principles, to stand up. "Rise, you idiot" the old bird said, feathers ruffling in frustration. "Don't make this harder on yourself than it has to be! Sitting there contemptuously makes you look guilty!" Jack didn't listen and had to be forced to his hind legs. Even Santos, who was usually too daft to realize where trouble lurked, had the good sense to stand and show the court some respect. Intimidated into silence, for once the fat farmer had nothing, however pointless, to say. Both he and Jack were feeling the weight and majesty of the court. It pressed down on all sides, assaulting them from every angle, as it was designed to. In this at least, Helgayarn, Brunnhilde, and Betty knew their business—which was why they chose the redwood as the ideal location in which to convene court. One of the few remaining trees left standing after the high winds and even higher tides, the Witches thought it the capital location in which to practice their brand of law. Now, to be sure, some of their reasons were practical. For instance it was, as stated before, adjacent to Sequoia Estates—or what was left of the development in the wake of Junior's noble defense of his mother. Thus there were rooms handy and to be had for the various witnesses, relevant experts, and court functionaries who'd be brought in just so this cir-

THE CHRISTMAS RABBIT

cus could roll. There were the Australian jurors and their alternates, and deposers galore, it seemed, from the four corners of the world and beyond—all of whom were brought in at great expense to testify before the court as to how they and those around them had been made to suffer in the wake of the terrible tragedy which the prosecution claimed was the direct result of actions perpetrated by the defendants. All these witnesses had to be housed somewhere, even if "somewhere" had long since been considered substandard and was one step away from being condemned. Even the Witches themselves were quartered at the sequoia, having kicked the current tenant out of the presidential suite, as their custom-made Winnebago covered wagon on which they'd four payments left, had been totaled in the previous tumult and those Insurance Dicks wouldn't pay up. Their carrier, Repressive Insurance of Mesozoic Mesopotamia, whose acronym was RIMM, rather than do the decent thing and settle, cited some hidden and arcane clause buried deep within their policy which exempted Repressive from "any and all acts of The Powers That Be or any actions or inactions indirect or otherwise, resulting from said Powers" actions or inactions thereof, whether naturally occurring or supernaturally brought about, and not withstanding outside agitation or influence by farmers, rabbits, or their progeny, ongoing or intermittent, and without regard to severity, within the confines of said planet, Earth (although back then they called it Mungo) in which said vehicle is licensed and authorized to be insured, etc. They had lawyers of their own, and this wasn't the first claim they'd ever denied and certainly wouldn't be the last—but it did establish the standard for all its future offspring and misbegotten stepchildren—those Prudentials, Mutual of Omahas, Allstates, and all the other guarantors of security who would follow the example of the pattern established by accepting as collateral the hard-earned savings of their respective beneficiaries while at the same time working in earnest to deny them those same benefits when they were needed most. It was a great way to make money back then and remains so today. In fact, so utile were they in the performance and engagement of this particular sort of usury that folk back in Olden Days, when denied their rightful claim by a Repressive adjuster, rather than whine, moan, or go into lengthy detail regarding its particulars, instead referred to such screwing with a bitter smile, as having received a RIMM Job. Wieners.

Yet most of the Witches' reasons for choosing this particular site were practical in no way whatsoever and stemmed from a further desire on their part to flex their muscle in a big way that others were sure to take note of. It was one of the few remaining trees left standing in the wake of *Hurricane Junior*, and it did stand next to Sequoia Estates, making it both convenient and handy as well as large and roomy. It had, however, one debilitating feature. Despite the recent upheaval, the old redwood still stood hale and hearty. Solid to the core, it was green and still growing.

Well, thought the trio, *this won't do at all*. They reasoned that already having settled everyone into the sequoia, and having paid for the rooms in advance, they'd be damned now if they'd up and move the whole shebang to the other side of the forest for the convenience of obtaining proper gallery space. The hearty old redwood would just have to do, wouldn't it? Besides, with so few of its brethren left standing, it would surely be missed once they finished up with it and its rotten and ruined hulk toppled over. A final punishment to those folk from the immediate area, both two-and four-legged, who looked with wonder upon the mighty tree as it stood guard in the forest. Those tree huggers, reasoned the Witches, were the same folk who were witnesses to all this damned silliness between the farmer and the rabbit and who therefore should've had the common sense to put a stop to it before it got so crazy and out of hand. The trio felt that the locals had it coming. Therefore they'd take their tree and use it to spite them. So they hollowed it out. Charred and seared it from the inside out, using a secret magic that they employed at special times only. It gave off a noxious reek that hung in the air like old farts and corruption, and its sourness could be smelt and tasted throughout the forest and beyond. Even those in Australia with sensitive smellers found themselves holding their noses. From top to bottom, old redwood had been scoured and burnt out. Cored, like a sour apple. There were perches and benches attached and drilled into its newly hollowed-out sides, starting at the base of the bole and continuing up to the topmost branch. It was simple, utter abuse and carnage—and done in the name of progress and order, and it is a lesson to those of us who live Nowadays. Today, just as it was back then, the power of the law is a destructive force if placed in the wrong hands. Therefore we should be careful, very careful, about whom we let wield it.

But back then, as is most often today, nobody gave a cattle crap about being careful. They were too busy watching their backs, looking after their own skins, while trying to line up on what they thought would be the winning side. Therefore every perch, seat, stool, stand, bench, and lounge chair was occupied. In the ordered silence following the call to court, the mere breathing of all those men and animals created an echoing din which the tree, like the woodwind it now was, reverberated and threw back, causing a constant and underlying hum. Both Jack and Santos looked up to see all the humming faces—and there were hundreds, looking balefully down at them. Is it any wonder that they were claustrophobic and dizzy?

The jury was sworn in and the trial got underway. Because of the volume of witnesses brought in to offer testimony, proceedings lasted for weeks, during which time the two old birds for the defense sat meekly by as their senior partner, the peacock, ripped them apart, feather by feather. Not once did they object to any of his outlandish allegations, nor did they challenge a single piece of evidence despite Jack's impassioned pleas to "do something"! Instead they buckled their beaks while quietly whispering convoluted concepts of legal strategy in the ears of their clients. The fix was in, and since all three ambulance chasers had bar fees due that month and since such fees were paid to The Powers That Be who, being the only judges for miles around, were naturally the heads of the bar, the hacks were taking no chances and ensuring for themselves that the wheels of justice remained properly greased.

After hearing the evidence, most of which was trumped up, the jury retired for a mere fifteen minutes and returned with a verdict of "Guilty, Guilty, Guilty."

One "guilty" was bad enough. Two was even worse. But a triple "guilty" repeated as it was for emphasis and effect all but ensured that the four defendants would have their gooses cooked—and so they would have were it not for one curious happenstance. The Witches pronounced sentence. "Death by dismemberment!" they uniformly decreed, with Betty lending to the declaration her, "Yah!" A hush fell over the gallery. Perhaps those in court were expecting the sentence to be carried out then and there... But up popped the guardian ad litem to ask, "What about the children? This is no good. There's no justice here! What about them?"

Even in Olden Days, the courts always employed a guardian ad litem to ensure that the interests and welfare of little children were not lost in the legalistic bamboozle and trappings of the wheel of justice as it turned perpetually onward. The children being referred to were not Junior and Laddie because no one but Santos and his wife gave a cattle crap about them—but rather were numbered by all the sprites and waifs made homeless in the recent upheaval and who, in most instances, now faced the dangers of starvation and exposure to the elements. A low-throated grumble started in the upper tiers of the gallery as folk of all kinds, both two-legged and four, paused to give thought to this weighty question. It would be just jolly, they thought, to see the farmer and the rabbit drawn and quartered. But would such gratification serve to accomplish anything useful? Would it give them back their homes or put food in their children's stomachs? Most folk began to see that it wouldn't. The grumble became a groan, and as it worked its way down to the courtroom floor, echoing and trebling as it fell, became a full-throated roar. "What about our children? Feed our offspring! Protect our progeny!" There were many variations of this offered up and the roar of them echoed like thunder as they resounded throughout the hollowed-out tree.

Helgayarn shot Brunnhilde an inquiring glance, and she answered it with one of her own, which seemed to say, "You fool! You should have foreseen this!" Betty, chuckling heartily, merely said, "Yah!"

The din went on unchecked for some minutes until Helgayarn restored order by rapping her gavel with all force, breaking it asunder. Lightning leapt from its shards, bathing the interior of the tree and all inside with a cold electric light. Thunder boomed and rolled throughout the confines and all perches, benches, stools, and lounge chairs were suddenly emptied as everyone within fell from their seats. There was, after all, no point in having such power, if you couldn't display it from time to time. Folk quickly came to recognize discretion as the better part of valor and therefore collectively shut up. Staring out and up at the silenced crowd, as if her very glance would cause them to wilt and melt, Helgayarn made an appraisal of their predicament. It would seem, she grudgingly had to admit, that once again, double-dealing fate with all its perfidy, was about to stab them in their backs by robbing them yet again of both their standing and their satisfaction. "Well," she said, her voice screeching like a shrew, "we're all so fickle, aren't we?"

"Yah," agreed Betty while Brunnhilde silently nodded.

"So its food you want, is it?" The crowd, feeling emboldened by Helgayarn's question, answered in the affirmative.

Helgayarn and Brunnhilde offered the throng a glacierlike stare while Betty, looking on silently, quietly took notes. There were whole chapters being enacted for her book here and now! "Very well," continued Helgayarn. "If you prefer food over justice, then food is what the lot of you shall get and may your stomachs grow sick of it!"

It was a small-minded and mean-spirited thing to say to be sure, but then the Witches had always excelled in small minds and mean spirits. Situations like this just brought to the forefront their natural proclivities. In truth, they were scared silly. The crowd turned upon them, demanding food for compensation rather than The Powers That Be's unique brand of magistrature. It was as much as admitting that they had no confidence in the Witches or the arm of the law they represented, to provide them with adequate restitution for the damages they'd suffered. Implied in all that was the notion that the crowd thought the trio to be more than nominally responsible for the situation in the first place. And although Helgayarn, Brunnhilde, and Betty already inferred that, it was with growing unease that the trio realized this to be the first time anyone in the crowd was bold enough to make reference to their "involvement" no matter how convoluted or protracted the implication. This was how rebellions started. What might the agitators do next? Helly's initial thought was to kill them all and do so quickly. Defendants, attorneys, jury and witnesses—just wipe them off the face of the planet and leave no trace of them ever having been there. But somehow, she knew, word would leak out. It always did. Even the Witches weren't powerful enough to prevent that. The sea of cattle craps they'd be made to wade through in the wake of that obvious abuse of power would most likely drown them, and even if it didn't they couldn't very well derive any satisfaction from "lording it over" subjects who no longer existed. What fun was there in that? Therefore it was time to pacify and sedate. The crowd, angry and upset, could too easily turn against them.

"What kind of food do you require?" Helgayarn asked them. There arose much discussion surrounding this question. Some favored vegetables of various sorts, but since the only vegetable farmer for miles around was Santos and since his farm and the good topsoil that went with it were washed away like everything else, that idea was quickly rejected. Others held out for steaks done over the grill, teriyaki style, but one or two cattle in the crowd mooed out their strenuous objections to that suggestion, killing the idea as quickly as the previous one. Another idea, quickly voted down, was rock candy, as dentists, unlike doctors, were few and far between. One suggestion after another was offered up only to be shot down until someone with vision stood up and asked, "Hey, what about omelets?"

And that's how the whole business got started.

The trio quickly retired to their chambers in order to confer upon the matter. It was decided that there was too much at risk and that the stakes were too high to let the farmer have a hand in any of it. He'd screw it up, the Witches reasoned, as surely as young boys grew into old men—and that they simply could not allow. And so, citing an idiot clause within the law, they appeared magnanimous and seemingly let the dumb farmer off the hook while at the same time branding him with yet another nickname—"Clause," due to the loophole in the referenced law that favored idiots and simpletons, but that was okay, for surely upon his release, he'd rendezvous with those two snot-nosed brats of his, and when he did, the trio intended to descend upon the entire family like vultures and settle up with the lot of 'em! Quickly, quietly, and somewhere deep in the wood where no one else would see. The rabbit then would have to carry the ball

THE CHRISTMAS RABBIT

and bear the punishment—and so it was decided. They didn't make it easy for him either. They cast a spell and took away his pockets which made gathering for Jack that much harder. Of course, rabbits have never been very good cooks—in fact, so poorly do they perform this art that within its purview, they could be said to be kissing cousins to the redoubtable Mrs. Santos. Spies, yes. Thieves—even better. But there never has been, and probably never will be, a rabbit renowned for its culinary prowess. The Witches feared some accidental poisoning such as they had been made to recently undergo, and so a compromise was reached. Jack would not have to beat the eggs, merely deliver them. Let the recipients scramble their own omelets.

No magic powers were given to Jack to aid him in his task, and as everyone knows, rabbits do not lay eggs—they're just not built that way. Thus Jack had to be about the business of stealing them from various birds of a feather when such birds were occupied elsewhere. The first trio that he robbed were none other than Owl, Owl, & Peacock—thus returning to them in equal measure as good as he got.

Nutmeg was sentenced to live out her life with Jack, bearing him children and aiding him in his task. All this she did gratefully, thankful enough to be alive and inside her own skin. An affection, and even love, grew between the two, for Nutmeg got everything she ever dreamt of as Jack became the most famous of rabbits and for a time was well thought of by everyone. Everyone, that is, except Santos, who hated all rabbits on principle; the Witches, who had no principles whatsoever and therefore had no love for anything but themselves; and the Rabbits of Influence and their cohorts, who jealously felt that they had been robbed of Nutmeg and her exceptional talents and whose envy grew in proportion to Jack's fame and popularity.

But as was said before, no magical powers were given to Jack. And without magic or a reasonable equivalent, eventually, we all grow old and die. It was as true in Olden Days as it is today, and it's the same for rabbits as it is for men.

One day, much later, Jack finally stopped running. He would deliver no more eggs. His children, jackrabbits of later descent, would carry on for him. Some were more famous and some less so.

Some were even considered infamous, like the rabbit who one year delivered shad roe. It caused quite a scandal and the uproar that followed in its wake could be heard around planet Mungo. Yet shad roe are eggs after a fashion, and in the end, despite all the grumbling and hard feelings, nothing could be done about it. But whether famous or not, notorious or just plain nefarious, Jack's descendants carried on, and the tradition continued, however imperfectly, on down to this very day.

BOOK 2
Nowadays

CHAPTER I

The Dawes Meet Their Destiny

Lawrence Torrance Dawe walked up the worn and flinty path to check his traps. Overhead the desert sun beat down unmercifully, but he didn't trouble himself with that. Having grown up in the desert and having survived its myriad degrees of heat, the sun with all its power and majesty had over the years become second nature to him, a day-to-day occurrence which simply had to be dealt with. He considered it, took the appropriate precautions, and then went about his day.

Most desert-dwellers are fearful of the sun and give it the respect it's due. Not Lawrence. It hadn't beaten him yet and he didn't figure that it ever would. You might regard such apparent disregard as crazy and you'd be right. Lawrence was loonier than a jaybird. With two cans perpetually short of a six-pack and an elevator that didn't stop on all floors, one has to wonder how he ever survived and more importantly, what he was doing out there in the first place.

His skin, parched again and again, was the color and texture of old shoe leather and his dirty blonde hair was bleached virtually white. His eyes were a pale blue and had the annoying habit of not jointly focusing—each would track off on its own, making it extremely difficult to engage him in conversation as one could never be sure where his attention lie. Yet he was not afflicted with what we term "lazy eye." His eyes were always working, and for all of looking like he was a million miles away, he rarely missed much. Lose sight of where you are in the desert or fail to recognize a pertinent feature regarding landscape or surrounding, and you're dead. The desert rarely forgives. Lawrence knew that if not much else.

He moved along the path as quietly as an Apache. In fact, it was an Apache that taught him this skill of stealth in exchange for some much-needed water. Lawrence had plenty of water which no doubt accounts for, at least in part, his unlikely survival in a harsh and brutal climate that could kill as quickly as a cobra or as slowly and painfully as cancer.

Lawrence was a diviner. What he divined was water. If there was moisture within a hundred miles, he could find it. If it was hidden under the ground, then he knew just where to dig in order to obtain it. He often wondered if this were an acquired skill or if he'd been born with it. He wasn't entirely sure, but he supposed it was probably the latter. Except for his Apache marching instructor, he could not remember a single tutor in his early life. There were his parents, of course, but having been dead since he was seven, they did not get the chance to teach him too much. What skills he had, with the exception of creeping, he'd either been born with or picked up along the way. The desert has a way of making you self-reliant, even if your rocker's squeaky—and even if you're off it.

As he crept along the path, placing one foot carefully in front of the other, not a twig did he bend nor a grain of sand displace. He was silence. He went about his desert barefoot and had been doing so ever since childhood, having finally outgrown his only pair of shoes.

If his skin was like old leather, then the soles of his feet were like cured elephant hide. Tougher than nails, there was nothing in his desert capable of piercing them. His Apache marching instructor, impressed by the durability of his dogs, adopted Lawrence on the spot, making him a foster son and member of the tribe and naming him *Sáí Ézhaazhé*, which when translated from Apache into the language of this story means Sand Toes. So Sand Toes he was to all of the Apaches—although, to be sure, others called him other things for other reasons.

Beside him and walking nearly as quietly as he, strode his daughter, Lauren Tea Dawe. Lauren was a little cherub, both in looks and demeanor. Barely seven herself, she nevertheless went with her

THE CHRISTMAS RABBIT

Da on most of his outdoor forays, be they trap-checking, water-prospecting, or just plain sand-shoveling—something Lawrence did for God only knows what reason. And she kept pace with this madman by relying on those traits which were her mainstay here in the desert, to wit: long-suffering and patience and an identification with and affinity for that passage of biblical verse which admonishes children to honor their parents that their days might be long on this earth. Lauren took that passage to heart. Her mother was lost and presumed dead, and Lauren's short life had already taught her that you needed a prayer out here if you were going to survive. With Da running the show, there were many times she knew when she could've used the wing too. Instead she patiently put up with her Da's eccentricities while repeating over and over to herself that one verse of scripture. Her mother, when she'd been alive, had read it to her again and again while the two of them waited for Lawrence to return home from the desert and whatever he'd been doing that day. Shortly after her Ma disappeared, Lauren took that verse and emblazoned it upon her heart and soul. It became for her a daily prayer and litany. In a place like this with a Da like that, she needed both. "Da," she said as they walked along, "can we change my name someday?" She hated her name, and the two of them had engaged in this conversation before. She was secretly petrified that she'd been named after her Da. Her name engendered all sorts of nicknames, none of which she favored, and supposedly funny jokes, all of which she found less than amusing. But with a middle name like Tea, Lauren grudgingly learned to accept such teasing. At least her nicknames and the reasons for them weren't as bad as her Da's. *Oh God,* she thought, *thank you for that at least!*

In his wild-eyed but endearing manner, Sand Toes snapped his head back over his shoulder while never breaking his forward stride. Eyes focusing on his daughter, they finally came to rest somewhere directly behind her. "La," he whispered—and he always whispered when trapping even though whatever he caught, by the time he got back around to claim it, was either dead or so near to being on its doorstep that such slyness and desertcraft were unnecessary. "Now, whaddya wanna go'n' do that fer, lass? 'Tis a grand old name!" Sand

Toes, like his barely remembered parents before him and like their parents before them, spoke in a heavy Irish brogue, rolling thickly huddled consonants like beer barrels off the tip of his tongue. Lauren had a hard time keeping up with it and understanding what was said, even more so when whispered and especially when she was tired. Though it was barely noon, they'd nevertheless been at it since early sunrise, flitting here, pit-a-patting there, prospecting water and checking traps. Sand-shoveling, she refused to participate in, finding it both boring and of no practical value. She was right, of course, and even Lawrence only looked upon the chore as a pastime and hobby—practice as it were, for his great quest. Therefore he did not demand her company when engaged in that endeavor. Still, water-prospecting and trap-checking weren't easy, especially at the pace her Da set, and now the sun, nearly at its zenith, beat down upon her unmercifully, sapping her of both strength and patience. Lauren pulled her sombrero a little further down her forehead in a mostly futile attempt to cut the sun's glare while creating for herself a bit more shade. "I want to change my name because it's stupid! Whoever heard of a daughter being named after her Da? I should've been named after Ma!"

"Careful, lass," replied her Da, "Yer Ma, God rest her soul, was a Dawe too and a foine one at that!"

"Da—she was your third cousin!"

"Aye, that she was, lass," Sand Toes replied, "and a foiner par o' kissin' cousins there never was—o' that ye can be sure!"

"Well, I still think I should've been named after Ma," replied Lauren sourly.

"Oh, to be sure," argued Sand Toes, "and I'm supposin' girlo, that we shoulda named ye Larraine Tee Dawe, just like yer Ma? Then what a foine mess ye'd have found yerself in!"

"Da…" Lauren replied exasperated. "Lawrence T. Dawe, Larraine Tee Dawe, Lauren Tea Dawe—they're all the same. Would it have mattered?" Her Da offered her a condescending grin. "If that be the case," asked he, "then why change it?" Why indeed? In truth, Lauren could not think of a single reason worthwhile. A difference, which made no difference, was no difference. Yet she hated the name, if only for the funny way it sat on her and the fact that it or some version of it produced an inherited monogram—and from both sides of the family once sundered and then reunited in the unlikely union of her parents made it stranger still. Perhaps an entirely new handle was called for. She'd have to take some time to think about it. But not now. Now they were nearing the pool of standing water and therefore approaching their traps.

She halted at her Da's sudden signal and watched with anticipation as he stood upon his toes and with his nose tested the winds. It being noon in the desert with the merciless sun stifling the air and making it as thick as Styrofoam, there were no winds to test. But there was an odor that Sand Toes did not recognize, permeating the immediate whereabouts, coupled with a second scent which, owing to experience and repetition, he placed almost immediately. The latter smell was the stench brought about by oncoming death. You or I wouldn't have noticed it—especially from that far off. Our olfactory senses are not attuned and sensitized by survival in the desert and the harsh demands it places upon one's attributes. As city slickers, we do not need to continually draw upon our senses to ensure our survival. Sand Toes, however, used his nose every day and depended upon it in ways you and I would hardly give consideration to. We don't need our nose to find food. We can open the refrigerator door and find all the chow we can chew. When we want a drink of water, we just go to the nearest tap and get some. We use maps or ask directions (some of us anyway) when we're lost. Of course, since he met and married Larraine, Lawrence did all these too. Larraine taught him lots and not just about refrigerators and maps. But for years he knew nothing of such devices and depended almost entirely upon his smeller, always believing that the nose knows. Thus it was that Sand Toes knew he had caught something in his trap. Good. And as far as he could tell or smell, it was something different, something he'd never trapped before. Even better. There was nothing after all, like new food!

"What's for dinner, Da?" Lauren asked, recognizing his stance. Da could always smell dinner—even from way out here, and he could usually tell what it was.

"I dinna know," Sand Toes replied uncertainly. "Never hae I heard tell or smelled smell o' the likes o' this, lass." He sniffed again, pulling great draughts of air up his nose, which being clipped and having a perpetually red tip tugging increasingly upward, marked his descent for all to see—although if you asked him he would have stated that he was an Apache. Before meeting his wife and with the exception of his barely remembered parents, they were the only family he knew. "Stay back now," he continued. "Di' ye hear me, girlo? I'll not hae ye right on me backside when we be approachin' strange beasties—the likes o' which are unknown to ye or me. Could be a might dangerous. Then where would we be, aye? We might be fleein' back up yon path with our backsides a-draggin' behind us! Ganglin' about in terror we might be and about to fall into the clutches o' some dark and horrible ogre sent by Lucifer himsel'! Nae, ye best be hanging' back a ways now."

"But, Da," countered Lauren, "can you smell it?"

"Sure 'n' begorrah!" Sand Toes answered. "I said so, didn't I?"

Lauren looked at him patiently. "Is it dead then?" Sand Toes took another couple of whiffs. "It ain't well," he replied with a chuckle. "But still, lassie, ye never know—it could be musk and it might be faking'!"

"Oh, c'mon, you silly," Lauren laughed, "I'm a big girl now." She raced up to the bend in the path, beyond which lay their captured quarry. She beat her Da to the trap by just a single step. When they got there, they stopped short, brought to an abrupt halt by the sight which confronted them. "What is it?" asked the elder Dawe.

"I'm not sure," replied his daughter, "but I think it's a rabbit."

Sand Toes looked down at his daughter, his face an etching in skepticism. "There be nae such thing," he adamantly replied. "I've never seen one, I don't remember that me Ma and Da ever did, and the Apaches never mention 'em! Therefore I dinna believe they exist!"

"Da," Lauren replied in a fiery tone, "you don't know the Apaches half as well as you think you do. I promise that one day they're going to do something to disappoint you. And you hardly even remember your parents. I know more about Grandda and Grandma than you! Besides, I saw a picture of a rabbit in school once," she continued, gesturing at the pitiful thing which lay at their feet, "and it looked sorta like that."

THE CHRISTMAS RABBIT

Sand Toes offered his daughter a disdainful glare. Such a look said all it needed to say about how he felt toward *that* institution and those who ran it. He chose to speak his mind anyway. "Och, that place! What is it that they be learnin' ye there, I wonder? What good is it, aye? Are they learnin' ye t' find moisture? Are they teachin' ye t' build a better trap? Nae! Nothin' but a whole lot o' ciphers and grammer! The king's English, curse him, and geography—as if there were any place else other than this! Did yer ole Da have even one bit o' what yer dearly departed Ma liked to refer to as *edjucahsin*? Did he? Yer darn right he dinna! And did such a lack hurt the ole man? I think not, aye? Yer ole man's all right, ain't he?"

"Yes, Da," Lauren replied. "But I still say it's a rabbit."

"Well, maybe 'tis and maybe 't ain't. Either way, ye stand back, girlo, while I gets the job done." He guided his daughter to his rear and then knelt down to give his catch a careful inspection—close enough to get a cautious look but far enough back to beat a hasty retreat just in case. Grabbing a nearby stick, he gave it a gentle prod, which caused it to flop about weakly. Still alive then. Best to get it done quickly. But what was that lying beside it in the sand?

"La," he said, "are ye sure this isn'a some kind o' bird now?"

"Bird? Da, does it look like any bird you've ever seen? Does it have wings?"

"Not that I can make out, girlo," came the reply, "but it lays eggs!"

"What?"

"Oh, posh, lass! Don't be tellin' me that ye dinna know what an egg is! Chickens lay 'em all the time, and I'm telling ye that so does this rabbit!"

"Da, rabbits can't lay eggs."

Lawrence offered his daughter a triumphant smile. "Then this can nae be one, can it? It must be somewhat else altogether!"

"Da," Lauren replied with surety, "it's a rabbit. Now let me see it." She reminded him so much of Larraine, looking just like her with her wavy chestnut hair and freckles splayed so sweetly across the bridge of her nose, that he gave way and let her get close. Larraine, when she'd been alive, had always been giving advice and getting in his business—usually for the better. With his daughter bearing so close a resemblance, it made sense in his simple mind to continue the habit whenever possible. He missed his poor Larraine. Lost in a bizarre mining accident, she'd been taken away in her prime and now his daughter, who mimicked her unconsciously, was all he had left of her. He rarely refused Lauren much.

Looking down at the rabbit, Lauren could see that there was definitely an egg lying beside it. But such an egg! Lauren had never before seen its like. Not any larger than your average chicken egg, it was however multicolored with shapes of various sizes and hues emblazoned upon its shell. It must have been quite magnificent, thought the young girl, before it got cracked and broke. She wondered about what might have been in it as she stood there marveling at the various pieces of shell. She gave thought to how it could have gotten there while experiencing a sense of wonder as she observed its many colors. Some of those hues were entirely new to her, and she couldn't recognize them at all. But even the reds, blues, and yellows were subtly different than those shades with which she was familiar—as if each hue and tint had been blended anew to create a color fresh and never before seen. She glanced from the egg to the pitiful creature caught in their trap. The poor thing lay there panting and mewling weakly. Its grayish brown fur was all tangled and matted from the various thrashings brought about in its attempt to escape. One of its hind legs, from the top of its foot to the joint at the hip, was worn raw, abraded by the wire as it tore up and down the pitiful beast.

Lauren felt her heart breaking for the nearly expired rabbit, and in her sorrow for what she had helped cause, put two and two together, her ciphers aiding her at least in this instance, to come up with four...

"Da!" she exclaimed. "This is the Easter Bunny!"

"Och, do go on now, lassie!" her Da replied. "There be nae such thing as the Easter Bunny. That be just ole wives' tales. Posh and nonsense and ole nursery rhymes!"

"Well then," she countered, "what about the egg?"

THE CHRISTMAS RABBIT

"What about it? It's a chicken egg plain as day, lassie. Anyone can see that! Probably one o' ours."

"Da, we don't have any chickens. We only have roosters. Uncle Slim and Uncle Jim bring us eggs. If we had a couple of our own chickens we wouldn't need them to. We could grow our own!"

"I think that the chickens do that," Sand Toes replied with a chuckle, "although I never looked to be sure."

"Da!"

"All right then, enough! The damned roosters' prob'ly hae their own chickens in the back o' the barn anyway."

"Whose barn?" Lauren asked. "What barn? Anyway, Da, where we get our eggs and how we get em' certainly doesn't explain this." She bent down in a crouch, huddling over the poor creature and shading it from the grueling sun. "Give me the canteen. I'm going to save it."

"Och! Come now, Little La," admonished her Da, "we've had this talk before, girlo."

"Da—I hate it when you call me that!" she replied, meaning La.

"Never ye mind, missy," he said. "It's yer dear ole Da's nickname. It was yer dearly departed Ma's as well, and now its yers too—and all fer different reasons. Quite a family tradition, if I do say so meself. Now step aside, lass, and let your Da do his work." He reached for his canteen but grabbed his knife instead. Maybe he never reached for the canteen at all. Who knows? But Lauren would've liked to believe otherwise and so assumed his selection was a mistake. "Da, that's not the water."

"Moisture, lass. Moisture. And I know it's nae. Now stand aside."

"Please, Da," Lauren pleaded, and her voice so much like her mother's, melted Sand Toes's heart. "Let me save it."

Lawrence hesitated, nearly fumbling the knife and dropping it. As each day passed, Lauren grew more and more like Larraine. In voice and mannerisms as well as general appearance, she so unconsciously mimicked her mother that Sand Toes found it increasingly difficult to refuse her anything. And just like her mother, Lauren was right more often than not. But this? She knew the *way* out here, and the *way* was survival. Survival at any cost. She understood as well as he that the entire desert was a predator feeding upon everyone and everything. Predation was as natural as creation in this harsh land. Here was meat and new meat at that. Something different. Rabbit or whatever, it sure looked tasty. They usually caught snakes, tortoises, and other reptiles in their traps, creatures all leathery and stringy and not very tasty at all—not that dear Mrs. Dawe hadn't been able to do wonders with a dead reptile when she'd been around to do it. But culinary arts were skills that Lawrence had failed to learn. As for Lauren, she took no interest in them either. She was indifferent to what was set before her plate and had been since the loss of her mother. It was as if even back then she could sense, perhaps somehow even taste, the unusual meals that were about to come her way with her Da behind the frying pan and therefore determined then and there to turn off her taste buds. Sand Toes however enjoyed a good meal when he could get it and didn't like giving up so easily the rare one when it came along. "Girlo, are ye sure that be a rabbit?" he asked again. "And if so, how in the name o' Saint Paddy can ye be sure it's the Easter Bunny?"

"The egg, Da," she said. "The egg!"

"What o' it? 'Tis a chicken egg as I told ye before."

"I know, Da, but look at the colors! Where did it get such colors? They're beautiful! Have you ever seen a chicken egg decorated like this?" She picked up a good-sized piece of the ovate casing and handed it to him. It was just under a quarter of the shell and yet there must have been at least fifty different shapes of various colors upon its surface. The patterns were intricate and bespoke much effort.

"Och no, lass!" Sand Toes replied. "I know this well enough. It comes from the big city, it does, and yer Ma told me all about it." He began flipping the shell like a coin all the while being careful not to break it. When he failed he turned his attention back to his daughter. "It's called graffiti, La, and it's the plague o' the big city, or so yer Ma used to say. 'Twas one of the reasons she came back to the desert. That and getting started in the family business again." The family business was gold mining but more on that later. "Yer Ma used to say that people would go crazy in a riot of paintbrushes and

THE CHRISTMAS RABBIT

color, trying to turn everything into something it wasn't while trying to make everything else stand out! I mean look at this egg, or what's left o' it. So bright and cheery. Someone's been takin' liberties with it and now it shines through like a giant shamrock in a field o' daisies. Even broken, it's visible for a couple o' miles. No wonder it's cracked. Something spotted it from far off, came along, and ate it!"

"And left the rabbit?"

Lawrence offered his daughter a sour stare. "Perhaps he came later."

"Da," Lauren replied, "it's the Easter Bunny, believe me. Now please hand me the water." Sand Toes did so but not without protest. "It's all nonsense, lass," said he, "and yer in fer a big disappointment!"

Lauren looked up at her Da to offer him a reply. "Don't talk to me about nonsense," she said, "not with some of the things you believe! Leprechauns, elves, and whatnot! And if anyone but me knew about your most guarded secret...well, it's like Ma used to say—they'd pack you off to the brick house and throw away the key! So don't tell me about nonsense!"

"Okay," Lawrence replied, getting antsy and casting glances here and there. "Okay. But keep yer voice down—others might hear!"

"What others?"

"Any others."

"There are no others," Lauren replied, "at least not around here."

"Here or there," said Sand Toes, "the desert hears everything!"

"Oh please!" Lauren took the canteen from her Da. Not having a cup, she upended the jug, taking a big gulp. Trying hard not to swallow, she swished it around, running it over her tongue and between her teeth in order to warm it. The rabbit was so close to dead, she knew, that cold water poured all over it would most likely finish the job that bad luck and their trap had started. She undid the wire, freeing the poor beast, and then gently picking it up, held it next to her face while allowing a slow dribble of moisture to drip into its parched and arid mouth. As the water passed its lips, easing its scorched and burning throat, the pitiful creature mewled weakly then fell away into a fitful sleep. It seemed this rabbit had enough for one day.

"Well, girlo," asked a befuddled Sand Toes, "what are ye gonna do with it now?"

*****

Lawrence and Lauren made the five-mile trek from their traps to their home in just under an hour, owing mainly to Lauren's concern for their poor refugee and her subsequent admonishments to Da to make more haste. For once, she set the pace, and Lawrence found it surprisingly difficult to keep up with. Usually he had to slow down for her. Even with a full day of moisture-prospecting and trap-checking before him—and even with a little sand-shoveling thrown in just for good fun, he hardly ever moved at this speed.

Their home, when they came upon it, was exactly as they left it. Not surprising. Few folk lived this far out. They liked having their modern comforts, if not handy then at least accessible. Doctors and lawyers and such were too important to stray too far away from. Most folk liked having such conveniences within a day's reach. But even had an army descended upon the Dawe residence, it is unlikely that they could've done much damage to the place. The Dawes lived in an abandoned mine shaft whose ore had long since played out. It had been Sand Toes's home since as long as he could remember—even back to the time of his parents who had resided there too, and he refused, even after meeting Larraine, to consider living anywhere else. Left in its forlorn condition until Sand Toes met and married his wife, it was an exercise in caving in with rotting timber and littered with hidden shafts and hazards throughout the property. Larraine Dawe moved in and nagged her third cousin, "Come, husband," into doing some much-needed home repair. She made him rip out all the old timber and replace it with new beams of cedar and cherry which she had imported from somewhere beyond the sandlands. She admonished him to seal off all of the deeper shafts and to childproof their adits—she would raise no children, she told him, in a home that was either unfit or unsafe. She hounded him until he installed paneling on the walls and laid carpet on the floor. Water was easy for Sand Toes who, being a diviner, had plenty to spare. It then became a matter of plumbing—something beyond Lawrence's ken even if he'd been given the chance to study the trade. It frightened him, and he refused to have anything to do with it, perhaps secretly fearing that if Larraine had all the moisture she needed and moreover had it handy, she wouldn't need him. At the mere mention of spanning wrenches and elbow joints, Sand Toes could be counted upon to pack up his spade and head out into the desert deep for a lengthy sojourn and far-flung bout of sand-shoveling. Larraine, however, wanted her pipe laid. Having water when you wanted it was all well and good—especially out here, but cold showers beneath a bucket weren't doing it for her. With no one else to turn to, she gladly called upon the guy in town, another cousin, who did this sort of thing for a living and who was more than happy to lay her pipes.

From the mail order store, also in town, she ordered a series of "how to" books and set about the task of learning what was needed to rig her new home for solar power. She saw quickly enough that she would need help, and that left Lawrence because there were no solar guys in town. She thought briefly about calling the plumber, but laying good pipe takes lots of time it if it's to be done right, and Larry had already questioned her about the plumber's frequent and extended visits.

After the fiasco of trying to get her husband to lay pipe, Larraine dreaded the idea of trying to enlist his aid in the installation of solar paneling. She figured him likely to go off screaming into the desert and never return. She was surprised, therefore, when exactly the opposite occurred. Lawrence took to solar like an overgrown snail to a new shell. After years of fighting the sun just to eke out an existence, he was tickled pink at the thought of putting that big yellow bastard to work instead. He understood the technology and concepts once they were explained to him, as if born to them, and as a result Larraine ended up with a series of solar cells which guarded their home and stood about like sentinels in the immediate desert surrounding their mine shaft. Sand Toes, an expert with his nose and therefore a self-taught journeyman about winds and their subsequent uses, constructed a windmill as well, which pumped water through Larraine's pipes along with picking up the electrical slack that the solar cells were incapable of handling. They got all their supplies from the mail order store, and on their own they kept that business overstaffed and working overtime too. And all through this hectic period Larraine still found the time to dust her home from top to bottom.

Mineshafts, as anyone who's ever been in one knows, are great gatherers of dust and must. And as any homemaker can tell you, coal dust, gold dust, any dust is old dust when you're in a mine shaft. When you have to clean it up and get rid of it, it's even worse. Yet she tackled the job with a fervor, committed to her new husband and her new home. She'd go to work in town in the morning, help Larry with the paneling or the solar cells in the afternoon, and then dust at night, using a flashlight to see by until they got the power up and running. No stalactite or stalagmite went unpolished. Not one bat remained in its belfry or was left to hang in the rafters—they'd been turned out once and for all, and the dust went out by the cartload. In the old and abandoned air shafts, she had her lunatic husband who was the only one crazy enough in those parts to venture into them in the first place scale their uneven and moss-lined walls to install windows at their egresses. You couldn't look out them of course. They were far too high and too dangerous to reach, but a simple pulley system and some counterweights allowed them to be opened and closed from level 5, which the Dawes called home. It was the ground floor level and so called because there were another four above it. The original miners bore their shaft into the side of a mountain, striking both upward and downward apparently at the same time, in their unceasing efforts to suck the mountain dry of ore from the inside out. No one, not even Lawrence, knew how many levels there were below. Sand Toes couldn't guess. Larraine comforted herself with the knowledge that God knew. He was the only one discerning enough to see into things so deeply. Larraine let it be and had Sand Toes seal off all of the passageways leading to the lower depths with the exception of the main shaft which by necessity had to remain open in order to provide their home with needed ventilation. Eventually and with a lot of hard work, the couple turned their shaft into a dwelling that any miner, forty-niner or otherwise, would have been proud to call home.

As she passed through the adit and into the living room, Lauren let some of her concern fall away. Familiarity brought with it a sense of security as she stopped to turn on lights and turn off the radio. The radio was always on in the Dawe home, but in this instance, Lauren reasoned that unfamiliar sounds would only add to her charge's overall discomfort and fright. She needed to keep the rabbit calm and tranquil if she hoped to pull it through. The radio came back on.

"Da," she said, "turn it off! The noise will frighten it." Lawrence looked across the room, which was gloomy despite the lights. "But, darlin'," he replied, "me show's on." Lauren patiently considered her Da. All the shows were *his* shows. He loved the radio—so much in fact that he insisted that it remain on even when they were away. Television, on the other hand, scared the living daylights out of him. He refused to have anything to do with it and did not allow one in his home. God only knew why. Da could be so weird at times! But in this instance he would have to bend. There were graver concerns to consider, and it was not every day, La knew, that some lucky child somewhere got the chance to save the Easter Bunny and more so, she supposed, when that very same child had a hand in almost killing it. She reasoned with her Da. She pleaded. And then she finally demanded, explaining her reasons and giving just cause while Sand Toes went on about how they should be "eatin' the wee thing" and the best way to cook it. Finally he gave in and shut the radio off, all the while grumbling to himself about how a man's castle was supposed to be his mine shaft.

Lauren set the rabbit down as it was too weak to run and in any case had nowhere to go, and then racing to the linen closet, fetched an old blanket for the poor thing to rest upon. Stopping off in the kitchen, she paused to get a small bowl of water and a slice of bread in case her charge got hungry later and decided to try and eat. Returning to her patient, she bent down, folded the blanket into a comfortable bed, and laid the rabbit gently upon it, putting both the moisture and the nourishment close at hand. As she sat there looking down at the pitiful creature, another thought occurred to her, and jumping up, she ran off to the bathroom to rifle the medicine chest. Ah! There lay what she was looking for. She grabbed the bottle of peroxide, the Q-tips, and the Ace Bandage and returned to her invalid. Gently, taking up its wounded leg gently, she began to delicately cleanse and treat the abrasion with Q-tips dipped in peroxide. She chose peroxide over rubbing alcohol because the latter wasn't as painful when applied to an open wound. Still, the rabbit squirmed pitifully and mewled weakly as she performed her ministrations. Its cries, soft but keening nevertheless, were highly pitched and echoed throughout the mine shaft. "There there, precious," she said, trying to comfort it with tender words as she finished up. "I won't hurt you. This is for your own good, you know. I'm sorry that you got caught in our trap." After applying the astringent she gingerly wrapped the rabbit's leg with the bandage and leaving it to rest, went off to her bedroom for her own siesta. Out here in the desert, especially since the radio was turned off, there wasn't a lot to do in the middle of the day except sleep. Her homework for school was already done and it had been an exhausting morning anyway. Her patient wasn't going anywhere and she could use the rest if she was going to be any help to it. Laying herself down, she closed her eyes and fell peacefully into slumber.

Sand Toes did not. Here rarely fell fully asleep even when dog-tired. It was a survival instinct bred into him by his long and solitary life in this unforgiving wasteland. He never completely closed his eyes when he rested. Thus his dreams were bizarre and vivid and because of his instabilities, full of turmoil and confusion. He tossed and turned when caught in their torturous embrace. He dreamt this way often, and today he dreamt of the past.

CHAPTER II
Larry Meets Larraine

Lawrence met Larraine in the middle of the desert on a dark and windy night. That is to say, he saw her. Spied upon her actually. He was returning late one evening from a foray of moisture prospecting although he did not refer to it as such at the time. He had no name for it back then. He simply got thirsty, dug himself a hole until he hit water, and then drank. Heading south from a day up north, he came across the campsite of a large party apparently lost by the sound and look of them and with those strange mounts that his friends, the Apaches, had. Horseless horses—and some of them even had radios! Sand Toes dearly loved the horseless horses but hadn't ridden upon one yet. They went too fast for him and he'd always been afraid that in their haste they would carry him far away from his desert and from his moisture which, being from this hellhole, was his most-prized possession. Water was life, he knew, and although there wasn't much of it to be had out here, at least he knew where what little of it lay. Such knowledge was to him both a comfort and a security. Where might moisture be out there, wherever it was that his Apaches said the desert ended? According to them the world was a whole lot larger than just his desert. Sand Toes didn't know what to believe but had pretty much guessed that at least this much was so. After all, when his friends left on their horseless horses they had to go somewhere, and they sure as heck didn't stick around here.

Even before meeting the Apaches, he came on his own to the conclusion that his desert must have finite limits. The world beyond, was too overwhelming, too intrusive, and in this day and age could not be completely shut out and so left its mark, even out here in the timeless sands, by the cast off beer or soda cans and other unwanted debris that the rare traveler saw fit to discard as useless. Then there were the cloud birds, as Lawrence thought of them—strange silver eagles that painted the desert sky with streamers of white fluff in the wake of their passage high overhead. Straight lines of billowing white from one end of the sky to the other. They must be mighty eagles, he reasoned, to fly so high and fast, and yet from down here on the sand they appeared to the naked eye to be smaller than pigeons. Still they offered up a mighty roar as they passed high overhead. Whatever they were, he was sure they were no part of his desert. Lawrence knew this for a fact because nothing from the desert roared louder than he. Therefore they must have come from "outside," as did the bottles and cans—strange things that puzzled him greatly. They hinted of something beyond all this if he could ever travel far enough to discover it. He tried to find that something once or twice in the past but became uneasy when straying too far from familiar landscapes and known sources of moisture. His desert was too deep to walk out of, no matter how firm your resolve or fleet your foot. Thus he was forced to accept at their word the Apaches when they told him that there was more than just desert out there. But when they told him that most of the rest of what was out there was covered with moisture and that the moisture was so plentiful, those who lived nearby had renamed it, calling it "water," he softly chuckled. How could that be? Where did one stand or could one stand on water? There had never been enough of it in the desert for him to make the attempt. Still he didn't think it possible. All this talk of a place beyond with its water by the bucket load sounded like posh and nonsense. He tried to imagine for himself this place where according to the Apaches, moisture flowed like wine in things called rivers, or was held in giant cups called lakes, or even bigger bowls called oceans. According to the Apaches, men had gone and fouled up most of it so that it was no longer potable. Sand Toes endeavored to see in his mind's eye this place where there was *water, water everywhere, but not a drop to drink,* and couldn't bring himself to believe it—who, after all, would poison their own moisture? But for the sake of friendship, when adding their stories to

THE CHRISTMAS RABBIT

the few clues he'd been able to glean for himself, he allowed as how the Apaches' tales might be true. Then they told him that the "cloud birds" he occasionally saw passing overhead had people in them, and he had to laugh out loud. Imagine his friends thinking him gullible enough to believe that pigeons could carry people! Sometime later, after he'd met and married Larraine and had been taught by her to read, he stumbled upon a book of hers. It was a *Roget's Thesaurus*. He asked his wife about it. From the couch where she'd been breast-feeding Little La, she looked up to tell him that it was a dictionary of sorts. Lawrence by then had known what a dictionary was, and so curious, he opened it up. As fate, chance, and dumb luck would have it, he happened upon page 414.67–414.69. There were columns of words printed upon the page, each broken occasionally by a set of numbers and more words in bolder typeface. It was unlike the other dictionary, which Larraine had previously introduced him to. Puzzling it out, he soon came to understand that what he was looking at was a species listing of various types of the same animal—horses, cattle, and birds to be exact. Then he saw it two thirds of the way down in the first column—a listing for "passenger pigeons"! It seemed that the Apaches were telling the truth all along. From then on and despite Larraine's admonishments to the contrary, he believed every word that the Apaches said.

But at the moment he just stood in the shadows surveying the campsite and the weary travelers huddled around the fire. Like his Apaches, they seemed to know the secret of making the hot tongues, which leapt up from and ate dead wood. They had a small blaze going around which they tried to keep warm. He envied them their fire on this cold desert night but was even more jealous of their footwear. He held up a finger for every person he could see by the fire's light and when he ran out of fingers but not out of people reasoned to himself that someone in that bunch would surely be wearing shoes which would fit his feet. He decided to obtain a pair but since they were currently on the feet of the various campers to whom they belonged, it wasn't as though he could just waltz in and take them. That meant stealing them, which necessitated the capture and incapacitation of their owners before he could do so. He would have to set traps and snare them. He had never trapped for people before. Even with his Apaches, there'd been too damned few of 'em to bother making the effort, and since he trapped mostly for food and since he was many things but not a cannibal, it seemed like a waste of his energies and talent.

From his dim and hazy childhood when his parents had roamed the desert, sharing with him the gift of words, he pulled forth from that nearly forgotten memory the rudiments of a language that by now lay almost lost, in an effort to learn for himself what sort of errand it was that had brought these foot-clad strangers to his desert. Was it something specific or were they just tourists? Perhaps they were in some sort of trouble. He would have to listen carefully and with luck, maybe they'd use some of the few remembered words, helping him to figure out who they were and what they wanted.

They were arguing—that much was certain. Their voices rose and fell discordantly and amongst the jumble of verbiage that Larry couldn't even begin to guess at were the words *north* and *south* being shouted back and forth. Those were words quite familiar to Sand Toes, as were *east* and *west*—sounds his long-dead Da would use to describe direction. Lawrence remembered them and even now knew how to differentiate between the four. That had been an early lesson and one not forgotten. So they were most likely lost. Good. No one would know where to look for them when they went missing. It was lucky for them, although they did not realize it at the time, that Sand Toes didn't know just how lost they were or things could've ended up much worse. As it was, he hesitated when deciding upon just how lethal his people traps should be. *Perhaps,* thought he, *if they never returned to where they came from others might come looking for them.* That the lost ones themselves might come back after being robbed and wounded and with a whole bunch of their friends in order to exact their revenge never even occurred to him. He figured after getting caught in one of his traps these tenderfeet would be thankful enough to get away with their skins intact without bothering to cry over stolen footwear! Once let loose, he was sure they'd pack up right quick and never return.

THE CHRISTMAS RABBIT

Listening further, he heard the word *water* mentioned often. They were afraid of running out of it or had done so already. Even better. Their lack of moisture made them predictable and easily maneuvered. He'd bait his trap with some and see how many he could catch. Perhaps he should try and bag 'em all. Shoes, he remembered, had a way of wearing out. He therefore figured he better grab extra pairs while he had the chance. He slunk deeper into the shadows and silently began to dig.

Sand Toes got the basics of trapping as he'd gotten the basics of everything else, except stalking, from watching his parents eke out their survival. After they died, he had to take the meager amount of knowledge imparted to him and build upon it, making improvements on his own through a series of trials and errors and more often than not the latter of the two. But he did learn in his own way and time to become quite proficient at the endeavor. He even trapped the larger animals although they were a lot harder to find out here and so had to be hunted only in very specific places. His smaller traps, those set for snakes, lizards, and tortoises, could be set randomly in almost any place that he chose. For larger prey, he waited until he happened to be journeying in those particular areas aforementioned and only after coming across spoor indicating their presence, go to all the bother of constructing his pits. They were a chore to create, not always successful, and only good for the larger animals of which there weren't many, who could pull his measly wires out of the desert floor as easily as he could set them. The pits were covered and concealed, of course; else how could they work? Smaller animals, being so tiny and light, could scamper or crawl across their covers without collapsing them. Larger animals—and these included people, he supposed, although he'd never hunted them before—would cause the covers to cave in when trod upon; however, if not injured in the initial collapse, larger prey could simply jump up or climb out of the hole and escape. Therefore he'd have to dig deeply.

Years of moisture prospecting for survival and sand-shoveling for the sake of practice while training for his secret quest had taught him to be both fast and efficient in his digging and so before the night was half through, he'd excavated a pit that was thirteen feet long, thirteen feet wide, and thirteen feet deep, and being a sly desert creature skilled in the ways of sand craft, had only to be dug thirteen yards away from where the strangers presently rested. He'd stuck moisture at the thirteenth foot but that was to be expected. He'd smelt it on the surface and expected to make such a discovery. Moreover, he needed it if his trap was to be successful. Thirteen, however, had nothing to do with anything. It just happened to be. It appears here as a strange coincidence in a strange tale and perhaps the only true coincidence in this entire story.

This particular part of his desert was not a sea of rolling dunes, although they did exist some few miles to the north from where he'd just returned; rather, this specific piece of landscape was composed of hardscrabble, littered with medium-sized rocks. Sagebrush and mesquite, two plants that he needed to complete his construction, grew here in abundance, covering the desert floor like uneven carpet.

When he finished his hole he scrambled his way out and flitting silently here and there, gathered up the rocks, sagebrush, and mesquite he'd need to complete his trap. Over yonder stood a lone barrel cactus, and he quietly cut it down, hollowing out a portion of it to serve as a pail which he could lower into his pit and draw out moisture. He intertwined some of the sagebrush and mesquite, fashioning for himself a crude rope of sorts. This he attached to his cactus pail and lowered into the pit. When it hit the water at the bottom it sank like a stone. Once completely submerged, he drew it forth and used its trapped moisture to facilitate the construction of the pit's cover. First he took the remaining sagebrush and mesquite that he'd gathered and intertwining the two, constructed a rudimentary tarp with which he planned to cover his trap. Upon it he secured medium-sized rocks and boulders, pushing them most of the way through the tarp so that their tops were almost flush with the top of the tarp itself. He strengthened the whole construction by lashing various pieces of deadwood and branches—most of which were petrified, although whether by him or the desert itself I cannot say—that lay scattered on the desert floor. Such materials were hard to come by and Sand Toes had to prosecute a diligent search in order to obtain the necessary implements of construction. Once the crude cover was fash-

THE CHRISTMAS RABBIT

ioned it became necessary to disguise it. To this end he poured copious amounts of moisture on the various piles of dirt he'd unearthed and made mud. Then using his hand like a trowel, he covered both sides of his tarp with a liberal coating of it. This he knew would not only help to disguise the cover but more importantly strengthen it that last little bit that it might hold the weight of those fifteen or twenty people he estimated to be out there. Of course, it wouldn't *hold* their weight—at least not for long. It wasn't supposed to. But if he could get most of them standing upon it before it collapsed, he felt sure that he'd be able to deal with the one or two remaining on the surface.

Now he had to wait until the mud dried and hardened, but even at night such a wait would not take long. The desert air was so dry that even in the deep of evening it sucked moisture out of anything as quickly as Dracula drained young virgins. While waiting for his project to dry and set, Lawrence took the remains of the toppled barrel cactus and fashioned three lengths of tubing, each of about seven feet, and approximately the same circumference as a drinking straw. He used the gummy resins inside the cactus to seal and make them watertight as well as attach them together, using the resinlike glue. At one end of his tubing he applied liberal amounts of moisture to make it soft and malleable. Once done, he bent that end at a thirty-five-degree angle, enough to make it stick up when inserted through the underside of the tarp but not so sharp as to kink and impede the flow of moisture. He then set that aside to dry too.

Once the desert air had leached the moisture out of his various fashionings he made his final preparations. He attached the tubing to the underside of the tarp and poked the angled end up through it. Gingerly, he dragged his tarp over the pit, laying it down as its cover. The tubing poked up right through the center, with the rest of it coming out the underside of the cover, which was furthest away from the campsite. Next, he took sand and dirt, spreading them randomly over the tarp in order to make it look as much like the surrounding landscape as possible. The final touch came when he uprooted one of the few remaining sagebrushes and taking it, gingerly walked out on the tarp and planted it around the tubing while beneath his feet the petrified branches and deadwood creaked ominously. The planted sagebrush served to hide the tube adding that last bit of camouflage he felt his project needed. It looked like it was growing there and always had been.

It was fast approaching sunrise, so he quickly covered the remainder of the tubing and scattered the last of his piles of sand and dirt. At the tube's furthest end, he hollowed out a little delve to lie in and then covered himself with a thin coat of sand in order to remain hidden. Wrapped around him was the tanned and treated stomach of one of the desert's larger creatures, and because it was waterproof, he used it to hold his bait. He could draw captured moisture from within the stomach through an attached straw, which he'd also fashioned, and he did so now in order to test his trap. Drawing a mouthful, he pinched off the stomach's straw and then transferred the trap's tube to his mouth and blew. The little spout gushed water like oil from a well. It was working perfectly! Now, if he judged his trap's strength correctly, then just before everyone gathered upon it to get at the moisture, it would reach critical mass and collapse. The petrified branches would give way, the sagebrush and mesquite lashings tear asunder, and the rocks hidden within, tumble and fall as well as the people too. No doubt, some would be injured—perhaps even killed, but that was merely life and death out here in the desert where survival was the *way* and where one's own survival was *all*. It was too harsh out here and too unforgiving to overly concern oneself with foolish notions of altruism and "doing unto others"…even had Sand Toes been familiar with such a ridiculous concept.

As the sun crept over the eastern horizon, the camp's dwellers began to stir. Sand Toes knew that the fools would do just that. It was at night when they should've been about and moving, both to keep warm and to make way; but no, like the idiots he was sure they were, they had chosen to sleep at night instead. Out here in the desert, daytime was the time of rest. Now was the time when the experienced desert man sought out shelter in order to escape from the environment and its harsh demands. Trust an outworlder to be ignorant of that. In fact, it was critical to his plans that they be possessed of such ineptitude. Should he start the flow of moisture now, he wondered,

THE CHRISTMAS RABBIT

or should he wait? He decided to delay a bit longer. It was still relatively cool under the desert sky. The longer he waited, the hotter it would get, and as the temperature increased, so would his quarry's collective thirst. Thirst would make them desperate and desperation would lead to critical mistakes in judgment. Once that big yellow bastard got high in the sky, pounding the landscape like a giant sledgehammer, his prey would fall deep into the desert thirst and so be ready to believe in the unlikely event of unforeseen moisture.

Larraine Dawe tumbled from her tent. It had been a hellacious three days out here in the waste looking for Geronimo's lost gold mine. She and those she led were the descendants of the original Secret Society of Lost Gold Miners, so called because when their ancestors formed the Society they were so sly and devious in their orchestration of its aims that when they finally set out upon their quest none of their neighbors knew they'd left. Subsequently, when they got lost, no one cared they were missing. The original members of the Society were all descended from forty-niners. Not the football team although undoubtedly those San Franciscans are responsible for a lot of bastards out there, but rather, drew their heritage from the Alaskan gold miners—those few who'd struck it rich came back east and blew all their earnings. Wine, women, and song—they partied till dawn and then one day woke up penniless. Their descendants grew up as paupers, resentful of their parent's extravagances. Knowing that they couldn't remine their parent's squandered fortunes, these great-granddaddy Dawes convinced their brethren and next o' kin to join them in an effort to mine new gold instead. They immediately ran into a brick wall. It seemed that despite a very thorough and extensive search, there was no new gold to be found anywhere. Of copper, silver, and even platinum, there was plenty—but they were gold miners and so were unsure of their dubious skills when it came to mining new metamict substances. The gold in California had paid itself out years ago, and the Black Hills of South Dakota had been scooped up and stolen from the Indians by the "big operators." There was South Africa, of course, but it was too far from their collective reach, and back in the days of the great-granddaddies Dawe, it was known as the Union of South Africa (although not officially—that title was still a few years down the road)—a British protectorate. Since the original Society were all of Irish descent they could find little use in anything *British* and so decided to leave it alone. "Screw the English," was their collective opinion. It was probably all fool's gold anyway. This left the two elderly Dawes—although back then they were middle-aged—and the fools who followed them without a readily available source of gold they could plunder.

Frustrated almost beyond their ability to bear, the Secret Society was in danger of fracturing and splitting before it could rightly get started. There was talk among its brethren of scrapping the whole affair and embarking upon new careers. Discussed was that newfangled invention by Carl Benz called the automobile. Various members of the Society were of the opinion that soon said autos would cover the countryside like fleas on a swamp dog—especially in light of Henry Ford's proven ability to mass produce them and that servicing and repairing them might make the Society's members a fortune if they were wise enough to get in on the ground floor while there was still a ground floor to be gotten on. Airplanes were up and coming as well, and much talk was also given to entering this field of endeavor. The great-granddas, who didn't know squat about automobiles and even less about airplanes, were of the opinion that neither was likely to get off the ground. But whether such things did or didn't was immaterial to them. All the brothers knew was that they knew nothing about these matters and were in danger of losing their positions of leadership within the Society to the onslaught of newfangled ways, turn-of-the-century ideas, and modern contraptions. So they acted. They drew straws for the right to embark upon one last quest for gold. The winner would prosecute the search while the loser stayed behind in order to hold the Society together while awaiting the successful return of the other.

Larraine's great-grandfather drew the long straw. He headed out west for one last search of the precious metal. He stopped in a Nevada Tobacco store to get some directions and some chew. The store itself was a rickety old shack, and on the porch, sitting in a tired rocking chair nearly as dilapidated as the shack itself, was an old

THE CHRISTMAS RABBIT

Indian, ancient and wrinkled like weathered oak. "How," said the Indian to Great-Granddaddy Dawe as he mounted the porch steps.

"How what?" came Dawe's reply.

"How you doing?"

"Oh, just fine, I suppose."

The Indian gave Great-Granddaddy Dawe a long and measured stare, the kind a carnival worker gives his mark before taking him to the cleaners. "You be mining gold?" asked the Indian.

Great-Granddaddy Dawe was taken aback. This was supposed to be a secret mission known only to members of the Society. He was supposed to be traveling incognito. He reasoned if his purpose and goals were this obvious, then every tin panner and prospector from here to Timbuktu would soon be on his trail and looking to make a stake on his claim, should he ever find one. "What makes ye spout out such balderdash?" he indifferently asked.

"Your hat," replied the Red Man.

"Me hat?"

"Yes, your hat. It's a helmet. Moreover, it's a miner's helmet. The lamp set in the middle is a dead giveaway." He spit out a long stream of tobacco juice at Great-Granddaddy Dawe's feet and then, wiping his chin on the back of his sleeve, continued. "I didn't think you were going to the church social wearing a hat like that. Besides, ain't no white man's church around here for miles. Mining be your interest and gold mining at that."

Great-Granddaddy Dawe removed his helmet and holding it in his hand, examined it as if suddenly aware of both its presence and purpose. "Ye sound pretty damned sure o' yerself," said he.

"I know the look," came the reply. "Miners and their metals have been a plague to me and my people since Geronimo was a pup."

"So what o' it?" asked Dawe. "What's me hat to the likes o' ye?"

"You want gold?" asked the Indian. "Gold I've got. Gold by the wheelbarrow full and it's yours for the taking, kemosabe, if the price is right."

"So's ye've got gold for the taking, aye? Then why n't ye just dig it up fo' yerself and be done wi' it?" The Indian spit out another long trail of tobacco juice. "Can't," he replied.

"What's the matter," asked Dawe, "can't Indians dig?"

"Oh, we dig as well as the next guy," said the Indian. "It's just that if I go through all the bother of unearthing it, then as sure as buffaloes make cattle craps, the government will come along and take it from me. I'd rather be without it in the first place than get it only to give it up to the white man. You guys are so greedy!"

Great-Granddaddy Dawe paused to consider for a moment the Indian's last words. Something about them didn't seem quite right, but for all of that, he couldn't put his finger on anything specific. "What makes ye think ye'd hae' to give up yer gold?"

"Are you kidding?" asked the incredulous Indian. "It's always been that way. Ever since you people came ashore back where the sun rises, you've been pushing your way westward and taking for yourselves what's been rightfully ours. Manifest Destiny and all that other cattle crap, don't you know. The tiger hasn't changed his stripes—nor the leopard, his spots!"

"Ye dinna seem too upset about it," replied Dawe. The red enigma before him suddenly stood up and began to dance and scream. "Does this make you feel any better," he yelled, "do I seem sincere enough now?" Calming down, the Indian retook his seat. "Besides," he continued, "it does no good to bitch. Nobody listens, and you people are not likely to give it all back, are you?" Dawe allowed as how that was probably so. "Also," said the man in the buckskin tunic, "what goes around comes around. The Great Spirit's cosmic wheel turns ever onward. Everything in its proper place and time. You steal from us," and here the Indian started to chuckle, "one day somebody bigger gonna come along and steal from you—maybe give it all back to the red man. Then you fellas better watch out!"

An awkward moment of silence spun itself out as the two antagonists took the measure of each other. "So what is it," Dawe finally asked, "that ye be wantin'?"

"I want to do business," said the Indian. "Isn't it plain? I have a map that points the way to a lost gold mine. It's yours if you can meet my price."

This redskin, thought Dawe, is a bit too cheeky and overconfident to be telling anything but the truth. He never learned that

THE CHRISTMAS RABBIT

all truths, except for the Almighty's, are merely subjective. Still, he wasn't going to pay just anything for the map, and it was said that nobody bargained like the Irish—except maybe the Scots, who everyone knew were as cheap as the day was long. It was time to get down to brass tacks. "I never do a deal with anyone whose name I dinna know."

The Indian spit out more juice and then spit out the tobacco too. The plug, having been masticated to a pulpy goo, landed at his feet like a small turd. Removing his knife from its sheath, he paused to consider the Irishman as he cut himself another, inserting it between his gum and cheek. "The name's Geromino," he said.

"Geronimo? I have the honor of addressing Geronimo?"

"No, you idiot," replied the Indian. "Not Geronimo, Geromino. Geronimo and I are cousins, although to be sure—it's Geronimo's map!"

Great-Granddaddy Dawe displayed his skepticism again. "How then," he asked, "did ye come by it?"

"You don't believe me?" asked Geromino. "Is that it? Well then, I'll tell you. At the last family reunion, after the picnic, I got him drunk and stole it! The daffy bastard kept going on about the old days and how the red man was gonna rise again. 'Not in this lifetime,' thought I. 'The idiot will never use the map,' I reasoned and so I took it from him when he passed out."

"You stole it? I thought that Indians were supposed to be honorable men, that all those tales about dishonesty and thievery were just that—tales! Stories made up by men 'o less than reputable means, as an excuse to plunder and take advantage of you and your people."

"Generally, my people are honorable," replied Geromino. "But not me! Honesty gets you nowhere in this world. Look at what's happened to all my people because of their honor and their honesty. Not me! Instead, I try with all my might to do what's white—just like my pale-faced brothers!"

"So," said Dawe, "ye be a thief just like the rest o' us! How then, in the name o' Saint Paddy, am I to be trustin' ye? The map might be a fake!"

Geromino looked at him guilelessly. "Honor among thieves," he replied, spitting out yet another stream of juice. "Look, white man," he continued, "the evening's getting on, and the wife gets ornery when I'm late for dinner. Are we gonna deal or what, paleface? It's time to crap or get off the pot!"

Great-Granddaddy Dawe took a moment to think it over. He still held with his first assessment of the Indian and therefore believed him to be too cocky and self-assured to be telling anything but the truth. Dawe also reasoned that this was more than likely his last chance to find gold. If this didn't pan out he'd be left with a lifetime filled with drudge and weariness, cleaning carburetors and patching tires. So what, if anything, did he have to lose? Nothing.

"Okay," he replied, "I'm in. What be yer price?"

"A thousand dollars," replied Geromino. "Cash."

"A thousand dollars?"

"Yeah, a thousand. What are you, deaf?"

"Make it five hundred," Great-Granddaddy Dawe said, "and then sure 'n' begorrah we'll have us a deal—after all, five hundred dollars be a helluva lot 'o wampum!" The Indian gave him such a look of disdain that Dawe could feel himself wilting from the inside out. "Don't talk down to me, you son of a bitch," replied the Indian, "I speak the king's English better than you! The price is a thousand—anything less and you wouldn't take me seriously!"

That's true, thought Dawe. Who parts with a gold mine for less than a grand? Even then it was a steal. "All right," the old miner replied, "it's a done deal." He reached into his money belt and began to count out a big wad of bills. "Not here!" Geromino said anxiously while looking about to see who might be spying upon them. "There's palefaces everywhere! They blend in with the white sands of the desert so that you can't see 'em until it's too late." He looked about once again to assure himself they weren't being watched. "White man sees you giving me all that cash, and as sure as cattle craps draw maggots, he's gonna descend upon me like a fly on feces and rob me of my profit! It's best we go to the rear of the building and do our deal there."

THE CHRISTMAS RABBIT

They walked around the back, and as Dawe began to parcel out the cash, Geromino added one more condition.

"What be that?" asked the Irishman warily.

"I or my descendants," replied Geromino, "get 10 percent of all gold—mined, panned, sifted, or in any other way extracted from Geronimo's mine."

"Ten percent?"

"You're getting the mine for practically peanuts," argued the Indian. "In one day, if you know your business, that mine will yield you ten times the amount that you're paying for it. Ten times! A 10 percent surcharge for ten times the return on your investment hardly seems unfair."

Dawe shook his head. "Ten percent be too much by far," he replied. "I'll give ye 2, and that's more 'n' fair!"

"The mine's a family heirloom," replied Geromino. "Take that 2 percent, and stick it where the sun don't shine—I want 10!"

Dawe gave the Indian a canny appraisal, scrutinizing him from head to toe. He could see for himself that Geromino dressed none too richly. The Indian's leggings were threadbare, and his moccasins had holes in their soles. Dawe reasoned that the man was only a step or two away from pauperdom and likely to take almost any deal tendered. All this bargaining was mere posturing only. The Indian was desperate. *That leaves me*, Dawe reasoned, *with plenty o' room to maneuver.* "Two percent."

"Oh, c'mon," whined Geromino. "Let's at least haggle a bit! How about 8?"

Dawe made a show of biting his lip, as if giving serious consideration to the offer. "Three percent," he finally replied. Overhead a vulture riding the desert thermals passed above them while seeming to cry out, "Cheap, cheap, cheap!" as it flew by. *You got that right, oh, winged brother*, thought Geromino. "Three percent is a trifle," the Indian replied, "and shouldn't be considered a serious offer between sincere negotiators! How about 6?"

"I'll go 4."

Geromino rolled his eyes. A lousy 4 percent? But what could he do? White men were white men and weren't likely to change their color anytime soon. "Make it 5," he said reluctantly, "and we'll attribute the extra percent to Christian charity—an asset you white men claim to be full of."

"Indeed we are," replied Dawe, "and the deal is done!"

"Yeah," replied Geromino, his words dripping with sarcasm. "You and Ebenezer."

Dawe broke out in a grin. "An ancient scion of me family," he replied, "a patriarch and an ancestor t' be proud o'! Now where do I sign and where be the map?"

"The map is right in my pocket," replied Geromino, spitting out more juice, "but we sign no white man's paper! White man signs a paper, he breaks his word as sure as the moon rises and the sun sets! A handshake between partners is enough for Geromino."

So they shook hands and the deal was done. Immediately following its consummation Geromino fell over, dead. Great-Granddaddy Dawe interpreted this as an auspicious sign, sure now that his dreams about rewon riches were about to come true. Of course, he made no effort to try and find Geromino's family and inform them of their up-and-coming 5 percent. Instead, he retrieved the map from Geromino's pocket along with the thousand in cash that he'd just paid for it, got out of there before the body was discovered, headed back east, gathered up the members of his Secret Society and stuck out west yet again to find his gold. But even as Geromino died and his body fell to the ground, they were being spied upon by those who hid behind one of the outlying sand dunes. Not a paleface among them who would've surely stood out had they been there. These spies were the relatives of Geromino. They'd tracked that thieving Geromino to this dusty Nevada town with the intention of retrieving the map and returning it to its rightful owner and, in the process, giving Geromino's thieving behind the good butt-kicking it deserved. Great-Granddaddy Dawe however, through fate, providence, or more than likely just dumb luck, beat them to him and got the map first. So they patiently waited and watched, intent on having their revenge and making *somebody* pay for the theft. It would be years, in fact decades, before the Great Spirit's wheel came full circle to give them their opportunity. And it would not be them but their children's children who would take up the gauntlet after having the tale passed down faithfully from father to son, mother to daughter. Generations watched and waited, biding their time until fate finally relented and gave them their chance.

Of course, Dawe knew nothing of these matters, and he never located the mine either because what he also didn't know but should've guessed nevertheless was that Geromino was not Geromino at all but actually a sly opportunist named Horse Feathers, who was no relation to Geronimo whatsoever. The map however, was genuine and had Horse Feathers known that he would have never given it up, no matter the price. How he came by it, no one knows, but when he was found dead in a back alley, his pockets were empty. No map and no thousand dollars either. Great-Granddaddy Dawe figured that the old sod certainly didn't need the moolah since according to legend, only Dawe's distant ancestor, old Ebenezer, had ever figured out a way to take it all with him and the thousand dollars Dawe knew would go a long way toward financing his expedition. The Irishman made off with both the map and the money. But even back then the Dawes had trouble reading a street sign. An old map—dusty, scribbled upon, and filled with arcane runes and drawings—was way beyond their collective ken and abilities to decipher.

For years the Secret Society of Lost Gold Miners, under the generalship of the brothers Dawe, wandered the desert in search of their gold. They'd go for days, sometimes months, in one direction while battling heat, drought, thirst, and hunger as they rambled, only to lose heart and hope—and then head off in an entirely new direction in order to prosecute their search once again. They got hopelessly lost. The desert is a pretty big place and does not look kindly upon trespassers who enter it with the intention of removing something hidden within. The desert and all within it belonged to the desert itself and to the desert only, and it would be quite some time before the Dawe Brothers and their Secret Society figured that out for themselves—and even then the message would not sink in with everybody.

For forty years, they wandered about in the desert like Moses and the children of Israel. Great-Granddaddy Dawe and his brother upped and passed away, never to see the fabled "promised land" that the map supposedly pointed the way to, and so were buried alone and forlorn, somewhere out in the wide wastelands, leaving the reins of joint leadership in the less than capable hands of Granddaddy Dawe and *his* brother, both of whom were as inept as their sires and who despised each other despite their close family ties or perhaps because of them and therefore could never agree on anything. Together the two of them ran afoul of each other, reaching the end of their collective hopes and ropes.

Unbeknownst to either, or to the entire Society for that matter, their adopted country was now engaged in a great war with the Huns of the near east and the Japs of the Far East as well. The Society knew nothing of Huns or Japs—it seems that word of such things never made it that far west. They were ignorant of the world war and the way in which it was being prosecuted. They had no knowledge of tanks, battleships, or newfangled weapons. So when the United States tested its first atomic bomb out in the desert it goes without saying that such testing caught the Secret Society of Lost Gold Miners by surprise. Those few in the Society who survived the blast interpreted the explosion as a biblical sign. A warning to get out of there while the getting' was good. A pillar of fire by night and a cloud of dust by day was how it appeared to the Secret Society of Lost Gold Miners, who got collectively knocked on their cans by its tremendous concussion.

In the bomb's mighty wake, most realized they had no idea of which end was up or what they were doing out there. Interpreting the blast to be a sign from God telling them to get out and go home, the majority of them packed up and headed back east. Though not a navigator among them, and as a group lousy with directions in general, the bedraggled membership at least understood *east*. That, they reasoned, was where the sun came up and so they made their way in that general direction until they struck "Georgia by the Sea," whereupon they hooked a left and headed north, finally arriving back in New York and to the ramshackle tenement buildings which their fathers once occupied.

THE CHRISTMAS RABBIT

There were, however, a few holdouts in the persons of Granddaddy Dawe's brother and those few who sided with him. They too saw the explosion as a sign from above but attached to it an entirely different interpretation. A pillar of fire by night and a cloud of dust by day, they viewed the detonation as a heavenly sign from God himself, pointing the way to their gold. After all, had not God used just such a device to lead Moses and his band into the promised land, and had not Moses and his brother Aaron died along the way—just as the journey neared its end? They too had been wandering for forty years, having lost their "Moses" and "Aaron" in the personages of Great-Granddaddy Dawe and his brother. They, too, now had pillar and cloud to guide them. Surely, history was repeating itself in biblical proportions! The cloud and fire were heavenly messages to the Society, telling them that they were just so close and to not lose heart, to not give up running the race when they were, in fact, so near the finish line. The land of milk and honey could be over those yonder hills! A fight broke out between the brothers Dawe and their individual supporters for possession of the map and its secrets. Having given up the quest, Granddaddy Dawe nevertheless refused to part company with the map. He was, after all, the senior Dawe and so felt that the map rightfully belonged to him. He also held out, hoping against hope, for the day when he might return and pick up the trail once again, starting anew from where he was about to leave off. His brother and followers, unable to wrest the map from him, vowed to find the gold anyway, map or no map, using the pillar of fire as their only guide. So in the end, about thirty of the Society's men and women stayed behind in the desert only to be slowly poisoned by radioactive fallout and thus grow even flakier than their parents. The rest returned home.

But once the gold fever rots the roots of your family tree, you have the devil's own time trying to be rid of it. Thus after two generations of family life in the slums Larraine Dawe gathered up the remnants of the Secret Society's descendants and using Great-Granddaddy Dawe's map, which had come to her through inheritance, attempted yet again to restore the family fortune by finding the lost gold. Thus we find her stirring from her tent as the sun rose over Lawrence Torrance Dawe's corner of creation. "Hey, Slim," she said, "now that the sun's up, have another look at that map and see if you can figure out where in the name o' wonder we happen to be."

Slim, who had also risen, was up and outside looking around in the morning light at the place where he would most likely die. He was the rebirthed Society's chief navigator, principal mapmaker, and senior locator of lost gold mines, as well as the portliest person in that dismal bunch. Like his ancestors of old, he was lousy at figuring out directions (he once got lost in a shopping mall—a minimall at that), but he had no peer when it came to being portly, being the Society's biggest eater too. Though entirely useless for any practical purpose whatsoever, the Society kept him on nevertheless—both for his sense of humor and because of his direct lineage to Great-Granddaddy Dawe. He looked over the map while brushing a greasy shock of hair out of his eyes. Even this early in the morning the sun shone so brightly he had to squint in order to see it. "Nope," he replied, "haven't a clue. Somewhere in the desert would be my best guess."

Larraine spit in frustration before stopping to consider how much of a waste of water spitting was in a place like this. She'd been a spitter from way back, using the gesture both visibly and often in order to display consternation and anger. It was a habit, she now realized, that her newly found environment would force her to give up, probably much sooner than she would have preferred. What was she doing out here anyway? Why was she leading this motley collection of troops on what would no doubt prove to be a fool's quest and one which would likely see them all dead? More importantly, to her mind anyway, was the question of why the others elected to follow her in the first place. Most, if not all, had fairly decent jobs back east, and yet to a man (although to herself she said "person"—she was an even bigger woman's libber than she was a spitter), they threw away security and stability for one last chance at redemption and riches. Second and third cousins all and twice removed at that, they knew that such foolishness had once almost cut the family tree at its roots before it even had a chance to blossom. Surely if there were any gold out here it would've been claimed by now. But here they were along with her, trying to find it anyway. It made her wonder about old

THE CHRISTMAS RABBIT

family tales and legends revolving around the birthmark and the subsequent silliness said birthmark supposedly engendered. *Perhaps,* she thought, *there is some truth to the stories after all.* "That's great, Slim," she said. "Just great. Somewhere in the desert—don't suppose you could narrow it down a mite?"

"Don't suppose," Slim replied.

"Oh, give me the damned thing," she said and, rushing over, snatched the parchment from his hands. Staring at it while trying to decipher its mystic lines and runes, she realized that there could be no doubt about it—they were definitely lost somewhere in the desert. Wonderful. Just wonderful. "Hey, Jim," she yelled out, "what's our water situation?"

Jim was Slim's brother, almost as portly and no better with directions than he—but he was a smart-enough man to know his limitations, most of the time anyway. "We dinna hae a water situation," he replied. "We dinna hae any water! We be dry as a bone, lassie, and that's a fact, to say nothing o' the gasoline—which we be outta too!" Larraine hated it when he spoke in that tired Irish brogue he affected, although if the truth were told, the rest affected the same effect, to more or less the same degree, including herself. It displayed itself under duress—which in this family was often, echoing and rolling off their tongues like hollow salamis which, as far as Larraine knew, were Italian, only adding to her ambivalence.

The others, numbering about fifteen, began to stir and rise from their bags and tents, mumbling and stumbling as they shook off a night of broken and uneasy sleep. Larraine dearly loved her people without being offended by the possibility that she might care for them a lot more than they did her—at least at the moment. Whose goofy idea was it anyway to resurrect this silly Society with their deranged scheme of finding lost gold using a map most of her troop now believed was either a fake or a forgery? Who'd led them here? I did, she sadly admitted. I'd have done better to leave the whole notion dead and buried—which it soon again would be…at least the dead part. The rest would be scattered to the winds and the scorpions. Yet both singularly and as a group, they went along with her plan and, by unanimous decision, appointed her to oversee it;

she was, after all, Great-grandaddy's Dawe. Everyone in this wacky troupe—second and third cousins all, some twice removed—had been weaned and teethed upon family lore, some of which wove the tale of the ill-fated expedition of the first formation of the Secret Society—and what a cluster of cattle craps that turned into! And although all present suffered under the severest case of gold fever ever to have been diagnosed, none among them had wanted the responsibility of leading their fellows into another mess like that. Larraine hadn't wanted it either. She'd just come up with the idea of resurrecting. Never in her wildest nightmares had she seen herself as "in charge" of this fiasco. That was, after all, men's work, wasn't it? Despite being an avid women's libber, Larraine could nevertheless be a convenient one, easily disregarding and casting away dearly held ideologies and catchphrases when the need or desire suited her. But in the end, she accepted the mantle. To do less, she knew, would doom the second iteration of the Secret Society of Lost Gold Miners to a lifetime of city dwelling and tenement housing where they'd be forever trapped as they stumbled over each other and those around them in a futile effort to assimilate and "fit in." Since the ill-fated day when her grandda and those who'd followed him out of the desert had turned left at the Georgia seashore, heading back north to the city, it became apparent to those with whom they came in contact that these were people better left to themselves inasmuch as was possible within the stricture and confines of city living. They couldn't be avoided altogether, of course; there were PTAs, football and field hockey practices, neighborhood watches, blood drives, housing referendums, alderman's races, and all the other manifestations of "community" that go into making up a society at large. Yet no matter how large society grew, the Secret Society and the members who comprised it were forever trying to find their rightful niche within it. Though not exactly shunned by their neighbors, they were avoided nevertheless and not so much out of prejudice as prudence. Although not all members of the Secret Society shared the ancestral birthmark, its presence and aura made itself manifest to a greater or lesser degree throughout root and branch of the entire family tree. Normal folk like you or I, forced by circumstance to interact with them on one level or another, could almost sense imprinted upon them their stamp of strangeness. Such awareness operated on an instinctual level going virtually unnoticed in the consciences of "normal" folk, directing them to offer up the barest minimum of greetings considered polite when passing Society members in the hallways or waiting behind them in line. Coworkers did not ask them to join bowling leagues, and supervisors did not, as a general rule, promote them—unless, of course, the stamp of strangeness brought with it luck or the semblance thereof—and even then promotions were rare and usually insignificant. Larraine dealt with such adversity well or at least had until now. Perhaps, she thought, now would not be such a bad time to abdicate her position and hand over authority, step down and retire. Let someone else make all the mistakes and listen to the subsequent complaints that arose from making them. If she had only a day or so left to her, then Lord let her spend it in relative peace and quiet answerable to and for no one. That was it then. Just tell them she was all done up. Sorry, lads, but I'm fresh out o' tricks and all out o' treats too. Was there any malediction, insult, or ill meaning epithet any of them could give voice to which would mean anything to her in the face of the death they were about to undergo? Larraine didn't think so. She'd come to learn that mere language could take a person only so far and that for expressing some things, it simply wasn't adequate at all. Even "cattlecrappingchickenshit," should that be their final consensus, would be meaningless to her and willy-nilly now, rolling off her shoulders like water. Why was their opinion of her, once held so dear, so unimportant now? Was she so deep into the pangs of terrible and unquenchable thirst that other considerations ceased to have the hold on her they once did? Having never been this thirsty before it was difficult for her to say one way or the other, but she supposed it might be so. Still, it didn't feel all that bad nor was it particularly unbearable, at least not yet. Where were the mirages that she'd always read about as a little girl and which, according to her reading, were said to accompany such a demise as theirs, hovering somewhere out there in the desert haze, shimmering and indistinct like gossamer visions, misleading them, perhaps for their own good, as they faded away into unknowable nothingness? Perhaps when they finally arrived the mirages would cause them to see water, just as she was seeing it now, spring up as if by magic from that lone sagebrush over yonder. Wet and inviting, the spray reminded her of nothing so much as Old Faithful, spouting as it did, every so often. Water springing up from the desert floor had to be a miracle, but since Larraine didn't believe in miracles but only in a misguided sense of something that could best be labeled blind fate, she chose to treat the miracle as a mirage and therefore determined that she would pay it no attention. However, when the others saw it, she reconsidered. Could mirages be catchy? Could they be spread like colds? Larraine honestly didn't know, but she was still the leader; she hadn't abdicated quite yet, and while in that position for however much longer, she deemed it unseemly to go jumping the gun and humping off half-cocked for water that in all likelihood didn't exist. Let the others do the humping and the jumping. She'd sit right here.

Slim, Jim, and the rest were more than happy to let her have her way. A small stampede broke out as the stranded campers, like mad buffalo on the prairie, charged the fountain. First to reach the magic spring was Slim with his brother, Jim, following close behind and nearly bounding over. The others piled behind and around them, noisy, cursing, and jostling each other like New York City traffic.

From the entrance to her tent, Larraine observed the pushing and shoving when suddenly she saw the ground beneath the melee give way and swallow them up. This sight was accompanied by a loud crack as, unseen, Sand Toes's hidden shoring collapsed from the combination of weight and frenzied movement. The hidden rocks, falling with a terrific crash, sounded like the neighborhood bowling alley on a Saturday night as the stones smashed and rolled together while colliding violently among the helpless quarry caught in the trap. Rising up from the sound of the concussion were the frightened screams of the wounded and crushed. Three of the would-be victims of Lawrence's trap were lucky enough to be sufficiently close to the edge of the pit so that when it gave way, they were able to leap back and escape the cave-in, but their luck was short-lived. Sand Toes sprang up from behind them like a rattlesnake out of the sand and pushed them back in. One of the three broke a leg. Another bashed his head on a rock while at the same time managing to blacken his eye when it collided with a random elbow rising sharply out of the tangled wreckage of bodies waiting to greet him at the end of his fall. The third escaped entirely unscathed but then had the temerity to burst her appendix after everyone else was rescued, adding to the list the number of those in need of medical attention.

When the dust eventually settled, ten there were who could be counted as injured, six of them seriously enough that they required assistance in the form of conveyance in order to ensure their survival. Slim had the crap scared out of him and so lost twenty pounds. Nearly half of their advance team had been crippled due to injury with the remainder in none-too-good shape either and having to carry the more seriously wounded, person for person. It was a Chinese fire drill gone awry, and Larraine looked on in horror, witnessing it. Mirages, she knew, although how she knew she knew not, did not go off and suddenly swallow their victims whole, nor did dust-covered phantoms suddenly spring up from them to polish off the potential victims the mirages themselves missed. Larraine stared at the suddenly appearing apparition and thought to herself that it looked seemingly human, whatever it was. That is to say it had two arms, two legs, and a head, or so she assumed. Truth to tell, she hadn't gotten a good look yet, merely observed passing flashes, which suggested something vaguely hominid. It stood in the middle of a boiling cloud of dirt and dust while assailing her fellows from behind and attacking from good cover. It screamed and whooped like a banshee. Whatever it was and was doing, Larraine knew just what to do with it when it did it around her. Pulling back the flap of her tent, she reached neatly inside and removed a Winchester rifle with a large caliber bore which had hitherto rested comfortably against the side of her shelter.

Two quick shots fired in Sand Toes's general direction were enough to convince him to cease and desist. Larry didn't know much but he did know guns—even if he didn't know them too well. What knowledge he had of them he'd gained from the Apaches, and what he knew was that they were a whole lot better at bringing down prey than his traps and pits were ever going to be. Therefore, at the sound of those twin thunderclaps, he immediately ceased his efforts and offered up a prayer for his own skin to the Great Spirit while considering the person who held the thunderstick in her hands. He wasn't sure how guns worked—his Apache friends were careful in that, at least, to keep such knowledge from him; but he'd seen enough demonstrations of their power to know that despite their mysteries, they were more than capable of getting the job done. Knowing that much, Sand Toes turned around slowly to see who it was that had got the drop on him and was surprised when he encountered his long-dead mother. He didn't, of course, meet his mother. His mother, after all, was dead. Yet unbeknownst to either Larraine or Larry at that time was the irony of their shared heritage, going all the way back to Great-grandaddy Dawe and his brother, and from them to antiquity. The fact that they were once-sundered third cousins twice removed, or some such silly relation they would both figure out later. But she wasn't his mother, and Larraine certainly knew that. Sand Toes wasn't so sure because although he didn't know then, those wacky genes on both sides of the family were so inbred and intermixed, look-alikes were bound from time to time to crop up. In fact, in their family, look-alikes outnumbered spring daisies. It was true that Larraine wasn't a "dead ringer" for her lost aunt, once sundered and twice removed, but Sand Toes's recollections of his dearly departed matriarch weren't much more than half-forgotten memories that amounted to no more than barely remembered glimpses. The minor differences in form and manner between the two women were overlooked by Larry and more than made up for by wishful thinking. Sand Toes missed his Ma and had been missing her for what seemed an eternity. Could the dead come back? Sand Toes, who didn't have much in the way of book learning and who therefore did not give much thought to death's finer and more philosophical aspects, honestly couldn't say. Anything killed by his own hand or meeting its end while at the mercy of one of his traps had been eaten too quickly for him to put the question to the test. But he supposed it was possible and, moreover, hoped so.

For her own part, Larraine didn't know what to make of Larry's frank and open consideration. His eyes, the color of robin's eggs, seemed filled with both uncanny wile and unending innocence, each of which now lay bare at her feet. At one moment this maniac was trying to kill her family, and in the next he seemed ready to worship her. He must've been out in the sun longer than her entire troupe put together. "Freeze!" she yelled, and he did, although not at all sure of what she meant. For now he was just content to gaze...and to give pause to consider the longing ache in his heart. It could be his Ma, he supposed, and if not, she was still beautiful to behold and still holding the gun. "Who are you?" Larraine asked. "And what are you doing here?" The stranger kept his silence all the while looking straight up the barrel of her rifle with eyes that gazed from faraway those sights they beheld up close. *They're a deeper blue than mine*, she thought, *not unalike but so different nevertheless...as if they'd seen things.* Things she didn't think she necessarily wanted to know about. "What's the meaning of this attack?" But the stranger said nothing, just stood there, mouth agape, as if adrift in a daydream of his own devising. "Well," she prodded, "are you just going to stand there?"

It seemed that he was. Keeping her finger poised lightly on the trigger, Larraine slowly lowered her gun. A few yards stood between her and where the stranger stood by the pit, and perhaps, she reasoned, if she lowered the gun, he'd feel less threatened and be more amenable to communication and, God only hoped, cooperation. Her people were hurt and lying in a hole behind him. She'd need his help—both in getting them out of that hole and out of here. With the barrel pointed at the ground, she watched as the stranger slowly advanced, empty hands at his sides and plainly visible, only to fall at her feet a mere three feet away.

He gazed upward at her with eyes that seemed to stare back from someplace just beyond the outer rim of eternity. "Muh?" he inquired.

"What?"

"Muh?"

By now those few who remained uninjured began to haul themselves out of the pit. One of the first to pull himself up was Jim, brother of Slim. Slim was uninjured as well but remained entangled among the twisted limbs and muck, being too heavy to extricate himself from the morass at the bottom of the pit. Jim, on the other hand, once freed from the tangle of broken limbs, bounded from the trap as if shot from a cannon. Sensing trouble from behind, Lawrence immediately spun about and pushed him back in. Mother or no mother, gun or no gun, he wasn't about to let any of those shoes escape!

Larraine looked on in disbelief as Jim fell back into the hole. She'd never shot anyone before and had no desire to start now, but something had to be done. Leaping after Sand Toes, she upended the barrel of her Winchester and brought the stock crashing down on his skull, sending Larry to La La Land.

Again, Jim hauled himself out of the hole and with thunderclouds on his brow walked slowly over to Larry's unconscious form and kicking him repeatedly, swore in a brogue so thick that even Larraine was hard put to interpret his curses. She did, however, manage to haul him off their prisoner and get him calmed down whereupon the two of them began the business of removing the injured from the trap, all the while discussing among themselves the mysterious stranger in their midst and what it was he'd been trying to say. "I tell you, it was Mohair," said Larraine, referring to her jacket. It was cold in the desert at night, and she'd bought an expensive one for just such occurrences before undertaking this expedition. She was wearing it this morning in order to fend off the rapidly disappearing chill from the evening before. "Mohair."

"I dinna ken that," replied Jim. "The daffy bastard was saying *Ma* to be sure."

Larraine offered him a sour look. "Ma?" she replied. "That's ridiculous—do I look like his mother?" She did—even if neither she nor Jim knew it.

"This whole expedition's been ridiculous, lass, and that crazy son of a bitch just makes it more so. But by me own Ma, he said *Ma*, sure 'n' begorrah!"

"But why would he say that?" she questioned. "Maybe he was telling me to move over."

"While graspin' at yer britches?"

THE CHRISTMAS RABBIT

"Oh, all right then," said Larraine, giving in, "he said *Ma*. But that still doesn't explain why he said it. He looks familiar, don't you think?"

"Och, posh 'n' nonsense, girlo," Jim replied. "Yer been out in the sun too long."

"No," she countered. "I've seen him before—I'm sure of it. I just can't remember where!" Jim cast a tired glance back at the pit and at the injured bodies that still lay within. Above the sky was a cerulean blue, and against it vultures high in the air glided upon thermal drafts while gazing down at the potential dinner below.

"Well, there's nothin' to be done about it now," Jim said. "We've injured that need attendin', and we best be about our business. Peter and Sinead are seeing to our people, and we best go lend 'em a hand." Larraine looked down at their unconscious prisoner. "What about him?" she asked.

"Och, leave the daffy bastard to lie where he be. He's out colder 'n' a pub regular on the day after Saint Paddy's! He ain't doin' no harm where he be and he ain't goin' nowhere either!"

Larraine allowed as how that was probably so—she'd given him a good one—and turned with Jim to assist their fellows at the pit, pausing once more to examine their captive. Where had she seen him?

It took the better part of the morning to get all the injured safely out of Sand Toes's trap. Sand Toes regained consciousness about halfway through the endeavor and was immediately put under heavy guard, although not that heavy—Slim was still in the pit and they were having the devil's own time of it trying to figure out a way to extricate him. Being totally unprepared for such a contingency they found themselves lacking in any type of rope whatsoever which they might have employed in their undertaking. To be sure, Sinead, an Irish knitter from way back, had brought along her knitting needles and yarn, but such feeble accoutrements were not up to a task like this. Regardless of her many attempts at knitting and purling her flimsy fibers were never going to be strong enough to haul four hundred plus pounds of dead weight out of a hole thirteen feet deep. And though her needles were sharp and could be counted upon to provide a good goosing under ordinary circumstances, they were totally inadequate given their present plight despite the many jabbings Slim received in his anus. Frustrated and angry, Larraine confronted Jim and discussed with him the possibility of enlisting the stranger's aid in the resolution of their predicament. "After all," said she, "he dug the damned thing in the first place and it seems to have been pretty efficient. This can't be the first time that he's done something like this. No doubt, he's mastered the skill of getting his quarry out of the pit once he's gotten them in." She walked over to the prisoner who was sitting on the ground with his knees pulled up to his chin and staring dejectedly at his feet. Things had not gone his way at all despite the ingenuity of his trap. Instead of capturing them they'd gone and gotten the upper hand on him. Since he had no footwear to steal Sand Toes wondered just what it was that they were going to do with him, picturing in his mind's eye any number of horrible fates. Who knew? With no shoes to barter, would they end up taking his feet instead? How could Sand Toes be Sand Toes if they robbed him of his dogs?

Larraine gave him a light kick in order to get his attention. "What's your name?" she asked. Sand Toes offered her a puzzled glance by way of reply. She spoke the language of his parents—of that he was certain, but it had been so long since he'd conversed in that tongue he'd forgotten most of what he once knew and what little he did remember had to be spoken slowly and distinctly in order for him to make even the barest sense of it. And what words he did remember such as *north*, *south*, *east*, *west*, and *water* were going to be of little use at the moment.

"What's your name?" Larraine repeated. Again that puzzled stare. She changed tactics. Kneeling down in front of him, she gently took his hand, and placing it upon her shoulder said, "Larraine. My name is Larraine. What's yours?" She took her hand and placed it upon his shoulder and waited for him to reply. Nothing. She repeated the twofold procedure over and over until something in Larry clicked. His eyes lit up, and he nodded excitedly. He then pointed to himself saying, "*Sáí Ézhaazhé.*"

THE CHRISTMAS RABBIT

"What in the name o' God's hell is that supposed to mean?" Jim asked. "That were a proper Irish brogue if ever I heard one, but that be no language from the auld country that he be speakin' or as sure as the English are a blight on creation, I'm a fookin' Scotsman!"

Larraine could count on one hand the number of times in which she found herself in accord with her cousin. Now, like it or not, she realized that she'd have to start using the other hand because she reluctantly found herself in agreement with him once again. Yes, the English were a blight, and although Jim was never going to be a "fookin' Scotsman," the stranger did in fact speak with an Irish brogue yet used no Celtic dialect she'd ever heard. What was it? She called Richard over to join her. Tall and gangly, Richard was by all appearances ordinary, yet he had a sharp and uncanny mind which he'd trained for years, both in school and out, in the learning of languages. God alone knew how many different tongues he could understand and converse in. Even Richard himself, when he stopped to consider such matters, couldn't say for sure as some people regard various dialects of the same language as an entirely different tongue altogether while others considered such aberrations mere slang. He knelt at Larraine's side and offered a curious glance to the stranger. "What's up?" he asked Larraine, pointing as he did to the wounded he and Sinead were still treating. "I've been helping with the injured, as you can see, and we're kind of busy at the moment."

"I know, but listen up," said Larraine, "and tell me what you make o' this." She repeated the gesture, which by now Larry had come to understand, viewing it as a game of sorts. He eagerly gave his reply. "Well?" Larraine asked.

Richard offered her a puzzled frown. "I'm not sure," he said. "Get him to say it again." She had Larry repeat it another three times before Richard felt confident with his interpretation. "It's Apache," he said. "At least I think it is—although whoever heard of Apache spoken with an Irish brogue?"

Larraine looked at him, dumfounded. "Apache?" she asked. "He doesn't look Native American."

"No, he doesn't" agreed Richard. "I'll admit, it's a mystery."

"Well, what in the name o' Saint Paddy is he saying?" Larraine's frustration was mounting. It was getting late in the day, and if they didn't resolve this language puzzle quickly and therefore enlist the stranger's aid, it was likely to be their last day—late or not.

"He says," Richard replied, "his name is Sand Toes. Sand Toes of the Apaches."

"Santos?"

"No, not *Santos*. *Sand Toes*."

Larraine offered Richard a sour scowl. "What the kind of name is that?"

Richard examined Larry's feet, taking note of the multiple calluses and corns while slowly nodding his head with understanding. "Names in Native American languages," he said, "are often descriptive, portraying some event or character trait associated with the person who bears the name. Sitting Bull and Crazy Horse are two classic examples which come to mind."

"Okay, fine," she replied. "But Sand Toes?"

"Take note of his feet," Richard said, "and I think you'll understand how he comes by his moniker."

Larraine did as she was instructed and saw that their captive's feet were overly large, devoid of footwear, and heavily callused like old shoe leather. "Well," she said after completing her examination, "the name seems to be apt."

"Another example," queried Richard, "of 'if the shoe fits, wear it'?"

"Oh, funny," Larraine replied. "Very funny."

CHAPTER III

Two Lunatics Meet Each Other

Lauren awoke promptly at six to find she had slept the afternoon away. From the tormented noise arising from his tossing and turning, it was clear that Da still slept soundly—or as soundly as lunatics are able, which is to say not too soundly at all. She was used to his thrashings and took them as a matter of course. They were normal for Da and caused her not the slightest bit of worry. Silence would've concerned her more. She knew from experience that your average lunatic was mostly a danger to themselves and to others when they kept quiet. In their infrequent silences they allowed thoughts to build up inside them like molten lava in a volcano, with pressure added to pressure, until they suddenly exploded, raining down ruin and havoc in their immediate area. Not that dear ole Da would ever intentionally cause her harm—Lauren was sure that he loved her far too much for that, and yet the crazy predicaments and pickles in which he would often land them were most often preceded by one of his rare bouts of silence. She rolled out of bed and padded off to the bathroom to make her toilet and refresh herself with a much-needed glass of water. Outside the westwardly wandering sun splashed the entrance to the mine with a rosy glow of hue and color. As she passed by Lauren looked out and saw that a few early stars had sprung up for the evening to shine like diamonds laid out for display on a curtain of velvet. If only she could shine so! Tomorrow she would have to go back to school, leaving her charge in the precarious care of her Da. She had enemies upon whom she wouldn't wish that, but what could she do? Despite her many attributes and her marked maturity for one so young, she was still nevertheless a child and as such, subject to the whims of Da who, she knew, wouldn't mind one whit if she skipped a day of school here and there—except that it had been her Ma's wish when she'd been around to wish it, that Lauren attend regularly. Her Da would never gainsay his wife even after being "dearly departed," no matter how long gone, so Lauren resigned herself to another week away from home. If she were going just for the day then she wouldn't feel so uneasy. She thought that her Da could be trusted that much at least, even with new food so helpless and so close at hand. But since they lived out in the middle of nowhere and since Da didn't drive, daily commuting to school was impractical, if not outright impossible. Her Uncle Jim in his Land Rover, she knew, would drive out here from town in the early morning and take her back to attend classes for the week. She'd stay with him and Uncle Slim. Although she liked her uncles and looked forward to her visits, this was one time when she thought she might do better avoiding their company.

That she had to nurse the Easter Bunny back to health was a foregone conclusion. Bad luck, she was sure, would dog her the rest of her days if she ended up having a hand in killing it. She was confident in the identification of her patient, sure that her charge was that famous rabbit. Who else could it be? The multicolored egg she and Da found cracked and lying beside it was proof enough of the rabbit's identity—despite her Da's opinions on the subject. Da knew all there was to know about the desert but he didn't know everything. Not by a long shot. She wondered why the Easter Bunny, deliverer of provender to all children everywhere, was this far out and away from civilization. There was no one else around these parts except for her and her Da. Then it hit her. *The rabbit was supposed to be here, and the egg it carried was meant for me!* Dear Heaven! What to do? She'd had a hand in almost killing the bearer of good gifts! Once again she felt guilt envelop her in its merciless grip. It squeezed ever tighter, yet its hold upon her only strengthened her resolve. Somehow she had to save it and atone for herself. Somehow she had to make it up to the beast and show the poor thing just how much she appreciated its efforts on her behalf. She crossed over to the living room to inspect her charge, taking note along the way that the stalactites overhead were dripping water once again, a perpetual plumbing problem that given her Da's disposition toward such things was not likely to evaporate and go away soon. No doubt, she thought, I'll have to call the layer of pipe once I get back into town and arrange for him to make a house call. She came upon her charge and found that he was still sleeping. Yet she realized that he must've awakened at some point during the afternoon as the water bowl she'd put before him looked slightly less full while the crust of bread appeared to have been nibbled about the edges. She felt reassured. She reasoned if the rabbit felt well enough to eat, then it was probably on the road to recovery. It would just have to be kept warm and quiet. This was the desert, and therefore "warm" was easy. However, it was also the home of Sand Toes of the Apaches, and that made "quiet" another matter altogether. As if to confirm that thought her Da chose that very moment to wake up. "Lauren, me foine lass," he shouted, "what time is it, girlo, and has that chicken croaked yet?"

"It's not a chicken!" she replied. "I keep telling you, it's the Easter Bunny—and no, it hasn't croaked yet. In fact, I think it may be getting better!" She looked down at her patient. "I even think it's eaten something!"

"Food eatin' food," Lawrence replied bitterly. "'Tis a strange world, to be sure, that we be livin' in."

"It's only food if we see it that way," said Lauren, "otherwise it's a being, just like you or I, and subject to the same considerations!" She gazed over at Da, who'd tumbled out from his bedroom to join her, looking more disheveled and wild-eyed than usual. "You've been dreaming about Ma again, haven't you?"

"Aye, lass," Lawrence replied, "aye. Do yer dear ole Da ever dream o' anyone or anything else?"

Lauren bent down to gently stroke the rabbit's head as she considered her Da's question. "Sand-shoveling," she replied. "Sometimes you go on the whole night caught up in an endless nightmare about sand-shoveling."

"'Tis true enough, I suppose," said Sand Toes, "but even then I see yer dearly departed Ma in those too."

"I'm sorry, Da," Laruen replied. "Perhaps you'll see her in Heaven one day."

Sand Toes, who still hadn't learned his way out of the desert, doubted his ability to find such a place—even if he had a map which showed him how to get there, but he agreed with his daughter nevertheless. "Perhaps I will, lass. Perhaps I will at that. Fer to be sure, such a foine woman as yer Ma—that has to be where she's gotten to."

Lauren hated to see her Da possessed of such melancholy. She knew he missed her mother even more than she did. Lauren had her friends in school and others in town in whom she could confide and express her misery. With her Ma gone, her Da, she knew, had no one but her, and out of love was careful not to burden her with too much. There were his friends, the Apaches, of course, but she wasn't altogether sure that they were his friends after all and was of the opinion, though she kept it to herself, that they were play-acting for reasons of their own. Someday she knew, she was sure to unmask them and then scalps would roll! In the meantime, she'd settle for cheering the old man up. "Let's take a walk outside," she said, exiting the mine through the adit. Sand Toes followed at her heels. The sun had set completely and utter darkness stole over the land, which was only possible despite the myriad of stars hanging suspended in the sky, in an empty barrenness like this. Orion with his scabbarded sword was out tonight sparkling like emeralds. Also visible were Cetus, the Whale, Musca, the Fly, and hosts of others. "Look, Da," Lauren excitedly proclaimed as she pointed to the heavens, "there's Lepus the Hare."

"I keep tellin' ye, girlo, that there be nae such thing!"

"Da," replied his daughter, "we've been studying the constellations in school, and I'm telling you, that's the hare."

"Rabbits 'n' hares," Sand Toes replied, "here, there, and everywhere! On the ground or in the sky—they all be figments o' someone's overactive imagination. Mirages they be. Mirages and nothing more!"

"The constellations," Lauren asked, "or the stars themselves?"

THE CHRISTMAS RABBIT

"Why, both, lass," her Da replied as he lovingly stroked her hair. "The constellations because there be no lines up there to connect the dots and the stars because wishin' upon 'em dinna do nae good."

"Do you wish upon the stars, Da?"

"Every night, lass. Ain't come true yet."

"So do I. I wish that Ma would come back."

"I know, lass. It's a good enough wish at that, and you just keep on wishin' it."

With the deepening of evening a cool wind sprung up from out of the northwest bringing with it a chill, which would settle into a bone-freezing cold as the night grew older. Now was the time of the desert hunter. The desert sprang to life in this early cooling-off period as daylight gave way to night and the sun relinquished the heavens to the moon and stars. Those very same stars, upon claiming their ascendancy, shouted out to everything, inviting all of creation into the wide open under for the grand viewing. All desert folk, Lauren knew, accepted the invitation. Lizards were scampering about and snakes were even now slithering out of their holes. Desert toads with their bulbous eyes and deep throats engaged in a croaking chorus as they sought out food or one another for mating; making them ideal for killing since their teeny brains were focused only on what they were doing and were therefore easy targets as any snake slipping out of its hole could tell you.

Lawrence looked down at his daughter, watching her as she came alive to the sounds of the early-evening desert, and oh, how he longed to be out there in the midst of it all, hunting and in turn being hunted. True, there wasn't much out there capable of giving him a good stalking—with the exception of the occasional puma or sly scorpion trying to sneak up on him from behind, that is, but even these rare hunters had by now grown so familiar with his scent and the subsequent traps such scent seemed to impend that they by and large shied away, giving him a wide berth. Still, to be preyed upon from time to time, and if not that, to be cautiously regarded at least, was what Sand Toes lived for. Like the Easter Bunny, Sand Toes was in continual training for an important mission, one he'd taken on with a sacred vow shortly after the death of his parents. It was an enterprise that he intended upon seeing to its conclusion, however long the expedition took. And though it could be argued perhaps that our Rabbit of Later Days, now lying holed up and injured in a cave, had completed his quest, or at least had taken it as far as he was going to, Lawrence knew that his own pursuit was ongoing and that hunting and being hunted were merely part of a daily regimen that would not cease for him until his goal was realized and his search bore fruit. His quest hadn't come full circle yet. He was hunting the biggest game of all and knowing that someday such game must inevitably pass his way, trained unceasingly in order to be ready when it did. Sand-shoveling, trap-digging, water-prospecting, and hunting were part and parcel of his self-imposed regimen, designed to prepare him for his quest's ultimate culmination. Now was the best time to hunt and he longed to be out in the vast traces doing just that whilst refining his skills. "Come, lass," he said. "Let's be about this evening. There's bound to be food a' plenty down by the standin' water tonight."

"You go, Da," Lauren replied. "I have to stay here and take care of this rabbit."

"That thing?"

"Yes, Da," said Lauren. "That thing. And as I keep on telling you, that thing is the Easter Bunny. We have to save it. I have to save it!" She began to cry, weighed down by the burden of her charge and the worry which filled her at the thought that it might not pull through even yet—despite its apparent first steps upon recovery's road. "Please let me stay home from school this week and take care of it. Please?"

Lawrence looked down at his daughter, gently patting her head as he did so. "Lassie," he said, "yer Ma, God rest her soul, was dead set on yer schoolin', girlo—ye know that. She'd not take too kindly to it, be she in heaven or any place else fer that matter, should she ever find out that I had a hand in helpin' ye to skip!"

"But, Da," the young girl pleaded, "it may die if I'm not here to look after it."

THE CHRISTMAS RABBIT

"Di ye think yer dear ole Da is ignorant o' the intricacies o' frontier medicine, girlo?" he replied, teasing her with a mock look of indignation.

"Och, you'll just eat him!" Lauren said. "He's just food to you and once I'm well and away your stomach will get the better of you!"

Lawrence softened his features and reached out to gently stroke his daughter's hair. "Lauren, love," said he, "if 'n' savin' that wee beastie means so much t' ye, lass, then ye can count on me t' be doctorin' it up. It'll be alive and well, when ye gangle on home, come Friday. Ye have me word on it, dearie."

Lauren looked up and hugged him fiercely. "Oh, Da!" she exclaimed. "Do you mean it? Do you really?"

"I said so, didn't I?" Lawrence returned his daughter's embrace with equal fervor. "Now ye just be about the business o' packin' yer bag and gatherin' up yer schoolwork while I make me a quick run down to the standin' water and see if I can scrounge us up somethin' fer dinner."

Lauren did as instructed, first pausing to look in on her charge. The creature was awake but motionless, its eyes half lidded and its breathing shallow as it went about the painful process of recuperation. As Lauren reached down to pet it the rabbit made a feeble attempt to shy away, mewling pitifully. It quickly gave the effort up. It was still too weak.

"There, there," Lauren softly said. She reached out to gently scratch the poor thing behind the ears. "No one's going to hurt you here."

The hare heard and Lauren swore that she read contemptuous disbelief on its face. But that, she knew, was impossible, yet she credited anyway, the look itself and the unspoken thought that it presumably represented. This was after all, the Easter Bunny, and who knew what was possible with it or what it was capable of? Maybe talking wasn't beyond the reach of its abilities and even if it was, then perhaps it could at least listen to people and understand them. It did after all, deliver eggs. It certainly held her gaze, returning it eye for eye with what Lauren took to be insight and understanding. It was unnerving, be it Easter Bunny or no, to be scrutinized and regarded in such a manner by an animal. Most prey were dead by the time her Da got back around and checked his traps. Of the few left alive who could comprehend anything, most too weak to even move merely stared mutely back in bestial terror. Not this rabbit. It was different. Lauren could not have said just how or why other than talk about brightly colored eggs and her own hopes, but still there was something in its regard as it meekly submitted to her scratching that seemed to reach out and touch her down to her very soul. They were connected, brought together by preordained fates, past lifetimes, or common karma. Lauren didn't know how, just knew that it was so. And for her sake, perhaps this was best. Had she known then just how far back her connection with this rabbit actually went and through whom such a connection was made, she might've gone off running and screaming into the desert herself, never to return. The connection was not to be understood. It was rather merely to be sensed instead of necessarily being comprehended. Like déjà vu was this karmic connection that seemed to bind her and the rabbit together, as if each knew of the other through mutual pasts and common enterprise. Was that possible? Lauren couldn't say. But if it were possible, she knew that hers was the family in which such occurrences would most likely take place. The silly stories and far-flung lore passed down from one generation to the next and utterly venerated though not entirely believed were enough to convince her of that. These tales were handed down by her Ma, and when she'd disappeared, by all those third cousins and uncles, twice removed, who resided in the desert town where she went to school. These yarns were chock-full of bizarre ancestors caught up in the strangest of circumstances and engaging in the most unusual of actions. From magic carpet riders to those who wove them, it seemed that every weirdo who ever was, at one point or another married into this family or worse, was born directly of it. They left their own tales to carry on after them, and each was born with the mark, just as she bore it and her Da as well. And though her mother denied it to her dying day, Lauren knew that she, when she'd been alive to bear it, wore the stamp of strangeness too—just in a place too private to mention, let alone admit to. Larraine had filled her daughter's days with lore regarding the mark and those who bore it, all the while admonishing her to be ever on the lookout for, and wary of, its influences. The mark could be counted upon to land you in adventure and happenstance, which Larraine further explained to Lauren were not necessarily bad things if you were ready, lucky, and knew how to deal with them. It was true, Lauren knew, that few in her family had been so prepared but was that so grievous either? Despite their uniform lack of preparation and their continual predisposition toward bad karma and the misfortune that such karma presaged, most of the heroes and heroines in her family tree through blind luck or providence seemed to have made out okay. Few came to what you or I would call bad ends though to be sure, we wouldn't view their lives as success stories either. Yet despite the strangeness of their circumstances and their suspect pedigrees, they managed on the whole to muddle through their individual and collective predicaments. It seemed that notwithstanding its penchant for mischief, the mark looked out for its own. Most times.

And there, of course, lay the rub. Most times meant sometimes not. One could never be sure which times were those times and when *such* times would most likely occur. One just had to live them out and hope for the best. You couldn't count on 'em and Lauren's Ma, once living proof of that fact, had warned her that when dealing with the mark there was no picking odds or figuring chances. With the mark one just played the hand one was dealt while hoping against hope that deuces were wild. Well, she'd play it then for all she was worth and give the mark a run for its money! "Are we about to get caught up in adventure and circumstance?" she asked the rabbit. "Are things about to get flaky around the edges as I've heard they so often do?" The rabbit answered her questions with an all-knowing gaze that seemed to say that they were deep into such proceedings already.

The night wore slowly away while Lauren kept her lonely vigil. At some point in the evening Sand Toes returned, carrying dinner—two sidewinders and a horned toad, which he filleted, fricasseed, and promptly fed to Lauren who hardly touched the meal for fear of taking her attention away from her patient.

Dawn came, bringing Slim and Jim with it. The brothers pulled up to the mine shaft in a dusty and dented Land Rover, which they'd been driving for the last three hours and pushing to its limits, in order to arrive on time. Parking in front of the adit, Jim honked the horn and he and his brother got out. Before they could set both feet on the ground however, Lauren came running out of the mine with her books and bag slung merrily across her shoulder. Approaching them both she threw her open arms around each and hugged them affectionately. She loved each dearly and thought them both tremendously funny. Uncle Jim was funny because his brogue reminded her of Da. And though she knew her uncle's use of brogue was a mere affectation while her Da's was the real article, still she found the two of them incredibly humorous. Uncle Slim was funny because he was anything but. Despite having a good sense of humor about his size and weight, *funny* was not a word included in his lexicon. Still, he did try. He was quick with a joke or a riddle but most often forgot the punch lines, or if remembering them, engaged in their delivery with no sense of timing whatsoever. If he got the timing right then the punch line itself was inane more often than not. His girth and weight and his good humor regarding both were more than enough, however, to make up for his lack of comedic talent. Even today, Lauren knew, long after the event had occurred, a storyteller—often with her Uncle Slim's help—was apt to get a good laugh when relating to his audience the tale of how Uncle Slim came to be caught in one of her Da's traps, regaling them with the blow-by-blow synopsis of the production that came to be the Society's efforts to extricate him. In the end it had required all of their collective effort including that of the wounded, and relating the exercise in hilarity that it became was one of the chief sources of entertainment for the Society when drinking Friday nights at the pub.

"Well met," said Jim, returning her embrace with equal fervor. "But why be ye ganglin' about here and in such a hurry to be off? And where be yer Da, I wonder?"

Lauren released them and stepped back. "He's still sleeping, Unc," she replied, "and since he is, I thought it best not to wake him." Jim, who did not exactly see eye to eye with Sand Toes regarding most things, who in fact had been a rival of Larry's for the fair hand of sweet Larraine and who was as well that very same plumber who liked to lay other people's pipe when he'd been in town to do it and not lost out in the desert somewhere seeking in vain for fools' gold, could not help despite his misgivings and reservations toward Sand Toes, but appreciate young Lauren for her consideration regarding her Da and his desire to sleep in. Life out here was hard. Even Jim had to admit to that. Still it was unlike Lawrence, he knew—who had fast become a legend of surpassing oddity even among the Society, to be abed with his little lass about to be off. Sand Toes could always be counted upon to be up and about for Lauren's weekly departures. He made it a point to send her on her way with a kiss and a very protective embrace in front of the others, as if to assure himself and make the point to those looking on too that Little La was his daughter, all the while interrogating her chaperones as to their planned route back to town (there was only one), their expected ETA (their arrival time never varied), living conditions (she had her own room in her uncle's house), planned menus for the week (she ate far better in town than she ever did at the mine shaft), and time of return (again, never varying and never late). Sand Toes was a stickler for such details and could be counted upon to raise a ruckus if even the slightest deviation occurred in the proposed plan. He didn't trust them. That's okay, Jim thought, although truth be told, he was irritated by Sand Toes's suspicions. The secret Society of Lost Gold Miners didn't trust Sand Toes either. "Are ye sure yer Da's all right and not come down sick?" Sand Toes had the constitution of an elephant and everyone in the Society knew it. No one, including Sand Toes himself, could ever remember a day when he had been feeling poorly. "Perhaps I should just look in on him." Jim didn't give a cattle crap about Lawrence, and if it weren't for Lauren, could have just as well wished that the crazy sandman dropped dead. From that first moment when Sand Toes had shoved him back into the pit, Jim knew that he'd been pushing him out of the way in order to get to Larraine and furthermore had been doing so up until the day she died. Jim never forgave Larry his enthusiasm for the girl, believing that he himself should have been the one to marry Larraine and not this desert derelict who may or may not be his fourth cousin twice removed or whatever. Their shared lineage had never been successfully proven to Jim's satisfaction despite the mark—which no one but Larraine could claim to have seen. He, along with everyone else had to take Larraine's word, when she'd been around to give it, for that. Now it was too late. For Larraine's sake, the Society had accepted Sand Toes back into the fold, regarding him as a long-lost cousin despite his own reluctance to regain admission into the family, and of course, once done, there was no kicking him out. For no matter how much any of them might want to, such expulsions set a bad precedent and would send a signal to all concerned that anyone could be booted out for any reason whatsoever. Each of the Society's members were jealous of their standing within the family and did not, as rule, allow outsiders in. This, they rationalized, would minimize the head count within the Society itself and in so doing increase the size of their shares should they ever find gold. For this reason, they guarded their own memberships with the ardor that a lioness displayed when protecting her cubs. It stood to reason, therefore, that attempts to deprive a member of their membership within the clan were seriously frowned upon. But so what? Suppose he and that whacko really were related? Did that change matters any? Certainly not! Sand Toes may well have been Larraine's fourth cousin. Jim however, was her second and therefore should've been given first consideration! He had, after all, familial rights! But along came that interloper destroying the most precious of his dreams and desires, disregarding gold, of course, and sending them into complete and utter ruin. Jim felt that he owed Sand Toes much and if it were only for himself could've easily wished Larry eternally onward and perhaps even taken an active hand in sending him there. But there was Lauren to consider. For her sake, despite feeling fate had done him dirty, Jim knew that he could not participate in, or in any way wish for, an accounting with Lawrence. Like most everyone in the Society, Jim loved Little La while she in turn loved her Da like any good Irish lass should. To lose him so soon after losing her Ma would cause the poor lass too much anguish and Jim could not bear to be, even through the passive act of wish fulfillment, the cause of such distress. He cherished her. Didn't they all? The entire Society was enamored of her, and it was only their collective predisposition toward little La that guaranteed Sand Toes any community with the Society now that Larraine had been lost. To hell with arcane and outdated rules that governed the Society and its lifetime membership! If it weren't for Lauren, Jim knew, the Society would've voted en masse for this singular exception and thrown Sand Toes out! Larry was not particularly well liked and given their first encounter with him could anyone in the Society be blamed for harboring such ill will? Jim didn't think so.

Sand Toes wasn't sleeping. He was guarding the rabbit, which he honestly believed was a chicken. Well, perhaps not a chicken but definitely some sort of furry fowl that laid brightly colored eggs. And what was he guarding it for? Certainly not against escape. The creature, whatever it was—chicken, rabbit, or something else altogether, was still too weak to move around much. Escape, therefore, was out of the question. No, he was guarding it from them, Slim and Jim. Why? He wasn't exactly sure. They were not going to eat it—that much was certain. If it was forbidden fruit to him then it was definitely the poisoned apple to them as well, yet Lauren had been adamant on keeping their catch a secret and so he would do just that.

Lauren had no logical reason for hiding their charge but was responding to a gut feeling, which kept kicking her in the stomach, warning her not to disclose their find to anyone. "Leave him be, Uncle Jim," she said, outwardly meaning her Da but secretly speaking of the rabbit. "I'm sure if he's sleeping, he's tired, and needs it. He put in quite an evening last night of trap-laying and sand-shoveling, and he's no spring chicken anymore! I'm not surprised he's so exhausted—besides, look at the sky. The sun's already up, and if we don't get moving, I'll be late for school!" Neither Jim nor Slim were buying entirely, whatever it was that their niece was trying to sell. Both were too familiar with Sand Toes to believe that a mere night of trap-laying and sand-shoveling were enough to exhaust him. Say what you would about him, the brothers agreed that when it came to unbounded energy Sand Toes was in a league of his own; but neither relished the thought of having to square off with Sinead O'Toole, the Society's resident knitter and schoolmarm for having been the cause of Lauren's tardiness. Slim hauled himself back into the front passenger seat, the springs beneath him squealing in protest. The other two followed suit with Jim getting behind the wheel and Lauren climbing in the back. As she shut the door, Slim gave her a curious appraisal, regarding her intensely. There was something strange going on here, not an abnormal circumstance in and of itself, but he couldn't put his finger on it and that was definitely unusual. Usually the most composed and comported of children, Lauren was atypically nervous and fidgety. She kept looking back toward the mine and crossing her legs. Slim noticed that she kept crossing her fingers too as if to ward off the evil eye or dispel an onset of bad luck. A thought occurred to him, and he voiced it, "Yer Da has nae found gold, has he?" Brother Jim's eyes lit up like sparklers at the mention of the possibility. "If'n he has, girlo," he chimed in, "then by rights he's got to share it with all o' us. That gold belongs to the entire Society—no matter who's the one that digs it up."

Lauren laughed. No different than any other members of the Society, except her Da, of course, her uncles could be counted upon to have one-track minds. "No," she said between chuckles, "nothing like that. He's just tired, that's all. Now can we please get going before I get a demerit from Ms. O'Toole?"

The brothers gave in, reluctantly agreeing to her request. Jim backed the Land Rover around and headed off in the direction from whence they came. It was a three-hour trip and no shorter on the way back than it was on the way out. So of course, with school starting at seven, Lauren would inevitably be late, not arriving until at least nine, and though Sinead O'Toole would offer up a lecture to all three concerning Lauren's habitual tardiness on Monday mornings, the schoolmarm wouldn't push the issue. It was her opinion that Little La was the singular shining star in a classroom whose heavenly body, if you will, was littered with asteroids, all of whose orbits were slowly decaying. It was a terrible prejudice to hold—especially for a teacher, but what could she do? The yearly achievement tests didn't lie and with the exception of Lauren herself, annual promotion to the next grade level was a rare phenomenon. Such strictness on her part and such displays of parsimony when it came time to hand out passing grades and promotions, did not exactly endear her to the parents within the Society—but since few of them had been able to complete

THE CHRISTMAS RABBIT

grade school themselves their complaints and criticisms rolled off like water. She would be true to her knitting and true to her profession. So she would admonish the three of them to try and do better next Monday, secretly thankful for the extra two hours given her in which she endeavored without success to catch the rest of the class up.

From the concealing shadows of the adit, Lawrence watched his fourth cousins twice removed drive away with his Little La. He didn't want this burden which his daughter thrust upon him and the only thing preventing him from refusing it was the fact that Larraine, wherever she might be—and to this day, Sand Toes did not actually believe she was dead—would never forgive him for pulling their daughter out of school. He watched the Land Rover fade away in the distance, becoming part of the horizon until it appeared as nothing more than a mote of dust balanced precariously upon the edge of eternity; yet not until it slipped completely over the horizon's edge did he relax his vigil. Once gone, Sand Toes turned his attention to their captive who returned his regard with equal measure. "Well," said the madman, "it looks like it's the two o' us. One fer the other!" The rabbit turned its back on him and before hobbling over to its blanket to retire, partook of a small crust of bread and a cool sip of water.

*****

It was sundown of the same day when Jack Rabbit awoke with a start, feeling as though he were being watched. He was. He rolled over, only to be greeted by the wild-eyed stare of Sand Toes who sat on his haunches, contemplating his prisoner. Each took in the measure of the other with careful regard. For Larry's part, he'd never before encountered this creature's like while Jack realized he was looking into the eyes of a dyed-in-the-wool lunatic. Not liking what he saw the rabbit also realized despite the lunatic's slim build that the stranger before him bore an uncanny resemblance to someone whom the rabbit had never met but who was nonetheless well-known, having become a central part of lapin lore and hareish history. To Jack's eye despite being skinny, Larry had the features of one who was often mentioned in tales from yesteryear and who, from the rabbits' point of view, figured prominently in all of his trials and tribulations. Larry's was the face of an enemy, well-known and universally despised. Not *The Enemy,* mind you, but a foe nevertheless.

"So what happens now?" Larry asked, more to himself than to anyone else as he hardly expected an answer.

"That depends," Jack replied, "on you and what your intentions are."

Lawrence was about to respond when the significance of what had just happened occurred to him. No animal, caught in a trap or otherwise, had ever spoken. He knew what the others thought of him and accepted the fact that he might be crazy. There were enough oddities in his life or so he'd been told to at least credit the possibility. Yet he realized despite such insights and amateur diagnoses, animals should not, and furthermore *could not,* converse—and yet this one appeared to be doing so.

"Say again?"

Ready for a confrontation, Jack stood on his hind legs. "I said that depends upon you! What are you, deaf? Or just dimwitted?"

"Just dimwitted," Sand Toes replied. It was all he could manage. He pinched himself to see if he was asleep and lost in yet another of his bizarre nightmares. When he determined that he was indeed awake, he had to accept the fact that what he was conversing with was a mirage. If there were anything in the desert that truly frightened him, it was mirages. Having encountered them often before while on any number of desert sojourns, he knew that their manifestations augured nothing but trouble and were a sure sign that you were cracking your quackers. Aware of the possibility that years spent baking in the desert sun might have caused his brains to fry to the point where they were one step away from the consistency of scrambled eggs, Larry dreaded the thought he might end up in the nuthouse so early in life. For one thing, said house was sure to be far away from his moisture, and for another, said house, or so he'd been told by Slim, Jim, and countless others, was certain to disallow visitation by anyone, including family, in all but the most strictly

THE CHRISTMAS RABBIT

supervised circumstances. What would happen to Little La without her dear ole Da to look after her?

"Dimwitted, to be sure," said Jack.

"Be silent now, ye gangrel beast! Whatever rabbits be—and I ain't saying ye be one—they canna' be talking now, can they?"

"I'm not a rabbit." Jack replied caustically as he sat down comfortably on his haunches. "I'm a chicken, remember? You said so yourself!"

"Ye are nae bloody chicken. Chickens nae have lips!"

"Of course they do," Jack replied. "Only they're called beaks, and they'll peck the cattle craps outta you with those lips if you let 'em!"

Larry looked down at his charge dumbfounded. "Och," said he, "I must be mad, listenin' as I am to this drivel and balderdash!" A lizard, out for an early evening's stroll, scurried across the floor. Seeing it, Sand Toes shot out his hand like a coiled rattler and grabbing it, scooped it up and into his mouth with one swift motion. He chewed it with relish savoring not only its taste, which was both gamey and bloody, but its essential reality as well. Here was something solid and substantial unlike the apparition now confronting him. A talking animal was obviously an illusion with no substance and like any other mirage, with the exception of Larraine, a plague to be wholeheartedly and with the utmost determination, avoided. But could something without any substance get caught in one of his traps? No. Therefore, he reasoned, the apparition before him had to be real. It was here, after all. No denying that! But why? "What be yer business in these parts?" Larry inquired. "What be ye doin' here, and how is it that ye came to be caught in one o' me traps?"

Jack offered him a scowl while at the same time stamping his feet. "What am I doing? I'm just doing my job! Just following my marching orders, and this is the payment I receive for doing it!

Sand Toes took a cautious step backward. "Just what is yer job, I wonder? What is it, aye?"

"You fool!" said Jack. "It's delivering those damned eggs! This was to be my last stop upon a very long journey! Having completed it I was about to turn a paw toward home where I could have had congratulations and accolades piled upon me that the completion of such a task merits. Bunnies galore would've fallen at my feet. Does! Breeders by the baker's dozens! They could've all been mine. But you've gone and ruined that. Now I'll never finish." He stamped again not in anger but despair while his ears, which had been straight and stiff with righteous indignation, drooped sadly in defeat until they dangled in the dirt. Sand Toes was not impressed. Neither the beast's display of emotion or its having called him a fool served to move him one whit. Now that his wife was gone, Lauren was the only one capable of producing a spark of emotion in him. Of passions he had plenty, but genuine emotions were almost nonexistent. As for being called a fool, well, he'd been so handled so often by so many that this so-and-so who sat there before him could hardly ruffle his feathers for having said it. So Sand Toes continued his interrogation. "And me traps? If ye were just bein' about yer business then how be it that ye came t' be caught in one o' me snares? And who was the egg fer? No one out this ways was askin' ye fer it. Answer me now and be quick about it!"

"I've been lost in this hell for days now," Jack replied, "trying to make my delivery. Little food, no water—I was at the end of my rope and about to pass pellets. To be sure, I was hardly at my best. That's how you caught me. The thought of dying with the job left undone had me somewhat preoccupied. I didn't see your damned trap and so got caught. Big deal. Give me a little more food, water, and sleep, and I'll run circles around both you and your silly old traps! When I'm at the top of my game, there's not a thing in this desert that can touch me, including you!"

"And the egg?" Lawrence asked. "What about that?"

"It was for her," the rabbit replied.

"Who's her?"

"She's her!" said the frustrated rabbit.

"Who's she?"

"Crimeny!" replied Jack. "Her! Your daughter, Lauren! She's she! Did you think the egg was for you? You're a little long in the tooth to be receiving Easter Eggs—at least from me!"

THE CHRISTMAS RABBIT

Lawrence, who had never credited either the Easter Bunny or the ova he delivered as being real, was of the opinion nevertheless that mere age had nothing to do with it. He had his own past from which to draw an example in order to confirm that. He would not, however, gratify this four-legged hopster with an answer to its last question as such an answer would also require an explanation. *And crazy or not, I'll be damned,* he thought, *if I have to account to this little leporide for any of my actions or beliefs.* For now, at least on the matter of Easter Eggs and those entitled to them, Sand Toes would keep his own council. He sat quietly, contemplating the beast while waiting for it to continue. But the enigma had chosen silence too.

The evening was advancing when Sand Toes decided to break the deadlock. "So just what in creation am I supposed t' be doin' with ye, aye?"

Jack was nonplussed. He'd been around the block a few times by now, had seen much of the world, and was more than conversant in the ways of both rabbits and men. What did any man do with a rabbit once he'd caught it?

"Don't tease me, you bastard!" Jack said. "Just fry me or fricassee me or eat me raw for all I care! But hurry up and be done with it. You're beginning to bore me."

Sand Toes smacked his lips, his mouth watering as he contemplated Jack's suggestion. It was a noble idea and very generous of the beast, thought Sand Toes, to offer himself up so willingly. Would that he could take him up on the offer! But Lauren wouldn't understand. If Sand Toes was sure of nothing else he was at least certain of that. "Canna'," he replied. "Gi' me word on it. It's me Little La, ye see. She's been all in a flurry and ganglin' about ever since we found ye. Thinks ye might be worth a peck, she does, and so made me promise not t' eat ye. It's a promise that I'm nae likin' t' be sure, but one I'll be holdin' t' nevertheless."

"Then let me go!"

"Canna' do that either. Ye almost died out there last time. Ye'll most likely perish fer sure if 'n I be givin' ye a second chance at it. The lass would surely blame me. It'd be yer fault fer runnin', but

Little La would blame me. I won't be having her think poorly about her Da, no matter what you might say or want. You ken?"

Jack thoughtfully pushed his ears back and concentrated on the puzzle before him. There were billions of people on this ball of dirt, he knew, and he supposed that given that many it wasn't unreasonable to assume that he'd eventually get caught by one of 'em. That's why, he concluded, so few of the others before him had ever come back—the world was wide and definitely in the hands of the enemy—be that enemy man or some sort of foul beast, dog, fox, or stoat. Yet for all that he'd had the misfortune to be caught by this guy! Any other enemy would've had him in the gullet by now, making his demise relatively painless. This one, however, seemed bent on inflicting upon him agony after agony by prolonging his days and filling them with the god-awful torture of inane chatter. Well, he supposed, failure brought about its own rewards and punishments. "Then what's to be done?" the rabbit asked. "You can't watch over me forever. You've been charged by your daughter to care for me so that I'm healing and getting better by the hour. Once I'm feeling up to snuff and you take your eyes off me, I'm gone, mister! I'm gone and gone so fast that all you'll see of me is my tail rising up from a cloud of dust as I moon you when I leave!"

Considering this, Sand Toes allowed as how the beast was probably right. He couldn't watch it continually. The desert placed its own demands upon him and their fulfillment often required his time and attention elsewhere. Plus there was his own quest to consider, his own mission, which he had to train for on a daily basis remaining sharp and at the top of his form in order to have any chance of ever completing it. These demands left him little leisure to engage in the pastime of being a jailer to jackrabbits. Some other solution would have to present itself. "I'll think about it," he replied. "In the meantime, I've seen enough injured critters to be knowin' that ye ain't goin' t' be ganglin' off just yet."

"Soon though."

Not soon enough t' suit me, thought Sand Toes. But he couldn't very well say that, could he? For what few hours remained that evening, Larry left Jack to himself and went wandering about the flat pans of the desert. He thought best when he wandered because he invariably thought of Larraine when he did so, postulating her continued existence until it was she, not he, who did the actual thinking. He would imagine her and her practical, hands-on approach to tackling the posers and conundrums which beset him and then return home or to wherever the problem lie and follow her imagined suggestion toward resolution. Who can say how or why but nevertheless as an exercise, this application of madness more often than not produced positive results. Perhaps in his sojourns, he really had visions wherein the bygone Larraine actually conversed with him. Who knows? What we do know, however, is that Lawrence took a walk...

CHAPTER IV
Larraine Says Yes

With Sand Toes's help as he was already hopelessly in love with her, Larraine and Jim were able to extricate the wounded from the pit. Lawrence showed them how to fashion rope from the sagebrush and mesquite native to the area. With large pieces of dead and petrified wood and using mostly primitive and crude hand gestures, he explained to them how to construct levers and hoists. They needed both—plus all hands helping, in order to free Slim from the trap. It was hot and thirsty work and the moisture which had accumulated in the bottom of Larry's pit had long since given up the ghost to the cruel desert sun. For Larraine's sake, Sand Toes willingly shared his own supply with his captors and when that ran out gladly dug for them subsequent holes until he found more.

Larraine could hardly take her eyes off him. His familiar face seemed so recognizable to her that it was almost spooky while she found his eagerness to please, despite the harm he'd done, very touching. Jim never quite thawed. Larraine found Sand Toes to be singularly striking despite his long hair, shaggy beard, and generally unkempt appearance, although his name to be sure caused her difficulty. How, she wondered, did someone like him come by such a name? Richard said that it was Native American in origin, but the stranger before her certainly didn't look Indian. In fact, despite his heavy tan the stranger looked to be of Irish descent and furthermore spoke in a brogue—as if to confirm his lineage! But that couldn't be, could it? What would an Irishman be doing out here in the middle of nowhere? The fact that there were better than three hundred

THE CHRISTMAS RABBIT

Irishmen along with their Irish lassies too, back at the base camp which just happened to be out in the middle of nowhere as well failed to impress itself upon her. They had a reason, however silly her secret heart said that reason was, for being here. What possible excuse could this wanderer have for doing likewise? Did he know about the map? Larraine thought it unlikely but wasn't taking any chances. How did this enigma come to be here, she wondered, and was his arrival merely coincidence or were there more sinister purposes at work? Surely the trap in which he'd caught and almost killed her expeditionary force would seem to indicate the latter. But if so, then why was he so eager to come to their aid now? It didn't make any sense. None of it did and though Larraine was certainly used to that, found in this instance that such confusion troubled her. But addled or not, she knew the answers to the riddle confronting her would remain hidden until she could better communicate with the stranger before her. To that end, she began to reeducate Sand Toes in the rudiments of the English language—a task she viewed with some trepidation given the stranger's apparent lack of knowledge regarding the spoken word. She soon realized, however, that she was in error regarding his ignorance and that only added to the puzzle before her. Sand Toes picked up the rudiments of the language and even some of its finer points more quickly than he should have—too quickly in fact for his tongue to have been totally ignorant of it. It soon became obvious to her that her pupil had exposure to English at some point in his past, but when? And if she were correct in her supposition, then how had he come to lose or almost completely forget the language that she now suspected had once been native to him? Yet for all his apparent aptitude, one does not relearn a language that has long remained dead on one's lips in an instant. Larraine concluded that despite Sand Toes's remarkable progress, it would be a week at least before they could hold a meaningful conversation. That necessitated camping on the spot despite the injuries to her party, for she was convinced that being hopelessly lost, Sand Toes provided their only chance for finding their way back to the base camp from which they came—and only if she could relate exactly the predicament in which they found themselves while describing with accuracy the landmarks and surroundings that made up the base camp itself. She had to be clear with her descriptions, she knew, and Sand Toes his interpretation of them, if they were ever to find their way back. Such clarity in communication would take time. Determined to take the time as an assurance against further screwups, Larraine made the decision to remain there, informing the others of her choice. Needless to say, they were less than thrilled. "We canna' do it!" exclaimed Jim. "There be lads and lassies hurt that need tendin' to. We must git 'em back to the base, girlo. We dinna hae nae choice!"

"Fine," replied Larraine. "You take them, seeing as how you know the way. You do know the way, don't you?" Jim was at a loss for words. He turned to Slim, who shook his head as well as his paunch in answer to his brother's unasked question. "Don't look to me," the portly Irishman said. "I've already stated that I have absolutely no idea of where we are and in my opinion, one direction is as good as another—but we canna' just sit here. We need t' be ganglin' off!"

There was murmured assent throughout the camp. No one liked to sit idly by while their cousins, no matter how many times removed, lay suffering and in agony.

"Well, I'm open to suggestions," said Larraine. "Anyone who thinks that they can lead us outta here is certainly welcome to step forward and try—however, you take all of the responsibility, succeed or fail, should you make the attempt." No one volunteered. Larraine was almost sorry it was so. She was getting damned sick of all their whining and grumbling. "Such a brave troupe have I," she murmured to herself. Everyone heard her remark, and most offered her a sharp glance but no one dared speak up.

Peter O'Toole, one of the troupe who remained uninjured, had been an EMT a thousand years ago, or so it seemed to him, when they'd all been leading seminormal lives back in New York City, so it fell to him to supervise the care and treatment of the wounded as they were pulled from the pit. He tended to the cuts and bruises, the contusions and contortions, as best he could; but when it came to broken bones, he was totally undersupplied with splints. The expeditionary team's first aid kit consisted of a small bottle of hydrogen peroxide, some bandages, and a bottle of aspirin. He hesitantly

THE CHRISTMAS RABBIT

approached Larraine. A meek and mild man, strong-willed women intimidated him even under the best of conditions, which these hardly were. His Ma, God rest her soul, had been such a woman and, until the day she died, had taken perverse delight in making her will and whim manifest in her son's life. Peter missed her terribly but even in his sorrow counted it a blessing to be free of her nagging and faultfinding, criticisms, and suggestions. Now he was about to confront a woman who by her very nature and position of authority made his dear ole Ma seem like Rebecca of Donnybrook Farms. Reinforcing those personality traits, he knew, were the contingencies of the present situation—which didn't help matters any. "Ms. Larraine," he softly said, "please excuse me fer addin' t' yer worries any further, but I think ye should be knowin' that I have nae nearly enough o' the proper supplies to be treatin' all the injured." He waited for a response from his leader. When none was forthcoming, with a nervous gesture he shifted his stance and continued. "Ye see, ma'am. The only painkiller that we hae on hand be aspirin, which is hardly equal to the task—and as for splints and braces, we hae none o' those whatsoever. So that, as you can see, is that." He paused for a moment to let the reality of the situation sink in. "I can understand your unwillingness," he continued, "t' move until we can figure out some method of more accurately assessing our location, but ye hae to understand, ma'am, that if we dinna get 'em back to the base camp where I can treat 'em proper, then their sufferin's bound t' get worse. Those with broken bones are bound to get the gangrene. Some will likely lose limbs…others, lives." He finished by snapping his fingers and tapping his toes. He fidgeted from one foot to the other, grinding his teeth as he did so. His eyes darted around in their sockets, and he wished fervently that she would at least say something!

    Larraine gave him a measured stare and finally sighed. He was right, she knew, but so was she. It was a case of being damned if you did and double damned if you didn't, and Larraine hated such cases. She looked over at the remains of levers and hoists now lying useless in the sand since they'd extricated Slim. "Peter," she asked, pointing to the discarded implements, "can ye make use of any of those?"

"Surely," he replied, "though there be hardly near enough to splint everyone as needs it. We need more, and there ain't no more to be found as far as I can tell." Overhead, the vultures circling cried out raucously while casting eerie shadows on the campers beneath. Peter eyed the creatures with a certain amount of trepidation knowing that their increased noise and activity presaged dire consequences. Those scavengers could smell blood from miles away and it was the sour scent of approaching death that drew them hither. "Even if we had enough splints," said he as he kept a weather eye on the scavengers above, "moving them about in this wasteland without the means to dope 'em up while subjecting 'em t' the poundin' heat is bound t' mean the death o' some, if not most."

"So what's t' be done?" Larraine asked.

"With all due respect, ma'am," Peter replied, his snapping fingers now knotted in grannies, "I came t' ye, hopin' ye'd tell me! After all, ye are the leader."

"Well, you're the doctor—make a suggestion!"

"Move 'em or not, I suppose. It dinna make much difference one way or the other, does it? We're all likely t' die out here anyway."

Move them or not. As a suggestion, Larraine considered that it left a lot to be desired. She looked around and saw Sinead and Richard constructing a makeshift shelter from one of the tents in order to provide some shade and relief for the wounded and injured. Richard the linguist. Why had she brought him, of all people, on this expedition? Surely she would've done better to leave him at the base camp. He had no skills whatsoever that were of any benefit to her troupe in this particular instance. Still, when choosing from the membership those who would accompany her on this expedition, her gut feeling told her to include him. Like most in her family, she was used to riding her instinct and playing her gut. Suddenly she found inspiration and getting his attention, signaled him to her.

Leaving the shelter's construction to Sinead, Richard came trotting over to his leader. "What now?" he asked.

Sweat rolled off him in miniature rivers, completely soaking his clothing and making him look like something the desert puma had dragged in while at the same time causing him to smell infinitely worse. Larraine didn't care. At the moment and to her eye, he looked like Sir Lancelot and smelled like ambrosia. "I'll be needin' ye t' speak to the stranger for me," she said.

"You mean Sand Toes?"

Larraine rolled her eyes. "Yes, him!" she said, exasperated. "How may other strangers di' ye see?"

"That depends upon yer meaning," he replied while giving his fingernails a curious examination. He paused to remove some ground in dirt. "If ye ask me, we all be lookin' just a wee bit strange. Yes, definitely we be lookin' weird."

"Ye know what I mean!"

"Nae, Larraine, I dinna! I can hazard a fairly good guess but the circumstances in which we find ourselves warrant, in fact demand, more. I'm a linguist, ye see. Words, and the inflections used to utter 'em, often change for me, their meanings. I must therefore insist that ye be precise in yer choice of nouns and verbiage and in yer enunciation too."

Larraine offered the linguist a sour appraisal. She knew damned well that he understood exactly what she meant. This was just his way of temporarily asserting some measure of control over her now that she needed him. Yet she was too tired to argue and therefore let him have both his say and his way…this one time. "Sand Toes," she contritely replied. "Yes, I mean Sand Toes. I need ye t' speak to him for me."

"Canna'," he replied.

Larraine felt like screaming. "Canna'? Dinna ye mean will nae?"

"Look, lassie," the linguist replied, getting hot under the collar, "we both know that ye and I have not always seen eye to eye. In fact, we disagree more often than not. It be no secret that I dinna consider ye t' be the right person t' be leadin' this here fire drill, but then I find myself wonderin' if in fact, any of us be. So I let the matter rest. When I think that yer wrong I say so, and when I do, I'm not ashamed t' say it loudly. I know that ye've always considered me vocalisms t' be insubordination and an attempt on me own part, t' undermine ye authority—but believe me when I tell ye that they're not. Though it's not often I find myself agreein' with yer decisions

I nevertheless be respectin' ye for havin' the courage to make 'em. I give ye my grudgin' admiration for acceptin' the mantle o' leadership under conditions such as these—especially considerin' it is not a position ye would've chosen fer yerself had ye been allowed t' make the choice! I certainly don't want it, and I dinna know anyone else who does either. So despite our differences I think yer t' be applauded for accepting it agin' yer own better judgment." Larraine was trying to puzzle that statement out in order to determine for herself whether or not it worked itself into a compliment. She quickly gave the effort up, however, when Richard continued. "Therefore, when I be debatin' ye, takin' a position that be contrary t' yers, please understand that I do so not out o' envy or a desire t' undermine ye. Rather, I'm obeyin' the dictates o' me own conscience and simply speakin' o' that which I feel t' be the truth. I understand that we be in a desperate situation here and that despite our differences, we hae t' work together if we be goin' t' survive." He looked up at the circling vultures as if to emphasize his point. "But nevertheless, I say agin that I canna' speak to the stranger."

"What be this load o' cattle craps?" Larraine asked. "Di ye understand Apache or not?"

"Yes."

"Ye can understand what Sand Toes says?"

"To a degree, yes."

"Then if ye be so willin' t' help," Larraine asked, "what's the problem?"

"The problem dinna lie in speaking," Richard replied. "It lies in saying."

"Come agin?"

Richard looked down at his feet and then back up to the buzzards circling overhead. They were in dire straits, he knew, and he had to make his leader understand. But how? *Best be simple*, he thought. "My tongue has nae the muscles."

"Huh?"

He knew that she still wasn't getting it. How could he put what he was trying to say in words she'd understand? For a linguist it shouldn't be hard. "Look," he said, "consider a weight lifter who

THE CHRISTMAS RABBIT

works out on the barbells every day. He trains constantly, pushing his limits, so that at the height of his training, he's lifting a combined total of, let's say, forty tons daily. He's muscle-bound like Hercules, and he's at the top of his form. Are you with me?"

"Yes," Larraine replied, "I think so."

"Good." He paused for a moment to gather his thoughts. "Now take that same athlete, still at the top of his form and ask him to swim a hundred laps in an Olympic-sized pool. Chances are that he'll not be able t' do it. He has nae the muscles."

"I think you lost me," Larraine grudgingly admitted.

"It be the conditioning!" Richard replied exasperated. "He has the tools but lacks the ability because he has nae the experience. His muscles aren't trained that way. He knows how t' do it, but his body is not used to being worked in such a manner. He lacks the muscles. It's the same with languages, wherein inflection is everythin' and can change entirely the meaning of what be spoken. I understand Apache but do not speak it because up until now there's been no need. There's no one else in our insular little group who speaks the language, so there's never been an opportunity to put me knowledge to use. My tongue is not used to shaping and arranging the consonants and vowels in such a manner—even though my brain understands and can interpret the language. I'd stammer."

"No one else here speaks Italian or French either, but you seem to do okay with those!"

"I stammer slightly in those too," replied Richard. "But at least there's a commonality to them that lends itself to the English language. Given the time and lots of practice, I could make me tongue spit out passable Apache, but for here and now, me tongue is tied. Still, I suppose that I could make the attempt nevertheless, and though I'm sure to interpret most of what you say to our friend correctly, I'm nonetheless hesitant to do so. I'm certain t' get some o' it wrong through misinflection. Given our situation, those errors could prove deadly. I'd rather not have that responsibility upon me shoulders."

Larraine looked around in panic—not only because she understood what Richard was trying to tell her but also because for the first time she could remember, she found herself in total agreement with him. It was unknown territory, uncharted and even more mysterious than this desert.

"So we canna' even communicate?"

"I didn'a say that," replied Richard.

Larraine looked at him sideways, totally confused. "Just what is it that you're telling me?" she asked. "And please speak plainly. No cattle craps, if you don't mind."

"That's just what I've been tryin' t' do," Richard said as he cracked his knuckles to emphasize, perhaps, that it was time to get down to brass tacks, "and ye haven't been listenin'. Because of lack of exercise and experience, my tongue canna' form correctly, the necessary sounds and inflections needed to reproduce the Apache language. My brain, however, understands it perfectly and is more than capable of rendering it into English, a language with which my tongue is perfectly familiar and one which your ears at least have a working knowledge of. Ye'll have to communicate with him at the most basic level. Then I'll interpret, while at the same time evaluate his responses, to see if we're communicating clearly, okay?"

"Okay!" Larraine responded eagerly. "Let's do it!"

"Hold on," Richard cautioned, thereby checking her burgeoning enthusiasm, "there be one more thing ye have to know."

Larraine rubbed her eyes, displaying her impatience while noticing that the vultures had descended and were now circling lower than before. It seemed the carrion were slowly moving in for the feast and that, she knew, left her troupe with very little time to spare. "What is it?" she tiredly asked.

"This may not work anyway."

Larraine wanted to slap him. Slap him hard. Slap him in the face, punch him in the gut, and kick him between the legs. Twice. These were not, however, viable options in which to engage. She settled for a conciliatory reply instead. "What other choice have we?"

Richard agreed that their options were indeed limited and so consented to begin. They sat down in front of Sand Toes and using simple words in short sentences, with Richard interpreting and Sand Toes paying strict attention to them both, Larraine pantomimed and acted out her desires and needs, giving what film critics would have rated an Oscar-winning performance. Yet despite her pantomimes and portrayals, it soon became obvious to both her and Richard that errors and misunderstandings abounded. After a lengthy bout of emoting, which consisted of various gestures, contortions, simple sentences, and their subsequent interpretations, Sand Toes responded in kind. There was concern and worry in his eyes, and his Apache laced as it was with Irish brogue rolled off his tongue flooding the immediate area around them like a tidal wave. In his anxiety, he spoke much too quickly for Richard to be one-hundred-percent sure that he'd interpreted the total sum of his reply correctly. Still, the linguist knew that he'd gotten the gist of it. "He asks," Richard said, turning to Larraine, "if you be feelin' well."

"What?"

Sand Toes could see confusion written upon the woman's face as Richard relayed again his response to her words and gestures. The desert man spoke once more.

"He says," Richard continued, "that among the Apache, only two types of people behave like you. The first are those who are driven mad by the desert sun. They dance and prance about in the sand because the sun has fried their brains. It's the Great Spirit's way of rendering unto them visions. What are your visions? What do your eyes tell you?"

Larraine pointed at her eyes, making the gesture of seeing. She then indicated a wounded member of the troupe and fell to the ground, signifying, she hoped, expiration and death. She continued this pantomime, repeatedly pointing to each member of her ménage in turn, and then falling. When she'd accounted for each person there including herself, she pointed to the circling buzzards. She then made other gestures, which she hoped communicated the notion of carrion landing to feed on the corpses of the stricken and fallen.

Once again, Sand Toes responded, and Richard interpreted. "Yes," he said. "It's plain to see that you are in trouble. One doesn't need visions from the Great Spirit to understand that! One just needs to look at you in order to see what is as clear as the sun in the noonday sky. You're dying. All of you. As oblivion approaches, it brings with it madness and insanity, and so you and your tribe begin to dance the dance of death. I honor you. The Great Spirit has touched you with his mighty finger. You are sacred."

Larraine could see that they were getting off track before it could even rightly be said that they'd started the race. If the conversation in which they were engaged continued its present course they were bound to get nowhere, and she couldn't afford the luxury of just standing idly by. She had to slow down and think things through. She paused for perhaps five minutes, gathering her thoughts, and then tried again. "I'm not sacred, and I'm not mad," she gestured.

"Really?" replied Sand Toes. "Your actions speak otherwise. Only madmen would come this far out into the depths of the desert without an adequate supply of moisture. If you're not mad, then you must be the holiest of holies. And yet you say you are not. Therefore I must believe you. The holy cannot lie for through them the voice of the Great Spirit speaks and therein lies all truth. Yet if you speak the truth and are not mad and therefore not holy either then perhaps you speak with the tongues of men and are lying for reasons of your own. How is a simple desert-dweller supposed to unravel such riddles? You puzzle me."

"Ditto."

"Yes, ditto," Larry agreed. "I do not understand the word but agree wholeheartedly with the sentiment! As I said earlier, there are two types of people who act as you do. The first are those touched by the Great Spirit, which you say you are not. The second are Medicine Men, who commune with the Great Spirit continually. Are you a Medicine Man? If so, you must be one of great power and skill or one possessed of extreme stupidity because you dance the dance of rain and no Medicine Man, no matter how powerful, has made it rain out here since Hector was a pup—just doesn't happen. To command such things is beyond the best of 'em so it's all but been given up for a lost art—at least this far out. To be sure, it does rain on the rare occasion, but never on command. It's the Great Spirit's way of showing all of us just who it is that's really in charge. Any pleas or entreaties for him to do otherwise are the height of folly and being so, are absolutely worthless in their effect and so are surely the acts of madmen.

THE CHRISTMAS RABBIT

So you see, we're back where we started. You're holy and I'm blessed for having encountered you. Yes, holy. But are you mad—and are you a Medicine Man?"

Larraine's head was spinning. Sand Toes was a whirlwind of contradictions and miscommunications. How to get through to him? She tried again, using once more gestures and pantomimes. "I'm simply a woman."

"Yes," replied Sand Toes, eyeing her with longing and hunger. "I realized this for myself. That much is obvious and takes no visions, be they from the Great Spirit or the peyote button, to see. Yet a Medicine Woman flies in the face of tradition. Such a thing would be heresy. The role of Medicine Man is the sole province of men, and yet here you are, dancing the dance of rain better than any man could whilst claiming for yourself sanity and purpose for doing so. Therefore a Medicine Man you must be. But a Medicine Man you cannot be, being a woman. Such things are evil yet my heart tells me that you are anything but. So you see my dilemma. One is taught to avoid evil, to shun it entirely. Yet I feel that you are not wicked, just confused and lost despite your obvious power and skill. Still as I said before you could be for reasons of your own, lying to me. If so you would surely be an evil to be shunned at all costs. I've been fooled before by those who've purported to be good and true. I must be careful. I won't be fooled again."

"We're not tryin' t' fool ye," Larraine gestured in reply.

Sand Toes offered her a hearty chuckle. "Says you. But then what else would you say? Whether or not you speak with a forked tongue, it's the only answer you could possibly offer. We are at what the Apache call, a rock in the road. A branch in the trail where the path forks. One must choose the left hand way or the right. Only one path is the trail of truth and how is one to know which is which? One must follow one's own heart. I want to help you. After all, I feel partially responsible for you and your dilemma—although to be sure, you're trespassing in my desert and some would say that you deserve what you get!"

Larraine looked at him sharply, refusing to believe what she'd heard. "Of all the cheek!" she said. "To claim all of this wide open country belongs to you! Just who do you think you are?" She gestured and pantomimed furiously at Sand Toes, telling him what she thought of his pretensions toward ownership and ending with the revelation that this entire great tract was currently held in ownership by the United States government.

Lawrence looked at her in confusion. As Sand Toes of the Apaches, he knew nothing of the federal government and acknowledged no authority, including the Apaches, other than himself. Was he not, with the occasional exception of interlopers like those who stood before him or his Apache brothers who only ventured this far out once in a while for a brief visit, the only soul out here? Did he not roam the sands and wastelands in absolute freedom, hunting and digging at will? Yes, yes, and yes again! He was Sand Toes of the Apaches and beholden to none! But he was more as well. If only he could remember what that "more" consisted of. He felt that the siren before him who reminded him so much of his long-dead mother held the answers—and if not the answers then at least some of the questions. But how to proceed and how to reach a common plateau where each could feel confidence in the other?

"I have a solution," he said. He reached into his tunic and, producing a stone knife, made a quick slash and cut his wrist. Crimson blood, bitter and red, fell to the desert floor, its metallic scent filling the air.

"Suicide?" Larraine gestured in shock. "That's your solution?"

"Yes," Sand Toes replied, with Richard still interpreting. "And a damned good one at that. I cut myself and offer t' ye me own life's moisture. Ye should be doin' likewise then together we will mingle our fluids and become one."

Larraine was taken aback. The stranger had sliced his arm deeply, and blood gushed everywhere. Overhead, the vultures who could smell the plasma as it spilt upon the ground, took up again their raucous cry, giving voice to their excitement and their eagerness to feed. Larraine turned to Richard with an inquiring look. "What do ye think," she asked, "should I do it?"

Richard looked Sand Toes over thoughtfully, trying to judge for himself the stranger's intent and purpose. "Well," he replied, "it would certainly gain us his trust and we be needin' that if we're t' survive. However, at the same time we canna' spare the bandages."

"It wouldn't have to be a big cut, would it?"

Richard was about to reply when Sand Toes interrupted him with an answer of his own. Richard interpreted. "He says that ye must act quickly! To hesitate is to waste fluid and the desert abhors waste. Hesitation signifies doubt and there can be nae truth between those who be one, blood or otherwise, where doubt separates the two. Do it quickly and end yer uncertainty. Where uncertainty and doubt end, only truth remains. It would then be impossible for either of us to be false to the other."

Larraine knew that people caught in desperate situations were capable of anything, including doubt, dishonesty, and downright back stabbing, but thought it best not to point that out. "Yes, I understand," she said and, taking a small knife of her own, administered a tiny nick on the inside of her forearm, drawing forth a few precious drops of her bodily fluid.

Sand Toes gave her a look bordering on contempt. "T' do somethin' halfway," said he, "is t' nae do it at all." He grabbed her wrist and, before Larraine could so much as squawk, took ahold of his stone knife and sliced her deeply. He then reached into his pouch and removing from it a cord wound from the fibers of a mesquite plant, bound their injured arms together and began to chant. He indicated that she should do likewise, but since Larraine knew neither the chant's lyrics nor meaning, she merely hummed along as best she could.

After completing his mantra Sand Toes came out of his reverie, looked at her, and said simply that it was done, that their moistures were mingled, and they were now joined in fluids. He unwound the cord which bound them and reaching once more into his pouch, removed some leaves from a desert plant unfamiliar to her and a small animal skin that was wrapped around a greasy green substance which had the consistency of melted candle wax. This substance, also unknown to her, he used like a salve, applying it both directly and liberally to their wounds. It burned like fire but stopped the flow of blood immediately. Then taking the leaves, he wrapped them around their wounds, binding them with the mesquite cord. "These," he said, "will heal our wounds. The salve must be applied daily and the leaves changed as well. I will do this fer ye along with anything else ye ask."

Larraine gestured her thanks as well as she could, now that she was limited, at least for the immediate present, to the use of one arm. The other was both simultaneously numb and on fire and therefore useless. It took her many attempts, due to her incapacity, to get her message across but persistence prevailed and she finally succeeded.

"Yes," Sand Toes replied. "I can find more wood and mesquite so that yer other Medicine Man," meaning Peter the Paramedic, "can fashion more braces and splints for the injured. I need two o' yer best warriors t' journey with me. They must be hearty braves, capable of fast travel on little rations and less moisture because for yer injured, time grows short and when the need is pressing Sand Toes of the Apaches travels across the desert sands like wind." Larraine gave thought to his request and chose Richard and Jim to accompany him.

"I'll nae be doin' it!" Jim cried out when he learned of her decision. "I'll nae be placin' meself in the hands o' that madman! Ganglin' about in the desert with that piece o' work will likely be me death, girlo! Ye wouldn'a want that now, would ye?" He stared suspiciously at Sand Toes, sensing even then, a rival for the affections of the fair Larraine. "I will nae be doin' it, I tell ye. I will nae!"

"You will!" Larraine replied sharply. "He needs our help. I'm leader here, and I've chosen ye and Richard to provide the assistance he requires! As leader, that's me final word on it and ye'll be obeyin'—so get movin'!"

Jim grumbled, raised a small fuss, but in the end acquiesced. She *was* leader after all, and he helped elect her. What choice did he have? None, he realized. But that realization didn't mean that he had to like it and he didn't.

It was about an hour before the three of them set out. In that time, Larry dug them another water hole and gathered up a large amount of a desert plant familiar to him whose leaves had narcotic properties. He ground these up and mixed them with water while, through Richard, explained to Larraine and Peter their use and dosage. Still not entirely trusting of Sand Toes, the two travelers reluctantly decided to administer his medication nevertheless—they were down to their last two aspirin and a single alcohol swab and had no choice. One didn't need complete understanding of the English language to read the look of doubt that passed between the two as they meted out the medicine. Sand Toes saw it, read it, and interpreted it without any help from Richard whatsoever. "Ye still dinna trust me," he said. "Even after mingling our moisture yer heart doubts and ye see me as a wolf amongst sheep."

Larraine shrugged her shoulders, cautious before replying. "Ye did attack us from ambush," she gestured, "that be enough, I think, t' cause doubt in anyone."

"That was before we mingled moisture."

"True," Larraine gestured, "but such mingling and mixing are out of the ordinary for my people and I—"

Sand Toes interrupted her, speaking furiously. "It's out of the ordinary fer me too! What sort o' desert tramp do ye take me fer? I dinna go minglin' me moisture and mixin' me fluids with just anybody!"

Larraine was quick to see Sand Toes's misinterpretation. "I didn't mean it that way," she said.

"Oh! Ye be too high class t' be minglin' yer moisture with the likes o' me, is that it? Red man not good enough for ye, eh?"

Larraine offered Richard a puzzled glance. "Are ye sure he said that?"

"Pretty sure," her interpreter replied. "The exact wording is open to interpretation, and as I told ye, some miscommunication is bound t' occur, but yes, that be the gist o' it."

Larraine turned back to Sand Toes. "Yer not red," she said. "Yer white. You just have one helluva tan!"

"I be an Apache," Sand Toes shouted. "That makes me red!"

"As ye say," Larraine gestured soothingly, "but still I dinna mean it as ye took it when I said that such rituals were fer me an' mine, out o' the ordinary. I meant that as people, we dinna use them at all. We have hae other ways o' conveyin' trust in one another, and among us, it must be earned and proven. I want t' believe ye, but ye must understand that from my point o' view, ye hae a lot o' catchin' up t' do."

"So be it," replied the desert man, "but when I return with yer people, then perhaps ye'll be thinkin' better o' me…"

With those words, they parted, and Sand Toes headed into the deep desert with Richard and Jim in tow, to search out those necessities the Society's vanguard required to ensure survival. He set a pace both Irishmen found difficult to maintain, yet for Sand Toes, it was turtle speed. Out of necessity, he slowed down in order to accommodate the two outworlders in his charge. Also, they were traveling by day—something he avoided whenever possible because of the danger of exposure. But in this he realized he had little choice. The lovely woman's people were like lost babes in his wilderness. He knew that out here in his desert, it was the sickly and the young that succumbed most quickly to the fire in the sky and from his viewpoint Larraine's troupe was littered with both. He had to come to their aid and do so quickly—thus the daylight excursion, which was almost as unfamiliar to him as it was to his traveling companions.

Over the horizon and out of sight they sped, pausing only occasionally to partake of some food and moisture, which Sand Toes had brought along in his pouch. Richard and Jim were glad for the water and greedily accepted it. They were quick, however, to turn down his offer of jerked lizard and sun-dried scorpions, Richard offering up half-hearted excuses about having had a large breakfast. Sand Toes, who'd been spying on them since well before dawn, knew such posh 'n' nonsense to be the cattle craps that it was but refrained from remonstrating. This was not the time for powwow and debate. Let the outworlders go hungry if that was their choice. All he could do was offer, knowing that you can lead an outworlder to lizard, but you can't make him eat. In the desert, one had to be free to make one's own choices so long as one was willing to live by them and more importantly die by them when such choices proved ill. "One for all and all for one" didn't apply out here. It was everybody for himself, and he'd already broken that cardinal rule by offering his help in the first place. *Screw 'em,* thought he. They had work to do!

THE CHRISTMAS RABBIT

Eventually they reached a sheltered canyon, which due to the height of the cliffs surrounding it saw very little in the way of direct sunlight except at high noon. Small streams trickled from the canyon's walls only to run precariously down its face until they reached the floor of the canyon itself where they collected in tiny pools. These pools, along with the generous supply of shade, served to turn this sheltered coulee into an oasis out in the middle of nowhere. A variety of plant life grew in profusion. Various types of cacti, wildflowers, grass, and trees of many different species made their home in this secluded valley. Fragile seedlings, which would die anywhere else, grew and took root here. Animals of all sorts came to drink and luxuriate in the pools. It was, to Sand Toes, the most beautiful place in the world. Filled with a riot of color and scent unknown to him in any other part of his hostile world, the hunting here was more than easy and moisture, such a rare and precious necessity to survival, was here for the drinking. He therefore limited his infrequent visits to this Eden. Life here was soft. Too soft. To live here or even visit regularly would be to become dependent upon it, growing soft and comfortable too. To live here would mean being exiled here, trapped by one's own weaknesses and dependencies. One could quickly get used to the "easy life" and the idyllic existence with which this place tempted you. It was seduction, Sand Toes knew, that could all too easily prove fatal. Growing soft and comfortable here would leave one unable to deal with the harsh realities confronted when one left this utopia. So he parceled his visits out, coming here only once or twice a year.

Being well watered and nourished, the wood here was still in the form of living trees and not at all petrified—although they did discuss among themselves with nervous stirrings and whispers, the anguish they felt when the trio began chopping them down.

Three small trees, Sand Toes knew, would more than meet the party's needs for splints and braces and still leave enough for them to build stretchers too. It would be almost more than the three of them could carry back anyway unless he showed them how to build some sort of travois. He called a halt to the arboreal butchering in order to show them just how to fashion such a device. This was accomplished through much trial and error, as both questions and answers were often mixed up and misunderstood. Although he understood it well enough as he'd already pointed out, Richard's tongue spoke barely literate Apache, not being trained that way, and as a gesturer, he was never going to be anyone's preferred partner for a game of charades. They did, however, despite their many miscommunications, manage to construct it and had almost completed the task of loading when Sand Toes called a halt to their activity with a curt and cutting slash of his hands. Putting his nose to the wind, he sniffed quickly and then motioned for the other two to hide behind the accumulated pile of tree trunks and branches.

It was late in the afternoon. The cool breezes of oncoming evening brought with them the scent of food moving down the trail toward the sheltered valley. They were downwind of potential prey and so went unnoticed, at least for the moment. That would not remain the case however if he couldn't get those two idiots to stay quiet. The Irishmen, confused by his actions and suspecting him of some sort of tomfoolery, were whispering together like frightened squirrels and making a racket. Couldn't they smell food as it approached? Obviously not, or else they'd do a better job of keeping silent. In no uncertain terms and with a glare that promised a harsh rebuke, Sand Toes put his fingers to his lips, admonishing them to silence. When he saw he had their attention, he gestured for them to stay put. They signaled their silent understanding and he quietly left them to circle around the canyon, padding quickly and quietly like a desert cat on the prowl. At the entrance to the canyon he came to a tree and shinned up with the ease of a leapin' lizard while the other two, looking on from good cover, watched in awe as he silently scaled its heights, hiding himself in the middle branches. "He sure is a quiet fellow," whispered Richard.

"Aye, lad," Jim replied in a hush, "but 'tis the silent ones that need lookin' after, sure n' begorrah. But what di' ye suppose is goin on out there? Were we followed, and if so, by whom? Suppos'n it be one o' our own folk and he ambushes 'em agin? Di' we need more injured than we already hae? So I'm askin' ye, Mr. College Edjucashun, what's to be done about it?"

THE CHRISTMAS RABBIT

Richard's eyes remain fixed on their guide in the tree, too caught up in the going's on to be drawn into a lengthy explanation or protracted argument with his mule headed third cousin about what might or might not be happening. "I don't know," he mumbled reluctantly, "it could be anyone, I suppose."

"Ye dinna know? Well, a whole lot o' good an upper edjucashun did thee!"

Richard grabbed him by the collar. "Ye be nae Einstein either," he fiercely whispered. "Why dinna we just keep quiet like the man wants and wait and see what happens and who's coming, if anybody? It's probably nobody we know anyway."

Jim gave him a sour look but settled in anyhow for what was a very short wait as they both kept their eyes upon the "lurker in the leaves." After about five minutes they noticed a good-sized mule deer approaching them from the trail. Wandering into the shady glade, it would pass directly under the tree in which their madman lay hidden. It paused for a second or two, sniffing the air, testing the winds, and applying its heightened senses to scan the immediate area for hidden danger. Such caution on its part was second nature—not that such prudence and circumspection would account for much by day's end. Rather than second nature, wariness should've been the deer's primary concern. Had that been so, then perhaps the young buck might have survived the day. As it was, the deer was fast on its way to becoming sirloin tips. As it passed under his tree, Sand Toes sprang from the boughs to land full atop of it. His weight, coupled with the kinetic energy amassed in the gravity of his descent, brought the stag crushingly to the ground, its forelegs buckling with a dry snap, whereupon it quickly expired under the ministrations of Sand Toes's cruel and bitter knife.

One of the tenets that Sand Toes held to be true regarding survival in the desert was "waste not, want not," and so it was that two very sickened Irishman looked on in silent, abject disgust, as Larry lapped up the blood from his kill before it could seep into the dry desert floor. Signaling them to him, he gestured that they should join him. They declined his invitation, offering half-hearted excuses in the form of return gestures that detailed their religious prohibitions regarding such acts—they were both atheists, and their vegan predispositions even though the only vegans either knew were Las Vegans. Sand Toes thought them overly provincial but kept his opinions to himself and continued lapping. Upon finishing his liquid lunch he bathed himself in one of the abundant waterholes and when Jim and Richard's stomachs had settled down enough for them to be of any appreciable assistance, led them in his chore of butchering the kill. First he showed them how to skin it. Initially he gutted it, removing its organs and entrails. Although he knew that these had many uses he left them for the buzzards and other carrion eaters as he had neither the time nor materials handy to prepare and preserve them properly. Next he made a circular incision around the top of each foreleg where it joined the body. There was no need for him to make an incision around its neck as its throat had already been slit in the act of killing it. Then he connected the incision for slitting and the incision for gutting by slicing further up the carcass, through the breastplate, until the two cuts were joined together in a tee. He rolled the deer over on its now-empty stomach and peeled back the fold of skin around its neck. He took a fist-sized rock and wrapped the fold of skin around it. Next, reaching into his pouch, he removed some rope which he'd fashioned sometime before from the fibers of dried barrel cactus. In all, there was about eight feet of sturdy twine and he cut about two feet from that. He then took the six-foot length and tied one end securely around the fold of skin that housed the rock at the base of the neck. Afterward, he took the two-foot length and tied an end securely around the tines of one of the deer's antlers. He climbed back into the tree, making his way carefully out to the middle of one of its lower branches. When he reached his desired location, he told Richard that both he and Jim should lift the deer up to him while at the same time passing to him the other end of the two-foot rope. When they did so with much grunting and groaning, Larry took the rope's end and made it fast to the overhanging bough. Their trophy was now dangling suspended from the tree with its hind legs completely off the ground. Larry leapt to the desert floor and taking up the bitter end of the other rope, began to pull on the carcass of the deer while gesturing to the others that they should each

THE CHRISTMAS RABBIT

grab hold as well and do likewise. Together, the three of them pulled on the cord. As the trio took a strain, increasing their efforts and tugging in unison, the hide of the dead animal began to peel and pull away from its carcass like the skin off a ripe banana. Down the torso and right of the hind legs, the skin came away in one piece and with relative ease until the only parts of the animal that remained clothed were the forelegs and the head.

Larry laid the skin out underneath the animal and then lowered the carcass down upon it. It was then fast work to butcher the remains into crude quarters and then to quarter those quarters themselves. These eighths they wrapped completely in the deerskin to protect them until they could make their way back to the camp.

They loaded their prize upon the travois along with a little extra wood, filled Larry's water skin, washed the blood and grime from themselves, and then quickly set out upon the return trek. It was early evening now and Sand Toes guessed that they couldn't complete the return trip until sometime after sunrise.

It was Jim's and Richard's responsibility to pull the travois behind them while Sand Toes ran ahead, scouting the trail. The two complained about the chore bitterly, feeling it was only right that their guide do his fair share of the hauling. Sand Toes paid them no mind. He shut out their complaints, focusing all his attention on the task of leading them back while recalling the face of fair Larraine and using it as a beacon to guide his steps.

They journeyed the entire night, arriving back at the camp just as Larry predicted, soon after sunrise. Larraine was up and about and there to greet them. "Hey!" she exclaimed upon sighting them. "So there ye be! We were getting' a might worried. We all be near starving, and the medicine has about run out. We were about t' give the three o' ye up fer lost and try headin' back on our own. Where in this waste hae ye been?"

"Beats me," replied Richard. "Somewhere out thataway, be me best guess," he said, pointing doubtfully behind him as if unsure of just where he'd come from. "Ask the stranger where we've been. Only he knows."

With gestures, Larraine asked and Larry answered. Larraine queried Richard for an interpretation. "As close as I can make out," the linguist replied, "he says that we been o'er hill and o'er dale. Of course, there be no dales out here. Maybe he meant dune."

"Dune, dale, or dell," replied the relieved leader, "it's good t' hae the three o' ye back!"

"Aye, lass," said Jim, "and sure n' begorrah, it's good t' be back! Ganglin' about in the desert with that maniac is enough t' take the wind out o' anyone's sheets! But hey now, look what me n' Richard brought ye!" He removed the butchered carcass from the travois and presented it to her like a hopeful suitor presenting his sweetheart a birthday gift. "Fresh meat that be—and we saw t' it ourselves, we did!"

Larraine looked from the meat to her starving people and could've kissed Jim there and then, which was what he'd plotted for and which should've happened as planned had not Richard inconveniently chosen just that moment to speak up and utter something so ridiculous as the absolute truth.

"Actually," he clarified, "we hauled it, which is true enough, I suppose, but—"

"Quiet, Laddie!" Jim interrupted and then turning to Larraine, he continued. "Dinna ye be payin' no mind to the ravin's o' this one, lass. He's been out in the sun too long and holdin' conversation with the likes o' that madman there! Talkin' wi' him would drive anyone loopy! It be our deer, t' be sure, and that there lunatic had nothing t' do with it!"

"That nae be true!" Richard replied vehemently. "Sand Toes slew the kine! He gathered the wood and water as well and built the travois too!"

Larraine offered Jim a sour appraisal which he wilted under like an overwatered cactus. Then turning to Richard, she demanded a complete accounting of their adventures. The linguist obeyed, telling her about the trek across the sands which brought them to the hidden fairy land in the canyon. He related all of Sand Toes amazing exploits, ending with the riveting account of how he slew the deer.

THE CHRISTMAS RABBIT

"Really, Larraine," he said, "whoever he be and whether he be crazy or nae and despite the fact that we dinna get off on the right foot, we owe him a lot. Regardless o' his trap and whatever his initial plans were, I'm sure that without his help we'd hae all died by now from thirst and exposure and be pushin' up daisies."

"There be nae daisies in the desert," Jim chimed in self-righteously.

Ignoring Jim, Larraine looked over at Larry, who was standing off to one side watching the three engage in debate. He looked proud, she thought and displayed a certain cheerfulness at having been able to help. Still underneath that warmth and reflecting out from his eyes like an insane light, Larraine could see a certain wildness that she doubted she would ever completely understand or be able to control. She found this character trait both scary and attractive. There was an element of danger and unpredictability that wrapped itself around the stranger like a well-worn cloak, preventing anyone who would ever know him from ever understanding him. This mystic cloak that surrounded him, covering him in enigma, was sadly lacking in the male members of her troupe despite so many of them being branded with the mark. They were predictable and boring. And again there was that familiarity regarding his features, which drew her. Where had she seen him before?

Sand Toes returned her intense regard with a frank glance of his own, not needing an interpreter this time to get a fairly good idea of the thoughts running through her head. She would be his, he was sure of it! In fact, given the ceremony of mixing moistures, coupled with the aid and succor that he'd already provided, was certain that she was his already. But her people still needed his help. There were still splints to be fashioned and stretchers to construct for the wounded, as well as meat to prepare and sand to be shoveled in order to ensure an ongoing supply of adequate moisture. There would be time enough later, he reasoned, to settle issues of lust and obligation.

With Larry's ready assistance the troupe soon had everything in good order. The remaining splints were set, stretchers fashioned, meat cooked, and medicine made. Moisture was found and gathered and the company stood ready to set out for their base camp. It was time to resolve outstanding matters. He approached Larraine and began his negotiations. "I be Sand Toes," he said. "I hae provided ye with—"

"I canna' understand ye," replied Larraine with a gesture, "not fully anyway."

Sand Toes nodded his head, indicating that he understood that much at least. He pointed to Richard while motioning to Larraine that she should call him over to interpret. She did so, and Larry began again. "I be Sand Toes. I hae provided ye with meat and medicine and our moistures have mingled. My ways are the ways o' the desert. Brother I be to the snake and the scorpion. Every rock in this land, I know. Every cactus and sagebrush be mine. Where moisture flows, I know. My brother the wind, blows and upon its breath is borne the scent of many things—life and death and all that lies between. The death wind blows now. It blows for all yer people. Only I, Sand Toes of the Apaches, can save ye. I will lead ye t' moisture. I will guide ye steps, leading ye through the desert at night and return ye on the morrow t' the River o' the Risin' Sun—although tongues talking without forks might put that journey at just over a fortnight. Our fluids have mingled. I will lead ye and yer people through harsh lands, mining moisture as we make our way through desert and dustbowl by following the track of the moon, and ye in turn shall be me wife. I am Sand Toes. I have spoken."

Larraine looked from Larry to Richard and then back to Larry. "He's got to be kidding! Is he proposing marriage?"

"I dinna think that's quite right," replied Richard. "I think he means that by virtue of obligation and moistures mingled, you be his wife already!"

Larraine rubbed her forehead in consternation. "I'm flattered," she gestured, "but I must refuse."

"You have a brave already?" asked Sand Toes.

Larraine's cheeks flamed a crimson red. "Nae."

"Ah," replied the desert man. "I understand. I hae spoken out o' turn. Send fer yer chief that he may speak for ye, and together we will settle this honorably."

THE CHRISTMAS RABBIT

"I be chief o' this tribe," replied Larraine. "I lead me people, and I must refuse yer offer although I say again that I'm deeply flattered."

"Squaws canna' be chiefs!" said Sand Toes. "It isn'a done! No medicine women and no squaws fer chiefs! Why di' ye speak to Sand Toes with a forked tongue? I hae aided yer people. I will save them yet, but first ye must acknowledge me yer husband! I hae earned the right t' bring ye into me cave. Yer home will be mine—and believe me when I say I ain't kiddin'!"

"Please!" Larraine tried to reason with him while gently taking his hand in hers. "I be honored by yer offer, but I'm not completely me own mistress in this affair. My people be on a quest. A secret quest—and we've all sworn, one t' the other, to marry no one who's not a member o' our troop and party to our secret." She looked around helplessly, striving for something more to say. "It's a tradition that me people hold dear."

"A tradition, you say?"

"Yes."

"Then break it," Larry replied.

Larraine couldn't believe her ears. "I canna' do that," she replied while laughing nervously. "Besides," she continued suddenly skeptical, "I thought all you Apaches were such traditionalists?"

"Depends on whose traditions," Sand Toes replied. "Break it!"

Larraine shook her head. "I'm sorry," she said. "I canna'. It be bad luck to break a tradition."

"Yer a female chief!" Sand Toes exclaimed, rolling his eyes. "Such a thing flies in the face of tradition!"

"Depends on whose traditions," she coyly replied.

Sand Toes offered her a slight smile as a sign of surrender for he was sure as shootin' right about that. But with her violet eyes and her chestnut hair, she stood there shining so radiant in the late morning sun that his heart demanded he keep trying anyway. "Well, whatever yer creed be," he replied in a conciliatory manner. "It sure has brought ye a heap o' bad luck here! Yer lost with only the food and moisture that I've provided. Where will ye find more? How will ye and yours survive without the succor of Sand Toes?"

Larraine's temper began to boil for it seemed to her that this stranger with his antagonizing questions was casting dispersions upon her ability to lead. "Look here, buddy," she gestured sharply, "just who do you think you are anyway? We've come this far without yer help, and the fates be willin' we'll go further yet! If you be such a great leader then where be yer troupe? Whom di' ye watch over, aye?"

Sand Toes had to admire her grit. "Yes, you have come far," he replied. "But yer trail is as a dust mote blown upon the breeze. Soon the wild wind will die and your journey with it. Only Sand Toes of the Apaches can save ye. I lead no one because I'm beholden to no one. I roam the desert o' my own free will, answerable for and to no one—but acknowledge me as yours and I shall forever be bound to you. I have spoken. Say yes, and our trails will mingle. Say no, and Sand Toes, broken of heart, will walk off into the desert alone and leave ye here. Then, after seven sunsets, I will return t' bury yer bones or whatever's left of 'em once the buzzards get through."

"Are you threatening me?"

"You're just a squaw," Larry replied derisively. "Sand Toes dinna threaten squaws. He just tells 'em the way it is and expects 'em to use the common sense the Great Spirit gave 'em to see that it is so!"

Larraine considered. "Are ye blackmailing me then? Is that it? Is this blackmail?"

Sand Toes looked at her with eyes that were clearly befuddled. Blackmail was not among the few words he could recall in his native tongue. It was also a word that was nonexistent in the Apache dialect in which he was conversant, and as a gesture the word *blackmail* when used by Larraine was made up of a series of twists and contortions almost incomprehensible in their interpretation, leaving Lawrence, as was usual, basically buffaloed. "What is blackmail?"

"Coercion through means of extortion," replied Larraine. "It's the threat of a particular action or inaction unless prior rendition of another specific action or inaction is given by one party to the other—usually in the form of money."

Of course, this definition was not entirely accurate, but then Larraine had never claimed to be an expert on the contents of *Webster's Dictionary*. Still as a verbal reply to the stranger's question

THE CHRISTMAS RABBIT

her answer sufficed, although it was nonetheless complicated. As a gesture, however, it was absolutely frightening to the adopted Indian watching on in horror as Larraine, in the performance of its rendition, twisted herself up tighter than a pretzel, with arms entwined at odd angles over her head and behind her back while her legs, which she needed to complete the gesture, were passed up the front of her torso, over her shoulders, and underneath each arm, where they ended their peculiar journey wrapped completely around her body. Lying on the ground, she was writhing in agony while trying to enact her explanation.

Larry looked on in wonder as she began her gestured elucidation, but curiosity and intrigue quickly gave way to outright fear and terror as she began to screw herself up tighter and tighter with each passing pantomime. How, he wondered, could a person possibly do that and having done it, how could they reasonably hope to survive?

"Stop!" he shouted. "Enough, enough!"

But Larraine kept twisting and contorting, wanting her answer to be perfectly clear. Still unsure of her meaning, Sand Toes knew nevertheless that he had to say something in order to get her to stop. He took note that Richard was screaming in a panic, and both Slim and Jim were shouting fretfully too. In fact, the entire troupe cast apprehensive glances her way, and Larry didn't need an interpreter to understand those. He did the only thing he could think of—which was something that he'd never done before. He lied. "I think that I understand now coercion and extortion! I really do—honest Injun!"

Larraine took note of Sand Toes's panicked plea, coming to a quick and grateful halt. She lay there in a heap of tangles, her breath bellowing out in ponderous gasps as the sweat of exertion ran from her in streamlets and rills. With both Slim and Jim's aid, Richard began the arduous task of straightening her out one appendage at a time, beginning with her fingers and toes and unraveling their knots and twists. Then working their way up her arms and legs, the threesome smoothed out and made right her many tangles. This was accomplished on the part of the trio by performing a succession of convoluted and complicated maneuvers and bodily adjustments wherein the undoing of one series of knots often produced another set of tangles, as if by uncontrolled reflex. Larraine, suffering through this additional torture, cried out in agony at the onset of each manipulation. Peter the Paramedic was called over to assist, but given the complexity of her contortions, declined the call, offering up the feeble excuse that in real life he'd been a fireman and not a chiropractor. Eventually the task was accomplished and Larraine lay on the ground, sweat-stained, straightened, and parched dry by her exertions. "Water," she mumbled, "I need some water." Sand Toes immediately dug a hole.

When Larraine slaked her thirst sufficiently and had rested enough to continue their conversation, she gestured yet again, careful this time to use very simple words. Sand Toes wanted no further repetition of the horror just transpired but still felt he needed at least one point clarified. "Yes," he replied. "I understand now coercion and extortion." He was lying through his teeth and understood neither, but he reasoned to himself in this instance it was better to speak with a forked tongue than to be responsible for having this woman he loved twist herself like a wet noodle. "But," he said hesitantly, dreading her reply, "what is money?"

Larraine groaned, envisioning the sequence of complicated manipulations required to explain such an abstract concept. She reasoned that it might've been easier had she known the proper gesture for wampum, but she didn't. She couldn't hazard a guess as to its proper composition while at the same time not even taking into consideration that had she been familiar with the proper response, delivering it correctly and with the appropriate gestures, that such familiarity would have served to avail her little. Sand Toes was an adopted member of a western tribe. Wampum, being made up of sea shells and the like, was used almost exclusively by Native Americans living on the east coast and had long since fallen out of use anyway with the advent of the greenback. George Washington's familiar face was a much more accepted form of currency. Yet she doubted that Sand Toes would be familiar with him either. Still, the question had been asked, and she would therefore try to her best to answer it. So she began her complicated movements once again.

THE CHRISTMAS RABBIT

Sand Toes cut her off in midgesture. "Stop!" he pleaded. "Who cares about money? It probably has little value out here anyway so let's just forget it!"

Larraine uttered a sigh of relief while praising her lucky star and whatever gods there were that granted her this momentary reprieve. But nothing was settled, and she knew it. "So then," she gestured to Larry, "will ye be leadin' us out o' here?"

"Will ye accept the fact that the gods have made ye me wife?"

"Gods? What gods?"

In truth, Sand Toes didn't know what gods, if any, were responsible for the dilemma in which they all found themselves and having lied once already he found it subsequently easier to do so again. Therefore, in order to add legitimacy to his claim, he made some up. "Locktar and Bagdush," he replied, "the gods o' wind and fire. They brought me here and led me t' ye."

Larraine turned to her resident expert in Apache for confirmation regarding this preposterous turn in the conversation. "Dinna be askin' me," Richard replied to her unspoken question. "I just speak the language. I—"

"Ye dinna even do that," Larraine interrupted, her voice dripping sarcasm, "and I'm beginnin' t' wonder if yer interpretations are t' be trusted!" Miffed, Richard began to walk away. "Wait," Larraine apologized, "I'm sorry for snappin' and bein' such a witch, but surely ye can appreciate the rock I'm up agin' here." Richard turned slowly around to face her, putting his hands in his pockets and sighing. "Sure," he replied. "I guess that we all be little on edge."

"Thank ye," Larraine said.

"No sweat. But as I started t' say, I merely speak the language—I dinna practice the religion."

"Are there any references to these gods in anything ye've read or studied?"

Richard searched his memory before replying. Finally, he answered in the negative but did so with the caveat that his lack of recognition did not mean that such deities didn't exist, at least for Sand Toes. "As I said," he continued, "I'm nae expert in Apache religion."

"So there be no way then, t' tell if he be lyin' or nae?"

"None that I can think of," said Richard, "other than dyin' and waitin' around t' see just who or what shows up t' greet ye! Personally, I prefer ignorance."

"Great," Larraine replied. "What's t' be done then?"

"Go along with it."

"I canna'!" replied Larraine. "I hardly know him! We have nae been properly introduced or even been out on a date! He's handsome yes, but as me mom used to say, 'handsome is as handsome does,' and most likely, this fella's crazy! Our astrological signs may not agree. Our biorhythms may be different. We belong to different political parties!"

Richard laughed at her discomfiture. "I dinna think Sand Toes belongs to a party," he said, "and yer procrastinatin'."

"That may well be," Larraine replied flustered, "but I dinna—"

Richard cut her off, "Larraine, what are ye afraid o'?"

She looked at him incredulously. "Ye want the entire list?"

Standing off to the side while listening to conversations that were really none of his business, Jim decided that he'd heard enough and so determined to pitch in his two cents worth.

"Now just a damned minute, bucko," said he, "she dinna hae t' do this! Besides, marryin' out o' the family clan's forbidden—ye know that! We all took oaths, we did."

"Oh, do shut up, you ignorant ass!" Richard replied. "Canna' ye see that our lives be at stake? Our lives and the lives o' the three hundred others back at the base camp, whom I'm certain, are just foolish enough to wait until doomsday for our expected return. And that will na' happen if we can't get this fella to come to our aid!"

"I dinna call such an action foolish," Slim's brother retorted. "I call it loyal!"

Richard rolled his eyes and then turned his attention back to their leader. "What happens to them? Ye know they'll wait. The mark that most bear certainly assures us o' that!" Larraine looked doubtful, torn as she was between doing what she must in order to protect her troupe and what she wanted in order to safeguard herself. Richard looked on in sympathy, realizing that because she was caught in the middle of such bizarre circumstances, she could not see the obvious way out of them. "I told ye t' go along with it," he said. "I dinna mean to go along with it forever. Just let him think ye mean it and when he leads us back from whence we came ye can dump 'im."

"I canna'! Do ye mean divorce?"

"Sure. We'll even help ye."

Larraine looked uncertain. "But on foot," she said, "it may take days, even weeks, before we get back."

"So what?"

"So what happens in the meantime if he wants to, ye know, get intimate?"

Richard sighed in exasperation. "Then get intimate!" he said. "Do whatever it takes t' keep him happy. We be in dire straits, lass—"

"Don't call me lass—it's demeanin'."

"Jim does."

"He's me, dear ole cousin!"

"I come by the same blood—and just as legitimate!

"Yes, dearie," she replied with a soft chuckle, knowing him for what he was, "but whereas he be me third cousin twice removed, and you be only me second cousin three times removed one way or the other, then he be closer t' me than ye… See?" The wonder of it was that he did. "Besides," she continued, what matter's here is "ole and he be older, there's no denyin' that. He hae privileges."

"Whatever," he replied with a grin, acknowledging her joke that they both knew was no joke at all, but his smile quickly faded as he faced up to the dire circumstances in which they'd found themselves. "As I was sayin'," he continued, "our lives be on the line. Go down on him if ye have to! Believe me, we'll all look the other way."

"Easy fer ye," she said, "I nae have the choice!"

"None o' us hae a choice," said Richard, "and neither do ye."

With a half-hearted shrug, which caved in on itself until all that remained of it was a long-suffering sigh, Larraine reluctantly gave in. "Very well," she said. "I do, I will, and I am—although I'm nae very happy about it!"

And so it was settled. Lawrence Torrance Dawe, aka Sand Toes of the Apaches, took for himself a wife. Of course, never having had a wife before, now that he did, didn't know what to do with her. He stood there fidgeting in his lizard skins. Meanwhile an agreement had been reached. The troupe would begin necessary preparations for their return journey! The injured and crippled would be loaded onto their stretchers while what little the advance party had of consumable food and supplies would be plied upon the backs of the upright—they were getting outta here!

During the hustle and bustle, Lawrence with Richard to interpret, and speaking such a flood of Apache it would have drenched a desert had languages been liquid, danced madly about while pointing wildly at the sun. He was trying to get these stupid outworlders to take seriously for a moment, that big yellow bastard in the sky and to consider carefully, if they were capable of such deliberation, the hazards of traveling by daylight. All he got, however, from the few members of the troupe who deigned to approach him in order to extend their cautious and in some cases dubious congratulations, were vague recollections regarding past direction and dimly remembered landmarks of the days preceding their capture, when they'd wandered the desert, lost and at the mercies of their fates and their marks. By the time he danced himself silly trying to get those stone heads to see the light, he had a pretty good idea of where they'd been and how they'd gotten here. He was astounded that they'd managed to survive the journey, knowing that in their blind ignorance they'd traversed many dark and dangerous places within his desert, not the least of which was Witch Valley, a tract of such utter desolation that even he avoided it. Thankfully, he knew of another route that would take them back to their original starting point. It had the disadvantage of being the long way around but set against this risk was his knowledge that such a wayward path would avoid Witch Valley altogether, making the delay undeniably attractive.

It was high noon when the preparations for the journey were finally complete. It had been hot and thirsty work all the while with Sand Toes digging any number of holes in order to provide and maintain the necessary moisture for such excursion in this desert heat. Between shovelfuls, he tried to get them to see daylight, but they refused, stubbornly choosing to remain in the dark. *To hell with 'em,*

THE CHRISTMAS RABBIT

thought Sand Toes. They weren't going anywhere without him, and he was waiting out the day's heat, determined not to dare even an hour's travel in the desert sun. Through Richard, he told the others to give it a rest and to retire to their tents, that they'd start their return journey at dusk, and taking hold of Larraine, made move to do likewise. They were stopped, however, by some disaffected grumbling on the part of their charges. Larraine's people were tired and had had enough of this place. They wanted to leave and leave now and besides, all their tents had been previously packed on the travois and on their backs. Sand Toes would not hear of it. A journey under the sun would mean the death of most of them, and he'd sworn a vow to do everything within his power to prevent that. Since he seemed determined to stay regardless of what they said or how they felt, the troupe reluctantly gave in and unpacked their tents. "But what about the wounded?" someone said. "They be already made fast to the stretchers. What do we do about them?" Sand Toes paused for a moment to consider their predicament. "Throw a tarp over 'em'," he said, "they ain't goin' anywhere." He headed once again for Larraine's tent, and for the briefest of moments, she resisted. She'd never been with a man before and was not at all certain that she wanted the experience or adventure now. She deemed that her life had been overly replete with too much adventure of late to do the average person any good. The lust for adventure (not to mention gold) was responsible for her current predicament. What further pickles had lust and adventure in store for her behind those tent flaps? What positions and postures, locations, and bearings might she be forced endure? Larraine wasn't sure that she'd survive such enlightenment. She forced herself to remember that she'd made a bargain and had given her agreement. "I do, I will, and I am," she'd said, but there was still that within her which did not have to like it.

There was someone else who didn't like it either, and as Larry handed Larraine into the tent, Jim, with intentions of eloping with the bride, dove at them. "She be mine, I tell ye, she be mine!" After all, long before this, such a notion had at least been alluded to—in fact, it had been a much-tabled discussion on her part ever since they'd departed the tenements in New York, and so screaming and swearing, Jim had it in mind to kill Sand Toes and, if not kill him, at least fatten his lip. Fortunately for him, as Sand Toes was capable of snapping his back like a piece of petrified wood, his brother, Slim, rushed in to drag him away and, pulling him off them, sat on him. Using his prodigious weight to his advantage, Slim ground his brother into the sand, nearly suffocating him and, for the moment, squeezing the jealousy out of him too. Out it went in a wild *woosh*, along with most of the air in his lungs, causing him to pass out. By the time he recovered, regaining his feet and his jealousy, it was too late. The lovebirds had found each other.

*****

Sand Toes led Larraine inside the tent and sealed the flap. Motioning her to the far corner, he instructed her to lie down and then did likewise on the tent's opposite side. Larraine lay there for some moments, eyes closed and nervous with anticipation. She dared not even peep at her new husband and the preparations he might be making. Who knew, after all, what form Apache lust might take? Were there instruments to be employed? Salves or balms to be administered? Larraine didn't know and found her ignorance daunting. Just what would he do and more importantly, just what would he expect? She tried to prepare, steeling herself for anything, but when anything turned out to be the sound of snoring coming from the opposite side of the tent, she opened her eyes to discover that her newlywed husband was fast asleep. Asleep! *How dare he*, she thought, *how dare he be so rude and inconsiderate?* Erased were all her earlier fears regarding possibilities of what might transpire. Expunged were her previous concerns about positions and postures, locations and bearings. Obliterated were her worries about the application of salves and balms or the instruments used to apply them. Here she was, a woman on her wedding day—and a desirable one at that, and her husband of less than an hour had fallen asleep on her! It was insulting. No, more than that—it was degrading! Didn't he want her? Didn't he find her attractive? No doubt he'd undergone one hell of an ordeal in the last couple of days, trekking across the desert, gathering wood, meat, and moisture, and then hightailing it back. Anyone, she knew, would be fatigued after that, but this? Hadn't he demanded that she become his wife? Yes! And if so, then for what? To be ignored on her honeymoon? Nae bloody likely! She reached out with her leg and kicked him. "Hey!" she yelled. "Are ye just gonna lay there?"

Bleary-eyed from lack of sleep and just as confused as ever, Sand Toes rolled over to look at her and shrugged his shoulders. "I dinna understand," he said, "but now is the time for sleepin'. Tonight we must be on our way and start our journey."

Larraine scowled at his babbling. Knowing that he couldn't understand her or she him, she got ready to call for Richard but stifled her cry in midutterance, realizing that Richard's services would be out of place in her wedding bower, with two being company and three being a crowd. She'd have to make the enigmatic stranger understand with the tools she had handy. The gestures, she knew, for conveying the idea of 'do me' were relatively simple and presented to her no danger whatsoever. However, she was sick and tired of gesturing and the misunderstandings it created and therefore resolved then and there to try a more direct and simple form of communication. Slowly, one button at a time, she loosened her blouse, letting it fall softly to the floor. With a look of wanton abandon she unclasped the hasp of her bra and let that fall away too. She languidly looked into Larry's eyes, inviting him to do to her what to any normal red-blooded American male should be natural. Lawrence Torrance Dawe, aka Sand Toes of the Apaches, though no doubt red-blooded was not, however, natural or normal in any sense whatsoever and furthermore would not have considered himself American even if he understood the term. He lay on his side of the tent confused and staring at his newly wedded wife as she displayed with all their splendor, her mammalian protuberances. Uncertain as to what was supposed to happen next, he nevertheless felt powerful and unfamiliar stirrings deep within his core. Both hot and cold at the same time, Sand Toes broke out in a prodigious sweat as he shivered and nervously shook.

Larraine's doubts began to resurface. What was she doing playing the harlot and trying to seduce a man that she'd only accepted because of gravest necessity and even then under protest? If he didn't want her, rather than be insulted, shouldn't she accept his lack of desire as a blessing in disguise? Of course she should, that ever pragmatic and logical part of her being cried out. Her pride, though, sang a different tune altogether. Pride and the core of her womanhood, which resonated and responded to the primordial maleness that emanated from this stranger, cried out for a coupling. Torn between conflicting desires it's no wonder she was confused. Still, there was no denying that the stranger before her was handsome in a rugged sort of way. Oh, what the hell! She moved across the tent to join her husband and taking his hand, placed it firmly but gently, upon her breast.

The soft malleability of Larraine's mammary was a new sensation to Sand Toes, exciting him more than moisture-prospecting or sand-shoveling had ever done while providing a complementary contrast to the hardening in his loins.

"Ooh, baby!" would have been his description of the sensations, but since "Ooh, baby!" had no equivalent in the Apache tongue, and since he hadn't nearly the grip on the English language that he had on his wife's breast, he merely grunted. Although to be sure, he did so with enthusiasm.

Larraine was getting hotter by the moment and responded to her husband's touch with mounting fervor. They touched, they petted. They twisted in two as they explored the mysteries of each other. Larry's instincts coupled with Larraine's passion soon had the bride and groom rolling on the floor and entwined in a knot that did much to rival Larraine's tangles from earlier that morning.

They passed the remaining hours of the day doing the horizontal bop, the flip-flop, the sideways drop, and any other position that that their passions and imaginations gave reign to. The noise brought on by their exertions, their cooing and aahing, grunting and moaning, was such that the other members of the troupe from time to time peered from out of their tents only to stare at the lodging of the newlyweds and wonder just what was going on in there. There have been three known passions down through the ages, which all legitimate historians will agree have been the most ardent and compelling. Antony and Cleopatra, David and Bathsheba, and of course, Adam

THE CHRISTMAS RABBIT

and Eve (although truth be told, it was Arkie). This topped all three of 'em combined, and the violence of their wrestling caused a minor earthquake out in the middle of the desert.

Day gave way to evening and as the sun began its descent members of the troupe hesitantly approached the nuptial tent and scratched on its flap. "It's time t' be goin', dinna ye think?" said one, or "The sun's set, and we must be about our business and see t' our wounded," said another. There were many such comments and questions and the newlyweds' response to all of them was, "Go away, and leave us alone. We're busy!"

Such responses were followed, of course, by more moaning and heavy breathing on the part of one or the other. In the end, it was another three days before the company got moving—with the newlyweds hobbling along like they were among the injured. Bruised, sore, and content, Larry and Larraine led the troupe back to the base camp, having many adventures along the way, though to be sure, Sand Toes steered them well away from Witch Valley.

CHAPTER V

The Rabbit Digs Some Holes

At dawn, Sand Toes came home after daydreaming that night of Larraine. Her mirage floated off in the distance, shimmering and ghostlike as it wafted on the gentle breeze of a cool desert night. Her spectre was more than willing to offer up admonishments, criticisms, and much-sought-after advice. He could not, she told him, kill the rabbit. Little La would never forgive him, and neither would she. On that she'd made herself quite clear, mirage or not. Her no-nonsense stance left little room for a spousal chat or an exchange of ideas. What it left him with was a conundrum; if he couldn't kill it, he couldn't let it go either. That would surely kill it quicker than clubbing it and Larraine had already said no to that. Little La would be devastated, and Larraine—well, needless to say, her mirage had been quite clear—and as to eatin' it, wouldn't even discuss the matter. Just prattled on as Irish ghosts often will once they've got their dander up, about the Easter Bunny—even she was calling it that—and its importance to his own quest, a rather peculiar position for her to take given her grudging tolerance of the quest itself and her reasonable doubt regarding his quarry... For all of that, the beast was bound and determined to escape—it had said so! That the little fur ball was sly beyond description was self-evident in its ability to talk and therefore, once having made such a bold statement, had to be taken at its word. Sand Toes questioned the imagined apparition of his wife about the reality and subsequent credibility of talking animals and the existence of rabbits in particular talking or otherwise. She informed him that yes, there were indeed such things, but as for talking ones, who

THE CHRISTMAS RABBIT

knew? She certainly didn't! But she reminded him of their family's history, pointing out that stranger things than talking rabbits were woven into the fabric of that dear old blanket and the kinsmen whose tales were wrapped snugly within. Interspersed with her lecture on family folklore were her strict admonitions not to abandon his own quest, and again he wondered at that as she casually laughed off her telltale change of heart, saying to him, "It took bein' in the dark me handsome lad, t' be seein' things in a new light!"

Larry didn't necessarily see it that way. Sand Toes gave up trying to understand the capriciousness of life and death and the subsequent trickeries that both were capable of. No matter, he thought, for a few moments at least, he'd had Larraine back and that was enough. Never look a gift horse in the mouth—especially when they're as pretty as her! Instead, he found himself grateful for the visit however brief, as they stood there shouting at one another from a distance and in the dark. Despite his desert speed and his aptly named Sand Toes, Larry had long since given up trying to catch his dead wife's mirage. She always hovered off in the distance, beckoning yet forever out of reach. Long experience with mirages had taught Sand Toes that it was just their way. Seasons of fruitless effort had caused him to give up that particular quest years ago. He was content to receive the occasional visit, but to be able to stroke her warm skin once again while feeling her gentle heart pressed softly against him was all he desired. Yet whenever he made the attempt she faded like morning mist evaporating in the early sunrise—which was quite a trick since it was still night. Like a lonely ghost, she'd dematerialize wraithlike wearing a sad but sweet smile while saying in a voice which echoed as it faded that the time was not yet for such a reunion and admonishing him, as always, to take care of Little La until it was. Ever an anon or so it seemed, he would run after her fading image but, to date hadn't caught it. Her ghost was adroit at giving him the slip and there weren't too many things out there which could do that. Before fading she pleaded with him to reach some accord with the rabbit while insisting at the same time that he'd just have to take her word that its aid could prove valuable. Was he not finishing up plans for his biggest trap ever? Wouldn't that trap require a hole of tremendous proportions and were not rabbits spoken of as the best diggers of holes anywhere? Sand Toes—whose familiarity with rabbits was severely limited to one, if indeed it was a rabbit—honestly didn't know. All he knew was that for some reason he couldn't explain the rabbit made him uncomfortable, as if it might know something he didn't. But his wife's mirage, who grudgingly admitted to a similar discomfort despite never having met it, said nevertheless that such things must be and when Larraine said something it was so. Therefore he'd endeavor to do it. He'd strike a bargain with the rabbit, enlist his aid, and if Larraine were right, at last see the fulfillment of his near lifelong quest.

Entering the cave, Sand Toes found Jack sitting up and partaking nourishment. Another night of rest had done the rabbit a world of good. Still a bit stiff to be sure, he could hobble around now and Sand Toes knew that within a day or two Jack would try and give him the slip.

Crossing the empty cavern that constituted the living room, Sand Toes paused at a corner to pick up a miner's pickaxe leaning against the near wall and reaching Jack, raised it above his head only to bring it crashing down, shattering the rock at Jack's feet. The rabbit let his gaze travel from the head of the pickaxe, which had buried itself in the floor, slowly upward until he encountered the crazed visage of Sand Toes peering down at him from the gloom above. "So?" he asked with utmost calm although in truth, he was anything but. This lunatic before him had the look of someone whose brain had just burst its own bubble. His eyes, glazed and out of focus, darted to and fro, and he shook with a mild palsy. Blond hair hung in long, dank locks about his face, and his breath smelled of old toad. "So I could'a killed ye," the lunatic replied. "I could'a smashed yer head like a sour melon and left yer brains to spatter all o'er the rock o' me livin' room floor." He chuckled softly while half-heartedly raising the pickax once again as if to make good on his threat.

"So why didn't you?" asked Jack.

"I told ye yesterday," answered Larry, "I made me a promise to Little La."

THE CHRISTMAS RABBIT

Jack spit and stamped his feet. "That wouldn't have stopped you," he replied. "Surely you're cagey enough to talk your way around a broken promise?"

It was true. Sand Toes was indeed sly enough to do just that. But just because someone had the ability to do a particular thing it did not necessarily follow that such an act was the right thing to do. He would never break his word to Little La, no matter what this fur ball might say. Still, that wasn't the entire reason he refrained from killing, was it?

"Me wife counseled me that ye might be o' some use."

Jack regarded him with a measured stare. "The way your kid tells it," he replied, "your wife's been gone for near two years now."

"Is that all 'tis been? Seems like ages, it does. But sure 'n' begorrah, 'tis true, although she comes back fer a visit every now and then, does me dear Larraine."

Jack kept his eye on him, always cautious. Was this lunatic talking about ghosts, he wondered, or was this madcap spewing off about mirages? Did he want the truth either way? Jack decided that he didn't. Such curiosity on his part might lead that madman to believe the two of them had some common bond to be discovered, and having erroneously assumed that much might then further infer that together they could enter into an agreement of sorts leading to an exchange of confidences, giving way to solemn pacts and agreements rendered one to the other, that would have at their root a shared commonality which had never really existed in the first place. Jack wanted no part of such lies and as little to do with this psychotic as possible. Yet he realized that such an ideal wasn't going to be so easy. They were in close quarters and it was obvious to the rabbit that this brain damaged desert-dweller wanted something from him. What was it? And more importantly, at least to Jack, what was to become of him once his captor had from him whatever it was which he wanted in the first place? What would become of old Jack then? Welsh Rarebit, no doubt—a hearty stew in a stone bowl! Could he use his jailer's desire to his own advantage, twisting it upon itself until it provided him with some means of freedom and escape? These were the questions Jack wrestled with as he sat facing his warden.

Unfortunately, though his questions were many Sand Toes's answers were few. In fact, Sand Toes answers were none. He stood there looking down the handle of his weapon with eyes like old stone, saying nothing while at the same time saying everything and saying it in a language that only those dead eyes could speak. Jack was determined to be bold. "So are we gonna stand around all night," our rabbit of later days asked, "or are we gonna dance?"

Sand Toes returned the rabbit's measured stare, glare for glare. Surely this little hopster dinna think it was goin' t' be that easy, did he? Did the wee beast take him for that much of a fool? From his demeanor and attitude, it seemed to Sand Toes that he sure 'n' begorrah did! Let the wee idiot think whatever he wanted. The beastie would be that much easier to control and less likely to gangle off if he thought of himself as in charge of the thinking! "I'll nae be p'ckin' a fight with ye, laddie, at least not right now," Larry said, "but I will be needin' yer help."

"Well, that's different then, isn't it?" Jack replied evenly all the while dreading the endless possibilities that danced dark circles in the hidden corners of his endless imagination. "You've got it!"

Sand Toes merely stared. "And yer cooperation?"

"That too!"

"Unconditionally?"

"Yes, unconditionally," Jack replied. "Whatever you want." Sand Toes responded with a small chuckle which sounded to Jack like it was slightly inside, as if the madman before him were party to a secret that he'd do well to know about too. "What I'll be wantin," said the sand man, "is yer help in diggin' me a hole."

Of all the nerve! What the madman meant, of course, was a trap! After nearly killing him in one kind of trap this lunatic wanted his help in building another! "No sweat!" Jack replied. "Rabbits are great diggers! How deep do you want it? Two feet? Four? And how long? A yard or so?" Sand Toes rattled off the dimensions to the sound of Jack nervously grinding his buckteeth. *That's not a hole*, the rabbit thought, *that's a crater!* "Do you have any idea how long that'll take?"

"I'll be helping, ye," Sand Toes replied, "if that's any comfort. And I be something o' an accomplished sand-shoveler meself!

THE CHRISTMAS RABBIT

Together we'll get us the job done sure 'n' begorrah! We'll also have help from Little La when she comes ganglin' on home on the weekends. The three o' us should make out right proper. As to the time it'll take, the three o' us hae just under a month and half. It be mid-November already and we must be finished nigh December's end!"

"You are crazy!" exclaimed Jack. "Over the deep end, completely off your rocker, and loonier than a caged lab rat!"

Lawrence offered the rabbit a sly smile. "Perhaps," he replied. "But who's the daffiest, I wonder, the man with the plan or the wee fella that agrees t' follow it—and ye did agree, didn't ye?"

Jack looked nonplussed. "Well..." he stammered, "that is to say that I had no idea, but—"

"Nae buts!" Sand Toes replied harshly. "Either ye agree or ye nae be a rabbit o' yer word! Which is it? There'll be consequences no matter what ye choose!" Looking up at the madman Jack could've kicked himself in the behind with his own foot had it been able to reach, for having been so easily maneuvered. Hadn't he been warned early on in his training about such shenanigans and trickeries? Hadn't those Mad Rabbits and the might-have-been's who spoke in their name, tried to impress upon him this very same lesson? Day after day he'd been grilled, tested and tried, all the while being admonished to beware of such treacheries. He'd absorbed it all, or so he'd thought, learning his lessons well, or so he'd presumed, until he'd accounted himself an expert on such deceits and the men who practiced them. But would such an expert have ever been caught in the first place? *Probably not*, he admitted. It was vanity and ego, Jack realized, that misled him into believing that he was even conversant in such matters. Thinking well of himself he merely perpetuated the fact that he was the ultimate fool. So be it. He'd finally learned his lesson—even if he'd learned it the hard way and far too late. "Very well," he reluctantly said, "I did agree, and I am a rabbit of my word. So when do we start?"

Sand Toes could see that he had won the battle, at least for the moment, although he was not so foolish as to believe that his victory was either complete or permanent as yet. The beastie, he knew, would be on guard and ready to take advantage of any opportunity which might present itself that would allow him to back out of his agreement or more likely, escape. *Well and good*, thought the desert-dweller. It made their endeavor that much more interesting!

"Rest through the day," he replied, "we be off at night after that big yeller bastard leaves the sky."

"Can't wait," Jack sourly replied. He hobbled back across the living room to his makeshift bed of old rugs and torn blankets. Sand Toes watched him retire, making sure that the little critter went to its bed and to its bed only. It wouldn't do at all for the little hopster to be ganglin' off now when there was work to be done later. Once he was certain that the rabbit was settled in and sleeping, Larry made his way to the supply closet, which was no more than a smaller cave within the mine itself and gathered up the tools and materials they would need to complete the final stages of his quest. Soon now, he knew, with the beastie's help and a little bit o' the Irish luck, he would complete the mission that he'd set for himself so early on in his childhood. Yes, shortly now with the little hopster's aid and a smidgen o' good fortune, Sand Toes would taste the revenge that he'd so long anticipated.

Before Larraine had come into his life revenge was all that Sand Toes lived for. Revenge and of course a good thick lizard, nice 'n' crunchy with a cool sip of moisture to wash it all down. And he placed value in those only because they allowed him to survive another day in this hellish place, bringing him that much closer to his time of reckoning. Now with his Larraine dearly departed and not counting Little La, revenge was all he had left. When Larraine had been around to calm him and quell the fiery rage within, he'd been swift to set such bitter satisfaction aside so that its pursuance became more of a hobby than an actual full-time obsession. With his mania somewhat mellowed, he'd been able to lay aside for days at a time, the quest itself, living only for the love and joy he'd discovered in his new family. But when Larraine had been lost in the cave-in on Christmas Eve of two years ago, having nothing left to live for but Little La who ended up going away each week for school, his life once again became static and boring so he returned to his roots and to the quest that had occupied all his attention prior to that

THE CHRISTMAS RABBIT

blessed day when he'd trapped his wife and her scouting party. Now after wrestling with his loss for so long and talking to mirages while taking up again the chore he'd almost set aside for the sake of love, he was certain nevertheless that he could let it go still, had he been motivated to do so for his own sake—after all the bitterness within him had at its core a child's disillusionment. But there was Little La to think of now and despite her disbelief in the object of the quest itself and her objections in general to the idea of revenge in any form whatsoever, Sand Toes was nevertheless determined that she never be made to feel such sour disappointment.

*****

Jack awoke at sunset to find that he'd been encased in a harness that passed completely over his back and beneath his underside. It had four cutouts, one for each leg, which allowed him the freedom of movement but only to a limited degree for attached to the harness itself was a rope, the bitter end of which Sand Toes held fast in his hand as he sat on his haunches examining his captive. "What the hell is this?" asked the rabbit.

Sand Toes chuckled. "Insurance."

"Insurance? Who the hell's your carrier, Repressive of Mesozoic Mesopotamia? Screw this!" Jack bolted for the adit and the desert deep but was abruptly pulled to a halt as the mesquite rope drew taught to its final length, snapping him back like an out of control yo-yo and tumbling him end over end until he came to an uneasy rest, having had the wind choked out of him and lying sprawled at his captor's feet...

"Ye plan t' be ganglin' off somewhere?" Lawrence inquired.

"Screw you!" the rabbit sputtered in reply between painful gasps for lost air. "What the hell is this anyway? I thought that we had a deal?"

"We do," said Sand Toes. "I just be takin' some extra precautions t' be sure that ye hold t' yer end o' the bargain."

Jack struggled to his feet while craning his neck in order to look up at his jailer. "This wasn't part of the bargain," he replied. "You never said anything about leashes! I've never been made to work on a leash and I have no plans to start now!"

"Change yer plans then," Sand Toes said. "I did."

"Look, fella," Jack pleaded, "we don't need this. We agreed—"

"We agreed," Sand Toes interrupted, "that ye would be doin' what I tell ye to and I say that ye be wearin' the leash until I state otherwise!" He crossed the room and poured himself a glass of moisture. He drank it in three quick gulps and then continued. "I be needin' some sort o' guarantee, besides yer word, that ye will na be ganglin' off when me back's turned—for despite what ye say and regardless o' what we be agreein' t', I'm not altogether sure that I can be trustin' ye. It strikes me that yer full o' mischief and apt t' be a bit unreliable once I takes me eye off 'n' ye. Also I'm not too sure that I can be trustin' meself in this matter. After all, talkin' rabbits? I hae t' be crazier than a jaybird t' believe in 'em no matter what me dearly departed wife's thoughts be on the matter and if I be as crazy as I suspect then you be no more than a mere phantom or mirage and likely t' be takin' it into yer head to be disappearin' when I ain't lookin'! Little La would never forgive me if I let ye get way—so the leash stays put and that's me last word on it!"

"But it's itchy and uncomfortable," Jack whined, "and it's rubbing against the wound on my leg." These statements were true. Rope twisted from mesquite fibers and cactus is extremely abrasive and rough to the touch—especially on raw flesh which was about all that was left of Jack's leg. Sand Toes would not be moved however and determined that the harness would stay put. He acquiesced enough to compromise by padding the rabbit's leg with some cotton gauze from the first aid kit which Larraine had seen fit to stock the mine with when she'd first moved in. "Is that any better?" he mockingly asked.

"Hardly," said the hare, "but what do you care?"

"I dinna."

For some time the two sat in silence, each thinking wicked and uncharitable thoughts regarding the other. Finally Larry spoke up, saying that it was about time to get started and that they'd best be going about their business.

THE CHRISTMAS RABBIT

"I don't even know *our business*," Jack replied, "let alone how to go about it!"

"Never ye mind," came the reply. "Ye just be about the task o' followin' me and dig where I be tellin' ye to."

Jack ran a puzzled paw over his ear as he whistled through his teeth. "Whew," he said, "this is just great. Just Great!"

"Isn't it though?" Sand Toes honestly asked. "It be more 'n' just great. It be glorious! The grandest quest o' them all and ye be part o' it! Ye'll be thankin' me before too long, ye will. Ye'll have a page in the history book written about ye and be famous throughout the land!"

"I'm already famous," Jack replied, "and look what it's got me— the wrong end of a lunatic's leash! Give me anonymity any day and the quiet life of a simple rabbit. You can take this fame business and stuff it right where the sun don't shine for all I care."

"Well then, perhaps ye'll get yer wish," Lawrence said. "Yes, perhaps ye will at that. But not until the job gets done so let's be about our business whether ye understand it or nae!

"What be yer name, anyway? I dinna like titles and even if I were partial to 'em I'm not entirely satisfied that yer who ye clam t' be, regardless of what Little La might think."

"The name is Jack Rabbit," replied the hare, "but you can call me Mr. Rabbit."

"How's about I just call ye Jack, and we saves the *Mr.* for when ye've earned it?"

Jack offered Sand Toes a scowl as a reply. "And just what am I supposed to call you?" he asked. "Boss? Sir? Master? What?"

Sand Toes paused to consider the matter. He hadn't really planned on the rabbit calling him anything. By his own calculations he figured that once the work got started the miserable little beast would be too tired to spit much less engage him in conversation. "Well, me dearly departed wife called me Lawrence," he said, "and Little La calls me Da. But ye be neither and no relation whatsoever so you can be callin' me *Sái Ézhaazhé*." He gave the rabbit the unadulterated Apache.

Jack had confusion written all over his face. "*Sáí Ézhaazhé*," he asked. "Just what the hell is *Sáí Ézhaazhé*, and what's it supposed to mean?"

"The English translation," Lawrence replied, "is Sand Toes."

Jack stamped in fury while gnashing his teeth. "Santos?" he asked with a growl. "Your name is Santos? You looked familiar—I knew it! I'll kill you, you son of a bitch!"

"Not Santos," Larry said, exasperated. "Sand Toes. Because o' me feet." He displayed for Jack his pemmican textured soles covered with calluses atop of calluses. "I hae me the toughest arch in the desert, and it comes o' walkin' about all me life on me bare feet. Sand Toes."

"Oh," replied Jack. "Well, that's different, isn't it? I mean, if you were Santos and not Sand Toes, then I'd have to kill you despite our agreement, wouldn't I?"

"I dinna know. Would ye?"

"Indeed yes! I could never work for a Santos. If you were one of his I'd have to kill you."

"Well," Larry said with a chuckle, "ye could certainly try. But tell me, who be this Santos fella?"

"An enemy of long-standing," Jack said, "and one to whom, despite your wiry frame, you bear an uncanny resemblance. You have that same vapid and stupid look about you that he was supposed to have sported."

"Supposed to have sported? Ye mean ye never even met the fella and ye consider him yer enemy? And ye be callin' me stupid?"

"Yeah, you!" replied the rabbit. "Only an idiot like Santos would live out here in the middle of nowhere. Only a fool such as Ole Slomoe would find contentment here in this wasteland, wanting nothing better. Why don't you move to the city? Take in the theater or go to a museum?"

"I like it here," replied Sand Toes. "I like it here and I be happy... well, if nae happy then at least content and if nae that, then at least out here I know me place. Besides it might be as ye say, that only an idiot would choose t' live here. But if true then only a bigger idiot than he would choose t' come out fer an uninvited visit!"

THE CHRISTMAS RABBIT

To that Jack had no reply. There was no point, he knew, in arguing with a lunatic—especially if the lunatic was right. Just what the hell had been on his mind anyway when he'd first ventured out into this wasteland? The Mad Rabbits weren't watching him. There was no one keeping tabs. Surely he could've skipped the last name on the rolls and no one would've been the wiser. Why hadn't he? He didn't know and knew only that it was far too late to ponder such things now.

"So just who," Lawrence asked again, "is this Santos fella and why are ye mistakin' me for him?"

"Well, as I've said," replied the rabbit, "you have that look about you despite your lack of girth and as to the names, Santos and Sand Toes sound sort of alike, do they not?"

"I suppose," said Sand Toes, "as far as it goes. But any way the wind blows, I'm still Sand Toes. So who is this Santos?"

"As far as it goes," said the rabbit as he rose, "you should give up the poetry and stick to digging holes! As I've stated already, Santos is an old enemy, albeit one I've never personally met—but an enemy nevertheless! And that's all that need be said on the subject."

Sand Toes considered questioning his prisoner further but discarded the idea. There was no doubt that such questions would only subject him to more of the same malarkey and they had work to get done. There was no time for such posh 'n' nonsense and he still needed to test the skills of this little digger in order to evaluate its worth. This would help enable him to estimate the likelihood of the quest's success. He knew that the hare would be held back somewhat by the fact that it would be working in the dark, both literally and figuratively. Sand Toes was determined, for security's sake, to keep the rabbit ignorant as to the quest's specific purpose and ultimate goal. This would slow them down, he knew, unless he picked up the slack himself, which he was prepared to do in order to ensure secrecy. He would therefore keep the little beast in the dark until the last possible moment and admonish Little La, when with them, to do likewise. From Sand Toes's point of view the quest was to be treated as "top secret," and specific details as to its actual aims and purposes would be disseminated on a "need-to-know" basis. Too much information, he reasoned, was dangerous in the wrong hands. As his dearly departed wife had been fond of saying, loose lips sank ships, whatever they were, and the last thing he wanted was word getting back to that foolish Society regarding his plans and ambitions. He needed no help from them—of that he was sure. Nor was he inclined to share with them, the treasure he would certainly acquire once his quest's fulfillment reached its fruition. "Enough o' the talk," he barked, "let us be ganglin' off into the desert and dig us some holes."

The pair ran for hours with Sand Toes in the lead, holding the rope and dragging Jack behind as he jumped and hopped over rough scrub, leapt ravines, and scrambled up and down sand dunes. Throughout the long toil Larry hadn't even broken a sweat although Jack was nearly spent and exhausted. In a dash and even with his wounded leg Jack knew that he could run circles around his captor but rabbits are not built to withstand the demands of an extended jog and much of the instruction regarding the channeling of power, first propounded by the venerable Hareihito Rabakami, who'd long since faded away into legend, had been lost in the great span of years between Olden Days and now. Thus the strain was beginning to show. Added to the rigors of the run itself was the weight of the harness strapped about him and the subsequent restrictions it placed upon his ability to move about freely. Finally, unable to keep up the pace any longer the rabbit simply collapsed, flopping upon the desert floor. Sand Toes didn't even break stride but rather dragged Jack across the hardscrabble and rock. "Hey, you banana head," screamed the rabbit, "slow down, will ya? I'm out on my feet here!"

Sand Toes came to a reluctant halt. "I'll nae be slowin' down now," he replied, "and I'll nae be carryin' ye upon me back either! Besides, it only be about another mile. Surely ye can go that far, can't ye?"

"Perhaps," replied the rabbit through gasps for air, "but if I do, there'll be nothing left to dig with, dig that?"

"Dig what? We nae be doin' any o' the diggin' yet."

Jack rolled his eyes. It was bad enough, he reasoned, that he had to converse in the language of men; it was worse still, he felt, to be saddled in conversation with someone who was ignorant of modern idiom and vernacular. Bohemian peasant! It would serve the idiot right if he tripped over his own tongue and broke his vocal chords. *At least then*, thought Jack, *I wouldn't have to listen to him!* "I meant, do you understand? Can you dig it?"

"Do I understand diggin'? O' course I understand diggin'. Didn't I say so? Probably hae me more knowledge o' the art than ye do! Understand diggin'? Why, I was diggin' holes and findin' moisture when ye were just a bun in yer ma's oven! I—"

"Forget it," Jack interrupted. "Let's just be on our way and get there. Anything's better than listening to you and your ranting." Sand Toes and Jack set off once again, but at a decidedly slower pace. It was all Jack could manage, and his injured leg was beginning to stiffen up. They came upon a line of low hills through which, winding snakelike, ran the dried up remains of a pitiful brook, sere and desiccated, till all that remained of it was a cracked and barren stream bed. They followed the course of that long ago river weaving their way through the tired and ancient hills until at last they came to its mouth, which originated in an abandoned mine not unlike the one in which Sand Toes lived. The mine itself was set in the last of the hills, which ended in a hard packed valley of sand that fell away at their feet as they trod over it. A few small scrub oak, along with the inevitable mesquite and cacti, grew randomly out on the desert pan and provided the only greenery for miles. Everything else was colored in the dull tans and beiges of the endless desert. On the tops of the hills themselves nothing dared to grow because the sun beat down upon them unmercifully. Not even the occasional cactus seed, borne by the wind and carried to their slopes, was able to take root there. These hills and the incline they formed were as sterile as an operating theater and as harsh and unforgiving as well.

Sand Toes gazed into the murky depths of the mine's shaft, shedding a single tear which ran inexorably down his cheek and under his chin. "In there," said he, "is where I lost me sweet Larraine when the roof o' the tunnel came crashin' down upon her." He shuddered as a chill enveloped his spine, turning his testicles into ice. "She'd been restockin' the lower levels with food and moisture so that her bloody Society might hae both the supplies and means necessary to explore the deepest levels o' the chasm when there came a quake out there in the pan where I was tryin' to dig me a trap. The rumble brought down the roof o' the mine and the walls along with it. Filled the entire shaft almost. Diggin' her out proved t' be impossible so we never recovered her body. She's down there still, I imagine, restin' under all o' that rubble."

Despite a determined effort on his part to ward it off, Jack could not help but feel a moment of pity for this lunatic and the loss he so keenly suffered. Pity, however, tied his tongue, leaving him for the first time in his life with nothing to say. He mumbled and stammered until he finally spit out a weak word of condolence, totally inadequate, he knew, and from Sand Toes's point of view, hardly appropriate. "Ye'll nae be feelin' sorry fer me, Jackie lad!" said the desert man. "Besides, ye only be sayin that in the hope that sayin so will make the goin' slow—well forget it and get goin'!" Jack saw no need to respond to that last remark as, like it or not, he realized that it had to it the ring of truth.

"And down there," Sand Toes continued, "is where we'll be diggin' our hole and layin' our trap! Winter be comin'. Soon it'll deepen, and then we'll see!"

"See what," asked Jack, "and just who or what are we supposed to be trapping?"

"Just nae ye mind! Ye'll know when ye need t' and not a moment before!" With that last remark the travelers set off down the slope of the hill and onto the desert pan where they began their digging.

They didn't dig the great excavation, not yet. It would still be a while yet before they took on that chore. First Sand Toes had to measure Jack's mettle and determine for himself the fiber he was made of. To this end he assigned the rabbit a variety of tasks to be performed and holes to be dug, ranging from a simple ditch to an underground tunnel, and ending with a medium-sized pit.

Despite his belief in the overriding wisdom of his dearly departed Larraine and notwithstanding her mirage's ardent admonitions to him that the captured rabbit should be gainfully made use of, and taking into consideration as well the harness the rabbit was made to work in, it nevertheless became apparent to Sand Toes that

THE CHRISTMAS RABBIT

Jack was not half the digger he claimed to be. When delving out a ditch Jack didn't dig quite deep enough to measure up to what Sand Toes deemed a determined effort. When boring out the tunnel it was Sand Toes's opinion that the rabbit barely broke a sweat. The fact that Jack's tunnel was far better than anything he could've dug on his own given the same restrictions of material and movement served not to impress the adopted Apache in the least. The rabbit, he reasoned, looked far too composed after its exertions, with nary a drop of moisture on its brow, for him to have credited its effort. Unbeknownst to Larry, rabbits do not have sweat glands, being another of those physical attributes which The Powers That Be, or the Witches, as they were referred to by rabbitry everywhere, took from them when they robbed the first Jack of his pockets, and even had Sand Toes such an insight it's doubtful that understanding on his part would've served one whit to change his opinion of Jack or his underachievement. It was the opinion of Lawrence Torrance Dawe that no matter what one accomplished or how much, one did not deserve credit for a job well done unless one expended a little moisture to attain it. "Work smarter, not harder" was not a credo to which Sand Toes of the Apaches subscribed. Even though the rabbit no longer had the glandular ability to produce perspiration, Larry was nevertheless determined that the little beast would do some sweating before he was through with him and as far as the rabbit's pitiful pit went, it was Sand Toes's opinion that Jack's little hole was barely a burrow and one with no depth to it at that. They were three days into their digging drills, practicing performance and prosecuting procedure when Sand Toes finally gave voice to his displeasure. "What the hell be the matter with ye, Jackie boy?" he asked. "Ye be slower 'n' a cold toad with shoe booties on!"

Jack tried to puzzle out that last remark but quickly gave up the effort. In three days of working with Sand Toes, he'd come to realize that the madman was full of saws and adages that only made sense to himself. Perhaps the Mad Rabbits had they been around to consult could've deciphered his proverbs but the Mad Rabbits were weeks behind him on the backward trail and Jack despaired of ever discussing such dictums with them again. Adding to this despair was the discomfort brought about by the unwholesome diet he'd been made to subside upon. Having no taste for lizard or toad—fried, fricasseed, or otherwise—he'd been made to endure and gain sustenance from a diet consisting wholly of cactus from which Sand Toes had scraped away the spines and pricklers. Cactus is roughage piled upon roughage, piled upon roughage. It is like eating dried old hemp, and a consistent diet of it is guaranteed to lock the bowels of the hardiest rabbit like a set of vice grips on a screw. Jack's insides were now a set of channel locks and nothing moved within them or exited his orifice without the most strenuous application of effort.

"Whaddya mean slow?" he asked indignantly. "My guts are locked tighter than a drum with the food you're feeding me, you ration out water like a miser spends pennies—and we work in the dark! How's anyone supposed to perform under these conditions?"

"I get by," Sand Toes replied.

Jack stamped his feet in anger, although he avoided spitting. He had far too little moisture in reserve to waste what little he had on such extravagances. "Of course you do," he said. "You're eating old toad! It's so full of grease and oil that I'm sure you're more lubricated than the pole car at the Indianapolis 500! Everything passes through you like it was riding an oil slick! Besides, you've got the shovel."

Sand Toes looked at the implement in his hands, examining it as if it were a newly discovered treasure and just recently unearthed. He pored over the handle and studied the spade. "Well," he said, "perhaps I could fashion ye one, makin' it a bit smaller o' course, to accommodate yer size, or lack o' it."

"Don't bother," Jack replied caustically. "You'll just be wasting your time."

"Ye mean that if I go t' all the trouble o' makin' ye one, ye will nae use it?"

"Boy, *you are* stupid!" replied the rabbit. "Not won't, but can't! Compare your hands to mine. Do you notice any difference, sharp eyes?"

"Mine are bigger."

"No shit, Sherlock," replied Jack. "Could you point out anything more obvious? Take a good hard look at both your hands and mine and tell me what else you notice." Jack held up his paws, turning them this way and that, so Sand Toes could observe them from both sides. "Well?"

"Well," said Sand Toes hesitantly, "yer wearin' gloves and me hands be bare."

"Those aren't gloves, you dolt—that's my fur!"

"I can see that fer meself, ye know. It be as plain as the nose on me face that yer wearin' fur gloves—although why a chicken or anyone else fer that matter, would want t' in this heat, is beyond me ken." Jack gave his head a long-suffering shake. "You've got less brains than a bag of rocks! What else do you see?"

Sand Toes peered intently at Jack's paws. Suddenly the light of revelation lit his face. "I've got it," he replied, "Ye've only got four fingers!"

"Actually, they're not fingers," replied the rabbit, "but pray, continue."

"I've got five?" Sand Toes asked, uncertain.

"No, you've only got four," Jack said. "Keep looking."

Sand Toes studied Jack's paws again, scrutinizing them intently and scanning their every feature. Jack imagined that he could smell the wood burning and the smoke pouring out of his captor's ears as his frying mind tried to solve this simplistic and ridiculous riddle. Larry continued to examine Jack, attempting to define for himself a difference that was to Jack, patently obvious. After five minutes of intense scrutiny and concentrated contemplation, Sand Toes was still drawing blanks. "I give up," said he. "What be the difference?"

"Thumbs, you idiot! Opposable thumbs! You've got 'em—I don't! I couldn't grab hold of a shovel if my life depended upon it!"

Sand Toes looked at his own hands as if seeing them for the very first time. It never occurred to him to realize just what a valuable implement a thumb could be. "Ye mean ye canna' use tools?" he asked incredulously.

"Tools?" replied the rabbit. "What the hell are tools?"

Sand Toes was at a loss. How, he wondered, did one respond to that? It was a certainty that this rabbit was not as smart as he let on. "This is a tool," he said, holding out the shovel.

"Tools are shovels?"

"Aye," replied Lawrence, "but 'tis certain that tools be more 'n' that. They be anythin' that extends yer reach."

Jack was getting more confused by the second. "Explain," he said.

Sand Toes grabbed hold of his noggin frustrated, hoping perhaps to force a thought out of that hollow chamber which passed itself off as his head, by compressing his temples and squeezing one out like pus from a zit. "Let's see," he began, "ye can be extendin' yer reach in a variety o' ways. There be height and depth, increases in strength such as torque and leverage; any o' these can be examples o' the use o' tools."

"Yes, yes," Jack replied, exasperated. "That at least is so patently clear that even a simpleton could see it, but please, I need specific examples."

Larry's head swam as he tried to remember just how they'd gotten on this silly subject in the first place. How was it, he wondered, that someone could claim to understand a tool's function yet have no concept of a tool itself? Was that possible? He supposed that in his family it was not only possible but highly probable. Yet the rabbit was not part of his family—at least as far as he could tell, so where did that leave him? He concluded, correctly for once, that the rabbit knew nothing of tools, neither their specific variations nor their general applications, and was therefore just trying to cattle crap his way through a bout of ignorance. Sand Toes gave thought to the different tools that he employed—there were basically three. His shovel, which destroyed the ground by tearing it up in small tufts and scoops; his pickax, which destroyed rocks of various sizes by shattering them into even smaller pebbles of various sizes, and the ropes and snares he employed which destroyed life by killing their victims. Suddenly he lit upon a definition that his ignorant captive might understand.

"Tools," he said with authority, "are implements of destruction."

Jack rolled that definition around his little noggin to see if he could make sense of it. "All at once, and from seemingly nowhere, revelation's light shone from within. "Why," he exclaimed, "I see it now! Tools are weapons!"

THE CHRISTMAS RABBIT

A smile broke out on Sand Toes's face. "Sure 'n' begorrah," he agreed. "I believe they are!"

Once they reached a mutual understanding, once they came to a consensus, an accord if you will, the work proceeded at a much quicker pace—not that the definition of "tool as a weapon," no matter how vague it might be, was in any way germane or even semi-pertinent to the task at hand. It wasn't. Rather, the definition of a tool, as stated by Larry and inferred by Jack, was more akin to those initial agreements arrived at by the disparate parties who'd negotiated the end of the Korean War. No substantial progress could be made on the peace initiative by either side until an accord could be reached regarding the size and shape of the negotiating table around which the talks would commence. It was a frivolous compromise to be sure, the substance of which had nothing to do with the real issues at hand, but it was reassuring to both sides nevertheless that such diametrically opposed factions should agree on anything no matter how pointless, and it was comforting to both parties to come to the understanding that from such humble beginnings, they could only go up. So it was with Jack and Sand Toes. Their resolution as to the nature and makeup of tools and weapons was meaningless before the issues that confronted them, but it was self-serving in that it gave each of them a starting point from which they could proceed forward. Trust began at such points—although not always on the part of both parties at the same time and not necessarily to the same degree.

Despite any similarities between men and rabbits and notwithstanding the tutelage Jack received at the paws of the Mad Rabbits and might-have-been's upon whom he'd once placed so much reliance—and regardless of the fact that he came from a very long and distinguished line of lapins, who alone had any claim to the title "Easter Bunny" and who among rabbitry worldwide were solely entrusted with the task of carrying on the sacred traditions and dealing exclusively with men on behalf of rabbits everywhere—despite all this, Jack, like countless generations of Easter Bunnies, Mad Rabbits, and might-have-been's before was pretty naive as to the true nature of men and the treacheries of which they were capable. There was an age, to be sure, back in Olden Days and shortly thereafter, when rabbits in general and Easter Bunnies in particular, could be said to be as conversant on the subject of men and their subsequent double-dealings as anyone else in the forest. But Olden Days were a long time ago. Rabbits, Easter Bunny or otherwise, like most animals, have changed very little from then until now. Men on the other hand, have changed continually and it's universally accepted by everyone else that such changes have not been for the better and that the species has gone from bad to worse until Nowadays it's beyond any rabbit, Easter Bunny or no, to imagine for itself the callousness that men are capable of or the disgustingly low levels of behavior which they'll stoop to when they feel that their interests are being threatened. With men, the ends always justified the means—a tenet that few else in the animal kingdom would scarce condone, remembering in their lore The Powers That Be and the extremes to which a particular ism can be taken. All animals had enough of that truck ages ago and clearly weren't returning to it. So it was that even though Jack, who certainly should've had enough experience with men by now—after all Sand Toes wasn't the first person he'd ever run afoul of although admittedly he was the weirdest—to be on his guard, never forgetting the devils with whom he was dealing nor the treacherous depths to which their souls were capable of plunging when they felt that their interests were being threatened—and to hear them tell it they were always being threatened—took the desert madman at his word instead, and took him at his word regarding the shovel at that. Well, a body had to start somewhere. Jack viewed his mutual understanding with Sand Toes as a verifiable agreement, easily validated by either party and a first step toward a more mutually nourishing and personally satisfying relationship for each as they went about the business of erecting trust's bridges, often creaky, and securing trust's ropes, often frayed at the ends and worn in the middle, in order to transverse and overcome the abyss of discord and disbelief which separated the parties as they now stood, and the nature of tools was as good a place to start as any. Of course, all forest creatures hold with the value that once you give a promise you cannot take it back no matter what. If you could and if you did it would imply that such a gift was never yours to give in the first place and if that were so then

THE CHRISTMAS RABBIT

where did you get it? It was too confusing to keep up with or sort out but what it boiled down to was that you kept your word and an animal did and a person didn't...yet Sand Toes did anyway.

Truth to tell, the consensus reached with Sand Toes regarding the nature of tools and weapons threw Jack for quite a curve. He, like any other forest animal—which he most certainly was not—considered himself to be well versed in lore regarding men, and all the magazines and encounter groups worldwide said that men were a mealy-mouthed species, as apt to lie as not, and for no apparent reason one way or the other whether or not they did or they didn't. All of the articles, inserts, and sidebars in the plethora of self-help guides to interspecies interaction placed particular emphasis on dealing with *Homo sapiens*, warning their various readerships of the generally poor character traits and disreputable practices one could expect to discover and endure for having had even casual contact with such a freeloading, self-centered, all-for-me species. Even the definitive tome on this subject, the one read more often by more animals anywhere—*Help With Homos*—says quite clearly in its definition of *Homo sapiens* that they're to be steered clear of whenever possible, and that there is no help, either for them or you, should your steps become entwined. For the rest, it's just a breakdown of the word *Homo sapiens* itself and its subsequent definition.

> **Homo:** def: Fucking Queer. **Sap**: def: 1) idiot. 2) to drain or to draw from. **Ien(s)**: def: To be or not to be, depending upon tense; an animal adverb describing state of being or existence

Thus, according to that definitive guide which all the animal world takes refuge in when confronted with any number of the assorted trials and tribulations that are attendant to a life lived within the confines of human encroachment, *Help With Homos* defines human beings as those "Fucking Idiot Queers Whose Very Existence Is A Drain Upon Me." So knowing all this, it was a foregone conclusion to Jack that Sand Toes would grudgingly have to admit from the get-go that his words concerning shovels and tools were not to be regarded as gospel by any means whatsoever and so save everyone concerned a lot of bother and to-do later. This way everyone knew where everyone else stood in relationship to themselves and therefore what was expected of them and of each other. It prevented friction from occurring down the road—especially if the tires were well worn and threadbare. But Sand Toes promised and then moreover, kept his word. Where Jack erred was in assuming that such an agreement had any more substance to it than the actual words spoken to define it. Therefore, thinking they'd reached a watershed agreement, a diplomatic hallmark, Jack found himself to be full of the negotiating spirit and so launched into a diatribe regarding work hours, conditions, lunch breaks, benefits, and overtime wages. Larry just let him rattle on in the rear while patiently saying yes to whatever ridiculous demand the rabbit saw fit to give voice to.

Sand Toes didn't see their agreement as an agreement at all. To him it was a treaty and thinking so, viewed it and all that was said after in the same light—and that made all the difference in the world. Treaties, or so he'd been taught by the Apaches, were much more manageable than agreements, being far easier to bend, fold, mutilate, or simply rip up. Apaches, adopted or otherwise, through long and bitter experience with treaties and the mealy mouthed, two-faced sons of witches who wrote them, have come to realize that rather than being permanent, treaties are in fact, *made* to be broken. It's what they get written for in the first place. Having had so many broken on them for self-serving reasons at the hands of their co-signers, the Apaches had come to learn too late that it was far better, when it came to treaties and their subsequent nullifications, to be the breaker rather than the breakee. Breakees routinely got inundated in an avalanche of the breakers' cattle craps from which it became increasingly difficult to extricate themselves.

Well, not this time, thought Sand Toes. This time and with this treaty, he'd be the breaker and not the breakee. He'd make his adopted people proud with his ability to do unto others before it got done unto him!

Still, the two of them had their starting ground nevertheless and from the rabbit's point of view their footing was on solid earth. Now

THE CHRISTMAS RABBIT

working as a team they did their digging as if they had a mission, which they did—even though Jack, despite further negotiations, was no closer to discovering just what that mission was. That, however, did not stop the digging. Tunnels, trenches, and pits galore appeared on the arid pan at the foot of the hills, as if by magic. Sand Toes, in sole possession of the only shovel and acknowledged by all who knew him as a digger and shoveler of some repute, now found himself hard put to keep up with Jack and his exertions. Clouds of dust and sand surrounded each, enveloping them in a smog of dirt and soil that would've all but choked them had they not taken to wearing kerchiefs over their faces. When they completed a series of excavations Sand Toes would assess the depth, width, and length of each, as well as calculate the time that it took to complete them. He would note this information down in a little book, which he carried with him constantly. Once the data was recorded he would order that their efforts be immediately undone and the holes filled in.

Jack complied readily and without complaint. After all, they'd entered into an agreement, hadn't they? Such agreements, however vague and ill defined, made for partners and partners, Jack reasoned, always did as they were asked, having complete faith in the intentions and purposes of their fellow conspirators. All week long they worked like demons, digging holes and then filling them in. Then on Friday morning Sand Toes called a temporary halt to their efforts in order to pack up and begin the journey back to the mine which served him and Little La as home. They'd travel through the heat of day, Sand Toes explained, to ensure that they arrived by early evening and so be home, with supper on the table, to greet Little La and her uncles when they arrived.

For the briefest of moments Jack made as if to disagree but then thought better of it. Were they not after all, partners? Partners always compromised, he reasoned. Soon enough, he assured himself, he would get the chance being an equal partner in this venture, whatever it was, to be on the issuing end of the orders and give a few directives himself. He therefore acquiesced quietly and together the two of them, shouldering their bundles, began the trek home with Sand Toes leading and Jack following on the leash. It was hard being so tethered—especially now that they had an understanding, but the rabbit bore up under it patiently, perhaps realizing that trust developed slowly and that like Rome itself was not built in a day. At least Sand Toes was courteous enough to set a gentler pace for their return journey.

For his own part, Sand Toes was awash in a sea of confusion. Nothing unusual there—he floundered in such seas constantly. What was unique about this specific dip in that particular ocean, was that it was one of those rare occurrences where Sand Toes could see the confusion for himself and as we all know, seeing is believing. Believing however is not necessarily understanding and speaks not at all to the task of resolving. Resolving had a language all its own, and Sand Toes had barely mastered English. Confusion words though—Sand Toes knew and understood those well, along with perceiving that none of them, or all of them together for that matter, couldn't begin to describe the jumble of disorder and mental debris that made up the tangle of misimpressions, mixed emotions, and misguided interpretations that had plagued him since the arrival of the rabbit. And it must be repeated that to some degree or another, Sand Toes was almost always in such a state; yet this instance was unusual in that it was one of those rare moments wherein he could recognize the situation for what it was...almost. He could at least, in this particular instance, peer around the problem's edges if not necessarily see into the heart of it and this allowed him the rare insight that there might even be a problem, lurking like a sleepy snake in the insane forest of thoughts and ideas that grew and took root in his brain, providing for him the basis for how he saw himself and others; his dreams, his hopes, his beliefs and doubts, what was real and what was not. Yet even in slumber he could sense that snake, ever hungry for a victim, sleeping with one eye open while waiting for its chance to strike the unwary, who knowing no better, found themselves stepping on its nest.

The sleepy snake was doubt and Jack's unlooked for arrival had brought it slithering out of its hole. Sand Toes admired a good stalking but was nonetheless terrified as he gave thought to the viper that lie in wait for him coiled somewhere in the uneven underbrush of his tangled thoughts. He'd never run from anything, anywhere, anytime. But he'd sure run now, he thought, for the animal stalking him was himself and how does one contend with oneself? How does one do battle with the preconceived notions, beliefs, and biases, recognized or not, instilled by others or inferred from conclusions arrived at on one's own, that since the first days of their burgeoning influence have been driving a person as if he or she were an ox under the yolk, directed by runaway forces and exhorted to go this way or that? *The answer*, thought Sand Toes, *was simple. One flees and hopes like hell that he or she is lucky enough to live to flee another day!*

But even Sand Toes, who was accounted by all who lived in those parts as having the fleetest feet anywhere, could not run forever. Eventually even the swiftest of feet tire out and you're forced to turn and confront your own shadow. Sometimes you confront sooner rather than later. It all depends upon the nature of the beast from which you flee and the aggressiveness with which it pursues you, as well as the subsequent energy you're forced to expend in fear and flight as you attempt to flee from it. Anyone, even normal folk like you and I, are from time to time confronted with such monsters of self-doubt which seem to take root in the ground and rise up magically before us whenever we're compelled to examine the base causes of our own motivations and desires for self-fulfillment and weigh them against the perceived concerns and needs of others. In fact, with normal people like you and I, it happens all the time. Not because we're any smarter than Sand Toes—or he, us—although to be sure there are ham hocks out there who could offer him a serious challenge in the intelligence department, but rather by virtue or misfortune, depending upon your point of view, of the fact that we are inherently social creatures who by living in societies in the first place have those tendencies to mingle further enhanced by the social environment thrust upon us and so we puzzle out the riddle for ourselves and in our own way, using rote and repetition, construct relationships with each other by coming to terms with ourselves first, and generally these fragile links, these tenuous cords that we use to bind each other to ourselves, if not always fair, are usually sturdy and of good fiber although admittedly there are occasional snaps in the thread even so.

Family and friends, acquaintances and workmates, the asshole who stole my parking space this morning, and the idiot driving the wrong way on I-95 last night—being the chummy creatures that we are we can't help but bumping in to them on a daily basis. We have to rub elbows with them constantly, and such rubbing and bumping is apt to cause a little friction amongst the bumpers from time to time. It happens continually in such socially addicted animals as ourselves and by virtue of our sheer numbers and our constant encroachment upon each other's lives, we all get plenty of practice in sorting out the tangles and instances of self-doubt. We rub elbows and then find that we're rubbing each other the wrong way. Friction develops. Little conflicts arise, which if we're decent folk—and I'm presuming (perhaps foolishly) that most of us are—force us to examine the wellsprings of our own motivations to see for ourselves just how much give and take there is in the coils which absorb for us the shock of constantly being afflicted with one another. We give, we take, and we make concessions when we have to. Through it all along the way and never with the same lesson learned in quite the same manner, each of us comes to a sense of ourselves and thus learns to spin the fragile web of society that holds us all together. But as said before, threads can snap. Doubt is a daily companion with us—when you can walk into almost any public school in the country while having to run the risk of getting caught in the crossfire of a student shooting spree how could it be otherwise? When it's conceivable that any random postal employee could blow you and five others away just because you tried to mail a package with insufficient postage, why would any of us think differently? Doubt is our handmaiden. It walks with us continually as if to keep us company, all the while manifesting itself in a variety of poorly formed shapes and ill-conceived notions about who is who and what is what, forcing us to assess and then reassess each potential action and interaction with one another. We're therefore prudent about whom who we piss off. Prudence is only normal. Sand Toes was never prudent. But then he was never normal either, having been born entirely outside what you and I would consider society or even its immediate neighborhood. Gun-toting postal clerks and runaway school children are just two examples of society's web-snapping, and it's conceivable, I suppose, that had Sand Toes been one of us, a creature born in and to society, that he might have ended up as one of those broken strands and so come hurtling back upon himself and the rest of us, causing injury and perhaps death in his backlash and failure to adjust—so thank God that he wasn't born down the block! But the fact is, he wasn't one of us. He was one of him and one of him I think you'll agree, comes close to being one too many. Be that as it may, having grown up almost entirely alone he was free of such doubts and insecurities. Esoteric questions regarding social interaction, personal loyalty, and proper etiquette, never vexed him. In fact, such conundrums never even occurred to him until meeting Larraine. Oh, there were the Apaches, but since he saw so little of them these days they hardly counted. Besides what he learned from them were the rituals and rote practices involving certain interactions and the possible instances when certain reactions to those interactions were expected and what those reactions might be—in other words, the "hows" of relationship building, no pun intended, not the "whys." Sand Toes regarded the Apaches as his people but only because they'd been the only ones around. Also they'd given him a name after he'd long since forgotten his own and a name is an important thing to have even if you are a hermit and have no one to tell it to—at least you still have something to call yourself. They came around every now and then did the Apaches. They traded goods for moisture and were as friendly as people can be, I suppose, who've had their entire country stolen from them, but they were careful to keep their distance. For instance, when they met they powwowed with Sand Toes until dawn, passing the peace pipe, guzzling fermented cactus juice, and chewing a peyote button or two until everyone in the tepee was staggering blind stoned. But never would the last Apache pass out until he'd seen Sand Toes safely out the tepee's flap at the end of the night's festivities, making sure to tie it securely behind him as their guest staggered off into the rising sun. "Really, I dinna mind stayin' here," he'd say.

"No, please," they would always in turn reply. "We insist!"

Having by this time assimilated the "hows" of relationship building, he knew the proper response to such a reply and so left to be by himself and sleep it off. He'd done as much before and often for his own reasons so it didn't trouble him that the Apaches might like him to do so as well. Why they might want him to do so and other questions involving "why" never occurred to him until he met Larraine who showed him the hows and whys of just about everything. Thus even today Sand Toes remained mostly unaware of when he pissed people off and couldn't care less about it, even in the rare instance when he was cognizant of the fact. The desert, always a harsh task master, had taught him that survival meant looking out for yourself first because there was nobody else around to do it for you. Charity and love of neighbor were unknown concepts. Except for the occasional partying Apaches, there were no neighbors upon whom to practice such impractical extravagances. Charity and love of neighbor were luxuries to be practiced only when one had the time and leisure to do so and the desert afforded damned little of either. Having grown up with it and it alone, the desert had by now impressed upon him its sense of eternal loneliness. He was aware of its vast solitude. The desert made him cognizant of this particular feature by forcing him to sit up and take notice of it while the sun beat down upon him unmercifully and the vast tracts of utter emptiness assaulted him from all sides. At times, Sand Toes knew, the emptiness and solitude could literally be felt and be said to have weight as it bore down heavily upon his neck and shoulders while pounding into him the concepts of solitude and self. He had, through constant exposure to such sensations, grown so used to them that they wrapped themselves around him like a warm blanket on a cool desert night and therefore with the exception of first Larraine, and then Little La, preferred solitude over company, neither wanting or needing anyone else. He was by all accounts a hermit and apart from an occasional flirtation with curiosity regarding what occurred beyond his self-imposed borders, was content to let the world go its way so long as it didn't interfere with his own life and the way he wanted to live it. When it did Sand Toes was quick to set it right and put it in its place without suffering the merest qualm for having done so.

Sometimes things happened of themselves and you had to be able *and* willing to take advantage of them when they did, as in his

THE CHRISTMAS RABBIT

long ago first meeting with Larraine and her damned Society. They were in his desert where they had no right to be. They had shoes galore, which he'd coveted for himself. So he excavated a pit and constructed a trap in order to obtain them and did so without suffering the slightest pang of guilt for having done it. That was dog-eat-dog survival and he was good at it, having trapped and eaten a few coyotes in his day. Larraine of course and the love he came to feel for her became a mitigating factor in his dealings with the others. For her sake he put up with them, leaving them alone if they did likewise, but so ingrained within was this sense of solitude that even after marrying Larraine and moving her into his shaft, he rarely sought them out, preferring to stay at home when she and Little La went to town.

Sand Toes didn't need friends or the obligations they brought and he wasn't one for adjusting his values, habits, or beliefs in order to accommodate the feelings and opinions of others. Rubbing elbows to smooth over rough edges just wasn't in his nature. He had Little La, and she was enough. He sorely missed Larraine and the love she'd brought him, but she was gone now and even he knew that there was little he could do about that except visit her in his mirages and dreams. Friends were a burden he neither wanted nor needed. They interfered with his desert way of life as they tried with their chumminess and good will to subvert the desert's overriding ideal—self-preservation! It was hard enough in this place eking out a survival for two without having to worry or care about anyone else. Friends would force him uncomfortably and against his will, to confront certain aspects about himself that until now he'd done a good job of running from. Now along comes this rabbit, and he should've had no qualms or misgivings whatsoever about using it for his own ends but despite his best efforts to maintain his cold reserve and adversarial attitude found that three days of shared toil, digging holes and excavating pits, had sorely hampered his ability to maintain focus. Irregardless of his loud mouth and his tendency toward guff, Sand Toes knew that Jack had more on the ball and made more sense—at least to him, than any of the Secret Society's members—except, of course, his wife and daughter. In those three days they'd come to share an occasional joke at the desert's expense or a comradely cup of moisture as they surveyed the extent of their work. Much to his own surprise and personal discomfort Sand Toes began to care about Jack and his opinions, often finding himself actively seeking those opinions out. Was this the beginning of friendship and if so, what burdens might it place upon him? What sort of concessions might such friendship require? He had a certain idea in mind regarding this rabbit and the role, beyond strictly digging, that Jack might play in his quest to capture the ultimate quarry. Although Sand Toes didn't fully understand the concept of friendship he was familiar enough with the idea to understand that what he planned for Jack might not necessarily be something that one friend would do to another. What then? Sand Toes didn't know and was therefore drowning in a sea of turmoil and doubt and could only thank providence that he at least understood the "hows" of treaties (again, no pun intended). Treaties, he knew, had built in mechanisms written right into them for the absolution of guilt once the treaties themselves had been broken. Surely had they not then our country would've fallen victim to its own lofty pretensions by now. Sand Toes didn't know that but understood it intuitively regardless. That intuitive understanding however didn't prevent him from feeling like defeated cattle craps when he gave thought to Jack and the plans he had for him. It only gave him the misguided ability to rationalize them.

Mixed into this emotional soup was the certainty on Larry's part that fate had placed Jack here for a specific purpose above and beyond the delivery of Little La's egg and that whether he realized it or not, Jack had a preordained part to play in upcoming affairs. How else could one credit the existence of a talking rabbit—if indeed he was a rabbit, which Larry was not fully convinced of yet—coincidence? Certainly not! Therefore Jack's participation was a role that no matter how much Sand Toes sought to direct would nevertheless evolve for reasons of its own, forever beyond his personal control and perpetually out of his reach and understanding. Just what did that portend and what subsequent questions did it raise regarding who was in charge here and who was not? Sand Toes was sure that he would not enjoy discovering the answers to those riddles—even if he'd been lucky enough in this instance to have puzzled out the questions. He wrestled with the dilemma during their return trip with no answers or solutions forthcoming. By virtue of constant conversation Jack kept Sand Toes from seeking out the advice of Larraine in one of his daydreams. Every time she came swimmingly into focus, gliding toward him out of the shimmering horizon like a mirage blown upon the desert's hot breath, Jack would up and ask another question or offer an unsolicited observation regarding this matter or that, thus ending Larry's reverie and ruining any chance that he might have had for spousal discussion. At any other time, Sand Toes would've sorely resented such intrusions and made plain his feelings about them. This time however he did neither, taking unusual pleasure for himself in the rabbit's conversation. Why, he wondered, was that?

They followed the line of unbroken hills throughout the day until they gave way to the gypsum plains beyond. Upon reaching those endless tracts they made a left at Broken Rock, heading north for the last leg of their journey home. The sun beat down upon them, the Great Spirit's sledgehammer of heat and light, pounding and grinding them into the desert sand and Sand Toes had to show Jack how to cover himself up in order to avoid the worst of it and so be spared the agonies of dehydration. They stopped often for moisture, which Sand Toes found by digging holes in the appropriate places. New to the desert, Jack invariably drank too much, too quickly, and too often and so was inevitably overcome with cramps and shivers, compelling Larry to carry him in order to keep to his schedule and make it home in time to greet Little La. Normally, such a weakness as Jack currently displayed would rouse Larry to anger. He had no patience for city slickers or "outworlders," as he termed them, those desert tenderfeet who encumbered by ignorance and lack of experience had no business being out in the wastelands and who could be counted upon as sure as cattle craps littered a cow field to so complicate and lengthen a desert journey as to make its undertaking hardly worth the effort in the first place. This however, was a special circumstance—was this rabbit not his new friend? Even so, for the briefest of moments Sand Toes did away with the silly notion of possible friendship and regardless of Jack's perceived importance to the successful undertaking of his overall plan, was ready to treat him as the soft outworlder that he certainly was and leave him out in the middle of nowhere to bake. After all, it wasn't as though he hadn't tried to warn him. Time and again at every stop to obtain moisture, Sand Toes had offered the rabbit a word of caution. "Hey, laddie," he'd say as Jack eagerly drank, "ye be takin' in too much o; the moisture there, bucko. Take ye smaller sips and drink slower." Questioning whether or not there was enough water in the whole wide world to quench a thirst like his, Jack would reply that his dehydration was his own business and that he was fully capable of making his own decisions regarding the matter. Sand Toes had once heard that you could lead a dumb horse to water but you couldn't make it drink. Perhaps that was true but apparently it didn't apply to rabbits! "Hae it yer own way," he said, knowing full well what would be the inevitable outcome of the hare's stubbornness and ignorance. Now riding in the crook of Larry's arm, Jack was again in the throes of another attack of cramps and shivers. Lawrence looked down on him without pity. "Dinna be losin' it, Jackie boy," he warned. Puke on me jackass and I'll skin ye alive and use yer fur fer me mop!"

"I'm not a jackass," the rabbit replied weakly through a shiver, "I'm a jackrabbit!"

"That may be," said Sand Toes, "but ye be actin' like a jackass sure 'n' begorrah!" Jack mumbled an incoherent reply as he drifted off into an uneasy sleep.

He awoke to the coolness of the mine's living room floor. So they made it back, it seemed, and apparently in one piece. Somewhere from back in the mine, probably from the kitchen Jack reasoned, could be heard the shuffling and movement of Sand Toes as he prepared dinner in anticipation of Little La's looked for return. The grating sound of metal upon glass assaulted the rabbit's ears as Sand Toes opened assorted jars and emptied their contents into stone bowls. Jack took note of a high, piercing screech. Some desert-dweller, he supposed, unlucky enough to get caught in one of Sand Toes's traps but not nearly enamored of the good fortune to die instantly was now having its luck catch up to its fortune as Sand Toes ended its luck, good or bad, once and for all. The rabbit's clever ears picked up the sound of meat sizzling on the coals and following that his nostrils were assaulted by the oily scent of great horned toad being fried and fricasseed in a cast iron skillet. The greasy smell, borne as it was upon the roiling smoke bellowing out of the kitchen was unpleasant to a vegetarian like himself causing his queasiness and general discomfort to return. His stomach rolled sickeningly and in a wave of nausea he felt his gorge rise. Sand Toes heard Jack's pitiful thrashing about as the rabbit wrestled with the odor while his stomach did battle. To assure himself as to Jack's well-being, Sand Toes popped into the living room to check on his charge. Jack saw him enter. "What is that god-awful stink?" the rabbit asked squeamishly. "It smells absolutely foul!"

"Stink?" replied Sand Toes. "Stink? Why that be toad in the skillet, laddie. There be nothin' like the smell o' old toad that be fryin' in the pan! T' be sure, I likes me own raw but Little La, God love 'er, will hae nothin' t' do with such hearty eatin' as that! Wants her food cooked, she does—just like her dearly departed Ma before her. So's I cooks it. Therefore dinna be castin' any dispersions or unwanted criticisms regardin' the smell o' my good cookin'!" Jack merely groaned. He hadn't the energy to do anything else. "Have you got a stick of celery or something?" he asked, hoping that a little wholesome food would quiet his disgruntled abdomen.

"Nae celery," replied Sand Toes. "Nae bread either fer that matter. Lauren will be bringin' all o' that back with her when she returns with her uncles. In the mean time we make do with what we've got. Would ye be interested in tryin' some toad now?"

"Ugh!" was Jack's reply.

"Ugh it is then," Sand Toes answered indifferently. "It'll just mean more fer me 'n' La when she gets back!" He gazed with longing back toward the kitchen where the old toad was still sizzling in the skillet. "I suppose," he said reluctantly, that I'll hae t' set a plate or two fer me cousins, although why I bother I dinna know. The ungrateful sods are never polite enough t' eat what I serve 'em! But Little La says that despite their lack o' manners I hae to be courteous! Hae ye ever heard tell o' the like? My Little La says that such niceties and posturin's be nothin' more 'n' civilized and necessary. A waste o' my time and good cookin' is what I say! But she loves her uncles, she does, and so I put up with 'em and let her hae her way."

"Well, aren't you a prince?" replied the rabbit.

CHAPTER VI
Lauren Says "Nae!"

Little La arrived back at the mine in the company of her uncles, Slim and Jim. With their usual punctuality they returned just as Sand Toes was finishing up the business of fricasseeing old toad. A draft blowing up from the depths of the shaft and out the adit carried its gamey odor to the three travelers who using their noses, followed the scent home. "Ack!" said Jim. "I believe yer old man's cookin' up the frog agin'! Don't he ever feed ye anythin' else?"

Lauren laughed. "It's toad," she replied, "and yes, he serves up other food too—when we can get it. You know that there isn't much to choose from way out here and we have to be content with what God provides us." They hit a chuckhole in the desert floor that with any other three passengers the Land Rover would've glided over, but Uncle Slim was one of the three and Uncle Jim was another. Their prodigious bulks and the concurrent weight that went with them were already tasking the automobile's shocks and springs to well beyond their rated limits so that they creaked and groaned at the least little bump. "Ack!" Jim said again as his head bounced off the Land Rover's roof. "Aye, that one hurt, it did." They drove for another couple of minutes in silence, each lost to their own thoughts until the mine's shaft became visible. *Not long to go now*, thought Slim sitting in the back seat. *Best t' hae another go at it before we drop her off.*

"Listen, La," he said, "yer uncle and I both know that old toad is about all that the two o' you can come by. Is nae that why we always load up the back o' the wagon with the provisions and essentials that the two o' ye need t' be getting yerselves through the week? O' course 'tis! Yer family, ye know. We wouldn'a want ye t' starve."

"And that be nothin' but the truth," Jim chimed in. "Nothin' but the gospel accordin' t' Saint Paddy, sure 'n' begorrah!"

Lauren gave her uncles a long-suffering glance irrespective of the tender thoughts that she harbored toward each. She loved them dearly and knew that they returned her sentiment while understanding that they had her best interests at heart even though they often erred in their assumptions as to just what her best interests might be. This was an old conversation for the three of them and one in which they engaged every Friday evening as they made ready to drop her off. "I know you don't want me to starve," she said, "but I'm not starving now, am I?"

"Looks can be deceivin'," Jim replied weakly. They'd lost the argument with her before it had even begun. Still, there was nothing to do but press on. "Lassie," he continued, "we're o' knowin' that ye nae be starvin' out here, just as we know that yer Da be providin' ye toadies and lizard gizzards all regular and timely. But, girlo, old toad day in and day out—it just ain't healthy." Slim nodded in agreement. "Ye be needin' a bit o' variety, La," he added.

"We don't eat old toad every day or lizard gizzards either! Sometimes we have rattlesnake and if we're really lucky and one of 'em gets caught in Da's traps, we even get to feast on vulture! Da calls 'em desert chickens on account that he says they're so cowardly. I wouldn't know. I don't trust 'em far enough to find out! But you know Da, he'll trust anybody once."

"We know that, La," replied Slim. "We know that but—"

"But what?" interrupted Lauren, pressing her point. "You're right. It's still not enough variety so Da makes sure that at least once a month he goes back to that place where he killed the deer when you all first met."

"I shot that deer," Jim corrected, his voice puffed with pride and belching braggadocio as if he'd overeaten on it at lunch. "Just ask anyone who was there—they saw it!"

Lauren and Slim conspired together with a smile, both knowing that Jim was divulging less than the truth. That was Uncle Jim, an

THE CHRISTMAS RABBIT

Irish storyteller in the grandest of traditions. "And furthermore," he continued, lecturing his niece and applying the gloss and wash of the little white lies he employed by rationalizing to himself that such lies preserved a greater truth, "'twas the day we met yer Da that I bagged me that bucko. Ask yer Uncle Slim. He remembers!"

"Sure n' begorrah, I do," Slim replied with a hearty chuckle, his ample sides rolling merrily with the joke of mimicking an old brogue that in truth he had no use for. "I remember it well, and I tell ye 'twas the day after that or 'twas nae day at all that Sand Toes killed the stag. The day after. 'Twas the day that we met when he trapped us all. Then 'twas the day he slew the kine. 'Twas the day after that, being the third day in all that he married Larraine—and I'm sure ye'll be rememberin' *that* day, aye?"

Jim bristled, and his face scrunched up. He didn't like being reminded of past mistakes and failures and more importantly, could see for himself where this conversation was heading. "Enough!" he said quickly, his hands chopping a slashing gesture as he called for silence. "'Twas the day after then—just as ye say!" They drove on in silence for the briefest moment of time, the merest passage of seconds, before he changed the subject. "Well, well," said he, "here we be and already at the mine at that! By the blessin' o' Saint Paddy, who would'a believed it?" Although they were drawing nearer to the adit, they were still some hundreds of yards from actually being at the doorstep. Slim laughed once again at his brother and his poorly contrived attempt to avoid the truth and admit to the facts of those fateful far-flung days.

"'Twas two days from the day we met Larry," he said, teasing his brother and playing him like a tuna caught on a hook, "that he married Larraine!"

"He dinna like t' be called Larry," Jim replied sharply. Then glancing at La, he softened both the look on his face and the words on his tongue. "He prefers," he said soothingly, "t' be called Sand Toes."

Lauren's face tightened in little knots. She had no use for the Apaches, at least those she had met, and quickly leaped to her Da's defense. "He does not," she retorted perhaps a little too quickly, knowing for herself just how full of cattle craps her reply was. Her Da lived to be Sand Toes!

"La," Slim said in a placating manner, "I be understandin' yer reluctance t' admit the truth o' it. I'm nae sure that I like the Apaches meself or if they even be real Apaches at that. But there's nae denyin' that yer Da prefers his adopted people over his own Irish ancestry and in particular the Dawe family tree as identified by the mark—"

"That's never been proven t' me own satisfaction!" Jim cut in. "I've never been in the way o' seein' it, and neither hae ye! Where is it, I ask ye? Where is it, aye? Not on his face, like yerself." Slim's eagle talon was on his left cheek. "It's nae on his nose, like me." Jim's was on the very tip of his nose, shining like a beacon, and had he antlers, would have allowed him to pass himself off as the son of a very famous reindeer. "And it's nae on his leg, like Little La's either!" Lauren had the cutest little mark on her left calf. As birthmarks went, the Society wholeheartedly agreed that it was one of the finest, standing out boldly as it did, clearly defined and gaily colored. Most thought it meant that she was destined for great things. But then they'd all thought the same about her mother too.

"Enough!" said Slim, his impatience mounting. "Tell me, brother dear, did anyone ever lay eyes on Larraine's mark in order to offer up proof, both to themselves and others, that it even existed? Nae!" They hit another chuckhole and again Jim's head bounced of the roof. "Ack!" he cried once more. "I'm getting' tired o' bumpin' me noggin! Why n't ye do us both a favor and lose some o' that extra weight ye be carryin' around like a sack o' potatoes?"

"I like my weight," Slim retorted, "and so does everyone else, and you, dear brother, are tryin' t' change the subject! I ask ye agin, did ye or anyone else fer that matter, ever see Larraine's mark?"

"She always maintained that it was on her private person," Jim mumbled quietly.

"What was that? I did'na hear ye?"

Jim shot his brother an evil look. "I said that she always maintained that the mark was on her private person!"

"Well then," Slim replied, "did ye nae believe her?"

"O' course I believed her! Larraine Dawe was the truest woman that ever was! The leader o' our Society and a real corker from foine Irish stock! She would'na lie about a thing so important as the mark—not hers or anybody else's fer that mater. If she said that her mark was somewhere on her private person than ye can rest assured that's where it lie!"

Then ye took her at her word?" Slim asked.

"T' be sure," Jim replied. "Although I would o' preferred seein' it fer meself—then I would'na hae this one's Da come along and throw his monkey in me wench!"

"True enough, I suppose," replied Slim, "and a good toss it was, sure 'n' begorrah! But dinna ye mean wrench?"

"Whatever."

"There be nae use in cryin' over the milk that's been spilt," Slim continued, "or in tryin' t' turn back the clock either. What be done, be done and had Sand Toes not come along when he did then we'd all be dead and nary a Dawe, inside the Society or out o' it, would've gotten t' see Larraine's mark. So when, dear brother, are ye goin' t' let it go? Ye've got to, ye know. If not for yer own sake then for Little La's. Ye be her uncle after all and eccentric or nae, her Da be her Da! This feud between family, which I might add has its roots in yer jealousy, is unseemly. It's especially uncomfortable for the little one here."

They drove on for some seconds in utter silence, each of three wrestling with their own thoughts. Finally, Lauren spoke up, hoping to close the rift between the two brothers.

"It's all right, Uncle Slim," she said. "When it comes to Da, I know that Uncle Jim can't help but feel the way he does. I understand, and it's all right."

"Nae, lass," Slim said. "You're a smart one—the brightest bulb on the tree, but yer young yet and ye dinna know enough about the human condition t' be makin' such pronouncements." He stared at his brother. "Well?"

"Well, what?" Jim asked sharply. "Do ye want me to tell ye that he won fair and square? Well, I will nae! I remember well enough how he maneuvered the lot o' us with that blood bondin' ceremony into lettin' Larraine marry him. 'Twas an unfair advantage, that was! He had us over a wheelbarrow and knew it!"

"That be true," answered Slim, "but it also be true that as far as the rest of us were concerned, she was under nae obligation to endure the unendurable once we were safe in our own territory and on familiar ground. She could've left him then and there and done so with all o' our support! It's a matter o' record that she chose t' stay with him. At some point somewhere out there in the desert, she fell in love and that's the truth o' it. It was then, if you remember, that she claimed him as one of our own, a long-lost relative probably, and no doubt descended from Great-granddaddy Dawe's brother, while claiming that he too bore the mark, and again in a place not readily visible to the eye."

"Said she," said Jim.

"Ye did'na believe her?" Slim asked incredulously. "Ye just claimed a minute ago that Larraine Dawe would never lie about the mark. Are ye now sayin' that she would, and if so, why?"

"Oh, all right then!" Jim reluctantly conceded. "Perhaps he hae the mark. But 'tis certain that mark or nae, he nae be me own kind o' Dawe—he be some other kind!"

"And what kind o' Dawe be that?"

"The kind that causes dissension amongst the clan! The kind that splits the family and stays put when others say go!"

Lauren gave Slim a conspiratorial wink then turned her attention to Jim. "Oh," she said teasingly, "do you mean as an example, my great-great-granda?"

"Which one?" Jim asked cautiously.

"The one who stayed put."

"None other," replied Jim.

"Well, surely," said Slim, "ye canna' blame Lawrence—"

"Sand Toes."

"Och, all right then! But certainly ye canna' hold Sand Toes responsible for the misdeeds o' his ancestors—if they even were misdeeds. After all, his great-grandda stayed while ours along with his side o' the family, came back east. Now look at us! After all that feudin' on their parts—here we are all back in the desert agin and trying

THE CHRISTMAS RABBIT

t' retrace the footsteps o' our great-grandsires! Do ye not find that t' be the least bit ironic?"

Jim considered for a moment, his brother's insight. "Nae," he replied, "absolutely nae. It be normal fer this family!"

"Point conceded," Slim said. "But beyond admitting that Sand Toes is part of the family—which by the way ye've just done, surely ye must acknowledge the possibility, given how things have turned out, that perhaps events might've gone better if our ancestors had remained together, staying put out here as a family and not splitting the tree as it were, down the trunk. Who knows? We may hae even found Geronimo's Lost Gold Mine by now."

Jim offered both his brother and his niece an incredulous look. Could they really be that naive, he wondered? Could they be that foolish? Slim possibly. But it was a shock to him to discover that Lauren, whom everyone regarded as clever beyond her years, could be likewise disabled. "Ye be outta yer bloomin' minds," he said. "Has Sand Toes ever found the gold, I ask ye? Not the least little nugget o' it—and he be roamin' around this desert all o' his life! The last o' his side o' the clan and madder n' a hatter! Do ye not think that had our great-granda stayed we wouldn'a be in the same shape? We'd all be bloomin' fruitcakes, aye?"

Neither Slim nor Lauren had an answer to that supposition which was just as well. They'd pulled up to the entrance of the mine. In a cloud of dust the Land Rover screeched to a halt in front of the adit. The commotion of their arrival brought Lawrence running out of the mine as if he were late for a fire. Any noise not natural to the desert always set him on edge, which most who knew him agreed he was constantly tiptoeing upon anyway. "What be ye doin', ganglin' up to me doorstep in such an uproar," he cried, "and where be me, Little La?"

"I'm right here, Da," Lauren replied, sticking her head out of the window so that Sand Toes could see her. Lawrence relaxed somewhat at the sight of her but eyed his cousins suspiciously nevertheless.

Jim looked to Slim, who was too busy looking to Lauren for help, to be of much use in the confrontation that seemed to be looming. "Whaddya think we're doin' ya daffy bastard?" he asked. "We're bringin' yer daughter back home—just like we always do!"

Sand Toes continued to stare at the two brothers, his eyes clouded with doubt and giving the pair the once-over whilst eyeing the infernal machine that they rode in. He didn't trust it or the brothers who drove it—not since they'd popped the hood a few years back to show him and to brag about, the two hundred horses underneath the hood. Sand Toes had looked for the life of him, staring intently down at the engine and the block upon which it rested but had been unable to discover for himself so much as a single pony. He distrusted anything he couldn't see and everything that had anything to do with these two, especially the thinner one—the plumber who liked to lay other people's pipe! "Why nae be droppin' the lass off a couple o' hundred yards from the door and be done with it?" he asked. "Then the two of ye could be ganglin' on yer way all right n' proper without botherin' the likes o' me!"

"Sure n' begorrah!" replied Jim. "And as soon as the lass so much as stubs a toe whilst walkin' betwixt there and here, ye'll be sayin' that it was our fault fer not seein' her all the way home! And then ye'd never let her out o' the house agin to be seein' her uncles or the rest o' her family, I'm sure!"

Little La looked to her Uncle Slim, who merely shrugged. It was the same conversation week in and week out whenever they brought her back. Each of them knew that Jim and Sand Toes were never going to see eye to eye on anything as both had the eye for Larraine when she'd been around to keep an eye upon. That Larraine discovered she'd only had eyes for Larry just made matters worse as Jim was never able to find the eye for anyone else. Now each had eyes in the backs of their heads and were continually looking into the past. Had each of them been able to use the eyes God gave them and look forward instead of seeing through the ones they'd invented for themselves—those prejudicial peepers of hindsight and subjective bias which caused both of them to draw inward while reflecting upon bittersweet memory, then perhaps their relationship might've been different. As it was their ongoing tunnel vision marred their perspectives. Now at a predictable impasse, the two glared at each

THE CHRISTMAS RABBIT

other wickedly, neither willing to bend a bit or give an inch and each determined to remain steadfastly anchored in their mutual distrust and suspicion, leaving Little La, as usual in the position of arbitrator, to negotiate if not an outright peace then at least a temporary truce, honored until after dinner whereupon her uncles would return to town and the Society which made it up. "Da," she pleaded, her voice honeyed with the sweet sounds of conciliation and respectful compromise, "we can't just let them go home without feeding them. What would Mother say? And besides, they've oodles of foodstuffs for us in the back of the wagon, including your favorites, strawberries and watermelon!"

    Sand Toes licked his lips as he tried to peer beyond the front seat of the Land Rover and into the back of the jeep where Slim was seated, guarding the treasures. Finally, he grunted out a reluctant assent and allowed as how the two of them should join he and his daughter at table. "There be enough fer everyone," he said shortly. "Fricasseed toad, fresh off the spit with a lizard hollandaise—me favorite!"

    Jim and Slim turned a withered eye upon each other resigning themselves to the unavoidable. With Lauren's return, every Friday saw the inevitable meal served with garish gusto by Lawrence Torrance Dawe. Sand Toes, as he liked to call himself, had been serving it to them once a week for nearly two years, ever since they'd taken up the duty of returning Lauren home for the weekend in Larraine's stead. After almost one hundred reluctant servings, they should've gotten used to it. But how, each wondered, does *anyone* develop a taste for fricasseed toad fresh of the spit with lizard hollandaise? After two years of being subjected to this cruel gruel on a weekly basis, the brothers could only agree that it tasted progressively worse with each anticipated serving. Green and slimy from the scum floating on top to the broken pieces of charred and burnt flesh resting uneasily at the bottom of the bowl, neither brother had ever managed to finish his allotted portion and each despaired of ever doing so. Still despite their reticence they were required as a show of good manners to try nevertheless—if only for Lauren's sake, and it was that necessity that got the two of them out of the car and moving.

Lauren ran to her Da who scooped her up in his arms and gave her a heartfelt hug, being careful not to crush her in the process. "La," he quietly whispered in her ear as he held her to him, "what be ye thinking about, invitin' the likes o' these two t' table when we be havin' a dinner guest already?"

"You mean the chicken?" she whispered innocently in his ear.

"I mean the rabbit," he replied with a quip. "A rabbit is what he be and a talkin' rabbit at that!"

"Talking?"

"Sure n' begorrah," Sand Toes replied secretively. He looked beyond her to ensure himself that the two brothers remained out of earshot. "The damned beast be ganglin' about the mine and talkin' yer ear off if ye be lettin' it!"

Little La allowed a momentary look of triumph to shine forth. Her Da's revelation was proof that their charge was indeed someone special, someone of consequence. Who else among animals other than the Easter Bunny could converse in the spoken word? No one, that's who. Now she was sure of the identity of their guest…just as she was sure that they could not avoid having her uncles for dinner regardless of the circumstances dictated by the unlooked for appearance of their unlikely visitor. Uncles Jim and Slim had been rightly suspicious when she tried to spirit them away from the mine at the beginning of the week. It had required all of her skill in misdirection and manipulation to allay their doubts and reservations. To push the Irishmen out and send them on their hurried way once again could well prove disastrous. For the life of her, she couldn't say just why this was so but felt it intrinsically nevertheless. Gut feelings and instincts, she knew, were phenomenon that folk in her family were brought up to give credence to. So be it. Her uncles would know that a talking animal might be worth more than all the gold in Geronimo's mine, therefore she and her Da would just have to make the best of the situation while hoping that their guest had the good sense to keep his mouth shut! She explained this both quickly and quietly to Lawrence as he held her in his arms. She then motioned for him to put her down.

THE CHRISTMAS RABBIT

The sun was slowly sinking beyond the western horizon, painting the desert a violent orange as Lauren led the three men into the mouth of the cave. They entered the living room to confront Jack, who was sitting up and regarding them skeptically. Who were these folk and why were they here? The young lass, of course, he knew, but who were the other two? Were they part of Sand Toes's quest—whatever that was, and if so, what role did they play? More importantly, if they were part of the quest in any way, shape, or form, then what in the name of the seven suns did Sand Toes need him for? He eyed the pair intently, giving each of them the once-over from top to bottom, when he noticed that displayed prominently upon each of their faces was the mark—the stigmata—the battle flag which called him to war upon the descendants of his ancestral enemy. There it was, and as plain as the noses on their faces! The skinnier of the two had the eagle's talon, done in red, shining prominently from the end of his proboscis like a beacon in a lighthouse. The fatter one had it on his cheek and it shone forth with equal resplendence. Jack had never seen the mark before nor did he know of any other living rabbit who had. Centuries had passed since those days in the Old Forest. Generations of ancestors had fallen asleep and gone to ground since the mark had last been seen. Ages had swept by until now all a contemporary rabbit had to rely upon was rumor and handed down tales (only half believed until this very moment), which served to encompass the legend regarding the mark and those who bore it. But they were enough, and Jack was ready. The battle would be taken up once again!

Since the days of the first Jack and the kangaroo court, which forced such a demanding and untoward sentence on generation after generation of Easter Bunnies-to-be, jackrabbits called and charged with carrying out the court's demands had been undergoing the training necessary to accomplish their sentence. Such training included the learning and constant refining of the philosophy of Zen and its concurrent martial arts, which were so necessary to their cause if they were to prosecute their sentence and in so doing, become brave new rabbits in a tired old world. Through ages of practice, they refined their philosophy, incorporating into it the physical skills of karate, judo, jujitsu, and just plain biting—skills necessary both to their own survival and the accomplishment of their hellish mission on the road, until centuries of instruction culminated in the presence of our rabbit of later days who was accounted by rabbitry everywhere as being the most skillful in these arts of any rabbit save the venerable Hareihito Rabakami himself—the first ninja rabbit in known history and one for whom, it was said, the mold was broken, and thank God for that!

Jack struck with a fury.

From a sitting position, he leapt into the air, pivoting in midjump to deliver a punishing side kick to his enemy's groin, toppling him like an old tree which had long since rotted at the root. It was poor Slim, who, being closest to his antagonist, suffered the humiliation of the blow. But Jack didn't stop there. Bouncing off Slim's groin and using the force of the blow to ricochet and rebound, the rabbit turned warrior flew through the air once again to deliver a rabid attack upon his second enemy. A roundhouse kick to the sternum caught Jim by surprise, knocking the wind out of him and doubling him over. Not wasting a second, Jack leapt once again and, citing a Zen koan, chanted a mantra, which marshaled his energies and brought them into focus. He bit down hard for biting's sake and sheared a piece off of Jim's cheek.

The fury of his onslaught occurred in the space of a second or two. Slim was laying on the floor, writhing in agony. Jim was gasping Irish profanities and panting in torment. Lauren looked on in shock and worry while Sand Toes merely sat back enjoying the show. But the rabbit wasn't done yet. Intending to do his victims even more harm than he had already he prepared to hurl his harea at them but Lauren, coming out of her stupor, put the quash on that. No one, not even the Easter Bunny, caused harm to her family and got away with it! With his back turned toward her and his concentration divided between his two enemies the rabbit made an easy target. Lauren simply grabbed him by the scruff of his neck and threw him across the room whereupon he crashed into the far wall, stunned and temporarily out of fight.

"Nae!" La screamed at the rabbit who was making a valiant effort to regain his feet and press the battle. "Nae!" she screamed

THE CHRISTMAS RABBIT

again at her Uncle Jim whom she could tell was getting ready to exact his revenge by returning blow for blow with interest. "Nae!" she yelled yet again as she leapt upon her uncle Slim, smothering him with her own body and stopping his writhing, which had she allowed it to continue, would soon cause him to roll over the rabbit, crushing it for sure.

"Kill the beast, lassie!" gasped Jim while eyeing the rabbit warily. "Kill it, I say, n' be done with the bloody thing! 'Tis a menace, sure n' begorrah!"

The three antagonists caught up in a war of two against one, had each for the moment retired to a neutral corner, though La knew that such a halt to hostilities could not go on indefinitely. The Easter Bunny was eyeing her two uncles with a look that clearly spoke of murder yet to be committed while it was plain to the young girl from the looks on her uncle's faces, that nothing would please them more than rabbit skinned, cleaned, and deep fried in the pan. For once, had he known it, Jim would've been surprised to discover that there was at least one thing that he and Sand Toes could agree on. The moment of revelation was lost however as Lauren quickly took charge. "Enough!" she said to the trio while at the same time remonstrating with her Da for not having broken them up in the first place.

"Nae my fight," reasoned Lawrence, trying to placate his daughter. "Best not t' be mixin' in the affairs o' others as I've told ye often enough." Sand Toes looked at Jack and then at his two cousins, while allowing himself a hearty chuckle. "And besides, La," he continued, "from the state o' those two, it be pretty damned certain that our guest here be one tough SOB! There be nae percentage in runnin' afoul o' someone as contrary as that! It could just as easily hae been yer Da there—and holdin' his gonads too, instead o' yer Uncle Slim. It ain't seemly fer the host t' be gropin' about his privates when there be guests to entertain. Just ain't proper, it ain't."

"Thick headed Irishman," Lauren mumbled to herself and turned her attention back to her uncles. "That goes for the two of you," she said, pointing to them. "And two times two for you!" she said to Jack. All four were thoroughly chastised. Both her Da and her uncles knew from past experience that La T. Da was no one to mess with and that within her, emotions ran deep. Getting her riled was something one did at one's own risk; even Jack, who knew little of La, could discern from what little he did know that this little lady was no one to trifle with. The four kept a discreet silence. "Now then," she said to the chastised quartet, "we're going to have dinner just like we do every Friday and everybody, and I do mean everybody, is going to get along, no ifs, ands, or buts! Family will eat at the dining room table just as always and you, Mr. Rabbit, will hop on over to your blanket as quick as may be—and no trouble out of anybody!"

The three men were as quick to the table as the rabbit was to his quilt. Slim or Jim might have remarked that it was passing strange indeed that a mere animal should understand their niece as well as this one apparently did and yet the look on her face and the tension in her posture communicated quite clearly her desire and left little room for extraneous conversation. Her red hair was ablaze while her violet eyes burned with a fire to match and you would have had to have been a dumb slug, they reasoned, one rung below an earthworm on the evolutionary ladder, to have not discerned for yourself her resolve regarding the matter at hand. Her look and body language bespoke volumes, announcing themselves with the utmost coherence and clarity. So it wasn't passing strange at all, they reasoned, that the rabbit should get it—and even if it was, strange they both knew, was only to be expected in this house where weird was only normal.

After she had everyone seated in their proper place she petitioned her Da to say grace. Sand Toes did so, as always praying to the Great Spirit, which caused both her uncles and the rabbit to squirm. Her uncles would have preferred that he pray to the God of the Old Testament while invoking the name of his son as an added blessing. Jack, on the other hand, regarded any god or spirit who allowed such events to play out as they did and therefore land him in the morass he was in, as not so great and not worthy of mention. Lauren set about serving the meal only to discover that during the fracas the dinner had burned. Thinking quickly, she added to the pan some cayenne pepper and curry powder and then announced to the diners that rather than their usual Friday evening fare of fricasseed toad in a lizard hollandaise, that they were to be treated instead to a new

THE CHRISTMAS RABBIT

dish—blackened toad, done up Cajun style, in a lizard hollandaise. The uncles shared a doubtful look while taking their obligatory serving in order to be polite. Lawrence however, greedily licked his lips while salivating in anticipation. Blackened toad done Cajun style in a rich lizard hollandaise—now there was a dish that made one's mouth water!

Over on his blanket, Jack looked on in half-concealed disgust as the four diners contemplated their evening meal with varying degrees of enthusiasm, all the while being thankful that he himself was a vegetarian. *Are they really going to eat that?* he wondered. The oily aroma as it wafted up and off the dinner plates was making his head spin and his stomach bark with the violent rumblings of oncoming sickness. But the dinner proceeded as Friday dinners at the Dawe home always did. Sand Toes and his daughter attacked their portions with hardy gusto while Slim and Jim looked on in abject horror, ready to recoil in an instant's notice should their food jump up from its plate and attack them instead. In an effort to appear good mannered, if only for appearance's sake, each said a silent prayer to the God of the Old Testament—who alone was powerful enough to protect the brothers from what lay before them, and then took the necessary taste of the gastrointestinal nightmare which lay uneasily upon their plates. Each brought to their mouths the merest sliver of old toad, the tiniest taste of lizard hollandaise—just enough to present the barest minimum of courtesy to their host and hostess. Table talk was kept to a minimum for a number of reasons, the chief being that Sand Toes, even in the best of moods, was not what one would call a conversationalist. Still, curiosity got the better of the two uncles, and so the conversation, such as it was, went. "Ye new pet," asked Jim as he twiddled his toad on the tines of his fork, "where did ye git it, I wonder? How was it caught, aye? And who in the name o' Saint Paddy ever heard o' a rabbit that fights with the fury o' Bruce Lee?"

"And it's smart," chimed in Slim, "smarter than yer average hare. Hell's bells, that rabbit's smarter than yer average bear—and that's sayin' quite a lot!" He too twiddled his toad with an equal lack of enthusiasm before continuing. "What's it doin' here, I wonder?" What's its purpose—for purpose it must surely have. I would'na wonder that the damned thing could talk if it had a mind to." This observation caused Lauren and Larry to shoot apprehensive looks at the rabbit. Mercifully, Jack remained silent. Both father and daughter instinctively knew that revealing the rabbit's oral abilities and therefore having to explain to the brothers its linguistic dexterity within the context of the revelation regarding its identity and fighting skills, which they found surprising themselves, would only lead to trouble. Lauren knew that her uncles would report such a disclosure to other members of the Society, who always being eager to get rich and to get rich quickly, would see in their charge a golden opportunity for big bucks should they reveal and be able to prove his existence to the rest of the world. Lauren refused to have the rabbit made a mockery of or to be in any other way put on display.

Sand Toes didn't give a cattle crap about displays, mock or otherwise. He only knew that he had a mission to fulfill, a quest to complete—and this rabbit figured prominently in his ability to conclude it. To reveal the rabbit's identity before his quest had a chance to bear fruit would likely mean its ruination for lack of execution. Let them get the job done first, reasoned Sand Toes, and then they'd see about revealing who was who and the potential monies to be made in revelation! He'd worry about his guilty conscience later. Money, he knew, had a way of assuaging such feelings and though he had no use for it himself, through his dearly departed Larraine had come to understand its importance in the outside world and realized that Little La would need plenty of it if she were going to go to college as Larraine had always insisted. Higher education, she'd told him, wasn't cheap. Besides, he further reasoned, if his request bore fruit, if he nailed his trophy to the wall, then perhaps there'd be enough money made to buy Little La a university of her own—maybe even two.

"So whence came the rabbit?" Jim asked again.

Sand Toes looked at Lauren and merely shrugged. He wouldn't credit their inquiry with a lie and saw no percentage either in telling them the truth. He might have told them a half-truth or part of the whole truth but real truth was itself, subjective. Open to interpretation and constantly fluid, truth was as malleable as silly putty and just about as reliable. Besides, he didn't know the whole truth.

THE CHRISTMAS RABBIT

Beyond finding Jack in his trap, Sand Toes had no idea of where the rabbit came from or when, so how was he supposed to answer questions regarding whence? Besides, he still wasn't entirely convinced that Jack was a rabbit anyway, despite his daughter's protestations and the rabbit's own remonstrations. For all Sand Toes really knew, Jack could still be a chicken in disguise. Such doubts on his part left Lauren to come up with an answer. "We found it in one of our traps," she said. "It was almost dead when we came across it, and we've nursed it back to health."

Jim gave Slim a knowledgeable look. "In yer traps, aye?" he asked. "And how came it t' be there, I wonder? Where had it come from and where was it goin'?"

La looked to her Da for help but could see immediately that there would be none forthcoming, at least from that source. She decided to brazen it out. "I don't know, Uncle," she replied. "Why don't you ask it yourself?"

Jim gave her a sour look while his brother admonished her not to get flip. "It's as plain as the noses on yer faces," Jim continued, "that the two of ye are concealin' somethin'. There be more t' this here rabbit than meets the eye! What secrets does it know? Is it good at findin' gold and can it dig it up once it's been found?"

Lauren bridled in anger. "Gold, gold, and more gold," she said. "That's all you Society folks ever dwell upon. There's more to life than gold and those who dig it!"

"Fine then," replied Slim. "We'll let the matter go for the moment. Answer for me this then, if ye will—where did the wee beastie learn to fight like that?"

"He's rabid."

The brothers shrugged while offering each other a shared look of concern. Anything was possible, they supposed.

"This here hare is a simple rabbit," said Lauren. "He's our rabbit. He's my pet, and I'm going to keep him and that's all there is to it—no more, no less!"

"But ye canna'," said Jim.

"Can't what?"

"The rabbit. Ye canna' keep it."

"Why not?"

"Because everyone knows," said Slim, "that wild rabbits die when kept in captivity."

"Well, this one won't!" Lauren said, tears flowing both from anger and fright. It couldn't be helped. Despite maturity beyond her years, she was still nevertheless a little girl who became frightened and angry at her uncles' implications. Her tears became rivers of mortification as she considered the possibility that she might cause the rabbit harm. Having nearly murdered it once she did not want to be held responsible yet again for its untimely demise." He'll live—just you wait and see!"

"Now ye gone and done it!" said Sand Toes, the flames of his ire ignited. "Ye've gone an upset me Little La and ye know that I will na' stand fer that! Begone, the both of ye, or else I'll be grindin' yer bones to make me cornbread!" He rose up suddenly, towering above the brothers in a threatening display of impending violence. He considered himself a patient sort—one had to be patient in order to put up with the myriad of trials the desert threw at you, but threats to Little La or anything else for that matter which caused her the least amount of agitation excepting, of course, his own actions and eccentricities, were not to be tolerated and could be counted upon to set him off like a roman candle on a short fuse. The brothers knew it too. Just as they knew that singly or together, neither were a match for Sand Toes when his dander was up. A long life of fighting against the desert in order to eke out a survival had strengthened and toughened him beyond belief. It had hardened him beyond measure until he was too robust and resilient for any five Society members to tangle with and hope to come away even. He was a wild man whose instincts and proclivity toward violence were kept in check only by the love of his lost wife and his concern for his daughter. The brothers considered the situation both quickly and carefully and got the hell out of there. Through the adit, down the path, and to their awaiting Land Rover, they ran like foxes with their tails on fire. "We'll be back," shouted Jim to the darkness behind him as he fled. "Just ye wait and see!" This threat, of course, was no surprise to Sand Toes who knew that they must come back on Monday in order to return Little La to school. Of course they'd be back, he reasoned, how else would his daughter get there? "We'll be back," Jim yelled again as he started up the jeep. "We'll be back and we'll be bringin' the whole lot o' us t' be sure! The whole Society will hear o' this—ye can count on it!"

The brothers drove off in a fury heading across the harsh sands of the desert for the relative comforts of home. Throughout their entire journey they spoke of Sand Toes and Lauren, of the goings on in their cave, and the advent of the strange little visitor. No doubt there was a mystery here and the rabbit was a shrouded figure, an enigma wrapped in impenetrable robes of concealment who lay hugger-muggering like some enigmatic skeleton in a closet who holds within its bony hand the key which would solve some cryptic puzzle. How else could they explain their niece's strange behavior and attempts at concealment? Until now, the brothers knew that Lauren had always treated them fairly, mediating between them and her Da honestly and with an open hand which hid nothing from either. Now however it was clear to both brothers that their beloved niece, Little La, was keeping secrets. What might they be, the brothers wondered? Together they discussed the matter from all possible angles, examining each and every facet. Being who and what they were however, and given that they were part of an unruly mob that for years now had been unsuccessfully trying to fulfill a quest of their own, it's not surprising that the brothers should arrive at the conclusion they did. They had, after all, mentioned it previously. Gold! Somehow and in some fashion, the rabbit had discovered gold, and now father and daughter were privy to the secret and unwilling to share it with the Society as members in good standing were supposed to. Where did the gold lie, and how was it to be gotten and dug up? Were they to delve in the ground for it or were they going to pan for it in some as yet undiscovered stream? If the latter then the brothers knew that such a rivulet must be indeed well hidden for the desert gave up or revealed very little surface water. Did such a stream flow underground? Perhaps in their cave and if not, then perhaps in Geronimo's lost one? Had the rabbit discovered it? And suppose the gold lie hidden in neither? Where then might it be? The brothers gave thought to those early days in their association with Sand Toes when lost in the desert he'd led them to hunt in that fairy land of growing trees and flowing streams and rills. Could the gold lie there? And if so could they find the hidden land on their own? To this day no one but Sand Toes knew how to get there. Would they be able to find such a tract by themselves and if not would they have to spy Sand Toes out until he led them to it? Suppose the gold lie not there at all but hidden someplace else entirely? What then? Suppose, God forbid, that it lay buried in someplace altogether inhospitable and dangerous? Suppose in fact, that the gold was located somewhere deep within the confines of Witch Valley? What to do then? They couldn't just waltz in and take it, could they? Even Sand Toes shunned that place! Three desperately old crones lived there, or so said he, and they carved into mincemeat anyone who got caught in their net. What was the use of such gold regardless of how big the lode, if one was not left alive to spend it? In and amongst all these questions lay the brothers' doubts and concerns about the rabbit itself and to this puzzle the two often returned. How had the rabbit found the gold and what was it doing seeking after it in the first place? What kind of rabbit wanted gold anyway? Whoever heard of such a thing? How were Sand Toes and La extracting the necessary information from it? Were they torturing it and if so, would calling the SPCA avail them of any practical use or would such an alliance necessitate that they give all their newfound gold to charity? Could they torture the rabbit themselves and compel it to reveal its secrets? And if so would they be able to understand such a confession? After all neither one of them spoke the language—if indeed there was a language to be spoken! Did Sand Toes, who knew well the ways of the desert and the languages of those who dwelt in it, speak lapin? The answers to these questions as well as a host of others remained enigmas to the brothers as they drove through the desert night discussing such matters and their possible resolution. Whatever the answers were the brothers determined that the entire Society should be made aware of their discovery and that together they should force Sand Toes and his daughter to hand over their charge and make known to them its secrets. There would be an accounting. They drove on, sight unseen or so they thought, and the long miles passed as they headed toward

THE CHRISTMAS RABBIT

their home. But Slim and Jim had been living in this harsh land, if only at its fringes, long enough to have known that nothing stays hidden in the desert. There is no place to hide and sound carries far. Thus it was that unbeknownst to them their trail was perceived and their conversation overheard. All their hopes and fears, all their concerns regarding enigmatic rabbits and those who were party to their secrets, were laid bare before the eyes and ears of two very distinct sets of eavesdroppers.

Away in a haunted valley, three witches who for ages had existed undisturbed, guarded by the mere rumor of their presence and the possibility of their impending wrath and who had patiently waited out the slow passage of the ages in order to exact their moment of revenge, now took note of the brothers and all that they said. Helgayarn, Brunnhilde, and Betty laid their plans for a long anticipated revenge while in hills not too distant, cast out members of an Indian tribe nearly expunged at the turn of the last century by the avarice of the white man, gave thought to the greed in their own hearts and to lost treasure, rightfully theirs, which had been sold out from under them for a song by a no good relative long dead and deservedly so. Smoke signals went up—a sign by them to marshal their forces for the coming battle. It seemed then that there would be an accounting indeed—but not at all like the one which the brothers had envisioned.

*****

Back at the mine and unaware of any of this, father and daughter confronted the rabbit.

"Just what were ye thinkin' o', Jack?" asked Sand Toes. "Now ye done gone and almost quashed the whole plan! Not only have ye roused the suspicions o' Slim and Jim, but sure as cows are makin' cattle craps out in the pasture, ye've gone and done sent 'em an invitation to gangle on out here with all o' their relatives." Sand Toes and La were seated in the parlor having drawn up chairs by the rabbit's blanket. Sand Toes had a bottle of fermented cactus juice from which he took a long pull every now and then in order to calm his nerves.

Society members always made him uneasy and soon he knew, they'd descend upon him with all their to-do and bother like flies on cattle craps, all buzzing about, digging for gold and disrupting his plans. At any other time he could have made do to deal with them or barring that simply taken Little La on a sojourn, fading away deep into the desert where no one could find him and in so doing wait out their silliness until the situation settled itself. He had no master or equal out on the timeless sands and they would never have located him until he was ready to be found. But December's end was approaching fast and he felt instinctively that this December would at last see the culmination of his quest—provided he could keep the hounds at bay long enough to get the job done. "Agin', I ask, with ye knowin' what's at stake, how could ye play such a fool?"

Jack returned his gaze evenly. No desert rube was going to brow beat him! "That's the point, banana head," he replied. "I don't know what's at stake! You never told me! You just said, 'Jack, dig a hole here,' or 'Jack, dig a ditch there.' Just what the hell are you up to anyway?"

Lauren looked on in astonishment. Despite what her Da had whispered to her when she first alit from the car with her uncles—an absurdity which she only half believed at the time and notwithstanding her own hopes and desires, she'd been doubtful when her Da secretly boasted of their guest's linguistic abilities. But now there could be no doubt, for if seeing was believing then hearing was doubly so. The rabbit was speaking! No fooling around—this rabbit carried on like it really had something to say! "You're talking!" she exclaimed. "You're really and truly talking!"

Jack looked at her deadpan. "Of course I am," he replied with thinly disguised patience. "Didn't your old man tell you so?"

Lauren nodded, still amazed.

"So what's the problem? Can't believe your eyes? Your ears? What?"

"I must be dreaming," she offered up to no one in particular.

"Are you?" Jack spat. "Well, okay then, if you're dreaming then please wake up and let me out of your freaking nightmare! I'm just a day tripper in this bad dream and don't deserve the abuse!"

THE CHRISTMAS RABBIT

Lauren looked on, both in puzzlement and in shock. The rabbit, she thought, seemed inordinately rude and abrasive—not to mention overbearing, for one whose life they'd saved. She made a point of telling him so.

"Ha!" Jack replied. "Saved me! Goodness gracious, sure you did. Saved me after almost killing me. Spared me, I guess, so I could wind up as your old man's ditch-digger."

Lauren scowled. No one talked that way about her Da! Her face flushed and her eyes became hard as adamant. She got up from her chair and looked down upon the rabbit severely. "Catching you in our trap," she replied, "was all a misunderstanding, as you well know! How were we to know you were the Easter Bunny or that you'd even come along? It's not as though you're a regular visitor to these parts! For all we knew, you were an ordinary hare. A rabbit of no consequence whatsoever!"

To Jack's mind, all rabbits had consequence—some more than others! He stamped his feet and spit wickedly. "Back off!" he yelled. "I know judo and last time you got lucky! As for what you just said, oh that makes me feel ever so much better! Had I been a garden-variety rabbit then no doubt I'd be in the pot by now. I'd be making myself comfortable within the confines of your stomach! Thanks for kindness and charity! Thank you too for pointing out to me that should I ever come across any of my non–Easter Bunny relations to warn them most wholeheartedly to avoid your kindly ministrations!"

The trio confronted each other in uncomfortable silence, each feeling as though they had a particular point to make but unsure as to how to make it. Finally, Sand Toes could stand the silence no longer. His daughter was being chastised by this little whippersnapper, and he would leap to her defense. "If ye were a garden-variety rabbit," he said, "then ye would'na even be here! There be nae gardens this far out—o' that ye can be sure. Small patches o' tumbleweed and mesquite, aye, and occasional bunches o' cacti, but nae gardens. None. So if ye were a garden variety rabbit ye'd be somewhere else entirely, now wouldn't ye? In a garden most likely is me own guess, whatever the hell a garden be." He looked at his daughter who knew lots more about such things. "La, darlin'," he asked, "what be a garden?"

Lauren looked long-sufferingly at Jack, who looked patiently back while wondering to himself how on earth a little girl like this survived out here with a father like that. *It's true*, he reasoned, *God really does look after drunks and small children.* It was the only answer to the riddle confronting him that made any sense.

"Da," Lauren said while offering her father a tired frown, "You're not helping matters any."

"Well, I ain't hurtin' 'em, am I?"

"At this point," Jack replied caustically, "that'd be hard—even for you!"

Sand Toes scowled and made a fist. Jack immediately assumed the crane stance, forelegs raised up with paws bent down. He balanced on one leg while raising the other up to hip level. Such a stance spoke volumes about his determination to defend himself for rabbit legs do not bend in the same manner as yours and mine and therefore such posturing does not come easily to them. It had taken Jack years to learn and become adept. It took hours of unflagging effort and Zen meditation on his part just to imagine it, thus training his joints and muscles to actually move in a corresponding manner as to be able to achieve such a stance was the effort of a practiced master. He was ready now for any manner of attack no matter what form it took and when that bastard came at him he'd strike with authority, hitting low and knocking the son of a bitch's balls off!

"Nae!" Lauren shouted out, sensing the impending battle. "Nae more fighting! Fighting doesn't do anyone any good and besides, we're all friends here. Sort of."

Jack looked warily from her to his would-be antagonist. "Fine with me," he said. "Just tell Joe Frazier there to put his dukes down."

"Da," Lauren pleaded, "it's okay. There's no need to fight."

"Sand Toes demurred and reluctantly unclenched his fist. He could always make another.

"And speaking of fighting," Lauren asked Jack, "why did you whip on my uncles?"

Jack looked at her incredulously. "I know an enemy when I see one," he replied.

"On that, we agree," said Sand Toes.

THE CHRISTMAS RABBIT

"Da, you're not helping again," replied Lauren while trying to puzzle out Jack's answer. What had he meant about recognizing an enemy? Surely he had never met her uncles before. The rabbit's attitude was enigmatic at best. He gave away nothing. The picture-perfect puzzle, his mere appearance here, presented to Lauren the most challenging of riddles. She thought for a moment about her Ma, gone nearly two years now, and how they used to sit in the living room each morning discussing the possibilities of such beings as Jack while they waited for Da to return from trap-checking, sand-shoveling, or whatever it was that happened to occupy that particular evening's sojourn. While denying emphatically the existence of that other giver of children's gifts, Larraine Dawe had always steadfastly maintained to her daughter her belief in the existence of the Easter Bunny. It was one of the few sources of contention between her Ma and her Da. Each believed in the one but denied the existence of the other. Now sitting in her living room and confronting the reality of the fairy tale, Lauren wondered if in fact her Ma had ever believed in the Easter Bunny. It seemed more reasonable to assume that Larraine Dawe had instead presented a false front of belief for the sake of her daughter who because of her Da's crazy quest, was denied the pleasures most children enjoy which were brought about by the annual visits of that other giver of gifts; said giver being the recipient of Da's pent up antagonism and as such the object of Da's quest, was denied even verbal mention within the Dawe household. Larraine, when she'd been around, had no doubt wanted to shield her daughter from such madness. Therefore she feigned belief in the one because necessity demanded that for sanity's sake, she deny the other. What would she say now, Lauren wondered, if she could see that such posturing, done for whatever reason, had its basis in improbable fact? She'd probably say, "I told you so." This reminiscing, however, did nothing to relieve her current dilemma. "Why do you think my uncles are enemies?"

"It's as plain as the nose on the skinny one's face—who by the way, isn't skinny at all and whose nose isn't ordinary by any means."

"No," Lauren replied as her Da looked on in his usual state of confusion, "it isn't."

"Then my meaning," Jack continued, "should be just as plain."

It wasn't, but Lauren saw no point in giving that away—at least not yet. The rabbit had, for all appearances, settled down, and could even be said to have reached that emotional plateau were one might regard him as amicable. Lauren could see no percentage in ruining that mood by antagonizing him.

She took a drink of her own cactus juice, unfermented of course—Larraine, when she'd been around to do it, had laid down strict rules regarding underage drinking and Sand Toes saw fit to adhere to them—and wondered where from here, this conversation should proceed, and whether or not it was going anywhere at all. She determined that it did indeed have a destination but that said port of call could well end up being an anchorage embroiled in storm and hurt and so decided to tack off on a different course altogether. "So," said she, "my Da has got you digging holes and ditches, has he?"

"Yep," replied Jack. "Somewhere out in the desert though don't ask me to tell you where." He paused to look at Sand Toes. "He says that it's top secret, and besides, I could never find the place on my own anyway. Truth to tell," and again he looked at Lawrence, "I'm surprised that he can find it out there in that intractable wasteland. So like it as not, we'll most probably be digging somewhere else next week."

Lauren scoffed and laughingly shook her head. "Not likely," she replied. "My Da knows these lands and the desert which makes them up as though he were born to them—which he was. If he has a specific place for you to dig then dig there you shall." She paused for a moment to consider the implications of her last statement. Which implications were which and what kind of effect would they have on the lives of those she cherished? She was none too eager to find out but fretted remaining in the dark as well. The trouble you could see coming was the dilemma most easily dealt with. It was when trouble crept up from behind and blindsided you that you really found yourself in a pickle. Therefore necessity placed its demands upon her, forcing her to cast aside personal fear for the greater good. She had to confirm what she already knew in her heart. The lives of too many, not the least of which was her own, were in the balance. "So if you can't tell me where you're digging, could you at least tell me why?"

THE CHRISTMAS RABBIT

Again the rabbit looked at Lawrence, who in turn stared at the ceiling pretending indifference. "Nope, not for sure anyway. Your Da hasn't seen fit to tell me anything specific, but I gather from what he has said and more importantly what he hasn't, that it involves the culmination of some grand scheme long planned and prepared for. The pits and ditches remind me of traps, very large and very deep. So I assume that they're snares of some sort, but as to what sort, I'm clueless."

Lauren looked down at the rabbit in dismay as darkness wrapped itself around her soul, spilling concurrent fear throughout her. Chills ran up and down her spine, her forehead bled cold and clammy sweat, and she shook as though convulsed. So it was true then and her worry was well founded. Her Da, despite all notions of common sense, which she had to admit he had very little notion of at all, and regardless of prudence and courtesy to one's guests, which he never gave a damn about anyway, was attempting to enlist the Easter Bunny's aid in the silly and probably dangerous business of prosecuting his quest. She knew well enough what time of year it was and they were deep into the season when his sought-after prey, if such prey existed at all, was most likely to be found. Now armed with the knowledge that Jack and her Da were digging pits in her absence and that these pits, by the rabbit's own admission were trenches of enormous size and depth, she came to the conclusion that such holes could be only practical for the capture and containment of her Da's perpetual quarry. For the rabbit's sake, as well as her own and her Da's too, she had to have this out with the old man right now! There could be no delay for each day of hesitation brought with it the possibility of confusion and chaos as her Da's plans neared fruition. Even worse yet, what would her Da do if her mother had been right and so subsequently tempting fate Sand Toes strove to grab hold of his life's dream only to find that said dream was a dream within a dream after all and therefore impossible to capture and latch on to? Might not that realization send him over the edge forever? Surely it would! What would happen then? Would anyone lingering about be safe in the aftermath of Sand Toes's world as it came crashing down around them? Would even his Little La remain unscathed? Probably not. Therefore necessity demanded action, however unpleasant, and act she would! "Da!" she screamed at the top of her lungs, forcing Lawrence out of his reverie. "What is it, La?" he asked. "What be the matter with—?" But he cut himself short, thwarted no doubt by the look of fury that flashed from the hard and unyielding eyes of his daughter. "I...," he mumbled apologetically, "that is to say, we...or rather me, or most likely us—"

Gazing upward at his countenance, Lauren's laserlike eyes pierced his heart, laying bare at her feet all his plots and intrigues. He tried once again to explain but she cut him off. "I know what you're up to," she said. "It's as plain as day that you've enlisted Jack in this silly quest of yours. Well, I won't have it! We almost killed him once, but fate saw fit to give us a second chance. I won't tempt it again, do you hear me? And I won't let you tempt it either!" Father and daughter glared at each other while the rabbit looked on, trying to puzzle out for himself what was happening. Breaking the silence, he finally spoke up. "Don't I have any say in my own fate?" he asked. "As a player in this game, whatever this game is, shouldn't I be able to contribute to the discussion?"

A simultaneous "Nae!" was offered to him by both, with Lauren's slippage into brogue an indication of her anger. Jack shook his head and offered them a tired chuckle while he made a show of washing his paws of the affair and throwing in the imaginary towel. "Settle it yourselves then!"

"We will!"

Father and daughter were in a face-off where each contended with the other for possession of a hockey puck named Jack. Locking skates in the center of the rink, their sticks brandished, neither was about to skate into neutral territory and a way had to be found to break the ice. At last Lauren hit upon a plan. She examined it from all sides, picking it apart and scrutinizing every detail until finally pronouncing to herself that her plan was indeed good. And it was. That is, as far as plans go. And therein lay another of our tale's rubs for plans more often than not, never go far enough and rarely take into account all factors and contingencies that inevitably impact them. As is more likely they are woefully deficient in one facet or another,

THE CHRISTMAS RABBIT

lacking any number of proposed resolutions to the various and often numerous parcel of chance events, either foreseen or unaccounted for, that as a matter of course and inexorable in their own way, collide with the original intent of the scheme and in so doing, dash it to wee pieces. Thus most plans, imperfect as they are, are forever falling short of their promise. It's part of the human condition and we have so many examples from the long years of mankind's history to parade before ourselves that consulting even a partial list of failed proposals and those who drafted them, in order to compile a reference book, would be a lifetime achievement. Be that as it may, there were few reference books in the mine anyway. Sand Toes, on general principals didn't believe in them and therefore wouldn't allow most in his home. Having grown up in the desert practically on his own and in so doing amassing for himself and by himself his own store of knowledge however misguided and impractical, and furthermore having acquired such lore by the realization and correction of past mistakes made mostly from ignorance, came to view reference books and self-help manuals with a distaste that bordered on disgust. If you couldn't figure it out for yourself then it was the opinion or Lawrence Torrance Dawe that the lessons learned from such tomes were pointless and probably useless too. So left with no reference manuals to speak of or any other sources of expertise upon which to rely, Lauren took hold of fate's wheel and attempted to chart her course. But as the old saying goes, all things end up back where they started. The wheel turns on and on until it comes full circle whereupon despite one's best efforts to the contrary one finds that they've been running in place and that they're back at the beginning without having gone anywhere at all. Nothing changes as fate and destiny impose their will upon the universe, molding and shaping it as they see fit. The exact parameters and design of something so grandiose defies mortal definition despite all of our attempts to do just that. Yet the shape retains memory and purpose, for fight against it as we often will, pushing its envelope and seeking to make it over in our own image, it always snaps back to its original intent and form like a malignant rubber band.

    Despite many long talks with her Ma regarding this very subject, Lauren knew none of this for sure yet believed most of it anyway. Now standing in the living room and confronting her Da she thought back to all those evenings spent in her mother's company, each waiting for Da to return from wherever the desert night sought fit to send him. Often she'd just sit at her Ma's feet whilst Larraine regaled her with sermons and pronouncements about the nature of fate in general and its specific attributes when applied to the Dawe family in particular. Larraine would recline in her rocker, peeling beans maybe or just knitting and complaining to herself and to La as well that she was never going to get this purling business down despite the O'Toole woman's instruction. They'd discuss each other's day, how Lauren did at school and the progress Larraine and the others were making in their effort to locate Geronimo's lost mine. Eventually as always, the conversation turned to the Dawe family tree and the arcane history, which served as its root and upon whose bole the entire structure precariously balanced. From root to branch nothing and no one were ever at rest. The winds of fortune and fate blew and the Dawes, second, third, and fourth cousins all, twice removed or not, were blown with them. Larraine lectured her daughter in this vein daily. She wanted Lauren to understand that fate had a way of sneaking up on a person—especially in this family. Just look at how she met her husband! It was a theme much expounded upon and La T. Da paid attention to every word while determining for herself that fate was never going to get the drop on her. She'd be forever vigilant and ready! Larraine would have been proud had she been around to see the conviction her daughter displayed with regard to such matters while bitterly regretting in the same instance that there hadn't been enough time to instill in her the vital lesson about the many ways to skin a cat. There were at least fifty-three known ways to do so and Fate being familiar with them all knew a few that weren't even in the book. Therefore if your destiny is outrageous fortune and bizarre circumstance then rest assured that Fate will find a way to get you there and most likely make you pay for the ticket. It doesn't have to sneak up on you from behind although it excels in ambushing the unwary. It puts on a different face for each of us, never appearing the same way twice. Therefore it often stands in the middle of the road right in plain sight but unrecognizable nevertheless, unseen and virtually

THE CHRISTMAS RABBIT

invisible, until we stumble blindly into it despite all of our attention and vigilance. Fate is a bear trap always on the lookout for a misstep.

Lauren made such a misstep now unaware that as she did her feet were in fact taking the first steps upon a path from which there'd be no detouring. Yet who can blame her? Certainly not I. Even Larraine, had she been available to lay blame would have in this instance, found her daughter's logic flawless. It's what she herself would have done had she been around to do it. She'd always argued with Sand Toes about the legitimacy and pertinence of his so-called quest. He would defend both the means needed to accomplish the task and the end result that such fulfillment would bring when completion and success were realized. She would retort loudly that it was mere foolishness while keeping to herself the uneasiness that wormed its way quietly through her, freezing her tummy and making her nipples hard with worry as she contemplated her husband's expedition and the ensuing ramifications that would rain down upon them like falling rocks should he succeed. For although she had no faith in the quest itself, either in the reality of the undertaking's object or the right of anyone to pursue it, she realized nevertheless that if it could be done, if such a thing were indeed possible, then her husband, Lawrence Torrance Dawe, aka Sand Toes of the Apaches, was just the guy to see it through—and she wasn't sure she wanted either herself or her daughter to be in the general vicinity if and when he did.

In this ongoing debate with Sand Toes Larraine continually sought out allies who shared her opinions (they weren't hard to find) as she tried to enlist their aid in her attempts to convince him to cast such silliness aside. Those few who cared enough to take the time and offer some assistance were never listened to. Sand Toes invariably shrugged them and their suggestions off. These busybodies were after all, the same people who sought after hidden gold in the middle of the desert despite generations or ongoing failure and general lack of success. It was the opinion of Lawrence Torrance Dawe that you couldn't get much wackier than that. Slim and Jim never bothered to make the effort. So as a seeker of aid Larraine would well understand her daughter's desire to do likewise although like it as not the only 'likewise' available to Lauren was Jack who in this instance would likewise be like Larry and who would therefore not likely be much help in dissuading her Da whether Little La liked it or not. And had she even the barest inkling of Jack's attitude and predisposition regarding the matter she would have liked it even less—in fact, she wouldn't have liked it one damned bit! "Da," she said, "you have to tell him about the quest. He has the right to know and decide for himself about this foolishness."

Sand Toes looked at Jack, who merely shrugged and offered up his paws in a gesture of supplication. "He's a critter," said the desert man, "and critters nae have rights."

"He's more than just a critter," his daughter replied. "He's the Easter Bunny! Renowned amongst rabbits and men—he has more than just the right. He has the prerogative!"

Prerogative? Now what was that? Sand Toes had never heard the word before. It must be one o' those newfangled words that his daughter was learning at school. *Begorrah*, he thought, *aren't there enough words already?* Too many than was probably good for most folk—and yet with this overabundance of verbiage most people still had trouble expressing themselves and saying what they meant, thus giving way to the desire to invent more words, which only added to the confusion. He thought of asking his daughter the meaning of *prerogative* but didn't want to yield the advantage. How he longed for Larraine's dictionary. Sitting right there on the table it was the one reference book, along with her thesaurus, that he allowed in his home! All he had to do was reach for it. But that too, he reasoned, could be taken for a weakness. Instead he chose to attack. "Easter Bunny," he mockingly replied. "I thought you said he was a chicken!"

Lauren offered her Da a sour glare. "You said that, not me."

"Well, okay then," Sand Toes replied disdainfully, "so I did. The Easter Chicken he be, and Easter Chickens have nae rights whatsoever!"

"I'm not a chicken!" said Jack. "I'm a rabbit, both well-known and regarded, considered brave and the hardiest amongst the hardy. Chicken indeed! What do you take me for, some sort of 'fraidy cat? You think that just anyone who hops around on four legs gets to be the Easter Bunny? I assure you, friend, that it just ain't so! There's

THE CHRISTMAS RABBIT

hard training involved. Oodles of it! There's enforced marches, short rations, and little water. There's martial training! Most can't cut it and of the few that do, most never return. Believe you me when I say, I'm no chicken!"

Sand Toes looked on skeptically. Something didn't add up and he knew what that something was. For his daughter's sake he'd kept his silence, but now Little La and her charge were backing him into a corner and it was time to fight back. A rabbit Jack might well be and considering he was a talking rabbit that probably made him unique. But the Easter Bunny? Sand Toes had his doubts and thought that pigs with wings were much more likely.

"If ye be the Easter Bunny," asked he, "then why be ye here?"

"Jiminy Cricket!" Jack replied. "Haven't we been through this once before? I've already told you—I came to deliver to your daughter her egg!"

"In December?" asked Sand Toes. "I dinna know where ye be hailin' from, Jackie lad, but in these parts, Easter comes in April—so 'tis already well-nigh past or a long time comin' dependin' upon where in the calendar ye be standin' if ye take me meanin'."

Jack did, as he looked about helplessly, embarrassed to be called upon the point. "Well," he stammered, paws twitching and tail shaking, "it's kinda like this…you see…there's only one of us at a time, sort of, and there's lots of children and hardly enough eggs for the taking—let alone time enough to deliver 'em all. I have lots of stops to make and with nary enough hours in the day to make 'em! Plus, there's rivers to cross, cars to dodge, predators to avoid and a host of other unlooked for interruptions—any of which can set a poor rabbit back and put it behind schedule and ah, well …"

"Well, what," Sand Toes asked sharply, "just what are ye implying'?"

"I'm just saying that it takes time! More time than it used to, or so I'm, told. Therefore, Easter Bunnies don't strictly deliver in the Easter Season anymore. It's a year-round occupation!"

"But the eggs," replied Sand Toes, "surely they dinna last until next April?"

Jack looked at him out of eyes ridden with guilt. "Well," he stammered, "you see, I hide 'em well, and since no one bothers looking for them until early spring, they stay pretty much hidden."

"With all o' that graffiti on 'em? I'm doubtin' it!"

"Well, maybe a few get found," Jack conceded. "After all, I'm just the Easter Bunny, not Superman."

Sand Toes continued his skeptical appraisal. "And where di' ye get the eggs, I wonder?"

Jack looked from Larry to Lauren, hesitating before he replied. It wouldn't do the girl any good, he knew, to hear the truth of that! He'd have to try and talk his way around it. "You see," said he, "I acquire them."

"Acquire them?" queried Sand Toes. "What the hell does *acquire them* mean?"

"It means that someone lays them and I *acquire them*!"

"Who does the layin'?"

"Whoever."

"Whoever?" asked Sand Toes. "Are ye tellin' us that ye dinna hae a regular supplier?"

"Nae!" Jack replied sarcastically as he offered Sand Toes a venomous look. "I acquire in job lots, so I shop around for the best deals!"

Sand Toes stared intensely at the rabbit as if doing so would enable him to peer through his body to beyond the other side of his soul where Sand Toes suspected, lie the whole truths which made up the half-baked lies his guest tried to serve up. No one would ever accuse Mr. Dawe of being in any way worldly whatsoever and even he would admit if pressed on the point, that he didn't know cattle craps about how things were done beyond the borders of his own land but even so, to his own mind, the rabbits protestations didn't add up. He had to credit the idea of a talking rabbit—after all he had one in his living room. Furthermore, for the sake of Lauren, he could further postulate that a talking rabbit must indeed be the Easter Bunny. But a talking rabbit with the copious amounts of cash necessary to do all the *acquiring* needed to deliver ova to the millions of children that Lauren had told him lived beyond the borders of his

THE CHRISTMAS RABBIT

desert? That seemed to Sand Toes, highly unlikely. Where would any rabbit, Easter Bunny or nae, get that kind of moolah? How would he earn it and just as importantly, how would he cart it all around until he could find a vendor upon whom to spend it? It wasn't as though Easter Bunnies had checkbooks or credit cards. Surely, if he were *acquiring*, as Jack so vaguely put it, then he was doing so on a cash-only basis.

"Ye nae be tellin' the truth here, Jackie boy."

"Whaddya mean?" asked the rabbit. "Of course I'm telling the truth—rabbits never lie!" But of course he was fibbing. Lying and thieving have gone hand in hand since before even Olden Days and rabbits on down the ages have perfected both, turning each into an art form. Sand Toes, however, wasn't fooled. Not for a minute. "It be all posh 'n' nonsense, Jack," he said. "Posh 'n' nonsense. Where does a rabbit get the money needed to be *acquirin'* millions o' eggs? And how does he deliver 'em all, I wonder?"

"Millions?" replied Jack. "What are you talking about?"

"There be millions o' kiddies," Sand Toes shot back. "None o' em as sweet as me Little La here, mind ye, but dear enough, I suppose, and all deservin' o' an egg or two come Easter. So how about it? Are ye getting' to 'em all?"

Jack uttered a short laugh. Leave it to someone like this desert rube who rarely strayed far from his cave and never left the wastelands at all to make such naive and erroneous assumptions. "Of course not," the rabbit replied. "There's far too many of the little shavers out there to do that! Only the best of the best get my eggs—everyone else gets cheap forgeries, laid out no doubt, by parents too proud to admit that their children are anything more than merely ordinary. And as far as the best goes, well, it's only the best Christians at that. Not everybody's a Christian, you know." Sand Toes knew it but let him continue anyway. "There's Buddhists, Hindus, Muslims, and Confucianists," said the rabbit. "Not to mention Shintoists, Theosophists, Reincarnationists, and Scientologists, as well as Yogis, Jews, and out-and-out Pagans—and that says nothing of the so-called Christians themselves—why there's Baptists, Protestants, Seventh-day Adventists, Episcopalians, Mormons, Latter-Day Saints,

Jehovah's Witnesses, and more besides, with each of them thinking that they alone have the lock on the truth and what it means to be good—as if something as big as God could be held within the palms of their hands. All the while each of them denigrate the other and threaten those who choose to believe differently with an eternity in hell—and that says nothing about those mackerel-snapping Catholics! Boy, if ever there was a religious denomination whose children were less deserving of an egg come springtime it's those wine-guzzling sheep herders and their big boy over in Rome! Who is God anyway, what is he? There are other forces in the wide universe who rightly or wrongly, might attribute to themselves such a lofty title—I know, I work for three of them…although they've been somewhat silent of late."

"Where's Rome?" inquired Sand Toes.

"Over that way," Jack replied, pointing east, "thousands of miles away. Well beyond your desert and across the water!"

"Water?"

"Yes, the Atlantic Ocean! But that's hardly the point. Near or far, there are so many belief systems out there that one poor Easter Bunny going it alone could not possibly service them all or the petitioners who embody them. I have to draw the line somewhere and I say that with the exception of those mackerel-snappers, all the rest have their own holidays and their children can do for themselves! And as far as those damned Catholics go—they own half the world already and have a lien on most of the rest. The last thing their children need is one of my hard-to-come-by eggs!"

As Jack launched into his tirade about religions in general and Catholics in particular, Lauren felt herself bridle. Sitting there and having to endure his pompous oration she found that it was almost more than she could do to contain her anger and keep her peace. Far be it for anyone, she thought, to mock another's faith—there being so few faithful in any religion to begin with. Only God could judge what was in a person's heart. Only he had the right to determine which beliefs were valid and which were not. It was incumbent upon the rest of us, she felt, to be a bit more open-minded and tolerant of one another's beliefs. Why even the Apostle Paul, as her Ma had read to her out of the Good Book, when touring the kingdom of Greece and seeing for himself all the statuary depicting what were to him foreign and false gods, nevertheless had the good graces to compliment the locals on their abundance of religion. If it was good enough for him then it was certainly okay with her and should've been likewise for this damned rabbit, who being the Easter Bunny and therefore an ambassador of peace and goodwill, ought to have known better. Jack was concluding his diatribe on inferior religions, giving the Catholics what he felt was their just desserts, when Lauren, unable to contain herself any longer, exploded. "Wait just a darned minute!" she yelled at him. "Where do you get off saying such things? Have you ever been to Heaven? Can you judge?"

Jack looked at her confidently while smoothing down his fur. "Nope," he replied, "can't claim that I have—however I've been to hell, or at least its nearest equivalent. So I guess that makes me some kind of judge."

"Hell?"

"Yeah. Hell on earth. It's called Bayonne, New Jersey, and a more godforsaken place you'll never visit!"

"Oh please!" Lauren replied, her eyes rolling in their sockets. "You can do better than that!"

"I'm not kidding," said Jack. "Just ask anyone who's been there. They all say the same thing. Bayonne is hell on earth."

"We don't know anyone from Bayonne," Lauren said.

"Well, there you go," answered the rabbit. "How can you say that I'm wrong when you haven't even been there and furthermore don't know anyone who has? Don't I at least get the benefit of the doubt?" Jack offered the lass a smug stare, resting comfortably in the knowledge that he'd trapped her far more efficiently than one of her Da's own snares. "Well?"

Lauren returned his scowl before replying. "I suppose," she said, "that I must provisionally agree—about Bayonne anyway, since I've never been there and am not likely to go anytime soon. This religious bias however, smacks of prejudice and I think its unseemly, not to mention dangerous, in someone such as yourself. After all, mere Christianity, as a panacea to the world's problems, is hardly a universal cure-all, is it? A lot of harm has been done under that banner. I know. I learned about it in school!"

"And most of the damage," Jack replied, "was done at the hands of those damned Catholics! They've been pushing their beliefs upon everyone who's gotten in their way for almost two thousand years now and in so doing, wiping out indigenous cultures and belief systems as they go happy-assholing along while singing 'Onward Christian Soldiers'!"

"Not true, not true!" countered Lauren. "Just look at all the carnage wrought in settling this country. By and large that wasn't the Catholics. It was those Puritans and their damned ethic!"

"La, my love," interrupted her Da, "dinna curse. Yer dearly departed Ma always said that cursin' was unladylike, although that never seemed to stop her."

"Sorry, Da."

Jack looked up at the two of them while formulating his reply. How could he make her see his point? How to get her to see the truth about religions, Christian or otherwise? "In this particular place," he said, "and at that particular time, yes, it was the Puritans and their 'damned ethic' as you so quaintly put it. But this is only a small corner of the wide world and even on this continent the mackerel-snappers had first go at it. It was them that started the ball rolling here. After all, it was that Italian Catholic Christopher Columbus and his whore, Isabella, who 'discovered' this new world. And so began the enforced conversion and wholesale slaughter that enabled the Puritans to have someplace to go and exploit—and by the way, those Puritans were once Catholics themselves! No doubt, Puritans past have much to answer for yet the damned mackerel-snappers are pretty much running roughshod over the rest of it. Them and the Muslims. It as though they were flies, and the world was one big ball of cattle craps. But all religions have committed similar atrocities in the name of the 'truth' as they saw it, or the god they envisioned. I know, I've been out in the wide world and seen a thing or two!" This wasn't, of course, strictly true. Despite being the Easter Bunny and notwithstanding the inordinate amount of training and hardship he'd undergone in order to win for himself that lofty title, Jack wasn't nearly the world-class traveler that he made out to be—the world itself being much larger than his pretensions. But this little slip of a lass wouldn't know that either.

"Well, it doesn't seem fair," Lauren said. "Neither your religious biases or your elitist tendencies toward egg delivery."

"I can't help what you think," replied Jack, "but even the Easter Bunny has rules that have to be followed."

"Well, I don't like it!" Lauren replied sharply.

"No one asked you to," countered Jack. "You're entitled to your own opinion just like anyone else. Just remember that opinions are like cattle craps—most of 'em stink!"

"Whoa there, Jackie boy," said Sand Toes, his anger rising. He stood up suddenly and leaning over the rabbit, threatened him again with his cocked fist. "No one talks to me Little La like that and gits away w' it! Ye be apologizin' right now, ye hear? Or you 'n' me will go a few!"

Once again and as quick as a snake, Jack assumed the crane stance. Let the mad Irishman make his play! Lauren flung herself between the two. "Both of you sit down," she said, steering Jack into a neutral corner. "And you," she continued as she pointed to her Da, "back in your chair!"

Sand Toes did as he was told, but not before trying to defend his actions. He got no further than "But..." when Lauren cut him off. "No buts," she said. "Fighting never solved anything—regardless of whether or not the Puritans, the Catholics, or anyone else for that matter ever learned the lesson or not. There'll be no more fighting in this house—especially on my account!"

Jack looked up at her sheepishly. "So what happens now?" he asked.

Sand Toes offered him a wicked grin. "Well, I for one," said he, "think that we be ganglin' off course. We still ain't resolved the egg business." Again he looked at Jack, sizing him up like a shark eyeing a wounded tuna. "So it be thousands o' eggs ye be deliverin' instead o' millions—is that right?"

Jack shuffled his hind feet nervously before replying. "I suppose," he stammered, "though truth to tell, I never stopped to take the time and actually count 'em."

"But thousands—that be in the ballpark, aye?"

"I'd imagine so," Jack replied shortly, his eyes downcast with nervous embarrassment. "Yes. Now can we drop it?" He thought he'd steered them away from this divisive topic, but apparently Sand Toes seized upon such matters like a rabid dog biting a muskrat and wouldn't easily let go. "Not yet," the adopted Apache gleefully replied. "Thousands is still lots—a whole bunch o' lots! Where be ye getting' them from, I wonder?"

"I told you," replied Jack nervously, "I acquire 'em. The truth is, I buy 'em. Got me a chicken back on the farm that sells 'em to me wholesale."

"One chicken?"

"She works overtime."

"Baldersdash!" Sand Toes replied, his voice made flinty with sarcasm. "Ye'd need a barn full o' chickens and all o' 'em layin t' beat the band to git that many! Who supports 'em all, I wonder, and how are the eggs paid fer?"

Jack was trapped like a rat in a corner with no way out but to offer up the truth. The young lady wouldn't like it, that was sure. Oh well, he'd tried his best to avoid this unpleasant reality. If Lauren were forced to give up some of her misconceptions, heralding the end of childhood and innocence, that wasn't his fault. Lay the blame on her jerk of a Da who didn't know when to let well enough alone.

"I steal 'em! Okay?"

The living room lay in uneasy silence as Lauren sat there staring at Jack, crushed and disheartened. The bearer of good gifts was nothing more than a common thief, and she his accomplice for having succored him and received stolen property. "You make off with them?" she asked incredulously. "You pilfer them?"

Jack returned her look of disbelief with an indignant gaze of his own. "*Poach* would be more the word," he replied. "That's what you do with eggs—poach 'em! What did you think I did, lay 'em? In case you haven't been taught yet about the birds and the bees and by inference, rabbits, hares can't lay eggs, not being built that way. So yes, I poach 'em."

"Well, I never!" replied the exasperated little girl.

"I'll bet that's true," countered Jack, "but then you never had to. You're not under official edict to get the job done! One never knows the depths one is capable of sinking to until one is forced to swim in morality's fickle seas! Maybe it's about time that you grew up some, got out and saw a bit of the world!"

"Maybe," Lauren bit back, "but if that's the way the wide world turns then maybe, I'm better off confined to the desert. I don't want your ill-gotten egg and I'm sorry I ever accepted it, cracked or not! Whom do you steal them from anyway?"

"Robins, sparrows, starlings, or whatever bird is at hand or in the bush. Even chickens if some dumb farmer is foolish enough to leave the henhouse door unlocked. Although I prefer robins as their eggs come prepainted—saves time when you're on the road."

"I think that's disgusting," replied Lauren.

"Nobody asked you!" retorted Jack.

The trio offered each other the cold comfort of hard stares as uneasy silence spun away into nothingness. It seemed to the young lady that there was no more to say, at least on the subject of stolen eggs, and for that, Lauren was grateful. It was Jack who finally broke the silence. After all, someone had to, and since father and daughter seemed unwilling, Jack reluctantly put his best paw forward. "So," he ventured, "you two now know all of my deepest and darkest secrets. What are yours, and what's this mysterious quest?"

Sand Toes looked pleadingly at Lauren, unwilling to divulge to this stranger the object of his bizarre venture.

Lauren was upset with Jack for ruining her illusions about the nature of giving and gifts in general. The whole meaning of Easter Eggs and their talismanic symbolism had been shattered by his revelation regarding thievery. Deep in her heart, she wanted to punish him on behalf of all the unborn flocks of sparrows, starlings, chickens, and especially robins, who because of his misdeeds would never live to see the light of day. There was a thing in the world called justice, and Lauren was of a mind to see that it was enacted to its fullest with regard to this thieving little critter. However, she also realized that caught up in the throes of self-righteous anger a zealot, taking matters into her own hands, might take such retribution, whether the guilty party deserved it or not, too far. Allowing Jack to hop blindly into her Da's outrageous enterprise might well be an example of that. There were axe murderers out there, she knew, who didn't merit that kind of misery. So she nodded to her Da, indicating that he should proceed.

"Are ye sure, La?" he asked. "After all, the beastie's nae more 'n' a common thief and therefore canna' be trusted."

"There's nothing common about me," Jack asserted. "I'm a rare thief indeed, a pilferer and poacher of the most extraordinary means!"

Sand Toes looked at him sideways before continuing his plea to Lauren. "Why, he nae be even family, and even yer uncles dinna know the whole o' me plans."

"True," replied his daughter, "but they're not part of the plan, and he is. Just tell him, Da, and we'll let him decide for himself."

"But he may say nae, lass, and I'm thinkin' more and more that I'll be needin' him before it's over."

"You'll just have to risk it," she replied. "After all, fair is fair— even for those who aren't very fair themselves." She offered Jack a searing appraisal, under which he withered. He didn't think that it would matter to him one way or another what this child's opinion of him might be. Yet much to his surprise, he found that it did. For ages past, children all over creation had always adored the Easter Bunny, looking forward to his coming and counting the days until his impending arrival. Now he confronted a child who wanted nothing to do with either himself or his sordid business. If word of this got out to the wide world then where would he be? Up the proverbial creek without a paddle, that's where. Only this creek would be no mere slipstream, it'd be the equivalent to the Colorado. He'd be ruined and with a reputation irreparably damaged he'd be unable to complete his quest. What then? He'd be forced to return to his warren, alone and forlorn, only to face the anger and derision of the Mad Rabbits. Worse yet, he might be turned out alone to face the wide world by himself. What then? Although they hadn't been seen for years upon years now and therefore existed in rabbit lore more as matters of myth and legend than of actual fact, there were three certain someone's, he knew, who, upon hearing of his downfall, might just decide to pay him an unwanted visit… And though it was certainly no fault of his own that the task he'd been given was what it was, this knowledge did little to ease his conscience. He had, after all, volunteered for the job—in fact he'd competed hard against others of his kind in order to be awarded it. That the roots of such a desire and the position it led to lay so far back within convoluted time and myth so as to further absolve him from personal guilt did little to ease his conscience either. Therefore he was more than relieved when Lauren turned her accusing eyes away from him and brought them to bear upon her Da who nodded his unwilling acceptance. "Would ye like t' hear a tale?" asked Sand Toes.

The rabbit was in no mood for tales—especially a story told by Sand Toes whose fables, he knew, were littered with arcane symbols and confusing metaphors while being chock-full of morals which could be barely understood, let alone agreed to. But he reasoned to himself that anything was better than once again withering away under the laserlike scrutiny of the madman's daughter. "Sure," he reluctantly replied. "Why not?"

"I was born in the desert," Sand Toes began. "Me, Ma, and Da were likewise sired. I dinna know this then o' course. In fact, I dinna know lots o' the tale until I married me sweet Larraine. She it was, who after marryin' me and movin' into me cave, went through old manuscripts and bits o' parchment left by me parents and so pieced together fer me the tale, tellin' me fer certain who I was and who I was descended from. I barely remembered any o' it, and even today most parts o' the story remain cloudy and dim, castin' mere shadows in me memory. But what I do remember, I'll be relatin' t' ye now."

*****

Sand Toes was born on the night of the full moon, which had nevertheless eclipsed, and was christened Lawrence Torrance Dawe. His great-grandda was indeed the brother of that same Great-

Granddaddy Dawe, who purloined the treasure map from the corpse of Horse Feathers, Indian con artist and entrepreneur, which supposedly pointed the way to Geronimo's lost mine. It was after the two great-grandas died, and their sons took over joint generalship of the Secret Society that the United States tested its first atomic bomb somewhere out in the Nevada desert. One son took it as a sign from Heaven to return eastward to the barrios and slums of New York City while the other regarded it as an omen to stay put. It was from this latter brother, his granda, that Lawrence Torrance Dawe, later to be known as Sand Toes of the Apaches, was descended. The one brother who returned east did so with the map, and the other remained with all of his followers, directionless and without a clue as to how to proceed. But since neither brother nor those who followed them were very adept at map reading anyway, perhaps the lack of such made little difference. Be that as it may, one left and one stayed and the one that stayed progressed, some might say descended, from just plain flakiness to out-and-out lunacy as did those who elected to remain with him. This wholesale lunacy grew exponentially as it passed on to their descendants, the first generation of Dawes born to the desert—a harsh and forbidding wasteland where no white man in his normal mind had any business being anyway.

By the time his grandparents had raised children of their own and passed onward, the few remaining members of the Society left in the wastelands were first and second cousins all. They all had the same last name, and many of them shared similar first names too. Had their surnames been Lapp, they could've all passed for Amish—certainly they were inbred enough to carry it off. Out of the remaining group that now barely numbered twenty, Sand Toes's Da chose as his wife, his own second cousin, Lulu Ludlow Dawe. The name suited her to a tee because true to her handle, Lulu was indeed a lulu. Daddy Dawe loved her dearly, and to give him due credit, he'd chosen as his bride the most comeliest and rational of women left to him. There can be no doubt when it is said that Lulu was a knockout. Just like Larraine, her later third cousin twice removed would one day come to be, Lulu herself was a throwback and a carbon copy (at least in looks) to a certain meretrix from days of yore. There was no

THE CHRISTMAS RABBIT

doubt about it. Just as there can be no doubt when I say Lulu was the most rational of women left to choose from that such rationality was merely a matter of degree—which in this family only meant a slightly lesser degree of insanity, hardly to be measured and barely to be noticed.

Not every Dawe in the remaining twenty were enamored with Daddy Dawe's choice of mate, and most of the grumblers had accused him of incest, although by this time and with this particular family, such choices had become part of the family crest. The truth of the matter was that most of the other Dawes, male and female alike, were eyeing Lulu greedily for themselves. They wanted her and wanted her badly. Songs were sung by all and sundry, extolling her beauty and fulsomely fulcrumed figure. But Daddy Dawe, believing that incest was best, stuck to his choice. There was screaming and shouting by all involved with harsh words and curses bandied back and forth. Finally Daddy Dawe and Lulu each pointed to the mark—that strawberry-colored blemish shaped like an eagle's talon that both shared. Others in the twenty were likewise tattooed but not only did Daddy Dawe and Lulu share the mark, but each sported it in the same place, on their big left toe. This, they claimed, was a sign from the fates that they should be joined in wedlock, and no one there was going to dispute that. Still they grumbled. "Ill fortune will come o' it," they said, "just ye wait and see!" The couple were resolved nevertheless in their march toward matrimony and when the rest of the family considered their determination to go through with it, threatened to leave them alone in the desert high and dry. When they consummated the marriage, the remaining Dawes did just that, marching off into the wastelands en masse, only to wander about aimlessly until they all perished in a sandstorm, proving to themselves at least, that trouble did indeed come from such close unions. Daddy Dawe and Lulu knew nothing of their cousins' misfortunes. Left alone, high and dry, it was just the two of them out there in the wastelands and despite being mapless, neither wanted to give up the search for Geronimo's lost mine. Each felt that the mine was near and that discovery was merely a matter of time. They stumbled upon an abandoned mine shaft and, thinking that they'd hit pay dirt, settled in and set up shop. The shaft proved to be barren and empty but the setback only strengthened their resolve. Where there was one shaft there were bound to be others and the couple used this abandoned one as a base camp from which to set about and explore the surrounding area in the hopes of discovering more. They were simple but happy and that's more than can be said for most folk, incestuous or not.

The year was 1953 when Lulu gave birth to a son, naming him, of course, Lawrence Torrance Dawe—just like his Da before him, his granda before him, and his great-granda before him. There was such a thing as tradition and this generation of Dawes aimed to chart their courses by it! The birth itself came as a surprise, both to Daddy Dawe and especially to Lulu, who thought that her swelling belly was merely a manifestation of trapped gas, pent up and locked deep within her bowels. She hadn't broken wind for nearly nine months, and a constant diet of lizard and old toad are enough to constipate anyone as well as cause a daily occurrence of morning sickness, so who can fault her? Certainly, Daddy Dawe held her blameless, doting as he did not only upon her but upon their newborn son. And what a son! He was crawling within two months and walking within six. When he cried, his screams were louder than the desert winds, causing minor sand slides in the neighboring dunes. His feet, overly large for someone so small, were already callused and covered with respectable corns. He outgrew his shoes faster than Daddy Dawe killed the number of lizards necessary to tan leather and make new ones. Looking at him, both parents, taking pride in their progeny, knew that their son was destined to do great things.

It was the winter of 1960. Larry was seven, and yule was fast approaching when the Dawes met a stranger wandering alone in the desert. The first person that the family had seen in almost ten years, his name was Bob, and he was a beatnik from San Francisco who'd come out to the wastelands on a pilgrimage of enlightenment. The beatniks, forerunners of the hippies, had descended upon San Francisco like horseflies to a pile of cattle craps so that by the autumn of 1960, they were thicker than molasses and suffocating each other with their mere presence and body odor until most could barely breathe for lack of oxygen and clean air. There was talk amongst the beatnik community of branching out, of getting the hell out of San Francisco and seeking enlightenment somewhere else since there seemed to be so damned little of it in the city on the bay. Most opted for San Diego or San Clemente since San seemed somehow so important, but Beatnik Bob, as he introduced himself to the Dawes, was having none of that, simply striving for sans beatnik altogether and so headed straight for the desert. If there was enlightenment to be found anywhere, he felt that the desert with its vast amount of sunshine would surely be the place in which to find it. He got more than he counted on, for just like our Rabbit of Later Days, he got himself lost in the wastelands, wandering around aimlessly and enlightened, while at the same time dying of moisture deprivation. When he stumbled into the Dawes' mine shaft, Beatnik Bob was a shadow of his former self, emaciated and wild-eyed. He babbled constantly and loudly—so loud in fact he was nearly screaming. Thus Daddy Dawe and Lulu heard him coming long before they ever saw him. He spoke to those who weren't there, arguing vehemently with them in between singing duets. Daddy Dawe and Lulu, thinking that Beatnik Bob's behavior was all well and proper, took his ranting and raving in stride and as a matter of course. They had, after all, been engaging in similar activity for years. Here finally was a brother after their own hearts! They took him in and under their wing, nurturing him back to health with lots of moisture and old toad. Bob took to their ministrations as if born to them. By December's onset, he'd progressed to a semblance of his former self—which only goes to show just how far he'd deteriorated. His blonde hair, cropped short to compliment his goatee, had regained most of its luster and his brown eyes sparkled like polished onyx. Mass helpings of moisture and old toad served to him three times a day, as Lulu was a stickler about proper meals served in appropriate amounts and regular servings, had helped to put some of the weight back on him that the desert burned off. He no longer talked to those who weren't there although he kept up the duets since the Dawes told him that they sounded so good—especially the unseen singers who were doing the harmonizing, "Wow, like groovy," he'd reply to their praise, or "Cool, man, and real solid," whenever either Dawe would ask for an encore. Sometimes Daddy Dawe and Lulu would join in with Beatnik Bob and the disembodied voices to create four- or five-way harmonies, or they'd just hum a tune while Beatnik Bob scatted along beside them.

"Doowahpahbahdoowopdoowah."

The Dawes were never sure what all that "doowahping" meant but dug that crazy beat nevertheless. Lawrence, only seven, looked on confused. "Da," said he, "what does *doowahpahbahdoowopdoowah* mean?"

"I dinna ken it," replied the elder Dawe, "but I knows that I dig it! Ask Robert."

Little La did as he was told and was informed by the beatnik that it meant "groovy, solid, and just so full of cool and soul that it was ready to burst." The boy looked around apprehensively as if expecting *doowahpahs* and *doowahs* to come exploding out of thin air, which they often did, so much in fact that he took to ducking and dodging them in order to avoid being hit.

One morning, while Daddy Dawe was out moisture prospecting and Lulu was in the kitchen preparing lizard eggs for breakfast, Little La asked Beatnik Bob what was to him a question of utmost importance. "Mr. Bob," he inquired, "do you believe in Santa Claus?" They were two weeks away from Christmas, according to Daddy Dawe—although in reality the holiday was two weeks gone by (the Dawes, as well as being lousy readers of maps were poor judges of the passage of time too), and Santa, Daddy Dawe had told him, was going to bring him a new pair of shoes, which as usual he needed badly.

"The jolly old elf?" replied Bob. "Of course I do! That's one cool cat, man, real cosmic and karmic, you dig? Brining all those presents to all the little dudes and dudettes the world over, I think he's like, supremo!"

"Me too," said Larry. "Da says that he'll be bringin' me some new shoes before the year's out."

"Then no doubt," replied Bob, "you'll have new boots on your feet come January!" Lulu brought breakfast to the table, admonishing them to eat their lizard ova. "After all," she said with a cackle, "an

THE CHRISTMAS RABBIT

egg a day keeps witches away!" Then she laughed to herself, leaving Beatnik Bob to wonder what she meant.

Late that morning Daddy Dawe returned bearing a strange plant that neither he, Lulu, nor Larry had ever seen. Bob, however, burnt-out beatnik that he was, recognized it immediately. "Oh, too cool, man!" he shouted. "Can you get more?"

"Sure 'n' begorrah," replied Daddy Dawe. "I found plenty o' it. But what is it, I'm wonderin'?"

Beatnik Bob stared at him in disbelief. "You mean to tell me that you've been living out here all this time and don't know what this is?"

"That's what I'm meanin'," replied Daddy.

"It's peyote," said Bob, "and just too cool! I was wondering what we were gonna do for kicks—now I know. Too cool!"

"Peyote? What be peyote?"

"Mother Nature's acid, man!" came the fervent reply. "Too cool and real hep. Let's chew some buttons now and get real high!"

"Acid?" asked Dawe fearfully, afraid of getting scalded. He quickly dropped the plant while looking uncertainly at Bob. "Acid? Be ye sure?"

Beatnik Bob laughed out loud, nearly splitting his sides in good humor. "Oh man, I'm sure," said he. "This is just too far out!" He paused to count the buttons on the plant. "Yeah, man, it's acid," he continued, "but not like caustic acid. It's tripping acid, real groovy and mellow. It'll send you places that you've only dreamed about going to. It'll float you on a cloud, man, like a soft summer breeze."

Daddy Dawe had his doubts. Summer breezes, at least those that he'd become familiar with, were anything but soft, let alone groovy and mellow—whatever the hell *they* were. Summer breezes in these parts tended to be harsh and hard, wearing away the skin off one's body and sucking from it, precious moisture. By now, Lulu had joined them, curious about the plant too. "Tripping acid?" she asked. "It be sendin' ye on trips?"

"Only the best," replied Bob. "Only the best!"

Lulu, who'd spent her entire life in the desert, considered the notion of going on a trip as something to look forward to. It would be grand, thought she, to get away for a while and take a small vacation so long as she was assured of returning—after all they still had a mine to find and plunder. "How far will it take us?" she asked.

Again Bob laughed. "That's the beauty of it," he said. "No one knows. It's different for everybody. Maybe you'll fly to the moon, tasting colors and seeing music on the way. It's real bitching stuff! You'll soar!"

Tasting colors and seeing music. Lulu liked the sound of that! Still there was a bit of uncertainty yet to be resolved. "Would these be solo flights," she asked, "or could we all fly together?"

"We'll make it a party trip." Bob replied jovially, "and all fly together!" With that, he began culling buttons from the plant and lining them up for consumption.

"What about Little La?" asked Daddy Dawe, "Can he come a' flyin' too?"

Bob looked sadly down at Lawrence. "Oh no," he admonished his parents, "this trip is strictly for adults—no kids allowed!"

Lulu looked fearfully at her husband as the thought of abandoning their child played itself out in her imagination. Left alone, he would surely fall victim to scorpions, pumas, and sidewinders. No journey was worth that. "But we canna' just leave Little La!" she remonstrated. "One o' us has t' stay behind and look after the lad!"

"Relax," Bob said soothingly. "We're going on a trip but we're really not going *anywhere*. We'll be right here with him the whole time. It's all in the mind, man, all in the mind."

Both Daddy Dawe and Lulu looked at each other doubtfully. It was beyond either to understand how they could go on a trip and remain in the same place all at the same time. Still, if Bob said that it was so, they mutually reasoned, then it probably was. After all, he hadn't lied to them yet.

From the plant that Daddy Dawe had brought back, Bob was able to cull thirteen buttons. He divided them evenly, keeping the odd one for himself, which he promptly chewed and swallowed.

"Now this is what you do," he said. "Just follow me and keep eating these buttons. Soon you'll be in La La Land!" He popped another in his mouth, chewing and swallowing it while waiting for the Dawes to do likewise. When they complied, he ate another, and so did they.

"They taste a might bitter," observed Daddy Dawe.

"They're supposed to," instructed Bob. "That just means they're fresh and potent. Man, we're in for the trip of our lives!"

The trio had consumed all thirteen buttons—four apiece—plus Bob's remaining dividend and yet no trip seemed imminent. "I dinna feel as if I'm going anywhere," said Lulu. "I think that I'm stayin' right here, like it as nae."

Bob softly chuckled. "Give it time, love," he said. "Give it time. All good things come to those who wait. That's from the Bible, if you can dig it, and bitchin' groovy."

"The Bible?" asked Daddy Dawe. "What be that?"

"You know," replied Bob, "the Bible—Adam and Eve and all that!"

"Adam and Eve? I canna' say as I ever heard o' 'em."

"Living way out here," observed Bob, "I'm not surprised."

The trio sat facing each other in a triangular circle, waiting for their trip to commence while Larry, alone in a corner, stared at them apprehensively. What was this trip they were taking, and would they be gone long? If so, would such a sojourn interfere with his plans for Christmas? He hoped not. He'd been looking forward to Christmas all year and was getting downright antsy with anticipation as December waned. He'd be sorely disappointed if he had to miss it on account of his parents' travel plans. He hadn't missed one yet and had no intention of doing so now. Every year he and Da would wait up on Christmas Eve for the arrival of that jolly old elf, Santa Claus, because Da had told him that Santa brought presents to all the good lads and lassies the whole world over, and Little La knew himself to be one good lad. Hadn't his parents always said so? But each year he had fallen asleep before the jolly elf arrived only to awaken the next morning to discover that the treats and snacks he'd so carefully laid out the evening before had mysteriously disappeared and been replaced with presents. *But this year*, he thought, *will be different*. He was seven now—practically a grown-up and fully capable, he knew, of lasting the whole night and staying awake in order to greet that holiday reveler upon his anticipated arrival. Would Santa bring his reindeer? Of course he would! How else could he get around? After all, the North Pole was a longs ways off, or so said Daddy Dawe, and Santa needed his reindeer like miners needed pickaxes. Each was a mighty tool in the hands of the other. Both, Larry knew, extended the reach of the respective user and allowed him to get the job done. The fallacy in Little La's logic, of course, was that there had been generations of Dawes before him, all armed with pickaxes, shovels, miners' helmets, lanterns, and various hooks and ladders—yet despite the copious amounts of armament and the collective extension of reach that such armament allowed, they had yet to slay their collective dragon. Little La knew none of this and even if he'd had wouldn't have cared one way or the other. All he knew was that Christmas approached and that Da told him Santa would bring him a new pair of shoes. Everything was ready and had been taken into account. All the preparations had been made, including the Santa Snacks, chiefly composed of Lulu's famous Toadhouse Cookies, which had been fermenting in a vat for weeks and were nearly ready. They were a favorite of Daddy Dawe and Little La too. He was hard put to keep from eating up the entire bunch but he dearly wanted those shoes! Again he thought of the reindeer. Flying caribou! What a wonder they must be. If I stay awake all night to greet him, will Santa offer me a ride in his sleigh? That, he knew, would be better than a pair of shoes any day! "Da," he tentatively asked, "how many more days 'til Christmas?"

"Four," Daddy Dawe replied. "Now shut ye trap! I be waitin' fer me trip."

"Lawrence Torrance Dawe," admonished Lulu, "dinna ye be talkin' to the wee lad so!" She gestured to Little La, inviting him to come forward. When he did, she lovingly took him in her arms, holding him gently against her ample bosom. "Well, what di' ye expect?" replied Dawe. "The little blighter's been buggerin' me for weeks about it! If I told 'im once I told 'im a thousand times—Christmas will come as sure as the Fourth o' July!" And it would. Unfortunately, for all concerned, Daddy Dawe and his lovely wife would not be there to greet the Advent, having missed it already by nearly two weeks and since they were about to embark on an ill-conceived trip from which there would be no returning their poor timing and inadequate travel plans are cited here only as a footnote.

Beatnik Bob began to sway where he sat, humming off-key and staring vacantly at his navel. "I'm folding into myself!" he exclaimed with joy. "I'm turning inside, out. Just too cool!" Then he began to laugh like a loon, and it seemed to Little La, sitting there in his Ma's lap, that he'd never stop.

Daddy Dawe knew nothing of folding or even spindling for that matter but was aware nevertheless that something was indeed happening. The panorama of the desert which lay before him exploded in a riotous orgy of color, blending like taffy and shifting like quicksand until reds and greens ran together, making themselves into pastel blues, while yellows looked on impotently and screamed in silence. The sky itself seemed to press down upon him while the earth rushed up at his feet. A high-pitched whine invaded his hears like the swarming of a billion bees, causing him to tremble and shiver. "I be buzzin'!" he cried out. "I be buzzin'!"

"Of course you are," replied Bob. "It's acid!"

"It's God-Almighty strange, is what it is," said Dawe.

"Yes, isn't it?" agreed Lulu, chuckling. "But pleasant enough just the same." The peyote was beginning to course through her, playing upon her imagination as though it were a finely tuned Irish harp. Although she saw no music nor tasted any colors, elves—which, being of Irish descent she deemed leprechauns, appeared magically before her, introducing themselves as Pixie and Dixie. She made small talk with them, reasoning to herself that if she were able to disarm them with her charm they would think they'd made a new friend and, lead her to their gold, which she could steal when they weren't looking.

The wee folk spoke of ingots and nuggets. Lulu cleverly stuck to the weather. They spoke of bullion and plate. Lulu complimented them upon the finery of their attire. They concluded with rainbows and pots of gold that lay at the far side of them. Lulu pretended polite indifference. *What rainbows?* There were no rainbows in the desert. Rainbows needed air saturated with moisture and the desert atmosphere had too little of it to spare for such extravagances. Yet when she looked off to where Pixie and Dixie were pointing, there it was slicing an arc through the clear blue sky. And what a rainbow! Although Lulu had never seen another with which to compare it she was sure nevertheless that this one was uniquely singular, both in dimension and hue. It stood out garishly against the desert skyline as it shimmered and pulsated in Day-Glo colors, most of which she'd never seen before nor even heard tell of. The bow itself, which began at the top of a fifty-foot butte located out in the gypsum plain some thousand yards from her doorway, traced an unending arc through the heavens as it climbed ever upward. She'd heard in her childhood that the other end of the rainbow was always beyond the horizon and perhaps this one concluded in the same fashion as well, but one could never tell by looking at it. Rather than end somewhere in the vague distance it seemed to go on forever.

Magical folk, like elves and leprechauns, with their greatly enhanced abilities and generally broader worldviews find ordinary folk like you and I and even eccentric folk like Daddy Dawe and Lulu to be dull and boring company and so tire of us easily whether we're tripping on acid or stone cold sober. Therefore it wasn't very long before the two sprites grew bored with their conversation and made ready to leave. "We hae t' be ganglin' along and get back t' our gold," they impishly, said. "Follow us if'n ye dare!" With that they hopped off and skipping along their merry way, paused every twenty paces or so in order to turn about and offer Lulu come along gestures. Lulu wasn't going to let an opportunity like this pass her by. "Da!" she exclaimed.

Daddy Dawe turned his lamp-lit eyes to her, as did Beatnik Bob. "What is it, my love?" he asked, as if from far away.

"Look!" Lulu replied eagerly. "Di ye not see 'em?"

"See who?" In truth, Daddy Dawe saw no one out there. Neither did Beatnik Bob. Each was lost in their respective heads or what was left of them as the peyote fried their minds. In a sea of sand, Daddy Dawe saw the ocean rolling in. Comber after comber broke with a roar upon the imaginary beachhead of desert sand which lay before his feet. Foam and spew of the purest white splayed itself around and about him in an unending procession of miraculous moisture.

THE CHRISTMAS RABBIT

Beatnik Bob, looking at various cacti, saw saxophones and trumpets instead, all spitting out music while swaying to a groovy beat that was just way too cool for him to actually grasp and take note of.

"The leprechauns!" cried Lulu. "The leprechauns and the rainbow! Di ye not see 'em? Over there. Over there!" She pointed the way. Once she did the men's respective visions fell apart, shattering like fine crystal fallen to the ground as they broke into shimmering flakes, only to fragment into desert dust, whereupon they were replaced by Lulu's fanciful reverie. Now all three of them saw the leprechauns and the rainbow to which they were headed. "Too cool," screamed Beatnik Bob joyfully, "just way too cool!"

"Yes," Lulu merrily replied, too overjoyed at the prospect of gold to be overly concerned with their guest's use modern slang in her son's presence. "Da," she said, "they're headed over the rainbow t' count their gold! I know—they told me so!"

"Gold?" asked Dawe. "They hae gold?"

"But o' course they do." His wife replied. "After all, they be leprechauns, aye?"

"Aye," her husband eagerly replied. "We must be ganglin' off after 'em. A leprechaun's gold be a treasure trove indeed!"

"I'm coming too," said Bob. You could buy lots of enlightenment, he knew, with a third share of that treasure. Lots of enlightenment and all of the mescal, LSD, peyote and high-tension booze that one burnt-out beatnik could ever hope to consume.

So the trio left Little La at the mine with instructions to stay put until they returned and then set off to give chase. The leprechauns seemed none too eager to get away for they paused and often came to a full halt, singing out encouragement whenever one of the trio stumbled or faltered. "This way!" they laughingly shouted out. "This way!"

At the base of the butte the leprechauns pulled on their noses and simply floated up the face of the cliff, reaching its summit with very little effort. Daddy Dawe, Lulu, and Bob tried to do likewise but quickly discovered that acid trip or not, such magic as the elves employed was not available for their use, and so had to painstakingly climb up the cliff face the old fashioned way, employing hand and foot. It was a dangerous ascent with disaster awaiting them in every handhold. Often the trio despaired of ever reaching the top while worrying needlessly that the leprechauns would have magically disappeared once, and if, they did. But eventually they scaled it and found that their worries were baseless and without substance. Their magical guides were awaiting them. "This way!" they again shouted. "This way!" Then they ran up the rainbow as quick as lightning and vanished.

It took less than a nanosecond for the trio to decide what to do. There was gold waiting for them at the other end of the rainbow if they were brave enough to follow and anything that a midget could do they were sure to be able to do better. "Last one up is a pile of cattle craps!" cried Lulu, taking off in hot pursuit with Daddy Dawe and Beatnik Bob following close at her heels...

The trio plunged off the cliff and plummeted to the ground below totally unaware of the danger racing up to meet them. From the mine's adit Little La looked on in horror, an unwilling witness to their untimely deaths.

They all landed headfirst in the sand below, buried up to their hips with their legs lightly swaying and their feet barely twitching. By the time Larry reached them, all bodily motion had stopped. They were as dead as doornails. Lawrence left them where they protruded out of the ground and returned to the mine to mourn their passing. He cried for a day and a half and then returning with his Da's shovel, buried them. But he left Beatnik Bob as he was with his head in the ground and his feet pointing skyward, in order to punish him for the misery he'd wrought.

Alone in the desert, Little La wondered what to do and what would become of him later. Da had shown him the rudiments of moisture prospecting and how to set a rough trap. But was such knowledge enough, he wondered, to enable him to survive? Would he be able to eke out an existence using the minimum of lore left to him? If not, then who in all this wide wasteland would come to his aid and rescue him? No one, that's who. He would die here—just like his parents, only more slowly and miserably. In the depths of despair and at the lowest emotional ebb to which he was capable of

THE CHRISTMAS RABBIT

sinking, Little La suddenly found that his soul, which had heretofore been empty and bleak, was suddenly filled with light and new hope. Christmas was only two days away! Santa Claus, when he came, would surely rescue him once note was taken of his pitiful condition! Yes, Santa would save him!

Little La waited up through Christmas Eve and all through Christmas day, patiently anticipating his rescuer's arrival. But Santa never put in an appearance. Maybe he's been delayed, thought Larry. Maybe ole Rudolph's nose burnt out, and so they've lost their way. Sure, that was it. I'll wait another day. And so he did. And another. And another. And another. By New Year's, Little La had to accept for himself the fact that Santa wasn't coming this year, if ever. It seemed that Santa only looked after good little lads and lassies who had parents. Orphans obviously, no matter how needy or how well behaved, were of little concern to him. Little La couldn't know that not only had Christmas passed him by but that New Year's Day had done likewise. He didn't know that his parents had been lacking somewhat in their ability to track time and were therefore continually out of date. In fact, Santa, lost in the desert too, had overflown their mine some fifteen days ago and the reindeer, downwind of the Toadhouse Cookies, caught scent of them and so stampeded in midair, taking off like bats out of hell in a harness. Therefore it would be years before this deficiency regarding holidays and the dates upon which they fell, was corrected and Larraine would be the one to do the correcting. But by then so much time had passed and so many bad feelings had accumulated that such a correction ended up making little difference one way or the other.

With the misadventure of that long ago Christmas an uncontrollable hate for that jolly old soul who abandoned lost orphans infused itself within Sand Toes, becoming deeply ingrained and cancerous, spreading from head to toe and filling him with an unholy desire for revenge, which would become the mainstay of his existence out there in the great wide empty, providing him with the energy and determination necessary to ensure his survival. He had to live, he reasoned, in order to be assured his day of reckoning.

*****

"And that," said Sand Toes to Jack, "be me tale." He looked at the rabbit keenly, taking in his measure. "Now that ye be in the way o' knowin'," he continued, "will ye be o' the mind to hinder me in achieving me goal?"

"Hinder you?" cried Jack. "Let me get this straight—you tell me that you're after the Tortoise, Old Slomoe himself, and you want to know if I'll hinder you?" Sand Toes, unsure of who or what Old Slomoe or the Tortoise might be, nevertheless nodded his reply. "Hinder hell!" replied the rabbit gleefully. "I'm only too happy to help!"

BOOK 3
Olden Days

And so Jack Rabbit, found guilty by jury and condemned by witches, took to delivering eggs as penance. First however, he had to get 'em and since he couldn't lay 'em—despite a prodigious amount of initial effort, stole 'em, instead. What else could he do? Sentence had been handed down and punishment executed. Being a jackrabbit he occupied one of the lowest rungs upon life's ladder wherein he was prey to just about everything everywhere, except of course Santos, who only prayed that he'd seen the last of him. Added to this misfortune was the cheap trick played upon him by the Rabbits of Influence in their abandonment and subsequent banishment of his person—an effort to avoid for themselves an embarrassment of their own making. He therefore found himself helpless with no manifest destiny or subsequent change jingling in his pockets as he no longer had pockets. Thus he complied, however reluctantly and not without protest, to official decree.

Santos, however, was let off the hook. But it wasn't as if The Powers That Be didn't want his hide too. They would have done him in twice over just for the pleasure of doing so, but since they could think of no punishment more fitting than suffering through daily bouts of his wife's questionable cooking, saw fit to let him go. There were murderers out there who didn't deserve that. Besides, Helgayarn, Brunnhilde, and Betty kept hoping that Old Slomoe would lead them to his snot-nosed little sirelings who'd wreaked such havoc with their recipes and in doing, nearly killed them too. When he did find them, who knew? They knew, that's who. They'd settle with those little truants and their parents too. The Powers That Be's lives would span nearly forever so they could afford to waste time daydreaming and indulging themselves in poor poetry and even baser forms of self-gratification as they waited patiently for the karmic wheel to turn its course and provide the proper moment to strike. No doubt the dumb farmer was just keen enough to realize they were keeping watch upon him from afar, explaining his reluctance to bring his kiddies in from the cold. Sooner or later he'd get around to feeling that the heat had died down and when he did he'd make his move—then watch out!

The Witches assumed again, and we know what happens when we assume, don't we? It happened to them too. In fact, it happened to them a helluva lot more often than it happens to us so we shouldn't feel too badly when we find ourselves in the same boat—and don't go telling anyone that I told you so either because even in these days, even in Nowadays, the Witches still have their ways of finding things out, and I wouldn't want it to get back that I've been criticizing them!

Upon completion of the trial Santos took it upon himself to infer that his release only provided further proof of the moral correctness and justifiability of his war with the rabbits. After all, it was Jack who'd been punished while he had been turned free. It stood to reason therefore that the forces of law and order were on his side. Nothing could've been further from the truth. They were not on his side but rather on the sidelines, keeping an eye on him and waiting for him to screw up whereupon they would descend upon him like three tackles on a tight end.

Santos realized none of this. He simply didn't know where his children were. He'd gone and lost them in the previous uproar and boy howdy, wasn't the wife peeved about that! It had after all been a simple plan and arranged in haste, so when he searched the forest or rather what was left of it, looking high and low for trails of breadcrumbs, radishes, and even rocks, he found no sign, nor heard the slightest rumor of, Junior and Laddie. It seemed that they had disappeared off the very face of the earth. He searched for his children continually and when he wasn't searching went around bragging to anyone who would listen that he'd gotten the better of all of them, both rabbits and witches.

The Powers That Be were not amused; however they let him continue such ranting, recording each insult for posterity and stor-

THE CHRISTMAS RABBIT

ing them up like squirrels gathering nuts for the winter. They were almost eternal, had nearly forever, and so could afford to be patient. In the meantime there was nothing for the trio do but keep one eye on him and the other eye on Jack while making sure that the rabbit went about the business of carrying out his sentence. This however, proved harder to accomplish than any of the threesome were willing to admit for although Santos remained blissfully unaware of the trio's scrutiny, Jack saw right through 'em. He knew he was being watched by the three hawks and so moved to upset the Witches collective apple carts. He'd win in the end, he knew. As sure as Cattle made Craps! In the meantime however it was safest to obey the law and carry out his sentence—although not necessarily in the manner the Witches assumed he would and certainly not where they could see him…

He began his circumvention by digging for himself his own system of interwoven and underground information networks composed of secret runs and tunnels, which surfaced among dead logs throughout the forest or what was left of it. He hid these so well that even other rabbits were unaware of their existence or that they were being used as such. In undertaking this endeavor he had the reluctant but nonetheless resigned assistance from his newly acquired wife Nutmeg, who now being a pariah herself, had no one else to turn to and therefore little choice. At first she tried seducing her way back into the comfortable paws of those infamous Rabbits of Influence but they promptly, although grudgingly, threw her out. There were too many skeletons in their respective closets already as well as stolen vegetables in their pantries, to run the risk of sheltering her and so after carefully considering her offer for all of two seconds decided to put as much distance between themselves and the tramp as possible and in so doing, avoid potential scandal.

Jack tried to do likewise but upon reflection came to the conclusion that it was either Nutmeg or no one and Nuts, as he would playfully come to call her, was better than no one at all, although it would be some while before he could bring himself to trust her far from his sight. Even when digging, he took extra precaution to ensure that he was always looking over her shoulder.

When he wasn't busy keeping an eye on her or digging a tunnel himself, Jack took to spying on chickens and other various fowl in order to get a handle on and feel for, this whole business of egg laying. Hawks and sparrows, eagles and chickadees, he took to watching them all, fearful that he might miss an important clue. *Damned witches and their protracted sentences*, thought he. Why not make his penance something that he could accomplish and why not punish the Tortoise too? Why was Old Slomoe let off the hook? Surely it was as much Wideass's fault as it was his own for not sharing in the first place. It would've been fairer, Jack knew, had he been sentenced to delivering vegetables instead of eggs. He knew nothing of ova other than their general shapes—and as for producing them, he was totally at sea. Of course, he knew nothing about producing vegetables either, but at least with the latter he was accounted an expert, if only by himself, at stealing them. Santos, he knew, would soon plant another garden to replace the one destroyed in the previous disaster and then there would be vegetables for all and sundry. They'd be much easier to get than eggs and more wholesome too. There weren't many out there, Jack knew, who could eat eggs all day long and stay happy and healthy while doing so. For one thing, an egg is an egg no matter who lays it. Chicken and chickadee alike, Jack knew that once you cracked the shell and scrambled the yolk they all tasted pretty much the same. And any egg, he realized, was bound to be a crack-open can full of cholesterol and other offensive stuff that would over time, harden arteries, causing strokes, heart attacks, and generally sour dispositions. Vegetables, on the other hand, came in a variety of shapes, sizes, and colors, could be counted upon to have distinctly different tastes and were almost guaranteed to be cholesterol-free. There'd be no hardened arteries there, thought Jack, and everybody's mail would move just fine. But what could he do? It seemed that nobody cared for him or his opinions, being content to merely get their eggs and scramble 'em. So he watched and spied and took notes. He observed egg laying and production in all its various stages. He took note of the many procedures employed by any number of avians of different wing and feather and found that the methods used by each were as similar as two peas in a pod. They all went at it the same way. Maybe,

THE CHRISTMAS RABBIT

thought he, eggs in birds were akin to kidney stones in everyone else and thus were the result of improper diet. He got himself a journal and wrote down his observations on what the various cacklers, croakers, and crooners were ingesting in an effort to discover for himself clues to egg laying hidden in avian eating habits. When he had a cookbook of sorts, filled with the most often-used and best-loved recipes for birds of a feather, he started eating what they ate in an effort to ovulate. He went on his infamous *crash diet,* or so it came to be called by folk who were around back then, because no folk, whether two- or four-legged, bald-headed or bare-breasted, had ever heard of such a silly thing as dieting—except, of course, when invited to the Santos's for dinner. Then it was diet for your life. The whole idea of not eating, of starving oneself when there was food to be had, was an alien concept. Back in Olden Days, if you were smart you ate what food you could get when you could get it as an assurance against those times when there was none to be had and most folk thought that those times occurred often enough with The Powers That Be so mixed up in everything; also everybody, whether they were two-legged, four-footed, bald-headed—or all three together—knew that one's diet dealt with what one ate. Thus *dieting*, by inference, must deal with what one is eating. How then, could something that meant eating also be used to describe the act of not eating? It was a nebulous concept at best, would obviously not work and so, thought everyone, doomed to failure. What few friends Jack had left—and they were acquaintances really, tried to engage him in conversation regarding these matters in order to better understand for themselves, his intentions, methods, and modus operandi. In the wake of the uproar there was little trust to be had and that's probably why most of them tried to draw him out with their impolite inquiries. But I'm certain that one or two succumbed to simple curiosity. After all, no one who couldn't lay an egg had ever attempted to do so anyway. It was one of the premier endeavors of those times and if successful those in the know knew that it would change the face of the evolutionary pace forever.

One of those taking an active interest in Jack's experiment was the Shoe Lady, who kept close scrutiny upon him as she contemplated whether or not egg laying was any easier or less painful than natural child birth, which through uncounted repetitions, she'd come to loathe and despise. Even the Witches were keeping a close eye and jotting down notes. So folk from all over questioned him long and hard in order to better understand this newfangled concept called dieting. It soon became apparent to most that though the word *dieting* meant not eating, usually for the purpose of weight loss and was therefore a misnomer since a *diet* dealt with what one ate and how was one supposed to lose weight if one continued to eat in the first place—that *dieting* as Jack meant it, had nothing to do with weight, either in the gaining or losing. As near as they could tell it was a weightless *diet* with no clearly defined goals, poorly planned, and thus bound to flop. All it dealt with was changing what one ate and replacing it with what someone else ate. There was no gram or calorie counting and there was no mention made of whole-wheat bran whatsoever and who in hell would expect a *diet* like that to work anyway? Changing what one ate just to change what one ate was a stupid idea, and most folk back then knew it. There was a natural balance to things back in Olden Days, despite The Powers That Be and their many attempts to tweak it. Folk who were smart respected that balance and paid it the attention it deserved. Certain species ate certain things at certain times and even certain subspecies of same species ate certain subthings substantially. No one but people ever messed around out of their own food group. Everyone had their own nutrient sources and liked it that way, competition in the food chain being stiff enough as it was. Such a system ensured that the chain was unencumbered by weak links, such as wolves eating all the chicken food instead of the chickens themselves and only if they could get 'em. Only people, the uncultured buffoons that they were, took to invading another's food group in order to purloin nourishment. Meat, both red and white, which they dined upon for the sole excuse of having two kinds of wine; vegetables, fish, and a variety of nuts, berries and grains. It seemed to most folk that the slobs would eat anything. Worse yet, not only did they eat out of their food group but they went foraging for food out of their own areas as well, often importing such smarmy items as lobsters from Maine or

THE CHRISTMAS RABBIT

black caviar from the Baltic Sea. No one, even in Olden Days, liked slobs—especially when they put on airs and tried to show off. But Jack wasn't people and it caused quite a stir that he should want to act in the remotest way like them. Some felt the whole ordeal was merely a ploy on his part, a ruse affected in order to accomplish something else entirely. They came to the collective conclusion that as such there would be no *diet* and therefore no *crash*...and yet that's exactly what happened. It was inevitable and Jack should've known better. But it was his first attempt at *dieting*—it was anybody's first attempt, at least as they understood him to mean the word, and like his long-standing enemy Farmer Santos, he was winging it, which would've been okay had he been a bird in the first place. After all, birds wing it all the time—in fact, that's all they do when they're not busy laying eggs. But Jack wasn't a bird. He was a rabbit and there were other rabbits out there who would've argued that. Be that as it may, accepted as one of their own or not, rabbits cannot eat bird food. A diet consisting mostly of worms, slugs, ticks, and raw fish does not agree with them. In fact it does just the opposite, waging inside them what could best be described as gastrointestinal guerrilla warfare.

The crash occurred when Jack's bowels locked up and imploded, causing rabbit turds, which were normally hard, round, and easy to deal with, to come ushering out of his anal orifice like the Erie Canal, compelling those nearby to duck and run.

As Jack contemplated his insides, acutely aware of the complex intestinal intrigue to which he'd subjected himself, the agony was such that it certainly felt to him as though he were laying eggs, so despite the prodigious cramps, gasses, and subsequent discomforts, found himself elated as he thought he'd hit upon the looked for solution. Still, after culling through the craps nary an egg was found.

After having nearly half his body weight simply "run away" (and believe you me, half his weight was a lot to a rabbit like Jack and if you don't think so then try losing a proportional amount of weight yourself and see how well you do), he came close to dying. But it was Nutmeg, ever practical, who later that same day hit upon the solution. Cleaning out their hole after a decidedly heavy day of craps, she paused for a moment, torn between utter bewilderment and dumbfound resignation, listening in as her husband, lying curled, cramped, and dejected on the cold earthen floor, uttered weakly to himself that the explanation to egg laying had to be lying somewhere, hidden perhaps in a missing avian recipe which he'd failed to take note of.

What happened next—and I'll be the first to admit that the upcoming events are based at least in part, upon my own conjecture—is that Nutmeg reached her nut, having attained what anyone, I suppose, would say was the reasonable limit in what a hare like her was expected to handle from a hare like him. We guys, well most of us anyway, know that we're not always the best catch that you ladies might've reeled in. Most of you no doubt, feel from time to time you could've done better. And the fact that from time to time you might even be right doesn't help to ease your aggravation the least little bit. When you're angling, however, sometimes you can't land the biggest or the brightest fish and simply have to settle for the one that bites. That's us. Love us or leave us, we're the only choice you have. And as one of us, I feel that I can speak for most of us when I tell all of you that from time to time you're no bargain either. Such assertions however, even when mentioned with the best of intentions and the sincerest of gestures, coupled too with heartfelt devotion honestly expressed, only lead to further arguments amongst us regarding division amongst the sexes and whose role is what and why. We have our opinions and you have yours. It's best, I think, if we leave it there. I am willing to admit however, that I, and by inference us, are not always as attentive to you as we should be. Perhaps we're not always as emotionally open as you would prefer, walling ourselves off as we often will with our petty male distractions and chauvinistic attitudes, thereby erecting barriers all of you perhaps, find sometimes difficult to breach. To give you all your due I'll further admit that sometimes we take it a step beyond this and rather than build barriers which you're forever trying to knock down, we end up digging frigging moats instead. They're wide, these moats, and deep, except of course where there are dangerous shoals and oh God, there are plenty of those. You'd almost think that these moats were, in fact, bays with names like Narragansett, Biscayne, and Fundy. Treacherous seas for

THE CHRISTMAS RABBIT

sailors such as yourselves to chart a course through. We fill 'em with our sharks and squids, the psychological and emotional reptiles of our own frustrated male egos, which we deny having in the first place, and then dare you to swim across them. If you do then that's where you'll find us, drinking beer, watching contact sports, farting out loud, and telling bad jokes—often about you. That's just the way we are. There's no helping it and there's no changing it either. We're often late for dinner, we forget anniversaries and birthdays, we frequently don't shave and most of us dress like slobs once you get to know us. The best of us are content to let you handle the majority of the house work if you're willing, even if *you're working* which most of you are Nowadays, although most weren't back then. Which brings us back to Nutmeg because none of us have ever argued with any of you that we as us, got a better deal than you as you, when whoever it was apportioned out the divisions and roles to those allotted sexes which we avoided arguing about earlier. No matter how poorly any of us has ever behaved toward any of you now or then, not one of us could ever argue convincingly to anyone including ourselves, that you as you, got the better of that arrangement. In other words we as us, have to collectively admit that in the division of the sexes and with the exception of seahorses, that you ladies got shafted. Someone was paid off, I think. Maybe even The Powers That Be. But here nevertheless was Jack, making himself sick and making a mess as well and all the while pissing and moaning about how hard it was to lay eggs—as if anyone in their right mind would want to. Nutmeg went off her deep end and started screaming at him. "That's the biggest load of cattle craps that I've ever heard tell of," she yelled, "except for the load lying at your feet which I'm cleaning up now—and you're full it!"

It was true, Jack knew. He was full of it. So full in fact that he felt ready to burst and knew that he was not likely to rid himself of this burden anytime in the near future. Groaning, he replied, "But Nuts, what's there to do? I have to get eggs somehow. I haven't even laid my first clutch yet and already I'm a month behind on deliveries."

"You idiot!" replied Nutmeg. "Do what comes naturally and stop being so birdbrained! Has it ever occurred to you that even if rabbits could lay eggs that it would be the female who did so? That's true for the birds and the tortoises and they lay eggs all the time. So don't go digging for yourself holes where there aren't any carrots because that's just bound to fail. Go out and steal 'em!"

In truth, it had not occurred to Jack that being a male, his efforts to bear fruit might end in failure. "What you just said about birds and tortoises," he asked, "do you mean to say that I should be getting Slomoe's wife to do the laying?"

"Did I say that, you fool? I said, steal 'em!"

"Steal 'em?"

"Yes, steal 'em." Nutmeg scathingly replied. "What are you, deaf? You can't be deaf with ears like that!"

Jack looked at her through languid and tired eyes, shivering as another bout of cramps and nausea wracked his aching torso. "No," he replied weakly. "I'm not deaf, just sick. Really sick."

Nutmeg's reply was to offer him a sarcastic chuckle as a measure of sympathy. "Well, I'm really sick too," she said. "I'm sick of all this crap!"

"And well you might be," he replied, "but I don't know anything about stealing eggs—vegetables are my forte."

Nutmeg displayed a decidedly wicked frown. "You don't have a forte, Jack," she said. "While I'm down on my knees trying to clean up this mess, I'm still waiting for my carrot! Besides, stealing is stealing, whether it's vegetables, eggs, or whatever. The same basic skills apply. The only type of theft that's different is white-collar crime, and since you have a gray collar, you needn't trouble yourself about it. Anyway, to be really good a white-collar, crime you need the use of a personal computer with many gigs and lots of RAM, and they haven't been invented yet. Just stick to what you do best and steal us some eggs. I want those witches off my back!"

"You and me both."

"Then do it!"

Jack considered her demand. "Okay," he replied, "I will."

*****

THE CHRISTMAS RABBIT

For Jack, the hardest part of egg thievery was scaling the trees in order to reach the nests and purloin the hidden treasures within. He was however fortunate that the violence of the preceding storm, which came to be known by everyone everywhere as *Hurricane Junior* was so great that it toppled all but the hardiest of timber forcing most birds whether they liked it or not, to build their nests closer to the ground. Thus very little climbing on Jack's part was actually required. Some slight shinnying on a rare occasion in order to reach the top of some fallen log or toppled trunk made up the extent of his day. Still shinnying is not something that rabbits do well and much practice was required of him to master the talent. Jack understood as well that just because there were few trees left standing at the moment did not mean that on some future date they wouldn't spring up again like lice—and who knew how long he'd be doing this? Perhaps forever. So he sought out the various scalers and ascenders and learned from them what skills and lessons they were willing to impart. From mountain climbers to social climbers, he left no source untapped. Each had their own theories and instructions and Jack partook of them all. From the mountaineers he learned the value of conditioning and training; from the evolutionary climbers he learned the art of patience and how to deal positively with negative setbacks when such climbing led to dead ends; from the corporate climbers he learned to show no mercy to those whose shoulders he stepped upon while engaged in his endeavor; and from the social climbers he learned never to look back from whence he came until at the end of his training, having mastered for himself a wide variety of skills and disciplines, was accounted by all who gave a damn about such things, as the most skillful scaler anywhere…and still most eggs were to be found close to the ground.

Once a handout is given and once a person or people become used to getting it, such a thing tends to snowball and gathers up a life of its own as it feeds off its momentum, growing exponentially. So it was with Jack and his eggs. Despite their collective desire for omelets most folk living back in Olden Days never believed for a minute that Jack and his ova would actually become a reality. The majority took it to be just another foolish pronouncement on the part of The Powers

That Be, which probably wouldn't work out nearly as well in practice as it did in theory. So they were collectively surprised when it came off even better than planned—at least at first. But folk took their eggs for granted rather than putting them in a shoe and beating them and so ended up with them all in one basket. In other words, they got greedy and not being satisfied with just one egg, demanded more. "Three eggs," they said, "are the minimum needed to make even the merest of omelets. Three eggs, some diced ham, peppers and onions, and maybe a little rosemary or thyme for seasoning."

This lack of appreciation did not, of course, occur all at once or altogether. Even snowballs take some finite amount of time to gather momentum and roll. But after a couple of years of single-egg delivery, the recipients of Jack's efforts became dissatisfied with their lot as they demanded of him even more eggs and the garnishes to go with them. During a spare moment—of which he had few, Jack took the time to file a grievance with The Powers That Be, complaining about the varied injustices inherent in the whole affair and pleading for redress, whilst humbly asking them for a ruling.

The Powers, in true witch fashion, promptly wrote him back, basically telling him to get lost. If people wanted more eggs for their children, then it would just have to be his business to get them, wouldn't it? They ended their letter by rudely telling him not to bother them anymore with such petty cattle craps as they were all extremely busy at the moment and couldn't spare the time to trouble themselves about eggs or those who ate them. Betty, of course, post-scripted an enthusiastic, "Yah!"

Resigned to the inevitable, Jack reluctantly accepted the fact that he would just have to make more and larger deliveries. By now he and Nutmeg had produced two litters of their own and were well on the way to producing a third. Jack took his two eldest sons from the first litter, Peter and Cottontail, and set about training them in the arts of egg thievery and delivery with the idea that once they were fully trained they could help him out with the family business and in turn train others to do likewise. He had it in mind to turn over the whole affair to his progeny and retire early. It wasn't too long before he had a staff of twenty, and then fifty, and then even a hundred—

THE CHRISTMAS RABBIT

and he needed every one of them. Why the Shoe Lady and her feral breed alone—a mob nearly in and of itself, accounted for over half his gross. Other folk were multiplying too and Jack found that he needed every egg that he could lay his paws on just to keep pace with the birthrate—which, of course, caused trouble…

For the sake of peace and harmony, as they'd had their own encounters with The Powers That Be and were therefore sympathetic, birds throughout the forest, when first told of the trio's pronouncement regarding eggs and those who were to receive them, were willing to turn their collective heads the other way and let a few youngsters go by as Jack initiated his efforts in thievery. However, when their eggs began disappearing by the nest load they began to feel that they were being unjustly burdened and so complained, both in chorus and loudly.

But as with so many other social programs promulgated and promoted by any number of bureaucracies, triumvirates, and politburos on down through the ages, the "Great Egg Scramble," as it came to be called, conceived and hatched by The Powers That Be, ultimately proved itself to be flawed and with a shell half-cracked, in that one small portion of the population was made to suffer for the greater good of everyone else. Being witches, Helgayarn, Brunnhilde, and Betty made great bureaucrats and politicians too, being blind to their own shortcomings from as long ago as Way Back, and like all influence peddlers and pencil pushers anywhere or anywhen, refused to see the deficiencies in their enacted pronouncements so long as their plans worked on paper, were statistically correct, and were capable of execution. If a policy met these criteria then common sense input on the part of the constituents upon whom it was fostered went largely unread and mostly ignored. The wheels were turning so roll baby, roll.

The birds cackled, cawed, and screeched until they were blue in the beak and all to no avail. The program was working, at least for most folk, thereby proving that criminal rehabilitation was indeed a viable option that laws promulgated could in fact be enforced, and the decree would stand as written thank you very much. If the birds didn't like it why they could just fly south for the winter! But thanks to The Powers That Be and another decree of theirs, namely seasons, so many birds were in fact already availing themselves of this option that it was not looked upon by the few that remained as a reasonable redress to their grievances. "Pretty birdbrained," was their collective opinion... "This plan is for the birds!" they would often claim when gathering in flocks to discuss their lot. Not finding any redress in legal recourse the birds took the law into their own talons and began to resteal the eggs stolen from them. This proactivity on their part cut down the amount of ova available to Jack for delivery. Each child's ration was reduced from three eggs to one and a half, until once again their parents began to complain about the size of omelets.

It was Cottontail, Jack's number 2 son, who in his spare time amused himself by painting various abstracts with multicolored dyes, that hit upon the solution that would return the status quo to stat. The birds, he realized, were reclaiming their eggs nearly as quickly as he and his family could steal them and would continue to do so unless a plan could be devised to confuse and befuddle them, whereupon the birds of a feather, flocking together, would most likely give the whole affair up. Cottontail reasoned that if a method could be found for disguising the eggs so that it became impossible to tell who's was whose, then it was likely that no bird would claim any egg for fear of raising a chick that wasn't its own because as everyone knows chicks in their teenage years are nothing but trouble.

Not being able to tell one egg from another and therefore which chick was which, Cottontail correctly assumed that the whiners and cacklers would soon chicken out like the chicken shits they most certainly were and cease their efforts. To this end he began disguising the stolen booty by painting abstracts on their individual casings while teaching his brethren to do likewise. As anticipated, the birds gave up their efforts to reclaim their lost children and took to roosting closer to the nest in an effort to safeguard their progeny. What wasn't expected however, was the popularity these newly disguised and highly festive ova earned for themselves. Folk just loved 'em, as most being dirt poor to begin with could never have afforded such fancy artwork had they gone to the gallery to actually buy it. Now they had the comforts of art and culture added to the convenience of home delivery along with a readily available food supply that cost them nothing. They began thinking of themselves as quite chic in their good fortune and this newly formed opinion of themselves caused Jack to become more popular with the two-footed crowd than he'd ever wanted to be. The snowball was indeed rolling and all he could hope to do was balance himself atop it while at the same time attempt to juggle his newfound celebrity status. It became so bad he soon found that he couldn't even step out of his burrow without someone suddenly approaching and demanding of him either an egg, an autograph, or both. In a desperate attempt to appease his adoring public Jack took to autographing his eggs even though he was neither responsible for their production or the subsequent artwork with which they became emblazoned and world famous. No one cared. All anyone knew or gave thought to was the fact that his eggs were suddenly the rage and the "in" thing and that having a Jack original meant that you were somebody. Everybody wants to be somebody, that's only natural—and there isn't anybody who likes being nobody. Especially Farmer Santos, who despite all his bragging now found himself in a position in which he was almost totally ignored. Being maligned and made fun of, he thought, had been bad enough; but to be totally disregarded was even worse. Folk knew he liked to talk about how he'd gotten the best of everybody, inferring as they listened that such statements included them too, but Jack, true heart that he was, kept his opinions of himself to himself while delivering eggs to all and sundry—and such eggs! Had anyone ever seen their like? Certainly not! Folk in the know knew even then that when Faberge's came into existence they would hardly compare in form or beauty to these pieces. And what did Santos bring? Nothing but braggadocio and oft-repeated stories, most of which were boring, and all of which people had no real use for or interest in anyway. And not even a single parsnip to go along with them to ease the disappointment and despair of being forced to listen to twice-told tales. No one much cares for twice told tales despite Hawthorne's success with them (And even his weren't all that popular until after he was dead so what good did they do him?) since having been told twice, everyone knows how they're going to end. People need drama and suspense.

It's true today and was especially so back in Olden Days when there was so little going on in the way of diversion—unless of course you counted the miscues of The Powers That Be whose diversions tended to be so disastrous that folk by and large tried to ignore or forget them entirely. But now they had ongoing diversion and drama in the regular and routine delivery of Jack's eggs. If Santos couldn't at least match the effort let alone surpass it, then why should they bother giving him the time of day? He had no more vegetables, thus the reasons for his silly war with the rabbits were nullified and he therefore no longer provided even good sport. Folk were completely bored with him and even Mrs. Santos, despite her short stint as serving wench for The Powers That Be, found that she was shunned by all including her quilting bee who otherwise would've been hungry for juicy tales regarding the Witches.

Time passed and the couple's situation declined from bad to worse although truth to tell the fall was short. Something, Santos knew, had to be done. A plan was needed to stifle Jack and his ever-increasing popularity. But what? As usual the farmer hadn't a clue.

It was Helgayarn, Brunnhilde, and Betty, The Powers That Be, who got him off his duff and moving. They too were not happy with Jack and his unlooked for success. They had planned on him to fail, for of course, rabbits cannot lay eggs and therefore, they reasoned, he would be forced to purloin them. They were just waiting for the recipients to get used to the idea of receiving them on a regular basis, knowing that as the population increased and the demand for them grew, at some point a level of threshold would be reached which would be impossible for the rabbit to surpass. Those who lived upon the far fringes of the forest and beyond would certainly get left out of the rabbit's loop and as a result, fail to get their ova. Then would come the complaining for sure. This would give the trio a chance to step in and a) restore order by ensuring that deliveries continued to remain routine and regular and in doing, gain for themselves the goodwill of the masses, and b) get a second chance to punish that rabbit for stealing—once for himself and once for that silly farmer who in and of himself was too damned opprobrious and deplorable to condemn and castigate. So they were totally unprepared for Jack's success. They figured on him to steal an egg or two and then get caught—just like he did at Farm Boy's. If Old Slomoe could get the best of him then surely the birds, when given their chance, would carve him into mincemeat. What they forgot to take into account was that Santos had help, namely them; and during that incident Jack was thinking with his penis. Now Nutmeg was the only one who did any thinking with that and she had her own thoughts on the subject. That was fine with Jack. She was the expert anyway.

The Witches also counted upon the birds, with their beady little eyes and their snooping and gossiping ways, who were always into everybody's business, saw everything, and took delight in spreading a tale as far as their puny little wings could carry it, to spy out Jack early in his endeavor and rat him out to the world. But Jack had paid attention in climbing school and all those hours of tutelage at the hands of experts who for whatever their reasons had nothing better to do than teach Jack how to get one rung ahead of the other guy, had apparently paid off. These heightened and sensitized skills in combination with his own natural talent for sneaking and thieving had made him virtually undetectable, thus enhancing his chances for success. Also he took to wearing camo fatigues in order to remain well hidden. His interwoven underground information network composed of secret runs, tunnels, and dead logs scattered throughout the forest was well hidden and established. He was firmly dug in. His sons and daughters, little egg thieves all, were being guided by his firm paw and led by him personally—and he and Nutmeg were pumping them out faster than he could train 'em. Cottontail and Peter were experimenting with waterproof dyes in an effort to deliver eggs that wouldn't run when left outside in the rain. He'd learned about this mistake soon after Cottontail started "graffitiing" his eggs with watercolors and since then had his two eldest firmly applying the paws of technology to the problem because no one liked a runny egg. Everybody knew that once eggs started running you had the devil's own time catching them. Often they ran all the way home and you then had to resteal 'em. So a dye that resisted running was important and therefore had to be manufactured if their enterprise were to continue as a successful endeavor. Jack had no doubt that his boys would succeed. His two eldest, Peter and Cottontail, were geniuses and were acknowledged by all as the very Einstein's of rabbitry. Jack knew that they could show that wisenheimer Junior a thing or two if they ever met him and no matter what one had to say about Nutmeg there was no denying that she produced fine children. So Jack was confident that the solution to the runny eggs would present itself, and from there his warren could only go up.

The Powers That Be, however, were intent on bringing him down. Basking in the limelight of unlooked for success and popularity, the trio felt that Jack was getting a bit too cheeky to put up with for too much longer. Imagine him autographing his eggs like he was some famous artist of the surreal and abstract or worse yet, some twentieth century movie star and mercy my—that was still ages down everyone's collective calendar pages! Until then, such idolization and fan adoration, thought the Witches, belonged solely to them. In the eyes of his recipients, he and his deliveries were the first and only of the trio's schemes to ever come off as expected, and even better than expected at that. Since no plan before this that they'd ever devised came off half as well as promised, folk on the receiving end of a job well done were certainly not going to give them credit for one now. Instead they gave all their applause to Jack and his rabbits, who in receiving it whether reluctantly or not, were in effect stealing the Witches thunder as readily as they made off with eggs.

Helgayarn, Brunnhilde, and Betty spent agonizing days and weeks discussing Jack and his unlooked for success and what could best be done about it. Thought was given to killing him and his entire family—after all, there were plenty of other rabbits out there. They knew therefore that they could get away with it and not be accused of practicing genocide but in the end realized that success would leave no one but them to make the deliveries and none of the three wanted *that*. Simple maiming was put forward as a possible solution but in the end was rejected for the same reason. What they needed was a way to short-circuit the hare's operation while being able at the same time to distance themselves from the sabotage. That way when the whiners started to mumble and grumble as whiners could always be counted upon to do, the trio could look them boldly in the eye and say, "Get lost—it's not our problem!" But with everyone so enamored of Jack and his deliveries, it was proving difficult for them to enlist anyone of any worth who could get the job done. Thus Santos.

*****

One day, some years after Hurricane Junior, as Santos was in the midst of doing battle with a crop of weeds intent on choking the life out of his newly planted garden, three visitors approached him in secret in order to make him an offer. Mrs. Santos was away for the day, having received an engraved invitation to attend a gathering of the world's most famous chefs. It was a fake. Not the invitation, mind you—that was real enough, having been printed on bona fide parchment with gold ink and raised letters, and having been delivered by UPS—but the gathering itself. It was a ploy on the part of The Powers That Be, who wanted to get Santos alone and who for their very lives, had not the courage to face another ordeal at the hands of his wife and her dubious culinary prowess, for surely had she been present she would've offered them refreshment as befitting a good hostess, and they, of course—for the sake of good manners—would be compelled to partake of it. They'd cheated death once at her hands and were not at all sure that they were powerful enough and lucky as well, to do so twice. And for what the trio had in mind they knew that it was better to approach the dumb farmer when he was alone and with no one being the wiser. The less others knew the better off they'd be. They'd even be better off than that, they reasoned, if they could find anyone, anyone at all besides the dumb farmer, to play for them the part they had scripted. But even though people were by and large much more innocent in Olden Days than they are today, they were not as a rule stupid, unless of course you considered the farmer who was by and large the largest person in those parts and certainly the most foolish too.

The trio came upon him as he was engaged in a tug o' war with a deeply embedded and entrenched group of weeds—a war in which the weeds were winning. The Witches had traveled incognito so as to avoid recognition and journeyed downwind of everyone in the area so that no one would be able to smell 'em either. Even the rabbits, with their secret runs and interwoven network of underground tunnels and spy holes hidden throughout the forest were unaware of their presence. Jack was the only creature for miles around with enough wit to have detected their arrival but alas, he was at the other end of the wood and waiting for a chicken to fly the coop so that he might steal her eggs.

After much tugging, pulling, and grunting, Santos achieved a partial victory when a single weed finally consented to be parted from its place in the ground. Suddenly its roots let go, causing the farmer to topple over backward and go rolling in a heap of cloddy earth and sandy topsoil. He came to an abrupt halt, only to find himself staring at three pairs of feet. He gazed upward past three sets of knobby knees, continuing on past three sets of sagging breasts, until his eyes rested upon the countenances of three unwholesome yet strangely familiar faces. "May I help you?" he hesitantly asked.

The trio looked at him as if examining a slug. "Perhaps," two of the three replied in unison. "It depends upon whether or not your wife is around." The three looked at each other, looked at him, and then scanned the immediate area with a marked sense of unease as if to ensure themselves of her absence. It had been their experience of late that you could never be too careful and having been badly burned once were quick to learn that the burned hand teaches best.

"Oh no," replied the farmer, "my good wife is away for the day. She's a famous chef, you know!"

The trio relaxed visibly. "We know."

"Well, anyway," continued the farmer, "having garnished for herself a reputation for being a culinary wizard of the highest order, she's been invited to attend a get together comprised of fellow "culinartists" of similar caliber. She's even the keynote cooker! Why do you know that she once even prepared a meal for The Powers That Be?" At this reminder of their near demise the trio blanched, their skins turning a sickening shade of gray. However, this feeling quickly passed, only to be replaced by one of euphoria as they realized the wench was miles away and so at least for the moment, incapable of doing them harm. "We know that too," they said while letting their disguises fall away.

"Yah!"

Santos cowered at the sudden change in their appearance. They shifted their shapes and their camouflages and costumes melted away into nothingness as they assumed their true forms. The farmer gasped out loud. Although he thought them ugly to begin with, they were nothing compared to the horrors which stood before him now. Then he realized just how horrible they were as he recognized *who they were*. He cut his gasp short and jumping up, bowed to them like a courtier. "My ladies," he groveled, "what a pleasant surprise to see you!"

"Shut up, fat boy," said Helgayarn. "We're here on business, not pleasure."

"Yah!" agreed Betty.

Santos looked nervously from them to the sea of weeds growing in his garden. "You're here because my latest efforts to grow vegetables have not borne fruit, aren't you?" he asked. "I swear to you—I've tried everything I know of and don't have a single brussels sprout to show for my efforts. Thinking that the soil might need fertilizing, I inundated it with cattle craps, but alas, all I have to show for my hard work are these damned weeds! Did you ladies fair happen by per chance, or have you come to aid me with a bit of magic?"

"Oh, do be quiet you old fool," said Brunnhilde, "and listen! We're here on business. We've already said so, and if you cleaned the cattle craps out of your ears, you might have heard us too. Business. And our business has nothing to do with you and your silly old vegetables!"

"Oh," said Santos, looking crestfallen. It seemed that in the wake of the past disaster, he'd gone and lost his green thumb. But he supposed, he'd just have to keep trying. "Well then," he continued, "if you fair maidens will pardon me for having fallen and inadvertently gotten in your way, then I'll beg your further indulgence whilst humbly asking that you step aside as the three of you are standing in my weeds."

The Witches looked at each other, rolling their eyes. "Perhaps this wasn't such a good idea after all," said Brunnhilde.

"Yah!" replied Betty.

"It's a lousy idea," said Helgayarn, "and it stinks more than a cattle crap stew! But what other choice have we? Who else but Old Slomoe here, will go along with it?"

"True," replied Brunnhilde. "We've really no other options."

"Yah!"

"Well, all right then," said Helly, "let's get on with it, be done with it and get the hell out of here before anyone sees us!"

As Santos listened in on the trio's three-way conversation his sense of confusion, always enormous, grew even greater. It was obvious, even to him, that the Witches were here for *something* and that the something they were here for concerned him. But if not vegetables, then what? They said that it was business but taters, carrots, and such were the only business he knew and if one looked at his garden and observed within it all the weeds growing both in profusion and preponderance, one would conclude that it was a business that despite his bragging, he did not know well. So why were they here? Were they finally going to impose sentence?

"Listen, fatso," said Helgayarn, "we don't give a cattle crap about you're difficulties with weeds and vegetables! We're here to cut you a deal!" Her companions nodded their heads. "A deal?" asked the farmer. "What sort, and for what?"

"Well," replied Brunnhilde, "for some time now it's been apparent to us that you've had no success in recovering your lost children. We've heard rumor of you searching the forest high and low for them as well as seen you for ourselves from time to time. We know that your wife is none too happy with you either for having gone and lost them." She paused for a moment to let that sink into his thick head. "So tell us," she continued, "would you like them back, and would you like us to help you find them?"

"Would I?" exclaimed Santos. "You bet your ass I would!"

The Witches offered him a threefold scowl for his impertinence, and the farmer mumbled an abject apology as he took note of their frowns. "I mean to say," he haltingly continued, "that of course, I'd

THE CHRISTMAS RABBIT

be most honored and extremely gratified to receive your most noble and welcome assistance."

"That's better," Helgayarn said shortly. "We understand your excitement but that's no reason to be vulgar!"

"Again, my apologies," the farmer replied.

"Apology accepted," Helgayarn said. "But to get back to the business at hand, I'm sure that even you must realize that the three of us are very busy at the moment—especially in light of all that's happened recently. There's a whole world to set straight with a long way to go and a lot to do before it gets there. To help you would only delay that noble purpose." She paused, glaring at him intently over steepled fingers, as if sizing him up. "What we need to know," she continued, "if we give of ourselves, lending to you both our precious time and infinite resources, would you be amenable to doing likewise?"

"Of course!" Santos said eagerly as he joyfully rubbed his hands together, unable to contain his excitement. With these three on his side and lending their talents he was sure to have his children back in no more than a fortnight! Then perhaps the wife would desist from giving him the "cold shoulder" as it were, and he'd no longer have to sleep on the couch. "Anything you want," he said. "Anything at all!"

"Fine," replied Helly. "What we want from you is that damned Jack, and we want his head on a platter!"

"Yah!" cried Betty.

"Even better!" said Santos excitedly. "Even better!" But then his face fell yet again as it folded into itself with frustration and worry.

"What's the matter, eh?" asked Helly, taking note of his unease. "What's the matter now?

"Well," said Santos timidly as he looked to his three patronesses, "you ladies must have noticed that catching and killing rabbits has not exactly been my forte."

"Yah!"

The farmer spewed out yet another weak apology and then awkwardly pushed on. "But I'll do better," he continued, "I promise! I'll get a bigger club—just you wait and see!"

"You dumb ass!" replied the head witch. "Don't be so literal! Did I use the word *kill*? Did I say that? No, I didn't, did I? Don't you think we know what you can and can't do?" She rolled her eyes in frustration while taking a deep breath to calm herself. These actions however proved to be of little use. Still she continued. "A simple killing would be too merciful for the dirty little beast—and no one would ever accuse us of mercy! What we want you to do is embarrass him! Thwart his plans and steal his eggs! If he has no eggs to deliver then folk will get to grumbling again and soon they'll come to despise him almost as much as they do you! Once that happens, the three of us will step in and see to it that egg deliveries get put back on track by appointing some other hare as chief rabbit. Then *we'll* kill him! We'll reclaim our lost popularity and we'll have you to thank for it! Believe me, you'll be richly rewarded."

Fool that he was, Santos did believe them but saw a flaw in their machinations nevertheless. "That Jack is pretty sharp," he observed. "Won't the dirty little beast catch on to what I'm about and figure out that I'm stealing his eggs?"

"Not if you're careful," said Brunnhilde.

"Yah!" agreed Betty.

"Besides," Brunnhilde continued, "he'll most likely blame the birds anyway. They are after all, whom he's been stealing from in the first place...although we haven't been able to prove it. We know it for a fact—we just haven't been able to catch the sneaky little leporide! Steal back the eggs and collect for us solid proof that he's been making off with them in the first place and we'll set aside all our other endeavors and turn our considerable powers toward finding your children. Now, ain't that a deal?"

Santos looked at the trio, and they at him, as he weighed their offer, evaluating it from all sides and angles—at least those sides and angles that he was capable of assessing. But in a deal like this with witches like that any such agreement would have at its minimum fifty-seven different sides, angles, and facets. Santos, as usual, missed most of them and saw only the two, which to him were the most obvious—getting even with the rabbit and getting back his children.

"Well," asked Helgayarn, "is it a deal?"

THE CHRISTMAS RABBIT

"You ain't just whistlin', Dixie!" the farmer replied. "It's a deal!"

"Then what are you waiting for?" asked Helgayarn.

"Righto," Santos replied with good cheer and took off running. But he stopped fifteen feet down the road and abruptly came about. With abject humility and head bowed he plodded wearily back to The Powers That Be.

"What is it," asked Helgayarn, staring at him while trying to keep in check her growing impatience, "what's the problem now?"

"Actually, my lady," Santos replied, "there are two."

"Two? Good gravy! Well, I suppose you'd better come out and tell us what they are."

"Yah!"

Santos gazed fearfully at the three dour dames, unsure of how to begin or whether or not to say anything at all. So much was riding on their goodwill or lack of it. He'd had no luck in locating his children and until today had concluded that such an endeavor was hopeless. Junior and Laddie were gone forever. Then out of the blue came these witches offering him the deal of lifetime if he could just hold up his end. But he couldn't and to give him the credit he deserved, at least this time he realized it. Still, there was nothing to do, he supposed, other than to voice his concerns and hope that the trio could offer suggestive and innovative solutions to address them. "The sticking points are," he said, "(a) I've never stolen anything in my life and wouldn't be at all sure as to how to go about it, and (b) even if I were a thief extraordinaire, I'm told that Jack has his entire family, which now numbers in the hundreds, they say, working collectively on this damned egg business. There's no way that I could keep up with them all."

Helgayarn, Brunnhilde, and Betty looked at each other in dumfounded amazement. The farmer, against all odds and chances to the contrary, was absolutely right. Betty had a heartfelt desire to take out her journal and make note of the extraordinary event. No one anywhere, they knew, could ever remember being present at such a singular and uncommon occurrence. The farmer being right happened about as frequently as the Harmonic Convergence, and the next one of those wasn't due to arrive until AD 1994! The trio immediately went into a private huddle, forming a triangle of sorts, with arms on each other's shoulders and presenting their backsides to the embarrassed farmer. They were deep in trouble and knew it. Worst of all, given who they'd chose to work through, should've foreseen these difficulties themselves. Thank our lucky stars, they thought to themselves, that no one else was around to take note of our short-sightedness! "Well," whispered Brunnhilde, "the pellets are about to hit the wind now!"

"Yah!" Betty worriedly replied.

"Just what are you going to do about this, Helly?"

"Me?" replied Helgayarn. "Why me?"

"This was your idea!" Brunnhilde whispered sharply.

"Yah!" agreed Betty.

"So what of it?" asked Helgayarn, her voice laced with bitter desperation.

"What of it?" Brunnhilde nearly screamed. "You're the big witch! The head honcho—that's what of it! It was your idea to use Old Slomoe and you got us into this. Now get us out!"

"How?" Helgayarn asked desperately.

"We don't know how! That's what we have you for. Think of something!"

Helgayarn peeked up from their huddle to look around anxiously. "I don't know, my dears," she said. "I'm fresh out of tricks and haven't any treats either—wait!" A wicked smile spread across her morbid features as she drew her conspirators even closer. "Oh, I've got it," she whispered slyly. "I've really got it this time!" She lowered the tenor of her voice even further until she spoke in the barest of whispers. No one could've heard her except for Brunnhilde and Betty who were huddled so closely. Even I'm not sure of exactly all that was stated, suffice is to say that when she concluded laying out her spur-of-the-moment plan, the trio broke out in peals of girlish laughter. "Oh. It's delicious, sister!" exclaimed Brunnhilde. "Absolutely scrumptious! Let's do put your idea into action!"

"Yah!" agreed Betty. "Yah!"

The trio broke from their private conference to approach the farmer. All three displayed sickeningly sweet smiles upon their visages, which on normal people like you and I would have been deemed frowns. Just looking at them gave Santos butterflies in his stomach the size of pterodactyls. But he would've endured tyrannosaurs in his tummy if doing so meant a chance of reclaiming his lost children. So he gamely stood his ground, preparing himself for the worst the trio could dish out. He was, therefore, surprised when he got a temporary reprieve. "Listen, you," said Helgayarn, "against all odds—for once you're right. But don't let it go to your head! Stealing Jack's eggs by yourself is simply out of the question, so we've come up with an enhancement to our plan. Just you stand tight a while and keep that fat mouth of yours shut! We're going away for a bit to gather you up some help, so don't move from this spot until we return. Understand?"

"Most assuredly."

"With you," Helgayarn replied bitterly, "nothing is assured. But it can't be helped, although we're going to do everything in our power to change that. Just don't you move till we get back!" With that, the trio marshaled the forces and called up a whirlwind, darkening the skies in the immediate area and turning the pastel blue into a sickening shade of purple, resembling a bruise. The purple alternated to violent yellow as the wind increased in strength. The few trees still standing toppled over backward while small shrubs and flowers were uprooted and sucked into the maelstrom. The weeds though, hardy as ever, maintained their firm grip in the ground, impervious. The farmer's hair and beard stood on end while dust and nettles blown about by the gale assaulted him, stinging his eyes and filling his oral and aural orifices with crud. Blinking erratically, his cheeks wet with tears, the dumb farmer looked on in awe as the trio whisked themselves away.

*****

How long did he stay rooted to that spot, obeying the last dictates of The Powers That Be? These days no one really knows for sure and I'm not going to try and make fools of you all by pretending otherwise. Some say it was so long while others say it was even longer.

I've heard conflicting reports. Some say a month, some say a year, and some say even longer than that. But however long the passage of days or even months, rest assured that it was a goodly amount of time and that he never moved from the spot. Not once. Never and under no circumstances; rooted himself to the ground and stayed there. Hardly moved a muscle. Barely breathed a word. Scarcely blinked an eye. He ate there, drank there, crapped and peed there too. He met there with whoever happened by for whatever reason they happened, and those who happened by for no reason whatsoever but who were merely passing through. He had a deal. He wasn't quite sure just what the deal was since the Witches seemed to append it just before departing but whatever its terms, he didn't dare break them for fear of losing his only means of finding Junior and Laddie—and part of the deal was that he stay put. And so he remained, stuck fast to that very spot while rationalizing his action as that very form of discretion which is so often the better part of valor. Thus he put all of his energies toward honoring the one part of the contract he did understand and so avoided the possibility of unintentionally violating some hidden and arcane clause within its body of which he wasn't even aware. It was a sly move and as such went completely unaccounted by him as having been so, but was employed rather, as an act of desperation. To solidify his bargaining position, he had Mrs. Santos, when she returned, bring to him two sticks which he used as props so that he could sleep there standing up. Upon delivering his stilts his wife inquired as to what kind of hare brained scheme he'd become involved in, but remembering the trio's admonitions to keep quiet, he maintained a discreet silence.

 For a short time, Santos regained some of his lost notoriety as folk from all over, when not sitting on or eating their eggs, came down to his valley in order to throw rocks at him and hurl sticks, tell bad jokes and call him names. Day and night, as best he could, he stood there still as a statue, absorbing the abuse and taking the punishment. Through wind and rain, snow and hail, he remained there motionless. Various tormentors tried to get a rise out of him by bull baiting and brow beating but he was having none of it. He stood there oblivious to it all… Yeah right. And pigs fly and cattle never

THE CHRISTMAS RABBIT

crap. It never happens that way in real stories either. The folk in 'em make up all that malarkey in order to get you and I to like 'em when we run across them in the pages of a good book. In reality he took to hurling insults of his own at those who threw first. When this proved itself deficient he offered up sass from the get go in order to get the opening shot in. To hell with them, he thought. He had powerful allies now and his day of reckoning was surely coming!

The Rabbits of Influence and their suck-up cronies put in an appearance as well, poking fun at him, giving him the finger, shouting obscenities, and generally making a nuisance of themselves. It was a lot to endure and as he'd taken too much for too long determined that he would return each injury and insult twofold. Let the rabbits have their day. Soon, he knew, the Witches would arrive with their promised help and when they did he'd take after the little leporides and have his revenge!

One day, while his wife was off cooking, his two-legged tormenters were off partying, and the Rabbits of Influence were off feeding themselves—a much more complicated chore than in seasons past as there was no garden to raid anymore, The Powers That Be returned. They came in a brand new Winnebago covered wagon that was even plusher than the one they'd owned previously and which they'd received as a gift from those cheap dicks at Repressive Insurance of Mesozoic Mesopotamia. The trio had finally negotiated a settlement out of court with those cheapskates by using their influence while in court to nearly bankrupt them. Every time someone sued Repressive for damages, whether or not they were right or wrong and regardless of whether the suits were justified or trivial, the trio invariably found for the plaintiffs, causing Repressive to turn nearly belly-up. The CEOs, chairpersons of the board, stockholders, adjusters, and everyone else who had an interest in the company pleaded with The Powers That Be for impartiality—but Helgayarn, Brunnhilde, and Betty were having none of that. It was their intention to drive those cheap dicks into the ground for their impertinence in denying the original claim and so they would have until the folks at Repressive, resigned to the inevitable, waved the white flag of surrender by dangling the new Winnebago before them, free of charge and waiving the deductible they would've had to pay had Repressive honored their original claim to begin with. Therefore, having proved their point while getting a new wagon in the bargain, the Witches graciously consented to relent.

Behind them and bringing up the rear were hundreds of wee people; various leprechauns, dwarves, sprites, gnomes, and picts, which The Powers That Be saw fit to group under the general classification of Elves. These were to be Santos's helpers in his campaign to discredit Jack. The Witches gathered them up from the four corners of the earth—it was square back then—and some of them had obviously magical powers which they were instructed by the trio to use in an effort to aid the farmer. Some were green and some were gray. Some had rings on their fingers—all six of them in fact, and bells on their toes. Some were beautiful to behold and some, especially the dwarves and gnomes, were downright ugly. But what did that matter? They had a job to do after all, and this wasn't a beauty contest anyway.

As they came marching up, Santos breathed a sigh of relief. His wait was finally over, and thank you very much for that! He'd been propped up in one place for far too long now. His muscles were cramped and atrophied, his feet were sore, and, oh, mercy, how he needed a bath!

As Helgayarn, Brunnhilde, and Betty approached, they took note of the farmer's position and posture.

"Amazing," said Helly quietly to the others. "That jackass has literally not moved from that spot since we left him! What do you make of that, Bunny?"

Brunnhilde eyed her sister tersely while formulating a scathing reply. Helly knew that she hated to be called Bunny but insisted upon using the nickname anyway. It really pissed her off, and it was about time that she said something to the old bag about it! At the last moment however, she elected to maintain a discreet silence. Now was not the time, she reasoned, to start a futile and probably pointless argument concerning a nickname that Helgayarn was unlikely to give up. She instead gave her attention to Helly's question. "Well," Brunnhilde replied, "the Tortoise is certainly obedient anyway."

THE CHRISTMAS RABBIT

"Yah!" agreed Betty.

Helgayarn rolled her eyes. "Cattle craps!" she said. "We knew that already, didn't we? But the damned fool didn't have to take us so literally for Pete's sake! Who knows what kind of attention he's been drawing to himself? Why, I'll bet folk have been coming here from miles around just to get a glimpse of him! You both know as well as I that success depends upon secrecy. How secretive can you be when you're drawing that much notice—not to mention flies—to yourself?"

Brunnhilde shrugged noncommittally. "There's nothing we can do about it now," she said, "and after all, we did tell him to wait *exactly* where he was."

"Yah!" said Betty.

The blood, or what passed for it in three sour dour dames as they, rose to Helgayarn's face, turning her skin green. Her eyes bulged, and her temples throbbed angrily. "Are you two implying that this is our fault?"

"Well, no, of course not," Brunnhilde meekly replied. "No one in their right mind could be expected to wait so long and in one place at that. Nor should anyone else require them to do so. But perhaps we should have considered that whom we're dealing with isn't in his right mind to begin with and is never going to be, and made allowances. Gave him some leeway. Something else. I don't know."

Helgayarn offered her two confederates a decidedly sour scowl as the trio approached even closer. When they neared within ten feet of the sorry farmer, they came to an abrupt and sudden halt. The stench emanating for Santos was almost unbearable and they found they could draw no closer. Behind them lines of leprechauns, fairies, dwarfs, and midgets began stumbling one over the other as they were forced into an unexpected halt. Grumbling to each other, they picked themselves up off the ground, brushing the dust and loam from their clothing as they did. Their angry chatter was a high-pitched whine that grated upon the ears of The Powers That Be. Helgayarn admonished the unruly mob to hush, whereupon the miniature army fell into a reluctant and uneasy silence. At another command from her the assemblage seated themselves on the ground in a disorderly fashion to begin the tedious business of waiting upon their fate. They had no idea exactly of what they were in for—the Witches had merely formed them up and given them their marching orders, but rumor of Santos and his war with the rabbits had spread even as far away as the secretive and isolated places from which they'd come, and of course everyone everywhere had heard about the infamous trial. Now, taking note of the feral and grimy visage of the farmer the elven army started to silently bemoan their fate as the wisest among them began to perceive, at least in part, the role the trio would cast them in.

Damned witches, they all thought. It was always the same. Leave it to the big folk to paint their asses into a corner, which they inevitably did, and then expect the wee people to bail out their boats! World without end, it spun ever onward, and such things had always been, would always be, and at least as far as the elves could see, were not likely to change for the better anytime in the near future. But they kept their mouths shut because Helgayarn, Brunnhilde, and Betty were no mistresses to trifle with. They'd all learned that lesson the hard way some ages ago when the trio turned them into sprites—but that in itself is another story and one which we have no time for here. Being however magical folk and therefore fashioned somewhat in the image of their mistresses, their elven minds lay open to the trio, enabling the Powers to sense their dissatisfaction despite the uniformity of their silence. Thus Helgayarn was aware of their quiet complaining and to stifle it, offered them a frightful frown that would curdle new milk. Thoroughly chastised by her implied warning, the wee folk settled down and gave themselves over to happy thoughts.

Having settled those whiners, Helgayarn once again turned her attention to the disheveled personage of the pitiful farmer. *My word, how he stinks*, she thought. *He's covered in dirt and filth!* She took note of the heaps of brown piles that surrounded him. It couldn't be, could it? "Sister," she asked disbelievingly of Brunnhilde, "are those what I think they are?" She pointed at the mounds, unable to believe her own eyes.

Bunny saw them too. *Unbelievable*, she thought. Yet seeing was believing, or so it was said, and there could be no doubt that they all

THE CHRISTMAS RABBIT

saw it; therefore, like it or not, they were forced to accept it. "I think so," said Brunnhilde. "They're piles of dung."

"Oh, cattle craps," Helly moaned.

"No," Brunnhilde disagreed, "just plain dung."

Helgayarn shot her a sideways glance. "Why he hasn't even moved to relieve himself," she exclaimed, "let alone take a bath! And that smug smile on his face—he's actually proud of his deeds!"

"Well, you must admit," Brunnhilde replied distastefully, "whether you like it or not, that such fortitude and obedience requires a certain amount of determination."

"It doesn't require determination," Helly fired back. "It requires desipience and dimwittedness in the highest degree!"

"He is the farmer."

"I suppose," Helgayarn reluctantly agreed. "But really!" She turned her eyes once again to the clod, despising him. "Well," she asked sharply, "what have you to say for yourself?"

"I did what you asked," Santos replied. "No, I did what you ordered! Can I go take a bath now? In case you haven't noticed, I'm rather soiled."

Helgayarn offered up a sarcastic chuckle. "That's like saying the Grand Canyon is a mere hole in the ground (which at the time, it was)! Do you think that a simple bath will suffice? My word, you're caked with layer upon layer of grime and filth and the flies are buzzing around, alighting on and off you like you were a cattle crap creamsicle! You're in danger of becoming a stinkbug yourself or even worse, a dung beetle! How can you stand it?"

"Believe you me," replied the farmer, "it ain't been easy."

"I can well believe it! Yes, by all means go get cleaned up and make yourself presentable, if that's possible, before you return." The farmer gratefully turned away, eager to comply. "Wait a minute," said Helgayarn. "A mere mortal such as yourself would need a ball-peen hammer and some blasting powder to get that amount of crud off. Simple washing won't do. You'd better take some bath attendants with you."

"Bath attendants?"

"Yes, you fool!" She called out to the crowd of wee folk seated behind her. "Two of you imps come forward—I don't care who—and help this idiot clean himself up."

No one moved. No one volunteered.

"Now!"

Reluctantly, two junior sprites, Pixie and Dixie, about as low on the elven chain of command as two poor fellows could get and still remain elves, stepped out of the pack and presented themselves to the trio.

Actually, they were pushed from behind. "Yes, m'lady?" one asked. "How may we be of service?"

"You heard me," Helgayarn said, tapping her fingers impatiently upon the sides of her legs. "Be about your business and get this idiot cleaned up!"

"Oh," said Dixie, who was so named because he was from Alabama and therefore a Southern elf, "I don't think that we have nearly the magic or skill to accomplish that! Surely, y'all will be wanting more senior and powerful elves for so vast an undertaking."

"You'll do just fine," Helgayarn replied shrewishly. "Just you get him cleaned up. Grab yourselves a couple of scouring pads from out of the Winnebago and some Janitor In A Drum. Take him down to the river and turn to. And see to it that you don't foul up the water!"

"But, m'lady, we—"

"Move!"

Under protest, the two elves, along with their charge, moved slowly off toward the river in order to carry out their assigned task.

"And don't be afraid," Helgayarn called after them, "to employ whatever magic you need to get the job done. I want him cleaned up and quickly—no matter what it takes. And have a care for that river!"

Forlorn, the trio headed off toward the river as Helgayarn turned her attention back to her sisters. "Do you believe that fool?" she asked. "Who in his right mind would allow himself to get so soiled and befouled?"

Both Brunnhilde and Betty were at a loss to provide a response. What all three of them forgot was that Santos was enduring the unendurable for the sake of his children. It'd been so long since the trio had raised children of their own that they forgot how parents through love of progeny, will wade through any amount of crap for the sake of their offspring. It goes with the territory and children from Olden Days on down to the present have excelled in landing their parents hip-deep in it. There just went the walking proof although the Witches were too self-centered to see it. "Well," said Brunnhilde, eyeing the slowly receding forms, "do you still think your plan will work?"

"Our plan!" Helgayarn hissed.

"Oh, very well," Brunnhilde retorted. "Our plan! But will it work? Anyone foolish enough to stand in craps for that long can hardly be depended upon to pull something like this off!"

Helgayarn scowled again. "You're the one who said he had determination," she replied.

"True," countered Brunnhilde. "But you correctly pointed out that it isn't determination that our farmer is endowed with but rather desipience and dimwittedness in the highest degree, and upon reflection I'm inclined to agree. So again I ask, will it work?"

"Yah!"

Both Helgayarn and Brunnhilde gave Betty a glare. "Who asked you?" they jointly said.

"As the silent partner in this three-ring circus," Helgayarn continued, "it's your job to stand there and be quiet!"

Betty meekly bowed her head and wisely shut up—but not before making a mental note to record this insult in her journal.

"Well?" Brunnhilde persisted.

"It better work," Helgayarn replied. "It's the only plan we've got. If it fails we'll all be up the river, sans paddle!"

Brunnhilde cringed as she thought about the last time they'd been forced to navigate their way through those dreadful waters—the great "washaway" in the cataclysm of Hurricane Junior. "Oh my," she said in despair, "anything but that!"

"I wouldn't worry too much," replied Helly, reading her mind. "The snot-nosed little truant has gone into deep cover and isn't likely to surface until we drag him out into the light. And when we do, we'll be sure to have all of our potions and elixirs securely out of reach! In the meantime, all we have to worry about is Santos and that little leporide, Jack—and that's why we've brought the army along. If anyone can get it done, they can."

"What happens if Farm Boy tries to take credit for their accomplishments?"

"He'll play along and keep mum," Helgayarn replied. "After all, he wants his children back, doesn't he?"

"I hadn't thought of that," admitted Brunnhilde.

"That's why I'm the boss. The big witch!"

Brunnhilde offered her a skeptical appraisal. "Well then, Your Witchiness," she sarcastically asked, "where are they?"

"Who?"

"The farmer's kids! Junior and Laddie, or whatever their names are!"

Helgayarn replied to Brunnhilde's skepticism with an incredulous look of her own. "Where are they?" she asked. "How should I know?"

"You mean you've no idea?"

"Of course not! Haven't we all had enough to do without bothering to search for those rug rats? Have any of us actually been looking for them? We assumed Old Slomoe would know where he sent them. Well, that's what we get for assuming! They'll turn up though—have no doubt! And if they don't, then we'll just have to find them."

Brunnhilde shook her head with worry. "Suppose we can't," she asked, "what then?"

"We'll find them, don't fret about it!"

"Yah!"

Brunnhilde eyed Betty vindictively. "Oh, do be quiet, you!" she said. Turning her attention back to Helgayarn, she repeated her question. "But suppose we can't?"

Helgayarn threw her hands up, frustrated. "So what?" she replied. "By then, the elven army will have accomplished its mission. But if they don't and they get caught, which in turn causes another scandal, the fallout will be credited to Santos while the three of us fall back on plausible deniability. Everyone will be so upset, feeling that they've been cheated, that they're sure to come gunning for the old clod. Therefore he'll be so busy trying to keep his buns out of the burner that he won't have time to give thought to broken promises and breaches of contract! He'll consider himself lucky enough to get away with his skin still on, and if not, what's he gonna do, sue us?" This remark caused the other two to giggle gleefully. Peals of laughter ushered forth from their pallid lips to fall gratingly on the ears of the nearby elves like old fingernails scouring a chalkboard. As their laughter slowly fell away, Brunnhilde grew somber yet again as another thought struck her. She tried her best to hide her agitation, but Helly was aware of her discomfiture nevertheless. "Well," she asked, "what's bothering you now?"

Brunnhilde offered her a timid glance while formulating her reply. "Suppose we can?" she asked.

"Eh?"

"Suppose we can," Bunny repeated, "find them, I mean. What then?"

"Jiminy Cricket!" said Helgayarn, shaking her head. "You do go on, my dear, don't you?"

"Well, just suppose," Bunny offered weakly. "What then?"

Helgayarn stared at her in disbelief. "Why, we kill 'em!" she said. "The kids, the farmer, the wife, Jack, Nutmeg, their kids—we just kill 'em! After all, we're going to have to do it sooner or later."

Brunnhilde looked at her uncertainly. "I know," she replied doubtfully, "but it hardly seems fair, does it?"

"Mama Mia!" Helgayarn said to herself. Was she really hearing this? "Fair? What did 'fair' have to do with anything? Life isn't fair, and I'm here to say so and say it loudly!"

"I know," Brunnhilde replied, "but—"

"No buts!"

"One but please?"

"No!" replied Helgayarn adamantly. "No buts!"

"Very well then," Brunnhilde retorted. "No buts. Just an if!"

Helgayarn drummed her fingers against her legs as she tried in vain to marshal her patience. "Well?"

"What if we miss?"

"Huh?"

"What if we miss?" Brunnhilde asked again. "After all, we've done so at least twice now. Once when that little snot first let loose the hurricane and again at the trial when things got so out of hand. So again, I must ask, what if we miss?"

"Then we miss!" Helgayarn said loudly. "So what?" Old age will get them all in the end—it always does. Now, do you have any more ifs or buts? Because I'd really like to do some quiet thinking and planning while we still have time."

"No more ifs or buts," Brunnhilde said reassuringly. Just a couple of ands."

"Ands?" Helgayarn nearly screamed. "Ands? Between your ifs, ands, and buts, I'm never going to get a moment's peace…"

And so it went, hour upon hour and day upon day, with Brunnhilde questioning, Helgayarn answering, and Betty offering an occasional, "Yah!" when she could get a word in edgewise, while down at the river the two elves went about the arduous chore of getting the farmer cleaned up. From time to time, the trio's arguments were interrupted by the moans and screams of Old Slomoe, the sounds of his agony being borne upon the breeze and wafted on the wind as Pixie and Dixie applied magic, jackhammers, and whatever else came to mind in order to chisel away the dirt, crud, and layers of crap with which the farmer was encrusted. It was a painful ordeal, both for the farmer and the elves and not one soon accomplished—much to the consternation of all concerned. But eventually, after seemingly untold days of effort applied and innumerable gallons of sweat expended, along with buckets of the aforementioned Janitor In A Drum as well as innumerable bottles of Lysol, Ajax, Borax (and not just the twenty-mule team but the whole heaping' herd), and whatever other cleanser happened to be handy, the job was at last completed.

Santos, Pixie, and Dixie stumbled wearily up the lane as they slowly made their way back to The Powers That Be. The threesome were unrecognizable, as none of them looked the way they did before the ordeal began.

The other trio, that Triumvirate of Terror and Testiness, known formally as The Powers That Be, had since backed themselves into a

THE CHRISTMAS RABBIT

triangle with each on the alert and facing outward. It was a classic position of defense known and practiced from the dawn of time. The Witches had assumed the stance when the farmer's wife exited her kitchen shortly after they'd sent him off to get cleaned up. They mistakenly assumed her still at the conference of "culinartists," and had they known she was about, would've made themselves busy elsewhere. The fates only knew what she'd been concocting but thankfully the odor of such culinary culpability surrounded her as she exited the kitchen door. The stench, powerful as it was, preceded her like an ill begotten herald of doom and therefore the trio were adequately warned of her presence despite being upwind at the time. Such a stench gave no regard to winds either their ups or downs. It ignored all boundaries and attempts at confinement. Houdini had he been alive back then, would have been envious of such a miasma as there was nothing, absolutely nothing, which could contain it. Thus, having ample warning of her impending arrival, the Witches took the necessary precautions and triangulated. It was, after all, survival. "What the hell do you want?" they screeched. Even Betty managed a multisyllabic articulation—she was that frightened.

"My ladies fair!" replied Mrs. Santos, surprised that they should be there. "What good fortune brings you here?" She paused, eyeing them greedily and coveting their presence. Perhaps, even after Junior's fiasco, it was not too late to garner for herself a second chance and so ingratiate her personage back into their confidences. A good meal—that's what the trio needed! Some wholesome food would surely go a long way to repairing the damage done by Junior and help restore her former position! "Are we chance met?" she asked. "Or have you journeyed all this way just to ample some more of my good cooking?" Having asked the question, she uncovered the lid of a tray she'd been carrying and upon the silver dish lay a meal fit for a farmer. Haggis. The trio wilted. "Oh, I know," said Mrs. Santos, mistaking their fear for curiosity, "that you've never seen haggis quite like this, for where would you? It's my own special recipe! It's been baking for a while now and should be ready. I'll admit, it's a bit gamey—but tasty nevertheless. Do try some!"

Keeping themselves triangulated, the Witches began to back away as a unit, slowly while never taking their eyes off her for fear of their lives.

"Now don't go running away until you've tired some," said Mrs. Santos, full of pride at a job well done. "It's another one of my husband's favorites, although why I even bother with such effort when he's gone and lost our children, I'll never know." She inched a little closer. "I've also brought dessert," she said, displaying yet another dish. "Blood pudding—and look, it even has clots!"

That was it. Weakened first by smell and then assaulted by sight, the trio found that they lacked the strength to retreat any further. After all, how could mere witches defend themselves against a horror like this? They hadn't the stomachs for it and although their bodies were willing their spirits were weak—hence another bout of full-fledged, far-flung, upchucking. Gasping between hurls, Helgayarn warned the farmer's wife to approach no closer, to get away from their presence, and to take her poisons and alkalis with her when she did.

"Well, I never!" replied Mrs. Santos, slightly miffed. "I wonder what's gotten into you three?"

"Nothing!" replied Helgayarn acidly. "And we'd prefer keeping it that way!"

Although nearly as dense as her husband, Mrs. Santos knew when to take a hint. She strolled off with head held high and her meal proudly held out in front of her. Flowers wilted as she passed while trees despaired and dropped their fruit. Even the weeds, tenacious as they were, withdrew into themselves, sinking slowly back into the ground from whence they'd sprung; yet of these matters Mrs. Santos took no note. Her pride had been injured just once too often and she determined then and there that this would be the last time she ever offered those ungrateful witches so much as a canapé!

That had been days ago and Mrs. Santos, much to the relief of The Powers That Be, had yet to put in another appearance. Still the Witches kept to their formation. In circumstances like these with an enemy like that no precaution was too minor or too trivial. Thus they were still triangulated when Santos, Pixie, and Dixie returned from the river. They stumbled in weariness while The Powers That Be eyed them skeptically, sure that the three were about to relate to them the trials and tribulations they'd been made to undergo whilst engaged in their massive clean-up effort. Hah! Santos, Pixie, and Dixie, they knew, had it easy down by the river while *they*, on the other hand, had been made to suffer through the real ordeal. The farmer and his cleanup crew would get no pity from them! "It's about time, you three!" Helgayarn said harshly. "You've no idea of what we've been made to undergo while the three of you have been off skylarking!"

"Yah!"

"Double-dipping yah on that!" Brunnhilde agreed.

"Could it have been as bad as this?" asked Santos, taking off his hat and outer garments to reveal a body, which was beet red, scratched, and completely devoid of hair. "These idjits," said he, "pummeled and pumiced me over and over until they removed my top three layers of skin and robbed me of my animal fiber!"

"Animal fiber," queried Brunnhilde, "what's the hell is animal fiber, eh?"

"Hair!" replied the farmer testily. "All my hair is gone. From the top of my head to the tips of my toes—gone! I've lost my lustrous beard, and now I'm bald. It's embarrassing—I look like an egg!"

Helgayarn glanced at Pixie and Dixie and then returned her attention to the Tortoise. "Fine!" she said with a snap of her fingers. "It's fitting that it should be so considering eggs are at the heart of our troubles!" She gave him an appreciative glance. "Stop whining," she continued, "it'll all grow back eventually."

"Oh, I doubt that," said Santos. "I doubt that very much! I'll never be hairy again. Alas, doomed to a life of depilation! What will my hares say?"

"You mean heirs, don't you?" asked Brunnhilde.

"Heirs, hares," replied the farmer. "Let's not split hairs over a question of spelling!"

"You could always purchase a hairpiece," ventured Bunny. "At least until you grew your own back."

Santos dared to scowl. "You mean a wig?" he asked incredulously. His vanity wouldn't allow it, and he bridled at the very thought of affecting a hairpiece in order to convey a sense of hairdo. It was too hairy a concept.

"Oh well," he said, resigned to the loss of his locks, "hair today, gone tomorrow. I only wish I'd ended up hareless rather than hairless!"

Helgayarn had listened to his hair-raising diatribe long enough. She'd had it with such silliness, was fed up with the whole affair, and had always had a hair-trigger temper anyway. She made use of it now. "Shut up!" she yelled. "This harebrained conversation is getting us nowhere. The question before us is what to do about the hare and whether or not you have hair is not germane to the issue!"

"It isn't?" asked the farmer.

"It isn't," came the witch's terse reply. Santos fell back on comfortable confusion. "But you said that it was," he challenged.

"I did?" asked Helly.

"You did," said Santos.

"I most certainly did not!"

"Yes, you did when you told me that looking like an egg was fitting, given the task at hand! Therefore, whether you like it or not, I'd say being hairless is definitely pertinent to these issues in which we find ourselves so deeply engrossed!"

"There's nothing deep about you," Helgayarn sarcastically replied. "Everything about you can be measured in a hairsbreadth! Except, of course, your middle—which is as wide as the Erie Canal! How do you put on and maintain such girth while eating the food you do?"

"What do you mean?" asked the farmer.

"Your wife's cooking," replied the witch. "Her recipes should be bottled and sold under the common label of diarrhetic!"

"Oh, they're not that bad," said Santos defensively.

"The hell you say," Brunnhilde chimed in. "We know better—we've had the misfortune of trying one or two!"

"One merely has to lower one's expectations," replied the farmer, "and fine tune their taste buds."

"So that's the secret to gaining weight on the Santos diet, is it?" asked Helgayarn.

"That and lack of exercise," Santos replied. "It helps to be a couch potato."

"Good gravy," Helgayarn commented tiredly, "we're getting offtrack."

"Nothing new there," Santos replied under his breath.

"What was that?"

"Oh, nothing. Nothing at all."

Helgayarn eyed the farmer suspiciously. "It better be nothing," she said. "Now put your clothes back on. I find your obesity disgusting!" Santos complied while the trio looked on distastefully. "Say," said Brunnhilde, watching him dress, "what's that thing on your face?"

"Thing? What thing?" asked Santos self-consciously, fearing that he'd grown a wart. "You mean my chin?"

"No, no," replied Bunny. "Above that, above it!"

"You mean my cheek? That's my cheek."

"Don't get cheeky with me," the witch replied. "I mean that thing *on* your cheek! That spot. What is it?"

"Oh, that," replied the farmer off-handedly, as if it were a matter of no great import. "That's just my mark. Most of the Santos men have borne it—although not all in the same place. Even some of our women have been likewise tattooed. It's what sets us apart from the common folk!"

"You're certainly uncommon," remarked Helgayarn. "But do you mean to say that you all have it?"

"Most of us," the farmer replied tersely, feeling both piqued, that the big witch was obviously not listening to him as he had to repeat himself, and embarrassed that he should be discussing in the first place so personal an attribute which until his loss of hair, had always remained hidden. "Sometimes it skips a generation or two. Or sometimes it will appear on some offspring but not on others—like Junior and Laddie, for instance. Laddie's got it but Junior doesn't. Don't know why really."

The trio shared a conspiratorial glance. Each knew about the deceitful Dawes, even if the dumb farm boy didn't. "And what about

Laddie," asked Brunnhilde, "does he bear the mark in the same place?"

"No!"

"Well?"

"Why do you ask?"

"Because knowing where it is," said Helgayarn, "will help to both locate and identify him, won't it?"

"Perhaps," replied the farmer, the tremor in his voice giving evidence to both his nervousness and embarrassment, "but then, perhaps not. Laddie has the mark—however, it's not located in quite the same place."

"Where is it then?"

"It's not here!" cried Santos, pointing to his cheek. "It's not here!"

"Where then?"

"On his bum," the farmer barely whispered.

"What was that? We didn't hear you."

"On his bum, I said! Smack-dab on the middle of his ass!"

"My!" exclaimed Helgayarn. "We're certainly not going to get that close!"

"I should hope not!" the farmer replied ardently. "Still, one has to wonder just how the heck you're going to find him."

"Leave that to us," said Helgayarn. "You just concentrate on upholding your end of the bargain."

"My end? What's my end?"

The trio collectively rolled their eyes, resigned to the fickle pickle which fate had put on their plate in the personage of the fat farmer.

"I told you," Bunny whispered to Helly, "that this would never work. Farm Boy has all the attention span of a parsnip—he'll never pull it off!"

"Yah!"

"But we've all agreed that we don't have any other choice," replied Helgayarn tiredly. "And as you've so rightly pointed out, Bunny, my dear, what he lacks in focus, he more than makes up for in determination."

THE CHRISTMAS RABBIT

"Desipience," retorted Brunnhilde. "Desipience and dimwittedness in the highest degree—these are the Tortoise's only qualities!"

"Perhaps," replied Helly. "But even these may serve in the end." She turned her attention back to Santos, taking his measure one final time while offering up a silent sigh.

Well, she thought, there's nothing can be done about the situation now. This is the flawed clay with which we must shape the perfect vehicle for our revenge and only such skillful artisans as ourselves are capable of the molding! She continued to regard the farmer while wishing fervently for some other way, any other way, to pull off what they were about to attempt. Finding none, she reluctantly answered Santos.

"Your end," she said, "is humbling that damned rabbit! Hasn't that at least been made clear to you?"

"I suppose," replied the farmer haltingly. "But, my ladies, as I've already tried to point out, of eggs I know little and of thieving, even less."

"Aarrgh!" screamed Helgayarn. "You dimwitted, dunderheaded dingaling! Look around, you fool! Can't you see all the help we've brought you? Elves, leprechauns, and sprites galore—with a couple of picts, gnomes, and dwarves thrown in for good measure! They'll steal the eggs, you idiot! With his eggs gone missing, Jack won't be able to keep up with his deliveries. Folk will get uneasy as their children go without their omelets. Uneasiness will give way to unhappiness, which in turn will give way to out-and-out anger as their children go hungry. When the situation reaches its boiling point, that's when you'll step in!"

"I will?"

"Yes, you will!"

"How?"

"By claiming that you can do better. You'll challenge the rabbit to a race. A race to deliver the eggs, which you'll win, of course."

Santos had his doubts. "A race?" he asked. "I hate to admit it, but if any of you've followed my conquest of the rabbits, you may have noticed that I'm not too fleet of foot. In a race against Jack, I wouldn't stand a chance."

"Don't you think we know that?" Brunnhilde asked shrewishly. "The fix is in, just don't you worry. We've seen to everything. Taken into account all possibilities. You just do your part, and everything else will fall into place!"

Looking upon the miniature army, Santos felt a vague uneasiness worm its way into his bones like the chill of a mid-December morning. He had a funny feeling that he wasn't being told everything; that there was more to this harebrained scheme than he was being led to believe. He was right, of course. Even if he couldn't see these things he was nevertheless correct in intuiting them. But what could he do? All of his attempts to find Junior and Laddie had ended in complete failure. Perhaps, he thought, if I'd spent more time searching for them and less time bragging about past accomplishments I might not be in the position in which I now find myself. It was a point whose validity would not be challenged by any rational mind so of course his own questioned it incessantly and upon examination's completion determined instead that he was merely a victim of circumstance and that the blame lay elsewhere. Now there was no help for it, he supposed, but to go along with the scheme while hoping that things turned out for the best. "They do look like quite a throng," he said meaning the elves, "but can they accomplish the task and do they come with references?"

"Can they accomplish it?" asked Helgayarn in disbelief. "And do they come with references? Dolt! They're elves and such and therefore magical in their own right. They could steal the very sun from the sky if they put their minds to it—and if we let 'em! And as far as references go, they have us! What other references do you need?"

"Well, I'd be much happier," the farmer replied timidly, "with a more objective opinion."

"And we likewise," retorted Brunnhilde, "would be much more content it we hadn't been roped into this whole affair to begin with! Just you remember, fat boy, that it was you and that silly business with those damned rabbits that stirred up all this trouble in the first place. We've had nothing but headaches and heartaches—not to mention heartburn itself and the most unbearable gastrointestinal maladies, since this ridiculous fiasco began. Consider yourself lucky that my sisters and I don't turn you into a gnat and squash you. You deserve no less and certainly more!"

"Yah!"

Santos bowed his head, cringing in fear. "I do, my ladies," he replied. "But—"

"No!" Helgayarn shouted. "No more buts will I entertain this year. I'm up to my butt in *buts* and will not stand for another. You have your army, and you have your marching orders. Now get going and march!"

"You mean, I've been drafted?"

"Exactly. You're the general in our shadow army and your mission is top secret. Now stop farting around and get busy!"

There was nothing more to be said even if the farmer had the wit to say it. For the time being, manpower would be the only aid forthcoming. As far as strategies went, the Witches were of no help whatsoever, remaining totally closemouthed and silent. They would not help formulate or plan his campaign. They were holding close to their hearts the notion of plausible deniability, a well-known tool of statecraft and one which they figured to employ should the situation go south—a prospect they admitted to themselves that was more than likely with Santos holding the reins of generalship. If the pellets hit the wind they wanted to be able to deny any knowledge as to Santos's intent. It wasn't quite the truth. In fact, it stretched the truth to its outermost limits, but then plausible deniability has always been good at stretching such truths and the Witches knew it. So under silent protest Santos gingerly hobbled off, taking care not to rub his abraded skin against the harsh woolens he was wearing, and gathering up his army proceeded to plan and make ready the second campaign in his war with the rabbits.

*****

One day, not very long after Santos had his tryst with the Witches, Jack Rabbit called together the various and sundry members of his family in order to discuss a matter of extreme import. Jackrabbits from all over the forest and descended from Jack and

Nutmeg came from the four corners of the land in order to participate in the Great Council. Peter and Cottontail were there as were Flopsy Doodle, Noel, Bellamy, Rabbitboodles, and an army of others. Although Jack and Nutmeg had very little in the way of leisure time, what small amount that they possessed they put to productive use in the arts of conceiving and raising children. Not content to rely upon her own expertise in this matter Nutmeg sought ought an expert in the person of the Shoe Lady and with her, compared notes on the various strategies and conceptions in the art of conception itself, as well as guidelines, methodologies, and the contrivances necessary to ensure the healthy growth of the extended yet nuclear family. But so great were Nutmeg's skills in conception and crowd control it soon became apparent to the Shoe Lady that the student had outpaced the master. For once, the Shoe Lady found herself in the position of taking instruction rather than giving it.

Nutmeg's daughters, Flopsy Doodle, Bellamy, Noel, and Rabbitboodles were quick to learn the lessons of their mother and apply them in their own lives so that when the council convened Jack and Nutmeg found themselves the patriarch and matriarch of an extended family that numbered well into the thousands. There were gathered children, grandchildren, and great-grandchildren galore. There were nieces, nephews, and out-freyn cousins too. There were so many relatives to account for and bloodlines to keep track of that it became impossible to tell who was who and by whom they were related. Associating a specific name with a particular face became all but impossible. The two founders of this dynasty had trouble remembering all of their own children's names, let alone their kitten's kitten's kittens—still the couple presided over the entire magilla, ruling it with iron paws.

"This meeting is called to order," Jack said loudly, quieting the crowd and bringing it into some semblance of order. His pheromones spoke with authority and conviction and soon the masses settled in to hear the pronouncements of "Our Father." The intervening years rested comfortably on the hare, aging him like fine wine, which lying untouched in a cellar, set apart and undisturbed, mellows slowly until it reaches a full-bodiedness and bouquet unsurpassed by more recent vintages. Nutmeg, on the other hand, had learned well the arts of her tutor whom she soon eclipsed and found that the secret to longevity lay in good sex and lots of it. Thus the Great Council found her as fresh as a spring daisy and still endowed with the vibrancy of youth for which she'd once been world famous.

As Jack Rabbit called the meeting to order the crowd settled down and in to turn their collective attention to the "Abraham" of their clan. "We've many subjects to cover," said Jack, "including methods of collection and distribution, artwork and dyes, accounting, recipient roles, and of course, loss prevention. No doubt you've all heard the rumors circulating throughout the warrens regarding an army of wee folk who are restealing our stolen booty. Some of you claim to have caught glimpses of these folk yourselves while others disregard the sightings entirely, blaming such losses instead on inefficiency and lack of a good work ethic. Certainly, there are two sides to every coin and arguments of both the 'puritans' and the 'sightseers' each have merit. Therefore, we will enter into a discussion regarding these rumors and what, if anything, might be done about them, but first we will clear the agenda of other subject matter. Any objections?"

There were none, and the rabbits eagerly wagged heads and twitched noses in agreement. They were excited about the prospect of discussing rumors and participating in innuendo. Such things appealed to rabbits back then just as they do today, and for them such scuttlebutt and supposition are as much sought after as food itself. "The first subject," said Jack, "to be taken up is collection and distribution, and to report on these important items, I'll turn the podium over to my illustrious son, Peter."

Peter, being the eldest heir amongst the hares, was a rabbit of some prominence and the spitting image of his sire. Nevertheless as he rose to the podium the crowd greeted him with half-hearted applause and some quiet grumbling. Everyone gathered knew already how to collect eggs and distribute them. They wanted to get into the meat of the rumors. Peter took the dais and sent out an interrogative pheromone or two in order to sample the mood and get a sense for his audience. Their reply was noncommittal at best. "I've nothing new to report," said he, "on the collection of eggs or their distribution either, other than to reiterate that someone or something has definitely been replundering our plunder." He hopped off the stage and resumed his seat.

Jack rose to his hind legs, speaking angrily. "That's it," he asked, "that's all you have to say?"

Peter twitched his nose uncertainly while offering his father a few ambiguous pheromones as recompense. What more was there to relate? There'd been no breakthroughs in collection technology or in distribution methods either for quite some time now—only setbacks in the latter. "Father," he replied, "I've nothing more to add and no report to make, other than to reaffirm that someone is stealing from us."

"Well, as I said before," Jack replied sharply, "we'll take up that item in its proper time!" This pronouncement was greeted by further rumbling on the part of the extended warren. It was silenced quickly however by a severe look from Jack and an admonition from Nutmeg to her children, grandchildren, and great-grandchildren, two and three times removed, to show "Our Father" the respect that was his due. The crowd fell into an uneasy hush. They had much to say regarding the purported little egg thieves but would for now, bite their tongues and stifle their scent glands and in so doing keep in check their flinty replies laced with harsh pheromones and impolite adjectives that children did not, if they were smart, use when conversing with their parents—especially Jack. With regard to such matters and despite the years of mellowing, he had very little patience for such things and all of them knew he was no rabbit to mess with. "Next on the agenda," continued the head hare, "are those items concerning artwork and dyes and I want you all to pay close attention here because through the diligent efforts of my good son, Cottontail, I'm happy to report that we've resolved the problem of runny eggs. Cottontail?" The forlorn rabbit took his place at the podium with even less enthusiasm than his elder brother. Through much effort and application on his part coupled with exposure to various toxic and nontoxic dyes, paints, and pigmentations, Cottontail had indeed solved the problem of runny eggs and subsequently the artwork with which they became emblazoned was now a permanent fixture upon their casings. For a short while, the sought-after solution had worked like a charm. Since the eggs were now permanently dyed and graffitied there was no way the aggrieved avians could ever hope to identify their lost chicks. The new process had stopped the running and the complaining and everyone seemed to be happy except, of course, the birds. But who really gave a cattle crap about them anyway? Yet soon the runny egg riddle, as it came to be known, resurfaced—for despite the permanency of the artwork the ova began to disappear once again. It was beyond Cottontail to discern for himself how the birds had managed to identify one egg from another. It should've been impossible. He concluded that such must indeed be the case and subsequently laid responsibility for the thievery at the doorstep of some as yet undiscovered and mysterious entity. "The dye is a success," he said, "and our stock is permanently tattooed. However, such effort seems to have been in vain for someone is making off with our eggs nevertheless." He thanked his audience for their attention and quickly quit the podium.

"Crimey!" Jack commented from his seat. "Can't we be quit of that subject or at least take it up in its proper forum and at the proper time?"

"Father," replied Cottontail, "we can't reject what is no matter how much we might wish it to be otherwise."

"Huh?"

"The truth can't be denied. Someone or something is making off with our booty before the recipients get a chance to harvest it for themselves, and it seems to me sir, with no disrespect to you intended, that the only matter of importance we have to discuss is what we're going to do about it!"

"That'll be enough out of you, young hare, hear?" Find your seat and be silent!"

"But—"

"Now!"

Cottontail, who knew better than to argue, took his seat.

"That's better," said Jack, trying his best to maintain order and remain civil at the same time. "Now," he continued, "on to the next order of business. For a report on accounting we turn to my cherished daughter, Rabbitboodles."

Resigned to the inevitable, Rabbitboodles nevertheless made her way to the lectern. Her white fur coat, speckled with gray spots and mottled, could not keep away the onset of chills that beset her as she gave thought to her report and what her father might make of it. Unlike most jackrabbits whose ears although long tend to stand straight up, she and her sisters Flopsy Doodle and Noel were graced with ears that hung down along the sides of their heads, almost completely covering their faces. If only they could truly conceal me, she thought to herself, then I might've escaped my father's notice and not been called upon to deliver my report! But there was nothing for it, she deemed, other than to wade right in and get it over with. "Thank you, fellow rabbits," she began. "It's a pleasure to be here." She sent out a few pleasing pheromones in order to pacify a restless crowd but they were largely ineffective. Not that her brethren were insensitive to such things—far from it. Had they been insensitive or even inclined to impartiality then surely such scents would have played better to the crowd there gathered. But because they were endowed with acute perceptions regarding pheromones, hormones, and scents in general, they were not easily fooled when someone tried to pull the wool over their noses. They all knew that the nose knows and their noses knew cattle craps when they smelled 'em. Because of the nervousness brought about by her father's presence, coupled with the overall ambivalence regarding her report in general, the release of pleasing pheromones that carried with them the scents of tranquility and composure were completely beyond Rabbitboodles capabilities to produce. Thus, when she spoke to the crowd of her pleasure in addressing them, her scents belied her. She was lying through her scent glands and those gathered could smell the lies on her. They were fidgety which only added to her overall ambivalence and they were all conversant in her accounting methods anyway. But sensing that it was near the noon lunch break and knowing that the crowd were eager for their midmorning fare, Rabbitboodles settled in and spoke her piece. "Accounting methods regarding inventory control and reconciliation remain largely unchanged," she said. "We steal an egg and add a mark to the credit side of the tally sheet. Then we deliver that egg to the designated recipient and add a mark to the debit side of the ledger. At the end of the day we subtract the debits from the credits and end up with zero. Nix, nil, naught, squat, nada, zilch, and doo-dah!" She wiped the nonexistent perspiration from her brow before continuing. "So at the end of a hard week's work, we've nothing to show for our efforts which is, I'm sure, exactly what The Powers That Be had in mind when they sentenced father to this unconscionable act in the first place." She paused for a moment to look out over the podium at the sea of faces gazing up at her intently. Heads were nodding, noses were twitching, and tails were wagging in agreement as she spoke to them of the obvious. She relaxed, sensing in them their concurrence. Her juices got flowing and her blood, going. She was now hot to trot—if it could be said that rabbits were capable of such action—yet she was ready to hop, skip, and jump nevertheless. She warmed to their sudden enthusiasm, her nervousness regarding her report giving way to unbridled anger as she regarded the Witches and what they'd unfairly done to her and hers through the unwilling and undeserved vessel of her father. "Still," she continued, "zero is zero and for all of that does represent a balanced book and so, I suppose, we should all be grateful." She looked out at the sea of heads with ears of varying lengths, shapes, and attitudes, nodding in reluctant agreement. "But such is no longer the case!" She emphatically stated. "Now, we've got positive numbers on our tally sheets and negative eggs to show for them!"

"Damned right!" cried out one rabbit lost in the crowd.

"Double damn on that!" cried another. The murmuring and whispering had started again as the rabbits began to grumble to one another about the loss of booty.

Jack looked over at Nutmeg who merely shrugged her shoulders, when Rabbitboodles began to speak again.

"Now," she said, "we steal an egg and make a mark in the credit side of the ledger while delivering it to the recipient by placing it upon their doorstep or perhaps in their basket, yet before they claim it someone else makes off with it. The job being incomplete, we can't transfer a mark to the debit side of the ledger because we can no longer account for the egg which as everyone knows, is still ours until properly claimed." She paused for breath. "I must tell you," she continued, "it's an accounting nightmare. I wish Peter and Cottontail," and here she paused yet again as she cast the two hares a baleful eye, "who deem themselves so clever about such things, could invent a solution—a new type of math, perhaps. One that deals with the abstract notion of negative eggs accounted for positively. Chaos Theory. Even Lotus 123 would be a help if they were clever enough to come up with it. But I suppose such things will have to wait until the advent of the personal computer—speaking of which, are you to any closer to a resolution regarding that?"

The brothers traded guilty glances with one another. "No," replied Peter, "but we think we've finally worked the bugs out of the abacus."

"You think?" asked Rabbitboodles.

"We're not sure," said Cottontail. "That is, it works in theory but the little balls keep getting hung up on the wires and as far as advanced mathematics go, the abacus is never going to do for such complicated mathematics as hyperbolic geometry, infinitesimal calculus, or spherical trigonometry. Therefore, coming up with an acceptable chaos theory that we can all sink our teeth into is quite beyond us at the moment."

Rabbitboodles shook her head in disgust. "Well, there you have it," she said. "We're delivering eggs that we can't account for and someone is making off with them despite our best efforts to the contrary—and there's no accounting for that either!" Having said her piece, Rabbitboodles marched off the podium with conviction and with her head held high.

Reluctantly Jack reclaimed his position on the dais. He was hesitant to do so after the impassioned speech of his eldest daughter for fear that further words on his part would only add fuel to the fire, inciting the crowd to additional and louder outbursts. He looked out timidly upon the sea of sons and daughters who sat there gazing up at him expectantly, as if waiting for him to add further to, and expound upon, the words of their esteemed elder sister. But he was having none of it—at least not until all other issues, relevant or not, were discussed and debated. Rabbitboodles, he knew, had incited his children's passions regarding The Powers That Be. That mania, he realized, was never buried far from the surface and in their anguish, his children's children's children were just like himself. The fruit, as it were, didn't fall far from the tree. Still, he had to make them see that if they were ever going to win this battle with the Witches, they had to fight an indirect struggle, a guerilla war, with hit and run tactics that never directly assaulted their enemies, while hoping to eventually wear them down, for their foes were far too powerful to oppose outright. Therefore laying blame for all their troubles at the feet of The Powers That Be, though perhaps justified, was nevertheless poor strategy. He had to teach them that discretion was often the better part of valor. It was a lesson whose instructions had been hard for him to absorb and perhaps his resistance to learning them was incidental to their troubles. He didn't want his children repeating his mistakes. They needed, he realized, some time to cool off and reflect upon all that had been said. Thus he reached his decision.

"Let's break for lunch," he proclaimed, "and reconvene in an hour." It was simple, to the point, and not at all unexpected. The sun was high, moral low, and rabbits down to the last kitten, were hungry indeed. They quickly dispersed, hoping off quietly with a favorite sibling or a preferred cousin in order to lunch together and discuss amongst themselves the implications of the important issues thus far propounded.

Peter, Cottontail, Rabbitboodles, Flopsy Doodle, Bellamy, and Noel, all kittens of Jack and Nutmeg's first litter, sought each other out for solace and some quiet reflection but alas, such was not to be as their parents descended upon them in a rage, corralling them in a corner before they could make good their getaway.

"You kittens should know better!" said Jack vehemently. His ears stood up stiff as planks. His fur was spiked and his eyes blazed fire. "You're shaking the family tree to its roots so that sour apples are dropping all over the lawn!" Nutmeg nodded her agreement while twitching her nose in order to display her dissatisfaction with the lot of them. "That's right," she declared, "and I won't have children of mine carrying on in such a fashion. It's unseemly, that's what it is—and moreover, it's dangerous!"

Rabbitboodles, by far the most headstrong of the litter, looked to her brethren for support but saw none forthcoming. She therefore took up the banner alone, allowing her cowardly siblings to cringe meekly behind her. "We've spoken nothing but the truth!" she sharply replied. "We've stated the facts and you both know it!"

"And we've said nothing at all!" cried Flopsy and Bellamy jointly. "We've just sat there on our haunches and listened, being perfect little pitchers with big ears!" Finding courage in their joint declaration, they haughtily twitched their noses while holding their heads high.

Jack shook his head. "Whether you've told the truth or not," he replied, "or whether you've said nothing at all is hardly the point. It's as plain to your mother and I as the noses on our faces that your inflamed speeches are inciting fiery passions amongst family that would be best left extinguished!" He admonished his eldest with the most severest of glances. "And as for you two," he continued, nodding at Flopsy Doodle and Bellamy, "your tongues may be silent but your glands are going a mile a minute, spitting pheromones into the crowd, inciting them, goading them, and egging them on! Are you all so foolish as to bring this house of cards tumbling down on our heads?"

"But, father," asked Rabbitboodles, "what else are we to do? For too long now we've chaffed under the yoke of The Powers That Be! For too long we've gathered and delivered ova at the behest of that trio and what have we to show for it? We're shunned by other rabbits who laugh at us behind our backs!" The others nodded their heads, feeling that Rabbitboodles stated the matter succinctly. "Oh, I know," she continued, her dander up, "that the recipients of our efforts are quite fond of their eggs and of the artwork with which we decorate them and that because of this they claim to hold you in the highest regard. Haven't we all seen them clamoring after you for an egg and an autograph? But let that supply of edible artwork fall off for an instant, as it's doing now, and your admirers will quickly come about and present themselves to you as adversaries. They'll turn on you and on us, like ballerinas pirouetting! We'll be hoist upon our own petards and the ironic part will be that it won't be our devices that cause our undoing, but rather those of The Powers That Be! Damn them for all eternity for the trouble they've caused and damn that silly farmer for making such a fuss over a few lousy turnips! And damn his offspring too while we're at it!"

Jack put a halt to her tirade with an abrupt slash of his paw. "Hold your tongue," he replied, "and silence your scent glands! Your pheromones are leaking out indiscriminately." Rabbitboodles struggled to regain her composure, finally succeeding in bringing her glands into good order. "Damn who you will," Jack continued, "but do so quietly and to yourself only and in so doing, leave Old Slomoe's kids out of it! I've met them, you know, and for people they ain't half bad."

"But, father," said Peter, summoning up the courage to come to the aid of his sister, "the way folk tell it, it was the eldest of Slomoe's children who caused the disaster immediately preceding the trial, and had he not done so, then perhaps The Powers That Be would have demonstrated leniency when conducting court." Again heads wagged up and down. There could be no doubt that Junior was a name reviled and held in contempt by all. Jack thought back to that time preceding both the hurricane and the subsequent trial. He remembered having engaged the eldest of the two children in conversation and how the lad had freed him from the cage in which the Witches had him imprisoned. He remembered as well, admonishing the lad to take his younger brother and flee for their lives and how Junior, despite the good advice he'd been given, elected instead to return to the Winnebago and attempt a rescue of his mother. It was foolish to have done so but looking back Jack allowed that had the situation been reversed, with his own mother in the clutches of The Powers That Be, he might've done likewise. "He did battle with the Witches," said Jack, "and with them there's no telling where the truth of the matter really lies. Most likely both he and his mother were in danger of losing their lives. It's not the first time such things have happened and The Powers That Be are not called "The Witches for nothing!"

The children looked down at their feet, embarrassed, while quietly accepting the rebuke of their father.

"And as far as damning the Witches goes," said Nutmeg critically, "that's just plain foolishness pure and simple. Whether they deserve it or not, such curses, spoken aloud, are dangerous. They have their ways of finding things out, you know, and take both insults and threats to their persons to heart, acting upon them quickly and cruelly! Yes, we've been unfairly put upon, and yes, we've chaffed under their oppressive yoke and for no good reason at that, but let your father and I, who feel just as you do but who've more experience with regard to these matters, guide your steps while formulating our overall strategy. Otherwise you hasten the ruination of us all."

The children were stunned into silence as was Jack. They all knew that Nutmeg, although great at oral, was nevertheless not one for long-windedness and yet there she stood, having just given the speech of her life. Even she, to whom actions had always been louder than words, allowed herself a moment to be impressed by her own oratory.

"Well," said Jack, shaking off his stupor, "I guess that says everything!"

No one saw fit to disagree.

Meanwhile, the rest of the children, lesser children, and great-grandchildren twice removed were off in a field nibbling flowers and sampling dandelions. Common meals like this were usually fraught with such laughter and gaiety as rabbits, when in a gathering, are wont to indulge in. This day, however, their mood was somber and subdued as the little lapines conversing amongst each other, engaged in serious conversation regarding the events of that morning. They talked softly in groups of two or three, sometimes trading one fellow for another from this group or that in order to form a more collective opinion with regard to the implications of the morning's pronouncements. It was a regular rabbit roundtable such as had never occurred before and one that was not likely to take place again. Ever. An outsider, given the chance to look in on this strange occurrence, would have thought in terms of a conspiracy—what with all the whispering taking place and the sly and sideways glances that every rabbit present stole in order to assure themselves and their fellows that such goings on were not being overheard or spied upon. But in truth there was no conspiracy, just general confusion and disorder as each, one to the other, made comments like, "Do you believe that?" or "Phew! What a pheromone! I wonder what brought that on?" or even "I can't believe that Peter and/or Cottontail and/or Rabbitboodles, would have the nerve to carry on so and say such things!" As each statement was uttered and each notion of confusion brought forward and admitted to, there was a general wagging of heads and twitching of noses. The rabbits, one after another, held forth in agreement, with pheromones flying. "What's to be made of it?" someone asked.

"I don't know," came the hesitant reply, accompanied by its requisite pheromone.

"Do you think they'll take action?"

"I guess they'll have to," someone else answered. "What other choice have they?"

"Well, I suppose," said another, that's what they're all meeting about. Still, I wouldn't want to be in their paws. 'Our Father' looked pretty pissed!"

"And well he might be," replied yet another. "Father Jack almost lost control—not only of himself but of the council too and not just once mind you, but several times!"

And so it went as the lunch hour wore on. Hares swapping opinions, engaging in scuttlebutt, and being about the business of unbridled speculation and rumormongering; and if the issues confronting them weren't of such paramount importance then they would've been having the time of their lives.

Lunch came to a close and Jack reconvened the council. Rabbits young and old hesitantly took to their seats as if afraid to hear the decrees of the head hare. They needn't have worried. Nothing had been determined and Jack had no pronouncements to make whatsoever. He merely called upon the next speaker, which though a relief to most was certainly a disappointment to some. "We'll turn our attention now," said Jack, "to the next item on our agenda which is the recipient rolls. To present her report, I give you my good daughter, Flopsy Doodle."

Flopsy, who was almost as headstrong as her twin sister Rabbitboodles, found that she'd grown tired of this pointless affair and like the others wanted only to take up the important issue of loss prevention, so she nearly leapt to the podium in her eagerness to get her report over with. Ironically, besides the matter of loss prevention itself, hers was the only subject on which there was any new or pertinent information to be disseminated. She didn't waste any time therefore in expending the unnecessary effort needed to offer up lackluster greetings or misleading pheromones, but rather got right down to business and directly to the point. "The roll," she stated emphatically, "is growing. Like us, people have babies too, although not as quickly and certainly not as many at once."

"Amateurs!" someone from the crowd shouted out. "Amateurs one and all!"

"No doubt," replied Flopsy. "Yet we should be thankful nevertheless for their lack of expertise for despite their amateurish approach to matters pertaining to procreation there can be no doubt that their numbers are growing. As their offspring increase so does our responsibility toward them. More children means more egg deliveries. If all things were equal I shouldn't be too worried. But they're not. The humans may not have our reproductive skill, but they live far longer and their young remain children far longer too. A human baby and one of us, both born on the same day, do not age at the same rate. A human baby born today will still be a child and thus a legal recipient listed on the role, long after most of us are dead and buried. As more of them achieve reproductive status, their birth rate will grow exponentially. It's nothing to concern ourselves with in the short term and since we'll all be dead by the time threshold level is achieved, I guess it doesn't really concern us at all but mark my words, there'll come a day in the not-so-distant future when our descendants will be unable to make all of their required deliveries, regardless of their accounting methods or any improvements that we, or they, might make in the area of loss prevention." There was subdued silence as each member of the gathering considered the implications of Flopsy's statement.

THE CHRISTMAS RABBIT

What would happen when the theoretical threshold was reached and their descendants, through no fault of their own, became unable to complete all of their deliveries? On that not-too-distant day, when demand far outweighed supply, what would The Powers That Be say and more importantly, what would they do? All at the Great Council knew that the Witches were just waiting for something like this to occur so they could pounce upon the warren and inflict even further punishments. There'd be hell to pay, they knew, and the Witches would be holding the IOUs. Not a pleasant prospect. Not pleasant at all.

Peter stood up to ask the question which was on all of their minds. "Any idea of when this theoretical threshold will be reached?"

Flopsy afforded herself a long pause before replying. There were so many variables, she knew, that fixing even an approximate date was next to impossible. "You have to understand," she said, "that there are, or could be, any number of mitigating factors which by themselves or taken as an aggregate, could affect the advent of threshold, thereby hastening or delaying it."

What was this load of cattle craps? Was it yes or was it no? Was it sooner or later? Peter decided to try again. "Such as?"

Flopsy gave her brother an evil look while sending a sour smelling pheromone his way for having the temerity to try and pin her down. "For instance," she reluctantly replied, "there's the coming Ice Age that we've all heard tell of. It may come sooner or it may come later or it may not happen at all. Who can say? Suffice it to say, if it does occur that it's bound to cut into their birthrate."

A nameless face from somewhere deep within the crowd spoke up. "I disagree," said she. "If what you say is true and the Ice Age cometh, well, we all know that there's only one thing to do when it's cold outside. That's why so many babies are born in spring!"

"I hadn't considered that," Flopsy admitted, "and along with that they may get better at birthing and their females become more fertile. Such happenstances may hasten the date. Who knows?"

But Peter was not to be put off so easily. "Say all things remain equal," he asked, "what do your figures indicate then?"

"They still remain pretty vague and inexact," replied Flopsy, "but as near as I can tell, all things being equal, the threshold date should occur somewhere within the next one hundred to one thousand years."

For a moment, there was stunned silence, but only for a moment as the quiet gave way quickly to raucous and unbridled laughter. For rabbits, whose short life spans were seven to ten years at best, such passages of time were almost incomprehensible.

Peter wondered how many rabbits there'd be on this far-flung theoretical day and so took up his abacus and did some quick ciphering. He'd been around long enough and had sired enough children with his own mate to assume some givens. First, he reasoned through experience that any given doe could breed and produce about every other month and that the litters produced averaged about six kittens apiece. To simplify matters, he hypothesized that each litter of six would produce an equal number of males and females. Though not strictly true in the particular, he realized nevertheless that when viewed as an overall and in terms of the long run, such a hypothesis held firm. He knew of no males anyway, that were lacking for nookie, therefore although not exact he was sure his reasoning would bear up under scrutiny and at least it gave him a starting point from which to proceed. Okay, he thought, let me hypothesize one doe as our target breeder. She does the wild thing and after thirty days or so gives birth to six kittens, three does, and three bucks. She then rests and recuperates for a month while weaning her kittens, who in turn are ready at the end of that month to breed themselves.

So now he had one doe, which he designated as target 1, or T1, plus 3 more does who all breed again and who produce three does each for a total of twelve does. He moved the requisite number of beads on his abacus to account for his math. They all rest for a month and then begin the breeding yet again so that the next iteration of his equation could be expressed as $T1 + (T2 \times 3) + (T3 \times 9) = 36$ does. T's 1-4 end up producing 153 does. T's 1-5 produce 612 does. T's 1-6 produce approximately 2,448 does give or take for at this point he further theorized that one would have to account for some rate of attrition…

THE CHRISTMAS RABBIT

And so it went with Peter carrying out his equations while sliding the beads on his abacus furiously until they rattled like maracas as he threw himself into his math. Conservatively then, at the end of two years' time, he found himself with a base population of does that numbered almost two and a half thousand and all ready to breed like cattle the following month. At a minimum, he knew that according to his sister's calculations they had at least ninety-eight more years to go before the theoretical threshold in human population would be reached. Taking into account the aforementioned attrition, as well as other unlooked-for natural disasters, and factoring in the unwholesome influence of The Powers That Be, he decided to err in favor of conservatism by multiplying his 2-year total by itself and then by 98, so that his final iteration produced approximately 1,751,846,342 rabbits, which was a conservative number to say the least and which accounted for does only. And according to his sister they might still have another nine centuries of this malarkey to undergo. He tried to carry out his equations to account for those nine hundred years but his abacus reached a threshold of its own and ran out of beads. The strings broke from the mathematical strain and little round beads went bounding off in tandem as he looked on in dismay. And suppose, thought he, that people were capable of reproducing at even a tenth of the rate that he'd hypothesized for his own kind? That would still leave millions of recipients to account for and there could never be that many people, could there? There simply wouldn't be room enough for 'em! Peter took pains to point all this out.

"You're wrong," said Flopsy after he'd finished his tirade. "My calculations show that there will indeed come a time when our world is littered with the beasts. They'll encroach upon our territory and everyone else's too. It's only a matter of time."

"Well, I wanna see the math," Peter sharply retorted.

"And so you shall," Flopsy replied, "but not today. We've no time for it at the moment and we've still much else to discuss."

"Fine," said Peter, reluctantly giving in. "But there's another flaw in your reasoning besides your questionable math."

Flopsy raised an eyebrow while emitting an incredulous pheromone. "And what might that be?"

"You've not accounted for evolution," replied Peter, and the possible effects that it may have on your projected outcome. For instance, after a thousand years of breeding we're talking about billions and billions of rabbits. Evolution is bound to have made changes in us by then. It's conceivable that our distant cousins may not even be rabbits anymore—at least as we understand ourselves—and that says nothing about men! Who knows what the hell they'll be like after all that time or what they'll want. And as for the birds, perhaps they won't even be birds anymore or laying eggs any longer. After all, they were once dinosaurs a long time ago or so they'd have us believe. Perhaps in your hypothetical future eggs will be a thing of the past! What then, eh? What then?"

"How the hell should I know?" Flopsy retorted angrily. "What do I look like, a soothsayer? Whatever will be, will be. *Que sera, sera!* But rest assured that no matter how much or in what way we each evolve, the Witches are not likely to commute our sentence. Somehow, some way, they'll find the means to continue punishing us!"

Again heads nodded in agreement as rabbits one and all heard the truth of her words and scented the flawless accuracy of her pheromones. Even Peter was compelled to agree for he knew that when it came to The Powers That Be and their inclination toward mischief and misery, that they were as constant as the tides and would continue to trouble them until shrimps learned to whistle.

Flopsy quit the podium to utter silence. Not a grumble or even a discontented whisper was to be heard. She'd given her brethren far too much to think about and all their energies were being spent in a futile effort to absorb it.

Jack rose to reclaim the dais once again. "Well," he said, rubbing a paw across his bewildered brow and back down one ear, "you've certainly given us a heap of pellets to chew, and I say that we save that particular snack for another day entirely. Any objections?" There were none as no one wanted to examine too closely the picture that Flopsy had painted—except, of course, Peter, but he was discriminately ignored. "Good," said Jack, pretending not to see his eldest son his waving paw, "let's move on then to the final item on

THE CHRISTMAS RABBIT

our agenda—loss prevention. I'll chair the discussion and begin it by opening up the floor to general comments and observations. Just remember to raise your paws and wait your turns!"

The rabbits did indeed raise their paws, waiving them like kites in the wind but as for turns, they decided to forego such order and harmony, opting instead to speak out en masse. With an eagerness bordering on mania, they took up their chatter, which consisted of a perpetual plethora of twitching noses, squeaky voices, and wagging heads. Pheromones flew in such profusion that the very air around the mob grew pasty and thick with scents and minute excretions, causing the weakest among them to swoon where they sat and fall away into a dead faint brought on by sensory overload.

Seated directly behind Jack upon the stage, Nutmeg felt the impending presence of those pheromones as well. They assaulted from all sides her sense of smell, making her nose runny. The various sensations they produced within made her run first hot, then cold, then hot and cold simultaneously. She shivered and quaked and was in danger of fainting. Defying an onset of dizziness and struggling for balance, she reached out nevertheless to pull frantically upon Jack's tail.

"Do something, you fool," she rasped, "before they all end up drunk as sots!"

"There's no danger of that," he replied. "They'll pass out before that happens. In the meantime, stick your head down by your tail and between your legs. It will help center you and fend off disorientation. You might try pinching your nose too, but since we have no opposable thumbs, good luck. Cover it with your paw instead and try to ride out the storm!" Nutmeg took his advice as there was nothing else to do and she was too dizzy to argue anyway.

Eventually, the last of them fell victim to the onslaught of their own olfactory's and passed out. Weary beyond all measure, Jack crawled over to Nutmeg and taking her in his arms, fell away into a deep slumber. His last thought before his mind danced off into dreamland was that he should make an effort to stay conscious so as to wake his extended family up and not allow them the luxury of sleeping off their overindulgence. He was himself, however, too wasted to make the effort.

*****

Jack awoke the following morning to the sounds of his clan as they shook off the last dregs of sleep and stupefaction. "Oh my word," he heard one of them say, "my head is killing me!"

"Quite so," said another.

"Indeed!" replied a third.

They were all, including Jack, going through the agonies of pheromone withdrawal, which is analogous to a hangover in you and I. The nausea and pounding would have been quite familiar to either one of us. If you've ever overindulged and with champagne in particular, then you know whereof I speak. Their stomachs rolled and fluttered while their heads cried, "Ave Maria," and their mouths, dry as tombstones, felt like their tails, all stuffed with cotton. They staggered and belched as they slowly picked themselves up off the ground. They farted continuously and in each other's faces at that. Jack looked down upon his brood and felt for them no pity, none whatsoever. They'd done it to themselves, he reasoned, and managed to catch both him, and Nutmeg up in their mish mash while they did it! But hungover or not there was work to be done and issues to decide, plans to make and actions to take. "All right," he yelled although it hurt his head to do so, "we've all had our fun and we all understand now, the price we must pay for having it." Heads nodded weakly and meager whispers of agreement were reluctantly uttered, but nary a pheromone was cast. It seemed that one and all, the entire family had enough of stimulating scents…at least for the time being. "So," Jack continued, "are we ready to proceed in an orderly and businesslike fashion?" Multiple heads wagging in a forlorn manner from side to side indicated that they were anything but. "Father," Peter uttered weakly, "I think that we all need some time to walk this off, get some food in our stomachs, and have some coffee." Rabbits, of course, do not drink coffee—it's one of man's vices, and therefore they want no part of it. However, when in the throes of a pheromone

THE CHRISTMAS RABBIT

hangover, they brew a special tea, medicinal and made from herbs and roots, the exact nature of which they keep secret and to themselves. So secret in fact, that even The Powers That Be know nothing of its existence. I was only made aware of it by chance. I happened to be out traipsing through the woods one day and stumbled across a hare that had just undergone a similar ordeal as the one previously described although not nearly to the same degree or proportion, who was in the act of brewing it. I tried to interrogate it as to the contents but it simply sniffed at me disdainfully while knocking over the kettle and then half-heartedly hopping away. I never found out the proper name for this particular brew just as I remain unaware of its specific ingredients. Suffice it to say, however, that it works on them like a good strong cup of coffee on us—especially when subjected to the agonies of a real katzenjammer. And believe you me, at that particular time and in that particular place, their katzens were jammed. Still, I do not know this remedy's name and therefore refer to it as "coffee" merely for the purpose of clarification.

Jack glanced at Peter and then surveyed the rest of the crowd. "No coffee," he said. "Do you hear me? No coffee!" It was high time, he felt, that his children learned the lesson of overindulgence. When you sated yourself like a glutton, you paid the price. He knew that everyone here, on down to the last little kitten, were soldiers in their battle with The Powers That Be and that soldiers by virtue of their trade needed to attain a certain level of spirituality in order to be successful and still live with themselves while participating in the acts they were forced to commit for having engaged in the vocation of soldiering to begin with. For as any soldier worth his salt knows there's a lot of guilt to be absorbed. Having a solid spiritual grounding, Jack knew, helped one to accomplish this. The attainment of such a lofty state was something Jack knew as well since he'd absorbed the lesson after reading *Zen and the Art of Primitive Tool Repair*. It lies in abstinence, fasting, and frugality. Such wanton displays of gluttony and self-indulgence as those engaged in by his troops the day before only served to mitigate such efforts at spiritual enlightenment by compounding guilt, thereby making atrocities, which are often a soldier's daily fare, much more difficult to engage in and complete and therefore were never to be condoned and had to be dealt with harshly and in no uncertain terms. "Now get yourselves cleaned up," he said. "Brush out your tangles and straighten your whiskers! You look like a pack of rabble, not rabbits! Mother and I will return shortly and then we'll take up where we left off yesterday. But this time we'll do so in an orderly and discreet manner!" He gently took hold of Nutmeg's paw and made ready to leave.

"Where are you going?" someone shouted.

Jack turned back momentarily to confront his family and offer them an incredulous glance. "Are you kidding?" he asked no one in particular. "We're going for a cup of coffee!"

*****

Jack gave his family about an hour. That was more than enough time, he reasoned, for them to get their craps together, brush out tangles, and realign whiskers. It also allowed him the space to brew a belated cup for himself and Nutmeg. She thanked him gratefully for hers and sipped it slowly, savoring each bitter drop and the restoration it imparted as it coursed its way through her tired body and aching head, bringing with it new life and vitality, so at the end of the hour she felt almost better. Not quite, but almost. They sat together for some moments sampling their brew in quiet contemplation but unable to keep her worry to herself, Nutmeg finally spoke. "Jack," she asked, "about last night, what do you think?"

Confused, Jack shook his head while blinking. "Whaddya mean?"

"That orgy of madness," she replied, "had at its roots, fear and uncertainty. Do you think that there's any truth to the rumors? I mean, after all, an army of little people running throughout the forest and stealing our eggs—that's a little improbable, isn't it?"

"Not any more than an army of rabbits," he replied.

"So you believe it?"

Jack paused before answering in order to carefully consider his reply. "I don't disbelieve it," he said. "To tell the truth, I don't know what to think. Something's going on. After all, our eggs have gone missing."

Nutmeg looked at him thoughtfully while running a tired paw across her face. "Do you think it's the You-Know-Whos?"

Jack considered the Witches and their penchant for mischief. "Probably," he replied. "They'd love, after all, to cause trouble. But are they directly involved? I rather doubt it. It wouldn't do for them to be caught having a hand in thwarting their own judgments. They're probably working from the sidelines and using that dumb farmer as their errand boy."

"Santos?" asked Nutmeg incredulously. That idiot couldn't even tie his own shoelaces! Surely the theft of our eggs is beyond him."

"Maybe he has help," Jack replied.

"The wee people?"

"Maybe."

They resumed their silence, each giving consideration to the events of the evening before. After a few more moments passed Nutmeg spoke yet again. "Jack, about last night, do you think we should've?"

"What?"

"You know, do you think we should've let the situation get so out of hand?"

Jack took a sip of coffee before replying. "Don't see how we could've stopped it," he said.

"Oh, we could've stopped it," Nutmeg replied matter-of-factly. "We certainly could have done that and you know it!"

Jack gave her assessment some consideration. "Yes, I suppose we could have," he reluctantly admitted. "But even now, I'm not so sure it would've been the right thing to do."

"How so?"

"Because even though parsimony is best," he replied, "especially when partaking of such things as pheromones, there are times, particularly when we're uncertain or afraid, when it's better to sate ourselves on them. At such times if we wallow in our pheromones while giving vent to our fears and uncertainties, we allow worry and doubt to run their full course. It's painful, to be sure—especially the aftermath and the hangovers. But once we work through those we're often capable of seeing for ourselves that we were able to survive such bewilderments despite being in the midst of their maelstrom. Such doubts inevitably fade away while we continue on. Therefore we end up learning that although fear may gain control of us temporarily—if we're brave, then nothing can conquer us forever."

"That's very un-rabbit-like," she laughingly replied.

Jack chuckled too. "Well," he said, "those Rabbits of Influence with whom you were once so infatuated, used to say that I was the most un-rabbit-like rabbit they'd ever run into!"

"How true," Nutmeg answered sweetly. "How very true." She gave her husband a heartfelt embrace, hugging the hare until he thought he'd choke. He basked in her ministrations while she smoothed out his fur and curried his ears. "Darling," she asked, causing his ears to perk up as he'd never heard her refer to him so tenderly before, "darling, I've something to confess to you."

"Oh, what's that?"

"It's like this," she replied, uncertain as to whether she should continue or not. Doubtful, she nevertheless stammered her way through it. "The day that you first returned from your trip to New York, I…uh, well, that is to say, at the behest of the Rabbits of Influence, I was lying in wait for you in order to spring their trap! They were looking for a scapegoat to take the blame for their raids of Santos's garden and they offered me a lot if I went along with their plans, while at the same time threatening me with the reverse if I refused to play ball!" There. She'd finally worked up the courage to admit it. The truth, however bitter, was finally out, and it was time to let the pellets fall where they may.

"I know," he said, offering her as he did a heartfelt smile. "I know that you were waiting to trap me, and I know that you were coerced into doing it. But it's done with and over, and we'd both be better off forgetting it."

"You knew?"

"Yes," he replied. "Not then, of course, but I found out shortly afterward. Junior told me all about it in the garden on the eve of the hurricane. The Rabbits of Influence had been bragging to anyone who'd listen, I guess, about their handiwork and about how they'd made a sucker out of me by using you as the lollipop. Somehow the tale made it back to the lad. Quite a resourceful young fellow he was, as I remember."

"You knew and took me in anyway?"

"Nuts," he lovingly replied, "as I recollect events back then, it doesn't seem to me that I had much of a choice!"

"Oh." Nutmeg felt her poor little heart breaking but took some small comfort in the rationalization that heartbreak was the least she deserved for such a betrayal.

Jack took note of the sorrow reflected in her tear-stained eyes and longed to ease it. "But even if I'd had a choice," he said, "I would have taken you anyway. I loved you back then and still do today."

A grateful tear ran down Nutmeg's cheek. "Do you mean it?" she asked, unable to bring herself to believe him.

"Yes, my love, I mean it."

"Oh, Jack," she said, throwing her paws around him, "I don't deserve you!" She wept openly because she knew it was the truth. Suddenly she pushed herself away. "But there's more," she continued. "After their scheme blew up and before the trial itself, I tried to worm my way back into their confidences. I was betraying you again. They promptly told me to get lost however—although not exactly in those words, and it wasn't until they'd completely rejected me that I made my way reluctantly back to you and only because I had no place else to go." She was crying wholeheartedly now, gushing rivers of tears, which were completely unfeigned.

"I know."

"I resented you, Jack, for the trouble I'd let myself become embroiled in." She paused to stare dejectedly at her feet. "I was blaming you so that I wouldn't have to confront my own guilt, and I went on resenting you for the longest time. In fact, I don't think that I fully let go of my bitterness until last night as I watched you preside over the family. I realized then that you were doing this as much for my sake as you were the children's. I'm sorry for you—that you had to endure such bitterness. But now that it's truly purged, I can honestly say that I'm happy with my lot, witches and eggs excluded, of course, and that I'm proud to be your mate." She paused a moment. "I love you, Jack. I love you with all of my heart." He heard the sincerity in her words, and despite her hangover, she followed them through with a pheromone or two that he might smell her candor as well.

Jack felt his heart leap for joy! How long had he waited to hear such words? How long had he stayed in this one spot, never fleeing from it or shirking his penance in order to get that one chance to smell such scents? It seemed like forever. "And I love you," he replied. And he did. But he still didn't trust her, at least not completely. Not that she wouldn't do now what she thought best for him—he believed she would. Furthermore, he felt that she was willing at this point to attempt moving heaven and earth in order to do for him what she felt was right and in his best interest. That was devotion and love and he knew it. But her fickleness, he knew, would lead her to misconstrue what was best, causing her to color those perceptions with her own subjections. Jack remembered coming across a book of adages written by some king who lived days away from the forest. People, he'd been told, held this king in high regard, marveling at his wisdom and doting upon his every word. Not having much use for people in general Jack should have felt likewise about the king and his proverbs. But despite the rabbit's inherent prejudices the king's wisdom struck a chord within Jack, which resonated. One piece of advice particularly caught his attention, making its home in his heart. It went as follows:

> Look, says the Teacher, this is what I have discovered. Adding one thing to another to discover the scheme of things—while I was still searching but not finding—I found one upright man among a thousand but not one upright woman among them all.

Maybe that was so for the women of men. Jack couldn't honestly say as he'd been intimate with so few. But it certainly rang true for rabbits who by nature and design went about on all fours most of the time anyway; and it seemed especially applicable to Nutmeg!

THE CHRISTMAS RABBIT

The rabbits reconvened in a semiorderly fashion, the hares having split hairs and straightened tangles; there were however not a few who did too poor a job on their whiskers. Jack let it pass. There was no point in berating them about such a trivial matter. This was war after all, not a beauty contest. "Shall we try again," he asked humorously, "to pick up where we left off?" No one spoke up. Everyone remained silent for fear of inciting another pheromone frenzy. Outwardly Jack appraised them with a critical eye while secretly pleased that they'd seemingly learned their lesson and were proceeding cautiously.

"Let me sum up for you then," he said, "your incoherent babble of the evening before. The majority of you are of the opinion that there is an army of wee folk in and about the forest and in the lands beyond, who are involved in a campaign to plunder from us our hard earned booty, is that correct?" A chorus of heads nodded their agreement. Glands, however, were kept in check. "Does anyone have anything further to add before we decide on a plan of action?"

The crowd continued their silence. What more was there to say? Many there had caught glimpses of the sprites and there could be no further gain in denying them.

Jack shook his head derisively. He'd expected better of them—especially Peter and Cottontail who accounted themselves so smart. Well, it just goes to show, he thought, that being a genius doesn't necessarily mean you see what's plain, apparent, and in front of your nose. "Besides these alleged wee folk," asked Jack, "has anyone stopped to consider whether or not another party or parties are involved with these thefts?"

The rabbits looked at one another, both confused and uncertain. What was "Our Father" driving at? Who'd seen anyone else? As far as they knew, no one.

"Have any of you even considered the possibility that this might be a very well planned and executed conspiracy?"

"Of course it's a conspiracy, father," replied Peter. "Most of us agree that there are wee people and that they're stealing our eggs. Wee people, not wee person. *People* are plural, indicating the presence of more than one. When you have more than one conspirator involved in a plot, you have, by definition, a conspiracy." Peter looked smug as heads all about him nodded their affirmatives. Did "Our Father" think that they were stupid?

Jack offered Nutmeg a tired chuckle before turning his attention back to his children. "No, I don't think that you're stupid," he said, reading the looks on their faces. "A little dense maybe and a bit too big for your britches—if any of you wore britches, that is. And certainly you're all a bit wet behind the ears if you can't see for yourselves what is most certainly before you!" He paused for a moment in order to let that remark do its work for him but as he gazed out at the sea of blank faces, realized that it wasn't going to be so easy. "Well?"

"Father," spoke up Cottontail, "I think it plain to see that we don't really smell what you're sniffing out."

"Oh, that much is certain," the head hare replied. "If you did then I probably wouldn't even need to be here."

Most gathered there allowed as how that was probably so.

"Has anyone asked themselves," Jack inquired, "why the wee folk, if they exist at all, are even here in the first place? What I mean to say is that this isn't really their neck of the woods, is it? They come from foreign parts mostly and those lands are a good ways off. So why would they bother?"

"To steal our eggs!" someone from the crowd shouted out. "That much is obvious!"

Jack tracked the author of that statement down, glaring at him until the little lapin wilted under his gaze like wet lettuce. "That much and that much only!" Jack said adamantly. "If any of you could see past the noses on your faces, we wouldn't be having this meeting right now. We'd be out collecting our eggs or having accomplished that, be heading for Pompano Beach for a well-deserved vacation! Instead we find ourselves here and having to waste our valuable time in an effort to solve a riddle whose answer is as plain as day! Why would wee folk want our eggs? Everybody knows that they eat lembas and ambrosia. Eggs hold no interest for them. So why are they stealing them?"

"Perhaps," ventured someone in the crowd, "they're patrons of art."

THE CHRISTMAS RABBIT

Jack offered up another frown. "Don't any of you find it the least bit improbable that there's an army of wee folk out there acting upon their own initiative and stealing our eggs?"

"No more so than an army of rabbits!" someone else gamely shouted out.

"Exactly," retorted Jack. "That army of rabbits is us, and who do you think is responsible for our sad state of affairs?"

There were many there who felt they knew the answer to that, but being both afraid and embarrassed, held their tongues while meekly looking down at their feet. *Why you, father*, many thought. *It was you, after all, who got caught in the farmer's garden. You.*

Jack saw through to their innermost hearts while reading the accusation plainly written upon their faces. He seethed in anger, almost gave vent to it, and with supreme effort checked his wrath at the last possible moment. They were in their own indirect way almost correct, he supposed, and he'd as much as admitted this to himself the day before. But there were wheels within wheels turning, and his children had to be made to see who was rolling them. "The Witches!" he yelled. "The Witches put us in this position, and as sure as cattle crap, they're the movers and shakers behind the wee folk too!"

A concentrated and consternated, "Hmm," broke out amongst the crowd as one rabbit after another realized what should've been obvious from the beginning. That once again they were being maneuvered and manipulated by powerful forces and were beset by hidden and invisible enemies. Once again, they were finding themselves upon the short end of the stick. Heads wagged in unison, noses twitched in agreement. And before Jack could stop it, pheromones began to fly. "Hold there, I say! Hold! There's no point in provoking our pituitaries! We all remember how far that got us yesterday, don't we?"

They did. With reluctance, they restrained their passions and brought their glands into good order.

"Father Jack," asked a grandkitten from four litters out, "if the You-Know-Whos are behind this as you say—and it makes perfect sense to me that they are now that you say it, then what can be done about it? Can we trap them, do you think?"

"A good question, lad," replied Jack, "and one that deserves an answer, and that answer is no. At least, not directly." The crowd began to grumble. What then, they wondered, was the point of this conversation? "First off," Jack continued, we can't confront them directly because doing so would be tantamount to putting our heads in a lion's mouth. They're too tough to take on in a fight and doing so would be suicide. Worse, it would be genocide, for they'd surely kill us all."

This insight was acknowledged by the collective nodding of somber heads. Father Jack spoke the truth and no one there needed the further assurance of confirming pheromones to know it. "But there's another reason," said Jack, even more pertinent than their obvious power, for a strategy on our part which employs an oblique attack. Your mother and I have been discussing this matter, and it is our opinion that rather than controlling the wee folk directly, the Witches are instead making use of Old Slomoe, using the Tortoise as a go-between in order to provide distance for themselves from this affair. It's Santos, therefore, whom we must engage! We must take up arms once again and attack our enemy of old. Only in so doing can I foresee any hope of confronting The Powers That Be and thwarting their plans."

Rabbits of all shapes, sizes, and colors began twitching their noses and nodding their heads, as engaging their enemy of old was a notion they could all sink their teeth into. And if, as Father Jack claimed, The Powers That Be were the puppeteers pulling the strings in Santos's latest campaign to harass and embarrass them, then an assault against the farmer would allow them to repay in good measure the insults and injuries fostered on them by Helgayarn, Brunnhilde, and Betty. They would fall back on tried and true tactics, harassing the farmer from ambush and attacking him with their wicked little teeth. It had been tried with success before and what had worked once would surely succeed again. Beleaguered and beset, Santos would soon fall into familiar confusion and in so doing quickly relent of his current campaign against them. Pithecanthropus Wideass, whom they considered to be the very bane of their existence, would soon crack and crumble from the commensurate pressures brought about by the savagery of their combined attacks. As he fell apart, so would the machinations of The Powers That Be. It was a simple plan, they all knew, and one easy to implement…except for one sticking point…all those wee people. What were they going to do about them? The Powers That Be, they knew, would not risk the scandal which would ensue were they to be discovered as having been involved in this affair. The wee people however, who knew what they might do or what risks they might take? Who among the crowd gathered could with any accuracy predict either their intentions or the depth of their involvement within the conspiracy itself? Were even Peter or Cottontail, or for that matter "Our Father" himself, wise enough to define the parameters of their marching orders or the limits and restrictions which were placed upon them? Were there any limits? And if not, what kind of trouble did that spell? It was clear to the rabbits that The Powers That Be meant to triumph in this affair by whatever means possible. It was also obvious to them, just as they were sure it was plain to the Witches themselves, that by inducting the farmer and including him within the ranks of their conspiracy that the trio were severely handicapping themselves and their efforts. Why would they do that? Perhaps, concluded the rabbits, The Powers That Be had determined for themselves that they'd simply no choice. But would three such sour sirens so intent on securing their own supremacy no matter who suffered or what was at stake, stack the odds so singly against themselves? The rabbits thought not. Thus the inclusion of the wee people whom analysis on the part of the rabbits would seem to indicate were under no constraints whatsoever. It was the only way, the rabbits knew, that the Witches could hope to crawl out of the pit into which they'd fallen by involving Old Slomoe in their affairs in the first place. How could mere rabbits contend against such as adversaries as wee people when the latter were under no constraints regarding the rules of war? The methods of pack hunting which the rabbits had employed with such success and utility would not avail themselves against such enemies. For one thing, it was assumed, correctly in this instance, that there were far more of these folk than there were of the farmer, who could be accounted for by all present with one digit on their paws. The farmer was just one whereas his suspected cronies were an army in and of themselves and in terms of size almost rivaled the rabbits in numbers alone. The rabbits would be forced into one-on-one confrontation or something so similar that trying to define it in terms of rabbit to elf would be pointless. They'd have to stand toe-to-toe with the little bastards and engage them single-handedly. If each rabbit had for themselves a mere farmer to contend with there would be no problem and all there knew it. But though the little folk were far smaller than Santos, that didn't make them any less intelligent. Hell, there were rocks out there, the rabbits knew, that could run circles around Old Slomoe! Certainly the wee folk were capable of at least that and probably more. The rabbits could count upon the Witches stacking the deck, therefore the wee folk were in all likelihood magical, just the like the dames who employed them and how does one fight magic?

These matters were discussed in great detail by the family and most members had an opinion to offer or an observation to make. Those that spoke did so eloquently and from the convictions of their own beliefs, yet nary a single pheromone was emitted.

"We need the guidance of an expert," someone shouted out from the crowd. "Someone who's fought battles aplenty and who's used more than simple pack strategy to win 'em!"

"Here Hare!" came the crowd's enthusiastic reply. "Here Hare!"

"We need a professional," someone else imputed, "a warrior who loves battling for battle's sake. A wandering adventurer with no known allegiances who can be bought and who's devotion can be assured for a price!"

"Here Hare! Here Hare!"

"A tough guy," this same someone went on, "a real radical who won't be afraid to mix it up with the likes of our enemies. A soldier of fortune, a mercenary. One mean hombre with a hair across his ass about fighting those who'd hassle hares and who's not too particular about his enemies. A warmonger and a bully boy! A gorilla and a goon!"

"Here Hare! Here Hare!"

THE CHRISTMAS RABBIT

Jack looked out upon the sea of wagging heads and twitching noses, considering the idea. "To what end?" he asked. "Would you have this hooligan fight our battles for us?"

"Here Hare! Here Hare!"

"What about honor," asked the head hare, "and the ideal of fighting one's own fights?"

"What of it?" came the reply. "We're all too busy delivering eggs to get ourselves caught up in such silliness."

"It's our fight," Jack replied, slightly miffed. "We should fight it."

"Why?"

As he looked upon the crowd, Jack realized he didn't have a single argument with which to respond. Yes, he wondered, why should we do the fighting for ourselves? Hadn't the Witches done Santos's fighting for him on that long ago day when he'd been trapped in the garden? Yes. And didn't the Rabbits of Influence use Nutmeg to do their fighting for them when they'd made a scapegoat of him? Yes. And during the trial itself, hadn't the Witches employed the venerable law firm of Owl, Owl, & Peacock as their hired guns, using them as the front line in their battle with both Santos and himself? Yes! And weren't The Powers That Be even now employing both Santos and the wee people as foot soldiers in their continuing war with him? Yes! Yes! And Yes again! It suddenly dawned upon Jack that the smart generals, the ones who were accounted sly and crafty by their enemies, had always been slick enough to get someone else to do their fighting for them. They were adept at getting clods to take the licks that should've rightfully been theirs! Such had been the case from the dawn of creation and such practices weren't likely to change anytime in the near future. Why, even the serpent, if the old tales were true, had manipulated Adam and Eve, using them to fight his fight with God. If such tactics were good enough for that old snake, then why not likewise with rabbits? Why not?

He nodded his head in approval, giving an enthusiastic okay to their suggestion. The gathered rabbits in turn offered up cheer upon cheer with much "Here Haring." Jack allowed them to vent their enthusiasm but then raised an admonishing paw to silence them.

"Where do we find such a mercenary?" he asked. "And more importantly, how do we buy him off? If he wants hard currency we haven't got any! The best we can hope to treat with is acorns and eggs and is a mercenary of the caliber we seek likely to be had for such pay?"

The crowd looked about restlessly. They hadn't thought to consider such aspects. That's why, they supposed, they had Father Jack to look out for them. It was "Our Father," they knew, who was here to ask the really difficult questions and to clearly define the issues at hand while putting them in their proper perspectives.

"What do you suggest?" they all asked in chorus.

"I haven't a clue," Jack replied bitterly. Well…so much for "Our Father"!

"Perhaps, father," suggested Noel, "we should concentrate first on identifying a likely candidate. Even if we can get our paws on all the money in the world, such cash will avail us little if we cannot come up with a warrior upon whom to spend it. Maybe we should make our selection first and negotiate payment later."

There was another round of nodding heads and twitching tails as well as ongoing choruses of "Here Hare! Here Hare!"

"Seems sensible to me," someone said.

"I agree wholeheartedly," said another. And so on and so forth. Like most folks of Olden Days and even more so folk in our own time as well, it seems that rabbits have never had a problem with the notion of "Buy now, pay later." Like most of us, they foolishly believed that any problem could be solved with good credit.

"What about Sergeant Sergeant?" asked Peter. "He's a soldier and quite proficient at it, or so I'm told."

"Here Hare!" roared the crowd. "Here Hare!" All there had heard of the ant farmer who lived a ways west of them. A retired drill sergeant from the Marine Corps, he'd been spending his retirement planning a campaign of his own devising while training and commandeering an army of ants whom he hoped to lead into battle and conquer the world. Whereas Alexander merely ruled Persia, Sergeant Sergeant would not rest nor be content until the whole ball of dirt were in subjugation and lay at his feet. And of course, he had an army of his own which he could lead into battle on their behalf. To the rabbits at the council, he seemed the perfect choice. Jack, however, quickly put the quash on that selection. "No, no," he cried, "that lunatic simply won't do at all, not at all, I say!"

"Why not?" Peter asked in rebuttal. "He's a soldier, isn't he?"

"Yes," replied Jack. "But he's also a farmer, and farmers are never to be trusted. Never. Besides, in training his army, he's done no more than mimic our own strategies of pack hunting and attacking in force. We've already agreed that such a battle plan is not equal to the task at hand. But even if it were, and he was victorious in applying it, remember, all of you, that a farmer is a farmer is a farmer; and once he won the battle, he'd simply turn his army loose on us. He has his own agenda, you know, and we'll never turn him aside from his dreams of conquest no matter what the offered price."

So much for that idea. The rabbits thought long and hard as they strove to identify another likely candidate but could come up with no other alternatives. Sergeant Sergeant was the only warrior they knew of; thus, much against their will, they were forced into a prolonged and protracted silence.

The uneasy hush dragged on making its presence amongst the group felt like an unwanted and unwelcome intruder that inserts itself in your space, wrapping its cold and tenebrous fingers around your throat like an icy claw and with sadistic glee, chokes the very life out of you. The rabbits were suffocating in their own impotency and silence. It stretched out like warm taffy, enveloping them like pasty goo until one rabbit finally spoke out. This hare was hardly ever heard from. He was a quiet fellow who spoke only when he had something worthwhile to say unlike most of us, who rarely know when to keep our mouths shut. His name was Grasshopper, and he was so monikered because he loved to prance about and play in fields of green and no one, absolutely no one, could match him in a foot race. All through the Great Council he'd kept his silence. He could have said much, he knew, but since it was all being said for him by others, and since those others were older and presumably wiser than himself, elected to maintain a discreet silence, listening only. After all, someone had to! But now the host was at an impasse and he therefore determined that the time had come for him to speak out, put his best paw forward, and participate in this powwow. "Father Jack," he began, but was immediately cut off.

"Who are you, eh?" Jack interrupted. "I've never seen you before!"

Grasshopper looked about at the veritable throng around him. "Is that unusual?" he asked. "Aren't there many here that you've never met personally?"

"I've met them all," replied Jack. "I don't remember half of them once I do and of the half that I do I've discovered I like them half as well as I ought! But still, I've met them all. Of that I'm quite sure—or was until you spoke out. Who are you anyway? What's your name?"

"Grasshopper, sir. My name is Grasshopper."

"That seems right and proper for a rabbit," Jack said. "What's your question?"

"Sir," replied the young coney, "I haven't a question but if I may be allowed would like to offer up a suggestion."

"A suggestion?" uttered Jack. "Do you mean advice?" The junior rabbit meekly nodded his head. "Aren't you a little wet behind the ears," Jack continued, "to be offering up advice?"

"Perhaps," replied Grasshopper. "But you know what they say—out of the mouths of babes... And since no one else seems willing or able to do likewise, then perhaps you shouldn't be so choosy!"

Jack sniffed disdainfully. "Could be," he contritely replied. "Could be." They stared at each other for some moments until Jack spoke again. "Well, get on with it, lad," he said. "If you're impertinent enough to offer up advice then you better go whole hog and render it!"

Grasshopper hesitated before replying, nervous in his inexperience now that it came down to it. "Well, it's um—like this..." he stammered, "as, ah, many of you...hmm...here know, I'm...ah, the fastest hare hereabouts." There was a chorus of nods and twitching noses from those who knew him. Jack, however, viewed his statement with skepticism. After all, how could one so young be so accomplished? "And I'm not bragging," the young hare continued, sensing Jack's doubts, "but mention it only to point out that as the swiftest it often falls upon me to deliver our eggs the furthest afield. Upon one such happenstance, I found myself in Japan and—"

"Japan?" Jack cut in. "Where's Japan, eh? I've never heard of it!" He was lying of course. *Zen and the Art of Primitive Tool Repair*, that voluminous tome given to him by Thor Rowe, makes mention of Japan so often you'd think it was a travel brochure. He pretended ignorance, however, in order to test the veracity of the young speaker before him.

"It's a ways east of here," replied Grasshopper. A journey of many days over land and a couple of hours of swimming to boot!"

"What of it?" queried Jack.

"During one of my sojourns there," Grasshopper said, "while delivering my eggs, I heard stories from the locals about a famous warrior and wizard who lived alone like a hermit atop Mount Fujiama (which back in Olden Days was nothing more than a sand hill). It was related to me by natives who dwelt within its shadow that he lived atop the mountain in absolute solitude, a mystic and warrior aesthetic, practicing and perfecting his martial art. It was further related that as a youth this warrior had fought many great battles and had never been defeated. He was rumored to have killed a hundred opponents all at once and with one paw tied behind his back, whereupon it was said that he retired from the art of actual dueling. It presented to him no challenges worthy of his skills and so instead, gave himself over to thoughtful introspection while refining his martial theories. Perhaps he's grown bored with engaging in such esoteric endeavors and would welcome the challenge of putting his theories and skills to the test. If so, he might consider our plight and come to our aid."

Jack thought it over. "Sounds like a likely candidate," he said. "But would such a man be willing to help rabbits?"

"That's the beauty of it!" Grasshopper excitedly replied. "He's no man at all but rather a rabbit, just like ourselves!"

"A rabbit?" came Jack's incredulous reply. "A rabbit, you say? How come such a fellow never participated in the raids on Santos's garden? After all, such raiding sounds within his bailiwick!"

"Well," replied Grasshopper, "Japan's a long way to come from in order to take part in such silliness and even if it weren't, this fellow being a loner, is pretty much used to going his own way. I doubt he'd display much patience when it comes to taking orders and directives from the Rabbits of Influence and their ilk."

"Why then," asked Jack, "should he feel disposed to taking our directives?"

"We could frame them as petitions and requests," suggested Grasshopper, "rather than shout them out as orders. Being both polite and subservient while at the same time playing to his ego, which I'm sure must be massive having won for himself so many battles, would go a long way toward inducing him to do as we ask."

"What's his name," asked Flopsy Doodle, "and do you think you could find him?"

"His name," replied Grasshopper, "is Hareihito Rabbakami and yes, given that he's so well-known in those parts, I'm sure that I could locate him and convince him to come to our aid. But we have to act quickly. Japan's an awfully long journey and with the continental drift, draws further away with each passing second. Someday it's going to be impossible to get there!"

The choking silence of impotency surrendered itself to the quiet contemplation of anticipation as each rabbit gave thought to Grasshopper's proposal and its relative chances for success. Jack and Nutmeg, with their backs to the crowd, conferred quietly and in private for some minutes. Finally, they turned about and facing Grasshopper, gave him both permission to go and leave to recruit. "Set out today," they said. "Leave this very moment, and don't stop to pack! Return to Japan, find this warrior, Rabbakami, and bring him back here to us!"

"I will, father," he replied, and he did…well, sort of. But it was almost too little too late, for the trap was about to be sprung.

*****

Farmer Santos had been planning for this great day for months. Perhaps planning wasn't the right adjective. Old Slomoe never planned for anything; rather he was adept at riding the winds of fortune, both good and bad, while letting them carry him where they would. So it is more accurate then to describe his actions as unwittingly propelling him forward until he came face-to-face with this watershed event.

For an entire season, while under his generalship, the elves had been stealing a goodly portion of the rabbits' eggs and securing them in a magical room which only they could gain entrance to. Even Santos, when he tried, could not gain access into this fortress. Its magical door had been cast in iron—which was a feat in itself since back in Olden Days they'd barely entered the Bronze Age—and could only be opened by turning the magic dial on its face. The dial was round and engraved upon its rim were numbers starting from 0 and ending in 99. Since Santos could barely count past ten, the dial presented him with an unsolvable enigma. One had to turn the dial this way, and then that way, and then this way again in order for the magical door to open. Only the elves knew how to do it and that was just fine with the farmer. He didn't want the damned eggs anyway and had no idea of what to do with them now that they were in his possession. He couldn't return them to their original owners. They were tattooed with graffiti and unrecognizable. Nor could he give them away to their proper recipients as listed on the roles since he didn't have access to those lists and therefore had no idea of who the recipients might be. And even were he to make the attempt, assuming, of course, that he could defeat the door, then like it as not he'd be branded a thief himself for having possessed them in the first place. It was intolerable. But even magic rooms, it seemed, contained a finite amount of space and that space was rapidly filling up. It was not strictly what the Witches had in mind, he knew, when they'd first set him upon this task. In fact, it could be construed, he supposed, as being in direct confrontation with their schemes and designs since when they'd last met, although giving him their permission to steal eggs, offered no insight regarding their disposal, encouraging him instead to simply harass and embarrass. But to what end? And what to do with the stolen ova? Early on in the campaign he'd tried asking The Powers That Be for further clarification regarding the matter but they, hiding behind their cover of plausible deniability, ignored his requests for advice, making themselves unavailable for council whenever he sought them out and instead referring him to the good devices of the elves. *To hell with it*, he thought. He was tired of others assuming that he couldn't carry his own weight. He managed his girth just fine, thank you very much, and so what if he needed a girdle?

Like any good civilian who fancies himself a four-star general, Santos took to standing far in the rear of the battle lines as he received reports and updates from the actual grunts whose business it was to do the dirty work. Let the professionals who knew their business, he reasoned, be allowed to go about it without having to contend with interference from amateurs. It would be his task, he further reasoned, to take credit for their labors when the appropriate moment came. That moment however, seemed evermore distant as the elves amassed ova only to hoard them in the safe. Other than the thefts of the eggs, this second war appeared to be a stalemate. Finally, Santos and his helpers found that they could proceed no further as the magic room was full. There would be no more thieving because there could be no more hoarding. The Witches, he knew, would not appreciate it. "What can we do?" cried the farmer. "We can't just stop now! We've a rabbit to harass and three ladies—I use the word loosely—to whom we're committed! Can't you build another magic room?"

The elven smith who'd designed the first one stepped forward. His name was Hephaestus. He was old for an elf, and he looked it—which was unusual in their kind as most, at least the comely ones anyway, never seemed to age past adolescence. But Hephaestus was bent and twisted like the roots of an ancient oak. His skin was mottled and dark like the bark of an old chestnut, and it was streaked with black—ground-in soot, no doubt, from the fires of the mighty forge he'd employed to cast the iron door. Actually, the forge wasn't much more than a barbeque pit located in Santos's backyard, but since forges at that time were something of a rarity, then anything consisting of a bit of lighter fluid and two sticks to rub together would have been deemed mighty indeed. Hephaestus's arms and shoulders were massive as a result of the constant strain he subjected them to whilst employed at the forge and operating its bellows. They were also out of proportion to his legs, which were skinny shanks, all bone and lacking meat. His spine was a corkscrew that ended up at the top of his shoulders in an obscene hump, causing his upper half to hunch over and bow from the onerous burden of the added weight. His right arm, when at rest, remained drawn to his side and twisted at the wrist so that the palm of that hand was forever facing upward with its fingers perpetually twisted in a forbidding claw. His hair was both dirty and lank and hung heavily upon his shoulders. His gray eyes were wide and bulbous, the right one being afflicted with a constant and disturbing twitch. His odor was sour and stale. His feet smelled and had fungi growing between their toes. His eyebrows were thick and bushy and his beard was gray and grizzled and each were lice ridden. His skin was pocked and covered with open sores, which oozed pus. His breath was a miasma, both foul and rank and he was missing his front teeth. Yet for all that, he was a jolly fellow who performed his assigned tasks without complaint. "Squire," said he, although none of the elves including himself felt that the farmer merited such distinction, using it only as a means of address since they had to call him *something* and "Pithecanthropus Wideass" was not an honorific which could be made use of if any sense of chain of command were to be preserved, "it took all of the iron ore that I could gather in these parts to build for you the one magic room that we have. To gather more, we'd have to search far afield, drilling into the very depths of Mungo herself. I'm not sure she'd appreciate such an invasion. Still, we could certainly do it; but even unopposed, it's bound to take time—time enough, I warrant, for those pesky rabbits to replenish their supply of eggs. Then we'd be right back where we started.

 Santos looked at Hephaestus and thought to himself that here stood one sorry soul that was surely in need of a vacation, but since unions and the rabble rousers who organized them were far in the future so was "time off," however much deserved. "We have to do something!" the farmer cried. "You lads were supposed to be my aces in the hole, the cards up my sleeve. Now, instead of aces I find that I'm holding all deuces! What of your magic? What of your power?

"Don't you have any ideas at all?" He looked on in exasperation as his multitude of short-limbed serfs and puny peons whispered amongst themselves, swapping ideas and exchanging alternatives. Finally, one of the wee folk spoke up. "Nope," said he. "We haven't a clue. We're not here to think, just do. It's your job to do the thinking."

"Then we're really in trouble," Santos said under his breath. Frightened by his lack of rumination and his inability to formulate the merest of plans as to how to proceed next, the farmer was nevertheless saved from himself when two excited elves came running up through the crowd. It was Pixie and Dixie who at his bequest had gone off to the other side of the forest in order to spy out Jack and his rabbits and determine for the farmer if the head hare and his family were planning any counterstrokes to their elven mischief. Excited and agitated, the two pushed their way through the crowd to throw themselves at the farmer's feet.

"Squire!" they cried. "Squire—we have news! News!" They looked quite a sight, being decorated with leaves, brambles and the flora of the forest. It was camouflage and it was a skill that the duo could have taught Jack a thing or two about had they been so inclined or otherwise employed. "The rabbits, sir," said Pixie, "are all gathered together in one place!"

"It's true," said Dixie. "They're having a meeting—a great council, or so they choose to call it. The beasts are all in one spot and therefore vulnerable. While Jack has his entire family before him, I say let's embarrass and humiliate the little rodent. We should attack!"

Santos eyed them doubtfully. "I don't know," he replied. "I've never been much good at that sort of thing, and besides, it all sounds rather violent, doesn't it? Someone could get killed, and although I'm all for that—so long as it isn't me, that is, The Powers That Be have strictly forbidden killing. I'd hate to go against their wishes and then find myself on their bad side."

"Geez, Louise!" cried Pixie, who'd had enough of this silly affair and who like the rest of the elves, looked forward to its speedy conclusion. "Their bad side, as you so quaintly put it, is the only side they have—and you've been on it since this whole business started! You're at rock bottom now with no place left to go but up! But when

I say attack, I'm not referring to actual battle and the killing such battle implies, but rather seizing the initiative. The way to embarrass Jack is to maneuver him while in front of his family, into a corner from which he cannot escape. Use his pride against him and you can expose him as the little miscreant we all know him to be!"

"I can?"

"Most assuredly."

"It sounds like a plan," Santos admitted. "But what is the plan exactly and how do I enact it?"

"You challenge him," said Dixie. "Am I not correct, brother," he said to Pixie, "that this is exactly what you had in mind as well?" It was, of course, since they'd discussed the matter thoroughly on their return trip.

"Indeed, brother!" replied Pixie. "Indeed it is. I find it simply amazing how great minds think alike!"

"It amazes me not in the least," said Dixie, "but rather, I credit the confluence of such cognitive processes to be the by-products of roads likewise traveled."

"Well, it amazes me," commented Santos, although perhaps it shouldn't, "that the two of you have managed to lose me already!" The two elves were pontificating, and their oration was chock-full of three- and four-syllable words. Santos didn't know that many two-syllable words, thus his confusion. "Challenge him, you say? Challenge him to what—a game of tiddlywinks and two out of three falls?"

Pixie and Dixie looked to each other as if to confirm one another's thoughts. "A contest," they replied. "A contest in which there can be no doubt of his expertise and skill—which when you win will therefore engender concerns regarding his proficiency in such endeavors since he will suffer a humiliating defeat at your hands. You'll challenge him on his own ground! Meet him in his own arena!" Santos looked at them suspiciously. Had they gone too far? they wondered. They had been rehearsing this last piece line-by-line, and speaking it in unison had perhaps made it sound a bit too contrived. But since "rehearsing" and "contrivance" are both multisyllabic, they needn't have worried. The meanings of each were beyond Slomoe's ability to comprehend. His suspicions arose from his own doubt in himself. He'd been boasting a lot in the recent past about how he'd gotten the better of everybody but then braggadocio is something that self-doubters often engage in. It helps them, I think, to fend off self-perceived inadequacies. It's not surprising then to find that Santos was the biggest braggart in the forest. "What in the name of the four winds," asked he, "do you have in mind?"

"A race," replied Dixie. "A great race wherein you challenge him to compete with you in a delivery of eggs!"

"A race? Are you out of your elven minds? I'm certainly not one to go about praising his attributes but even I know that on his worst day Jack could run circles around me—backward! I couldn't hope to win such a contest."

"That's most certainly true," said Pixie. "If left to your own devices, you'd surely fall flat on that ample behind of yours! But you won't be relying upon your skills. You'll have all of us in your corner and on your team! We'll run such interference for you, creating mayhem and havoc that the hapless hare will literally be running in circles. You can't help but win! And when you have and all his children gather together to question amongst themselves their father's abilities, we'll swoop down upon them and settle this silliness once and for all! Then we can all go home."

"What about The Powers That Be?" Santos asked nervously. "Although I do recall them mentioning some sort of race themselves, I gathered nevertheless that it would be a contest of their own devising, taking place at a time of their own choosing. This is bound to make them angry!"

"Only if you lose."

"I always lose!"

"That's because you've never had us!" Pixie and Dixie replied, pointing at themselves and their brethren. "We'll win this war for you and once we do and your mastery of Jack and his rabbits is proclaimed throughout the forest, why then the Witches will fall over each other in their efforts to align themselves with you. You'll be a hero!"

Santos had never been a hero before. He'd been a zero more often than he cared to remember but never a hero. The idea appealed

THE CHRISTMAS RABBIT

to him. The temptation of such recognition and all it would imply caused him to ignore whatever small amount of good sense fate saw fit to grace him with. "Yeah!" said he, getting caught up in the elvish fantasy. "Let's do it!" So they hashed out the details, discussed possible divergences in their plans and made counter-plans to confront them. When all was settled, they sent Santos to Jack in order to personally throw down the gauntlet.

*****

"Look at that, Father," cried Peter as they watched Grasshopper disappear over the hill on his way to Japan. "What he doing here?" As they watched Grasshopper take his leave of them, they saw as well the stumbling form of Santos come trundling into view. "Ho!" cried the farmer. "Ho, ho, ho! It is I, the redoubtable Santos, come to challenge Jack Rabbit personally to a contest of skill and daring. It is I, come to determine once and for all time which of us is the better of the two and to put to final rest all questions of guilt and innocence while determining forever, who has the right to grow vegetables and who has the right to eat 'em! Dare you face me?"

"I wonder," asked Cottontail, joining the conversation, "what this is all about. I've certainly heard tales in the past of this idiot blindly falling into one of our traps and getting waylaid. But never before have I heard tell of him boldly marching into our den, as it were, and looking for trouble. Surely, even he must realize that he's about to get set upon." As if to give credence to his observation, hundreds of rabbits began to hop in an ever diminishing circle about the farmer like wild Indians ringing a wagon train as they closed in while preparing to pounce en masse and rend him bloody with their sharp little paws and wicked little teeth. Bad News Bears be damned! It was time to turn the Tortoise turtle!

"Hold them off!" Jack whispered furiously to his two elder sons. "Don't let them attack! Something's not right here, and until we find out what it is, we'd best stay our hands. Don't forget the wee people. Just because we can't see 'em doesn't mean they're not out there!"

That was certainly true, the brothers reasoned, so obeying their father's dictates, they called off the minions and let the farmer boldly approach. When he came within ten feet of their father, the brothers prudently halted his advance.

"Stop!" cried Peter. "None may approach the head hare without permission!" Santos came to a halt while allowing himself a smirk. "Putting on airs, aren't we?" he asked of Jack. "Quite a little show for the kittens!"

"At least mine are here to see it, fat boy," replied the rabbit. "Where are yours?" Jack let all the contempt and disdain that he could muster echo within the confines of his last remark. As anticipated, it had the desired effect. Santos bridled. His cheeks flamed crimson and his eyebrows—or what was left of them, as they hadn't fully grown back in yet—fluttered like the wings of insane hummingbirds. He tried to stammer out a caustic reply but found himself stuttering meaninglessly instead, so taking three deep breaths in an effort to calm himself, he put forward his best smile. Somewhat relaxed now, he entered into the spirit of the engagement. "Oh, they're around," he replied. "I keep 'em well hidden so as not to be found by the You-Know-Whos."

"Yeah right." Jack chuckled. "Whatever you say. But they're not all you keep hidden, are they?"

Santos affected an air of saintly innocence. "Whatever could you mean?" he asked. "I come to you openly and in the full light of day, and you proclaim that I have tricks up my sleeve? Do tell!"

"Hey, Wideass," Jack replied," "it's me, okay? Me and my kind have been kicking your butt from one end of the forest to the other since long before my mate dropped her first litter! In spite of all this, now you come marching in here, bold as can be while knowing that if I just raise my paw you'll get more of the same and twice over at that—and you expect me to believe that you're not up to something? Where are your friends, eh? Where are the wee people?"

Santos maintained his angelic repose. "Wee people? To whom are your referring? I know of no wee people."

"The elves!" Jack shouted. "Those little pests from foreign parts that rumor says you've recruited. They're stealing my eggs. Isn't it

THE CHRISTMAS RABBIT

shame enough that I'm being punished for doing something that comes naturally? It's bad enough that I'm being punished wrongly for giving reign to natural tendencies—but I'm also getting the shaft because of you! Delivering these stupid eggs to folk who're too lazy to get 'em for themselves should be your job, not mine—after all, they're your kind!"

As he stood there, Santos felt an undeniable sense of euphoria as it coursed its way through his entire being. He felt both lightheaded and as fleet of foot as Jack himself. It seemed to him that he was walking on air while his eyes saw with a clarity that was to him heretofore unknown. These indisputable sensations he was experiencing were the tastes of victory and triumph. They warmed his blood, making him feel powerful. *So this is what it's like*, he thought. *I'll have to remember to sample more of this whenever I get the chance!* "Exactly!" he replied with bold satisfaction. "It should be my job, and I've come here to challenge you for it!"

"Eh?"

Santos rubbed his greedy palms together. "I said that I've come to challenge you for it. Surely you can't be deaf with ears like those?"

"Not deaf," Jack replied, "just dumfounded! So you want to go into the egg business, eh? Then go right ahead! I'll go get my lists and turn 'em over to you. The job is yours! You want the dyes too?"

Now it was Santos's turn to look dumfounded. This wasn't going as planned. This was a divergence that they hadn't accounted for although perhaps they should have. It was no secret to anyone anywhere that Jack chaffed under his sentence and that his brood hated their enforced labor and were therefore ever on the alert for ways to shirk it. Instead of craftily snaring the rabbit had he walked into one of Jack's traps? He fervently wished that Pixie and Dixie were here with him in order to salvage this train wreck but the plan they'd formulated required that the duo along with the rest of the elven army, remain hidden and in deep cover. Concealment was their main weapon and it would do no one except Jack, any good if they revealed themselves now. How to regain the edge? He thought back to the basic premise of their plan—that Jack, being embarrassed and humiliated before his progeny might therefore be maneuvered down a trail that he'd not travel otherwise. How to accomplish that? Embarrassment was the key, and with that realization, Santos had his answer. "It's all fine for you," said he, "to just hand over the lists while saying okay, run with it! But I don't really want your job either. All I'm saying is, wanted or not, I can do it better!"

"Fine," cried Jack, "then do it! Let me get you the lists!"

"No!" the farmer replied, shaking his head. "I don't want your lists—I want you both embarrassed and humiliated as partial payment for all the grief and misery I've been made to suffer! I therefore challenge you to a race to deliver those very same eggs, with the winner being accounted by all as the better man, or rabbit as the case may be. Do you accept?"

"I don't want to race," replied Jack. "I haven't the time to engage in such silly sport. You and your elves have seen to that! I'm way beneath my quota and far behind on my deliveries! Another time perhaps."

"You're chicken!"

Jack chose to misunderstand the farmer's accusation. "I'm not a chicken," he replied. "I'm a rabbit!"

"Let me put it plainer then," said Santos. "You're scared, and you're a coward!"

It was obvious to all gathered that you couldn't put it much plainer than that. Jack looked around at the sea of faces, taking note of his children's anticipation as they waited with baited breath to see what answer he would give to such ridiculous charges. There was only one answer which could be given. Jack read it all in their eyes and liked it not one bit that the farmer had maneuvered him into this. It set a bad precedent and he would have to be careful to ensure that such manipulations on the farmer's part were never allowed to occur again. It was a trap. Jack could smell it just as sure as he could sniff out the redolent and miasmic stench of sour cattle craps on a hot summer's day. But there was nothing to do now but walk into it while hoping that fate and circumstance would win the day for him. After all, not only his good standing lay at stake but the honor of all rabbitry was on the line. To refuse the challenge was tantamount to proclaiming to the world that he felt himself to be inadequate to

THE CHRISTMAS RABBIT

the Farm Boy. As the head hare stood there pondering this weighty dilemma Santos reached inside his suit and grabbing ahold of an iron mitt, hurled it with authority to the ground. "What the hell is that?" asked Jack.

"I'm throwing down the gauntlet!" replied the farmer. "As of now, the kid gloves come off!"

Jack rolled his eyes. The farmer was melodramatic at best and tiring more often than not. "Very well," he said. "I accept your challenge!" He bent down and grabbing the mitt, smacked Santos square on the knee.

Santos let loose a "Ho!" and a howl as he hopped about on one leg while gingerly holding his injured patella. "What did you do that for?" he cried.

"Because I couldn't reach your face! Now name the time and place…then take your wide load outta here!"

Santos had planned on challenging him then and there. What he hadn't planned on was racing on one leg and reasoned that even with elven help there was no way he was going to triumph at the moment. That one smart. It smart a lot! "Well, um, it's like this," he stated, "the proper way to engage in this sort of business, or so I'm told, is to have our seconds negotiate for us. As I look around, I see that you have seconds, thirds, and even fourths, on hand and ready to bargain. I however, ha, ha, foolishly neglected to bring my seconds with me, which of course gives you an unfair advantage. So I'll get back to you. See ya!" With that he hopped off as fast as his injured leg would allow. His retreating form suffered the agonies and humiliations of various catcalls and insults hurled his way by rabbits with ears erect and heads held high, all proud of Father Jack for boldly answering Santos's challenge. As the farmer disappeared from view, they raised a cheer and, lifting Jack to their shoulders, carried him about the warren amidst much yelling, whistling and shouting of, "Here Hare! Here Hare!" Jack let the nonsense continue a bit knowing his family needed the release after the buildup of such tensions, but when he deemed that enough was enough and that an appropriate amount of time and silliness had elapsed, called the fete to an abrupt halt. "Put me down, you fools," he shouted, "the party's over!

Get back about your business. Collect your ova and mix your dyes." Grumbling, the rabbits obeyed, setting him back upon his feet. "And you two," he said to Peter and Cottontail, "come along with me!"

The two brothers timidly followed at the heels of their father as he gathered up Nutmeg and led them through the crowd to the far end of the warren where the couple maintained a private hole. Jack paused at its entrance to survey the activity in and about his arboreal city, ensuring himself that the gatherers had left to gather and the dyers to dye. Everything seemed to be in order. As he led them down the passage, he let go a heavy sigh soured by a lifetime's worth of frustration that came from having been made a pawn of powerful enemies while knowing as he reviewed the tapestry of life and servitude displayed before him, that whatever the outcome of today's silliness, his days on this earth were surely numbered. Santos he could handle. The elves, though, were another matter entirely as were the Witches. There'd be hell to pay because of this race—whatever its outcome, and The Powers That Be, he knew, would be collecting the bill.

Settled for the moment in his hole, Nutmeg giving him an ear rub, Jack questioned his two eldest. "So," asked he, "whaddya think?"

Peter looked to Cottontail, who made a point out of looking the other way. "Frankly, father," replied the eldest brother, "I don't know what to think."

Cottontail nodded his head in agreement. "Ditto for me."

Jack looked at them while offering up a tired snort. "Ditto?" he asked. "The best either of you can come up with is ditto—and the two of you are supposed to be the Einsteins of rabbitry? Let me tell you—ditto is doo-doo. It's a cattle craps custard with pellets for sprinkles! Hazard a guess!"

"Well," Peter said tentatively, "it would seem to me that there's no obvious way Wideass could beat you in a foot race and as stupid as we all know him to be must nevertheless realize this and would never challenge you to one. But he did. Therefore, there must be more to this race than meets my eye, but there's nothing more to Old Slomoe than meets my eye but his girth. Consequently, I hypothesize that this race *isn't* his idea and probably *wasn't*. Am I making any sense?"

"Surprisingly, yes. Go on please."

THE CHRISTMAS RABBIT

"Since it *isn't* his idea then he couldn't have had it, could he? That can only mean that someone else had it for him. If we follow this train of thought then it stands to reason that whoever had it got him to put it forward as his own in order to create the impression amongst us that it was his in the first place, even though we all agree that it *wasn't*...don't we?"

"We do. Pray, continue."

"Where *was* I?"

"His idea that *was* and *wasn't* and *is* and *isn't*."

"*Isn't* it enough that I've taken it this far? Let Cottontail draw the conclusion."

"Me?" asked the junior brother.

"Yes, you!" replied Peter. "I've led you to the waters of hypothesis. It's up to you to tell us which way the currents flow!"

Cottontail looked around helplessly. "But I'm not a good swimmer!" he pleaded.

"Dog-paddle then," Jack dryly replied.

"Oh, very well! But where were we again?"

Nutmeg quit ministering to her husband in order to scold her two sons. She shook her paw at them while shaking her head in exasperation as well. "*Is* and *isn't*," she said, "and *was* and *wasn't* and the *two* of you are stalling!"

Cottontail offered Peter a sour look. "You really are the eldest," said he. "This should be your responsibility."

"Only by a minute or two," Peter smugly replied. "In light of that minimal difference my elder standing hardly seems worth mentioning, therefore pray continue."

Cottontail breathed a sigh. "Since we're all in agreement," said he, "that the idea for this race *isn't* Santos's and never *was*, we have to determine if we can, through logical means if possible while at the same time not being afraid to subscribe to inane theories should such logic prove fruitless, just whose idea this *is* or *was* and what we should do about it, yes?"

"I didn't invite the two of you in to shoot craps," replied Jack.

"Exactly! Since this *isn't* his idea and never *was*, can we conclude that the Witches are in some way responsible? I think yes, but only to a point. Certainly they're the authors of all our troubles and are somehow behind our present predicament, but are they so involved as to formulate a scheme such as this? I think not. Like Father, I conclude that they're pulling strings from deep under cover so that from this position, were they ever accused of being puppeteers, could wholeheartedly deny the charges. Besides this idea, if it's everything we think it *is* and *isn't*, is far too crafty for them to have thought up on their own. Oh, we all know that they're big and powerful and like to throw their weight around but this race, coupled with Santos's seeming assurance that he can win it, is far more complicated and convoluted than simple tides or seasons and we've seen how well the trio fared with those! No, this idea seems to me, too slick and simply too complicated for them to have even considered. That leaves us with the elves—whom no one with any credibility has even seen. Their strategies, therefore, and the motives which impel them, are equally invisible…"

And so the four-way conversation progressed. From one ambiguity to another, it descended in an ever-increasing spiral while the forces of darkness made their plans, hatched their plots, and tightened their noose.

*****

The first noose that needed tightening was the loop, which served as a buckle, on the belt that held up the farmer's pants. The old boy needed to lose weight and get in shape if the elves had any hope of accomplishing the task that they'd set. To this end, they had Santos running and jogging from one end of the forest to the other although most of his efforts were spent in tripping and falling. Santos was never very light on his feet and the elves were not about to change that no matter how many tricks they used or what magic they employed. Some things were constant, immutable, and eternal. They rejected dieting outright. If it didn't work for Jack then it wasn't likely to prove effective on him either. Besides, if Santos wasn't losing weight already from the daily fare his wife fed him then no change in his eating habits was going to produce the desired results. Still, the

THE CHRISTMAS RABBIT

elves kept at it. For months. For a time they took to assigning two of their number to ride along with him when he ran—one on each shoulder, to both increase his load and offer him encouragement as they put him through his paces with the idea being to toughen him up. They soon dropped that plan too. Elves don't weigh that much so there wasn't a whole lot of load to be gained and even if there were, no gains were gotten anyhow. Only a number of bruised and broken elves who fell victim to the overwhelming mass of Santos as he stumbled, tripped, and went crashing to the ground, usually with the sorry elves beneath him. They tried him on the StairMaster, aerobics, and tai chi. They had him lift weights, both free and dead, but to no avail. The only dead weight in the gym was him. Yoga, judo, and jumping jacks likewise proved fruitless. They experimented with the balance beam but it was unbearable, resulting in bruised bones for him and broken hearts for them. Not that they gave one whit for Santos or his injured pride but they were coming down to the wire and were fast running out of ideas. Some things, it seemed, were so soft and malleable that they defied anyone's efforts to whip 'em into shape and Santos appeared to be one of them.

One day Pixie called Dixie over to him for a conference. "Brother," he said, "it appears as if we're going to have to carry the bulk of this race upon our own shoulders."

"We already knew that, didn't we?" asked Dixie.

"I suppose," Pixie replied, "but I thought that we'd get at least a modicum of aid from the farmer. The way things are going however, we'll be lucky if we receive the barest of minimums! Therefore start drilling our brethren in the arts of ambush and sabotage. Take them out into the forest and hone their already considerable skills, as it doesn't appear that we'll be able to leave the least little circumstance to chance. Come race day, we'll have to be ready to harass and confound that rabbit."

"Has a date been set yet?"

"No, thanks be! The idiot made some sorry excuse about seconds when he had the chance to. That was fortunate for us. Had he set a date he probably would have opted for immediately and then we'd all be buried in cattle craps up to our ears!" Pixie allowed himself a tired sigh. "Has there ever been anyone, I ask you, as absolutely useless as that fat cow whom we shepherd?"

Dixie knew the answer to that question. But since he was sure that Pixie did likewise and was therefore being merely rhetorical in the asking, chose not to answer. No was no and could never be yes or even made to be maybe for that matter and pointing such things out, he knew, would only serve to diminish his brother elf's depressed spirits.

*****

As events were moving forward however erratically, in the camp of Farmer Santos, circumstances were unfolding in the warren of Jack Rabbit, which would only serve to further complicate and confuse issues, ending in the silly mess which we find ourselves today.

One day, long after Grasshopper had left the family to seek out Harehito Rabbakami, a stranger came walking up to the warren. Since Santos's ultimatum guards had been posted around its perimeter as the rabbits were ever on the alert for the farmer's second. Surely, thought the sentries posted on duty that day, this must be he. Although they were expecting an elf or maybe a dwarf—and certainly whoever this stranger was he wasn't one of those, it was as plain to the guards as the noses on their faces that he must indeed have come from the farmer. With the exception of Santos himself, a sorrier-looking soul they'd never before seen. His clothes were rags. He was unkempt and dirty. He stumbled toward them, weary and forlorn, on his last legs and by the look of him, at the end of his rope too. The outlying pickets broke cover, stepping out from behind concealing shrubs and bushes, to reveal themselves. The stranger paused and looking up, took note of them as they stepped into view. He started, as if not sure of what his eyes beheld. "Rabbits? Are you rabbits?" He broke into a run, hurling himself toward them but in his last extremities, tripped over his own two feet to go tumbling in a disheveled and ungainly heap which came to rest at their feet. "I ask again," he panted, "are you rabbits?"

THE CHRISTMAS RABBIT

One guard looked to another, who in turn looked to another, who in turn did likewise, none of them sure how to respond. Of course they were rabbits and anyone who could see for themselves could surely see that. But who was this? He certainly was a sight whoever he was, and since they weren't sure of that were therefore hesitant to reveal themselves. He didn't look like an elf but he could be in league with 'em! "Who are you?" one of their number asked. "And why seek after rabbits?"

The wayward stranger retched, clearing his throat of the dirt and dust which he'd swallowed in the violence of his tumble. "Not just any rabbit," he hacked, "but one in particular. I seek after a rabbit named Jack. Jack Rabbit, or Father Jack as I'm told he's called in these parts. Or simply, 'Our Father.'"

"And who told you that?"

"Grasshopper," came the forlorn reply. "It was Grasshopper."

The rabbits looked at each other in disbelief. Surely this wretched soul, squalid and unkempt, couldn't be Hareihito Rabbakaimi, could he? Apparently, he was. Who else but themselves knew about Grasshopper? "Where is he?" they yelled. "Where's Grasshopper?"

"Dead," the stranger cried. "Grasshopper is dead."

A mournful sigh was heard amongst the guards. "Did you kill him?" one of them asked.

"Yes," came the tired reply. "No...well, sort of."

That caused a bit of a stir, let me tell you, as the rabbits tried to puzzle it out for themselves. It had to be either yes or no, they reasoned, and whichever it was, it certainly wasn't "sort of." What the hell did that mean? "Who are you?" another of their number demanded. "Are you the one Grasshopper went looking for? Are you Rabbakami? You certainly don't look like a rabbit!"

The stranger pulled himself to his knees, looking around wild-eyed in fear. "Of course I'm not Rabbakami," he stammered. "Do I look like Rabbakami? Do I even look like a rabbit?" The guards allowed as how he didn't. "I'm a man," That much was obvious. "I'm samurai. My name is Nobunaga, and I'm Harehito's herald and personal retainer."

Retainer? What, wondered the rabbits, *did the stranger mean by that?* As far as any of them knew, a retainer was something you placed in your mouth to help straighten out buckteeth—of which there were plenty in the guards gathered. Nobunaga saw their confusion. "You know," said he, "retainer, servant, butler. His man Friday."

Friday? As far as the rabbits knew, it was Saturday, and Nobunaga, whoever he was, was a day late and a dollar short.

Exasperated, the forlorn samurai gave up trying to explain himself. "Never mind," he said. "It will all be made clear in time. I'm the herald of my master's impending arrival. It's a glorious day for you all! The great Harehito will soon be amongst you to shower you with his wisdom and his droppings while offering to you the protection of his strong shield and terribly swift sword." That sounded promising, thought the rabbits, but it still didn't answer their questions regarding Grasshopper.

"I'll answer all in good time," pleaded Nobunaga. "For now, however, I beg thee to take me to Father Jack that I might announce to him my master's arrival and make the necessary preparations required to greet such an august and revered personage."

The rabbits conferred amongst themselves until it was decided to take the stranger to Father Jack. Forming around him as his escort, they led him away through the woods and across the fields.

Jack was in a side hole down in the warren, a workshop really, where with Peter and Cottontail, he was reviewing the latest improvements to the run-free dye that Cottontail had invented some months earlier. "It's a quick-drying formula," said Cottontail as he showed them an egg emblazoned with the latest dye lot. "This new amalgam," he was quick to add, "dries and hardens much faster than those old inks we were using. I've added a little liquid sunshine to speed the process up and turn out our product faster, thereby making overall delivery time that much quicker. It's hoped that the quicker we can get the eggs to our recipients the less likely it will be that the elves will steal 'em."

Jack looked skeptical. "They'd have to cure pretty damned fast for that to happen," he commented. "Although since Santos issued

THE CHRISTMAS RABBIT

his challenge, egg theft appears to have dropped off. I wonder why, and more importantly, I wonder what he's up to?"

"Whatever it is," Peter sniffed, "I'm sure it won't be his idea." He held up one of the newly tattooed eggs and examined it. "Can we make this enamel flat instead of glossy?" he asked. "It's too reflective and shiny. It refracts too much light which will only make it easier for the elves to find when it's winking in the sunlight. Why make things any easier for them?"

"I suppose," replied Cottontail, "that I could add a little chalk or something to dull the finish but the recipients really like the way they gleam."

"Screw 'em! We're not doing this to satisfy their wants or desires. We're doing this because we've been ordered to. Therefore let us consider our own needs and desires, putting them above the petty likes and dislikes of those to whom we're forced to deliver. A less reflective surface will help to ensure that the eggs stay hidden until they're properly claimed."

"Really, Peter," Cottontail scoffed, "if Santos and his elves have it in mind to take our eggs, do you think the addition of a dull and nonreflective paint will in any way hamper their efforts?"

"It couldn't hurt!"

"Oh, very well," Cottontail replied, "I'll see to it as soon as this current batch dries."

"To hell with paints!" Jack said. "And to hell with eggs and to whom they're delivered! We have more important matters with which to contend! What's the farmer up to, I wonder, and whatever happened to that young coney we sent off in search of the warrior? He should've been back by now, shouldn't he?"

Peter and Cottontail exchanged glances, both of them aware that for some reason, which they could not fathom, their father seemed inordinately upset about their current condition and plight. Even though the elves had most likely put the idea of racing into the dumb farmer's head it would still be the dumb farmer nevertheless who did the actual running, wouldn't it? Certainly "Our Father" had no worries there. Even if Old Slomoe demanded to race one of his seconds whom they still hadn't seen yet, Jack could back out, crying foul, with no loss of honor. Or he could simply race. After all, how fast could elves be? And what of Grasshopper? Should he return and being the swiftest hare in the warren, could not Jack race him instead as his proper and legal second? The brothers traded a further glance, both feeling inadequate to Jack's queries as neither had been to Japan and therefore had no hypothesis to render regarding their young nephew and his probable fate. Each in his own mind was trying to formulate some hare brained answer with which to comfort their father when a commotion arose at the head of their hole. Loud voices could be heard coming down the shaft from the field above, echoing and resonating throughout the tunnel until they rang upon the walls of the workshop. "What's all the to-do, I wonder?" asked Peter.

"Go on up and see, will you?" asked Jack. "Unless it's important, I'd prefer not being disturbed." Peter hopped off along the tunnel, making his way quickly to the entrance. It wasn't too long before he came tearing back like a rabid dog, excited and agitated. "Father!" he cried, "Father—they've returned! They've returned!"

"Who? Santos and his seconds? Good! Let's have at 'em."

"No," exclaimed Peter, "not Santos but Grasshopper! Well, not Grasshopper either but Harehito Rabbakami! But not really him either—just his manservant. It's all very confusing, but I gather that Grasshopper did not survive the return journey. However, it would seem that he did accomplish his mission, managing to both get to Japan and enlist the aid of the warrior…or at least his butler. As I said, it's all very perplexing. Perhaps you should come and see for yourself."

Jack looked at him skeptically. "A manservant, you say? There's a strange rabbit out there acting as another's manservant? How demeaning!"

"Not a rabbit manservant," Peter replied, "but a man manservant! His skin is yellow and his eyes, black as coal, are mere slits in his face. It's a wonder he can see out of 'em!"

"What's this nonsense?" Jack asked, wondering whether or not his son had been indulging himself in too much fermented dandelion root. Yellow skin and slits for eyes! Really! What did they take him for, some kind of fool? But there was nothing for it, he supposed,

THE CHRISTMAS RABBIT

other than to go and have a look for himself. "Well, c'mon then," he exclaimed impatiently. He hopped along the tunnel, dragging his two sons in his wake. "Let's go see this Jap man for ourselves!" They made their way up the shaft and upon exiting the hole, confronted both daylight and the enigmatic presence of the foreigner in their midst. Jack was mildly surprised to find that the stranger's skin was indeed yellow and his eyes, slashes of ebony. "Who are you, fellow," Jack asked, "and what's your business here?"

The stranger turned toward him and bending slightly at the waist said, "Greetings. Be you the rabbit named Jack?" The head hare nodded. "Ah, so!" continued the stranger. "My name is Nobunaga. Unworthy and lowly servant am I to the great Harehito Rabbakami, master samurai and ninja extraordinaire! I come to you as the herald of his arrival, therefore make you ready to receive the great one! His advent is imminent! Prepare a great feast. Adorn your females with wreaths and garlands and usher them into his presence that they may present themselves to him as a gift befitting one of his noble stature, pleasing to his eye and worthy of his august attentions! Celebrate one and all. Your days of darkness and doubt are over! Your freedom from your oppressors is at hand, for Harehito is here! Deck the halls. Fa-la-la-la-la la-la-la-la!"

While all around him rabbits leapt for joy, whistling, shouting, and spouting out gay and spirited pheromones, Jack himself remained singularly unimpressed. "Where is old Harry?" he asked. "Where's the hare hiding, and why doesn't he show himself?"

Nobunaga looked ill at ease. "Believe you me, sire," he said. "Harehito hides not. He waits. He waits for you, as head hare, to come to him thus rendering to him the honor which his august stature merits."

"Hmm," Jack sniffed. "That so?" Nobunaga nodded uncomfortably. "Well, let's get something straight, bub," Jack continued, "no one comes waltzing into my hole while putting on airs. Nor does he get someone like you to do it for him. I'm the head honcho in these parts—the head hare here. Hear? If anyone's going to be doing any groveling it will be him with his face in the dust, not me! He may be a big deal where you're from but around here he's just another stranger in a strange land and as such, should be a little more polite. Have either of you got a visa?"

Nobunaga looked nonplussed. "A visa?" he asked. "I'm sure that I have no idea of what you're referring to."

"A visa!" Jack barked impatiently. "A passport with the proper stamps and documentation upon it! As foreign nationals, you need 'em in order to be here legally—plus a green card if you're going to be working. So have you got 'em or not?"

Nobunaga appeared even more confused than before. "I'm sure, sire," said he, "that we do not. No one ever made mention of them."

"Didn't the immigration folks or the border guards stop you in order to check your papers?"

Nobunaga returned his questioning glance with a look filled with pride. "My master," he said, "gave 'em the slip! No one sees Harehito if Harehito does not wish to be seen. My master has hareagei on his side."

"Hairy who?"

"No," replied the manservant. Not *hairy*, but *hare*—add in the *agei* and string it altogether. *Hareagei*. Anyway, my master is its master, and as such, saw the immigration folks coming before they even knew we were going and therefore was able to remain concealed. He thought it best, given the nature of his pending employment, to arrive unheralded."

"And sending you here ahead of him, shouting at the top of your lungs, bidding us to prepare a feast while offering up our daughters as a bribe is unheralded? Really! And what's this hareagei anyway? It sounds like a Japanese cattle crap!"

"Forgive me for saying so, sir," replied Nobunaga, "but only a round-eyed barbarian such as yourself would make so foolish a claim, however since you are a round-eyed barbarian, I'm sure that my master will forgive you nevertheless."

"Says you. Where's my great-great-grandnephew four times removed? Where's Grasshopper, and what have you done with him?"

Nobunaga nervously wiped his hands on his stained and travel worn kimono. "Me?" he innocently asked. "I've done nothing to him."

THE CHRISTMAS RABBIT

"Then what happened to him?"

"The same thing that happens to any of us," replied the forlorn samurai. "He ran out of time, or perhaps it's best to say that time caught up with him. It catches us all in the end, you know?"

"Not him," said Jack, "that young coney was too fleet of foot. The wind couldn't catch him! Therefore I don't see how time, which plods along at its own steady pace, could have overtaken him. What about your master, Harehito, was he involved?"

Nobunaga nervously shuffled his feet while Jack, looking on, took note that the retainer's brow glistened with nervous sweat. "I'm sure," said Nobunaga, "that you'd have to ask my master that."

"Well, that's gonna be kinda hard," Jack replied, "since you're master won't show his face. What's he expect me to do, write him a letter?"

"Again, I'm sure," said Nobunaga, "that all of your questions will be answered in good time if you exercise a little patience."

"You may have noticed," Jack rebutted, "that we're on something of a war footing around here. We're dealing with a fat farmer and a host of wee folk who are planning mischief of some sort and who are backed up by three sour old crones who've powers beyond belief. I'm hard-pressed on all sides and my patience has worn thin. Let your master come now or not at all. Tomorrow may be too late!"

"Give me leave then, sir, to go and get him."

"Leave." Nobunaga bent slightly at the waist and, spinning about, walked off the way he came. "What do you think?" asked Peter as he watched the departing samurai. "Is he the genuine article or not?"

"How should I know?" Jack replied, lashing out at his son. "What do I look like, the answer man?" He immediately regretted his loss of temper. His son, he knew, was merely trying to be of some aid. Peter couldn't help it, Jack knew, if he was still wet behind the ears. In a softer and more conciliatory tone, he said, "Grasshopper claimed that the Jap was a long ways off. From the looks of the stranger, I'd say that he's certainly traveled a great distance. I don't think that anyone could look so worn and tired unless he'd actually made the trip. But as to this Harehito, who knows? Where is he and why send a man, of all creatures, to treat with fellow rabbits? It's an insult is what it is! I don't like being insulted and I don't like being made to wait upon others! Perhaps this Rabbakami is on the up and up but I haven't even met him yet and already I don't trust him!"

"You think he's from the Witches," Peter asked, an incredulous look painted upon his face, "you think he's working for them?"

"Not at all," replied Jack. "No self-respecting rabbit would ever sink so low. However, just because he's not in their camp does not mean that he's pitched his tent in ours either. He could have his own plans and that, my son, is what we need to find out."

"How?"

"By letting him talk, assuming of course, that he ever shows his face. These big shots with their overinflated egos always trip themselves up in the end"

They stood there for some time debating the pros and cons of eastern vigilantes, whether real or imagined, when out off the corner of his eye Peter noticed Nobunaga returning from whence he came. Just to the rear of him and slightly to one side was a rabbit.

"Look, father," exclaimed Peter, "here comes that Nobunaga fellow—and see, there behind him comes a rabbit! Surely that must be Rabbakami." Looking off in the direction Peter indicated Jack saw that Nobunaga had indeed returned. He walked half-heartedly and with his head bowed as he shuffled along. Every so often the rabbit in his rear would kick him, knocking him to the ground. Nobunaga would fall on his face as the mysterious stranger looked on disdainfully. He'd wait impatiently for the samurai to regain his footing, allow him to take a few more faltering steps, and then wallop him again. Looking on, Jack realized that the scene being enacted before him defined the enigmatic duo's entire relationship. Nobunaga was a coward, and Rabbakami, if that's who this really was, was a bully. Well, Jack had met bullies before—namely Helgayarn, Brunnhilde, and Betty—and he wasn't impressed. Anybody could pick on somebody if that same somebody let 'em. Nobody, however, could pick on anybody if everybody stood up to him. Unfortunately for Jack, nobody was going to be with him when he met this particular bully. The head hare, for want of a better description, was head of state.

THE CHRISTMAS RABBIT

When such a one first met his potential commanding general it was appropriate that such a meeting take place in private in order to more effectively and confidentially negotiate the parameters of their working relationship. Thus somebody—at least in this particular instance—was more than likely to get an ass kicking; and that somebody was Jack if a third of the stories he'd heard about this foreign rabbit were even halfway true. Well, supposed the head hare, there'd be no helping it unless he could appeal, of course, to Rabbakami's sense of fair play. Unlikely. Therefore he'd have to listen carefully while taking his licks, hoping all the while to minimize his beating by tricking the foreigner. After all, Jack had contended with the best of 'em and how smart could this one rabbit be? "I'll be down in my hole," he said as he half-heartedly hopped off. "When the stranger arrives, send him and his retainer down to me."

"How will we get the man down your hole?" queried Peter.

Jack hadn't thought of that and the omission worried him. What else had he failed to consider? "Of course," he replied matter-of-factly, trying to cover his lapse, "I know that Nobunaga won't fit! What do you take me for, an idiot?"

"Of course not, father. It's just—"

"It's just nothing! We'll meet in the woods then. Well, away from everyone else."

"Should I come too?" asked Peter.

Jack gave his son's offer serious consideration. If the interview went bad, then it might be good to have an extra set of paws on hand to back him up. But if this rabbit was half the warrior Nobunaga claimed, then what good would a backup be? Not much. If he was going to get a lesson first hand on Rabbakami's military and martial prowess, he preferred that it be a private one. The warren could ill afford to see him suffer defeat at the hands of another.

"No," he replied, "send them on alone to the clearing over yonder, and no matter what happens or what you hear, keep away!" He grabbed ahold of Nutmeg and, taking her paw, led her over the field and into the aforementioned woods.

*****

The woods were thick but incorporated within them many clearings and in the middle of one, Jack sat on a bed of newly cut hay with Nutmeg standing off to one side observing as he approached, the enigmatic Harehito Rabbakami. Jack took note that the mysterious stranger walked upright on his hind legs rather than hopped, as was the normal way of all rabbits. *How does he do that?* the head hare wondered, for rabbits are built to walk upon all fours and two-legged traveling goes against their evolutionary upbringing. To Jack, it seemed that the very earth and the stranger were one. He appeared well grounded as he glided effortlessly forward, his feet barely leaving the ground. As he neared, Jack saw that his coat of fur, whiter than pure snow, sported the exception of a broad band of ebony encircling his middle. The fur on the top of his head was cut short and severe and stood up like a whiffle. His ears, both tall and straight, seemed to cut the very air around him. When the stranger approached to within a foot he halted, sat down, folded himself into the lotus position and bending slightly at the waist, said, "Ah, so."

"Ah, so"? "Ah, so" what? What was "Ah, so"? Was it some sort of greeting? To Jack, it sounded more like an oriental basting sauce taking advantage of a hokey pun in order to promote itself. "Ah, so," he tentatively replied, and before he could so much as finish his hello the stranger, reaching out from where he sat, cuffed Jack smartly across the face. The head hare went tumbling backward and perhaps would've rolled all the way over if Nobunaga had not stretched out a restraining arm to catch him.

"Hey!" said Nutmeg, fearful for her mate. "I don't know what they teach you folk back home but around here hitting hares is bad manners!" The stranger gave her a warning glance, admonishing her to silence.

Stunned, Jack shook the cobwebs out of his head to confront once again, this puzzling enigma. Again Harehito bent slightly at the waist. "Ah, so."

Jack considered that there was some sort of cultural misunderstanding occurring between the two but he'd endured too much already with too much at stake, to do anything other than at least try twice to bridge the ethnocentric divide separating them. "Ah, so?"

THE CHRISTMAS RABBIT

Whap! Harehito struck him once again, this time even harder. "What did I say, eh?" asked the head hare of no one in particular. "What did I say?"

"You fool!" Nobunaga shot back. "You're not being—"

But Harehito, raising a warning paw, cautioned the lowly samurai to silence.

"Ah, so," said Nobunaga, offering his master a slight bow.

"What is this," Jack asked confused, "a Chinese fire drill?"

Nobunaga looked on, taking note that his master's eyes became dark and flinty at the mention of those traditional enemies from across the straights. Risking his life, poor Nobunaga ventured to impart one last bit of advice to the head hare. In barely a whisper and speaking through clenched teeth, he warned Jack on pain of death, to never again mention those guys. "It really pisses him off!" Laughing nervously, he turned slightly to bow once again to his master.

Old Harehito wasn't fooled however, having grown tired of his servant's meager attempts at interference. With the speed of a striking snake, he reached out and walloped Nobunaga as well. And then walloped him again because the dim-witted samurai should've known better. He almost walloped Nutmeg too but held off at the last instant, knowing that it would be a sin to mar such a pretty face with the bruise he'd no doubt inflict. Also, this was a stranger sitting before him and Harehito hadn't determined yet just how far the stranger could be pushed. Along with being a mystic, a samurai, and a ninja as well, Harehito was also ronin, a mercenary who made himself and his skills available to the highest bidder. If he pushed Jack too far, there'd be no employment and he didn't want to end up having made this trip for nothing. He would therefore make every effort to save this lad some face, although of course as gaijin the lad had no face to save. It was a puzzle and being one, Harehito determined to proceed cautiously. But even so, patience had its limits. Bowing once again, he greeted Jack for the third time. "Ah, so."

For his own part, Jack wondered whether this misunderstanding had its roots in their seating arrangement, and so like the master before him, attempted to fold himself awkwardly. The rabbit from foreign parts laughed like a loon as Jack's limbs, unused to such exertions, denied his ambition's demands. Bending slightly at the waist, the master offered his fourth and final bow. If the round-eye didn't get it right this time he was gonna personally kick him from one end of this forest to the other.

Something thankfully, finally clicked. Without taking his eyes of the puzzling stranger, Jack bowed slightly, as had been demonstrated. He hesitantly offered a polite, "Ah, so." It was always better to be safe than sorry.

Harehito eyed him critically. This gaijin returned his bow as though they were equals. How impertinent! But perhaps it was only ignorance. The Tao taught that the way to enlightenment was through patience. Especially patience with round-eyes. "Thank you," he finally said.

"You speak my language?" asked Jack.

Harehito pointed to the forlorn samurai lying prostrate on the clover floor. "He does, doesn't he?"

"Yes," Jack replied, "but that's different."

"How so?"

"I'm not sure, really," Jack answered.

Harehito laughed approvingly. "Good!" he exclaimed. "That's the first reasonable thing you've said. To not know a thing is to know it intimately!"

"It is?"

"Assuredly."

"I don't understand," said Jack.

"A genius!" replied Harehito. "And a gaijin at that! Will wonders never cease?"

"I shouldn't think so," the head hare said under his breath.

The rabbits sat in silence as Nobunaga regained his feet. Each rabbit strove to take in the measure of the other. Jack was doubtful as to his next step, or how to put his best paw forward. Harehito, on the other hand, had a pretty good idea after conferring with Grasshopper, the reason for his visit and why he'd been summoned. For knowledge and wisdom, of course, and for training in those disciplines for which he was accounted master. What other worthy reason was there? He'd be damned disappointed if the fellow before him just

THE CHRISTMAS RABBIT

wanted an autograph. Harehito knew exactly how to proceed. The young fellow before him was to be applauded for his sand, but alas his answer to him must be no. Harehito had his own designs and his skills were strictly a clan secret to be passed on by him through direct bloodlines only and certainly weren't to be given away to round-eyes. Still, thought the master, it wouldn't hurt to demonstrate a technique or two before embarking on a foreign holiday. "So why, good rabbit, have you summoned me?" he asked.

Jack hesitated before replying. He knew that his answer had to be framed just so in order to appeal to this buffoon's ego, which of course he'd deny he had. It would have to play upon the master's vanity, which he'd doubtless gainsay too. "Master Harehito," he began, "word of your deeds and the excellence of your art goes before you like the prevailing east wind. Thus I, who have many rabbits under my care have sent for you that I might implore upon your mercy to come to our aid, rendering unto us in our hour of need, those skills and trickeries for which you are world-renowned! For see, great master, powerful enemies beset us and as all lapins know an enemy of one is an enemy of all." Harehito had his own thoughts on that particular subject but let the foreigner continue. "They attack us from all sides," Jack continued, "and press their assault from both the right and the left; from the heights to the depths our enemies assail us until we're trapped like rats in our very holes. Therefore we plead with you, great Rabbakami, to render unto us that which only you are capable of providing..." Jack admitted to himself that as a plea his was a bit windy, but even so it had a nice beat and he thought the old master might dance. As an added measure, he emitted a subservient pheromone or two.

Harehito however, was not impressed. He'd been subject to such malarkey before and often from the scent glands of his own clan who thought they could prevail upon him to offer up his secrets by merely flaunting family relations while flaying him with their silken tongues and sweet smelling scents. He hadn't stood for it then and wasn't going to put up with it now. "Cut the bull, round-eye," he replied harshly. "That's the biggest load of cattle craps any rabbit has ever been made to wade through! Speak in clear sentences without the camouflage of oral artifice and tell me plainly what you want—and keep your scents to yourself!"

His eyes flashed angrily while momentarily hurling his harea, his inner strength. The assault stated in no uncertain terms just what Jack could expect should he try to fool the master again. The head hare reeled from the unseen attack and for the briefest span of time he felt the full force of Harehito's harea as it emanated from the old master to be directed solely at him. His eyes bulged in their sockets while his heart fluttered like an insane kite blown upon an ill-gotten wind. His fur stood on end and his ears wilted like dead flowers. He writhed upon the ground as he tried in vain to draw breath. Dizzy and disoriented, a galaxy of stars paraded themselves before his shriven eyes. "Enough!" he pleaded, and the master relinquished his hold on him. Jack slowly regained his feet. "No more cattle craps," he promised though panting breaths. "The truth of the matter is that I and my people know very little of your skills. After all, Japan's a ways off from here and little of what actually occurs there ever makes its way back to us regardless of how great the tale or how mighty its heroes. I know you only through rumor as just one of my Warren has ever traveled to your lands and the tales he brought back, I'm ashamed to say, were regarded as haresay. But it's true—we are in dire straits. We need help, we need it fast, and based upon what little I'd heard you fit the bill. Rabbits, of course, should all stick together in times of trouble, so I summoned you here."

The master eyed him gravely. "That sounds a little better," he replied. "But I still don't know exactly what you want."

"To not know a thing," Jack said, "is to be intimately familiar with it."

A dark cloud settled upon Harehito's brow and his anger flashed like lightning. "Don't throw my isms back at me, boy," he warned, "or I'll make you eat 'em syllable by syllable!" An uneasy silence spun out as Jack stood before the master, chastised. "So what do you want?" Harehito continued. "Do you want me to teach you and yours my fighting skills? Is that it, eh?"

THE CHRISTMAS RABBIT

"Well, if it comes to that," Jack replied, "then I suppose that the answer is yes. But we were kinda hoping you'd do the fighting for us! You see, we have other matters which demand our attention."

"So you're a warren of cowards, is that it? Just like this poor example of a samurai who led me here!"

"Well, I wouldn't go that far!" Jack sniffed disdainfully. "We've had our share of scuffles but even so, there comes a time when you have to face the fact you've been outmatched."

Harehito shook his head. "There's never such a time!" he replied. "Envision defeat and it will surely find you. See in your mind's eye only victory and you will achieve it!" He paused for a moment to see what the round eye thought of that. Apparently not much, so he continued. "You want me to defeat for you, enemies whom you feel are too powerful to challenge yourselves, is that right?"

Jack meekly nodded his head.

"You mean like this?" asked the master. Suddenly he sprang up from where he was sitting and leapt through the air as if flying. He landed with all fours heavily impacting upon the chest of poor Nobunaga. Powerless, the hapless samurai was unable to defend himself as Harehito rained down upon him, blow after punishing blow, delivering a series of percussive strikes and kicks so quickly that his very movements were barely a blur. He brought every physical weapon in his arsenal to bear, employing deadly itemis, finger strikes, and spinning back fists. His hind legs became a windmill as they rendered unto helpless Nobunaga, roundhouses, sidekicks, and crescents until the herald lay helpless upon the ground, a bloody and disheveled heap. Not satisfied with such a paltry display of skill, Harehito then let loose his harea full force. It slammed into Nobunaga like a Greyhound bus, lifting him off the ground and hurling him, as the fiery winds of its essence, which cut like a scalpel, peeled away skin, layer by layer. Yet Nobunaga held on and held out, screaming in agony. Harehito rushed up to where the bloody samurai lay dying and employing the ninja technique of koppo, a specialized form of bone breaking, took up the samurai's neck and calmly snapped it. Nobunaga lay dead in his master's arms, his broken body reduced to so much bruised and beaten flesh. Harehito threw him down and his corpse tumbled away into the bushes and out of this tale.

Harehito turned back to Jack, expecting him to flee for his life, but the head hare bravely stood his ground. For a round-eye, Harehito knew, that took courage. His estimation of Jack went up a small fraction although he kept such regard to himself, his expression giving away nothing. The master just stood there, surveying him. He pointed at the shrubbery, which now concealed the expired samurai. Is that what you want me to enact upon your enemies?"

Jack shivered at the thought. "I suppose so," he stammered, "if it comes down to it."

"Forget it!" said the master. "Those techniques will never work. They're simple manipulations designed to inflict pain and death upon those with less power than yourself, not more. I haven't begun to show you the really juicy stuff! And I'm not about to either! They're trade secrets and not for round-eyes like you. Now be off—I want to contemplate my navel."

Inwardly, Jack allowed himself a small smile while outwardly maintaining a poker face. The master would help them. He knew it. Just as he'd known all along that if he let the old buzzard prattle on about his skills he'd eventually trap himself as had just happened. It was hard not to gloat, but Jack managed. How, after all, had Harehito known that they had enemies more powerful than themselves? Had he simply taken Jack's word on the matter? Doubtful. Therefore, Jack reasoned, the Jap must have an idea of whom we're really up against—beyond Santos and the elves, that is. And where did he get such intelligence? Obviously, there could be only one source and that source was Grasshopper who was conspicuously missing. Had Harehito done away with him in order to feign ignorance regarding their plight? Would he use such ignorance as a bargaining chip in order to gain certain concessions before agreeing to offer his services? Probably. And if so, what were those concessions likely to be? The mad rabbit's ego was tremendous Jack realized, but the fact that he boasted continually about his own prowess implied that there were some serious self-misgivings lurking within him as well; reservations regarding his skills and qualms about the validity of his position as

THE CHRISTMAS RABBIT

master. Harehito was always on the lookout to prove his superiority to somebody, generally somebody weaker than himself. Why else enact the sickening display just witnessed by killing poor Nobunaga who was obviously no threat to anyone? Harehito needed to boast and by boasting to do away with the self-doubt with which he did constant battle. Jack trusted his own assessment of the stranger but was there more going on here than met the eye and was the shallow dish standing before him empty or full? Jack didn't know but as had been pointed out to him previously, to not know a thing is to be intimately familiar with it. Grasshopper had met Harehito and had obviously spilled the beans. Harehito had subsequently gobbled them up and had come running from Japan, pushing poor Nobunaga before him as he came. Why? It was a lot of trouble to come all this way just to fight somebody else's battle. Did he know about the Witches? Jack had to assume that he did. Was the lure of battling those three enough to goad him into traveling such distances—especially when regardless of all the stated crap vis-à-vis the notion of envisioning victory, there was no guarantee that he could win? Was such a nebulous prospect, in and of itself, worth the risk and if not, then what was? And even if he were completely assured of victory—which only a fool would be when facing those three—would the attraction of such a conquest be enough of a temptation to warrant his undertaking such an arduous trek? Not if he were planning on returning to Japan once the battle was over. For if he did who was there in Japan to whom he could relate the tale? Certainly, he would boast of it if he found anyone willing to listen, but without eyewitnesses to glorify his deeds on the field such stories would lose much in their retelling. It would be merely his own word that such and such had actually happened. His listeners would have to take at face value, his tales and his own part in them. There would be naysayers and others who swallowed his yarns with a grain of salt. They would know that seeing is believing and that anyone can blow their own trumpet. Having a chorus blow one for you however is another matter entirely. Therefore if he were to return to the orient to boast his exploits it would be far better to have the confirmation of independent witnesses. Yet the one witness Harehito had in his pocket he'd just "hareaed" to death. It was doubtful that even in victory he'd get any of the saved to return with him while singing his praises. Despite the burdens laid upon them, Jack's rabbits were by and large content and not likely to give up the comfort of known and familiar surroundings in order to embark upon the unknown for the sole purpose of heralding the return of someone they hardly knew in the first place. True, from what Jack had seen, Harehito should he prove himself victorious on the field of battle, was more than capable of coercing a rabbit or two and forcing them to return. But would such witnesses, unwillingly pressed into service, be likely to relate with flowery praise, the glories of their slave driver? Wouldn't such acclimations likely be colored by resentment and ill will? Jack thought it likely. It was second nature to rabbits to hold such grudges—often their third and fourth natures too. Nobody likes to be pushed around, and not everybody was apt to be as spineless as the hapless Nobunaga. Harehito would know that. Therefore he couldn't be planning upon taking anyone with him when he left. Ergo he wasn't leaving and must therefore be planning on staying! Why? It dawned on Jack that despite his obvious prowess, Harehito—with the exception of the erstwhile samurai whom he'd just killed—had no one to lead; else he would've brought the army with him, wouldn't he? Suddenly the ninja rabbit's intentions were as clear to Jack as if the very blinders that seemingly covered his eyes were instantly removed. Harehito, once he won the battle, planned on taking over the whole ball of wax by usurping Jack's place as head hare. There'd be a bloody coup from which Harehito would emerge the victor. It was tempting for Jack to deny him his glory by simply abdicating. He'd wanted out of this dreadful egg business from the day it started. Left alone however with Harehito as the head hare, Jack realized his beloved warren would soon be reduced to nothing more than a pile of skinned pelts as the master lead them from one protracted battle to the next in his own quest for personal glory. You could use such egomaniacs to your own purposes however, as long as you reeled them in like fish while at the same time letting them think that they held the pole! "You mean that you won't help us?" asked Jack, feigning fright. "You mean to say after all we've been through you're going to turn a deaf ear and simply be on your way?"

THE CHRISTMAS RABBIT

"No and yes," replied Harehito.

"Eh?" It wasn't the answer the head hare hoped for let alone one that he expected.

"No, I'm not going to help you, and yes, I'm going to be on my way. Or kick your furry little butt from one end of the forest to the other if you don't let me be!"

Yeah. Right. Jack knew better than that. Harehito might indeed kick his butt backward, sideways, and inside out but he certainly wasn't going anywhere. Jack offered up his next gambit. "So be it," said he. "I'll be off then, as I'm sure you will—but I'd ask you a thing before we part if you'd be so kind."

The master stood staring at him. Outwardly he remained stone-faced. Inwardly he was a bit suspicious. What more could this gaijin possibly want? He should have been scared silly by now, passing pellets to beat the band. Instead he gamely stood his ground while displaying the effrontery to ask more questions. "What is it?" the master rabbit slowly asked. "What do you want?" Smiling secretly to himself while at the same time taking care not to emit a revealing pheromone, Jack asked the question that he hoped would bring Harehito's flimsy house of cards crashing down upon him. "Nobunaga—did you have to kill him?"

"Yes," the master replied shortly, pointing to the bushes concealing the discarded body. "That piece of cattle craps was a poor excuse for a samurai and had it coming!"

"Why?"

Harehito looked at Jack disdainfully, knowing that the gaijin before him was not worthy enough to hear the tale but couldn't resist the opportunity to brag. "I first met Nobunaga," said Hareinto, "some years ago in Shuzenzi Province. I'd just returned from a major ass kicking where, of course, I was the kicker. Nobunaga was one of the kickees—or would have been had he not chickened out just before the engagement. The coward turned tail and ran! An indifferent warrior at best, he beat feet and fled at the height of battle when it became clear to him that he and his rabble faced defeat. All around him friends and family bravely stood forth at the standards of their daimyos, preferring to die with honor rather than face the humiliation of capture, and as a consequence were slaughtered along with their lords and legions, having succumbed to the prevailing excellence of my martial art. Nobunaga managed to slip away during that great bloodletting and escaped for a time. That he was ultimately proven correct in his assessment of the tactical situation made little difference to those to whom he later offered his services. We Japanese hate a coward, and cowardice was the one quality which Nobunaga had more than his fair share of. No self-respecting daimyo would have anything to do with him. Even itinerant peasants and wandering beggars avoided his company. I chanced to meet him some months after the great battle. I came upon him, as I've said, hidden in a valley deep within Shuzenzi Province, a wanderer trusted by no one, homeless, penniless, and with dim prospects regarding his future." Rabbakami offered up a sigh as he contemplated the fortunes of the world and the strange diversions such fortunes were apt to take. Karma was a fickle mistress, and there was no denying that. "Bemoaning his fate," the master continued, "Nobunaga at one point considered *seppuku* but found that he lacked the fortitude and the follow-through."

"*Cepookoo*," asked Jack, "what's that?"

"*Seppuku*. It's the ritual act of disembowelment. The peasants call it *hara-kiri*, for rabbits it's called *harea-kiri*, and it's the only way for a transgressing samurai to atone for his misdeeds. It allows him to die with dignity and reclaim his lost honor. It requires that a second assist the transgressor by decapitating him after he's made the required two cuts to his abdomen. The second sees that honor is restored to the transgressor by assuring that decapitation takes place before he can give himself over to the agonies of the two cuts, thereby further disgracing himself. There are very few even amongst the bravest of samurai—with the exception of myself, of course—who, without a second, can retain their composure whilst in the throes of disembowelment and regain lost honor. Everyone back home however had heard of Nobunaga and his disgrace and all agreed that having a second, third, or even fourth would avail him little and that honor would therefore remain eternally out of reach. Disreputability and disparagement were forever his karma and those

THE CHRISTMAS RABBIT

whom he came in contact with refused to sully their swords on him. When I encountered him he'd been reduced to nothing more than a dirty and unkempt panhandler. His kimono was soiled and tattered. The blade of his katana was rusty and the hilt chipped and cracked. His *wakizashi*, the ritual small sword the samurai uses in harea-kiri, was conspicuously absent. It seems he'd sold it for a few bags of rice a couple of days prior to our encounter. He sat alone and forlorn in the middle of an empty field, crying for himself and the cruelties of the world, when I approached him. He disgusted me. But as it suited my design, I gave him purpose and gave him back his life! When that purpose, accompanying me here, was fulfilled, I took back what I'd given him. But *seppuku*? No way, round-eye! He didn't deserve that honor. I spit on him and his ancestors for ten thousand generations!"

Jack rolled his eyes. "You're a bloody, heartless bastard, aren't you?"

"In this veil of tears," Rabbakami soliloquized, "life is bloody and heartless. I'm here to point that out. That piece of walking cattle craps was a poor excuse for a samurai and got what was coming to him. Still, I gave him a warrior's death and that's more than he deserved!"

"You keep using that word, samurai. What's that?"

Harehito puffed up with pride. "A samurai," he responded, "is a warrior. Literally, the word means, 'to serve.'"

"So Nobunaga regained his samurai status by serving you?"

Harehito looked uncomfortable. He fidgeted a bit before replying. "I suppose you could infer that," he said, "but I point out again that samurai was an honor forever beyond him. He lacked the juice!"

"But not you?"

"Of course not!"

"Then you're samurai?"

"Of course," replied Harehito, exasperated. "What kind of asinine question is that? I'm Harehito Rabbakami, master samurai and ninja rabbit extraordinaire!"

"Right," replied Jack smiling. "I only wished for clarification. Whom do you serve?"

"Eh?"

"You're samurai, aren't you? And samurai means 'to serve.' So whom do you serve?"

"Well...I, ah, that is to say—"

"You must serve somebody, right? I mean, you can't really be samurai—at least as you've just described 'em—if you're not serving, correct?"

"I...ahh...I serve myself! Yes, that's it—I serve myself!"

Jack offered the master a skeptical smirk. "Sounds rather self-serving, if you ask me," he said. "Is such an attitude truly congruent with the warrior ideal? After all, everybody has to serve somebody, and nobody can serve anybody if they're too busy serving themselves, wouldn't you agree?"

"I don't know!" the consternated master replied shortly. He was near panic. "I'd hate to back myself into a corner!"

"You already have!" the head hare remarked gleefully. "How can someone who serves only himself serve anyone else? And if they can't serve anyone how can they be samurai? How can *you* be samurai? You can't! You're just a common thug!" He reached out and cuffed the master a good one as partial payment for all the blows that Harehito had rained upon him. Rabbakami, in shock and unable to believe that a mere gaijin would have the effrontery to treat him thus, made ready to return the blow; he gathered his harea and ready to hurl he suddenly halted, unsure of himself as his inherent insecurities so deeply suppressed and so thoroughly denied were nevertheless forced to the surface of his conscience to undergo the agonies of reluctant self-examination. Could the gaijin be right? Was he merely a common thug and no samurai after all? If so, from whence came his power? Was it even power? Was it mere illusion instead? A dream within a dream? A veil within a veil? Rabbakami remembered that life itself was a dream within a dream, never to be fully understood or predicted. But if that were truth then where did such truth leave him? A master had to know, had to understand, life and the forces that governed it. How else could he hope to control it? And yet it now appeared that after many years of self-delusion, he in fact knew nothing, understood nothing. Yet to not know a thing was to be intimately familiar with it. Was that true? It sounded now like so much empirical cant. What was the truth, reality or illusion? Or was illusion the reality or vice versa? Was versa even a vice? How could a simple rabbit, even a master such as he, be expected to puzzle out such riddles? And if these enigmatic questions comprised the basis for the inexplicable koan of life, then what was the point of ever reaching for the answer to solve it, and if no point in that, what was the point of life at all? Should he ask for a second at once? For years he'd been fooling himself into believing that he was master—a ninja and samurai saint. Now along comes this gaijin, who with a few well-placed words shakes those beliefs to their very core while pointing out the hypocrisies of his worldview and the lies inherent in his self-deception. The master was shell-shocked. More than that he was shriven, shattered, and shook up. Forced at last to confront his own delusions and finally compelled to face up to his heretofore denied fallibilities, he felt his self-confidence fall away to pieces like so much stale crumb cake. He stood there, shaking and unsure of his place in the world, a shadow of his former self whose arrogance and pomposity being cast aside, stands there revealed for all to see—a jumbled mass of doubts and inferiority complexes. "Master!" Rabbakami cried, for in turning the tables on the mad rabbit, Jack had in fact made a valid claim to his own superiority. "What to do? Help me to find the self that I've lost! Have pity upon me, and help me to be once again Harehito Rabbakami! I beg you please!" He threw himself at Jack's feet, weeping uncontrollably while spouting out pitiful smelling pheromones whose scents demanded of Jack sympathy, commiseration, and sought-after compassion. So sincere were such scents and so ingenuous that Jack had to harden his heart to avoid giving way to such sympathies while keeping in the forefront of his thoughts the fact that he had this sad sack buffaloed. It helped the head hare to remember that Rabbakami had surely used Grasshopper in a selfish plan to achieve his own ends. Turnabout was fair play, and certainly no more than this slant-eye deserved! "How can I be of service?" the head hare asked slyly.

"I've lost myself, Father Jack," Rabbakami replied. "I've deluded myself into believing that I knew all when in fact, I know nothing."

"To not know a thing," Jack replied with perverse delight, "is to be intimately familiar with it!" Rabbakami gazed up at the head hare in wonder, as if hearing those words for the very first time. Once they were the cornerstone of his beliefs, the very mantle of his life's ambitions, then they were exposed as the empty platitudes they surely were and yet uttered again by Father Jack, they rang to the sound of truth once more! Here then truly, was a master! One in whom Rabbakami could find fulfillment by simply abasing himself at the head hare's feet. "Tell me, master," he cried in near religious ecstasy, "how can I find enlightenment?"

"Be samurai," Jack replied, "and serve. Serve me!"

"Yes, master!" cried Harehito, happy to have gained for himself a noble purpose although there was enough of his central core left to resent his defeat at the paws of a gaijin. He was glad that both his enlightenment and humiliation had occurred in private.

But of course others did see and they reported these matters to those who'd sent them to spy such things out.

*****

Helgayarn, Brunnhilde, and Betty sat in their newly provided, custom-designed Winnebago covered wagon, complete with the new V-8 upgrade (Clydesdales again—but harnessed in a triangle for supposedly greater efficiency, and monster wagon wheels, designed specifically for off-road travel in out-of-the-way and hard-to-get-to places, which back in Olden Days meant everywhere) whilst sulking amongst themselves and whining about life. Things weren't going well for the trio whose plans once again were bearing fruit which they had not intended to grow. Despite their admonitions to the contrary, Santos and his elves were bragging to one and all about their exploits in egg thievery and there were tales of their deeds being told throughout the forest. Not only were they stealing eggs but for all intents and purposes seemed to be doing quite a job of it at that. The elves were responsible, no doubt, for the farmer's unlooked for success. But the trio hadn't planned on him being successful, which was why they'd cautioned him to silence in the first place. His performance, which was beyond their expectations and which certainly overreached and surpassed the limitations that they'd imposed, wasn't half as embarrassing to Jack as it was to them. How could they hope to maintain order amongst the masses when those in their direct employ took seeming delight in exercising their own initiative? Initiative was dangerous. It's exercise lead to thoughts of independence and if forest folk, following the dumb farmer's example, made use of initiative and in so doing began to have for themselves self-determining thoughts, then who would need them? Yet Santos, despite their best laid plans, tore up one side of the forest and down the other bragging to all who listen about his artfulness at sleight-of-hand and about egg thievery in general. Well, thought, Helly, we should at least be grateful, I suppose, that the farmer hasn't implicated us in his endeavors or cited us by name. Still if he were half as successful as rumor claimed him to be, where were the complainers who should have been raising hell by now? There should've been petitioners across the field and throughout the forest, all seeking an audience with The Powers That Be, and each ready to testify both individually and corporately before a Constitutional Cosmic Court if necessary, about the hardships they'd been made to endure with the cessation of ova dispensation; for had such whiners and complainers come forward then certainly they could've been made use of. But the crybabies were strangely silent; moreover they were conspicuously absent. By Helgayarn's estimation they should've been beating the trio's doors down and yet they were mysteriously missing. The situation presented itself as an enigma to the trio but in actuality there was no ambiguity at all. Back in Olden Days folk had gotten used to living with the broken dreams and failed promises of The Powers That Be. Excluding Hurricane Junior, both man and beast had by then been through so many disasters and plans gone awry such as "seasons" and "tides" to name just two, that another failure was deemed as nothing to lose one's hair over or get in a snit about. By and large folk had decided that it was more prudent to keep their silence regarding such miscues rather than give voice to their complaints, however legitimate their grievances might be. Why invite trouble? To give voice to such grievances would only provide the Witches with the excuse they needed to meddle even further and so compound an already aggravating situation. Loose lips sank ships and since everyone back then saw themselves as passengers in the same boat, most strove to keep it watertight and afloat. The only folk going out of their way to get an audience with the trio were the venerable law firm of Owl, Owl, & Peacock. As legal eagles and moreover birds of a feather, each had been subject to the plague of egg thievery, having had a number of ova stolen from their nests at one time or another. Being deep within the pockets of The Powers That Be—Owl, Owl, & Peacock sought to further grease the wheels of justice and keep them spinning by enduring what they perceived as more than their fair share of abuse and kidnap. They bore up under it well taking it like the men they weren't. But their collective burden was becoming more than merely onerous and bordered on downright ridiculous as they felt that their lineages were now in danger of out-an-out extinction. They hadn't even been paid their retainers yet for participating in that mockery of a trial some years back and for their patience regarding this oversight they were supposed to endure the hardship of child-napping as well? It was too much, they felt, for mere birds to bear. Therefore since they were forced to submit to such injuries they continued to likewise submit their invoices for legal services to The Powers That Be while complaining about egg theft. Whenever they submitted their bills the Witches returned them with a postmark which read, "Return to sender—address unknown." Helly had an answer for them though and was just waiting for the proper moment to deliver it. For the time being those birdbrains were merely an annoyance to be ignored. When they crossed the line, turning from petty irritations into active aggravations she would pounce upon them like a tigress and carve them into chicken cutlets! There were plenty of lawyers out there— too many in fact, and all were willing to suck up to the court in order to gain influence and consideration. Who needed those birds with their snappy and demanding beaks? So it was that the days of the venerable firm of Owl, Owl, & Peacock were numbered. But in the meantime Helgayarn, Brunnhilde, and Betty had bigger fish to fry. Fish like Santos and Jack. What, in fact, were they going to do? "Any ideas?" asked Helgayarn, her voice made sour with frustration. "Any

THE CHRISTMAS RABBIT

ideas at all? Because at this point, I'll even entertain foolish notions if the two of you can't do any better!"

Brunnhilde looked at Betty who returned her gaze with mute silence. Betty had a whole catalogue of ideas and quick fixes regarding their current predicament and how to best extricate themselves from its concurrent entanglements. She might have given voice to them or being unwilling to engage in such vocalizations at least written a few down for the others to see but instead chose to remain true to form, noting them down in her secret journal and keeping them to herself. Brunnhilde had no ideas whatsoever other than to say to Helgayarn, "I told you so," but that, she knew, would accomplish nothing more than setting the three of them at each other's throats. Now more than ever and with all the problems which beset them, they needed to maintain a unified front. With help from the wee people, Santos despite all odds to the contrary, had grown into an egg thief extraordinaire and was not afraid to brag about it either despite their trifold warning to avoid doing just that. *Helly*, thought Brunnhilde, *should have known better than to expect the Tortoise to keep silent about anything—especially a rare accomplishment!* Now because of his big mouth they were caught between a rock and a hard place as they could neither stop his stealing or his bragging. To do either would only legitimize him while at the same time implicate them in this sordid ordeal and they could ill afford that. Once implicated, they ran the risk of having to admit responsibility. Such an admission would prompt someone into demanding of them the redistribution of stolen eggs, which if done would thereby alleviate the very tensions and divisions they were working so hard to formulate. Divide and conquer, fracture and rule, had always been both their motto and their mainstay. At least Pithecanthropus Wideass had enough sense to leave their names out of it while traveling throughout the land and boasting of his exploits. But how long would he keep that secret? Not long enough, she was sure. If their names ever came up—and she was sure that eventually they'd be made mention of and that such citing was merely a matter of time—a major meltdown in the perceived relationship between themselves and those whom they sought to govern would certainly occur. Therefore it was time to act precipitously in order to avoid a crisis in confidence and an outbreak of chaotic complaints.

*****

One person who wasn't afraid to vocalize her dissatisfaction was the Shoe Lady. The brood she had living in her boot numbered more souls than populated most third world countries. All were registered recipients on the egg rolls and all had gone without a delivery for some time. Tired of waiting for packages whose arrival appeared unlikely, one night she shut up the shoe, took the evening off, and went to demand an audience with her cousins. Since she entertained all manner of clients from one side of the forest to the other and thus received news from both near and far, the Shoe Lady knew exactly where the Witches were and how to find 'em.

Helgayarn, Brunnhilde, and Betty were camped out in the barren tract of waste that had once been Santos's farm. Since it was so close to what had been termed ground zero in the aftermath of Hurricane Junior it remained entirely vacuous despite the resurgence of growth in the lands surrounding it. Not even weeds were hardy enough to spout stalks in the midst of that desolation. The farm and the immediate area about it were one big sand heap having suffered a complete erosion of topsoil, sporting not so much as a tree or bush or even a single blade of grass to provide cover and camouflage for those who might approach. Standing in the middle of that barren tract one had a three hundred and sixty degree view of the surrounding area with no obstructions to restrict one's field of vision. Thus it was that the terrible trio took note of the Shoe Lady's approach while she was yet a good distance off—not that intervening cover would have mattered one whit to the Shoe Lady. She was a giant killer from way back and it would take more than these three sour old crones to rattle her ribcage. When the Witches saw her approach they went into a mild panic. There were few things on Mungo that acting individually, could cause the trio to throw conniptions. Mrs. Santos, with measuring cup in one hand and recipe book in the other, was one. The Shoe Lady was another. She had a certain power of her own, did the Shoe

THE CHRISTMAS RABBIT

Lady—not to mention seemingly eternal good looks, which the Trio were unanimously jealous of. She was nearly as old as themselves but the Witches had to grudgingly admit that their cousin did not look a day over a thousand. It was an incredible display of magic on her part and Helgayarn, Brunnhilde, and Betty would have traded all of their lesser spells, charms, and incantations in order to become mistresses of its secret. All three knew, although they couldn't prove it, that eons ago their respective husbands had paid the Shoe Lady a clandestine visit and that such were her charms and seductive wile that all three men became enamored of her to the exclusion of anyone or anything else—including them! Thus it was that Helgayarn, Brunnhilde, and Betty *became* Helgayarn, Brunnhilde, and Betty.

The trio looked on intently as the siren made her slow but deliberate way across the wastes, avoiding the pits and mires with which it had become infested. She picked her path one careful step at a time, testing the ground before her by prodding it with a stick that she'd picked up in the forest earlier. Poke, tap, scrape, move—it was a slow process, tiring, and took hours. The Shoe Lady however, could afford to be patient. Time was the one thing, besides good looks, of which she had plenty. Still it irked her no end when she paused to consider what such dead time meant with regard to hours lost while on her feet when she should've been on her back and earning a living. The line to her boot was probably four feet wide by now and a mile long. But thanks to those three witches there could be no help for it and what must be done, must be done. The Shoe Lady cursed her three cousins roundly as she tested the ground in front of her yet again before placing another a careful foot forward.

"What do you think?" Helgayarn asked tentatively while she watched the Shoe Lady approach. "Is she here to make trouble?"

Brunnhilde offered her sister a tired sigh, the wrinkles of her face doubling and tripling as she did. "Of course she's here to make trouble, Helly. What other purpose could she have? I told you ages ago that we should have dealt with her there and then. Either killed her outright or invited her to join us. She's too full of possible consequence to have running around like a loose cannon!"

"Yah!" exclaimed Betty.

Helgayarn offered the Norwegian a sour glance. "Do you always have to be so damned agreeable?" she asked. "Don't you ever have an opinion of your own?"

Betty returned Helgayarn's bitter appraisal with a sour smile of her own. "Yah!" she gleefully replied.

Helgayarn shrugged her shoulders and sighed as she pushed a wisp of blue-gray hair out of her tired eyes. All the problems with Santos and Jack were beginning to take their toll upon her and these two were of no help whatsoever. Now on top of the current fiasco in which they'd become embroiled they were about to get caught up in another, she was sure. What did the Shoe Lady want, she wondered, and why show up now of all times? She'd have her answers soon enough, she supposed, as the Shoe Lady was even now approaching their front door.

There came a persistent and loud knocking.

Helgayarn looked to Brunnhilde who in turn, looked to Betty.

"Answer the door, you fool!" Helgayarn demanded of Brunnhilde.

"Yes, answer it!" Brunnhilde demanded of Betty while both she and Helgayarn stood there impatiently tapping their feet and nervously snapping their fingers. Betty stared at her compatriots intently while summoning all of her power in an effort to free her tongue of its palsy. "No way I'm answering that door!" she blurted out. "No way at all!"

Both Helgayarn and Brunnhilde looked incredulous. Neither had heard Betty utter more than a single syllable for centuries. To do so now spoke volumes to them about the plight in which they found themselves. With an angry gesture Helgayarn shoved the other two aside. "Crimeny!" she said. "Am I the big witch here, or what? I'll answer the damned door myself. She grabbed hold of its knob, pulling it open. "Cousin," she exclaimed, her voice dripping honey, "what a pleasant surprise, to find you've come calling! Do come in. Do come in! Brunnhilde, my dearest, put some tea on for our inestimable cousin!"

The Shoe Lady stood on the stoop peering into the Winnebago while eyeing the three of them suspiciously. Solicitude and good wishes from these three were to be regarded with extreme caution. These three, she knew, looked after no one but themselves. She entered warily, her face an etching in skepticism as she took note of every aspect of the wagon's interior while searching for traps—although common sense told her that such snares, if they'd been set, would not be so obvious. Nor would they likely be traps constructed to ensnare her person. More probable, they'd be Machiavellian ploys and subterfuges designed to limit her ability to act in her own self-interest. Still with these three one could never know for sure. They'd painted themselves into a corner over this damned egg business and so, she supposed, in their desperation were capable of anything. Well, let 'em, thought the Shoe Lady. She'd played such games with them in the past and more than once at that. Always she'd come out the winner because Helgayarn, Brunnhilde, and Betty were forever underestimating her while at the same time overestimating themselves. It was likely that things hadn't changed much. Looking them over the Shoe Lady determined that her best defense would be a good offense and therefore attacked. "Spare me the cattle craps, Helgayarn," she scathingly replied while pushing her way past them. "It's no surprise to you that I'm here. You saw me coming from a mile away. And as to your offer of tea the three of you will choke on your own brew before I allow such libations to my lips! Heaven knows what kind of mickey you might try and slip me!"

So, thought Betty, *that's to be her tone, is it?* Well, she had the answer for this husband-stealing strumpet! It was Betty's opinion that it was high time this particular tart be turned turtle. She pulled a hairpin, the point of which was sharper than a surgeon's scalpel, from the back of her head. The pin had been coated with the remains of Mrs. Santos's shark fin soup and a more toxic substance, Betty knew, was not to be found anywhere on the planet. One prick from her poisoned pin would likely send the Shoe Lady to the hell she deserved.

The Shoe Lady spied the pin in the witch's hand. So it was to be an obvious trap and a physical one at that. How foolish. "My people know where I am," she said to Helgayarn, "and when to expect my return!"

Helgayarn leapt in front of Betty holding her back and saving the Shoe Lady's life while at the same time saving themselves untold amounts of misery. Their cousin had come prepared and with seemingly all of her bases covered. Well, that was to be expected, wasn't it? The tart had always been a formidable enemy. "There's been a misunderstanding, my dear," said Helgayarn to the strumpet while at the same time giving her sister a baleful eye. "No harm was intended."

"Cattle craps!" the Shoe Lady replied acidly. "That witch was going to prick me with her poisoned pin!"

"But she didn't, did she?" countered Helly "And you have me to thank for that, don't you?"

The Shoe Lady offered the trio a dubious glance. "What do you want?" she asked.

"What do we want?" Helgayarn replied innocently. "It was you who came to us, cousin. But as to our wants, we want only to be of service to our redoubtable cousin. To be of service, that's all."

"Yeah, right," said the Shoe Lady, "and the sun sets in the east!" This remark cut the trio to the core causing all three to bridle and fidget as they'd tried long ago to accomplish that very feat but had failed miserably. "Even if your gesture is sincere," continued the Shoe Lady, "then no doubt such sincerity has reasons of its own for making itself available."

Helgayarn collected her composure before answering. Six breaths—three shallow, three deep, before she felt herself under control. Brunnhilde and Betty just stood there seething. "There's no doubt that what you say is true," replied Helly. "Just as you have your own motives for seeking us out. What remains to be seen however is whether your motives and our reasons remain inimical, one to the other, or whether an accord can be reached. Therefore tell us cousin, why seek you an audience?"

The Shoe Lady knew that the time had come to either put up or shut up and so laid her first card on the table. It would look to the trio like she was holding a weak hand but how could they know while she revealed her solitary deuce, that the rest of her cards were aces? "Eggs!" she declared. "I want my children's rightful share of the ova promised to them by official decree!"

THE CHRISTMAS RABBIT

Helgayarn offered Brunnhilde and Betty a smug smile before replying. They had her. They had her and it was going to be delicious! "Why come to us?" Helgayarn asked. "Surely you should be taking your complaint to Jack Rabbit. After all, he's the one responsible for eggs and their fair distribution. Go see him with our blessings, and may the fates smile kindly upon you."

Time to check, thought the Shoe Lady and in so doing draw the old crones out. "He may administer the law," she replied, "but as its authors, you three have the responsibility for enforcing it!"

"True," broke in Brunnhilde before Helgayarn could reply, "but we can't be expected to intercede in every petty grievance, can we?" She looked to the other two for confirmation and support. Slightly irritated, Helgayarn nevertheless offered up an affirmative nod. It was not quite the tack that she would have taken with their old adversary but she supposed that as a gambit, Brunnhilde's reply was serviceable.

"Yah!" contributed Betty.

"Why not?" countered the Shoe Lady, eyeing each of them in turn. "You interfere all the time when it suits you. Why should now be any different?"

Helgayarn offered their cousin a shark's smile. "Now you know that's not true," she replied, giving voice to the bald-faced lie. "We never interfere. We *intervene*. And such accusations on your part do nothing to further the diplomatic ideal, which I'm sure we all hope to achieve. But I forgive you cousin. Now go back to Jack Rabbit with our blessing and demand of him, your ova!"

"He hasn't got any," stated the Shoe Lady.

Brunnhilde feigned innocence. "Of course he does," she said. "He's been collecting them from all over the forest!"

"Yah!" replied Betty, adding her agreement to Brunnhilde's assertion while Helgayarn offered up an affirmative nod and smug smile as her reply.

The Shoe Lady returned one smirk for the other. Did they really think her that stupid? Did they consider her so naive as to be blissfully unaware of their machinations and intrigues? Well, thought she, it's time to burst that bubble! "I know," she said matter-of-factly.

The terrible trio looked on in puzzlement. "Of course you know," replied Helgayarn in an uncertain tenor. "You know that Jack Rabbit has eggs—now go and get them!"

The Shoe Lady laughed. "I don't know anything about that," she answered, "but I do know *everything* else!" It wasn't strictly the truth. There was plenty going on out there in the wide world that the Shoe Lady didn't know beans about; but about the great egg scramble, yes the Shoe Lady was cognizant of just about everything—at least as such matters applied to, and affected, her.

"I'm sure that I don't have the slightest idea of what you're referring to," Helgayarn replied carefully.

"Me either," Brunnhilde added with a nervous laugh.

"Yah." echoed Betty, her single syllable an exercise in desperation.

"Elves," stated the Shoe Lady.

"Helgayarn blanched. "Come again?"

"I said elves! Sprites, gnomes, dwarfs, and picts—you have them all working for Wideass! They're helping him resteal Jack's stolen booty!"

"I'm sure that we know nothing about that," Helgayarn replied skittishly. "Elves? What are elves?"

"Not what," countered the Shoe Lady, "who!" You know who they are because you drafted 'em and have 'em working for Farm Boy! I know, because all men—be they five foot one or one foot five, love to talk about how big they are while bragging of their exploits—especially little fellows with altitude issues and Napoleon complexes—and I've been seeing plenty of those lately! Hell, there've been so damned many of late and they've been such regular customers that I've had to set up and extra line and cut out a special hole in the heel of my boot just so I could accommodate them, keep the line moving, and do business! I tell you that I've never seen their like. Being tiny doesn't stop 'em from talking big. *Yak, yak, yak!* Crimeny—you'd think they'd just learned a new language and were trying it out!

"It isn't that I mind. They are after all paying for the time and for talking or at least listening, I charge double! But my, how they go on! And what the wee folk go on about is stolen eggs and how the three of you are up to your noses in yolks!" The trio desperately shook their heads in denial trying to gainsay the whore's accusations but the Shoe Lady was having none of it. "Don't try to deny it," she continued. "I've spoken to all of 'em! They've all been by for a quickie and they've all talked afterward—each and every one and I've got 'em all on tape!"

The terrible triumvirate were flabbergasted, out on their feet, and unsure of how to proceed. To the best of their knowledge tape recorders whether analog or digital, had not been invented yet and so they reasoned that such accusations if made public by their cousin, would come down to a matter of her word against theirs…and she was after all, a whore, whereas they were the law. Public opinion, they felt, would probably swing their way. Still though such devices to the best of their knowledge had yet to be developed, they had to nevertheless admit that often their knowledge was somewhat lacking and if anyone were to have within their possession a prototype of such a contraption that someone would most certainly be the Shoe Lady. Given the nature of her business it would be prudent no doubt, to employ such a device in order to maintain a firm hold upon her customers. Also her resources were almost unlimited. The Shoe Lady was a cash cow and hard cash, they knew, could buy almost anything. Furthermore, they reasoned, the whore might not even need such a device. Her word against theirs was indeed questionable but her word backed up by the testimony of hundreds of little people with inordinately big mouths coupled with the sworn statements of who knew how many other customers that might have overheard a particular conversation regarding eggs and their purloining while standing in line and waiting to be serviced would, they knew, doom them.

Just when the trio thought they'd seen their antagonist's final cards, the Shoe Lady showed 'em her last two aces.

"I have it on the best of authority, she said, that your precious Farm Boy has challenged Jack Rabbit to a race for the right to deliver eggs and that furthermore at the urging of the elves, is planning a surprise attack upon the warren with the intention of killing the little beast and settling the issue once and for all."

The trio blanched again. The Shoe Lady's accusations if they were true and why shouldn't they be—with that dumb farmer just about anything was possible—could only spell trouble with a capital T. Backed once again into a corner of their own devising, they fell back on the only option left to them.

"Cousin," they said ever so sweetly after conferring in private amongst themselves, "let us make you a deal…"

*****

"Kick, pivot, strike, block!" Harehito yelled and fully two hundred hares, handpicked in a manner of speaking, and chosen as the hardiest hares handy, tried their best to follow his directives. Most pivoted when they should've blocked or struck when they should've kicked and as a result found themselves sitting upon their cotton tailed little behinds and picking each other up off the ground. They were three months into training what Jack's rabbits publicly and proudly referred to as Rabbit 1, and privately, with fondness, as Jackhammer. When it became evident to Jack that Santos's seconds were not coming anytime soon he began to suspect treachery and so with Harehito's aid had organized the entire warren into militias, expecting an ambush of some sort. Rabbakami surveyed the tangled wreckage of twisted limbs and contorted postures while laughingly conceding to himself that Jackhammer was the biggest joke he'd ever heard tell of. "Wrong!" he yelled at his trainees, giving voice to his disgust. "Wrong, wrong. Wrong! Kick, pivot, strike, block! How many times do I have to tell you?" Once again he demonstrated for them the simple technique, revealing the apparent ease with which it could be performed. Kick, pivot, strike, block. It was like ballet—endowed with grace, enacted with fluidity, and performed with exactitude.

Of the few rabbits left standing, only Peter had enough presence of mind to pay attention as Rabbakami tried yet again to drill this simplest of techniques into their regiment. Rabbit 1 was the first wave of shock troops being established whose mission it would be to carry the war to the feet of their pesky little enemies before the teeny truants had the chance to do likewise. Harehito himself had been out once or twice on solo reconnaissance missions—just to get the lay of the land, ruffle a few feathers in their teeny weenie little caps, and let

THE CHRISTMAS RABBIT

them know there was a new sheriff in town. He had the scalp of one unfortunate elf displayed prominently over the entrance to his hole. Stamped into its forehead was the legend, "Harehito Was Here." As he stood there listening to the ninja Peter happened to catch a glance of the trophy hanging over the entrance to their visitor's quarters. It left him decidedly uneasy. He dwelt for a moment on the past and to those encounters, which compromised the initial battles between rabbits and the farmer. Though not alive himself back then, Peter had by now heard all the stories and had lived however vicariously, their glories. The rabbits, he knew, had done their fair share of butt kicking but they hadn't gone out of their way to kill anyone. The advent of the elven scalp hanging above the door changed all that. Peter wondered whether or not the elf, whoever he'd been, had believed in the cause he died for or had simply been caught up in circumstances beyond his control and as such, had merely been following the dictates of forces too powerful to deny. Probably the latter. Who after all, would volunteer themselves to take part in this?

Death. He could smell it around and about, as if it were lurking in the woods like some evil ogre, hidden, crafty, and waiting to claim him. If this Japanese lunatic had his way, Peter knew, then the grim reaper couldn't be too far down the road. Harehito wanted to marshal their forces and commit them to battle today, but Father Jack, in his wisdom, held off, knowing that they were far from ready. Harehito didn't care. All he wanted was a big battle with powerful enemies to defeat so that he could reinflate his ego which had been humiliated, humbled, and mortified by his loss of face to Father Jack. That hundreds of rabbits, perhaps even thousands, might have to die in order for Rabbakami to regain his lost glory was not a consideration that Harehito paused for even a moment to reflect upon. Good generals, the ninja knew, if they were ever to get anywhere in this life, had to be willing to expend lots of cannon fodder while embarked upon the journey—whether cannons had been invented yet or not.

Jack stood on a small rise watching with disgust, the carnage being enacted below as Harehito took to task one particularly reluctant rabbit, namely Cottontail, and slapped him a good one for not paying enough attention. Enough of that. "All right," yelled the head hare to the formation gathered below. "The lesson's over for the day. Everybody hit the showers and then get back to scrambling your eggs."

Harehito stood there looking up at Jack with mouth agape, unable to believe that this silly gaijin whom he was forced to acknowledge as master had called off his class without consulting him first. How was he to maintain control of the troops if civilian authority constantly overrode his directives? Although he was forced to acknowledge Jack as master he still held on to the hope that he'd be able to take over the whole ball of wax when the opportunity presented itself. He'd suffered defeat and humiliation at the paws of this vile gaijin and his ancestors cried out for revenge. It was a time honored Japanese tradition and one which he soon hoped to partake of. His humiliation had caused his harea to suffer oodles of disharmony and his karma would be forever misaligned and running in a corkscrew until he set the matter straight. He knew that as a Japanese, he could not live with such dishonor and since seppuku was not for him an option as he had too much to live for, then revenge dished out the sooner the better, was his preferred choice. In the fruit of time he'd win his rebellion, he knew, and claim for himself not only Jack's title of Head Hare, but that darling little Nutmeg too. What a looker! He was just waiting for the proper moment to take Jack out while at the same time make him a martyr to the cause. Every movement needed a good martyr around whom to rally. Harehito considered that he would have made the best martyr but martyrs, to be truly effective, had to be dead and old Harehito felt that he had far too much living to do before he'd be ready to fill that billet. Let the gaijin be their sacrificial duck. His children already viewed him as a noble cause anyway. The ninja was just awaiting the proper moment and the certain eventuality that Nutmeg would come to see in him whatever it was that she saw in that round-eyed fool. Surely she could see that he, Harehito, was by far the better rabbit. Sooner or later, he knew, that breeder would bounce around to his way of thinking. It was as clear as karma. But if that idiot was going to continue gainsaying him and interrupting his classes then old round-eyes just might meet with his fate sooner, rather than later. No one talked over him. No one. "With

THE CHRISTMAS RABBIT

all due respect, my lord," he said through gritted teeth, "just what do you think you're doing by canceling my class?"

"They're tired," Jack replied, hopping off his hill and down to the field below. "They're tired and need rest. Besides, we have our eggs to see to."

"Eggs?" asked a disbelieving Rabbakami. "How in the name of Buddha do you expect to keep the damned things if you're not ready to defend 'em?"

Jack surveyed the tangled wreckage of rabbits as they slowly picked themselves up and made their way to the showers. High in the trees surrounding the exercise area birds were nesting in the branches and looking down at the melee. *Spies for sure*, Jack thought and cryptically referred to by this Mad Rabbit before him as "Lurkers In The Leafs." Jack didn't see the point of correcting Rabbakami's grammar—the head hare had far too much on his mind to worry about such mundane matters as sentence structure and poor spelling. The "Lurkers In The Leafs" were there, no doubt, to keep watch on him and his and were on station at the behest of the elves or perhaps even The Powers That Be.

Well, thought Jack, there's no help for it.

Regardless of his climbing and scaling abilities Jack knew that if he attempted an ascension into the trees or sent others to do likewise, the birds would simply fly away. He supposed that he could ask Harehito to hurl his harea at them as well as a few noxious pheromones. That would certainly ruffle their feathers while knocking them out of their roosts but it would also tip the rabbits' paws, alerting the birds that the rabbits were aware of their presence. Such a revelation might force the issue, causing their enemies to move against them before they were ready. Maybe, with Harehito as their general, such considerations wouldn't amount to a hill of beans, but Jack was not disposed to ask the ninja for any favors. He wasn't sure that he approved of the way the mystic warrior and aesthetic treated his children and he certainly didn't like it that Rabbakami looked with lust upon his mate. But so long as the warren was in the position in which it found itself and therefore needed the lunatic before him, Jack supposed that such ill-mannered behavior would have to be overlooked.

He trusted Nutmeg by now with regard to such matters but held little confidence in the loyalty of Rabbakami himself and was therefore careful not to leave her unattended when the ninja rabbit was near. Turning his attention back to the 'Lurkers In The Leafs,' he questioned again his unease regarding them. Birds were stupid creatures, he knew, and one didn't bandy about the epithet "birdbrained," when fostering an insult upon someone else, for nothing. What, if anything, did birds know of battles or the martial arts employed in their enactment? All this must seem like nonsense to them, he reasoned, and therefore not worthy of report. But in that he was wrong. "Oh, I think we can defend them," he said to Rabbakami, meaning the eggs. "After all, we were doing just fine before you came along."

Detesting the necessary courtesies that the master-servant relationship forced upon him, Rabbakami strove to formulate a reply that was both polite and contrite. "So sorry," he humbly said. "You were? Then why, master, were you losing every third egg to those little truants?"

"I'll grant you," Jack replied, "that 'fine' is a relative term. It's true—we were losing one in three eggs before you showed up but now we're losing one in two! We have all these rabbits training and hardly any of them working, so what's the point? In expecting treachery, I understand the need for divisions of troops, but Rabbits 1, 2, 3, and 4? Crimeny—Jackhammer's size alone would lead one to believe that we're getting ready to fight the Battle of Babylon!

"What good is all this training anyway? Rabbits don't fight this way. We fight in packs. We gang up on our enemies like we used to do with Santos, and then we aggress. What worked before will work again."

Harehito offered Jack a sympathetic glance that was about as genuine as a three-dollar bill. "Predictability," he replied, has meant the annihilation of many an army. Your enemies will be expecting you to fall back on tried and true tactics and will therefore be prepared to defend against them. The excellence of my martial art is that there is no defense against it! Also your tactics assume that we'll engage only the Tortoise. There's the elves, you know. And there simply ain't enough of you to engage them using your inferior martial

THE CHRISTMAS RABBIT

art. Perhaps if we had another ten years in which to increase the size of our army such battle strategies might prove themselves to be of use." Harehito looked around the immediate area as if sensing unseen enemies. "But we don't have that kind of time."

Fool, thought Jack to himself. He felt like pointing out to "the master" that all he had to do was look up in order to be confronted with more enemies than he could possibly handle. How could one be aware of 'Lurkers In The Leafs' and yet nevertheless not see the leaves for the trees themselves? Jack thought back to his trip to the big apple and his encounter with Thor Rowe. He remembered Thor giving him that tome, *Zen and the Art of Primitive Tool Repair*. He also remembered the admonishment that Thor had delivered along with the volume itself. "Remember," Thor had said, "that any knowledge is imperfect knowledge. No truth is the whole truth. If it were, then by definition it would be lies. This book addresses among other things the concept of awareness, both of self and of others. But always realize that perfect awareness equals perfect paranoia!" Now, standing here and looking at this mad rabbit, Jack finally understood what the old hippie meant. Harehito, perfectly aware, was forever displaying the attitude that there were 'Lurkers In The Leafs,' whether he saw them or not.

Looking from side to side, the ninja rabbit continued, "There's those witches to account for too," said he. "And no pack, no matter how large, is tough enough to go mixing it up with those three. Not with the tactics you're espousing. Those old hags will make Welsh Rarebit out of the whole warren. So sorry, you need my martial art if you're to have any hope of surviving."

Yes, thought Jack, *we do. But what we don't need is you!* For the millionth time that day he wondered if it was possible to get the one without having to endure the other. "Regardless of what tactics we use," Jack replied, "I hadn't planned on any of us engaging The Powers That Be directly. That'd be suicide, pure and simple. Mass harea-kiri for sure!"

"It would be," replied the ninja rabbit with a chuckle, "for anyone else. But not for me! I'm Harehito Rabbakami, and I've never been defeated. Never! Why I even took on old Musashi himself!

Fought him with one hand tied behind my back, I did! Him with his two swords and his school of Two Heavens! He fought like a round-eye! I hurled my harea at him, knocking his pitiful blades right out of his hands! I was gonna hurl my harea again and finish the piker but then I thought to myself that such a pretender, traveling through the land as he did while billing himself the "Sword Saint" didn't deserve the honor, so I merely whipped out my war fan and hurling that instead, sliced him up into teeny weenie little ribbons! It all comes down to enlightenment and awareness. To be perfect in battle, one must strive for imperfection, to know a thing is to not know it; to not know it is become intimately familiar with it and vice versa. Mind, no mind. To be or not to be—that is the question!"

Jack had no idea what the lunatic before him was referring to but found himself wishing fervently nevertheless that Harehito would get the chance to prove his point. *Maybe then*, thought Jack, *we'll all be rid of him.* "That's the biggest load of Cattle Craps I've ever heard tell of," replied the head hare. "I've studied Zen myself, and I'm aware enough as it is. What sound does a tree make when it falls in the forest? How many angels can dance on the head of a pin? What is the sound of one hand clapping and what came first, the chicken or the egg? They're all koans. Riddles with no correct answers are of little practical value in the real world."

Harehito stared at Jack while disbelieving his very ears. How dare this round-eye impugn anything about him or his art? Though forced through trickery into acknowledging Jack the master, there came to Harehito as comes to every indentured servant, a time when mere contemplation of rebellion no longer serves to carry the day of the ego which drives it. And so it was with Harehito. His watershed moment had arrived. Useless? Harehito would show him useless! "This," he stated gleefully while striking Jack with an open handed blow and sending the poor rabbit end over end, "is the sound of one hand clapping! And it's about time that you learned it!" Harehito advanced on Jack, who lay stunned and prostrate on the ground, his mouth full of dirt and his cheek a red weal shining through gray whiskers. As Rabbakami drew near, he centered his harea and marshaled his pheromones. *To hell with the proper time*, thought he. Now

THE CHRISTMAS RABBIT

was the proper time! Jack surely would have met his end, and this tale not need telling, but at that very instant, an alarm broke out. It pealed throughout the trees and echoed throughout the secret network of interwoven tunnels. It rang and reverberated from one end of the forest to the other as it uttered its harsh and strident warning. They were under attack.

*****

From the moment it had been reported to Pixie and Dixie by the 'Lurkers In The Leafs' that Jack had won a contest of wits against the great Harehito Rabbakami whom all elves had heard of, and had gotten the ninja to pledge his fidelity and allegiance, enlisting his aid to train their militia, the two elves took it upon themselves to convince Santos of the need to attack quickly. They knew that two-fisted, double-dealing, blackhearted, son of a so-and-so Rabbakami from eternity and knew that he was not to be trusted in the long run no matter what kind of deal he purported to make with Jack. Most likely he was planning some sort of overthrow of his own. However that said nothing about the short run and there was no point, they knew, in giving that fanatic the time he needed whip Jack's rabbits into crack militias. Given those circumstances, an attack by the elven host could be costly. Also, if the ninja took over sooner rather than later, they'd face an army with him at its head, and they both favored running a race or facing an army with Jack as their chief opponent. Jack was civilized and could therefore be counted upon to abide by rules which could be turned against him. Harehito, on the other hand, was a law unto himself, and there'd be no predicting or accounting for the actions of such a confederate. So they began to drop hints to the farmer, to make suggestions and offer up plans and counter proposals.

"Why not show some initiative?" they asked. "To hell with Helgayarn, Brunnhilde, and Betty—lead us into battle and hence to victory! Show the Witches that there's more to you than your ample middle." Dixie turned back to his brethren gathered behind them. "Whaddya say, lads," he incited, "are y'all ready to rumble?"

There was a chorus of "Yeah's!" and "Right on's!" as the masses, caught up in Pixie and Dixie's fervor, took up the chant for war. "Sharpen your swords then," cried Pixie, "and see to your pikes and lances! Swing your staves and shillelaghs and bring forth your bastinados and battle-axes! To war, lads. To war!"

Despite the fact that he was nominally in charge, Santos who was never much of a leader to begin with, found himself caught up in the fury and the fervor of the moment. "Yes!" he cried. "To war! Let me get my club!"

"Best to leave it where it is," replied Pixie cautiously. "We don't want to hamper our column's advance by hauling dead weight."

On the night before Harehito's rebellion Santos and his elves made their way quietly through the depths of the forest. Elves can move as silently as rabbits when they have to and they had to if they were going to be successful with their planned ambush. They had Old Slomoe with them however and stealth was simply not a word to be found in his lexicon. Realizing a particular concept to be beyond an individual's ability to express, the elves further extrapolated that it was therefore beyond the realm of reason to expect that individual to implement it. For his own good then as well as their own, the elves bound and gagged the farmer while detailing twenty of their brethren to carry him upon a litter as they tiptoed their way through the wood. They reached their objective late in the watches of early morning, encircling the warren and positioning themselves for a dawn attack...which didn't occur until noon. Despite what you may have read in other tales, such as "The Elves and the Shoemaker," regarding the industriousness of wee folk and their penchant for turning out a good day's work by 6:00 a.m., the reality is that they're all lazy cusses who much prefer sleeping in until nine. Added to this lethargic attitude was the consensus among their masses that you couldn't fight a proper battle on an empty stomach. Therefore a good breakfast was called for before engaging in war. When it was realized, however, that no one among them remembered to bring the lembas and ambrosia, they decided to have poached eggs instead. But all the eggs were locked away in the magic room so another elven detail had to be organized to go back and get 'em.

THE CHRISTMAS RABBIT

After a late breakfast that would be better described as an early brunch the elves made ready their assault. They still had surprise on their side but untying the farmer to give him as nominal leader, the honor of spearheading their charge, gave away that edge entirely. It was a calculated risk that they hadn't fully considered. Pixie and Dixie's only concern was to have Wideass at the forefront of their charge in case matters got out of hand and the battle turned itself against them. Should that eventuality occur and the Witches get snitty about it, throwing one of their infamous hissy fits, then the two elves, having put Santos at the head of their column, could blame him for it going belly-up. They'd have enough on their hands, they knew, dealing with Rabbakami. They didn't need the added burden of three pissed-off Powers too! So Santos led their charge, tripping over a root as he did so and skinning his knee. "Ho! Ho! Ho!" he yelled in anguish, warning the rabbit sentries of the impending attack.

With the pealing of bells the confrontation between Jack and Harehito was forgotten. Rabbakami recognized the call to battle and relished the thought of pitting himself against opponents worthy of his mettle. Lying stunned on his back Jack comprehended none of this but had retained enough presence of mind to deduce that *something* was up.

"What's going on?" he asked no one in particular. "Have the pellets hit the wind?"

"In a big-time way, sonny!" replied Harehito. "It's Pithecanthropus Wideass and his elven eta! And wherever they are, you can be sure that the Witches aren't too far behind!"

"Are you certain?" Jack asked, still trying to shake off the ninja rabbit's attack.

"As sure as samurai shit sushi after supper, sonny," replied Harehito, "To arms! To arms!" And with that, the ninja rabbit sped off.

Jack regained his footing while he watched Harehito speed away.

Vulgar Bastard. *Two arms?* he thought. *Of course I have two arms—and two legs too! What's that lunatic talking about now?* As there was no answer immediately forthcoming he raced off to a tree in which he'd posted sentries. It was his intention to join them there.

Behind what would soon become the front lines, the tree offered him the best location from which to review the upcoming battle. As warden of the warren, head hare hereabouts, and leader of the pack, he was if only tacitly, commander-in-chief of all rabbits—and knew that the best place for a commander-in-chief, tacit or otherwise, was the hell out of the way where he couldn't interfere with the troops or the real generals whose business it was to command them. Let Harehito run the battle. The mad rabbit had been looking forward to this day since his arrival. Jack, on the other hand, would see to the civilians, who because of the recent call to arms numbered only two, himself and Nutmeg. Sometimes it paid to be head hare.

From all four sides of the forest the elves advanced in uniform columns. Row upon row of leprechauns, dwarfs, picts, and midgets marched in orderly fashion, each abreast of the other and with lances and staves held at the ready. Off to the east a battalion of gnomes stood their ground, maintaining their places while neither advancing nor retreating. The order of battle billeted them as the reserve force, to be used only if the fortunes of war were to turn against them. Otherwise, they were the mop-up crew, assigned the tasks of pillaging and raping, a gnomish duty indeed and offered to them because no one else in the elven army wanted anything to do with it. Elves are generally happy-go-lucky folk—rape and pillage does not sit well with them. Gnomes, being ugly and endowed with sour temperament, have the proper dispositions for engaging in such atrocities.

As the elven army advanced it began to encounter the front-runners and point guards from of Rabbits 1, 2, 3, and 4. Magical spears were hurled and enchanted maces swung. Each were endowed with various spells and charms of making to ensure that they found their mark and pierced their targets. But like their mistresses, the elves charms and magics were faulty and inconsistent so like their matrons the sprites missed their marks more often than not.

Rabbits galore skipped, hopped, and leapt over any number of slings, arrows, and darts to close upon their enemies, laying them open with their wicked little teeth. Pheromones flew in profusion, hareas were hurled whole-heartedly, and "Lurkers In The Leafs" were attacked with wild abandon. It was a regular free-for-all with rabbits and elves going toe-to-toe and head-to-head. At the forefront of the battle was the ninja rabbit himself, Rabbakami, hurling his harea before him and knocking down elves like duckpins. One dwarf hardier than most, managed to hold at bay Harehito's harea while at the same time swinging his stave, in an effort crush the ninja rabbit's head; so Harehito did him the old-fashioned way by blocking his strike and snapping his neck. He paused for a moment to spit in the face of his vanquished enemy while other rabbits fore and aft with both Peter and Cottontail included, were kicking elven butt in a similar fashion. But it wasn't a pitched battle or a one-way fight in any way whatsoever. The elves gave as good as they got, kicking their own butts and taking their own names. Many rabbits of fame and renown both male and female fell in the ensuing melee. Chief among them were Flopsy Doodle and Rabitboodles, Jack's eldest daughters, and Whiskers, an especially loved grandson—all slain by the wicked and unforgiving spears of the elves.

 The battle raged on through both day and night, waxing and waning, ebbing and flowing, as one side gained ground only to lose what ground it gained to a concentrated and well planned counter-strike from the other. Blood flowed liberally and red, staining the soil upon which it fell and turning it crimson—except where an elf lay wounded—there the earth turned green as elven blood has more copper, less iron.

 At one point in the fighting a platoon of dwarves captained by a gnome of vile disposition who was nevertheless a capable commander in his own right, took advantage of a rent in the rabbit left flank and finding a hole, waded into the rabbit rear with battle axes swinging and shillelaghs singing in an attempt to rout their enemies from the field. This left flank was composed of Rabbits 1 and 2 and two divisions each from Rabbits 3 and 4, accounting for nearly half the strength of Operation Jackhammer. It is said by those who know that a haragei master has eyes in the back of his head. A *hareagei* master, however, like Rabbakami, has eyes in the back of those eyes. So it was that employing one of the many applications of hareagei, Harehito sensed the danger to his forces from across the field and with harea hurling and pheromones flying, threw himself into the developing fray, coming to the left flank's aid. Ax-heads were shriven on their handles, staves and spears became twisted and warped in midflight, while dwarves and gnomes in bunches burned with ninja fire, the skin scorched of their teeny weenie little bodies as the ninja rabbit, employing hareagei, jaho, and his entire repertoire of dirty tricks, repelled the elven attack. As he stood there mopping up the remnants of this pitiful platoon Rabbakami took note of Santos to the rear of the battle, standing beneath his war standard, and directing the attack. With no regard to his own safety—it was, after all Pithecanthropus Wideass—Rabakami charged the standard of that blubbering ball of fat in the chartreuse suit, intent upon killing the son of a bitch there and then and so end the battle. But of course, that couldn't be allowed...

Ever since The Powers That Be concocted this inane plan where once again their goal was to set the silly farmer at odds with the rabbit, they were compelled for their own sake to keep a weather eye on both in order to safeguard against any permanent damages which might be done by one to the other in an overzealous display of enthusiasm and bad timing. Such monitoring was an effort on their part to ensure that this plan, like so many others, would not end in disaster by going belly-up before the hammer could be brought down. This effort proved only halfway effective which when considered in the privacy of their own persons and evaluated against similar endeavors that had ended in failure, could only be deemed as a total success. What reliable intelligence they were able to gather concerned Slomoe only. Jack was too cagey to be caught off guard and spied upon. The 'Lurkers In The Leafs' were operating independently and were reporting directly to the elves, many of whom the Shoe Lady had co-opted. As a result what information they were able to gather about Jack and his plans was second hand intelligence at best, with most of it being supposition based upon what Santos was doing. Still partial intelligence was better than none, they reasoned, and had to content themselves with what they could get. Therefore employing once again the venerable law firm of Owl, Owl, & Peacock, the trio drafted their entire staff of secretaries, paralegals, aides, and receptionists, and forming their own squadron of 'Leaf Lurkers' set out to

THE CHRISTMAS RABBIT

spy upon the farmer in the off-hand chance he should stumble across his children, unlikely as that contingency might be, and try to renege on his deal; or through incompetence, a possibility they regarded as much more plausible despite the aid of an elven army, bollix his billet, thereby ruining their plans for both. These spies were birds of a feather and reported directly to the trio as the Witches were picking up the tab for their services and would continue to do so for the duration. Owl, Owl, & Peacock, ever crafty in the ways of lawyers, judges, and witches, graciously offered to continue paying the salaries of those junior personnel on loan to The Powers That Be in an effort to ensure their continued loyalty, thus keeping the three partners "in the know" while at the same time safeguarding their backs and providing them they hoped, with a lever powerful enough to pry themselves out of the Witches claws. But Helgayarn, Brunnhilde, and Betty had been double-dealing, co-opting, and back stabbing for far too long to be taken in by such an obvious ploy, despite the cost benefits. The Witches knew that too much was riding on the outcome of this fiasco to put an untoward amount of trust in the allegiances of Owl, Owl, & Peacock. Lawyers, after all, are lawyers. The Powers That Be reasoned that given the enormous stakes the nod to caution was well worth the extra expense, especially since they had no intention of paying anyway, and so flatly rejected the firm's offer, shutting them down both promptly and in no uncertain terms. The spies would report to The Powers That Be and to The Powers That Be only. Any deviation in the arrangement, no matter how slight, would result in the immediate disbarment, disfigurement, and dismemberment, both corporately and literally, of Messrs. Owl, Owl, & Peacock.

So it was that while they were embroiled in negotiations with the Shoe Lady a certain leaf lurker flew like the wind toward the Winnebago bearing news that was both urgent and ominous. Alighting on the porch, it rapped its beak insistently upon the door. The bird was a fledgling sparrow named Arrow and so monikered because he always flew straight and true—something unheard of in the legal profession back in Olden Days and unknown Nowadays too. Its constant rapping intruded upon Helgayarn's concentration, forcing her to abandon for the moment her dialogue with the Shoe Lady. "Pardon me, cousin," she politely said. "It would appear that we have more company. Be a dear, will you, and allow me to answer the door?"

The Shoe Lady shrugged indifferently. What difference did it make to her one way or the other? These discussions were going nowhere.

"Bunny," asked Helly, "would you please see to the door?" Brunnhilde gave Helgayarn a withering scowl, despising the servant status her sister fostered upon her—especially in the presence of company! She was a witch herself and a big one at that—certainly not anyone's serf! So she passed the request on to Betty, who offered up a frown of her own while making a mental note to record the offense in her journal. She reached out to grasp hold of the doorknob when Helgayarn stopped her.

"Sister," cried the big witch, "you know better than to open the door without first asking who's there!"

Betty paused and looking back over her shoulder, offered the senior siren an icy glare coupled with a mute reply.

"Oh, do go on then," said Helly, her response made sour by pent-up frustration. Betty allowed herself a silent chuckle and with her wrinkled and liver-spotted hand grasping the knob, completed the task. The door opened and in flew Arrow Sparrow. Caroming off walls and windows, he announced himself to the four women with cries of, "News! News! News!" It was in bird language, of course—sparrowspeak, specifically—and although Helgayarn had no doubt that as such it was virtual pigeon talk to the Shoe Lady, she could not help but wish that the old whore was anyplace else. In their line of work, events often took an unexpected twist, with matters turning flaky upon the fringe. Often those instances followed upon the heels of such pronouncements as this—after all, no news was good news—and if it was indeed the case now that a pattern long repeated was about to be replayed, then Helgayarn preferred the Shoe Lady not be around to see so when it did. She had the feeling watching the sparrow flit madly about the room that such was going to be the situation now, and the less that others—especially this old harpy—knew of

THE CHRISTMAS RABBIT

their incompetence, the better off they'd be. But as usual, Helgayarn found they were caught between the proverbial rock and hard place. To allow the Shoe Lady to remain while allowing her to determine just how bad the situation had been bollixed was dangerous. Yet to ask her to leave would certainly raise her suspicions beyond the level at which they currently stood and the trio didn't need to add to those misgivings any more than they had to. What to do? In the end Helgayarn opted to let her stay. If the bird's message was half as bad as she expected then no doubt the Shoe Lady, relying upon her own resources, would find out anyway. Even in Olden Days, bad news rarely stayed within the family. Perhaps, thought she, I can bluff my way through. "So, little bird," she asked casually, "what brings you here and what's the good news?"

Arrow Sparrow ceased his erratic flight and alit on Helgayarn's shoulder. "No news is good news," he cried. "No news is good news, and since all news is bad news—*bad news!*"

Once again Helgayarn found herself rolling her eyes while offering Brunnhilde and Betty a tired sigh. Were things ever easy? she wondered. Apparently, in their case, no. "Of course you have news," she snapped at the sparrow, "and of course, it's bad—why else would you be here? Best that you spit it out and be done with it!"

"The farmer!" cried the bird. "The farmer and the elves are attacking Jack Rabbit!" Helgayarn took a moment to compose herself. This intelligence wasn't entirely unexpected, as the Shoe Lady herself had told them of this very possibility. Yet each of them, including the old whore, were of the impression that such an attack was in the planning stages and certainly not in any way imminent. Helgayarn figured they had time to forestall such a foolish maneuver. Apparently not. If the attack was allowed to proceed, and if it were successful, then they'd all look like idiots and Jack would be made into a martyr at their expense with the Shoe Lady looking on and laughing while showering them with, "I told you so's!"

Certainly that couldn't be allowed. Helgayarn looked at the whore, who in turn was eyeing her suspiciously, and knew she had no option other than to boldly brazen it out.

"Well, cousin," she said, "it would appear that you were right. Farm Boy is indeed attacking Jack at this very moment!" She chuckled and her two sisters, picking up on her cue, joined her laughter. "Can you imagine such silliness? I suppose that we'll have to put a stop to this inanity when we've a spare moment or two, although each of them no doubt deserves to get what the other intends to give. Still it would be uncharitable of us, don't you think, to do nothing at all?" Brunnhilde and Betty automatically nodded their heads while smiling and laughing. Helgayarn gave them both points for maintaining the charade in the face of disaster.

The Shoe Lady stared at them in disbelief. "The three of you are acting rather casually," she observed.

"Why shouldn't we?" Brunnhilde replied. "It's a minor affair at best."

"Yah!"

"Even I can see," replied the Shoe Lady, "that this is an unmitigated disaster!"

Both Brunnhilde and Betty, uncertain of their response, turned to Helgayarn for support. "Oh, I'd hardly call it that," the big witch said.

"Then a catastrophe!"

"Even that," replied Helgayarn, "gives such a minor incident more weight than it deserves. Still, I suppose that we must do something. Therefore we must ask you to run along whilst we consult with each other and devise our response."

"You want me to leave?"

"Absolutely."

The Shoe Lady eyed them wickedly. "There's more going on here," she said, "than you're willing to tell me."

"Nonsense!" replied Helgayarn in an effort to reassure her. She held her arms open in a conciliatory gesture. "But even you said that something has to be done so please allow us the privacy we need in which to do it! Do we look in your window when you're conducting business? Certainly not! So be on your way please, my dear, and thank you ever so much, both for your time and opinions! By the way—that idea of yours to pit the rabbit and the farmer against each other in a race is certainly a notion worthy of further consideration! Thank you for such a unique and novel stratagem!"

It wasn't the Shoe Lady's idea, and all four of them knew it. She'd merely brought them intelligence about a scheme that the three of them had been preparing beforehand, passing along only what she'd previously overheard. But Helgayarn wanted to stroke her ego. "We'll almost certainly put that gambit into practice and for suggesting it, allow you to participate with us in its enactment. Here's what we'd like you to do." Bending over the Shoe Lady's ear, Helgayarn whispered to her for some time. "What do you think," she asked the harlot, "will you do it?"

"That depends," replied the Shoe Lady, "considering the offer. I'll need some time to think it over."

"Of course, my dear," replied Helgayarn. "Of course. Perfectly understandable. In the meantime, we do have that situation that needs attending to, so if you'll excuse us?"

The Shoe Lady considered all of their posturing to be mere window dressing employed in an effort to disguise something which smelled like a load of cattle craps. But what could she do? She was in enemy territory and outnumbered three to one. Four to one, if you counted the bird. She had no option other than to back down and get out. "Very well," she reluctantly replied. "I'm going! Just see to it that you don't forget about me!" She didn't trust them—not for a moment—but was wise enough to know that sometimes in order to catch fish you had to let loose a little line. And when the fish were sharks it was best to put as much line between yourself and the hook as possible.

Doing a great imitation of Jaws, Helgayarn offered the Shoe Lady a predator's smile. "Forget you?" she asked innocently. "Never! Now goodbye, my dear. We look forward to seeing you soon."

"Yes, goodbye and good riddance," Brunnhilde said under her breath as the Shoe Lady took her leave. "We look forward to seeing you soon all right. Soon to be hung from a gibbet!"

"Yah!"

Helgayarn offered her two junior witches a scowl, then turning her attention to Arrow Sparrow, reluctantly asked him for all the details. Arrow walked across her shoulders and perching himself at the base of her neck began whispering in her ear. He told a tale of woe and blood, of dead rabbits and elves littering the ground like cast away garbage. He spoke of armies mustering and battalions charging, of rape and slaughter and violent death. As he related his tale, describing in detail the mustering of Santos's forces and the rabbits' stalwart defense, what passed for blood flowing in Helly's veins slowly coalesced in her feet, turning her normally pale complexion to a tincture that was beyond colorless, being pallid and absolutely ghastly. She shook like a leaf blown upon idiot winds. Her ears, buzzing with a high-pitched whine, caused her to be light-headed, and she swayed, dizzy and disoriented while her stomach turned somersaults. "Oh no," she muttered weakly. "Oh no."

Both Brunnhilde and Betty looked on in concern. "What is it," the former asked, "what is it now?"

"Same problem, new manifestation," Helgayarn replied, sick. "Once again, Farm Boy has taken it upon himself to place the bit in his teeth and in so doing has stampeded the herd!"

"Dimwittedness and desipience," Brunnhilde said in disgust. "Dimwittedness and desipience in the highest degree!"

"Yah!"

Folding her arms one over the other Helgayarn clutched at her torso, as if to offer herself both the moral and physical support needed to get through this fiasco. "I know," she tiredly replied. "I know."

"Then why…" asked Brunnhilde, but she was suddenly cut off by the big witch who, with a gesture, demanded silence. "Reasons and recriminations," said Helly, "are for later. For now we must be off to see if we can derail this runaway train!" With that, the trio gathered the forces, invoked the incantations, spoke the spells, and whisked themselves away.

*****

The Witches arrived upon the fringes of the battle and hid themselves in a tree to better observe the goings on. The scene unfolding before them was one of absolute carnage. Dead rabbits

THE CHRISTMAS RABBIT

and elves littered the field of slaughter like discarded trash, left to rot and decompose in the afternoon sun, their lifeless eyes staring up and outward at absolutely nothing while useless limbs lay bent, broken and twisted. The arid ground soaked up red and green like a sieve, making the earth spongy and damp while all about this horrible vista the terrible sounds of battle trumpeted as the high-pitched squeals of wounded and broken rabbits blended with the pealing screams and pitiful moans of mangled and mutilated elves, until they formed a strident and mournful dirge which echoed and reverberated throughout the valley. And still the war raged on.

"Well," a hidden voice shouted out above the cacophony, "are you three going to do anything about this?"

Startled, Helgayarn, Brunnhilde, and Betty spun about as if goosed, forgetting that as they did so they did it while hiding in the tree and as a result, overbalanced and fell off their branch, bending boughs and snapping twigs in the frenzy of their fall. They landed in a heap of tangled and twisted limbs as well as sprained digits—hardly to be noticed or made mention of in the violence occurring all around them. The indignity of their predicament was far worse than the physical trauma and that was one step shy of unbearable. "Oh, Helly," Brunnhilde moaned, gently pulling herself out of the heap they'd become and gingerly picking up her person while tentatively trying out each limb as she rose, "that hurt. That *really* hurt." From the middle of the pile and feeling every bit as injured, Betty was quick to agree. "Yah."

Helgayarn lay helpless at the bottom, gasping for air and crushed by the weight of the others. She could do no more than moan and that only weakly—it hurt too much to attempt anything else. Buried, she waited in stoic silence for her confederates to untangle themselves from atop her so she might attempt the improbable task of rising herself—an uncertain prospect at best. It felt as if every bone in her body were broken. Twice. Grunting, groaning, and bemoaning their fate, the twisted trio slowly pulled themselves up from the tangled wreckage of their unanticipated descent. At last Helgayarn regained her feet while carefully testing every toe as she did, in order to determine that each was still properly attached and therefore capable of supporting its load. It proved to be but just barely. Both thumb toes were sprained and therefore not fully able to support her avoirdupois, causing her to reel like a drunken Frenchman. Between gasps of pain, she looked about uncertainly, casting her gaze upward to the tree. "Did you hear someone?" she asked. "I heard someone or something. I know I did!"

"I don't know what I heard," Brunnhilde tentatively replied, "but I sure as shootin' smelled something!"

"Yah!"

"Damned right, yah!" the hidden voice responded. Those were my pheromones you scented. Good thing for you three that I didn't hurl my harea. I've been taking lessons!"

The trio gazed upward to discover Jack and Nutmeg swaying in the branches. "You can't climb those!" Helgayarn shouted incredulously, her brain refusing to believe the evidence of her eyes. Rabbits aren't built that way. How did you get up there?"

"Been taking lessons in that too!" Jack shouted back. How else was I going to carry out my unmerited sentence?"

"Unmerited?" shrieked Helgayarn, her face turning blue. "Unmerited? You have the gall to proclaim your innocence before us in the face of this?" She gestured behind her at the ensuing melee. "Hundreds of folk are dying out there!"

"As if you care!" Jack shouted back. "But it's only wee people. The real tragedy is all those dead rabbits. All my lost children! What are you going to do about that?"

"Do? Why should we have to *do* anything?"

"I didn't start this fight," Jack responded. "Me and mine were minding our own business and laying our eggs!"

"Rabbits don't lay eggs!"

"Figure of speech."

"You were stealing them!" Helgayarn shrieked. "Just like you stole those damned vegetables—which is how this sorry affair started!"

Jack offered the trio a tired sigh. "And by doing so," he replied, "if I did at all, stealing your thunder too—which is what this barbarity is really all about." He paused for a moment to scan the battlefield. "But who says I'm stealing? You've heard, no doubt, about my infamous crash diet? Maybe I've found a way to lay eggs after all. If a bird can do it, then rest assured, such an act is not beyond the reach of rabbits!"

Helgayarn regarded him doubtfully. Was it possible? she wondered. Could he really have done it? The evolutionary implications if indeed he'd been successful, were beyond comprehension. Beyond even belief. But no, even if such a feat were possible, still it was hardly likely to be fact. There were too many birds with too many kidnapped children for Jack's insinuations to have any more substantiality than mere wood smoke. "You're stealing," Helgayarn harped back. "You're stealing, and we know it!"

Jack uttered a bitter laugh—his view of the ongoing carnage was making him decidedly ill. "Prove it," said he. "Prove it if you can. You know damned well that I wasn't the only rabbit to pilfer a few turnips. So why pick on me? But even if I were the only rabbit who stole from the garden, so what? I was only doing what the Good Lord intended when he created me."

"Oh, him!" Helgayarn retorted, gamely trying to hide her discomfort at the mention of that particular personage while at the same time stealing uneasy glances both left and right, as if to assure herself that mere verbalization of such an august figure did not presage an immediate materialization. When none seemed to be forthcoming she relaxed somewhat. "I don't know that he exists or even cares one way or the other about such things!"

Jack flayed her with another chuckle. "Then why are you so jumpy at the mere mention of him?"

"Jumpy?" replied Helgayarn. "Who's jumpy? Not me! I'm anything by jumpy. I didn't leap outta that tree on purpose, fella. I fell, being startled, and landed on my tooshie! And don't think for a moment that I won't be holding you responsible!"

"Me?"

"Yes, you!"

"For gravity? You're holding me responsible for gravity? Crimeny—you witches claim to have invented the stuff and now you're blaming me for it?"

"That's beside the point!" Brunnhilde cried out in support of her leader.

"Yah!" agreed Betty.

"Glory and trumpets!" exclaimed Jack. "For once, and against all odds, you're right! It is beside the point. The point being that while we're here debating absurdities my folk are out there dying for the most insane of reasons—do something about it!"

Helgayarn gathered Brunnhilde and Betty around her in order to confer privately. The opportunity presenting itself before the trio was enormous but so was the risk. They'd have to tread carefully and with feathered feet to ensure that they didn't trip over themselves. They could let the respective factions kill each other. Then they'd be rid of the whole lot of them—ungrateful elves who didn't appreciate the gifts they'd been given, vacant and vacuous farmers who knew nothing, could do nothing, and were therefore worth nothing, and pesky rabbits who were always thieving and putting on airs. Hares in their hair…oh, to be rid of that misery! But could they afford such wholesale slaughter? Probably not, as allowing everyone to kill each other would leave the trio with no scapegoats left to deliver eggs. To allow just the elves to perish would be to waste a valuable resource, the creation of which represented years of untold effort and magic—to say nothing of leaving Farm Boy to his own defenses, which in light of this day's atrocities would surely end with the rabbits skinning him alive. That was a pleasure that The Powers That Be wished to reserve for themselves, to be relished at a time and place of their own choosing. They discussed simply indulging this fantasy and roasting him. They could take joy in that sought after satisfaction while citing this silly attack as their reason for invoking capital punishment. The elves could be dismissed as mere foot soldiers, unwilling pawns who were unfortunate in their fate to have blindly followed the flawed dictates of a foolish and power hungry general. Although it wasn't strictly the truth and was moreover a bald-faced lie, it sounded plausible enough and the Witches figured that most folk would buy it. The trio knew however, all about Pixie and Dixie and on some far-flung quiet afternoon, long after the dust of this day's madness had settled and when the trio could be sure that no one else was looking, they planned to settle up with those two and you could take that to the bank. The remaining wee folk wouldn't like it, the killing of two or their brethren, nor would they appreciate overmuch being spirited off in the middle of the night to be hidden away, perhaps in the bowels of the earth, forlorn and forgotten until this whole fiasco blew over. But at least they'd keep their skins on their backs. But no, such an option no matter how enticing, was no more viable than previous considerations in that it left Jack Rabbit in place and in charge of egg delivery without any system of checks and balances whatsoever. As a sheriff, Santos was by no means a Matt Dillon, but even the Witches were willing to concede that he was better than nothing—not much better and barely above board at that, but beggars, they knew, couldn't be choosers. Something was always better than nothing and leaving Jack on the field with absolutely no one in his way was tantamount to disaster. His egg deliveries and their fancy artwork had already afforded him far too much popularity and recognition for the Witches to not feel threatened. Such was his fame that were he left alone and unchecked the trio felt certain he would parley such advantages so as to position himself to one day rule the world! Then where would they be? Up the creek without a paddle, that's where, and landed in the biggest pile of cattle craps ever excreted! Surely their power and influence would fade away in proportion to Jack's own meteoric rise in prestige and popularity. Indeed they felt such events to be happening even now. They were becoming unpersons and nobodies in danger, they felt, of living out an uneventful existence, alone and entirely forgotten, out of sight and out of mind, only to be lost somewhere—probably in the desert. Before they let that happen they would act!

    Jack. What to do about Jack? Maybe killing him was the answer. He'd trained enough of his own in this silly egg business to carry on after him should he suddenly decease. And surely, Peter or Cottontail or whoever it was that ultimately took over this road show would be more amenable to their wishes, more easily bent to their wills, and therefore more than ready to respond with respect to the bidding of their betters. Kill Jack. Yes, that was the ticket! Do him now while nobody was looking and take that harlot of a wife out with him.

With no one looking on the trio could simply claim that the couple had stupidly fallen out of their tree, thus preventing martyrdom and the deification that would surely follow were the couple afforded that particular distinction.

Having finished their parley, the trio were now prepared to take action. They separated and circling the tree, began to gather the forces, invoke the incantations and weave the web of mumbo jumbo necessary to roast both Jack and Nutmeg as if they were spitted and hung over a slow burning fire.

Despite his misgivings and his overall heartbreak, Jack had to laugh and laugh loudly. Were there any others out there, he wondered, more inept than these three? And if not, if these three had indeed cornered the market in primal stupidity, how in the name of wonder had they ever risen to the vaulted and lofty positions which they now occupied? Did it mean that any idiot who had the good fortune to seat himself in the proper place at the right time could do likewise? Such a hypothesis had as the sum product of its equation, absolute and utter chaos with no hope of order and accountability in sight. Such theories, Jack knew, led to madness and insanity so he temporarily discarded them in order to better deal with the problem at hand. "I know what you know," he shouted down at them, interrupting their sorcery.

"Eh?"

"I said I know what you know!"

"That's impossible," Helgayarn replied shrewishly. "Nobody knows what we know!"

Jack thought it over. Despite their braggadocio and the obvious blowing of trumpets, he had to concede to himself that in this instance, the witch was probably correct. How could anyone know everything that someone else knew? Such deductive prowess was best left, he felt, in the hands of God alone, which he wasn't nor were these three either—regardless of their unceasing attempts to put on such airs. "Let me qualify," said the rabbit, "my misworded statement and rephrase it to say that *I know what you're planning*!"

"Impossible!" shouted Brunnhilde.

THE CHRISTMAS RABBIT

"Quite possible," remarked the hare, "and indeed, quite probable. You're forgetting these!" Jack pulled on his ears. "They hear everything and so overheard the three of you discussing your plans for me and my lovely wife. I have to warn you—it's a big mistake!"

"So what?" countered Brunnhilde. "It won't be our first!"

"I have no doubts about that," Jack replied. "Your list of mistakes is a mile long and five miles wide. Make this one however and it could be your last!"

"You're bluffing!" cried Helgayarn. "You've no power over us!"

"True," Jack shouted back. "Against you, I'm powerless. But I'm still not bluffing. Kill me and you'll have worse to deal with than this tired old rabbit."

Brunnhilde looked around uneasily. The rabbit sounded too sure of his position. "Nonsense," she said. "Whoever inherits from you will be more malleable to our will and control. We'll be on Easy Street!"

Jack looked to Nutmeg, who kept a discreet silence. She shrugged. It seemed that the Witches were forever doomed to learn lessons the hard way. "You're thinking, no doubt," Jack replied, "that Peter, Cottontail, or one of my lesser sons will step in to fill my shoes once I've expired."

"Rabbits don't wear shoes!" exclaimed Helgayarn.

"Yah!" agreed Betty.

"Another figure of speech. But even if I did, I certainly wouldn't want to be standing in yours upon the completion of my murder."

"Explain yourself!"

Jack offered the three wenches another tired sigh. Maybe, he thought, I should just allow them to kill me so I can laugh from the depths of hell as they try and deal with my replacement. But no, tempting as it was, there were Nutmeg and what few were left of his children to consider. He wasn't sure if there was a heaven or a hell but was positive nevertheless that hell was where he'd certainly end up if he left his family in the paws of a maniac! He pointed off into the distance.

"Look out at yonder battlefield," he said. "Do you see that white rabbit with the band of ebony around his middle knocking down elves like they were palooka dolls? That's Harehito Rabbakami, and he's one tough hombre! Unfortunately for you he's also the rabbit who'll take over if you do away with me. None of my children, you see, could possibly stand against him. I even have my doubts about the three of you!"

The Witches scoffed at Jack's assertions. Did he really think they could be swayed by such chatter? Rabid bears were mere cannon fodder in their grip! How much trouble could one rabbit be? In their conceit they forgot to consider that one rabbit, namely Jack, had already proven himself to be more trouble than the trio could handle.

Sensing that the Witches were about to resume their incantations, Jack tried one last time to admonish them to prudence. "Best look before you leap," he warned them.

"Oh really?" replied an exasperated Helgayarn. "You do go on, don't you?"

"Can it hurt to look?" Jack asked. "Can a couple of minutes one way or the other really make a difference?"

"Of course not!"

"Then consider my request as a condemned rabbit's last wish."

Helgayarn decided to be gracious. What could it hurt? Now or five minutes later, they'd be flensing the rabbit for their stew. "All right," the big witch replied. "We'll have ourselves another peek and see this famous warrior of yours." The trio climbed once again into the boughs of the tree in order to take advantage of height and get a better view of the battle unfolding before them. It didn't take a brain surgeon to distinguish Rabbakami from the various amateurs, both rabbit and elf, who'd taken the field. This was a real warrior no doubt, and his skills were self-evident. "Who is that fellow?" asked Helgayarn, more than just a little curious, although nervous and scared out of her skin perhaps would've best described her. That was one hell of a fighter out there, and watching him, Helgayarn began to give Jack's admonition some credence.

"I told you," replied the rabbit, "that's Harehito Rabbakami, ninja rabbit and samurai aesthetic. We brought him in to deal with the elves, and man, is he dealing. Look at that sucker go!"

THE CHRISTMAS RABBIT

And go he did. As Helgayarn, Brunnhilde, and Betty looked on, the warrior from Japan cut a path through the hosts of elves, breaking limbs and decapitating heads. In disbelief the trio watched as a battalion of gnomes, pushing back the ranks of rabbits, was met midway by a violent charge from the ninja. Preceding him was his harea, which he'd hurled beforehand in order to herald his arrival. It cut a path before him, ripping through the elves and flensing the skin of their bodies. With pheromones flying, he bowled over dwarfs, picts, and sprites, causing them to choke on their own vomit. Opting for crudity—it was war after all—the ninja rabbit also made use of his repertoire of physical assaults, delivering a series of punishing kicks, kites, and karate chops, which rained down upon his hapless victims like hard winter hail, breaking bones and bruising organs.

"Who is this fellow?"

"I told you once before," Jack replied, "he's—"

"Yes, I know what you told me!" Helgayarn interrupted sharply. "He's Harehito Rabbakami—but who the hell is that, and where does he hail from?"

"He is who he is," Jack answered back, "just as I'm who I am and you're who you are! He's a mystic warrior from Japan."

"Where's that?"

"Who knows?"

"Don't you?"

"Hell no," replied the rabbit. "All I know is that it's a ways east of here and many days travel."

"How did you ever find him if you didn't know where to look?" asked an incredulous Brunnhilde, secretly envious of Jack's more-than-masterful recruitment. If they had two of this ninja rabbit on their payroll they could storm the very gates of heaven! With even one of him in their pocket world domination would be a cakewalk... "And more importantly, how did you ever convince him to come to your aid?"

"One of my grandchildren," Jack replied, "who used to deliver eggs out that way heard tell of him while on his travels. So I sent him back to enlist the bullyboy! It wasn't all that hard, really. I simply instructed my messenger to say that we had a thorn (or three) in our foot while inviting him to come and remove it. His ego is such that he can't pass up a good fight so here he is and here you are!"

Stunned, Helgayarn merely shook her head. The rabbit's story sounded too far-fetched to be anything but the truth. "Who did you say found this fellow?"

"Name's Grasshopper," replied Jack. "My grandson, fourth or fifth generation, two or three times removed, I should think. There's been so many litters to date and litters of litters that truth to tell, I find it hard to keep up with who's who or to whom they're related and how."

Helgayarn scowled. "Bring this Grasshopper to me!" she demanded.

"Can't,"

"Can't or won't?"

"Both," the rabbit replied, as a tear slid slowly from his eye to run forlorn and alone down the side of his cheek. "My great-grandson, like my dear daughter Rabbitboodles, who lies lost in yonder engagement, now walks silently in fields of shadow. They're dead—victims of this ridiculous war and believe you me, somebody's going to answer for them!"

The trio took note of the unmitigated anger evident in Jack's eyes that had heretofore lay hidden and submerged. So great was his wrath that perceiving it for the first time the Witches powerful as they were, flinched in fear, taking an involuntary step backward and once again falling out of the tree. "This won't do," moaned Helly. *"This won't do at all!"* Sprawled upon the ground, she looked back up at Jack. "Surely you don't blame us?"

"Who else is there?" Jack tiredly asked. "Who gave Farm Boy his troops? Who set Old Slomoe about the business of stealing my eggs while giving him a free hand to employ whatever tactics he deemed necessary in order to pilfer 'em? One thing leads to another and that led to this!" He gestured to the hostilities occurring around them.

"Who indeed?" asked Helgayarn. "But why should you think it us?"

"Oh, c'mon!" Jack cried, his patience at an end. "Who else but you three have access to elves? If Farm Boy didn't get 'em from you then where did they come from? Surely you're not going to tell me that they just up and volunteered, enlisting in his cause of their own free will, are you? Anyone who knows him at all knows well enough to leave Old Slomoe to himself. Who in his right mind would willingly choose such misery? No! They were conscripted and coerced and being somewhat magical in their own right, who but the three of you would be powerful enough to bully them into such service? That they're taking his orders must mean they're following yours!"

"Your reasoning," Helgayarn replied, trying to bluff her way out of a corner, "is somewhat circular."

"No kidding! And therefore being so constructed, my contentions begin and end with the three of you!" Enraged beyond his ability to control, Jack put Harehito's lessons to good use and hurled his harea at them. The trio swayed, feeling dizzy and nauseous. But that was the extent of his attack. Those dour dames were too powerful to suffer any periculous effects at the paws of his meager skills. They'd had, after all, survived Mrs. Santos's shark fin soup.

Helgayarn stared at her antagonist in shock, barely able to believe her eyes or credit the ill feeling in her craw. "You would attack us?" she screeched. *"You would dare attack us? The Powers That Be?"*

"You came after me first," Jack solemnly replied. "Then when your scheme went belly-up, you set Farm Boy against me. When he proved inadequate, you brought in these hybrid hatchet men, these elven eradicators, to do your dirty work for you. From the moment you blundered into my business, inserting your busybodied selves into affairs that should've been left well enough alone, you've slowly been backing me into a corner from which I've had no choice but to fight back!"

Helgayarn was beyond livid. Brunnhilde and Betty had far surpassed outrage. How dare this little ball of fur impugn anything they did or their reasons for doing it? They were The Powers That Be and beyond the mere criticisms and petty condemnations of piddling mortals such as he. Hurl his harea at them, would he? Well they had a lesson or two to impart to this little leporide about the art of hurling hareas and class was in session! Helgayarn began to gather the forces once again but Brunnhilde the Levelheaded, discerning her intent, reined the old crone in. "No, Helly," she whispered sharply in her ear, "that won't do at all! Would you kill him now just to replace him with that maniac out there?" Helgayarn let out a frustrated sigh as she recalled the forces back. There had to be an easier method for getting her way. There had to! "So be it," she stated to no one in particular, her voice as cold as the open grave, "the rabbit wins this round."

Jack thought it the better part of prudence to refrain from pointing out to them that he'd been walking away with most of the rounds anyway despite the fact that a majority of you out there Nowadays might have the Witches ahead on your individual scorecards. But Jack knew that referees, just like lawyers, could be bought. The very fact that the Witches felt it incumbent upon themselves to even put in an appearance at this dogfight was evidence enough to the rabbit that he was winning (oh, but at what cost!) regardless of the carnage being enacted before him. Still, if the Witches insisted on maintaining the illusion that they held the upper hand, then who was he to argue with their misguided rationalizations? Right or wrong, they were still too powerful to gainsay openly or attack head-on. The only strategy of which he could avail himself was to engage them in an oblique attack, never assaulting them directly. Instead, he strove to strike at their sides and raid from the rear, hoping to wear them down through embarrassment and befuddlement. It was a tactic wherein the weaker with a good deal of luck, might hope to prevail over and vanquish, the stronger. Harehito would have termed it "Injuring The Corners," and despite the uniquely Japanese flavor of the contrivance, was nevertheless a technique that, through repetition, Jack had much more proficiency in than did the ninja himself. Practice makes perfect. But now a new strategy presented itself, and it was the mark of any good leader to be so fluid upon the field of battle as to allow for changing possibilities and opportunities. He'd been hoping for such a chance and planning for the contingency should it present itself, while never really expecting that such a likelihood would occur, for who in their right minds would ever conceive that the Witches would throw themselves into harm's way by boarding this runaway train in the first place? Harehito, he knew, would be more than delighted to injure all four corners on all three Witches, mak-

THE CHRISTMAS RABBIT

ing for a virtual boxcar of battlefield bruises and injuries. "No one wins anything," he said to them, "as long as that maniac is allowed to keep the field. He'll slaughter everybody. Look—even now he's taking after Slomoe!"

Turning their gaze to the carnage the Witches took note that indeed Harehito had spied out Santos and was even now making his way toward him, slicing through his elven body guard like a sickle through old wheat, intent no doubt, on carving himself some blubber. The terrible trio knew that the old fool could not possibly stand against such a battled hardened champion. The ninja rabbit would chop him into mincemeat, leaving the rabbits with no opposition in their *eggstravagant* endeavor and that, of course, could not be allowed. So summoning up a whirlwind, Helgayarn, Brunnhilde, and Betty whisked themselves away to the forefront of battle.

They landed in the middle of the melee, positioning themselves to stand between Harehito and his intended prey. The ninja rabbit, taking note of the threesome suddenly appearing before him, halted in midstride. "Witches!" he cried out, delighted. "At last! Opponents worthy of my mettle!" He lowered his head and with a roaring, "Banzai!" charged them, hurling his harea before him and hitting them head on. The trio were bowled over like three lone duckpins only to roll head over heels again and again through the blood soaked loam and mud. Bemired, Betty was the first to regain her legs, just to have them immediately cut out from under as Harehito pouncing, landed feet first fully upon her chest, collapsing a lung and knocking the wind out of her. As she fell the ninja rabbit grabbed her by the hair and pulling upward so as to extend her neck and expose her throat, delivered a series of rabbit punches to her esophagus. Choking on vomit and blood, Betty sank slowly to her knees, temporarily out of the fight. Meanwhile, Helgayarn had regained her footing and taking note of her sister's plight, leapt upon Harehito, encircling him with her arms, intending to fall upon, and crush him. But Harehito, using hareagei, was aware of her aim before she even knew her intent and so anticipating her attack from his rear, stepped into it to position one foot directly behind her as her arms closed about him. As she tightened her hold the ninja rabbit pushed off the ball of his forward foot while thrusting his shoulders and arms upward in the same instant. This caused Helgayarn to loosen her grip on him as well as stumble slightly to her rear. Using her own momentum for added leverage, Harehito arched his back, causing her to trip and fall over his rear foot. Before she could land in the loam yet again, the ninja rabbit leapt into the air and twisting full circle to gain added torque, delivered a powerful roundhouse kick to the side of her face, fracturing her jaw and knocking loose a tooth. As he landed, Brunnhilde, still on her knees, reached out with both hands to grab one of his arms just above the paw, her aim being to tear it out of its socket and make him eat it. Harehito, wise to that, stepped into her grip and reaching beyond her two-fisted grasp, grabbed at the extremity of his trapped paw with his free hand. He jerked his arm backward, pulling his paw toward him and forcing his elbow upward. As his trapped limb broke free of Brunnhilde's hold the rising elbow connected squarely with the bottom of her chin, snapping her neck back, causing whiplash, and sending her tumbling end over end once again. Betty regained her feet and was promptly knocked off them. Helgayarn pulled herself up only to find that upon doing so that she was immediately sent flying through the air, the victim of a judo toss performed expertly by the ninja rabbit. Aikido, Judo, Karate—Harehito made use of them all as he prosecuted his own little war against the trio while Santos just stood there helplessly looking on. The Tortoise had been temporarily forgotten as the ninja now had bigger fish to fry. He hurled hareas, excreted pheromones, and employed a hundred other ninja tricks in an effort to conquer his enemies. No mere mortal could have withstood such an onslaught for even a moment. But Helgayarn, Brunnhilde, and Betty were no mere mortals. They were The Powers That Be and as such had a bag of dirty tricks all their own and it was time to make use of them. They'd underestimated this rabbit while once again overestimating themselves. But no more!

 Bloody but unbowed, they gathered the forces. Incited the incantations, invoked the charms of making, and sent a tornado hurtling toward the ninja. It knocked over elves and rabbits alike in the violence of its passage. It tore up great tufts of sod, which moaned like lepers as they were wrenched from the earth. Blue and green

THE CHRISTMAS RABBIT

lightning flashed from within the bowels of its funnel and it stank of old loam and corruption. Many innocent foot soldiers from both armies were caught up in its winds, spun about in its funnel, and like runaway tops were blown away never to be found again. The tornado hit Harehito, picking him up and hurling him headlong into a tree. Its bole snapped like a dry toothpick, and Harehito came away from the crash with a terrific weal emblazoned upon his forehead.

    The combatants from both armies had by now come to an uneasy halt in hostilities with each side ceasing its attacks upon the other. They stood in rapt silence, watching in horrified wonder as the scene unfolding before them played itself out, knowing that the fate of the day would be decided not by them but by the four combatants now engaged in battle. Harehito again hurled his harea, this time at full strength and riding upon the wind of a caustic pheromone. It hit the harridans like a charging moose, blackening their skins and burning the blue-gray hair off their heads. In agony, Helgayarn let loose a high-pitched squeal. In all her years of witching she'd never had more reason to complain of injury. "Wait!" she screamed as Harehito was preparing to hurl more harea, "let's negotiate a truce!" She threw herself at the ninja's feet, begging for mercy while motioning her sisters to do likewise. Harehito had never before accepted surrender preferring rather, to simply kill his enemies. But he was nearly spent himself and out of tricks, ninja or otherwise. Better, thought he, to negotiate while he still had the upper hand. Besides, there were hundreds here to witness his mighty victory and surely some of them would carry the tale of his deeds back to his homeland and if not, well he planned on staying here anyway and it would be better to live and let live and so enjoy the fruit of his labor. His decision only served to show everyone, both then and now, that ego is the greatest enemy of us all. More of us get done in by our own overinflated opinions of ourselves rather than any external enemy we might face. We are, all of us, our own worst enemies...

    As the Witches knelt at his feet, Harehito offered them a flippant, "Ah, so." Knowing that she had the little leporide right where she wanted him, and realizing that he'd gone and hoisted himself upon his own ego, Helgayarn gave a knowing nod to both Brunnhilde and Betty who reading their sister's intentions, knew just what to do. The trio put their hands behind their heads in what is universally recognized as a display of surrender. As Harehito, puffed with pride, drank in their submission, the tricky triad removed from the burnt and blackened stubble of their once-glorious hairdos, their poisoned pins and, acting in concert, thrust unanimously, impaling Harehito with their darts.

"Ah, so this!" they cried.

The ninja rabbit took an uncertain step backward, a puzzled look of disbelief evident in his fluttering eyes. No one had ever gotten the better of him in a fight before. And even now no one had as yet. Instead, hubris had hurled at him a harea of its own. The pins, of course, were coated with the remains of Mrs. Santos's shark fin soup, and as stated before, a more caustic and vile substance was not to be found by anyone anywhere. Harehito swayed, struggling to stay on his feet as the poison raced through his veins. It gathered in the chambers of his heart, imploding the ventricles and crushing his aorta. His last words, or so they say, uttered in stubborn disbelief and spit out with the last of his great strength, were, "*Doku*? I didn't know that any of you round-eyes knew how to make *doku*..." Then he fell over like an embattled top that had lost its momentum and could no longer spin. His body hit the ground with a dull thud.

Silence reigned supreme in the wake of the battle as the Witches slowly pulled each other up off their knees. Each needed the assistance of the others in order to regain her footing. They were that weak. They were spent and tired beyond the ability of mere words to describe. Even the aftermath of Hurricane Junior had not produced in them such weariness. But they were still The Powers That Be. They were still the big witches on the block. They cast evil glances about them as they took in the day's carnage, each unwilling to accept, either individually or corporately, that they were in any way responsible for the horrors which presented themselves before them. Dead rabbits and elves littered the field like fallen leaves after an autumn storm. The humid air was stifling, made bitter by the coppery scent of spilt blood borne upon the ill winds which blew it. Seeking to wreak vengeance upon one and all for this day's madness the trio made ready to gather the forces, incite the incantations, and invoke the charms of making, but found that after such a horrific battle lacked the strength to perform even a simple card trick, never mind let loose the monumental magic which they now contemplated. Uttering a forlorn sigh with a promise to return and enact a grand retribution later, Helgayarn led her weary companions off the field and the trio hobbled their way back to the Winnebago, nursing their injuries and tending to each other's hurts as they went.

From opposite sides of the field, Jack and Santos appraised each other menacingly, both realizing that whereas they'd been mere antagonists in the past, they were now irreconcilable enemies while understanding that, as such, they still had more to fear from the trio who'd just quit the field than they did from each other.

*****

The Powers That Be were many moons repairing the damages inflicted upon both their persons and egos. Specialists were called in from far and wide to treat their injuries. A plethora of doctors and their attendant staff were forced to erect camp within the vicinity of the Winnebago and a virtual hospital had been built from the pop tents and lean-to's that had to be thrown together in order to accommodate them, making it the very first MASH unit ever and set up solely for the purpose of treating war casualties—of which there were three. Of course, there were many more but Helgayarn, Brunnhilde, and Betty reasoned for themselves that being witches, they were more than entitled to, and deserving of, individualized care and special treatment. Let the others, those wounded elves and rabbits, fend for themselves and find their own doctors! The surgeons present were needed here and here only!

There were podiatrists, pediatricians, and chiropodists on call. In attendance as well were various neurologists, and neurosurgeons, cardiologists, dermatologists, and thoracic reconstructive surgeons. Waiting in the wings, should they be required were a host of immunologists, gerontologists, and pathologists. In addition to all her other injuries, Helgayarn had as well, a fractured jaw, as did Betty, and some missing teeth too. Therefore no expense was spared to see that they had available to them a contingent of periodontists, orthodontists, radiodontists, oral surgeons, and plain old dentists. To round out this impressive crew and aid in their healing endeavors an army of support staff had been pressed into service as well. There were scads of nurses—practical, licensed practical, charge, and otherwise; there were paramedics, x-ray techs, radio and physical therapists, dieticians, and hospital administrators. To compliment these various quacks medicine men, midwives and other minor magicians were added to the payroll and available for consultation. They even had a veterinarian on call, and it was agreed upon, following a mass consultation by the claims adjusters at Repressive, that after the major hassle they'd just been made to undergo with regard to the newly furnished Winnebago, there was no percentage to be had in upsetting the applecart or rocking the boat by taking chances and providing less than adequate coverage. So they had a regular Mayo clinic set up and ready to run. A virtual John Hopkins established in the old forest back in Olden Days, yet because of the sheer numbers of those recruited to operate the facility, it became an inside joke among the staff to refer to it as simply Mass General…and still Helgayarn, Brunnhilde, and Betty would not condone to set so much as one foot within, demanding instead attention and treatment within the confines of their Winnebago. The doctors protested en masse, citing inefficiency and the higher cost of treatment related to such an excess. It was the world's first house call and the medicos did not appreciate participating in it. It set a bad precedent, they felt, and one in which they were sure they'd be years recovering from whilst being forced to practice door-to-door medicine. Under such conditions, how they wondered, would they ever be able to find the time to keep up with and engage in, the medicinal art of golf? One of those protesting was none other than that very same quack who presided over the birth of Junior and who through gargantuan incompetence, played a crucial part in the subsequent baby switching. His specializations were gynecology and obstetrics, none of which were likely to be required here and neither of which he was particularly proficient in anyway.

THE CHRISTMAS RABBIT

Therefore he was demoted to chief cook and bottle washer and was barely capable of those tasks either.

Everyone else got Band-Aids.

The various leeches, croakers, sawbones, and quacks offered up to the trio a host of diagnosis's, both oral, rectal, and otherwise. They performed biological diagnosis, clinical diagnosis, and differential diagnosis, which back in Olden Days was no different than anything else. There were biopsies, uroscopies, electrocardiographs, and electroencephalographs too. All of which only served to tell the Witches what they already knew—that they'd nearly had the living crap kicked out of them. But no doctor anywhere or anytime has ever made a living by handing in such mundane and overly simplistic medical evaluations and so both singularly and in consultation they pronounced that the trio suffered from such exotic and unlikely afflictions as dysentery, chicken pox, gonorrheal arthritis and locomotor ataxia. A second opinion had them suffering from angina, Fanconi's syndrome, and/or Rocky Mountain spotted fever. There were, of course, dissenters to both of these diagnoses, and they insisted that the trio's ailments could be directly attributed to such maladies as hypoglycemic shock, apoplexy, and sunstroke. But whatever the diagnosis or the alleged malady responsible for it, none of the medical staff could resist the temptation to offer up to the trio a miracle cure of their own prescribing. Armed with their cardio scopes, catheters, nebulizers, and needles, they prescribed a virtual overdose of various stimulants, depressants, antiseptics, antibiotics, and psychoactive drugs, all designed, they insisted, to lead the trio on down the road to wellness. The straw that broke the camel's back to coin a phrase, occurred when one physician, braver than the rest, dared to assert that what the Witches truly suffered from was an indisputable case of Farmer's Lung, while recommending as treatment, a high dosage of rabbit pheromones, to be administered directly via injection, in order to effect a cure. With that pronouncement, the Witches threw them all the hell out, daring them to bill Repressive Insurance of Mesozoic Mesopotomia for scads of untold wasted time and misdiagnoses, while in the meantime resigning themselves to aspirins and icepacks in order to effect a cure of their own.

As this incompetent advancement in medical science played out it caused within itself the retardation by a millennium or two, of the very skills, disciplines, and knowledge that its practitioners had hoped to propound. They set back by thousands of years a branch of learning that had only existed for a century or so, while throughout the forest and the lands immediately surrounding it folk waited in brooding silence for the expected yet unwanted, return of The Powers That Be. Man and animal alike kept to their respective places of dwelling whenever possible, whether such abodes were huts, holes, nests or mere hovels, for fear of venturing out in the open and therefore stumbling upon the Witches and in so doing, become the unwilling and unwitting victims of their presupposed wrath and unquenchable desire for retribution and revenge—for there was no doubt in anyone anywhere that the trio were mighty pissed off. Even Sergeant Sergeant and his army of ants were billeted down tightly and hunkering in holes. Egg delivery on the part of Jack and his rabbits had ground down to a virtual standstill while Santos had stopped even trying to grow vegetables, instead giving leave to the weeds to do with themselves as they would. The few elves left standing in the aftermath of the great battle had hidden themselves away in secluded caves and dens, refusing to venture outdoors when the sun was in the sky and only reluctantly deigning to sneak about after twilight. Even then they didn't dare wander too far away from their respective lairs and bunkers. The only person traveling abroad with any regularity was the Shoe Lady. With her clientele afraid of their own shadows and refusing to set one foot out of their own dooryards, she was impelled to take her act on the road. She had after all, mouths to feed—many mouths, and she couldn't fill them by standing on her feet and doing nothing. She needed to be on her back and working! Thus she went door-to-door, becoming the first whore who made house calls—the very first call girl—and she would agree with those aforementioned doctors that such a practice was pure misery. Yet for all of her efforts business continued slow and stagnated. There were too few men out in the wide world who were brave enough to risk detection on the part of The Powers That Be, by opening their doors. Those few who might have risked it remained nevertheless fearful of

THE CHRISTMAS RABBIT

their own wives and the revenge they'd no doubt exact upon them for having been caught cheating in the first place while in the amorous arms of the Shoe Lady. Santos, of course, threw his door wide open when the whore came calling but unfortunately for both, Mrs. Santos was home when she did and sent the prostitute packing by threatening the whore with a bowl of soup. However, the Shoe Lady's determination was such and her ongoing effort so great that folk back in Olden Days began to sing of her this song:

> *There was an old harlot who lived in a boot*
> *With too many young'uns and too little loot*
> *With no marketable skills which*
> *to keep 'em all fed—*
> *She lay on her back and sold booty instead!*
> *When fear of three witches*
> *kept menfolk at home*
> *She laced up her boot and she took to the road*
> *Selling her booty as she went door-to-door—*
> *There goes the Shoe Lady—*
> *one hell of a whore!"*

The translation of this tune has, of course, been corrupted by the passage of time as one generation to the next have handed it down and resung it throughout the ages, and certainly its central theme has been toned down somewhat as the song has been made into a child's rhyme, but thus goes the saga of the Shoe Lady, forever famous or infamous, depending upon one's point of view.

Yet the exploits of one however noteworthy or not, are quickly forgotten in light of the deeds of another. Thus it was when the Witches, feeling sufficiently recovered from having nearly had their asses handed to them by Harehito Rabbakmi, deigned to venture out again into the wide world, songs and speculations regarding the Shoe Lady and her heroic harlotries were temporarily buried, repressed, stifled, silenced, and eradicated from both mouth and mind. Helgayarn, Brunnhilde, and Betty had come forward from their Winnebago looking to exact their revenge upon the farmer, the rabbit, the elves, and anyone else who got in their way. They paid their first call to poor Farmer Santos.

Knocking upon his door one day, the trio demanded that he step outside and treat with them. In his own foolish way he pretended not to hear them. "I'm deaf!" he replied to their constant rapping. "Come back when I'm all ears!"

His remark only served to remind them of Jack, thus angering Helgayarn, Brunnhilde, and Betty even further. "Come out this instant, you toad!" shrieked Helly, who stood outside waiting with her sisters like three big bad wolves anticipating the suicidal pig. "Come out this instant, or we'll huff and we'll puff and we'll blow your house down!" Santos knew that they could do it too. Long-windedness was one of their few long suits. A little Hurricane in a Jar, some Snowstorm Soup, or even some Tidal Wave Tea would be more than sufficient to cause the collapse of his little hut. Even a cupful of Quaker Oats would be more than adequate! Therefore, he reluctantly threw open the door of his dilapidated dwelling and with many misgivings, stepped through it to stand on the front porch. There'd be hell to pay here and now, he knew, with this testy trio acting as collection agents! Helgayarn wasted no time in offering up polite amenities or greetings and instead got directly to the point.

"Where are your cronies?" she demanded, meaning the elves.

That all-too-familiar look of befuddlement displayed itself once again, upon the farmer's face. "My cronies?" he asked. "Aren't you my cronies?"

The three old hens became livid.

Brunnhilde, barely able to support herself and suffering the indignity of crutches replied, "Cronies? Are you implying that we're aged and ugly? That we three are both gruesome and an eyesore? Are we not, in fact, beautiful?"

Santos fidgeted about nervously. "Well, my ladies," he replied, desperately trying to extricate himself the morass in which he'd just firmly planted both feet, "beauty is in the eyes of the beholder, and mine are somewhat unreliable, succumbing as they have to the vicissitudes of age and the unwanted observation of things best left unseen." He was only thirty-six at the time, but it was true nevertheless that in his short span he'd indeed seen plenty.

"Unreliable?" shrieked Helgayarn. "Unreliable indeed—and not only your eyes sir, but your entire person—from the merest effort of that ungainly body of yours to accomplish the most insignificant of tasks to the very dubiousness and unreliability of your oaths, given to the three of us, to accomplish those very same aforementioned endeavors—you broke your word!"

"Yrr!" replied Betty, whose fractured jaw had been wired shut, thus significantly altering her one contribution to group conversation. Still she articulated the alteration with conviction.

"I may have indeed proven myself false," stammered the farmer, "but believe you me, ladies, that such prevarication, perjury, and out-and-out misrepresentation on my part did not come about through lack of effort!"

The Witches began to bridle, and Santos realized that once again he was misspeaking himself and was therefore being misunderstood. "That is to say," he pleaded, "that there was indeed very much effort on my part to comply with the terms of my parole, to wit—embarrassing that hair-raising hare! Indeed, much forethought and sweat were expended by your faithful servant to bring about this very goal—but alas, forethought has never been my forte (and in my own defense I did warn you of that) and so endeavors requiring such talent tend to slip away from me. They develop a momentum of their own, getting out of hand, if you will, and thus end up moving me, rather than the reverse!"

"That's your excuse?"

"It's the only one which presents itself at the moment."

Helgayarn offered the farmer a scowl. "Did we, or did we not," she asked, her voice laced with venom, "warn you not to go about the forest bragging of your abilities with regard to hare harassment and egg theft in general? Did we not warn you of this?"

"You did."

Helgayarn offered Brunnhilde and Betty a vindictive smile before continuing. "And did we not further caution that you were not to seek physical harm against the rabbit?"

"No," Santos replied, "you didn't."

"What?"

Santos closed his eyes in recollection. "Your exact words to me, as I remember them, my lady, were 'don't kill him.' Obviously, I haven't done that. Furthermore, if I misconstrued 'don't kill' to include 'don't harm,' it's also obvious that I haven't done that either. In fact, I've done nothing whatsoever. I've accomplished zilch, zippo, and doodah. But given my track record, surely you were expecting no more and perhaps a good deal less!"

"More or less—it makes no difference!" screamed Helgayarn. "There are dead elves and rabbits throughout the forest and egg delivery has ground to a halt!"

"Well, as to dead rabbits," replied the farmer, "that was strictly the elves' idea. I merely went along for the ride. Being something less than a self-starter, I excel in such things as bowing to the crowd and going whichever way the wind blows—but you knew that. And as to dead elves, who really cares about them? They breed almost as quickly as rabbits and will soon replenish their stock. Have no fear—with a short passage of time you'll each again have plenty of little people to push around. As to egg deliveries, if such things have ceased then I've accomplished the task you set for me, have I not? Therefore, in light of my unlooked for success, I must ask you, where are my children? Have you found them yet? Have you even been looking?"

Helgayarn was momentarily nonplussed. Brunnhilde however was quick to take up the gauntlet that her senior had dropped. "Of course we haven't been looking for them!" she chided. "We've been far too busy trying to enact damage control—with regard to both ourselves and the situation in general—to prosecute much of a search for lost truants!"

"Yrr!"

"Furthermore," she continued, "our agreement with you was predicated on the bargain that you would help us first. Despite the delay in egg delivery, it's patently obvious to anyone with eyes to use them—and here I include you regardless of your testament to failing vision, that you've been more harm than help!"

"Yrr!"

THE CHRISTMAS RABBIT

Brunnhilde offered Betty a grateful nod. "Thank you, my dear," she said, "for your support." Turning back to the farmer, she continued, "Yes, deliveries have stopped, but the main goal, that of hare razing embarrassment, has yet to be accomplished. Folk the wide world over have come to see that little hopster as an unwilling participant in the slaughter just enacted. Furthermore, because he delivered to them their eggs and was thought well of for doing so, they—with the exception of birds that is—see him now with the loss of so many children, as a martyr to these events, caught up in them against his will and propelled by forces beyond his control! He's more popular now than ever!"

"Yrr!'"

"Well, isn't he?" the farmer innocently asked. "A martyr, I mean. In fact, aren't we both? I just wanted a garden, untouched by any hand save my own. He, on the other hand, in trying to rob me was merely obeying the dictates of the Rabbits of Influence, whose influence ever since has been somewhat declining. Their star has fallen, as has mine, while Jack's sun has risen, albeit in a cloudy sky." The three witches bridled at the implied accusation. "Perhaps," the farmer continued nervously, "this whole mess could have been avoided had I the generosity to offer him a carrot or two when I had the chance."

"We'll never know, will we?" asked Helgayarn in an effort to control her anger. "Had you, hadn't you, would you, wouldn't you, will you, won't you, can you, can't you—these matters are all behind us now. We have to deal with matters the way they are and the way they are is that all of us—including you, are up to our necks in cattle craps! So my question to you is, what do you intend to do about it?"

"Me?" Haven't I done enough already? Surely you've a big enough disaster on your hands that the last thing you should be looking for is my further involvement! Why take mere disaster and escalate it into outright catastrophe? Haven't the three of you got enough briars in your britches already? Are you gluttons for punishment?"

"We must be," Helgayarn tiredly replied, "since we insist on treating with you! But you're all that's left to us and so we come, however reluctantly, to commandeer your aid in our efforts to set right what has gone wrong."

"But what can I do," replied Old Slomoe. "Surely the resolution of this affair one way or the other is far beyond any meager abilities I might possess."

Helgayarn looked at him slyly. "It would be," she said, her voice dripping honey, "If you didn't have us to help you."

"Oh no!" Santos vehemently replied. "I've had your help before, beginning, of course, with those damnable fruit lights, and your 'aid' has caused me and mine nothing but trouble! Children gone, farm destroyed, and my wife beating her breasts regarding the poor choices I've made both before and after. No, I've had quite enough of your *aid*, thank you! How much more could I possibly be expected to endure? Aid? It's more like interference, I'd say! Stick to tides and seasons, why don't you, and I'll help myself. Thank you indeed!"

"It's not as though you have much choice," warned Brunnhilde.

"Yrr!"

"There's always a choice," replied the farmer defiantly. "I can choose to refuse! Damn the torpedoes and full speed ahead! Send you packin'! Burst your bubbles! In other words, bite me!" It was, without a doubt, the bravest stance the farmer had ever taken. But for all that just as ill-considered as any of his prior choices for when bullies invite you onto their sandlot for a game of ball you can always say no. Just make sure that when you do you leave yourself enough room to run and get away. If you don't, then it's probably best to ask them which position they prefer you play, shortstop, infield, or first base. Santos knew nothing of baseball, however, and despite his experience with them, damned little of bullies either.

"A poor choice is no choice at all," replied Helgayarn while offering him her patented shark's smile. She was getting ready to feed. "Yes, it's true—you could refuse our wishes. But what then? Surely you must realize that in the wake of the pogrom previously enacted, that certain charges against you are likely to be brought up by Jack and the remainder of his warren. Accusations of war crimes, I should think, and other such nastiness, are bound to follow. Who will preside over such deliberations, do you think? No doubt, another Constitutional Cosmic Court will have to be convened with the three of us overseeing its proceedings. Would it not behoove you, therefore, to have friends in court? Champions of your cause who could render rulings in your favor?"

"Why would you do that?" Santos asked suspiciously.

"Why not?" Helgayarn replied. "Surely, if you help us we'll do likewise for you."

"For your own reasons, no doubt."

"No doubt," agreed Helgayarn. "But haven't we done as much in the past? Think you back to the last trial. Both Jack and yourself were equally guilty, however marginal that guilt might have been, yet we punished the rabbit and set you free. Have you never wondered why?"

"Of course I have," replied the farmer. "But my imagination has never been up to the task of comprehending the machinations of you three. Besides, I thought it better in the long run to not delve too deeply into the matter. Never look a gift horse in the mouth!"

"How true. And yet the reason we acted the way we did good sir, is that in all sincerity we'd much rather have you as a useful ally—that usefulness, of course, always being called into question—than a useless enemy. Surely we've proven ourselves by now? Even in light of your broken promises and botched attempts, still you find us standing beside you and we'll continue to do so for as long as you play ball in our park." Helgayarn paused for a minute to let her words to do their dirty work while Santos continued to puzzle out metaphors regarding baseball. "You'll have once again," she continued, "your friends in court should such friendship prove necessary as it most likely will, and my word that when this issue is settled once and for all, we'll apply our unceasing efforts in the endeavor to locate your children. You have my word on it!"

Santos eyed the trio dubiously, knowing full well that the word of a witch or a lawyer was about as solid as the shifting sands of Krakatoa and as full of hot air too. "Suppose," said he, "that having to undergo once again the scrutiny of a trial, I turn state's evidence instead and indict you three? You did after all, put me up to this—from that very first fruit light to the battle just enacted. What would a jury think, I wonder, in light of that?"

Helgayarn's eyes were like pieces of flint, gray and granite as she considered him and his implied threats. "Who knows?" she replied softly. "A jury is apt to think anything. But consider, being yourself impoverished you'll have to throw yourself upon the court's mercy in order to retain counsel and whom, do you think, we're likely to appoint? That's right—ever handy and always malleable Owl, Owl, & Peacock—all of whom are old hands at this sort of thing, being birds of a feather who know a hawk from a handsaw when it comes to jury picking and tampering. As court appointees, you understand that their final allegiance will always be to us? In light of such potential back-door dealing, how much credence, do you think, is likely to be given to your outrageous claims?"

Crestfallen, Santos reluctantly submitted as he found himself forced to agree with the trio that indeed, a poor choice was in fact, no choice.

"Very good," said Helgayarn, relishing her victory over the clod. "Yet perhaps we're getting ahead of ourselves. It may be that the whole nastiness of court and the lengthy trial involved can be avoided altogether, yes?"

"How?" asked Santos, jumping at straws. "How might that be?"

"If the rabbit," Helgayarn replied, "could be truly embarrassed and humiliated beforehand, then public opinion which is all for him now, might swing the other way, yes? The public is forever fickle with its praise, on the one hand bestowing it upon the undeserving like it were manna from heaven, and they, the angels responsible for its dispensation, while on the other, withholding it from those poor schleps whom they deem unworthy of such accolades, as if they were the very demons of hell and charged with the task of inflicting minor misery. No one likes a loser, Farm Boy, and if Jack could be made out to appear a loser even once, then surely public outcry, which is in his favor at the moment, would sour and turn against him. The fickle public, which only pretends to be so enamored with him and his eggs, would fall upon him like a pack of rabid wolves—especially if they'd put all their worth and wealth behind an effort to support him!"

"What are you getting at?" Santos asked uncertainly.

THE CHRISTMAS RABBIT

"Why the race, you old ass! That silly race you so foolishly challenged him to without consulting us first! Now there's nothing to be done but follow through with that challenge. You'll defeat him in the race. Humble him in his own ballpark."

Again the farmer found himself wrestling with major league metaphors. "I've been through all of this once before with the elves," he replied. "It simply can't be expected that one so clumsy upon his feet could ever hope to come out the better in a race with the rabbit. He can run circles around me backward! He wouldn't even break a sweat while defeating me in such an encounter. Give me something that I *can* do, and don't set me up for inevitable failure again!"

"You won't fail," Helgayarn replied reassuringly.

"Oh? And why not?"

"Here's why," replied the big witch, and drawing the farmer within their circle of three, began explaining to all of them in hushed whispers, the details of her plan.

*****

One day not too long after the big battle, having seen to the burial of such august personages as Rabbitboodles, Flopsy Doodle, and of course, Harehito Rabbakami, and having completed the policing of the battlefield and starting once again the business of egg thievery and delivery, the rabbits were surprised to find coming into their warren, a delegation of the two-footed in order to negotiate the terms of the race with Jack. At the head of the procession were Helgayarn, Brunnhilde, and Betty. The trio were followed by the remainder of the elves whom they'd discovered hiding in their holes, and were led of course by Pixie and Dixie who marched with their heads bowed, having been thoroughly chastised by The Powers That Be. Beside them and walking glumly, strode the inestimable Farmer Santos, still unsure of himself and his role within this silly scheme the Witches had concocted. They'd been marching for days to get here while living off of canned rations as it was agreed by all—with the exception of the farmer, that for the greater good Mrs. Santos and her cooking utensils should remain behind. As the delegation moved toward the head hare's hole they took note in passing of the training still being conducted by the tattered remnants of Rabbits 1, 2, and 3—all that remained of the shock troops comprising Operation Jackhammer, with 4 having been completely wiped out. It was evident to the trio as they looked out upon the training that Harehito, before passing onward had disseminated enough knowledge of his art to ensure the rabbits were forever "battle ready." That, they knew, would undoubtedly become a can of worms which they'd be forced to open later.

Upon taking note of the oncoming procession, both Peter and Cottontail, who'd been appointed by Jack as junior wardens of the warren and who found themselves guarding the doorway to their father's hole, raced through it and down the tunnel in order to forewarn him of the incoming delegation. Jack and Nutmeg had secluded themselves from all outside contact, being both busy and intent on starting a new litter in order to replace those lost in battle. It was difficult work for the couple despite its obvious delights, as the act of conception brought to the forefront of their memories the recollection of children recently fallen. Still as mere exercise it was a blast and Jack was busying himself with it when his two sons burst into their boudoir. "Crimeny!" Jack exclaimed, drawing the covers over himself and Nutmeg. "Don't the two of you know how to knock?"

Nutmeg was mortified. It was one thing to put on a show for her peers as she'd once done when in the employ of those infamous Rabbits of Influence. But it was another thing altogether to be caught in the act of screwing by her own children—even if they'd been screwing themselves for some time now and had their own litters to show for it. It was more than embarrassing. It was humiliating. But Peter and Cottontail apparently had taken no note, either of her plight or predicament. "Father," cried his eldest son, "we've got trouble. Trouble with a capital *t*, and that stands for witches! Even now they're approaching your door and have brought with them the farmer and his pesky elves."

Jack had been expecting just such a development. He'd even been looking forward to it in a macabre sort of way. The final scene, he knew, in the play that was his life, was about to be enacted. "Very

THE CHRISTMAS RABBIT

well," he softly replied. "Go back above ground and see to them. Serve 'em tea and crumpets and treat them as their position merits. We'll be along shortly." Peter and Cottontail turned to leave when Jack suddenly called them back. "Belay that," he said. "If you treat 'em as their position merits they'll take such treatment as an insult, no matter how well deserved. Better to just serve 'em the tea and cakes and act polite while doing so!" The two rabbits offered their father their reluctant acknowledgment and headed out of the hole. "This is the final hand, isn't it?" Nutmeg asked while licking her fur and cleaning her herself in order to appear more presentable before The Powers That Be.

Jack looked toward his mate, his eyes filled with heartbreak and pity. What will become of her, he wondered, after this day's madness plays itself out? "The last hand," he agreed, "the last hand in a high-stakes game."

"What are we holding?"

"Deuces," Jack replied. "Only deuces—but no matter. The game was always rigged, with no way to win. We both knew that." Nutmeg began to cry unabashedly. "We can run!" she pleaded. "We can sneak out the back door and run. Catch the train to New York if it's back in service, get lost in Central Park, and hookup with that Thor Rowe person you're always talking about. From what you've said, he doesn't much sound like the kind of fellow who'd harass hares. He'd have a thing or two to say about the schemes concocted against us! Surely he'd hide us. Let's disappear!"

Jack took hold of her, crushing her to him. "And what then, my love?" he asked. "Where do we go from there? And what becomes of our children when we're not here to answer for them?"

"The same thing that'll happen to them if we stay! Their destinies are their own, and we'll be gone either way. Disappeared or outright dead, we'll be beyond helping them and their fate is no longer in our hands. In New York we can have more children—we can start a new life, far away from witches and farmers and Rabbits of Influence! Away from the plagues that have so hounded our lives!"

"But not forever," Jack tiredly replied. "Eventually, one of them will find us. If we flee, they'll make it their business to hound and dog us till we're run into the ground. Those wolfhounds of the Witches will pick up our scent before we even make the train. They'll chase us down and eat us as sure as cattle makes craps."

"But Farm Boy's children got away," she said. "The Witches never found them."

"That," replied Jack, "is because along with almost everyone else, including the Witches, the two lads were washed away in the flood. In its aftermath, Helgayarn Brunnhilde and Betty have been too busy, I think, to spend too much time looking for them. Besides, they're Farm Boy's kids, and say what you will about him and his offspring, fate itself seems to have taken a singular interest in their affairs, guiding and leading them for purposes of its own devising. I don't think that Slomoe's children, if they're still alive, were ever meant to be found, and that it's beyond even The Powers That Be to locate 'em. No, they'll never turn up until some far distant day when Santos himself and likewise us rabbits, have all but forgotten our original purpose in life. But such is not the case for us and ours. The Witches will hunt us down while punishing our children for our cowardice in running. They'll skin us alive while proclaiming to all who look on that such treatment was wholly deserved for two fugitives from justice—and what hare here looking upon such an atrocity would have in his heart the nerve to gainsay them or having it, have in addition a hide tough enough to protect such a heart and keep it beating when the trio turned upon him for having stood up? No my love, its better this way. Better that I should go up and bravely face them. Here, now, or in New York, my life's a closed book anyway. Better that the final paragraph reads that I died with my boots on."

"But you don't wear boots!" Nutmeg argued, her voice caught between tears and laughter. "None of us do. Our boots are built in!" She laughed again. Then cried. Then laughed. Then cried yet again, all the while Jack holding her ever so gently, allowing her emotions to run their course. "A figure of speech," he replied. "I seem to be full of 'em these days. But if I 'die with my boots on' and am brave, then perhaps my actions will save my children and, more importantly, you. You and they are all that matter now."

"I won't live in a world without you!"

THE CHRISTMAS RABBIT

Jack shook her harshly. "Don't say that!" he shouted. "Don't you ever say that, and more importantly, don't you ever do it! After I'm gone you're all that our children will have left of me—the only wisdom standing between them and those three lionesses who're ready to eat us for dinner—so don't you even consider it! You owe it to them to carry on, and if I'm to die, then you owe it to me as well!"

"But I want to be with you!"

Jack smiled and again gently hugged her. "In time, my love," he said. "In good time, you'll stop running too. You can join me on the other side of this life then. I'll be waiting for you, I swear it."

"You promise?"

"With all my heart. Now make us some coffee. We'll drink a private toast to our lives and to our love."

"What about the Witches? They're waiting."

"To hell with 'em. They'll wait. They've waited this long, haven't they? A few more minutes won't kill 'em. If it would I'd take an hour!"

Nutmeg bustled about the hole, gathering cups and brewing coffee. Fraught with worry but resigned to the inevitable she tried her best to put on a brave face while carrying out her husband's last wishes. There was no point in crying, she knew. It would only serve to further burden Jack in his last hours. There'd be plenty of time for mourning later. To help bolster him and herself too she gamely tried to make light of their predicament.

"Do you think," she asked, "that those three incompetents will get caught up in their own net?"

"It's certainly possible," he replied with a small chuckle. "They've done as much many times before."

Nutmeg allowed herself some slight laughter but then the darkness descended once again, blackening her very thoughts. "Do you suppose," she asked hesitantly, "that they plan to kill you outright or do you think they've something more sinister in mind?"

"Probably the latter," Jack said gravely. "Even they can't just out-and-out whack me without cause and technically I haven't done anything other than get in their way. They may not even have a specific plan in mind with regard to my killing. They may be here simply to further their efforts in my ongoing embarrassment. It's possible, you know. Not likely since such efforts on their part have failed dismally. But it's possible. But you know how the schemes of those three go. Such machinations on their part are always getting out of hand and beyond them with the result being that someone almost certainly gets hurt or killed. Surely this time will be no different and their contrivances, whether they mean them to or not, will work to cook my goose. I'm dog meat one way or the other, and it only remains for me to see to it that my death counts for something, that it saves my people and, if we're lucky, topples that trio's tree house in the bargain."

*****

Above ground where the sun still shone, Helgayarn stood with thunderclouds on her brow, as did Brunnhilde and Betty who were likewise stormy.

How dare that rabbit keep us waiting!

Helgayarn was of a good mind to hurl a harea of her own, a caustic fireball of sulfur and brimstone right down his hole and burn them out. That would put an end to his impertinence! But she kept such self-indulgent thoughts in check. There was still no benefit, she knew, in making a martyr out of him. Too many saw him as one already. Rather let him fall in disgrace, the has-been champion of all those silly egg lovers who'd come to admire him and his artwork. Then she could kill him. Or better yet get those same eggbeaters who'd once so adored him to do her killing for her! She chuckled. Life was surely grand when you were a big witch.

Off to the side and in the company of Pixie and Dixie, stood Santos shuffling about nervously. "I don't much like this," he whispered to the elves. "Neither the waiting nor the beginning—and as for the ending, well this plan is even more sour than one of my wife's stews! It'll doom us, I tell you, and we'll be lapping up bile, all of us, before we're through!"

"Be quiet, you fool!" Dixie admonished harshly. "Do you want those three to hear you?"

THE CHRISTMAS RABBIT

"Of course it stinks," whispered Pixie, forgetting that he and Dixie had put forth a similar stratagem themselves. "But you've issued the challenge and thrown down the gauntlet!"

"At your suggestion!" replied the farmer.

Dixie eyed the fat man critically. "Who's loonier?" he asked. "The visionary who drafts a plan or the maniac who dares follow it? There's no help for it now. What's done is done!"

Helgayarn cast a glance their way. "What are you three mumbling about?" she demanded. "Nothing of importance, your worship," Dixie meekly replied. "The good farmer was just pointing out that the hour is getting rather late. Perhaps you'd like us to make camp?"

Helgayarn was just about to give him her reply when Jack and Nutmeg emerged from their hole. "So!" she said turning toward them instead, her voice dripping venom. "The great Jack Rabbit, head hare hereabouts and warden of the warren deigns to grace us with his presence. And in his company—the harlot! So much the better!"

Knowing that they wouldn't kill him here and now Jack decided to display a brave face and answer fire with fire. "Put a lid on it, you old battleaxe," he replied. "If you're here to treat, then treat! But do so in an appropriate manner or shuttle your tired old behinds back home!"

Such a display of insolence was more than Brunnhilde was willing to take. Even though she was on crutches she leapt at him with the intention of finishing him off once and for all. Such effrontery and impertinence could not go unpunished! She almost succeeded, catching everyone, including Helly off their guard with her unanticipated response. But Helgayarn caught her in midair at the last moment. As she did she looked down to take note of the rabbit's flight in the face of her sister's oncoming wrath but was surprised to find him gamely standing his ground. "You've got brass balls, sonny," she grudgingly admitted. But such accoutrements will only carry you so far!"

"They'll carry me as far as I need to go," said Jack. "But it's not my balls that'll carry the day for me. It's my keen sense of the dramatic and my certainty that you want something of me. Something more than mere death—which of course you could've had anytime."

Helgayarn considered the hare carefully while pondering for the briefest of moments the notion that she should invite him to join them. Before her stood one sharp cookie, she knew, and much could be made of him if he were a willing ally. But alas, her answer to her own question had to be no. She was sharp enough herself to realize that too much blood had been spilt and most of it from the veins of rabbits, for him to ever consider such reconciliation. Besides even were he to entertain the offer, what would her sisters, insecure in their own positions, make of its tender? Would they see it as a threat? Possibly. Would they consider him a menace to their own positions within the inner circle? Probably. Would he become a bone of contention? Most definitely! And there were already enough bones in their skeleton closets without adding more to the pile. Their three-sided triangle was overcrowded already without adding to it by making it a four-sided rectangle. They were The Powers That Be, The Terrible Trio, The Trinity of Terror, The Witches, and The Big Three! If they took on an additional partner now they'd have to change titles, honorifics, and monikers. This would necessitate the printing and publication of new and divergent business cards, placards, and general announcements—and ad men, even back in Olden Days, didn't come cheap. It would require as well the forgery of the appropriate law degrees and diplomas from the proper schools, which would all have to be signed, counter-signed and attested to. Then of course, there would have to follow a coronation and the attendant silliness that would encompass such a ceremony and Helgayarn, short on time and under pressure, could not afford to indulge herself in such nonsensical poppycock. Another time perhaps, with another rabbit maybe, but not this one and not today. Still, it was a waste of a good resource, she knew, or would've been had she not already thought of a peachy plan which made perfectly good use of this little leporide nevertheless. "You're pretty hep, for a little fur ball," she said without hiding the admiration in her voice. "No, we won't kill you, but we will demand that you stick to your agreement."

Jack looked at her suspiciously. "Which one was that?"

THE CHRISTMAS RABBIT

"Why, the one you made with Farm Boy to compete in a race. Let it be a contest then. You against him over a course of varying terrains with the winner being he who can deliver to a preselected and randomly chosen set of recipients as many eggs as possible. Winner takes all. Loser takes nothing!"

"Take all of what?" Jack asked. Take all further responsibility for egg delivery? I've already got that. Lose what—my esteemed position as head hare in charge of procurement and delivery? If that's what's at stake, then indeed I do have nothing to lose. I forfeit! Santos wins. Now go home."

"Ooh, but it's not going to be that easy." Brunnhilde laughed, joining the conversation.

"Yrr!"

"How's that?" Jack asked, turning his uneasy gaze to the others.

"Word has spread throughout the land," said Brunnhilde. "Farm Boy's been bragging about his challenge and your acceptance! Heard you really threw the gauntlet at him—well, for my money, you could've thrown it twice! Bets have been placed. Monies wagered. Folk have laid everything they have on the line for you, giving you ten-to one odds.

"That's ridiculous!" Jack replied. Why would folk risk everything they have on such folly? Wagering such stakes is for the simple-minded."

"How true," Helgayarn replied with a smile. "How true."

"Yrr!"

"Still, they've gone and done it," Helgayarn said.

"I don't believe it," Jack replied incredulously. "Even people aren't that stupid!"

"Oh, contraire, Master Rabbit. Oh contraire! People will bet on anything, believe me. Anything at all. Why, there'll come a day—I've seen it—when their very lives willed be filled with such silliness. In the not-too-distant future their energies will be focused almost entirely upon gambling of one sort or another. Poker games, keno parlors, bingo clubs, lotteries, stock markets, cockfights, and frequent flyer miles. The world will be full of such inanities and mankind will bow down to the gods of chance who rule them. Oh yes, they'll literally swim in the seas of such speculative ventures!"

"Perhaps," replied Jack, "Perhaps one day it will be as you say. But why here and now, and why, for the love of heaven, bet on me?"

"It's in their blood, silly," said Helgayarn. "They love taking risks. They're nourished by the excitement such recklessness affords. As to why they'd bet everything on you? Who knows? Perhaps in your deliveries you've impressed them with your speed and fleetness of foot or maybe they considered your contender and determined for themselves that given his reputation for foolhardiness and failure, you were a hands-down winner, an odds-on favorite, with no chance of losing. Either way, bets are placed and fortunes wagered."

Jack shot a quick glance at Nutmeg who merely offered a shrug as reply. Such things were beyond her ken. A cold wind arose and blew across the open field, rustling the trees on its border and rattling them like dry bones. The scents of bitterness and despair were borne upon that wild wind and Jack could smell both keenly, just as he could sense the noose closing about him. "If they're all so sure of themselves," he asked, "and likewise of me, who then in the name of wonder did they ever find to bet against me? Who'd be foolish enough to bet against ten-to-one odds?"

Helgayarn smiled dangerously. "Be careful, Jack," she replied, "about whom you deem foolish. You may end up eating your words! As to who took the bet—we did! We guaranteed the wagers. And we're not stupid. We think the farmer has a good chance of winning. Even as we speak we have our cousin, the Shoe Lady, out collecting bets in between house calls. She's holding the moolah, Jack and it's quite a pile! Since the race has been wagered upon, if you choose to forfeit then all those betting on you, which is just about everyone, lose. They won't be happy, Jack. In fact, they're apt to be quite angry and come hunting for your head—yours, Nutmeg's, and all the rest of these little snivelers you call family. Crowds are fickle Mr. Rabbit—especially when they've lost money. They can turn in an instant. Believe me, I know. I've seen it happen. Hell, I've had it happen many times! Such turnabout isn't pretty. Are you big enough, I wonder, or tough enough, to fend off the mob when it comes roar-

THE CHRISTMAS RABBIT

ing after you and hunting your hide? I don't think so." She began to laugh while rubbing her hands in satisfaction. "So you'll run," she continued. "You'll run as if the very devil himself had lit his fire beneath you, and you'll do your best to beat that dumb clod standing over there. But you'll lose. In the end, you'll lose. I know. We've arranged it!" She stood there looking down on him, uttering wicked laughter while her sisters joined her. Their braying struck a discordant melody, a high-pitched squealing like three pieces of old chalk rubbed the wrong way on a blackboard, screeching and sour. Trees quivered and ears rang. Glass shattered. Jack felt his stomach roll from the onslaught of the dreadful pealing, the bile inside it churning and threatening to choke him as he contemplated the pit of quicksand that the witches had so easily maneuvered him into.

"Where?" he asked weakly. "And when?"

Helgayarn stopped laughing long enough to smile triumphantly. "Why, right here, of course," she replied. "The race will begin right here. As to when—let's give it a week, shall we? That'll give our cousin ample time to collect *all* the wagers while allowing you enough leisure and leeway to settle your affairs—of course, you're in charge of snacks and refreshments!"

*****

On the day of the great race, a storm, small but mean nevertheless, its clouds amorphous gray sponges weeping rainwater and wet misery from beneath them as they passed, came rolling in from the north to make war upon the sun. It cared little for races or those who ran them, being busy as it was, attending to matters at hand. It was in a race of its own, seeing how far it could run before it finally blew itself out and the sun caught it up and killed it. The sun, with its talons of fire, was a relentless son of a bitch, pursuing it constantly, and the storm knew it. So it had enemies enough at the moment without offending anyone on the ground—especially The Powers That Be, yet in its final death throes it nevertheless managed to do just that while upsetting everyone else too as it cried in waves of sorrowful self-pity, remembering glory days gone by when it rolled on lightning and roared with the trumpeting of thunder! Race day was Friday and the storm knew that had this been last Tuesday it could've showed them all a thing or two—witches, bureaucrats, and the betting public! But as it was in fact Friday and not last Tuesday, it was running out of both time and itself. It was drying up, its race run, and the good fight fought; and for something which professed to have no interest in contests, races, and other silly notions, it strikes me as just a bit obsessive of it to have expended its short life running one. Some psychologist no doubt, could have explained to it the meaning of its fruitless cross-country marathon, which presented itself now as only unanswered questions regarding the nature and folly of pointless competition. But although there were doctors aplenty—including psychologists, as evidenced by the swarm of lettered men that had descended onto the field to practice their art and shake their juju sticks for the Witches in the aftermath of the elven battle—always billing their time, of course, to Repressive Insurance of Mesozoic Mesopotamia—there were to date, no 'Weather Wizards' as there are today; no pontificating three-lettered individuals spouting boastfully from the well of their dubious expertise about storms, their tracks, or their causes, while presenting to televised audiences their maps and graphs for general viewing and claiming to anyone foolish enough to listen that they could predict a storm's future by charting its past… and still have the nerve to get it wrong nine times out of ten. As if charting anything was that easy!

Weather Wizards—who, with their three lettered titles, their supercilious claims, and their arrogant boasting that because they'd spent their collegiate lives studying such beings and now professed the ability to track them, understand their motivations, predict their comings and goings, and who, therefore, by inference, should be able to tell a storm and those whom it assaulted, what it all meant—this fruitless ambition to run away wild, raise havoc and burn itself out as it sailed off into oblivion and self-destruction. Such pontificating fools were not tolerated back in Olden Days. Back then, no one would have put up with such half-assed predictions and third-rate fortune telling from such bold-faced liars as we've come to accept today. Even The Powers That Be weren't that brazen! Therefore hav-

THE CHRISTMAS RABBIT

ing no Weather Wizards in whom to confide and resenting the indignity it was being made to suffer under the cruel ministrations of its enemy, the sun, the storm spent its last hours alone and unloved, crying its crocodile tears of woe for the short miserable race it had been made to run while never for an instant pausing to consider that had it slowed down just once, in order to take stock of itself and the world below upon whom it shed tears, it might not have had to suffer these final indignities at all, that it might have found a way to continue with life had it merely learned to live and let live. Instead it grew ever more frustrated while expending its final measure of bitter tears upon those below, as if seeking some last minute revenge upon a dimly seen and poorly perceived enemy. The blowhard blew in great gusts shaking the leaves off trees and ripping the petals off flowers while torrents of rain assaulted the forest and the lands about. It's fury, so often like our own, wasn't aimed at anyone in particular and yet most gathered beneath suffered nevertheless as folk invariably do when forced to contend with someone else's self-pity. Folk were wet, uncomfortable, and resenting the storm's intrusion into what promised to be a fun-filled day. But being die hard gamblers and addicted to the excitement of spectacle, most opted to ride out the rains of self-pity and stay for the race despite it being the kind of day that had it occurred in our day, would have necessitated the cancellation of any sort of sporting endeavor regardless of the predictions and analyses of the prevailing Weather Wizards… With the exception of football. Football fans are absolutely crazy in their fanaticism regarding the game, enduring the harshest weather in order to support their team. Even the most ardent of wagerers back in Olden Days would have failed to understand such fervor and devotion. Be that as it may those days were not Nowadays. They were Olden Days and back in those days nothing got called off for anything. Exciting events like races and the festivities attendant to them were rare in their occurrence and were never postponed regardless of earthquakes, famines, plagues, or hell come high water. A little rainstorm no matter how unruly could hardly be expected to put a damper on the day's events.

 Folk came from all over the forest and from miles around to witness the magnificent contest. They came from as far away as Africa and China and a few of the wallabies and koalas who'd sat on the last Kangaroo Court had even sailed in from Australia, which with the continental drift continued to slide further and further away. It was a dangerous journey to be sure, but the excitement of the contest and the incredible odds to be gotten from the bookies at the betting booths, were such that no one felt they could afford *not* to make the journey and therefore attended the race despite the dangers and hardships encountered in getting there. Folk brought with them their entire store of worldly possessions bundled upon their backs in loose faggots, to be used as collateral against their ten to one wagers. They were looking for good odds and the attendant payoffs and could have had them had they been of real gambling ilk, but one look at the farmer and they bet conservatively, wagering their fortunes on Jack instead. The witches covered every bet no matter how large or small with the total value of the wagers ultimately placed equaling a whopping hundred dollars or so. Now that may not seem like much to you and I, living in Nowadays as we do, but remember, this was Olden Days, when a penny was worth more than a pound and inflation has played hell with the dollar ever since.

We've all heard the tale of the great race. It's been told and retold over and over until the story we hear today is hardly a true relating of those events as they actually occurred. The great race. Also known as the race between the Tortoise and the Hare. It didn't run its course as you've heard tell. By the time Aesop heard the tale and passed it on in its modern form to the likes of you and I, much had been omitted and the tale itself had already become so corrupted and filled with self-serving half-truths and out-and-out lies as to be unrecognizable from the actual facts as they really occurred. For instance, we hear Nowadays that the hare lost. He didn't—although he didn't actually win either. Or we hear that the tortoise won. That's a misleading statement at best and probably passed down to the likes of you and I because at the end of the day he was the only contestant left standing. Here's what really happened:

In the dim watches of dawn before the two contestants took the field. Wet and miserable, The Powers That Be, in their ongoing effort to fix the race sought Santos out and, finding him, pulled him aside in order to impart to him, some magic dust.

"What's this?" he asked wearily as he reluctantly took the baggie they'd adroitly slipped him. They were doing their best to be sneaky as they were nearly in plain view of those early arrivals, both two- and four-legged, who were even then pouring onto the field in order to claim their seats for the race's commencement. Menfolk from the four corners of the earth were seen in the company of bears and bison, lions and leopards, weasels and water buffaloes too. We were all of us back then, much easier to get along with, more similar in thought and attitude and more like-minded when it came to those pastimes which had at their heart community involvement, participation, and the chance for neighborly disagreement. Back then four-legged folk and those who flew for a living were just as indiscreet and outrageous as we, placing foolish bets and taking unnecessary chances for the mere thrill of doing so while giving no thought to the ramifications and consequences of such foolish behavior. The group mentality was ever prevalent within the encounter group itself. Looking around to make sure that they were not being taken note of, Helgayarn whispered to the farmer viciously. "It's magic dust, you idiot!" she hissed as she shot swift glances, first to one side and then the other, assuring herself their conversation remained private. "You lay out a line and snort it. It'll make you faster than the wind. You'll fly baby, fly!"

This dust was a magical concoction of their own devising and distilled from the essence of the coca plant, a weed native to the floral family of Erythroxylaceae, which grew both wildly and abundantly in some far flung third-world place called Columbia. Indiscriminate men in our own time produce and peddle a similar product from the same plant but what it rivals in kick it lacks in magical quality. Without magic, the substance, being restricted nowadays as it is to limitations of mere science and chemistry, becomes dangerous and addictive. However, the men who peddle it don't care. There's moolah to be made in the selling of that white powder and those making it don't give a damn that their gains are ill-gotten and derived through the exploitation and eventual ruination of their fellows who fall victim to it. Although if the truth were told and such were the consequences of their magic dust, then in all likelihood the Witches would not have been overly concerned about it either. "Snort it?" asked Santos. "How does one snort it?"

Helgayarn rolled her eyes, which had grown dizzy with the many repetitions of this action in the past few months. "You sniff it, you fool! You take it up your nose. Now be quick about it before anyone sees you!"

"Oh, I don't know," replied Santos, nervous and uncertain, "getting dust up my nose always makes me sneeze! I'm sure that this magic powder of yours whatever it is, is bound to do likewise or worse, and if I'm sneezing, then I can't be running for you see I'm one of those fellows who has trouble doing two things well when doing both at once."

"You can't even do one thing well—and even if it commands your entire attention!" quipped Brunnhilde.

"Yrr!" agreed Betty.

"But you'll do this," continued the middle ranking witch, "or we'll see to it that you never run anywhere anytime ever! Now take a snort!" She ground the little white rocks into a fine powder and held them under the farmer's snout. "Inhale!" she commanded.

In an effort to obey, Santos strove to snuffle the substance up his sinuses. He got the merest amount into one nostril, hardly enough to endow him with any magical benefit whatsoever, when as predicted, he broke out in a fit of sneezing. Great blasts of spit-laden air sputtered out from him as if his lungs were mighty bellows and his nostrils the forges, housing the very fires they fanned. His sneezing blew the magic dust every which way in a great tumultuous cloud. As it billowed forth there happened to be passing by, a small herd of caribou intent on placing bets and taking their seats for the great race. The dust cloud settled upon them and they began to breathe it in through their wet, black noses. As the powder entered the reindeer it penetrated their nasal cavities and sinuses, coursing through their veins like a runaway express train, endowing them with magic and enchantment. They began to float, and one of them, a poor stag named Rudolph who'd ingested more of the substance than the others, and who was more sensitive—both to its magic embellishments

THE CHRISTMAS RABBIT

and caustic properties—found that his nose turned from midnight black to fire-engine red; in fact, you could even say it glowed.

Helgayarn shrieked. "Oh no! Oh no, you fool! You blew it away and now it's rained down upon the damned deer! Oh mercy! We're doomed! We're doomed, I tell you!"

And they would have been if it were not for Brunnhilde the Levelheaded. Gathering up Betty, she took after the herd of caribou and, using a bit of rope that she just happened to have handy, lassoed them and brought them back to where Helgayarn stood berating the farmer. The big witch temporarily refrained from scolding the sod and turned her attention to her sisters and their captives.

"What's to be done with them?" she asked, pointing to the reindeer. "We can't have flying caribou gallivanting about, raising a ruckus, and making trouble for us, can we?"

"I thoroughly agree, sister," said Brunnhilde. "Let us keep them penned up for now and then we can serve them up as venison steaks after the race. They'll make a grand entrée for our victory celebration!"

"Yrr!"

The thought of a good haunch of bloody red meat thoroughly appealed to Helgayarn, who anticipating the victory feast to come, had been fasting for three days. The caribou, needless to say, were not overly enamored of Brunnhilde's suggestion, preferring as they did to hold on to their own haunches, and began to snort and grumble amongst themselves. They pulled and tugged on their reins and it was all Brunnhilde and Betty could do to keep them in check and prevent a stampede. The deer were desperate and, as we all do when we feel threatened, strained at the bounds of their captivity. But these were the Witches who held them hostage and mere resistance coupled with animalistic grunts and nasally enhanced snorts would avail them little in winning their freedom and escaping their fate. A plan was needed instead. A devilish stratagem that played into the trio's own schemes and desires for the race ahead. It was Rudolph, that slippery stag and cunning little caribou, who devised the plot that would provide for the herd, their one hope of salvation…and other reindeer have held it against him ever since.

"Yes, you can eat us," cried the little stag. "You can boil our bottoms in bayberry oil or roast us slowly over an open pit! What, after all, can mere caribou do to deter you? If you desire it then it is our destiny to be done in, both stag and doe, and served up as delicacies at your great feast—only please, we beg you, don't let the farmer's wife prepare dinner! Even reindeer rate a better end than that!" He turned to his fellows—there were about eight of them—to see if they were in agreement. They were, as far as it went, but felt nevertheless that it did not go nearly far enough, and they were unanimous in their opinion that as their spokesperson, they were expecting far more out of old Rudolph than merely being spared the humiliation of ending up as one of Mrs. Santos's main courses. He'd have to do far better than that, they whispered, if he didn't want to get punched in that shiny little red nose. Loudest in their objections were Comet and Cupid, who each had a doe, a deer, a female deer, waiting for them back home. As both were expectant fathers they were looking forward to returning after the race and learning in their absences, what sort of deer their does had dropped. "I'm not done yet!" Rudolph replied to his herdlings vocal complaints. "I've much more to say and a proposition to make!" Clearing his throat, he turned his attention back to the trio, who stood there regarding him while salivating as they contemplated him and his fellows served upon bone china with a complimentary Chianti. Such thoughts, Rudolph knew, so pleasing to the trio's palettes, needed to be derailed and redirected before all of their gooses got cooked. "Yes," he continued, "you can most certainly serve us up for dinner but then what have you got? One meal and one meal only with maybe some leftovers—and lot of gas to follow as digestion runs its natural course. And that presupposes you win, allowing your victory celebration to go forward."

"Win what?" asked Helgayarn. "We're not racing. We have nothing to win or lose."

Rudolph offered her a conspirator's smile. "Well, you know your own business better than I," said he. "But it seems to me that as the guarantors of all wagers, you have far more to lose than anyone else. I submit therefore, that you have some plan for fixing the race and that such plan consists in large part, of the magic dust which we

THE CHRISTMAS RABBIT

inadvertently consumed. Can you get more, I wonder? And can you obtain it in time to do any good? After all, Columbia's a long was off—even for the three of you!"

Brunnhilde offered Helgayarn a nervous glance. "The little fellow has a point," she replied, and I'm not just referring to his antlers! When fat boy sneezed our plans went up in smoke. Without the dust he hasn't a ghost of a chance to win this thing no matter how much interference Pixie, Dixie, and the elves run for him. We'll be paupers by nightfall!" Helgayarn uttered a tired sigh as she contemplated the eventuality, knowing that its realization would mean their ruination. "You obviously have some sort of plan," she said to the caribou. "Best you tell us its details, and we'll see for ourselves if it can be made to fly."

Rudolph stamped his hooves nervously while clearing his throat once again and hacking out phlegm. My but that magic dust was irritating! What he was about to suggest was a dangerous ploy. One filled with many pitfalls, most of which would go undetected and therefore unprepared against since there simply wasn't the time to plan for them. If only, thought he, rain delays were something that could be made use of, but alas, as stated before, such contrivances in delay and deferral had not been invented yet. Therefore they'd have to improvise as they went. Yet it seemed to Rudolph that despite his spur-of-the-moment plan's deficiencies, of which there were many, it still provided he and his fellows with a far better alternative to being carved up and served on a plate au jour should they instead stand around like sheep, doing nothing and meekly submitting to slaughter. "It like this," said he. "Your dust was that idiot's ace in the hole, and he literally blew it. He blew it our way, and there's nothing can be done about that now except, perhaps, to put my fellows and I in harness while letting us pull him along for the ride. We're fleet of foot, you know, and now, thanks to your powders, can fly too. We'll be unstoppable!"

Helgayarn offered Rudolph an ugly scowl. "What do you take me for," she scathingly asked, "a fool? The betting public will never go for it. This is a race between the Tortoise and the Hare only. It isn't supposed to be a team effort! If you can't come up with something better than that then you'd better start preparing dinner!"

"But there's more," replied Rudolph. "First off, there's nothing in the rules we've seen posted that says we *can't* join the farmer. The topic isn't covered because it was never considered! Therefore we have a loophole—a catch-22! And we can make use of it. Now certainly those who've placed wagers against the farmer will object to our participation if we give them the chance. But we won't! Upon leaving our little powwow the herd and I will immediately go over to the betting booths and make a big show of wagering all our worth on Jack and his anticipated success, and we will, of course, walk to the booths, not fly. There's nothing to be gained in giving away our advantage. Once we make our wager we'll promptly offer up our services to the farmer and it will be you three, who having witnessed our wager, that will object the loudest to our offer. But folk will think, having bet upon Jack, that this is an attempt on our part to insert ourselves into the race in order to sabotage the farmer and assure our payday. Since they've all bet the same way they'll see our interference as an opportunity of assuring their payday too while putting it to the three of you in spades—but only if you three put on a convincing display with regard to your feigned objections."

Helgayarn considered the scheme. Though not without faults she had to concede that as a piece of subterfuge thought of on the fly, it was pretty well reasoned and though she'd never admit it, was a plan she would never have conceived on her own. Was she so close to these events, she wondered, that she was incapable of viewing them objectively? She chided herself. What nonsense! She was the Big Witch. The leader of The Powers That Be and therefore objectivity was by inference, her middle name! As proof of that, she pointed out two obvious flaws in the caribou's plans. "If you bet against yourselves and win," she said, "you'll lose everything you have. What do you gain by that? And if we make a big show of objecting to your inclusion in the race and then reluctantly acquiesce, will not the betting public smell a rat?"

"Perhaps," replied the reindeer. "Perhaps. But having so ardently endorsed our participation they could not very well back away, could they? In changing their minds they'd look like hypocrites!"

"What of it?" asked Brunnhilde. "We do such things all the time!" As The Powers That Be, they were among other things, lawyers and politicians and were therefore constantly changing their opinions and positions in order to meet the needs of the moment and the exigencies of the day. "Why wouldn't the betting public do likewise?"

"Yrr!"

"They might," agreed Rudolph. "They might. But although they may hold to a differing opinion within the privacy of their own homes, each of them nevertheless when in the company of friends professes a general disgust of lawyers and politicians in general and a specific aversion to the three of you in particular!" The trio looked at him menacingly.

"Hey," the stag laughed nervously, "I'm not saying anything that the three of you don't already know! But it's my contention that since they profess such dislike they'll never—at least where they can be seen doing it—act in any way like you! They'll simply never change their position, claiming that such stalwartness on their part is a matter of principal. Their principles will become the gallows upon which they hang themselves and you three will walk away, reluctantly, of course, with their money in your pockets after giving them what they wanted despite your stated reservations and objections about having done so. You'll be able to say, 'I told you so,' while keeping their moolah as an objective lesson to the lot of them about the evils of gambling itself and the particular price to be paid when engaging and being party to, race tampering! You see? We fix it, and they bear the blame and burden, which ends in you taking their money while walking away from this sordid affair smelling like roses. Everybody wins!"

"Everybody, that is, except them and you," replied Helgayarn.

"Come again?" Rudolph asked nervously.

"If we win then everybody else loses—including you!"

"Well, I wouldn't go that far," replied the young buck. "Certainly those who bet against the farmer will lose their shirts—"

"As will you!"

"Better our shirts than our hides, which we'll certainly lose should you decide to skin us alive and roast us." The caribou paused, in the act of picking at a cuticle—which was an act only since hooves don't have 'em. "Besides," he continued, if we win this race then perhaps the three of you will be so generous as to show some magnanimity by recouping our losses. It would after all, be the least you could do."

Helgayarn chuckled. "Not likely," she replied. "We're not known as the Witches for nothing! No, I think it a far better thing for you to accept your losses. Were we to return such a wager then surely the betting public would utter cries of protest, citing collusion on our parts while filing against us all, charges of race tampering. Whereas should we keep all wagers then we maintain the appearance of neutrality while imparting to yourselves as well, those valuable lessons regarding the evils of gambling and race tampering, and the risks in particular, of trying to bribe The Powers That Be!"

Rudolph scowled. "Well, you can't blame a deer for trying," said he. "So what do you think, have we got a deal?" He looked both to the Witches and to his four-legged brethren, knowing that without their wholesale approval and reluctant compliance such a scheme was not only impractical but pointless. Comet, Cupid, Donner and Vixen, as well as the others, were smart enough however to realize that they had very little choice and therefore snorted out their grudging acceptance. All that remained was for The Powers That Be to give it their final seal of approval.

One party who'd been left out the scheme's planning stages chose this particular moment to speak out. From off to the side where he'd been left largely ignored, Santos made known to the conspirators his opinion. "I don't see that we have anything to lose," he cried out gleefully, "and I could certainly use all the help I can get! These reindeer look like stalwart fellows to me, and I'm sure they can be counted upon to give their all toward the successful conclusion of

THE CHRISTMAS RABBIT

our endeavor. Let us accept their offer of assistance with the assurance that together, we cannot fail!"

"Oh, do be quiet, you old ass!" retorted Helgayarn. "We'll do what we'll do and well do it on our own say so without any input from the likes of you! Just you stand there and wait upon our good pleasure—and while you're waiting be so kind as to remain silent!" She drew Brunnhilde and Betty aside for one of their infamous huddles. "What think you on this," asked Helgayarn, "does this crackpot scheme have a chance of pulling itself off?"

"I'm not sure," Brunnhilde whispered secretively while stealing glances about her to ensure herself that no one, including Santos or the reindeer, could overhear, "but it sure looks to me as if once again we've painted ourselves into a corner—"

"Yrr!"

"And it would seem to me," she continued after offering Betty a dirty look as payment for her unwanted interruption, "that once again we do not have much of a choice, do we? The old sod can't possibly beat Jack in a footrace without the aid of outside assistance and we simply haven't the time to journey to Columbia, gather the coca plants, and with them prepare more magic dust in order to assure victory. The tortoise will certainly lose to the hare if we allow things to remain as they are." She breathed a tired sigh while at the same time allowing her sisters to read the look of concern etched on her face. "Yet I'm not at all sanguine or confident in those damned deer! They can probably hold up their end of the bargain, but what then? Can we count upon their discretion to remain silent after the fact? I think not! If they're bettors then we must assume that they're braggarts as well and therefore cannot be relied upon to keep secrets, at least not for long, and this is one secret we can't afford to let slip! We need a back-up plan. One that accounts for them after the fact!"

"That's simple," replied Helgayarn. "After the race, we kill 'em and eat 'em anyway. Dead deer tell no tails, yes?"

"Don't you mean tales?"

Again Helgayarn found herself rolling her eyes. If this went on much longer, she knew, her orbs would likely go into orbit. "Whatever!" she tritely replied. "But even so, I must say I'm not at all comfortable with this scheme. Think back if you dare, upon our other machinations that for one reason or another, and often due to unforeseen consequences, failed to bear the intended fruit. They came to naught or 'elsewhat' despite all the planning and counter-planning because we didn't consider all the ramifications and possibilities inherent within those plans. We didn't cover all our bases, didn't account for every possible contingency and therefore our schemes went belly-up! I wonder, therefore, if we're not miscuing again as we're now considering one of the wackiest schemes ever, and moreover, it's not even our own stratagem, but rather the subterfuge of some silly-assed stag, and being such, we've had no opportunity to consider its unlooked for eventualities, entanglements, and ramifications even if we possessed the foresight to do so! Is this wise, I ask you? Or are we simply drawing an invisible noose tighter about our own necks?"

"I don't see how the noose can get much tighter than it already is," Brunnhilde reluctantly replied.

"Yrr!" agreed Betty, happy at least that there were volumes occurring here for later inclusion in her journal.

"So you're saying we should go along with it?"

"Since most of our other schemes never worked out in quite the way we expected them to," replied Brunnhilde, "then yes, perhaps it's time we tried our hand at total improvisation, working straight from the hoof, if you'll pardon the expression, and see where simple extemporization takes us." The other two looked at her doubtfully. "If it takes us up that fabled river once again," she continued with a grimace, "well, we've swum in that stream before and if forced to, no doubt can do so again."

"That's not very comforting!" Helgayarn replied doubtfully. "I'd prefer keeping my feet upon dry land and solid ground!"

"Wouldn't we all?" asked Brunnhilde. "As it is, we're swimming in a sea of cattle craps now and so must make any effort however outlandish, to reach the shoreline! 'Farmer Fred' over there, is our only means of doing so and by himself he's a boat too full of leaks to put too much faith in. His compass is suspect. The likelihood that left to his own devices, he'd get lost at sea, is not a possibility but a

THE CHRISTMAS RABBIT

certainty. Therefore we have no choice but to utilize the reindeer as paddles—whatever the risks!"

"Yrr!"

"Oh, do be quiet," said Helgayarn and Brunnhilde in unison, "and let us think!"

Brunnhilde gazed at her senior sister while awaiting her response and wondering what her decision would be. Couldn't she see they had little choice? The race was mere minutes away and the decision regarding it needed to be made quickly. Something of her concern must have transmitted itself to Helgayarn for she suddenly straightened up, a look of haggard resolve displaying itself upon her countenance. "Very well," the big witch said. She pointed at both the farmer and the caribou, "Go check yourselves in, placing your bets of course before you do, and we'll be along shortly."

Santos and the reindeer made their way through the crowd, he to the starting line and they to the betting booths where the Shoe Lady, acting as an unwilling agent for the interests of her cousins, was busy overseeing a sizable group of her children whom she employed as betting agents, odds makers, bookies, and ticket takers. "Hey, Ma!" one of her daughters cried, taking note of the cloven entourage as it approached, "Get a load of this! Bet you've never seen deer like these!"

Rudolph, walking at the head of the herd, approached the booth. "Clam up, little sister," said the stag as he slapped his pence upon the table. "All or nothing on the rabbit to win with the best odds you can give me." The young lady was about to offer a puzzled reply when her mother stepped in to affect her rescue. "Listen Horny," she said, "this close to race time one to four are the best odds you're going to get. That means if you win you get back an additional 25 percent. And you'll only get those odds at the animal betting booths. These tables are reserved for people and people only." She paused to size him up. "Now move along, sonny," she continued, and place your wager with the appropriate bookie. That would be my son, Faldo, over there, who's located six tables down on the left." Glancing off in the indicated direction, Rudolph took note of Faldo busy at his table and taking the wager of Mssrs. Owl,

Owl, & Peacock who, although regarding themselves as "in tight" with The Powers That Be, were nevertheless not privy to this day's silliness and therefore, being birds of a feather and notwithstanding their ill-will toward him, were placing all of their eggs in one basket and betting heavily on Jack. The stag took note that a goodish crowd were converging upon this table, intent upon witnessing the confrontation between himself and the harlot, no doubt regarding the pending argument as just one of the many attendant festivities linked to the day's inanities. His plan was coming together perfectly. "What do you mean?" he cried out loudly so all could hear. "Can't a reindeer place a bet where he will? Why not this table? Isn't a caribou, just like a man, another of God's creatures, put upon this earth to take his rightful place amongst the whole herd? Am I not therefore to be accorded the same considerations as a mere man, who too often considers no one but himself?" Although the Witches bridled at the mere mention of such an august personage, there was much nodding of assent and vocalizations of "how true" from the gathering crowd. The men, however, were smart enough in this instance to keep their opinions to themselves. "I demand," Rudolph continued, "equal treatment under the laws of nature! Therefore I reserve for myself the right to place my bet at this booth and this booth only!"

The Shoe Lady shrugged. "Very well," she replied. "If you're willing to settle for less favorable odds in order to make some silly point regarding the equality of species that's your own damned business! Has the deer got any dough?"

"Yeah, two bucks!"

The Shoe Lady rolled her eyes. Just what she needed—Moe, Larry, and Curley all rolled into one. "Take his bet, daughter," the Shoe Lady said and then wandered off to supervise the gaming at the other tables.

Along the way, she encountered Santos down by the starting line. "Farm Boy!" she said with a delightful grin. Her copper hair cascaded down and around her shoulders and even in this morning's rain gathered unto itself what little sunlight there was, to shine like molten fire. Her violet eyes were limpid pools in which Santos could see his reflection drowning. Never had she seemed so beautiful, never had she appeared more attractive and desirable. "There's time," she said, "if you will and if you've the money, of course, for a little roll in the hay! Whaddya say, hey? A little nookie for good luck couldn't hurt, could it?" Santos was sorely tempted but knew that the Witches would tolerate no skylarking on his part this close to the onset of the race. More importantly, Mrs. Santos was somewhere lurking in the crowd while no doubt keeping strict watch on him. If she caught him in the Shoe Lady's pants, she'd no doubt press his trousers! "Reluctantly, I must decline," he said. "However, there is a delicate business arrangement that I wish you to act as my agent in."

The Shoe Lady was intrigued. "Oh, what's that?" she asked. "Looking for condoms, pleasure pearls, or a mistress on the side with which to idle away your hours after this silly affair is over? I assure you that I can act as your agent with regard to any or all three. Name your pleasure and I'll name my price!"

Santos found her frankness regarding sexuality to be somewhat disconcerting and was not surprised to find himself blushing as he considered her offer. "No, no!" he abruptly replied. "Sex is the furthest thing from my mind these days. I want to place a wager on the race."

The Shoe Lady looked at him incredulously. "You don't really think you can win, do you? That rabbit is going to run up your front and down your back. In the time it takes you to find even one egg, he'll have gone and delivered his whole basket! Why do you think the odds are so long in his favor? You haven't got a chance, Farm Boy. Save your money for a rainy day because after this day's proceedings fella, you're going to need an umbrella!"

"You don't understand," the farmer replied. "I wish to bet on Jack Rabbit to win!" the Shoe Lady pulled him violently aside. "What are you talking about? She demanded. "You can't bet on the opposition! It smacks of race tampering and hidden agendas!"

"You know me," replied the farmer. "When it comes to concealing things, I couldn't hide a needle in a haystack with any hope that it would remain undiscovered. Besides, the reindeer did it and—"

"And what?"

The farmer looked uncomfortably down at his feet. "Perhaps I've said too much already," he replied. "Yes, I believe I've spoken out of turn. Let us forget this whole silly business of contestants placing wagers and just run the race!"

The Shoe Lady, however, was not to be put off so easily. "Listen, Farm Boy," she replied, "there's something going on here that I don't know about, and as the official bookie and bagman for this daily double, I feel it's my right to be made aware of it! So you'd better start talking, tubby, before I start carving me some blubber!"

Finding once again that he'd managed to step into a big pile of cattle craps, Santos sought desperately for some means of extrication from the heap of doo-doo into which he could feel himself sinking. But as so often happens in life, once you step on such a mound, the only way to remove yourself from it is to muddle your way through the mire, however unpleasant, until you come out the other side. Only then can you go about the business of wiping your shoes off. So it was back then. Santos saw no way to resolve the matter other than admit to the truth while letting the chips fall where they may. He knew that the Shoe Lady, although not a witch, was nevertheless no one to trifle with. She was a giant killer after all, and that victory took no small amount of effort. Certainly she was beyond the mere likes of him to contend with and to give him his due, Old Slomoe knew it. And still he hesitated. Sensitive to his reticence, the Shoe Lady turned away from vinegar, employing honey instead, knowing that with such bait it was much easier to catch flies. "Listen, sweetie," she softly whispered, "why don't you just tell Auntie Shoe Lady what the big secret is all about, hmm?" She offered up a sultry smile before continuing, "I promise that should you do so, then after the race and in some hidden place, there'll be time for you and I to fulfill your wildest fantasies, and to do so far from the prying eyes of witches and wives, who are better off not knowing and who think they know for themselves, what's proper and what isn't. Do you desire threesomes? Foursomes even? Some of my eldest daughters are of an age now where they're ready to enter the trade. Perhaps I can arrange for you a liaison with one or two of them. You can be their first conquest—I mean customer! Would you like that?" Santos nodded vigorously, the

THE CHRISTMAS RABBIT

nervous sweat of unbridled anticipation running off him in rivers, and still he resisted, fearful of saying too much. Frustrated, the Shoe Lady fell back on practicality. "Listen, bub," she said, "you know who I am, right?"

The farmer nodded in the affirmative.

"And you know who they are?" she asked, meaning the Witches.

Again the farmer nodded his reply.

"And as I'm personally holding all the bets that they're guaranteeing, one can easily see that I'm in their employ, is this not so?"

"I'm not sure," replied the farmer. I'm in their employ so to speak, and I don't think they'd trust me with that much money."

"Of course they trust you," she replied smoothly. "They've wagered upon you like you were family! Well, I'm family too—their favorite cousin!"

The farmer nodded once again. He'd heard as much before.

"Then doesn't it make sense to you, since I'm part of the family and since we're all, including you, on the same team, that the right guards know what the left guards are up to? That the tackles protect the running backs and that the front line has the quarterback safely ensconced?"

Santos hadn't a clue regarding the Shoe Lady's metaphors or their specific relationships one to the other, as football, like baseball, hadn't been invented yet. But he got the vague idea nevertheless that what she was trying to describe to him was the essence of teamwork and yes, it did seem reasonable to him that being on the same side it therefore made sense in this darkest of hours and with so much riding upon the race, to have all of the team's roster working in concert in order to achieve its stated goal. With that realization, he began to blab and blubber, both long and loud—or would have had the Shoe Lady not admonished him to keep his sentences short, sweet, and nearly silent.

In the course of five quick minutes, the Shoe Lady had her answers and, once she did, was more than happy to place the farmer's wager for him. It was quite a hefty sum that he handed over to her care—a whole bag of gold, representing his entire profit from the produce stand that he'd operated before the advent of Hurricane Junior and the trial that followed. He'd been hoarding away his receipts one day at a time as insurance against a rainy day. Well, it was raining today, the Shoe Lady knew, and she was more than happy to hoard his profits for herself. Taking his gold, she left him standing there with the assurance that she would place his bet—and she would, but she would also place one of her own. Walking away, she allowed herself an indulgent chuckle, as she considered all that the farmer had told her. It was quite a plan and she had to admire the reindeer's cunning in conceiving it. More importantly, she grudgingly offered up to her enemies a modicum of respect for having the audacity to allow its enactment. It would have worked too if not for the intervention of fate, circumstance, and the farmer's big mouth. But at long last, after waiting patiently along the banks of the river for her enemies to glide by, the Shoe Lady stood at water's edge as the Witches were about to go floating past her in a rickety old garbage scow, full of leaks, and with most of its caulking rotted away. Whether the trio knew it or not, their boat was taking on water fast, and it would be a simple matter, the Shoe Lady knew, to finish the job and sink 'em! She hurriedly made her way to the betting booths and grabbing Faldo, placed the farmer's wager. She then adroitly handed him a slip of paper containing the instructions for her own. Falco read it and then looked at her in disbelief. "You can't be serious, Mother!" he whispered harshly. "This wager, as large as it is, represents everything we have! A lifetime of effort spent lying on your back for this? Even the Witches, who are betting all they have on the farmer, aren't foolish enough to take this sort of risk! Our odds would be tremendous of course because the likelihood of such an outcome is, strictly speaking, very unlikely indeed! Are you sure?"

The Shoe Lady offered her son a reassuring smile. "I place my wager based upon inside information! We're going to clean up! But remember, place the wager in the name of one of your sisters or brothers who's not working the booths—in fact, use my darling Faula, who's home abed ill, as our proxy. Place the wager in her name, and list her as an absentee bettor!" The Shoe Lady was doing what is known in gambling parlance as placing a "layoff" wager wherein usually a small amount of money is bet on an unlikely outcome because the odds of that outcome materializing are so incredibly high. If the outcome itself doesn't manifest the loss is trivial; if, however, the unpredictable becomes, in fact, the unforeseen, then the small amount wagered rolls itself over into a heaping pile that is more than adequate to pay off the other losses. That's the way "layoffs" usually worked. In this particular instance, however, the Shoe Lady was merely holding the wagers, not guaranteeing them and therefore had no bets to layoff. So perhaps it is best to describe her gambit as a "lay-on." A massive endeavor wherein she was about to lay a big one on The Powers That Be, not only because of her wager's size but also due to its audacity and her own surety that she'd placed a winning bet. Still, as a matter of principle layoff wagers were a good strategy and the Shoe Lady was surprised that The Powers That Be hadn't placed one themselves. Yet as bookie for the Witches, she was confident that they'd overlooked the strategy. Were they that sure of their plan and therefore of themselves? If so, then pride went before the fall and there was no doubt, at least in her own mind, that the trio would soon take a tumble.

    Jack and Nutmeg spent their last minutes before the race together and alone at the bottom of their hole. The noise of the revelry above resounded throughout their chamber, echoing and trebling off the walls as the carnival got underway overhead. Mock races were being held, both in preparation for, and as a warm up to, the main event, with their contestants exhorted by a restless and eager crowd to push themselves over the finish line. Hawkers of various sorts wended their way through the throng while shouting above the din and adding to the noise and confusion as they endeavored to sell their wares. One of the peddlers was none other than the very same program vendor who years ago had tried to sell his playbills at the great trial. He had new ones made up for this event and was having the same dismal luck in his efforts to sell them. The audience doesn't really need a playbill if there are only two actors upon the stage.

    It was still raining and therefore muddy. The constant tramping of the crowd, both two-footed and four, had caused the ground underfoot to become slick, treacherous, and in some places, boggy like quickmire. So there was much slipping and sliding and laughing at those who did. One woman, intent on trying to find her children lost somewhere amid the gathered throng and therefore not paying too much attention to where she placed her feet, had them slip out from under her and in so doing inadvertently knocked another woman over. Both came crashing down upon the trampled loam beneath their feet to the general amusement of the crowd looking on. Bemired, both regained their legs whereupon the second woman, in a pique of anger, knocked her innocent attacker off her feet yet again and back on her bottom. The crowd roared. As the first woman began to rise the second pounced again while the crowd encouraged them both with catcalls, hoots, howls, and of course, more laughter. Scratching and clawing, biting and pulling, the two women fell upon each other only to go rolling over and over in the muddy soup upon which they battled. It was the first known mud-wrestling match ever and just like today, the males gathered back then were engrossed in it. In their ferocity the two antagonists tore at each other's clothes, exposing one another's breasts, which covered in cold wet mud, caused their areola to swell and their nipples to stand erect and at attention. The men were hooting and salivating as they eagerly awaited their final exposure. Even back then, even in Olden Days, men being the Neanderthals they still are today, have always felt threatened by the genuine display of affection that only one woman can give to another—a friendship built upon trust and the shared experience of similar trials borne and endured—those trials being, of course, us. We don't like it when Sally confides in her best friend, Mary—especially if such confidences reveal or make reference to, some shortcoming within ourselves. As a sex, we're much happier if Sally keeps her mouth shut and Mary minds her own damn business! True friendship on their parts, and genuine affection, scares the cattle craps out of us. For some reason, we men feel threatened by such displays and for reasons that we can't explain. You ladies now reading this, ask yourselves whether or not I'm right. Just how does that man of yours feel about your best friend? And you men? Be honest. Isn't that bosom buddy of your wife often the biggest pain in the ass in all creation as she sticks her nose into where it doesn't belong while encouraging your spouse to do and say things that you'd rather she left unsaid and undone? Don't all you men reading this agree with me when I say that what that uppity crotch really needs is a heaping helping of what we've got dangling? That'd surely straighten her out! In our view women have no business inserting themselves into the middle ground of friendship, becoming bosom buddies like we do. Their boobs get in the way. We fear such friendships, avoiding them when we can and breaking them up when we can't. We'd much rather see our ladies polarized and at either end of relationship's spectrum. Love or war—that's what we men want of our women! No middle ground called friendship for our girls—but let's have them frigging or fighting and only if we can look in on the fun! It was so even back in Olden Days and from then until now things haven't changed.

The high-pitched screech of battle along with the thunderous roar of the simpletons who stood upon the fringes egging it on, blended and mixed with the general noise of the fairlike atmosphere occurring all around them to echo and reverberate throughout the length and breadth of the entire warren and down its tunnels, causing minor quakes and cave-ins along the span of its walls. "What in the name of wonder is going on up there?" Nutmeg asked Jack. "Are they rioting? It's more tumultuous than the great battle or even the trial—and you remember how noisy they were!" Jack lovingly stroked his wife's ear. "I wouldn't worry too much about it, my love," he replied, "its only men carrying on and doing men things. I'm sure that the animals gathered above are adhering to at least a modicum of respectability. But men? Nothing's beneath them. They've always been that way and so have their women! All a rabbit can do is put up with them, deliver their eggs, and stay out of their way."

Nutmeg looked around the dim interior of their hole, taking note of another cascading slide of soil. "It feels like the end of everything," she said. "Like the whole world is coming down on top of us and the very stars themselves are trying to smother us! Why can't they give us a moment's peace? And why us? What did we ever do to deserve this fate?" She clung to her mate tightly, weeping as she did. "Oh, Jack—I'm so scared! In a few minutes you're going to leave me to run this awful race and I know, *I know* that I'm never going to see you again. What will I tell the children? And the children's children and their children?"

Jack sighed. "Our children know the score as it stands," he replied. "As do their children and their children's children. It's only the very young who've no idea as yet what this really means and what it portends. So you must be there for them, my love, their matriarch after I'm gone, to watch over them as they grow while ensuring that the deeds this day, done out of honor and necessity, are not lost to the vagaries of time and subjective narration. As the little ones grow tell them of this day, of what really happened here, and how their sire, Father Jack, ran the good race, fought the good fight, and in so doing, died that they might live."

"Has it really come to that? Are you really going to die?"

As Jack looked at her while lovingly stroking her fur, his heart nearly broke in anguish. How he wished he could spare her the agonies of this day and the miseries yet to be enacted. But no, he needed her to be strong, both for herself and their children, and to carry on for him after he was gone. "From the moment that the great trial got away from them," he said, "we always knew that the Witches were ever plotting and conniving to bring about my ruination and demise—and that hullabaloo with Harehito didn't help matters any! So I'll run their race but I can't run from them, not forever, and not from fate either. It's faster than I."

"But you're faster than the farmer," she countered. "Surely you'll be able to run circles around that lard ass even if they bind one of your legs."

"True. Which is why I'm positive the Witches have something particularly devious and nasty in mind in order to ensure victory."

"Why can't they do likewise to the Tortoise?" Nutmeg asked. "That's what I want to know! Why is he allowed to get off scot-free when to my way of thinking he's responsible for all of this nastiness in the first place? A miser, he is, a cheapskate who'd rather start a war and embroil us all in this quagmire then part with a couple of measly turnips! Why isn't he being held accountable?"

"Can't you see that will never happen?" Jack replied. "He's their scapegoat—the pawn through whom they do their dirty work and as such, will only be sacrificed in order to save their own skins. That day may indeed come in some far-flung and unforeseen future, but I

THE CHRISTMAS RABBIT

doubt that it will be today." He gave his mate a final hug. "Come, let us walk for the last time, up our hole and greet together, the doom which awaits us." He took hold of Nutmeg's paw and began to hop off toward the entrance but for the briefest moment she held him back. "Are you okay, my love," she asked. "Are you scared?"

"I'm more terrified than I've ever been of anything," he replied, "but I can't let them see it. Help me, Nutmeg my dear, to be brave, to show them all just what it is that a rabbit's made of." He stood there shivering, alone in the world in spite of her comforting presence, while Nutmeg crushed him to her. "Then lean on me," she replied. "Take strength from my love for you, knowing that even in death, something of me will always be with you—just as I'll take comfort in knowing that a piece of you will reside always, within the well of my heart." Then together, paw in paw, they hopped up their hole to face the day.

*****

The crowd, now gathered at the starting line, stood fidgety and restless, eagerly anticipating the onset of the great race. As Jack emerged from his hole, he was greeted as the odds-on favorite with a tremendous roar of approval. He looked about, taking note that Santos had positioned himself upon a wagon behind the starting line and in the rear of a bunch of hoofers. "What's this?" he protested. "This is between me and Pithecanthropus Wideass and no one else! Get those ringers out of here!"

Helgayarn chose that very moment to make her way through the crowd, her victory smile stamped indelibly on her features. "Here now, hare!" she laughingly shouted. "There've been some last-minute additions to the lineup! My sisters and I tried our best to voice our objections to their eleventh-hour inclusion, but the betting public would have no part of it. It would seem that they put an inordinate amount of faith in your ability to outrun just about anyone and everything!" She eyed the assembled bettors while rendering a vicious scowl. "Have it your way then," she cried out to them, "and let these herdlings hoof it for the farmer. But since you're so sure of your champion's abilities, I'm certain you won't mind paying out twenty-five to one should he lose!"

Thinking that the fix was in, the crowd scoffed at her bravado and dared her to make it fifty-to-one. The big witch, in a rare gesture of conciliation and cooperation, complied. As far as Helgayarn was concerned, the day's events were going swimmingly. "There, you see?" she said to Jack. "Your fan club is behind you all the way. Now don't disappoint them!"

"I don't give a cattle crap where they stand—behind me, in front, or off to the side! I don't like it, I tell you, and under the rules of general contests and races, I'm filing an official protest!"

"Oh really!" exclaimed Helgayarn, putting on airs. "One would think you thought having such a team gave the farmer some sort of advantage! Remember, master rabbit, that this is Wideass we're talking about, and if anything, these herdlings merely serve to level the playing field! Besides, in pulling the farmer along, look at what they have to ferry as well." She indicated the great wagon upon which Santos sat and which the reindeer were harnessed to. It was the trio's Winnebago, and they were loathe to loan it out, but on such short notice, there was nary a sleigh to be found. They considered doing away with the reindeer as a team and reharnessing their Clydesdales, but the V-8, caught up in another of their mistresses whacky schemes, were preoccupied that day, busy negotiating a contract with some nascent beer company in an effort to become their official spokespersons and mascots. The Winnebago, being the latest design, was assembled in large part of various balsa wood alloys to allow for better mileage and as such, was much lighter than it appeared. To further reduce the load the Witches directed the elves to empty it of all its nonessentials. Out came the AC hookups, the microwave oven, the sink, the stove, the pay toilet, the assorted spells in various stages of making, and anything else that might slow the farmer down. It was stripped to bare bones minimum, and by the time the elves were finished, it was a hardly more than a simple prairie schooner, a country covered wagon. "So are you the head hare around here," Helgayarn needled, "or are you merely chicken? If so, you can always forfeit!"

THE CHRISTMAS RABBIT

Jack gazed about him to take note of the anxious looks displayed upon the faces of those who'd wagered upon him to win. A forfeiture would bankrupt them. As one, they all grew gray with fear, their blood settling in their feet as they contemplated a prospect that had heretofore gone unconsidered. As much as he wanted to, Jack simply couldn't walk away. It would give Santos the victory and by proxy, The Powers That Be. If it were merely defeat, then Jack wouldn't have hesitated one moment to throw in the towel. But there was more in store than mere defeat if he gave up. There would be death, he knew, at the hands of an angry crowd for any action so chicken shit as towel-throwing, which would cause the loss of their aggregate fortunes. He hadn't sought their encouragement, either vocally or financially, but now reluctantly had both and couldn't walk away from either no matter how much he might want to. The crowd wouldn't let him. If he tried they'd turn upon him in an instant and most likely kill him. Then his death would accomplish nothing. He either had to win this race or die trying. If he won—all well and good. But if he died trying, then at least he'd be remembered, by those who witnessed his effort, as a martyr to his cause and to them as well. The price of martyrdom, he knew, was the cost he needed to pay in order to assure the continuation of his family line. "Me, chicken?" he replied with false bravado while spitting at the big witches' feet. "I'm not afraid of anything you can throw at me, you old battleaxe! The only reason you're using Slomoe here is that you're too old and decrepit to keep up with me yourself! Your running days have long since passed, and the best you can do now is to hobble your tired old behinds down the road while making misery for everyone else!" Helgayarn turned a sickening shade of purple, towering above him and ready to strike. As she seethed she heard the crowd yell out its support for the rabbit, congratulating him on his display of chutzpah at her expense. She cast her gaze throughout the crowd, taking note of everyone and of who was saying what. *They'll all pay,* she promised herself. *Someday, they'll all pay.* But for now, she knew it best to stick to the matter at hand. She smiled at the rabbit dangerously. "Do you have anything else to add, my little friend," she asked, "before we enact this charade?"

"What could I add," replied Jack, "that an old bag with as little wit as yourself could possibly understand?" The crowd whooped and hollered, enjoying every minute of the exchange while Betty furiously jotted down notes which she would fully expound upon later in her journal. Perhaps, thought the onlookers, the rabbit was trying to goad the witch into killing him outright. That wouldn't be forfeiture. That would be interference—official interference—and being such they would all collect! Jack could die if he had a mind to. What did they care so long as they recouped their wagers? There would always be more rabbits, they reasoned, to deliver eggs, whether Jack lived or not. Let the rabbit go out with a bang! Better for everybody!

Helgayarn bent over to put her arm around Jack, as if offering him a loving embrace. "Be careful, my little footpad," she whispered, her eyes glinting and the hate on her face nearly palatable. "Because there's no need to kill you now when I can always destroy your family later."

"You'll do what you're going to whether I'm here or not!" replied the hare defiantly. He hurled some harea in her face. The crowd roared out its approval while Helgayarn screeched. Her grinding teeth flashed sparks. Her stringy white hair tinted battleaxe blue and just starting to grow back stood on end, and flashes of lightning could be seen erupting in the whites of her eyes. "Start the race!" she screamed. "Start the race! Start it now!"

Brunnhilde ran up to the contestants and handed each a map and a basket. When she got to Jack, she shook her head, almost in pity. "You're so dead, little hare," she said in a half whisper, "that you should consider yourself already buried."

"Up yours too!" Jack replied.

Jack took his place at the starting line alongside Rudolph who headed the team pulling Santos's wagon. Helgayarn climbed a hastily erected platform and admonished the onlooking crowd to silence. "These are the rules of the race," she cried. "Each contestant has an empty basket and a map with the names of one hundred recipients listed on the rolls. When I lower my flag, they'll hasten away, first to gather eggs and then to deliver them to the names on the map. Once completed the contestants will return here. The first one back wins

THE CHRISTMAS RABBIT

the race!" The crowd looked on in silence whilst the air itself hung heavy, pregnant with anticipation and dread. Sounds were magnified so that the mere snap of a twig or the rustle of a leaf echoed like a gunshot and thus competed with the roar of thunder overhead as the passing storm expended its final fury. The banner whipping in the wind, Helgayarn raised the flag like an executioner on the block, and brought it down with one swift stoke. The Great Race had begun.

Jack was first off the line, his hind feet tearing up clods of earth and mud, sending them flying into the onlooking crowd. A mighty cheer arose as he tore away, leaving Santos and the reindeer to wipe from their faces, the splatter brought about by his frenzied departure. With map in one paw and basket in the other, the head hare sped swiftly off into the forest.

At the crack of Santos's whip, Rudolph did likewise, pulling his fellows behind him. The wheels of the Winnebago, which had partially sunk in the mud, groaned in protest as they were forced from the complacency of rest and unwillingly pulled into action. Round and round they turned, gathering speed, until their individual revolutions could no longer be distinguished and their rotations became a blur. Of course, a great event such as the one described, drew a huge crowd that could not be contained within the mere confines of the starting line. Thus after speeding away from the initial throng the two contestants were forced to contend with intermittent spectators gathered upon the fringes of the course. Their presence, scattered along its length, made it hard for the contestants to cheat but not impossible. At one point, taking note of a break in the crowd, Santos exhorted his reindeer to take to the air, intent on flying to his magic room and thereby gather all the eggs he needed at once. This would save him the time, he reasoned, of having to gather them himself. But he arrived at the safe only to realize that he had no elves with him, who knew how to open the door. In a panic he twisted the magic dial this way and that but to no avail. Thus he had to double back to where he'd left the path and start anew, his search for eggs. This mistake cost him both time and distance, as Jack, a master climber and egg thief extraordinaire, was well into the collection phase of the race by then and had gathered for himself half the deliveries needed to complete it. Santos had never retrieved an egg in his life and the caribou had all they could do to pull the combined burden of himself and the wagon. Therefore as egg thieves, they would be of no aid to him. Thus we find him in danger of suffering an embarrassing loss but fortunately for him the Witches had enough presence of mind to anticipate this deficiency and so in the confusion of the race's opening ceremonies, secretly dispatched Pixie and Dixie, sending them both into the forest to prosecute his search for him. When they collected his quota, they overtook him in some secluded part of the wood, far from the eyes of nosy spectators, and made the transference. But it took time. Perhaps days. Perhaps weeks. Nobody Nowadays really knows for sure. The two sprites were gifted—this much we know. They possessed magical abilities—of that we're certain. But despite these formidable talents, when it came to gathering eggs, they were never going to be a match for Jack, who by now had years of practice. Practice makes perfect, and though he had yet to attain that lofty height Jack was nevertheless as close to it as anyone was likely to get and the two elves, with all their magic, should have know that even if they knew nothing else. So it was that when they made their delivery to Old Slomoe, Jack had not only finished his gathering but had completed two thirds of his deliveries as well. It seemed, to the rabbit at least, that the race was in the bag. The course was easy, the map was clear, and he was far ahead of schedule. It was too easy and the little leporide should have been aware that such was the case. But who reading this can blame him for his untoward confidence? He'd been expecting death or worse to manifest itself at some point during the running of this race but as yet it hadn't come forward. Now with the race nearly three quarters completed, he began to rationalize to himself that perhaps dour fate wouldn't show its face, that perhaps all aspects of the contest were on the so called, up and up, and most importantly, that perhaps for once, the Witches were going to deal him straight. Thus he kept his eyes on the road and on the road only, taking extra care not to stumble over an upturned root or a half buried log and so fall, breaking his last remaining eggs before they could be delivered. He was down to two eggs and upon their delivery would speed his way back to the finish line and to the open

THE CHRISTMAS RABBIT

arms of his loving wife and family. If anything untoward was going to happen, he reasoned, then it would've happened already. He kept his eyes fixed firmly ahead, both to the path and the task at hand and therefore did not take note of the treachery creeping up on him from the side.

Pixie and Dixie, elven mischief-makers extraordinaire, took note of his progress and began to pace him, one on his left and one on his right, with the intent of thwarting his efforts and putting a halt to his progress. As far as the rabbit or the farmer went, they cared very little for either and even less about the outcome of this contest or how that outcome would affect the two contestants. They were elves and as such had more important and magical concerns than this simple race and those who ran it. They were keenly aware however, of the old adage that shit rolls downhill and though not in the valley themselves, knew nevertheless that their mere association with the farmer brought them close enough to it that they'd be swimming with him in a high sea of cattle craps should he lose the race and their matrons not get their way. Therefore although under no specific orders from the trio regarding the race other than to collect for the farmer the required ova, they took it upon themselves to show a little initiative by going the extra yard and applying the added effort needed to assure both themselves and the Witches, who'd no doubt reward them, that the race reached its desired conclusion. Even with the aid of their eggs, the silly farmer was days back and miles behind. He would not see the winner's circle unless he received some unlooked for and unexpected assistance. But they had to be careful and whatever action they took had to be administered at just the right moment, as there were continually scattered groups of spectators strewn about the course of the race. A quick determination on their part led them to the conclusion that the audience was thicker and more numbered at the beginning and middle stages of the contest and rather thinner and less populated as the race neared its completion. No doubt those gathered at the final stages had elected to congregate at the finish line itself in order to witness the race's conclusion. This left the elves with miles of empty forest on either side as the race neared its terminus. So much the better. At one particular stretch of forest choked with a riot of trees and brambles growing so thick and dense they formed a wall alongside the path upon which the contestants ran, the elves struck. Racing ahead of the rabbit to get to this particular stretch in the road, they planted their trap in the middle of the path where it could be easily seen by anyone passing, then positioned themselves within the flora, using magic to blend in with the herbage, remaining hidden and unseen. As Jack sped along, he took note of the carrot, which the elves had placed in the middle of the path to lure him. He almost passed it by. Carrots were not a particular favorite of his, and even if they had been, there'd be plenty of time, he reasoned, to relish one or two after the race. But with the destruction of Santos's farm juicy carrots had been awful hard to come by of late, and so growing there alone, in the middle of nowhere with its green shoots rising invitingly out of the ground, it seemed to say, "Here I am—eat me…" After Hurricane Junior and the subsequent months of scratching out a living among the few surviving weeds that provided the barest of sustenance, a lone carrot, planted in the middle of the road was more than a mere rabbit was capable of resisting. He rationalized that the farmer was days away yet. He was, therefore, in more than in a comfortable position from which to "take 5." He'd had neither food nor water for nearly three days and the luscious carrot would provide both. He came to a screeching halt, backpedaling to where the unexpected bounty rose temptingly out of the ground like the Tree of Life. He paused, both to look around and listen carefully for any signs of Santos or the Witches, but could detect neither. He took cautious whiffs of the air about him as well but could detect no danger there either—the elves being wise enough to have plastered themselves with deodorant before embarking upon their chosen method of sabotage. For one brief instant his heart cried out to him to beware, to take note of the fact that a cultivated carrot, growing on its own all alone in the middle of the road was not an occurrence that happened by mere chance only and that such a happenstance could only be the byproduct of someone or something's careful forethought and planning; but he was too tired and too hungry to listen too long or too hard to that inner voice of reason which advised caution. Eventually that voice was drowned out altogether, and Jack dug up his death sentence. It looked like an ordinary carrot and it smelled like one too—but of course, it wasn't. It was a magical carrot, a slice of slumber on an orange stick. But Jack didn't know that although perhaps as you read this you're all of the collective opinion that he should have; and so, with gusto, he consumed his unanticipated bonanza, gobbling it down like a ravenous wolf in a henhouse. Upon finishing he quickly brushed his buckteeth and sped off upon his way. Soon he'd be at the finish line, the King of Carrots, with the world in his arms. As he sped along the course, the contents of the carrot sped through him. The elves had injected it with sleeping potion and as the poison worked its way through his system the poor rabbit began to notice the onset of extreme fatigue. His eyelids grew heavy and began to droop. His thinking became garbled and fuzzy with one irrational thought chasing after another. His sight grew dim, his hearing fell off, and his sense of smell lost its sense. He stumbled drunkenly, barely managing to protect his last two eggs. It took all his will and fortitude to regain his legs, and once he did, found that he no longer possessed the strength to keep them under him. He fell over in a swoon and passed out. The elves, it seemed, had done their work in grand fashion.

*****

"Whoa!" The farmer's hair and beard, which had by now grown back, were being blown about in the wind of their furious passage, getting in his eyes and nearly blinding him. "I said whoa! I can hardly keep up!"

Rudolph, the red-nosed reindeer, who had a very shiny nose, gazed back from his lead position in harness to offer the farmer a look of contempt. "You needn't keep up," he replied. "Just hang on! Even with flying, we're miles behind the rabbit, and it's our necks if we don't catch up!" He snorted disdainfully. "I don't imagine," he continued, "that you've stopped to consider whether or not there'd be room enough on the Witches' spit to roast both a farmer and eight reindeer? Well I have and I assure you that if there isn't, The Powers That Be will just up and get a bigger spit!" The lead caribou brought his gaze back to what lay ahead and summoning up all his energies, exhorted his fellows to even greater effort, crying out, "Now, Dasher! Now, Dancer! Now, Prancer and Vixen! On, Comet! On, Cupid! On, Donner and Blitzen!" The others, strapped in their traces, were too busy and too tired to take umbrage at the uppity little fellow who dared to presume and give orders. The farmer, however, thought the exhortation had a pleasant ring to it and a beat to which he could dance, and so resolved to use for himself, that very same rallying cry should the opportunity ever present itself.

They'd been flying for days now and delivering eggs. The end of the race was in sight but that damned rabbit certainly wasn't. Rudolph however, had the feeling that they were very close. His red and very shiny nose could almost smell him… Yes, they were damned close and closing. It wouldn't do to give up now, he knew. Victory was in their grasp—if hooves could be made to do so—and he could almost taste it. He was just a little hoofer, albeit a crafty one, and had his whole life ahead of him if he could bring this race off. A flying caribou with a glow-in-the-dark nose could no doubt write his own meal ticket in the world that lay ahead. All he had to do was survive the day and if that meant pulling the farmer and the others along behind him then that's just what he would do! His shining nose blazed, a beacon of light going ever before them and pointing the way like the eternal North Star. Its luminescence shone like the setting sun, illuminating the forest below which lay huddled in the blanket of oncoming night. So it was that as they passed overhead, the little caribou took note of the forlorn creature lying in a heap on the path beneath them. "Glory and trumpets!" he cried. "We're doubling back and circling in for a landing, lads!"

From his position on the wagon, Santos made known his objections. "Do you think that wise?" he cried. "We've yet to catch up with the rabbit, and this hardly seems the time to be skylarking and engaging in malarkey!"

"You just corral your caribou, fat man," replied the reindeer. "I'm the guide here, I'm the one with the nose that glows and the nose knows, so what I say, goes—and I say we're going down!"

THE CHRISTMAS RABBIT

They traced an arc in the evening sky, descending as they completed their circular roundabout. They were all, both farmer and reindeer, new at this sort of thing and as a result, their descent was more of a controlled crash than anything else. They hit the ground doing sixty. These were the best of reindeer but even the fleetest of caribou cannot run that fast. On the ground, gravity and friction hold them back and they're impeded by the relatively slow pace that their legs are forced to run. Naturally, legs that can only do forty have no business going sixty and so upon hitting the ground, went out from underneath them, causing the herd in harness to roll and tumble end over end until they landed in a tangle of traces, reins, and broken antlers. Upon landing the Winnebago hit a bump in the road, flipped over completely and sailed through the air end over end, to land with a mighty crash at the head of the tumbled and tangled reindeer. In the violence of the crash Santos was thrown completely off his buckboard, only to go sailing himself through the air and land with a terrific smash on his kiester. Picking himself up out of the wreckage, Rudolph took stock of the situation around him. "We're gonna have to work on that landing, lads," he remarked. "Too many more like that and we'll all be venison chops!" Surveying the immediate area he took note of the poor wretch in the middle of the road. Just in front of the Winnebago and lying next to Santos himself, who was occupied with trying to regain his feet, lay the forlorn form of Jack Rabbit. Rudolph threw off his traces and went prancing up to observe the little fellow. Following behind him were Donner and Blitzen. As they neared, one of the latter asked, "Is he dead?"

Thinking they meant him, the farmer spoke up. "I'm not dead, but I might as well be! Every bone in my body's got bellyaches! I'm wrenched, twisted, and bent like a spoon!"

"Not you, old ass!" replied Rudolph while pointing. "Him!"

"Who?"

"Him! By your feet. By your feet!"

Santos looked down, taking note of his old enemy. "Oh, him. Is he dead?"

"That's what we've asked you!" replied Donner. "You're closest. Can't you tell?"

"I'm a farmer—not a doctor!" Santos took note of the beatific smile, which spread itself across Jack's features. There weren't many, the farmer knew, who attained such bliss. Certainly he had never achieved such happiness and found himself to be just a bit jealous. "I think he's on dope," said the Tortoise. "No one's that happy naturally. He looks drugged and dead to the world." Resenting the peaceful state that his enemy had somehow achieved, Santos sought to end it. "Maybe we should wake him up," he said and began to shake him. "No, you fool," replied Rudolph who, bending his head, butted the silly farmer out of the way with his antlers. "If you wake him, he runs. If he runs, he wins and we all die! Screw that! Get your tired old ass on its feet and get moving! Straighten out the harness and the traces and install the spare wheel on the wagon since one of them has busted a spoke, and let's get the hell outta here before he wakes! We've just a few more deliveries and the finish line can't be but ten miles down the road. Move, fat boy—move!" Santos resented taking orders from one of the lower orders, but orders were orders—whether from high or low and as he was used to taking them anyway, whether orderly or not, did so now. Still, he voiced his objections. "But we can't just leave him here, can we?"

"Why not?"

"Well…" replied the farmer, "he might die for real, that's why!"

"And would you really care," Rudolph asked, "after having tried so hard and so often to kill him yourself? What are you becoming—a bleeding heart liberal?" Santos wasn't sure what Rudolph meant as liberalism, along with football and a whole host of other pastimes, which we've since created in order to deem ourselves civilized, had not been invented yet. Life was too tough on the frontier to indulge oneself in the active contemplation of such silly notions as liberalism and the fair and humane treatment of others. Folk back then were just learning how to be human. "Humane" and the liberalism it implied were still ages beyond their collective reach. It was hard enough, back in Olden Days, just being liberal with yourself. Still, Santos pursued his objection.

"Well, it doesn't seem fair, does it?"

THE CHRISTMAS RABBIT

"Fair?" Rudolph was beyond mere incredulity. "Life is a wilting rose drowning in the sullied and soiled seas of unfairness," he replied. "Injustice and inequity stain anything they touch—and they touch everything! Yet life goes on and un-sportsman-like conduct, foul play, and hitting below the belt are what get a fellow through it and out the other side! Better for him that he should expire here and now. If he wakes up and wins then the Witches will surely carve him to mincemeat after they're done with us. If he wakes up but loses, then those who bet on him will have his fur. Therefore let him die in his sleep. It's more humane that way." Santos saw the logic in the reindeer's words but missed the irony of an animal espousing the values of humaneness, as the concept had not been invented yet or at least realized by the bi-pedaled buffoons who at that time occupied Mungo. Still, he was uncomfortable with the idea of murder as a racing tactic. It smacked of poor sportsmanship. "Can't we just break his legs?" he asked Dixie. "He's not apt to go far then." The elf rolled his eyes. "Fool!" he replied. "What happens when he drags his cotton-tailed behind back to the finish line and reports the incident? No, better to kill him now and be done with it."

"No!" replied the consternated farmer. "I don't like it and I'll have nothing to do with it!" It was one of the few times in his life that Old Slomoe ever put the foot down, and because it was so heavy, it landed with a resounding thud. "I'm in charge here," he continued, "at least nominally. And what I say goes! What did ya drug him with anyway, and how did ya do it?"

The two elves looked at each other, faces lined with guilt, but kept one another's confidences nevertheless. "Trade secret," they jointly replied in a bare whisper.

"Say it again?"

"Trade secret!"

The elves, impatient with waiting and frustrated with Santos's sense of fair play, nevertheless agreed to let the rabbit lay where he lie, undisturbed and untouched, so that once the traces and harnesses were repaired and the new wheel installed, the farmer and his retinue of reindeer floated up and away and off to the finish line. "I hope," yelled Rudolph, leading the way and looking back over his shoulder, "that we don't all live to regret your good sportsmanship!"

The race would have ended there and then with the rabbit asleep in the road and to all intents and purposes dead, had someone else not been watching. That someone was the Shoe Lady, who sought to guarantee her proxy wager. She figured the Witches to try something like this, either directly or through one of their many stooges. She'd counted upon it like she relied upon the sun to rise each day. Events up to, and including the poisoning of the rabbit, were unfolding exactly as she'd predicted. All that remained now to ensure her wager was to wake the little fellow and let him finish the race. But not quite yet. He was too fast to be woken up too early. Let Farm Boy put a little more distance between them. She sat down upon a fallen log to contemplate the hare. *Poor little fellow*, she thought. She didn't know if it was his fate to die or not, but surely it was his destiny, as well as her own, to upset The Powers That Be and their collective apple carts! And for that, although she was likely sending him to his death by waking him, she offered up a prayer to the one god she was sure existed, that little fella might live to see tomorrow.

We've all heard the story of Sleeping Beauty. It's another one of those tales that seems to have become corrupted as it's been passed down through the ages. It often gets confused with Snow White, as they both end in a similar fashion, in that Prince Charming plants a smacker on the slumbering maiden and presumably, because she's so latently horny, awakes from that kiss to a world of bliss. That's the way we hear it told today because some sexist man, looking to further his own agenda, rewrote the tale in its current fashion. The truth is that Sleeping Beauty was not a beauty at all, just merely asleep. She was a he, and he was a rabbit. Prince Charming was, in fact, a princess, and boy, was she a beaut—being, of course, the Shoe Lady, the most beautiful princess in those parts. The only kernel of truth which stands up (although these days, it's implied rather than overtly stated) is the part about latently horny, which all rabbits—being the little sex maniacs they are—are! So it was with Jack. Thus, when Beauty bent over to plant a kiss on our sleeping prince, he was locked in a dream in which he and Nutmeg cavorted and played, rolling

THE CHRISTMAS RABBIT

amongst the wildflowers in an endless and erotic ballet. The Shoe Lady's kiss, when administered, woke him in an instant, and for that brief moment Jack was indeed blissful, until he remembered who he was, where he was headed, and what he was supposed to be doing. Then he began to shiver and tremble with worry, thinking he'd lost the race. The Shoe Lady read the distress etched upon his face. "Your race is not over yet, good sir," she said. "See! I've awakened you with a kiss, and there's still time for you to be off and about! Hurry now, and catch your enemy—win the prize and win the day!"

Jack didn't know chalk from cheese about prizes. As far as he knew, the only prize would be the price of his own skin, which he just might keep attached to his person if he were lucky enough to win this shindig. But that was prize enough for him, so stooping to kiss the Shoe Lady's hand, he thanked her profusely for coming to his aid then took up his discarded basket and sped off.

Never before or since has any rabbit run faster. Even Grasshopper on his trip to Japan had not attained such speed. Jack's feet hit the ground so hard and so often that his soles became lined with blisters and the blisters lined with bruises. Sweat ran in rivers out the pores of his skin, matting his fur and making it kinky. This was indicative of the enormity of his effort as rabbits do not normally sweat. His little heart was beating a mile a minute while tapping out a tattoo that sounded like playing cards clothes-pinned to bicycle spokes and his blood pressure was three hundred over two hundred—far beyond what would be considered healthy in a middle-aged hare, even back then. Blood tears ran from his eyes as his capillaries began to pop and spring leaks. His sweat turned to steam in the heat of his passage. His pellets normally round and hard, were a watery goo that ran a river out his anus as his insides broke down and ruptured. Just ahead was the finish line, and Santos and the reindeer were taking their time as they made their way toward it, putting one plodding foot ahead of the other while basking in the derision and boos of an unforgiving and un-sportsman-like crowd that was about to lose its collective fortune. Jack put on one last burst of speed to the cheers and encouragement of those who spied him coming round the last turn. Shouts of, "Go, boy, go!" and "Hang in there, hare, you're almost here!"

bolstered him and gave him that last little bit of strength needed to cross the finish line in a dead heat with Rudolph.

Pandemonium broke out with each side claiming victory. Loudest of all were the witches who couldn't decide whether or not to take their frustrations out on the farmer and reindeer for slowing down in order to bask in the angst of disappointed bettors, blowing what would have been certain triumph, or the bettors themselves who loudly held forth while claiming Jack the victor and demanding their winnings. The debate raged back and forth, to and fro, for half a day, with one side claiming victory and the other vehemently denying it. Accusations of race rigging and odds tampering were bandied about like bad jokes—although such slurs were directed at the elves, as no one quite had the chutzpah to level such charges against The Powers That Be. Folk wanted what they felt were their rightful winnings but no one wanted to die in order to obtain them—after all, only Ebenezer of old had ever figured out a way to take it all with him and he passed on without revealing the secret of how to do it. Folk wanted their cake but they also wanted to be left alive in order to eat it. Everyone with any interest at all in the outcome was heard from. Compromise solutions were propounded and put forward as well as offers to pay varying amounts of pennies on the dollar, only to be universally rejected by all concerned parties. Finally, peering into her rulebook, Helgayarn came upon a solution, which she felt would come closest to giving her and her sisters the victory they so desperately craved. "As big witch, head honcho, and chief judge," she stated, "I'm declaring this race a tie!" The crowd looked around in uncertain silence. What did that mean? Were all bets off? And if so were they to just go home, unfulfilled and dissatisfied, the mass victims of an ambiguous decision that neither left them with anything nor took anything away? Was this whole event then merely a waste of their collective time? Helgayarn didn't see it that way and was quick to point her reasoning out. "According to the rules," she said, "which any of you may obtain a copy of at the nearest betting booth for a dollar (a lot of cash back then as inflation was as yet an unheard of concept), in the absence of a wager placed upon race's

THE CHRISTMAS RABBIT

actual outcome, all ties go to The Powers That Be! That means we keep the money!"

A roar of protest broke out amongst the betting crowd. Demands for copies of the rules were put forward and eagerly accommodated by the trio. Besides Owl, Owl, & Peacock there were many other attorneys and shysters in the crowd who stood to lose their shirts if this rule were upheld so they pored over the legalese of the rule book while complaining to anyone who'd listen that the codicils and subparagraphs regarding the eventualities of ties and the subsequent distribution of wagers placed when such an unlooked for occurrence actually took place, were in extremely fine print and hidden so artfully among the various sub-clauses, riders, coda, and interlineations of the general rules of races themselves, as to be essentially invisible and indecipherable to the average reader.

"That's why," Helgayarn replied matter-of-factly, "we have lawyers."

This seemed to be her last word on the matter and she was eagerly anticipating her winnings when the final party was heard from.

"Wait!" cried the Shoe Lady. "The rules giving you the right to collect your winnings in the eventuality of a draw only apply if no one bet on a tie."

Helgayarn eyed her lesser cousin suspiciously. Would she really have the nerve to try and make trouble for them now when events were moving so precipitously? "What of it?" the big witch asked, affecting an air of motherly patience. Soon she would be rich, with all the manifest destiny in her pockets and the subsequent change too. She could afford to wait a few extra moments while acting this farce out to its foregone conclusion.

"A tie bet was placed."

"Eh?"

"I say," said the Shoe Lady, "that a bet on a draw was wagered. Someone bet on the tie—we have a winner!"

Helgayarn's brow grew dark like the storm that had passed days before. Lightning glinted in the depths of her eyes. Her skin mottled and turned gray. "Who dared to place such a deceitful and outlandish wager?" she asked, her voice grating like new chalk drawn across old slate. "Who had the temerity to put forward such an outrageous bet?"

The Shoe Lady indulged herself in a quiet chuckle. She had the old witch now. Ahh, the sweet taste of victory! Always in the past, the best she'd been able to manage against these three was an uneasy and indecisive draw, with neither side coming away the winner and no one able to claim an out-and-out victory. But even to come away with a stalemate against The Powers That Be was an achievement that anyone could be proud of regardless of how many giants they might have slain; yet an unqualified triumph, a no-holds-barred conquest…ah, that was a rarity so long sought after that she paused to savor its sweetness while she still held it in her hands. In order to claim such a victory she would have to share it with the crowd. That meant, in a sense, letting it go, and once she did that, it would never be completely her own ever again. So she tarried, holding her reply suspended within like the pronouncement of doom which it was, savoring its mellifluous taste, while preserving within herself, the memory of that special moment when her enemies at last fell to the devices of her cunning. "My darling daughter Faula holds the winning ticket! The purse is hers, and as she's not here to collect it, I, as her mother, will take her winnings for her!"

Helgayarn stood speechless, mumbling and shaking. It was Brunnhilde the Levelheaded who tried to prevail against the black tide rising up to inundate them. "Hold on there," she said, her voice a high-pitched whine made squeaky with nervous worry. "If Faula's not here, then how could she have placed the bet? No one, not even us, can be two places at once!"

"Yrr!"

"True," replied the whore. "But I never claimed that my darling Faula was anywhere. In fact, she's home and sick with the swine flu. Faldo, her brother, placed the wager for her and did it in my name. As her mother, I demand the right to collect her winnings!" the Shoe Lady offered the trio both her disdainful appraisal and the winning betting slip while the crowd looked on with resigned acceptance. Whatever the outcome, those gathered knew for a certainty that

THE CHRISTMAS RABBIT

it wasn't likely to go their way. *Cattails 'n' bulrushes*, thought they. *Whores and harridans—we're about to get screwed once again—and by both at the same time!* Yet all gathered hoped nevertheless that the dispute, since they were going to be on the losing end of it anyway, would go the Shoe Lady's way. Better, they thought, that she should triumph rather than The Powers That Be; for however much they regarded with distaste both the whore herself and her chosen career path, even her most vocal detractors had to admit that at least her profession was an honest one. You paid for what you got, and you got what you paid for, sometimes even more than you bargained for, and when that happened, did the purchaser really have any right to complain? It wasn't as if she were a hack or some whore available to only the highest bidder or client with the deepest pockets. Nor, was she some strumpet or floozy who lay down with the law, fornicating and carousing only with those who held power. No, the Shoe Lady's services were available to anyone, no matter what their race, religion, sexual preference, or economic status happened to be. She provided on a "pay as you go" basis and only charged for her services what the individual customer could afford. She even did pro bono work—charity fornication that lawyers, such as Owl, Owl, & Peacock deeply resented and objected to. It set a bad precedent since attorneys when they're screwing you, love to have their little paws in your pockets and seem incapable of withdrawing them. The Powers That Be were among other things, just big shot lawyers and whether or not any of the bettors saw any of their winnings, surely it would be sweet, they agreed, to see the Witches take a tumble.

"This claim will have to be investigated," stated Helgayarn matter-of-factly. She'd regained her composure somewhat and was now looking for a way to forestall the proceedings in the hope that fate, aided by delay, would somehow turn both its face and the tides of fortune toward them and stave off this unanticipated disaster.

The Shoe Lady however, knowing that one largely made their own fate, held such fortune firmly in her grasp and was not about to let go. "Very well," replied she. "Investigate to your heart's content. But do so, both officially and legally, I call for a Constitutionally Convened Cosmic Court!"

Upon hearing this, the crowd oohed and ahhed. Such a thing was unheard of. Although anyone could, in theory at least, request such a proceeding, no one but The Powers That Be actually did so, as it was the Witches' own bailiwick and who in their right mind would tempt fate by challenging them on their own turf?

Helgayarn flushed. "You can't be serious?"

"Indeed I am," replied the Shoe Lady. "I've a right to request such a proceeding, and I'm invoking my rights!"

"But it's your daughter's rights that are in question of violation. She needs to make such invocations on her own."

"Then I do so—as both her legal guardian and her representative!"

Smiling like a poisonous toad, Helgayarn replied. "If you're her legal guardian that can only mean she's underage and therefore enjoined from placing wagers due to her minority status. I therefore declare such wager to be null and—"

"No!" interrupted the Shoe Lady. The witch wasn't getting off that easy. Just who did that old hag think she was dealing with anyway? The Shoe Lady had chosen her proxy carefully, anticipating just such a response from her antagonist. "Faula's of legal age—being twelve years old now." Back in Olden Days, twelve years was considered to be the onset of adulthood and therefore "legal age" as life was so full of hardship and toil that most folk never saw twenty-one.

"I claim legal guardianship as her mother not because she's a minor but because she's incapacitated at the moment and can neither represent herself in such proceedings or present herself to claim her winnings! Will the court, regardless of a child's age, challenge a mother's right to protect her and look after her interests?"

Helgayarn scowled while silently wishing that she'd let Brunnhilde prick the whore with her poisoned pin when they had the chance. Had she done so then perhaps all of this might have been avoided. Might've been. Events had a way of unraveling for the trio like a wayward ball of twine being pushed across the floor by an insane kitten, so that one could never be too sure, she knew, which action was proper and which was not. All she could do now was try to bluff. "You don't really think you can win, do you?"

THE CHRISTMAS RABBIT

"I don't think," replied the Shoe Lady. "I know! I've won already. It's just a matter of going through the legal motions in order to ensure that the three of you don't renege on the agreement you made when you drafted up the rules for this race."

"Who will represent you?"

"That's my business. You'll know when the time comes. Just you worry about who will represent the state!"

"Very well," Helgayarn scathingly replied. "Court will convene in one month and—"

Again the Shoe Lady interrupted, "No delays! It's my daughter's right to a fair and speedy trial. We have gathered here already in order to view the race, all the Australian wallabies, koalas, joeys, and marsupials we need in order to convene immediately, another Kangaroo Court! Why wait?"

"Why, to give you time to properly prepare your case," Helgayarn gently chided. "It wouldn't be fair to put your claim on trial without the necessary time to prepare your arguments." The Shoe Lady laughed at the witch's desperation. "But I'm not the one on trial," she replied, "the state is, and I, representing my daughter, am entitled to fair and speedy jurisprudence. The law makes no provisions for such noncorporeal entities as The State." And it didn't. Back in Olden Days, even the law was a relatively new concept and being in its infancy stages, was littered with many unrecognized loopholes and inadequacies which infested it like runaway locusts in a newly planted cornfield. From the state's point of view—and at this time the state was Helgayarn, Brunnhilde, and Betty—this instance and its potential to cause scandal, since the Witches were incapable of covering the bets and never had any intention of paying out anyway, could well form the pedestal from which they might end up dangling. How could we be so stupid, they collectively thought, as to have not foreseen this? It came, they supposed, from having to define all aspects of the law, spiritual, physical, and legal. Things were bound to get confused and items overlooked as you moved from one aspect of the law to the next. The Witches decided there and then that when they got a free moment, if they ever did, they would diligently apply themselves to the separation and differentiation of the laws three aspects in order to better beat the bugs out of each. But for now they were faced with a dilemma. They looked to each other for guidance but found none. They couldn't just grandfather in a "fair and speedy" clause regarding the state in order to meet the demands of the moment. It would appear self-serving while at the same time lack the morality and eternal wisdom upon which the law was supposed to be built. Therefore they could only take care of this particular bug in the law after the fact by ensuring themselves once this fiasco was over that such a situation could never again rear its ugly head. But for now as had happened to them too often in the past, they'd just have to tough it out and muddle their way through yet another humongous pile of cattle craps.

"Very well then!" Helgayarn snapped prudishly. "May you have your fair and speedy trial, and may you choke on it!"

If anyone were going to choke, the Shoe Lady felt sure, it would likely be those three, who no doubt even now were dreaming up some plot or machination which if employed, would hopefully extract them from the sea of cattle craps they found themselves swimming in. That particular sea, however, was fathoms-deep, and because The Powers That Be had lead weights strapped to their ancient and wrinkled ankles, were sinking in it before they could even give thought to swimming.

The second trial was convened in the bole of the same hollowed-out redwood in which the first Kangaroo Court was held. It unfolded in much the same way as its predecessor, with hawkers and highwaymen trying to feed off the public while the Witches tried to control testimony and in so doing ensure that legal arguments leaned their way. But of course as was usual, Helgayarn, Brunnhilde, and Betty failed miserably. Representing the state were none other than the infamous Owl, Owl, & Peacock while the Shoe Lady elected to present her own case. There was never a doubt as to the outcome. She was beyond their collective birdcages by leagues and miles and what she lacked in legal finesse she more than made up for in outlandish and brazen courtroom theatrics. Witnesses were sworn in and testimony given. Everyone was heard from except one. In the hullabaloo surrounding the trial it seems that he was completely forgotten and

THE CHRISTMAS RABBIT

ignored, which was strange since so many of the events which led up to both the first trial and this subsequent hearing had as one of their chief participants, himself. But Jack, alone and neglected, lay at the finish line, dying in the arms of his mate, his bruised and broken body burst in a hundred places, being ruptured and torn from the exertions he'd put it through. His eyes, growing filmy with the onset of death, looked out upon their last sunrise as his life trickled away only to seep slowly into the ground where he lay. "My love," he uttered weakly, "did we win? Did we save our offspring?"

"Yes," Nutmeg replied bravely, hiding both her tears and the knowledge that despite a valiant effort on the part of her hero, he had, in fact, achieved nothing. The situation and their enslavement to it, would continue as such things always had, with his children and his children's children condemned to a future of eggs dropped along the way during a predestined and predetermined life of door-to-door delivery. "Yes! You've achieved the world!" And she wept openly and bitterly as, with her last lie, her mate died peacefully in her arms.

At the trial no mention was made of Jack's passing other than to confer upon both Peter and Cottontail the continuation of their father's sentence. Helgayarn, Brunnhilde, and Betty were too busy trying to save their own necks to bother offering up eulogies to fallen enemies no matter how well deserved. And truly, the crowd gathered in the gallery cared little or less. They were all reduced to pauperdom and being broke were interested only in the pledged assurances on the part of The Powers That Be that egg deliveries would continue on a regular and routine basis. Jack was dead and therefore of no value to anyone. It was determined by one and all that it was best if his family bury him and get on with the business at hand. Hard work and productivity, they reasoned, were the best tributes his descendants could confer upon him. Other than that, he was just another rabbit, and rabbits were like flies. There were always more of them than you needed or wanted. A crappy epitaph, no doubt—but better than no epitaph at all.

Meanwhile, realizing their fortunes were indeed lost and that with such forfeiture went the dissipation of much of their Manifest Destiny and subsequent pocket change, the Witches determined that this time the farmer and the elves too, for that matter, would pay dearly. They'd skin 'em alive and roast 'em over a slow fire. They'd grind their bones into cornmeal and make patty-cakes out of their remains. They'd hang their heads from atop the highest gibbet while hawking lungas at them when they passed. They were just about to do it too when someone buried deep within the upper tier of the gallery spoke out. Once again, it was the guardian ad litem. "But what about the children?" the guardian asked.

"Eh?" A similar question had been put forward at the last trial and its acknowledgment had landed the trio in the current mess they now found themselves. Both Brunnhilde and Betty, distraught and with worry etched upon their features, turned to their elder sister for guidance. Helly, however, was at a loss as to how to answer. It was a question that did not bear repeating. Yet it was repeated anyway.

"I say again," the ad litem reiterated, "what about the children?"

"What about them?" Helgayarn replied nervously. "They have their eggs, what more do they need? The children are no concern of ours. With our decree regarding eggs, we've already done more for them than was required. Do you want your sons and daughters to grow up spoiled?"

"Spoiled? With the loss of our fortunes our children have literally lost the clothes off their backs! Would a little charity, perpetuated to ease their suffering, spoil them so?"

The crowd had the temerity to appear indignant. "What are you suggesting?" Helgayarn asked darkly. "What do you want?" This was a bitter blow for the trio in that once again for the sake of a good appearance, they were going to be forced by circumstance to make some sort of provision regarding little whelplings for whom they cared little themselves.

"Shirts," suggested someone.

"Pants," stated another.

"Shoes," put forward a third.

And still someone else suggested toys for the children in order to idle away their hours and thereby forget for a time the misery which had been inadvertently thrust upon them. Then one supplicant with vision hit upon a brilliant idea.

THE CHRISTMAS RABBIT

"Hey," said he, "why not all three? With yuletide cakes, scones, and sweetmeats too! Presents—that's what our children need! Presents, all wrapped up in colorful packaging and sealed tight with gay ribbon! After all, eggs come festively festooned! Yes, let it be gaily colored presents so all our children will know they're both loved and appreciated!"

Helgayarn looked upon the crowd with disbelief. Had they let events get away from them again?

"Presents," she asked, her voice riddled with scorn and derision, "what makes any of you think your little bratlings deserve presents?"

"Our children deserve the best we can give 'em!"

"But it won't be you doing the giving," replied Helgayarn. "It'll be us, and we're not of a very giving nature!"

"We noticed that," someone else shouted out. "We've noticed plenty! But are you saying that you're not up to it, that there's something that needs doing that's beyond you?"

Helgayarn bridled. "Certainly not!" she replied indignantly. "Nothing is beyond our scope or purview. No task beyond our abilities!"

"Prove it!"

The Witches went into one of their all too familiar huddles as they were hoist once again upon their own petards. They discussed and conferred, planned and plotted. In the end, and since they no longer had Jack upon whom they could take out their frustrations, it was decided by the three of them to make a scapegoat out of the farmer and the elves rather than killing them outright as originally planned. To Santos was given the chore of delivering the presents that the elves would be sentenced to make; and added to that onus was the burden of banishment to the far north. To the ice lands he would go and with him his wife, the elves, and the reindeer—never to return except to make their required deliveries.

At first, those gathered to hear the sentence pissed, moaned, and complained, having none too little faith in the farmer and his dubious abilities. But since the Witches said it was so then it was such and all of their pissing, moaning, and whining would do very little to change the matter. They did, however, take some small comfort in knowing that even if the proposition went belly-up, as it most likely would with nary a single squib or sweetmeat being delivered, at least they'd be rid of the silly farmer and his retinue.

This final sentence marked the beginning of the downfall of The Powers That Be—although there'd be greater landslides still to come. Yet from that moment on, they've been fading away into obscurity on down to this very day. Nevertheless, if one is unlucky enough, one can still run afoul of them, and therefore I'm always careful and forever watching my back!

After the trial, the Shoe Lady, now fabulously wealthy, settled down into retirement, forgetting her own axiom, "If you don't slow down, then you'll never grow old." She did both and ultimately faded away herself although how, where, and when, I couldn't say. Her children, however, carried on after her, becoming male and female prostitutes all, and darling Faula, the Shoe Lady's daughter by that deceitful Dawe who'd had an affair with her while his wife was pregnant with Junior, even moved to New York where she met Laddie and, through love, became the vessel by which he passed on the Santos line while taking her name in order to remain hidden.

But Jack Rabbit's days were over, and indeed he would deliver no more eggs. His children, however, and his children's children and their offspring as well on down to the present day would continue running...

BOOK 4
Nowadays

CHAPTER I
A Witch Looks Back

Somewhere, lost to the vagaries of time and indifference, alone and forlorn while residing deep within the wastelands of the southwestern desert of North America, resided that trinity of terror, The Powers That Be. Their little corner of the world was named, by those brave adventures who dared trespass, Witch Valley. But since none of those hardy souls have ever come out alive and since the only one who had was Sand Toes of the Apaches, and since no one trusted him, the rest of us just refer to it as *out there*, and these days nobody knows what it's called. Even the Apaches have no name for it. However, the Witches had taken up residence in their new digs long before the Apaches got there and simply called it home.

When Helgayarn, Brunnhilde, and Betty first fled to the valley, it and the surrounding area were a garden paradise rich in fruit trees growing wild upon its plains, atop its hills, and throughout its dales. Grapevines flourished, rising from the fertile earth as they twisted their way upward in serpentine fashion, wrapping themselves around those very same fruit trees that grew alongside them, sharing the wealth of nutrients the rich soil offered up to both. Shade trees, such as elm and oak, blanketed the lowlands while conifer and other pines took root in the high mountain passes. The grass grew greenish and thick upon the plains and the herds of grazers frequenting it took delight in the bounty to be found and foraged. Wildflowers, in an orgy of both color and shape, rioted with abandon amid the grasses, springing up in their season like carefree jack-in-the boxes to splay the rich greenery in an overlay of blues and pinks, purples and yellows, reds and golds. The land was well watered, with rivulets chuckling merrily along their courses throughout its length and breadth, providing sweet water to both the plant and animal alike. Rains fell gently, the wind blew softly, and the sun in moderation, tenderly massaged the surrounding landscape with its nurturing and life-giving streamers of light.

Life was grand in those days and the four-legged folk within the valley strove hard—within the bounds of their own individual proclivities and eating habits, of course, to get along with one another and to live and let live. Birds sang gaily, crickets chirped merrily, and even snakes and other reptiles were generally predisposed to feelings of good fellowship and congenial coexistence.

All that changed, however, when Helgayarn, Brunnhilde, and Betty moved in. They hadn't appreciated at all being chased out of their home territory and by someone they'd considered an upstart at that, so when they arrived upon the southwestern plains of North America, were already in a sour mood and not disposed to meet the new neighbors. Upon viewing the harmony around them, the Witches moods descended from sour down through the ultimate depths of dour, until their dispositions settled and came to a comfortable rest within the confines of downright ugly and offensive, which was where they felt at home anyway. "This won't do at all!" Helgayarn sniffed disdainfully as she took note of her new surroundings. "It's too wholesome for my tastes! Look at all the greenery—ugh!"

"I'm totally in agreement with you, sister," replied Brunnhilde. "We'll have to do something about it!"

"Yah!" said Betty, whose lips had finally healed.

"What to do?" Helgayarn asked herself while surveying the immediate landscape. "What to do indeed!" She turned to her sisters. "Suggestions? Opinions?"

"Let's just whip up some Tidal Wave Tea," replied Brunnhilde, "and cook us a pot of Quaker Oats. We can give this ghastly place a quick makeover before anyone here even knows what's coming!"

"Yah!"

Helgayarn allowed herself an affectionate smile. It took a lot of effort, but she managed, because it was Brunnhilde, and Helgayarn had to admit that despite her many not-so-inconsiderable faults, the old girl did try hard. "That's an idea certainly worthy of consideration," she replied in a conciliatory tone, "but perhaps if we applied ourselves and really gave it some thought, we might perchance come up with something even better!" Out there in the wastelands, they had nothing but time to kill, so Brunnhilde and Betty reluctantly agreed.

They finally hit upon a recipe so horrible, so thoroughly hideous and appallingly awful, that to this day it remains unnamed and can be best described as a sort of malignant molasses, which incorporated within in it only the worst elements of Snowstorm Soup, Hurricane in Bottle, Quaker Oats, Tidal Wave Tea, Ice Cream, and various other plagues, pestilences, calamities, scourges, murrains, and epizootics that the Witches could throw in the mason jar. The mixture rumbled darkly within as Helgayarn secured the lid, taking extra care to ensure that it was screwed on tight. They let it sit for a century or two as the stuff took a while to ferment. As it lay trapped, confined within its glass prison and souring within its own spumescence, it caused the frame of their Winnebago to shiver and tremble in time to its disquieting pulsation. It could be seen breathing ominously while still inside the jar, anticipating its ultimate release. But that wouldn't be for some time yet. The Witches set it to the side in a far corner of the Winnebago, knowing that a watched pot never boils. Then they took up their walking sticks and went about exploring the new country to which they'd fled. During their travels they did their best to disguise their true natures, making friends with one and all and offering advice to those four-legged folk stupid enough to ask their opinion. Only sand-chiggers and other such vermin were smart enough to give the trio a wide berth as one scorpion can always recognize another.

Finally, the day of dread dawned when it came time to unleash the monster that for years lay dormant and waiting. It had been feeding upon itself and growing for decades upon decades until it reached critical mass and stood ready to burst from within the confines of its glass prison. Helgayarn and her sisters took the jar of poison out to the middle of the verdant plain, walking carefully and stepping cautiously as they did. It would do no good, they knew, to drop the damn thing now while they were still within its proximity. Hurricane Junior was an April shower compared to the tempestuous rage they were about to unleash. They carefully set the jar down on its base and backed away slowly, keeping their eyes fixed upon the unwholesome magma as they did. Even caged, such a temperamental tea was not to be trusted and certainly not to be toyed nor trifled with indiscriminately. Casual attitudes, they knew, put forward when handling such combustible concoctions were the cause of many a lost limb and digit, and The Powers That Be preferred keeping theirs attached to their persons.

When the pressure became too great and the lid of the jar finally ruptured, the malignant molasses came pouring out in a sick syrupy soup, dispersing itself slowly and inexorably over the land and choking all the trees and flowers as it spread. Mountains toppled, rivers ran dry, and the landscape cried in agony as it writhed in its death throes, until at last over the course of many decades, the land lay desolate—a dismal collection of death valleys, sand heaps, and sterilized wastes, where in time only the hardiest of cacti and tumbleweeds would take root. Where only the toughest of toads and the most resilient of reptiles would even dare attempt to eke out an existence. Over the millennia yet to be it would form itself into a barren wasteland that only Sand Toes of the Apaches would ever feel at home in. "Now this is more like it!" said Helgayarn with a measure of satisfaction. "Finally we have a hectare or two that's so inhospitable, so thoroughly devoid of life that perhaps at long last we'll find for ourselves some peace, some rest and relief from the irksome trials brought about by inane and incompetent farmers and pesky and perturbing rabbits!"

"Hear Hare to that!" replied Brunnhilde.

"Yah!"

And so it came to be that The Powers That Be settled down in the desert to a life of quiet semiretirement, keeping largely to themselves while letting the planet go to hell in its own hand basket. After all, they'd tried in ages past to steer an ungrateful world in a direction it refused to go while enduring as they did its endless whining and grumbling as it gave voice to its umbrage and overall dissatisfaction

THE CHRISTMAS RABBIT

at having to be tutored and instructed by those who knew better than itself.

Well, to hell with it, thought Helly. *Let the world suffer the indignities of wayward farmers and smart-assed rabbits—and may it choke upon its own desires while doing so!*

Now here in the southwestern desert, ensconced within her cave which lay dead in the center of Witch Valley, as she sat contemplating these matters, Helgayarn's mind turned inward, taking her back along memory's twisted and tortured trail, forcing her to review the events which led up to this desolate existence while she waited out the slow passage of years for just the right moment to at last enact her final revenge.

*****

As related earlier, the Witches' downfall began with the culmination of the Great Race. Despite their best efforts to the contrary, Jack Rabbit when he died, was martyred, while Santos, banished to the Northlands and sentenced to deliver presents, achieved unlooked-for and unanticipated success in the pursuit of his unwanted endeavor. With the aid of both magical elves and reindeer, he set off upon an annual yuletide quest. The elves had built for him a magical sleigh with a bottomless hole, which enabled him to carry all the presents at once, and the speed of his caribou allowed him to complete his deliveries in single evening. For a long time his fame and popularity grew as every child everywhere, along with their annual allotment of ova, could now look forward as well to the routine and yearly delivery of brightly wrapped gifts.

In an effort to stay out of each other's way and reduce the lingering tensions of past animosities, it was agreed upon by all that each party would render their gifts at a certain time of the year, enabling one party to prepare their presents while the other was engaged in the act of delivery. Because Santos was banished to the cold lands, it was determined in subsequent negotiations that he would restrict his deliveries to the height of winter while the rabbits would schedule their deliveries at the onset of spring. Thus they avoided crossover conferrals while staying out of each other's way and, in addition, confined their combined deliveries to both separate and seasonally opposed times of the year so that little kiddies didn't get all their gifts at once, which had that happened, might've led to a lack of appreciation on their parts for one gift over another. The mutually agreed upon plan seemed to be working well, at least in theory. But as that venerable rabbit of days gone by, Flopsy Doodle, had predicted, the human population was growing and would soon reach a threshold level where even with the magical aid of elves and reindeer, routine and annual deliveries that reached and accounted for everyone would soon become an endeavor which became impossible to complete. And of course, Jack's rabbits had nothing but their ingenuity and the strength of their own legs to aid them in their particular sentence. Helgayarn Brunnhilde, and Betty were of a mind to let matters play out—it would serve all the recipients right they knew, and their parents too, if the farmer, the rabbits, and those who'd come to venerate them and their efforts were forced to eat a little humble pie in the face of their deliverers' preordained failures. But further reflection upon their parts determined for the trio that although such humble pie would be the result of the recipients' own baking, they nevertheless would bear the blame, as the architects of this scheme, for its ultimate failure. Their stars had already taken a meteoric nosedive, and they were of no mind to see their reputations sink further into the seas of neglectful indifference. What was needed, they knew, was a measuring bar of sorts that would separate the deserving from the undeserving and thereby reduce the number of potential recipients to a more manageable level. They came up with what they thought was both a unique and viable plan. They would amend the two sentences of their respective indentured servants so as to limit their deliveries to the deserving only. This left much to interpretation, they felt, and had the benefit of killing two birds with a single stone. First, it would make their ward's sentences more manageable and more readily accomplishable. Second and more importantly, it would sow the seeds of division amongst the recipients and their parents that such classifications as 'deserving' and 'undeserving' inevitably give rise to. No one likes to be told they're of lesser value than someone else or that the someone to whom they're being compared is cut from finer cloth or formed of purer clay. We all like to think—although it certainly isn't true—that we're all at least as good as the next guy, if not better, and this illusion we propagate about ourselves goes doubly so for our children. All of us are not created equal. Some are stronger, some less so. Some are wiser, and some never find wisdom no matter how much time and energy they spend looking for it. Some are kinder and more generous while many spend their lives hoarding their gifts. So if we're not all created equal then it stands to reason that the same holds true for our children, born with the same imperfections, who never seem to learn from our bad examples—and this was as true back then as it is today. To this end therefore, the Witches gave the farmer a crystal ball in which to view his recipients throughout the course of the year while his elves were busy making presents, so that he might determine on his own who was good and who was not. This would keep him occupied, they felt, since he had nothing to do up there but lie around in the snow while his underlings busied themselves with the tasks of manufacturing and wrapping. To Peter and Cottontail and all who followed after, they gave nothing, instructing them instead to make their evaluations while en route. But their amendments to their ward's sentences proved to be a complete failure. It's true that seeds of resentment were indeed sown, but the divisions the trio hoped to formulate never materialized, for after many years of trial and error, no more than three worthy recipients could be found upon the entire planet, and invariably they were never at home when the time came to deliver gifts. In their umbrage, the parents of those deemed unworthy banded together, each commiserating with the other that as individuals went, their children were being judged by too fine a scale and therefore were being unfairly denied their rightful due. The stockpiles of both eggs and presents began to overflow out of their bins and containers, littering the landscapes where they were stored while the parents, unable to admit to themselves either their own deficiencies or those of their children, in an ongoing effort to mask these faults, began buying presents of their own and decorating their own eggs, stashing them under trees and behind chairs, all the while perpetuating to their children the lie that they'd in fact been distributed by the famous farmer and the renowned band of rabbits. It was one of Cottontail's sons, a certain rabbit named Hopalong Cassidy, to whom fell the duty one spring of egg delivery and who was as well that infamous rabbit who elected to render unto the recipients on his roles, shad roe, which were technically eggs, who finally summoned up the courage to confront The Powers That Be with the deficiencies in their amendments. Having spent a month beforehand scouring the shoreline for castaway roe which an indifferent surf tossed carelessly upon it, having wrestled and fought many battles with various gulls and terns—birds of a feather whom it seemed had no trouble with, nor felt any guilt about, devouring someone else's eggs despite any losses in ova they themselves might have incurred—finally gathered up his treasures and began the journey to make his deliveries. As he roamed from one locale to another, evaluating the merits and worthiness of this recipient versus another and crossing each off the roles, the hot sun beat down upon not only him but the shad roe in his basket. They began to reek while thousands of flies, sensing in the roe's deterioration the malodorous magnificence of a potential proving ground in which to lay their own eggs, began swarming about both the basket and Hopalong himself, covering each in fly doo-doo while depositing their ova for pupation. Despite a valiant effort on his part, Hopalong Cassidy could not find but two recipients who, under the Witches' new guidelines, were deemed worthy enough to receive his eggs, which had by then grown so putrid and flyblown as to be unworthy of delivery anyway.

Screw this, thought Hopalong!

There was nothing in the ongoing sentence that required him to bear up under the burden of being festered with fly feces! He abandoned his efforts and instead sought out The Powers That Be to render unto them that which he held to be a legitimate complaint. At first Helgayarn, Brunnhilde, and Betty were of a mind to ignore Hopalong's plight and send him on his way but they could see from his defiant attitude that the rabbit was not going to go quietly without receiving some form of redress and in his current state the little lagomorph reminded the trio so much of Santos and his historic befouling that they determined then and there that they wanted as

THE CHRISTMAS RABBIT

little to do with Hopalong as was possible, and so handing him a gallon of Janitor In A Drum, instructed him to remove his person to the shores of the river and with cleanser and river water, busy himself with the chore of sterilization.

"And have a care for that waterway!" yelled Helly to his retreating form. "Don't be an idiot like the farmer and foul it up!" They then sent out such messages as could be contrived, both to Santos and to Jack's rabbits, amending their previous amendment and returning the status quo to stat. Another means of control, it seemed, would have to be contrived.

*****

Long after Olden Days but many moons ago nevertheless, while the Witches still resided in Mesopotamia and the population continued grow, inching ever closer to threshold level, The Powers That Be stumbled across another stratagem that they deemed worthy of use in their ongoing effort to control an untenable situation. They did not at first see it as such, but so intrigued were they by the relating of a tale told to them that they deemed it worthy to keep a further eye on the story's protagonist in order to better determine if such a personage could be brought under their control and made to be useful. It happened thus:

One day, while stewing some storms and quaking some oats, there happened upon them a group of magi returning eastward to their homes from a journey they'd made west while following the traces of a brilliant and unusual star they'd seen tracking across the heavens. The Witches had laid out before them their various mixing bowls and beakers in which were brewing the beginnings of Tidal Wave Tea, Snowstorm Soup, Quaker Oats, Ice Cream, and the like. The magi, along with their retinue of retainers, servants, and camels, came up and asked them if they might dip from their well in order to refresh themselves and their mounts before continuing on their journey. At first Helgayarn was of a mind to send them away. But she could see with her own eyes that there were glorious beams brighter than any fruit lights she'd ever been able to conjure up, shining from their faces, and therefore determined that such an occurrence as that which presented itself bore further investigation. "Help yourself," she grudgingly replied. "Water is fifty drachmas a cup—payable up front! And have a care for those camels—don't get any cattle craps in our water!" The magus looked about apprehensively. Fifty drachmas a cup! It wasn't that they didn't have the money—they were all moneyed men, but still the price seemed inordinately high—especially given that water, which flowed freely, was accounted by all to belong to creation itself. But they were far from their homes, and who knew when they'd happen upon the next spring? The eldest, whom we'll call Gaspar, replied to her demand for payment. "Water flows freely from nature," he said, "and as such is a gift from the Most High, to charge for it, especially excessively, is a sin against God himself."

Helgayarn offered the magus a scowl. "Oh, don't go mentioning him!" she replied disdainfully. "You won't find him strutting about in these parts! I'm the most high around here and I say fifty drachmas!"

Gaspar looked down at her from atop his camel. "Surely a compromise can be reached," he reasoned. "Would you not settle for twenty-five drachmas instead? After all, a bird in hand is worth more than two in the bush!"

Again Helgayarn scowled while waving her arms about her. "Do you see any bushes here?" she replied. "No! And no birds either! Fifty drachmas or good riddance to the lot of you! You're wasting our time!"

The second magus, a man of middle years whom we'll call Melchior, chose at that moment to speak up. "How about a group rate?" said he. "Twenty-five drachmas to water not only ourselves but our camels and servants too, and in return we'll impart to you a tale whose telling will enrich your lives!"

"It would have to be a saga of some import," replied Helgayarn. "Our lives are pretty rich already!"

The third magus, a young man whom we'll call Balthasar, chose that moment to lend his voice to the ongoing debate. "None live," he said, "who are so rich that they wouldn't benefit from hearing the tale we have to tell."

THE CHRISTMAS RABBIT

"Don't bet on it, bub!" said Brunnhilde while her elder sister looked on approvingly. "We're The Powers That Be! We've riches galore for the spending!" It was a lie, of course. They'd lost everything on the Great Race and were still well on the road to financial recovery. "We're up to our armpits in drachmas, dinars, dirhams, and dollars! We've got hoards of minas, talents, and shekels up our sleeves and stowed away in our piggy banks too! So believe you me, we're rich beyond measure."

"The wealth we would confer," replied Balthasar, "cannot be measured in talents and drachmas. Nor can it be evaluated by weighing it against dinars and dirhams. Slews of shekels and tons of talents will not buy for you, the riches we offer, for we would bestow upon you that most priceless of gifts, wisdom!"

Helgayarn looked at him darkly while preparing to strike him down for his effrontery. The cheek of this camel jockey to speak to them of wisdom! Were they not The Powers That Be? Who else in all the world could lay claim to such insight as they? She began to gather the forces and make the mojo, but that light shining from the three magi's faces gave her pause. There was something very mysterious and otherworldly about these three. They carried themselves as though in possession of a gift from heaven and, owning such, presented no fear when facing them. The magi gave the impression that possessing such a gift, whatever it was, made them not only their equals but their superiors! What nerve! *Well,* she reasoned, *I can always kill 'em later after I've discovered for myself this great secret of theirs.*

"Very well," she reluctantly replied. "We'll agree to your terms if, and only if, the set price is fifty drachmas for the lot of you—and only if upon hearing your tale, we deem it worth the price of our water, agreed?"

"Fifty drachmas," said Melchior, "boy, you and old Ebenezer!"

"My hero," Helgayarn replied sardonically. "Have we got a deal?"

The three wise guys, of a mind anyway to spread their Gospel for free, agreed to the terms.

"Good," replied Helgayarn. "Money first, tales second, water last."

"Would you prefer payment in gold, frankincense, or myrrh?" asked Melchior. "We have all three."

"Better make it gold," stated Helgayarn. Perfumes abhor us!" The wise guys measured out the appropriate amount of metamict substance and were about to begin the relating of their tale when Helgayarn gestured them to an unanticipated hush. "Before you tell us your tale," she admonished, "we'd better hear first a brief history of your life so that we can better evaluate for ourselves who you are and where you come from and therefore more accurately judge the veracity of your yarn. Who are you three anyway? What are your names, eh, and who's that fellow over there seeing to the camels?" She pointed at a lone man sitting amongst the trio's baggage who appeared, at least on the surface, to be the wisest of them all—at least he knew well enough anyway to keep his mouth shut when in the presence of his betters!

"That's a tale long in telling," replied Balthasar. "Our camels, as well as ourselves, could die of thirst before its entirety was related to you. Perhaps we should stick to the point."

"Perhaps you should do as you're told!" countered Helgayarn. "But do feel free, of course, to sketch us a synopsis—so long as you answer our questions—abridging where you will in order to shorten the length of your recital. We understand well enough that you and your camels are thirsty!"

Gaspar looked to Balthasar, who in turn looked to Melchior, who in turn looked back at them both. Each displayed upon his countenance a look of long-suffering and foreboding tension. As a rule, wise guys and magi did not allow themselves to be so easily pushed around. Both Solomon and Socrates, they knew, would have volumes to say about the way in which they'd allowed themselves to be manipulated. But they reasoned that such manipulation had been allowed to occur for the greater good of spreading their newly discovered truth.

"Well," the eldest of the three began, "we come from a ways east of here. My name is Gaspar, but being a man of some fame and renown, I'm also known in certain circles as Hor and Kagpa. Traveling with me here is Melchior, who's also referred to within these same circles as Karsudan or Badadakharida. And with us, of course, is this wise young man named Balthasar, also known as Basanater and Badadilma. About two years ago—"

"Wait a minute," Helgayarn interrupted. "You're getting ahead of yourself. What about that fourth guy over there—the one amongst the camels—who's he, eh?"

Both Gaspar and Melchior looked uncomfortable at the mention of their unnamed traveling companion, and neither was forthcoming or quick to reveal his identity.

Eager to insert himself once again into the conversation, Balthasar took their silence as an opportunity to speak up. "That's Lui Shang," he said, "a wise guy from the far orient."

Helgayarn rendered a quick appraisal of the lone camel jockey and then returned her dubious gaze to Balthasar.

"He doesn't look at all Chinese," she remarked doubtfully. "His features are rather Euro-Slavic. What's the truth here?"

"His mother," replied Balthasar in spite of his companions shooing gestures, "married a great round eye who was nevertheless named Frederick, the Marginal, who fathered him upon her. Thus Lui Shang is known in most circles as Frederick the Marginal, the II. It's an onerous appellative to be saddled with as you spend your days walking the earth—especially if you're deemed a wise guy like us, so he simply refers to himself as Fred, and he's the wisest of us all. At least he has the good sense to stay out of the public eye while at the same time avoiding useless conversation. Therefore he rarely gets mentioned!"

"Indeed," replied Helgayarn scornfully. "Continue."

Gaspar offered his younger traveling companion a scowl before resuming his tale. "As I started to say," he furthered, "about two years ago, while attending to our own knitting, we chanced to look up and saw in the sky a bright and luminous star shining high in the heavens which had never been there before. And unlike other stars, which seem to hang motionless in space, this one moved steadily westward, as if it were seeking someone or something out. Being all of us, amateur astronomers and astrologers, we knew this to be unusual and decided to follow the star to see where it led. Our journey took almost two years to complete and we soon ran out of funds—we hadn't prepared ourselves for quite so long a trek! But we made a living and a damned good one too, by telling fortunes along the way, interpreting the heavens, and performing tricks with cards and dice. Finally we ended up in Bethlehem, a suburb of Jerusalem, in the country of Judea where—"

Again Helgayarn interrupted. "Judea," she asked, "where's that, eh?"

Gaspar had the good graces to not look overly perturbed at her many interruptions. "A ways west of here," he replied. "In the land of Palestine."

"Oh, you mean Canaan," said Helgayarn, preferring the country's older name.

"Whatever," replied Gaspar as he fought the manly fight to maintain patience. "In Jerusalem, within the suburb of Bethlehem, we came upon a simple hut with a newly married couple who had born to them, the Son of the Most High!"

Most High? What was this ridiculousness? She was the most high and she hadn't borne any children in ages! How could anyone lay claim to such conceit? Moreover, how could anyone else be so foolish as to propound it?

"The mother," Gaspar continued, "is both meek and mild. The stepfather is a man both forthright and honest—but the Son! There's a lad the world will take note of! Only two years old when we happened upon him and already filled with the wisdom of the ages! Surely he'll be a king someday—the King of Kings! He'll rule forever, I tell you, both the earth itself and the very heavens above it. Meek and mild like his mother, he's his father's son nevertheless! He is, I tell you, the very Son of God!"

Helgayarn would have laughed at such an outlandish tale but for the light emanating from the wise guy's face. That light did not spring up of its own accord. Something, or more likely someone, was responsible for it. But God's own Son? She had her doubts, both in the Son and in God himself, who if he'd existed at all, hadn't put in an appearance for ages. But still, there was that light shining out from the wise guy's faces. If one were not a Power That Be like she, one

THE CHRISTMAS RABBIT

would almost describe such an effervescent glow as '*holy.*' Bah! Still Helgayarn knew that anyone capable of making such an impression at such an early age could well grow into someone who would have be contended with on down the road. She decided therefore not to waste her energies on killing the magi but instead took their money, gave them their water, and sent them on their way packing.

As the wise guys, along with their baggage man, faded away into the eastern distance, Helgayarn turned her gaze to her sisters. "Well," she asked, "what did you make of all that malarkey? You think there's any truth to it?"

Brunnhilde and Betty shrugged. "Who knows?" replied Brunnhilde. One can't simply take the word of three wise guys. Perhaps we should investigate."

"Yah!" agreed Betty, unaware of what she'd just consented to.

"Yes," said Helgayarn. "I think that for our own sakes, we should. We don't need any pretenders coming along with the intention of usurping our positions!" It was decided by two of them—much to the third's objections, of course—to send Betty to the land of Canaan to see for herself what the brouhaha was all about. Helgayarn chose Betty over Brunnhilde because of her monosyllabic impairment. It was thought by the big witch that being limited to one word, the little witch would not be capable of giving away too much. Helgayarn packed her a lunch before setting her on her way with this final admonition. "This is a fact finding mission only," she said. "Make your way to this Jerusalem unobserved, blend in and see for yourself what this little truant is all about. Record what you see in that silly journal of yours, and come back here to give us a report. If, however, even half of what those wise guys said proves to be even one-third of the truth, then kill him. Do you understand?" Betty nodded her reluctant agreement while looking forward to the far-flung day when she would be the Big Witch. Then she'd give the orders and others would do the marching!

"And walk there," cried Helgayarn to her retreating form, "don't whisk up a whirlwind and fly! This'll give you more time to better prepare yourself while thinking about the best means of approach!"

Betty set out for Palestine from Mesopotamia early one Sunday morning. By the following Wednesday she got so lost within the endless tracts of the Arabian Desert that she ended up completely turned around and heading east instead of west. This error in navigation produced a thirty-year delay in her arrival as she had to circumnavigate the globe before finding her way to the little town of Bethlehem. It was a long walk, and she was both footsore and world-weary upon completing it. She arrived in Bethlehem only to find that the young truant had grown into a man and had moved to Nazareth, which lay some eighty miles to the north as the crow flew. Betty was sorely put out and her feet were already barking like rabid dogs, but she had her marching orders and what was another eighty miles when she'd already circled the globe to get here? So she started out, thinking that this, the last leg of her journey, would prove to be an easy one. But she was wrong on both counts. It was neither her last leg nor easy. The territory itself attested to its difficulty to traverse, as she had to wend her way through the valleys and passes that made up the meandering route through the foothills and mountains that littered the lands of Jericho, Arimathea, and Samaria. Eighty miles became two hundred as along with indirect routing, she managed to get lost more than once while traveling through unfamiliar territory. When she crested a mountain summit, she froze in the chill air. When she wandered through the lower valleys and passes, the Judean sun beat down upon her like a sledgehammer, baking her like sour apple pie. She tried to gather the forces and make the mumbo jumbo in order to summon up a rain cloud, but for some mysterious reason, she was powerless in this strange land and unable to impose her will upon it. Some other presence, which she could barely sense, seemed to hover over the land itself, inhabiting it and stifling any attempts by outsiders to impose a will upon it other than its own. Betty's dimly perceived awareness of this mysterious presence was disconcerting. It went beyond disconcerting; it was downright eerie bordering on creepy. Never before had she experienced such a sense of insignificance while in the presence of something so barely defined yet so seemingly omnipotent. In her anxiety she flitted from rock to rock, stepping quietly and keeping to the shadows where she

THE CHRISTMAS RABBIT

could. Finally, she arrived in Nazareth hot, dusty, and all but done in. After making certain inquiries, she ascertained the location of the young man's home but upon arrival discovered that he was out of town yet again and could be presently found partying at a wedding feast in Cana. *My word*, she thought, *doesn't this guy ever stay in one place?* Cana was a pretty good hike from Nazareth, and both of Betty's footsore feet objected strenuously to the further toil about to be imposed upon them but she was a witch who had her marching orders, so off to Cana she marched—a trek of another ten-mile crow flight which, upon her legs, stretched itself into twenty. She arrived thoroughly spent, only to find the wedding reception in full swing. People were dancing, songs were being sung, and there was merriment being made all over. However the reception was by invitation only, and being a witch, she wasn't on the guest list. She therefore limited her appraisal of this young wannabe from the fringes of the party where along with many other uninvited guests, she was allowed to sit and observe the goings on from the other side of the barriers which had been erected in order to separate the Who's Whos of Jewry from Who's Nots. Still the outsiders looking in were richly provided for, as the families of both the bride and groom ensured to it that the foodstuffs which they and the wedding party were enjoying were distributed as well among the uninvited crowd. There were sweetmeats and trays of olives passed among those gathered on the far side of the barrier. They shared as well, in the racks of lamb and the loaves and fishes, while the wine—not the best quality, mind you—flowed liberally among them. In order to be polite and not draw attention to herself, Betty sampled a little of each. None were particularly to her liking; what she really craved was a good pork chop or a spare rib, but there would be none of those here! And the wine, being somewhat thin, tasted more like water than anything else.

From the fringes of the crowd where she looked in on the party while sampling her loaves and fishes and washing each down with her watered-down wine, it became readily apparent to Betty just who the target of her observation was. He sat, with his mother presumably, enjoying the feast—but doing so with a measure of restraint while all about him other guests were drinking and partying to beat the brass band. Once he looked past the crowd gathered inside to those gathered without, and it was clear from the look in his eyes where his sympathies lie.

How foolish, thought Betty, to be filled with empathy for the have-not's!

It was always better to align oneself with winners than to choose up sides with the losers.

Well, he'd learn the hard way, she reasoned.

His eyes fell upon her, and a knowing grin displayed itself briefly across his handsome features. It was a benign smile that seemed to incorporate within it a look of sympathy more than anything else. How dare he be sympathetic of her! She was Betty, a Power That Be!

She had just about had her fill of this young man, determining for herself that she'd seen all she needed to and that the lad didn't amount to a pot full of beans, when a cry went out from the hosts of the party that they'd inadvertently run out of wine. Of food there remained plenty, for being a wedding reception the invited guests had been doing more drinking than eating. One of the hosts approached the young man's mother, spoke quietly in her ear, and she then turned to her son. Betty, a good listener of long-standing, pricked up her ears in order to take note of their conversation. "The wine's run out," said his mother. "Please do something about it!" The young man looked at her patiently. "I can't help that now," he replied. "It isn't my time yet to perform miracles." The mother chose to ignore his objections and, calling the servants to her, instructed them to do whatever her son asked of them. The son looked at her and lovingly sighed. "Very well," he replied. "For you, Mother, because I love you." He noticed off to the side of the festivities a number of empty water pots, capable of holding about thirty gallons of water each. "Fill them with water, and bring them to me," he said. The servants did as instructed. He placed his hands upon the casks and, looking upward, called out for his father's blessing. *His father? Why would he do that?* wondered Betty. His father, a carpenter by trade, was back in Nazareth, Betty knew, putting the final touches on a roof he'd been hired to repair. Old Joe was miles away from Cana and unable to hear his son's pleas no matter how loudly voiced. And even if he were capable of hearing

THE CHRISTMAS RABBIT

such odd requests put forward from such lengthy distances, did this young man really think his father could do anything to grant them? Carpenters worked with wood, not grapes. They were carvers, not vintners. And even if carpenters were capable of both, no carpenter could turn water into wine!

After reciting his benediction, the young man instructed the servants to take a cupful of the water to the master of ceremonies that he might taste it. The leader of toasts sampled the offered cup and upon doing so called the bridegroom over to congratulate him on his forethought in saving the best for last. "Usually," replied the toastmaster, "a fellow in your position lets flow the good stuff early while there's still some level of discernment about our wits! Then later when we're all *faced* and nobody cares, let's flow the Boones Farm and the Manischewitz! But you, my friend, have done exactly the opposite, and may the God of our fathers bless you for it!" Betty was doubtful as she listened in on this malarkey while the new wine, being passed from one reveler to another, was continually praised by all who sampled. Water into wine—how foolish! Obviously the lot were already as drunk as was good for them and the young man had merely taken advantage of their inebriation in order to perform some sort of mass hypnosis. A flimflammery of the first magnitude and although plainly a trick of some sort, Betty had to admit that as stunts went, this one was a doozy. But then the wine passed her way and for the sake of politeness, she sampled it. It was both red and delicious. It tasted of grapes and wild berries, and it had a kick that although potent and heady was not the least bit intoxicating. Instead, it invigorated and refreshed! It went to the head, clearing it of inebriation while providing warmth to the body and restoring the vigor lost in a wild night's worth of partying. Those gathered on both sides of the barrier found new energy in its imbibing and a cleansing of the spirit that brought with it the desire to dance until dawn— and indeed, those gathered Hora'd, Yeminited, Ha'eer Beafared, and Na'Ale Na' Aled until well after the sun came up. As Betty looked up from her cup she took note of the young man vigorously dancing with a group of his friends who deferred to him as if they were disciples. He paused briefly his dance of the Ha'eer Beafar and offered her again that benign and sympathetic smile. Unable to help herself, Betty returned it and then fled. She had much to think about regarding this young man. Wine which tasted like water and water like wine? How were such things possible?

From then on, and for about a year afterward, Betty followed the young rabbi as he went from place to place and town to town, preaching sermons and delivering his message of love and forgiveness while comforting the hopeless and healing their ills as if by miracle. She watched carefully for his sleight of hand but could find no trace of it—and being a witch she knew what to look for. Of his message, Betty had not the tender or contrite heart to understand or agree with it. There was much he was saying about the blessings of the meek and the poor. *C'mon now*! The downtrodden and disenfranchised. He spoke often about an eternal life, following after the confines of this one if his listeners would but believe in him and his message. He taught them lessons in metaphor, speaking often of grapevines, olive branches, and seeds sown in both good soil and bad. How Betty wished he would speak in plainer language that she might better understand what he was trying to say! But the man himself—there was no denying him! He fed thousands with a couple of dead fish and a few loaves of bread. He healed the sick—both those sick in themselves and those sick of each other. He made the deaf hear and the blind see. Those who'd been crippled for life were given the ability to walk. Those mute suddenly found that they could sing like sparrows! The winds and waves seemed to obey his commands. Betty herself had seen him walk on water and once even raise the dead—a stunt she and her sisters had been trying to pull off for eons without success! *Who is this guy?* she wondered. Who is he, and how long will it be before he comes after me and my sisters, demanding of us our obedience and worship? It was obvious to Betty that something had to be done about this fellow before too long. She remembered Helgayarn's admonition to her should half of the magi's claims prove themselves to be even one third true. Now, seeing for herself this mighty man of power who nevertheless carried himself with such humility, Betty deemed that the magi's claims and boasts were not even the half of it! She again gave thought to Helgayarn's instruc-

THE CHRISTMAS RABBIT

tions but hesitated, unsure of her own power in the face and fact of this man while knowing that it would take a bigger witch than herself to get the job done. She needed to get back to Helgayarn and Brunnhilde right away and report her findings. And no way was she walking back—there wasn't time enough for that! She summoned the forces, invoked the charms, mumbled the mumbo-jumbo, and whisked herself away in a whirlwind. As she ascended into the storm, she took note that the young rabbi was looking up, observing her as she fled, and with that beatific smile still displayed upon his countenance, he shook his head in sorrow while watching her depart.

*****

Helgayarn and Brunnhilde busied themselves in their rock garden, pretending to grow stones while worrying fretfully about Betty. It'd been years since she'd gone off on her fact-finding mission, and she should've returned long before now. After all, the land of Canaan was only a few hundred miles away, and even with walking round-trip and staying there a bit to gather facts, such a journey shouldn't have taken more than a year or two tops! So to keep her off their worried minds and out of their troubled thoughts, they busied themselves erecting a Zen garden, placing their stones in exactly the right places and positions while affording themselves the necessary time in *time to waste*, meditating upon each stone and its proper placement. It was often months before either picked up a rock. Zen gardening was a meditative skill they stole from the rabbits who had studied the art under the venerable tutelage of Harehito Rabbakami. They could show that little leporide a thing or two about Zen gardening now, they reasoned, had he still been around to do so. Whereas Harehito planted fist-sized stones to define the limits of his rock orchid, Helgayarn and Brunnhilde placed within their stone arboretum boulders and minor-sized mountains—let those damned rabbits try and top that! Upon completion, they sat within its confines during the long years of Betty's absence, meditating on their rocks while trying within their mind's eye to make them grow. But distraction and ever-increasing worry regarding Betty hampered their ability to grow rocks, and since many were monoliths already and needed no urging on their parts, decided to leave well enough alone, the rocks having met their efforts with silent indifference.

Having finally given up on the rocks for being the stupid stones they were, Helgayarn and Brunnhilde decided to turn their attentions to their lost sister. They were packing a bag with the idea of setting out on their own in an effort to find her, when the skies above them flashed lightning and pealed thunder. "Well, it's about time!" said Helgayarn to Brunnhilde as she looked up at the gathering clouds. "The old girl must have stopped off for a long lunch!" Betty rode a bolt of lightning down to earth and came crashing in a gibbering heap at the feet of her sisters. Her hair was disheveled and stood out on end. The long journey coupled with the Judean heat had completely bleached the blue tint out of her stringy locks, and she was in dire need of both another rinsing and a permanent. Her eyes displayed a wild look in their irises as if she were a lone deer lost on the highway and caught up in the headlights of oncoming traffic. Upon landing she immediately rolled over on her back and, raising herself up on all fours, proceeded to scuttle madly like an insane and upside down crab to the front door of the Winnebago.

"What's gotten into her?" asked Brunnhilde. "If I didn't know any better, I'd say she was scared—right out of her Bermuda shorts!"

"It certainly does appear that way," Helgayarn replied, eyeing her truant sister. "Betty, my dear, what's gotten into you? You look like the cat who just swallowed the canary—and then choked on it!"

Betty flipped over to become a crab who now stood right side up and began to cackle and gibber. Helgayarn eyed her sister with concern. *What in the name of Jiminy Cricket was going on?* "Did you finally make it to Canaan?" asked the big witch. "Did you find the young lad those three wise guys were so on about?" Betty offered them a palsied nod as a reply. In her current state, even her monosyllabic articulation seemed to have deserted her. She flipped back over and began to scuttle once again toward the Winnebago.

This won't do at all, Helly thought. We need to get the old girl rested and cleaned up if we're going to get any useful information out of her. A good cup of tea, offered with tenderness and accompanied by a solicitous scone, would do wonders, no doubt, to restore the old girl's spirits!

First, however, the poor dear needed a bath and some cleaning up. The layered grime and the overall impression of dishevelment which wrapped itself around her like a tenuous shroud did not quite put her in the same company of such soiled personages as Old Slomoe and Hopalong Cassidy, but she was well on her way to giving either a dirty run for their money. So Helgayarn and Brunnhilde gathered her up, took her inside, and ran for her a warm and comforting bath. As Brunnhilde cleaned the soil while dressing her minor cuts and scrapes, Helgayarn applied the blue tint to her hair and administered the permanent. But such a wreck was Betty, so thoroughly grimed and tousled, with her stringy locks so completely shaggy and matted, that the makeover her sisters applied took a month to administer and as many changes of bathwater as there were days in the month to facilitate. Finally, after cleaning her up, they fed Betty her tea and scones and then promptly put her to bed. In her exhaustion and fright, she slept a fortnight. Helgayarn used the opportunity to search through her dirty clothing in order to retrieve and read her journal. She eyed with some resentment the earlier entries which she skimmed over that were both numerous and critical of herself and Brunnhilde. How dare the little witch be so secretive and at the same time so uppity? *Well,* Helgayarn reasoned, *there'd be plenty of opportunity later to take Betty to account about that!* But for now she was more interested in her later notations—those dealing with the fellow of whom they'd all been so lately concerned. It seemed that Betty had written reams about the young Hebrew, compacting them within the few remaining leaves of her journal while reducing her entries to pint-sized paragraphs embodying puny parcels of picayunish penmanship that sat peculiarly upon the pages therein and which couldn't possibly be true—with all of it having been squeezed together as one sentence ran into the next, while paragraphs were piled one atop of the other like castaway cordwood which had been stacked in heaps and left out to dry in preparation for a long, harsh winter. Such a prosaic style made her observations much harder for Helgayarn to translate and decipher. Added to these not-inconsiderable difficulties was the fact that Betty kept all of her notations in shorthand—which didn't make matters any easier for Helly who was both long handed and long-winded. She determined therefore that either she was missing the linguistic key which would enable her to unlock the little witch's rantings or Betty must indeed have been off her rocker by the time she'd arrived in Judea, as none of these fantasies which she'd just finished reading could possibly have any basis in fact.

After sleeping like a stone and lying in her bed like a log cut down dead, Betty chose at last to finally wake. She opened her eyes to the comforting gargoylish presence of her two sisters who sat solicitously on either side of her while tending to her needs and awaiting her return to consciousness. Brunnhilde had, by now, her own chance to read Betty's journal, and a look of uncertain worry displayed itself upon her pale features as she gazed anxiously down at her sister. "How are you doing, my dear?" she asked. "Are we feeling any better?"

Betty mumbled a weak reply, "Yah."

"Would you care for a bit of soup?"

Betty looked at her two sisters fretfully. Her concern was self-evident.

"No, no," Brunnhilde replied with a gentle chuckle. "It's not Mrs. Santos's shark fin, just plain old chicken noodle—and straight from the can at that. So you needn't worry about any incidental or accidental poisonings! Here, let me help you sit up." She adjusted Betty's pillows while Helgayarn slowly spoon-fed her the broth. "That's good, eh?" asked the big witch.

"Yah."

"Here, have some more then."

Betty did as she was told, allowing Helgayarn to ladle it into her oral cavity. When she'd finished the bowl she looked up and saw that Helgayarn was considering her carefully. "Betty, my dear," Helgayarn gently insisted, "the time has come to talk about your journey, and to discuss amongst the three of us just who, or what, you may have encountered over there. Do you feel up to it?" Betty offered a noncommittal shrug. She'd be more than happy if the subject never got mentioned again. "Betty, darling," Helgayarn said, taking note of the

THE CHRISTMAS RABBIT

unease displayed in the depths of her sister's eyes, "you must understand, my dear, how important it is that we get to the bottom of these matters. All of our Manifest Destiny and its subsequent pocket change could hang in the balance. Our fames, our fortunes—why our very standing within the tapestry of governance and our positions as Powers That Be's may very well ride upon both the factualness of these matters which you relate in your journal and our response to them! Do you understand?"

Betty offered her sister her reluctant reply. "Yah."

"So then," Helgayarn prompted gently, "these observations you've written down, are they true?"

Betty nodded her head. "Yah!" she replied.

Helgayarn looked apprehensively at Brunnhilde. Their sister, it seemed, had slipped into the seas of madness. "Everything?"

"Yah!"

"The water into wine?"

"Yah!"

"The healing of the sick?"

"Yah!"

"The calming of the winds and the pacification of the seas?"

"Yah!"

"The restoration of the lame?"

Yah!"

"Well then, certainly, this walking on water," Helgayarn continued, "was a fabrication of sorts!" Betty shook her head violently from side to side. "You actually saw him do it?"

"Yah!"

"What about raising the dead? Surely, you didn't witness that, did you?"

"Yah! Yah! Yah!"

"Okay, my dear," Helgayarn replied. "Okay, we believe you." She tucked Betty's blanket up under her chin and readjusted her pillows. "Just you rest a bit for now," she said, "while Brunnhilde and I prepare the three of us some dinner." She gestured for Brunnhilde to follow and rising up from the bed, proceeded to the living room, shutting the door behind her. What she needed was to hear Brunnhilde's own evaluation of Betty's veracity. She sat her sister down on the other side of the living room table. Taking her own seat, she offered up her query. "Well, what do you think? Has she gone bananas?" Betty offered a shrug. "She's always been a bit off her rocker. But this? She believes she's telling the truth, that much is certain."

"If Jack Rabbit has taught us anything," replied Helgayarn, "it's that nothing is certain. Do you hear me—nothing!"

"Well, let's suppose," Brunnhilde replied, "that for the sake of argument, Betty is indeed telling the truth. What does it mean with regard to this 'rabbi' as she so quaintly terms him? Can a mere man hold within his hands, such power?"

"Of course not!" Helgayarn replied matter-of-factly. "It's all smoke and mirrors—has to be!"

"But suppose it isn't?"

"Oh, don't start with your *buts* again! I had enough of those last millennium to last me through the next one!"

"Fine!" replied Brunnhilde. "But we both know that there's a grain of truth in every lie. And suppose this isn't a lie? In fact, suppose this grain of truth turns out to be an entire crop of wheat? What then?"

"Well, it certainly won't be that!" Helgayarn replied indifferently. "After all, either of us could have just as easily performed any number of those tricks! Taking the walking on water for example—any third-rate magician armed with a good pair of water wings and a Coast Guard approved flotation device could've just as easily pulled that one off!"

"True," Brunnhilde agreed. "But Betty's journal states that he was only shod in sandals and the Coast Guard hasn't been invented yet!"

Helgayarn offered her a sour look. "Well, what about those loaves and dead fish?" she asked. "Either Betty seriously miscounted the numbers or the thousands there gathered couldn't have been too hungry!"

"Maybe they were dieting," replied Betty.

"Dieting? You think they were dieting?"

"How else do you account for it?"

THE CHRISTMAS RABBIT

"I don't," replied Helgayarn, "other than to say that Betty must've been on a diet herself, having taken a brain enema before she did her counting!"

"What about raising the dead?" asked Brunnhilde. "How does one fake that?"

"There are any number of ways! Perhaps this Lazarus fellow was just sleeping. Perhaps they cooked the whole thing up together as a publicity stunt! All that weeping at the grave stuff sure sounds like hammy posturing to me. After all, who, with so much power, would waste a minute shedding even a single tear for someone so meaningless? And as for the actual feat, we've never had a success, have we? What makes you think he has? It's theatrics, I tell you, nothing more. We'll put this guy on the Gong Show when they finally get around to producing it. Chuck Barris is gonna love him!"

"Well, I'm not convinced," replied Brunnhilde. Whatever else this 'rabbi' might be—he sure sounds like some fella!"

"Yeah right!" Helgayarn replied. "Harehito Rabbakami thought that he was the cat's meow too—and look what happened to him! He turned out to be nothing more than the horse's rear end! We fixed his wagon and we'll fix this fellow's as well!"

Brunnhilde shook her head. "Helly," she said, "Harehito almost fixed our wagons by killing us while performing the repair work! This fellow sounds like ten times ten Harehitos! I think we should proceed cautiously."

"Cautiously? You're overreacting, my dear. This fellow's a lover, not a fighter. Did you not read all of that malarkey he spouted out about loving thy neighbor and the blessings of the meek? Blessed are the poor in spirit for they shall see God. Indeed! Do you think God, if he exists at all, gives a cattle crap about them? If he did, they wouldn't be poor, would they? Gods want sacrifices, and the poor have very little in the way of turtledoves, sheep, and whatnot to be wasting them upon such extravagances! No, my dear, all this talk of love, along with his other ridiculous parables littered as they are with unintelligible metaphor and coupled with obvious theatrics, only point him out for what he is—a charlatan and a fake. We can take him, rest assured."

"I still advise caution."

"Oh, you do go on, don't you?"

Brunnhilde let her latent anger rise to the surface. It was time that someone put this witch in her place and since there was no one else but Betty who lay incapacitated in bed, that left her, Brunnhilde, as the someone to do it! "Listen, you overrated, mealy mouthed, buzzard's beak," she replied. "For too many years now, Betty and I have had to endure your tirades and your temper tantrums as you spouted off time and again over one thing or another! Okay, you're the Big Witch, so what you say goes. But all we've done is go from wreck to ruin, from bad to worse. It was your idea to come up with tides and seasons, your idea to try and make the sun rise in the west! Worst off, it was your idea to pit the farmer against the rabbit as a punishment to them both—and for the most part all of the other ideas that have followed in the wake of that fiasco have been yours too! Well, I'm sick of it, do you hear? I'm just up-to-my-ears sick of it! I'm not called Brunnhilde the Levelheaded for nothing, you know! This time we're doing it my way. We're going to proceed cautiously and test the waters before we go swimming in them, or by the stars, Betty and I will go our own way without you! You may be a big enough witch to take either one of us in a fair fight but do you think you could hold your own if the two of us ganged up on you? I doubt it. And while you were busy trying to deal with us, who'd handle this rabbi? You thought Rabbakami gave you a run for your money—wait till you feel the brute force, hurled at you whole hog, by both Brunnhilde and Betty! Ninja rabbits and hareas hurled will be the least of your bad memories!"

Helgayarn, nonplussed, was taken aback. She'd never before walked the slippery slopes of impending mutiny. "I didn't know," she replied in her best conciliatory voice, "that you had such strong opinions regarding these matters."

Brunnhilde let out a tired sigh. "Oh, Helly," she replied wearily, "you are the big witch—and for good reason, you are the mightiest amongst us, and as such we've always been willing to defer to you. But for once, just this once, couldn't we do it my way?"

THE CHRISTMAS RABBIT

Helgayarn looked at her suspiciously. "What's your way?" she asked.

"My way," Betty replied, "is to go see for ourselves first what this Hebrew is all about and then decide what to do about him. Let's not go off half-cocked, as it were, blind in our tunnel vision, only to discover that once again we've waded bare-breasted into a sea of cattle craps!"

Helgayarn reluctantly conceded. "Oh, very well," she replied. "I think such snooping is taking the long way around an obvious shortcut—the low road over the high road. But for your sake, my dear, I'll agree to it!"

They let Betty sleep for another two days in order to recuperate and regain all her strength for the upcoming journey. When she awoke, they got her up and sat her down at the kitchen table. "Betty dear," said Helgayarn, "we know you believe everything you've related to us in that journal of yours but frankly darling, we're having trouble swallowing it. We want to go to Judea and see for ourselves this rabbi who seems to have impressed you so. And we want you to come with us as our guide so that we can more easily find him!"

Betty shook her head vehemently while rising from the table in an effort to flee to the safety of her bedroom. Helly caught ahold of her and gently sat her back down in her chair. "Easy, my love," she said soothingly. "There's nothing to worry about. Both Betty and I will be there to ensure that no rabbi rattles your rib cage! But we have to see for ourselves, dear, and we need you to show us the way!"

Betty gestured for a pencil and a piece of paper. Retrieving them, Brunnhilde placed them in her hands, whereupon she began to scribble furiously. When she finished, she defiantly thrust the note in Helgayarn's face. Checking her impatience, the big witch deigned to take ahold of it and read her sister's reply. "No cattle crapping way—you goose-stepping moron, am I ever going back there!" Betty wrote. "I'll draw you a freakin' map!"

"Now, Betty," Helgayarn replied patiently, "whoever this young fellow is—surely you don't believe all this 'Son of God' talk, do you? Who, after all, could be more powerful than the three of us?"

Again the junior witch scribbled furiously. "Him—that's who!" was her written reply. "And as to 'Son of God'—well, I tell you, the Jew boy's no son of your average Joe, that's for sure! Your average Joe is just a carpenter. I know—I checked him out! There's no way he could've fathered that kid! It just ain't in him!"

Helgayarn read the reply and then passed it to Betty. "Sons often exceed their fathers," she replied. "Just look at that Junior fellow and Santos!"

"Yah! Just look!" Betty wrote. "And Junior wasn't Santos's son either and we all know it!"

To that observation, neither Helgayarn nor Betty had an argument. Junior wasn't Santos's progeny no matter how much Santos or his wife thought differently. He was a Dawe done dirty—both by his real parents and the vicissitudes of fickle fate. Could the same be true of the carpenter's son? They'd never know for sure, Helgayarn reasoned, until they saw the fellow for themselves! But it was apparent from Betty's intractable objections that she and Brunnhilde would have to make the journey alone. "What are you going to do, my dear," she asked, "while we're gone?"

"Crawl under a rock," Betty scribbled. "Stay well hidden and out of sight! I've no doubt that remarkable fellow can see me—even here! I'll hide under one of your standing stones out there in yonder garden and keep a low profile! You two can go back to Judea and deal with the rabbi! You come away the winner in that and I'll shout out loud enough for the whole world to hear that you are indeed the Big Witch—in the meantime, make out your wills!"

Brunnhilde offered Helgayarn an apprehensive look. Always in ages past, either singly or acting in concert, the two of them had been able to bully Betty into agreeing with their decisions and going along with their plans, however misguided or misbegotten. To find her attitude both adamant and intractable spoke volumes to the number two witch about Betty's resolve and reservations. "Helly," she tentatively said, "perhaps we should just do as the old girl would seem to suggest and let the whole thing blow over. After all, how much trouble can one rabbi cause us? He may well stir up a hornet's nest in the time given him to walk this earth, but eventually as with all things mortal, both he and his works will pass away."

Helgayarn stood, staring at them both while tapping her fingers impatiently. "You want us to play chicken," she asked, "to turn the other cheek and ignore this Hebrew's effrontery? Is that it?" Brunnhilde shrugged. "Well, it ain't happening! We'll do it your way, investigate first and implement action later, but we're not going to hide like frightened hens in our coops while this charlatan goes about spreading false dogma and doctrine that steers the stupid even further away from their rightful allegiance to us! Our reputations, thanks to that idiot farmer and rambunctious rabbit, are already well on the road to decline and discredit. Before I'll let such a slide continue, aided by this upstart's homey parables and adages, which he backs up with cheap parlor tricks and theatrics, I'll draw my own line in the sand and confront him with a few maxims, mottos, and miracles of my own! Son of God? He darn well better hope so because he's going to need all the help he can get! Now pack a bag—we're off to Judea!" Brunnhilde offered a tired shrug but acquiesced nevertheless. After all, Helgayarn was indeed the Big Witch, and she'd given her word that they'd investigate first.

It took them days to pack on the presumption that a fellow such as the one they were seeking, despite his many homilies and teachings that seemed so sympathetic to the poor and disenfranchised, was bound to be found mixing it up with those who wielded the stiff arm of power and governance and who continually tanned themselves by sunbathing in recognition's warm limelight. After all, it's what they would have done. It therefore followed upon the heels of this presumption that such a fellow as the one they sought would be constantly sought after himself as a dinner guest and fellow reveler at the various fetes and cocktail parties being thrown in Judea at the time by those who governed it, among whom were both Herod Antipas and Pontius Pilate—both well-known to The Powers That Be as extravagant blowhards who liked to show off their wealth and position. So it was decided by both Helgayarn and Brunnhilde that in addition to simple peasant garb which they'd pack in order to blend in with the peons, that a suitable collection of evening gowns, business suits, ballet skirts, chitons, muu-muu's sarongs, sheaths, and Mother Hubbards were needed as well. To complement these and add to their creature comforts, they included an assortment of bed jackets, boudoir dresses, brunch coats, and peignoirs. Since they're were traveling to Judea where modesty in women was the rule rather than the exception, they also packed a large array of balmorals, bloomers, body stockings and brassieres as well as panties, petticoats, scanties, shifts, and shorts. To ensure they were properly shod and therefore thoroughly dressed, they packed into their suitcases' corners various sets of footwear, including desert boots, sandals, galoshes, getas, platforms, pumps, snowshoes, ski boots, and roller skates. Their jackboots they left in their closets—they would bring nothing with them that served to remind either of that pesky rabbit! To gird their waists they packed a conglomerate of baldrics, bandoliers, girdles, sashes, and bellybands. As an afterthought they threw in their cummerbunds as well in case they were called upon to don their tuxedos. To ensure their hands were well covered and the digits upon them properly protected, they packed a collection of muffs, mittens, suede gloves, baseball mitts and brass knuckles. Lastly, relying upon Betty's description of the temperature extremes to be found within the mountains of Judea itself, as a precautionary measure, added three changes of long underwear. One could never be too careful. "Well, that should about do it," commented Helgayarn as she sat heavily on her suitcase's lid while attempting to close it and snap the locks in place. Brunnhilde was just about to agree when a thought occurred to her. "Judea's pretty conservative, isn't it?" she asked.

Helly paused in the act of closing her suitcase in order to give her sister's question the proper consideration. "I don't know," she replied. "Certainly, they're not as liberal as old Babylon or as open-minded as present-day Rome, but as to conservatism, I don't know. Certainly, this rabbi fellow, whatever else he may be, impresses me as being somewhat of a free thinker. Why do you ask?"

"Well it struck me from the tone of Betty's journal that they must be of a conservative bent," replied Brunnhilde. "Therefore,

THE CHRISTMAS RABBIT

being so, I assume that when in public they expect that their women will go about with their faces veiled and their heads covered."

Helgayarn's shoulders slumped as she looked down and contemplated her overstuffed suitcase. It would be next to impossible to squeeze in so much as another sock. "Do you really think they'll notice such a minor oversight?" she asked. "I mean, after all, Bunny, all my dresses, especially the silks and chiffons, are going to be wrinkled as it is, and who knows if we'll find a Chinese tailor once we get there! We may very well have to do our own ironing and that's going to take time!"

"True," replied Brunnhilde, "but suppose they don't overlook such minor infractions in dress code, what then? We're supposed to blend in, and being chased through the streets because we're underdressed is not going to help us any in keeping a low profile. It will do us no good to be uncovered because of uncovered heads!"

"Fiddlesticks!" replied Helgayarn, knowing that it was pointless to argue with a witch—especially when the witch was right! So in one swift movement she both sprung the suitcase's locks and leapt out of the way. The portmanteau popped open like a cork jettisoned from a champagne bottle and all her packing spilled out from within like cheap wine overflowing. Chiffons, muu-muus, shifts shorts, panties, pumps, and bellybands all went flying. When everything settled to the floor she was knee-deep in clothing and facing the onerous task of having to repack.

Finally the chore was completed and the clothes resettled within their bandboxes. Added to the already-considerable sum of apparel and attire were the addition of various veils, scarves, kerchiefs, yashamaks, kaffiyehs, bowlers, bonnets, shakos, shovel hats, skullcaps, porkpies, pillboxes, beanies, berets, and baseball caps. Helgayarn was taking no chances. "There! I think that about covers the ballpark! We've every clothing contingency accounted for—and then some!"

She tried lifting her suitcase but found she could not raise it off the floor. "I'm going to have to drag the damn thing all the way from Jerusalem to Jericho!" she complained. "Sister, can you give me a hand with my baggage?"

Brunnhilde offered her a loud harrumph in reply. She was too busy sweating and straining herself as she attempted to hoist her own valise. "There's no help for it," Brunnhilde said. "We've packed only the essentials and barely enough for a weeklong visit at that. Let's hope we get our business done quickly so that we don't run out of changes in costume! I wonder if I should've packed my fez?"

"Don't you dare open that damned suitcase!" Helgayarn chided. "We can both do without a fez and if we find we can't we'll buy new ones when we get there!"

They dragged their boodle bags out of the Winnebago and down to the desert floor. "Betty!" cried Helgayarn, "Aren't you going to see us off?"

From over in the Zen garden, Betty tossed them a note which was tied to a stone. Upon it was written her adamant reply. "I'm under a rock," she declared, "and here's where I'll stay until the two of you get back. Have fun!"

"Oh, very well!" Helgayarn replied impatiently. "I haven't the time to deal with your foolishness!" She began to gather the forces, incite the incantations, and mumble the mumbo jumbo in preparation for summoning up a whirlwind when Betty, peering out from under her rock, broke the big witch's train of thought by suddenly jumping out from under her stone. She ran up to Helly and shoved another hastily written note in her face. "Aren't you walking?" She wrote. "You had me hoof it! What's the matter with you two?"

Brunnhilde looked to Helgayarn to provide the answer. Helgayarn offered her sister a scowl. "Betty," she finally said through gritted teeth and clenched fists, "it's better than five hundred miles from here to Judea—"

"It's a hell of a lot more than that if you take the route I traveled!" Betty replied, scribbling furiously. "But I did it! Too proud to walk?"

"No," replied Helgayarn matter-of-factly. "We're too good for it! Now, if you're not going to come, then please get out of our way!" Betty affected an air of disdain and with nose held proudly in the air, walked off and crawled back under her boulder. "Really!" said

THE CHRISTMAS RABBIT

Helgayarn to Brunnhilde. "What does the old broad expect us to do, lug our luggage all the way to Judea?"

"We may have to," replied Brunnhilde. "It's going to take one hell of a twister to carry both us and our baggage from here to Canaan. A virtual crosscurrent of both updrafts and downdrafts, an equinoctial gale of unparalleled proportions—a real williwaw! Do you think you can summon up such a windbag?"

Helgayarn, loath to admit inability to do anything, nevertheless looked down at their baggage while reluctantly conceding her sister's point. "Not by myself," she grudgingly replied. "But with a little help from you, chanting and invoking alongside me while singing in harmony, the two of us just might pull it off!"

Brunnhilde's blank-faced stare gave voice to her doubts. "All right," she replied, "we'll give it a whirl and see what we can whip up. But if we miss our mark and overshoot the damned thing we could well end up in Gaul or someplace even worse—how I hate those damned Frenchies! So let's both of us, be careful, agreed?"

"Agreed," replied Helgayarn.

So together they invoked the charms of making, incited the incantations, and mumbled the jumbo in their efforts to gather up a head wind capable of hauling them and their suitcases all the way to Palestine. The air grew thick and heavy as the winds began to increase and whirl around them. The skies darkened as clouds gathered overhead to pile one atop of the next. The air smelled of ozone as the cumuli above them rained down lightning bolts and hailstones the size of small hobbyhorses. Thunder boomed, and the earth shook. The barometric pressure fell so low it seemed impossible that it would ever rise again. Suddenly, dropping out of the clouds like an elevator in freefall, a funnel cloud of tremendous proportions descended upon them to lift them and their baggage up and aloft into an angry Arabian sky.

*****

Brunnhilde had trouble keeping her bearing and seeing straight while within the confines of their tornado. All about her dust and debris whirled about in a violent maelstrom. Nettles stung her eyes and abraded her skin. A lone camel, sucked up by the tempestuous void somewhere over Baghdad or thereabouts—caught up in the violence of the storm it was hard to tell—slammed into her, knocking the wind out of her and nearly knocking her out too, and she couldn't count the number of times she'd collided with her suitcase. It was a miracle the damned thing hadn't popped a lock or a hinge by now. If they had to go much further it was certain not to survive the trip.

"Helly!" she cried above the melee. "Are we near our destination yet? I don't think I can survive this tempest too much longer! I'm choking on dust, and I have sand granules impacted in my eardrums—it's gonna take a jackhammer to chisel 'em out!"

"I know," replied Helgayarn desperately. "My ears feel like loads of bricks too! But I don't think it's too much further. Look down below. If you can peer through the dust clouds, I do believe that flowing brook beneath us is the Jordan River. It can't be too much further now!"

Brunnhilde spit out a mouthful of sand. "I certainly hope not," she yelled. "We should've donned one of our kerchiefs as sand masks and dealt with this debacle in a more witchlike fashion—one befitting a Power That Be's. So help me Jiminy Cricket—if that damned camel collides with me one more time, I'm going to skin it alive, assuming this storm hasn't done so already! It's literally eating the flesh off my bones!"

"I know, my dear," Helgayarn yelled back in sympathetic reply. "Just hang on—we're almost there!"

There was a flash of lightning followed by a gargantuan boom from within the funnel, sending the duo whirling head over heels to crash, one into the other. "Jumpin' Jiminy Cricket!" cried Helgayarn. "Watch where you're going, will you? I've bruises and bangs enough already without having to wear your badges as well!"

"Up yours!" Brunnhilde vehemently shot back. "You think I can control where I'm going in this funnel cloud? I'm being tossed about like a two-headed drachma! It's a wonder we haven't crashed into each other before now!" Helgayarn was about to offer her sister a sour reply when she noticed through the whirling dust below

THE CHRISTMAS RABBIT

them, the outskirts of Jerusalem on the near horizon. "We'd better land here," she said, "and make the rest of our way on foot so as to arrive unannounced." Brunnhilde dreaded the thought of walking those last miles while dragging behind her overstuffed suitcase. But anything, she reasoned, was better than this madness. "Agreed!" she hastily replied. "Let's debark!"

They reversed their spell. The storm, after tearing across the Arabian desert siphoning sand and spitting out scorpions, came to an abrupt and sudden halt, pitching them into a sand dune a couple of miles southeast of Megiddo. They had to walk the two miles into town, dragging their valises behind them. At first they thought to make use of the camel but as Brunnhilde had foreseen, it was indeed stripped to the bone. All that remained was a meager skeleton and a couple of humps.

"Well, there's no help for it," said Helly, extracting herself from the sand dune. "We're going to have to hoof it into town before the sun gets too high."

Brunnhilde looked up to take note of the fireball in the sky. "It's already five minutes to twelve," she replied. "How much higher can it get?"

"Whatever!" Helgayarn shot back impatiently. "Just grab your bag and let's get going!" After much searching and subsequent digging the duo were able to locate their valises and, pulling each behind them, made their slow way to downtown Megiddo.

DON'T BE A FAG AND WALK A MILE FOR A CAMEL!
CAMEL CONSIGNMENTS AND SALES BY
ABDULLAH, THE MULLUAH!
ALL KINDS OF ASS FOR SALE AND CAMELS FOR HIRE—
BOTH NEW AND USED!
ONE HUMPED OR TWO—WE'VE THE CAMEL FOR YOU!
GREAT DEALS—HONEST PRICES!
LIQUIDATION SALE ON NOW—ALL STOCK PRICED TO MOVE!
GREAT MILEAGE—LOW MAINTENANCE!
THIS YEAR'S MODELS AT LAST YEAR'S PRICES!
CAMEL JOCKEYS FOR HIRE!

By Jerusalem standards Megiddo was a slum—a real barrio where only the poorest of the poor deigned to reside. "Mercy," Brunnhilde said. "It looks like Armageddon here, doesn't it?" Helgayarn looked around her. "Indeed," she replied. "It's a real dump all right. It makes the Old Forest, even in the wake of Hurricane Junior, look like the Garden of Eden. Thank our lucky stars that we're disguised. I wouldn't want to be caught dead in such a place!" As they neared the town limits they spied a lone tent upon its outskirts. Gathered about it and roped to fences were various camels and asses, presumably for sale. They took note of a sign which read:

"What do you think?" asked Brunnhilde, surveying the lot. Her countenance displayed her doubt. "Do we dare?" she asked.

"I don't see how we dare not," replied Helgayarn. "Anything is better than dragging our baggage behind us—we've undershot our mark! It's another fifty-five miles or so to Jerusalem, and who knows how many miles from there to Nazareth! We need to be about our business and find that rabbi. Still, those beasts look rather forlorn, do they not?"

"Forlorn is hardly the word," Brunnhilde replied dryly. "Despondent, despairing, and in disrepair would better describe them! But I suppose you're right—a rickety ride is better than no ride at all."

"How true," said Helgayarn. "But hush now. Here comes the proprietor! Let us not look too eager, or he'll drive up his prices!"

Approaching them from the flap of the tent came an old man wrapped in a burnoose. His face was a crag, both wrinkled and wizened, which supported upon it a bulbous and overlarge nose. He flashed a smile at them that would have been sunny had it not been missing all but three of its front teeth, which were crooked and stained with the vices of his many bad habits. He needed a bath and smelled of his stock. The odor of stale camels hung about him like the unwholesome miasma of cigarette smoke. "Good day, ladies," he said by way of greeting. "Something I can do for you?" He eyed them greedily, sensing that deep within their pockets lay untold drachmas and talents to be had for the taking.

THE CHRISTMAS RABBIT

"Abdullah?" inquired Helgayarn.

"The Mullah—that's me!" came the reply. "Abdullah the Mullah! Used-camel salesman!" He handed his card to Helgayarn, who reached for it cautiously.

It felt greasy and dirty in her hand. As she took the card Helgayarn scrutinized the salesman before her. "You're not from around here, are you?" she asked.

Abdullah the Mullah seemed to fidget. "Why would you ask that?" he answered indignantly. "Of course I'm from around here! You're the ones as look like out-of-towners!"

"Indeed," replied a sardonic Helgayarn. "It's just that Abdullah the Mullah doesn't sound very Jewish, does it? Semitic, no doubt, but certainly not Jewish."

"What?" replied the indignant salesman. "My name should end in Stein or Berg? What are you, some kind of racist?"

Helgayarn and Brunnhilde merely stood there appraising him while saying nothing.

Finally, Abdullah relented under their scrutiny. "Okay," he reluctantly admitted. "I'm half a Hebrew. Is that so bad? I'm a Samaritan, if you must know—and a damned good one at that!" There was an uncomfortable pause as the duo regarding him found that they had no reply. Abdullah, being the sly salesman that he was, knew nothing killed a deal quicker than prolonged and protracted silence. It was best to keep 'em talking, thereby getting them to reveal their wants and needs. "Say!" he suddenly spouted out, "are you ladies in the market for a good camel?

"Why? Have you got any?" asked Helgayarn.

"I've got dozens, here on my lot!"

"Perhaps," replied Brunnhilde in an offhanded manner, "we can't really say. It's a lovely day for walking and walk we just might."

"It sure is that!" replied Abdullah. "A lovely day, despite the storm that just passed through! I noticed you from afar coming in from the desert. It didn't catch you out there, did it? Terrible things, these desert dust storms—rise up all of a suddenlike and blow you all to hell if you're not careful!"

"Catch us?" replied Helgayarn. "We were right in the thick of it, bub!"

"I kinda thought so," replied the camel salesman. "You both look a bit disheveled."

"Disheveled? Why we're anything but! We're the Powers—"

Brunnhilde discreetly kicked Helgayarn in the leg before she could give away their identities.

"I, uhm, that is to say, that yes, we are a bit disheveled, now that you mention it—but not so much that we cannot continue on foot if a reasonable accord cannot be reached! How much for your used camels, sir, and do they come with warranties? What's their mileage and EPA rating? Do they have power steering or rack and pinion? Are they four-wheel drive or do they just go about on forelegs? Come now, and tell us about them!"

"They're all hoofers!" Abdullah replied with false sincerity. "Every one of them's a beaut! Each has been reconditioned, test-driven, and inspected. Low mileage—every one! And their all capable, when installed with optional saddlebags, of course, of hauling a load, which judging from the size of your boodle bags will come in handy!"

Helgayarn eyed the herd skeptically. "They all look a little weather-worn to me," she replied.

"Don't let their looks fool ya!" countered Abdullah. "It's the Judean sun—it plays hell on their finish coats! But underneath, nothing but prime stock—I guarantee it!"

"What about the power steering and the foreleg drive?" asked Brunnhilde. "Do they work?"

Abdullah offered her his best smile. "Smart lady. I can tell! You bet your jackass, that is if you had one, the foreleg drive works. On all of them! As to the power steering, they don't normally come so equipped, but for a nominal fee I can have my mechanic install a bigger bridle and bit. You shouldn't have any trouble."

"What's a nominal fee?"

The salesman laughed. "We can discuss that later," he replied. "A lot's gonna depend upon the particular make and model and you haven't made that choice yet. Tell me, are you planning on driving

THE CHRISTMAS RABBIT

around town or are you going out to the country? The only reason I ask is if your desert bound and traveling northward, you might want to consider paying the little extra and go for those models with the two tanks. Prevents running out of fuel, you know, in out-of-the-way places."

"Tanks?"

"Pardon me," he replied. "That's just what we call 'em around here. You probably refer to 'em as humps. Some models have one hump, and some of 'em have two. All are eco-friendly and run on water! Just take 'em to the nearest well and let 'em slurp up the gas! You can get a couple of hundred miles on a single tank and that's a savings you can take to the bank!"

"What about air-conditioning?" asked Helgayarn.

Abdullah offered her a long-suffering sigh. "Give me a break, lady," he pleaded. This is Judea! We're just west of Arabia and just north of the Sahara! Air-conditioning don't work in these parts. My advice is to carry a fan with you and stay well wrapped in your burnoose!"

Wiping the sweat from their brows, the two witches conceded the point. "Very well then," replied Helgayarn. "We'll take a couple of the duel tanked models. Whaddya want for them?"

Abdullah shook his head sadly. "Unfortunately," he replied, "I've only four of those on the lot right now and I've promised all four to a fellow named Omar, the tentmaker."

Helgayarn rolled her eyes.

"I did!" continued Abdullah. "Upon my honor! Omar even gave me a deposit to hold 'em for him! I suppose, though, seeing as how you're such refined ladies—dames who only travel with the best—that I could let 'em go to you anyway. You'd have to refund me his deposit, of course, plus a little extra to sort of smooth over his disappointment, if you take my meaning. But I'm sure that wouldn't be a problem to such well-off individuals as yourselves, would it?"

Brunnhilde regarded the salesman with disdain. "Let's just walk," she said to Helly. "It can't be that far!"

"Oh, you don't want to walk," replied Abdullah, "not in this sun—you'll roast in the Sinai sun! Where are you ladies headed anyway?"

Helgayarn and Betty, both uneasy with his inquiry, triangulated in one of their infamous huddles in order to confer, but without Betty, were unable to complete the formation. Frustrated, they abruptly broke apart. "We're headed to Nazareth," Helgayarn reluctantly admitted. "We've a mind to see something of the country."

"My jackass!" replied Abdullah. "You're looking for the rabbi!"

"Rabbi? Who's that?"

"Don't try to pull the camel's hair over my eyes," said the salesman. "Everybody wants a word with the rabbi. A word or a miracle." He looked at them suspiciously. "Say…" he inquired, "You two aren't lepers, are you?"

Helgayarn and Brunnhilde shook their heads.

"Good thing," replied Abdullah. "'Cause if that was the case I'd throw you the hell off my lot right now! We don't cotton to lepers around here. We've enough on our hands with the cripples and the beggars without having to put up with lepers too! Well, never mind. Folk around here will deal with their own problems, I suppose."

"Have you met this 'rabbi' fellow?" Helgayarn asked.

"Me? Nah—he don't get down this way much. Besides, he's always talking about the next life, or so I'm told, and I'm too busy trying to get by in this one without giving too much thought to the next. So whaddya say, you want them camels or not?"

"You still haven't told us how much."

"Two hundred and fifty talents each," replied the salesman without batting an eye. "And that's a deal!"

"Two hundred and fifty talents?" replied an incredulous Helgayarn. "That's highway robbery!"

"Ain't any highways around here," replied Abdullah. "Just dunes, deserts, and a few Roman roads. Two hundred and fifty is my bottom-line price, take it or leave it. If you take it, fine—I'll even throw in the saddlebags, the power steering bridles, and the bits for half price. But if you're too cheap then start walking—I've got date trees

THE CHRISTMAS RABBIT

to water and goats that need herding. In other words, I've spent all the time I'm going to spend on the likes of you. Put up or shut up!"

Helgayarn eyed him darkly while mumbling some mumbo jumbo. She'd strike this desert toad down in an instant for his temerity! Brunnhilde steadied her hand at the last moment while whispering in her ear and reminding her of their need to stay anonymous. "Besides, she added, "We've recouped a goodly portion of what we lost in the Great Race, and we've brought most of it with us. What's a few hundred talents to us?"

"It's the principle!" Helgayarn viciously whispered back. "This camel jockey knows he has us between a rock and a hard place and wishes to squeeze us. I'm used to being the squeezer, not the squeezee!" Brunnhilde the Levelheaded sought for a comforting reply. "Just let him have the money. For now, that is! Upon our return we'll make sure to pass this way and fall upon this Samaritan like the pharaohs of old—and when we do he'll be sorry we did! We'll squeeze the last dinar out of him like we were ringing a wet mop. He'll rue the day he ever dared try to take advantage of The Powers That Be!"

Helgayarn smiled. Brunnhilde's plan was delicious. First, the 'rabbi' as their main course. Then this little camel jockey for desert. It would be a feast fit for two queens! She turned back to Abdullah. "Very well," she replied, her shark's smile painted prettily upon her face. "We agree to your terms, five hundred talents."

Abdullah eyed her warily. "It's a thousand," he said. "Plus tax and title."

"A thousand? What in the name of the seven seas are you talking about? You just quoted us a price of two hundred and fifty talents each, you piker!"

"And so the price remains," he smoothly replied. "But five hundred talents only buys you two camels. With all that baggage, you're going to need all four at a minimum."

"Two will be just fine!" Helgayarn adamantly replied.

"Lady," replied Abdullah, "my camels are good animals, but they remain what they are—camels, not cranes and derricks! As it is, you're going to need a forklift and an anchor windlass just to hoist those damned bags atop their humps. I suggest that you break 'em down and load up the saddlebags, and even then it's going to be hard traveling for the poor beasts. But they're only camels so who cares, right?"

"We want just two," furthered Brunnhilde. "Don't try and take advantage of our good natures, mister. You wouldn't like us when we're angry!"

"Hah!" came the diffident reply. "I don't much care for you now! Foreigners who come in search of the rabbi! Why don't you go back to where you came from? Leave Judea to the Judeans and the rabbi to the Romans!"

It was Helgayarn this time who held Brunnhilde back. "You'll never make Nazareth," Abdullah continued, "with just two camels carrying both you and those trunks. They'll break down halfway between here and Mount Carmel! And I'll be blamed for it! You take all four or you take none!"

Helgayarn offered him a frown. "Just write up the bill, old man," she replied, "and be quick about it!" She walked away before succumbing to the desire to roast him.

Abdullah the Mullah, having closed the sale, scurried off to ready the camels, leaving Helgayarn and Betty to steam in the afternoon sun. As they stood there sweating they observed Abdullah directing his camel jockeys to outfit their beasts with the appropriate saddlebags, bridles, and bits, while he busied himself with his abacus, his quill, and a piece of papyrus, as he wrote up their bill. Presently, all was in order, and Abdullah returned, leading their train. He came to a halt before them and handed Helgayarn the bill. "Three thousand fifty talents!" she cried out in disbelief. "How did you ever arrive at that figure?"

"It's all itemized on the bill," said Abdullah innocently. "I've accounted for every dinar.

THE CHRISTMAS RABBIT

Helgayarn looked it over:

```
                    Abdullah, The Mullah
                   Dealer in Customized Camelry

1) 4 twin tank camels @ 250 talents per camel =    1000 talents
2) 4 bridles (half) price @ 25 talents per bridle =  100 talents
3) 4 bits (also half price) @ 25 talents per bit =   100 talents
4) 8 saddlebags (2 per camel) @ 100 talents each =   800 talents

Sub Total                                           2000 talents
Sales Tax (10%)                                      200 talents
Licensing & registration  50 talents per camel       200 talents
Insurance (Foreign Drivers w Family Discount
           Plan) 500 talents                         500 talents

60 gallons of fuel (15 per camel) @ 2 ½ talents
per gallon (tax included)                            150 talents

Grand Total:                                        3050 talents

Payable upon delivery

Cash only (no credit)

Come Back and See Us Again and Be Sure To Bring A Friend!
```

"This is outrageous!" she replied. "I'm not paying three thousand, fifty talents for these flyblown, flea-bitten humpbacks!"

"That's the price, lady—and I didn't even include the labor. My jockeys don't work for free, you know. As it is, by the time I pay 'em and refund Omar to boot, I'm barely seeing a profit! Don't be cheap like an Arab and try to chisel me down now—just dole out the dinars!"

"But that's most of our hard cash," complained Helgayarn. "What are we supposed to live on, our looks?"

"If so, you're gonna starve," mumbled the salesman.

"What was that?"

"Nothing," replied Abdullah. "Nothing at all!"

"Just pay the man, Helly," admonished Brunnhilde. "Pay him and let's get out of here. Nazareth's a long way off and I had hopes of spending the night in a decent Jerusalem hotel."

But Helgayarn refused to give in. "What about this fuel charge?" she demanded. "You're charging us for water?"

"Nothing's free, sweetheart and around here water ain't cheap!"

"Well, what about the sales tax then?"

"What about it?" asked Abdullah. "It's the standard 10 percent tax. It goes to fund the Roman roads. Everyone here has to fork over a few drachmas to the Caesars."

"Well, I refuse to pay it!" retorted Helgayarn. "I bow to no Roman toady!"

"You do," he replied, "if you don't want to end your days nailed to a tree! Around here everyone pays their taxes. A portion goes to Herod Antipas and a portion to Pilate. But the lion share goes back to Rome to fund the treasuries of Caesar himself. He's one greedy son of a bitch, and he doesn't take well, I'll tell you, to people who don't pay their taxes. He'll crucify you in a New York minute if you defy him!"

"Just let him try!" challenged Helgayarn. "I dare him! I double dare him! That Roman rube's got nothing on me! I'll carve him and his legions into mincemeat—just see if I don't!"

"If you say so, lady. In the meantime, the tax is two hundred talents."

"Just pay it, Helly," Brunnhilde whined.

Helgayarn looked at her evilly before returning her frigid gaze to Abdullah the Mullah. "What about these license and registration fees?" she snidely asked. "What are they all about?"

"Another tax the Romans have imposed for using their roads. It's the law of the Caesars—no unregistered vehicles on the highways!"

"I thought you said there weren't any highways!"

"I did," replied Abdullah. "The Romans, however, would beg to disagree. Personally, I don't grade 'em as much more than cobblestone carriageways whose traverse from Rome to Jerusalem is a journey juxtaposed with jumbles of potholes, ruts, and carelessly placed cobbles, making the trek from here to there, a tiresome drag.

THE CHRISTMAS RABBIT

Why, even here in downtown Jerusalem, the Romans have had their way and Main Street has become Main Drag! But as the saying goes, when in Rome—and we are part of the Roman Empire—do as the Romans do. Use the roads and pay the tax."

"Suppose we refuse to do either?"

"Lady," Abdullah replied with a sigh, "it's your own lookout if you want to stray off the beaten path and go wandering about in the wilderness. Who am I to say? But either way, you'll pay to license your vehicles or they remain parked in the lot."

Helgayarn made one last attempt to trim a talent or two from her bill. "What about the insurance?" she asked. "Surely you can cut us a break there. We're already insured after all, with Repressive Insurance of Mesozoic Mesopotamia—a very old and established firm!"

"No kidding!" replied the Mullah. "Same guys I use! Sure, I can take that off your bills. Got your cards?"

"Eh?'

"Your insurance cards! You got 'em with you?"

Helgayarn looked at Betty, who merely shrugged.

"I didn't think to bring mine," the junior witch said. "I never thought I'd need it. Didn't you bring yours?"

Helgayarn scowled. Turning back to Abdullah, she shrugged while displaying her empty hands.

"It would seem," she said, "that my sister and I left our cards back home on the dining room table."

"Really?" replied Abdullah. "Your insurance card is like your American Express—don't leave home without it. No card, no adjustment. Three thousand, fifty talents please."

Helgayarn gave up, gave in, and in the end gave out. "Can I use my American Express?" she asked. "I did remember to bring that."

"Don't leave home without it but don't expect to use it around here either," replied Abdullah. "Read the rider on the bill, lady—no credit!"

"But it's American Express!"

"Go tell it to Karl Malden—we don't take it around here!"

Helgayarn looked near tears. This Samaritan was going to get the best of her despite *her best* efforts to the contrary. Thank the fates that there was no one around to see her laid so low—and by a glorified "jockey" at that! "What about a check?" she asked. "Will you take a check?"

Abdullah had the nerve to look put out. "You mean a personal one?"

"Of course I mean a personal one," Helgayarn snapped. "Whoever heard of an impersonal check?"

Abdullah uttered a brief chuckle. "From an out-of-towner, drawn on an out-of-state bank? Get outta here!"

In the end, with no arguments left, Helgayarn reluctantly forked over the cash. As she handed over each individual talent it sighed as it slipped through her fingers, whereupon it sang out a merry tune when clutched by the greedy mitts of Abdullah the Mullah. The exchange of so much cash put a hurtin' on the duo's financial fortunes. They were planning on using most of that money to stay in swanky hotels. Now they'd have to settle for third-rate inns and stables instead, and they'd look pretty damned silly, they knew, sitting amongst the cows and goats while dressed in their evening gowns.

Bargaining is thirsty work especially when you lose. Helgayarn found that her throat was parched. "Could you spare a cup of water?" she asked the Mullah.

"Oh sure," came the reply. "That'll be fifty drachmas a cup ..."

*****

In the end, they paid for their water and a road map as well. Drawn on a piece of ancient papyrus and rolled up like a scroll, it was all but useless to the Witches as its roads and byways, cities and towns, alternate routes and mileage scales, were notated in Aramaic—a language that was even more puzzling to them than Betty's longwinded shorthand. But they assumed that the largest city on the map was Jerusalem and so headed off in a southeasterly direction. It was their plan to arrive at the City of David well before nightfall in order to prosecute their search for a good room. They still had some talents and drachmas on their persons, despite Abdullah's attempt to rob them of each remaining shekel, and planned to put them to good use.

As they traveled southeast, wending their way through mountain passes and traversing quiet valleys rich in olive groves, grapevines, and fields of wheat, they began to take note of the invisible yet omniscient presence, which Betty'd cited in her journal. There was a powerful undercurrent running throughout the land, which seemed to nevertheless hover above it. Therefore above them and below them and to either side as well, they were painfully aware of its presence. It humbled them in its quiet majesty, demanding that they bow their heads while keeping their big mouths shut. Such demands were hard on them both, but especially Helgayarn, who was used to holding her head erect while walking proudly and firing off commentary and snotty repartee whenever she felt so inclined. They plodded along, side by side, each atop of their camels, situated between the two humps, with their legs dangling over the sides and resting on the saddlebags. Their two baggage camels, one attached to each of their own beasts by means of a rope, shuffled along silently behind them. From time to time, they passed various peasants, wanderers, troubadours, tax collectors, and minor prophets. Each gave them a wide berth. For Helly's part, she wanted no truck with the locals. Let the peasantry blow! She was here to see one man and one man only. The Hebrews passing by, however, had a long history of oppression and affliction at the hands of others, and whether you argued that such misfortunes were a matter of mere circumstance or the result of having to lie upon beds which they themselves made, such bitter experience had taught them to recognize misery and trouble when they saw it coming. Therefore whenever a local took note of Helgayarn and Brunnhilde approaching while mounted atop their vehicles, he or she wandered off to the far side of the olive grove.

Jerusalem proved itself to be farther away than it looked on the map. They ended up passing that first night at the base of Mt. Gerizim, halfway between Megiddo and the capitol, an altogether inhospitable place. The night air was chill, the winds howled, and all about the Judean wilderness came the cry of wild animals, lions and wolves, to disturb their slumber. The camels were edgy and shuffled about nervously. There was no well in their immediate area from which to obtain moisture and they foolishly forgot to buy extra from Abdullah when they'd had the chance. So both they and their beasts went thirsty. In an effort to warm her body, which was chilled to the bone, and to convey some sense of security to the camels, which seemed to grow edgier with each passing minute, Helgayarn mumbled some jumbo in an attempt to ignite a fire. But as Betty had stated in her journal, such magics were mysteriously suppressed in this strange land, and she could not get a single stick she had Brunnhilde gather to so much as smolder. They spent the night cramped, uncomfortable, and cold, with little sleep and constantly on watch.

The rising sun which should've been a blessing to them revealed itself to be the opposite. From the moment it crested the eastern horizon it began to beat down upon both they and their mounts, broiling and baking them like Idaho potatoes. From the sky above it glared down menacingly as it hammered away at them while draining the moisture from both they and their camels, whose humps it could be seen, were shriveling away and drying up. The beasts panted and brayed out their protests at being led so foolishly by such inexperienced jockeys.

"I don't think we're going to make Jerusalem," said Betty, "if we don't find a filling station soon! Our camels are just about empty and I really need to take a whiz!"

Helgayarn offered Brunnhilde her dour appraisal. "Why didn't you go back at camp?" she asked. "Why wait and hold it till now?"

Brunnhilde looked nonplussed. "I should drop my drawers out in the open," she queried, "for all to see? I couldn't very well do that! I'm a witch—I have my modesty and reputation to uphold!"

"Bunny," replied Helly, "the land is empty. There's no one around for miles to see. There's just the two of us and you have nothing down there which interests me!"

Brunnhilde sniffed out her reply. "There's the camels," she said. "Who knows what interests them or how they get their thrills."

"Camels are only interested in, and thrilled by, water."

THE CHRISTMAS RABBIT

"Well that's what I was about to make!" the junior witch stated self-righteously. "I didn't want them sniffing around while I was making it!"

"Good grief!" replied Helgayarn. "I guess then that you'll just have to hold it till we get there! Now be a good girl, will you, and keep silent while we keep moving. Jerusalem can't be much further away. I'm sure we'll arrive there before too much longer." They plodded onward, passing the grueling hours beneath the torturing sun in uneasy silence.

About an hour before dusk they made Jerusalem, passing into the city through the Sheep's gate. The Pharisees and Sadducees gathered there to sit in judgment of the various cases brought before them, along with the traders and vendors who congregated at the gate as well in order to conduct business, eyed the couple warily as they passed under the arch. Jerusalem, being a trade center of the Middle East, saw its share of foreigners, including in the opinions of most, far too many Romans, but never had anyone seen anything such as the likes of these two. They were dirty, dusty, disheveled, and damn near done in, so it wasn't surprising then to find when they inquired after lodging that there was nary a room to be found. In addition to their questionable appearances, which brought with them their own difficulties, it seemed that Herod Antipas was in residence at his winter palace and was throwing a grand fete in honor of the Roman governor, Pontius Pilate, to whom he was ever sucking up. The party was to be held the very next night and therefore every hotel in Jerusalem had been booked the week before by the Who's Who of Jewry who'd received their invitations in the mail a week ago and who, for the life of them, could not come up with a reasonable excuse for avoiding such an unpleasant affair. Helgayarn and Brunnhilde sought lodging at the Hotel Hebrew but its manager, sniffing at them disdainfully while regarding their squalor, told them the Hotel was booked to capacity. From there they made inquiries at the Jerusalem Arms, where they were greeted in similar fashion and told the same thing. They then canvassed the Israeli Inn but were not even allowed to pass through the revolving door. Even the Holiday Inn, it seemed, was filled to overflowing. It was getting late on a Friday night, and they were getting ready to give up when they decided to make one last attempt. They inquired after rooms at the Bethsaida Bed & Breakfast, where on Saturdays, the Sabbath, there was provided for free a bountiful continental brunch complete with lox and bagels, but were told promptly to beat it. "Try one of the neighboring villages," someone suggested. "Perhaps you'll find a room there."

They wandered through the suburbs, getting denied lodging wherever they inquired of it until finally sporting saddle sores on their sterns the size of small softballs they came upon a third-rate inn situated in Bethlehem where the manager reluctantly deigned to offer them lodging. "I don't normally take in foreigners," he said, "especially dirty ones and especially on the Sabbath! All of Herod's revelers who couldn't find lodgings in downtown Jerusalem have booked every room I've available. I can pack you away in the manger for a talent or two, but only if I squeeze you in between the cows and goats! That's the best I can do. You want it?"

Helgayarn looked despairingly at Betty. It seemed that they didn't have too much choice. Jerusalem and its suburbs were crawling with footpads and hooligans this late in the evening and although such ruffians would normally have been of little concern to the duo, they were nevertheless wary of such gadabouts as with their arrival in this strange land they seemed powerless to act in their own defense. "Has it got running water?" asked Helgayarn.

The innkeeper laughed. "It's a stable, lady," he said. "Not the Ritz Carlton. It has a watering trough, and you're welcome to it."

Helgayarn sighed while forking over the two talents. "Just don't put us next to a pile of cattle craps," she pleaded. "Our lives of late have been nothing but one encounter after another with those!"

"Not to worry," the innkeeper replied jovially. "I've a nice corner tucked away that I've kept clean and cared for since I last let it out to the previous guests some thirty years ago. It just didn't seem right to me to let it get soiled and sullied after they'd graced it with their presence." Helgayarn might've wondered what he meant by that cryptic remark but was too tired and world-weary, too spent and saddle sore, to be overly concerned with such riddles. "Just see us there," she replied, "and water our camels. We'll be grateful for it."

The innkeeper led them to the stable, pointing out to them as they entered its one clean and cared-for corner. "That's your suite!" he said. "Have a good night!"

Helgayarn watched his retreating form disappear into the evening shadows. As soon as he was gone, she took note once again of that omniscient presence which seemed to envelop the entire stable. Wholesome and nurturing, it brought with it a refreshing sensation that was both cleansing and healing, and although Helgayarn and Brunnhilde were in dire need of both, they nonetheless found its influence repellent.

"My word," remarked Brunnhilde, "it's as though all the omnipresence that hovers about this forsaken land was gathered up in this very hut! What on earth do you suppose ever occurred here?"

Helgayarn nervously cast her gaze about, peering into shadows and scrutinizing nooks and corners, taking note of the cows and camels and assuring herself that they and they alone shared the confines of the hovel with the livestock and the livestock only. "I haven't any idea," replied the big witch. "But whatever it was it certainly has left its mark. You can almost taste the purity on your tongue. It's enough to make me gag!"

They settled down uneasily for the night, making beds out of straw and trying to get some sleep. But they couldn't fall off as the presence they'd sensed kept reasserting itself into their fitful attempts to slip into slumber. They kept bounding awake with a start just as they were about to nod off, only to spring up with hearts racing while feeling disoriented and slightly outside their own bodies. It was disconcerting. Moreover, it was frightening.

"This won't do at all!" Helgayarn complained. "I barely slept a wink last night out in that open wilderness. Now it appears that I'll sleep even less tonight!"

Brunnhilde, who was wrestling with the same difficulties herself, turned over to address her leader. "We'll get even less than that," she replied, "if a certain witch doesn't button up and keep quiet!"

They passed the night fitfully and only after each agreed to keep watch while the other slept. The best either could manage however was to doze restlessly while tossing and turning. A rooster crowed promptly at the crack of dawn, forcing them to give up the effort. They arose wearily, brushing the hayseed and chaff from off their clothing and out of their hair. Retrieving from their overnight kits their toothbrushes, they made their bleary way to the water trough while rubbing the weariness out of their eyes. Bending over the sluice bucket, Helgayarn's noggin collided with a head of cattle that had it in mind to perform the very same toilet.

"Moove over, lady," said the cow impatiently. "I was here first!"

Helgayarn, rubbing her forehead, rose up to confront the bovine. "Listen, bub," she said in its own language, "you'll moove before I do, got it? I'm a witch—you're just another barnyard animal. I have rights! My position gives me privileges and the right to first place!"

"Not around here it don't," replied the cow. "The rabbi says that the last shall be first, and the first shall be last! I had the honor, you know, of beating out a tune for him along with that lamb over there when the little drummer boy played for him all those years ago. My but those were good times!"

Helgayarn looked at the cow in disbelief. "You know the rabbi?" she asked. "You've met him?

"Oh sure," replied the cow. "Born right here, he was—in this very shed! What a night! I remember it like yesterday! People coming and going and everybody wanting a peek at him. And do you think he made a fuss over all the attention? Not one peep or complaint out of him, just a beautiful smile for everyone who beheld him! He was glorious, I tell you, absolutely glorious! You'd do well to remember the things he says!"

This was too much for the big witch. It was bad enough that those three wise guys should've prattled on so about the young man. Worse still that he should have had such a profound effect on Betty, but it seemed that even the cattle, who in her experience were normally pretty levelheaded except when stampeding, had succumbed to this upstart's charms, and had managed to do so while he'd still been

THE CHRISTMAS RABBIT

a baby! And now to be lectured about him by this Jersey cow that had the nerve to carry itself as if it were the dean of Columbia College and its manger the very halls of academia itself—well that was more than one witch should be made to bear!

"I'm getting out of here!" she said flatly to Brunnhilde, who stood off to the side, mouth agape, and nervously twisting her fingers. "I'll not stay another minute in such a coop as this where cattle craps are allowed to flow freely and where cows hold court as if they were rabbis themselves! What have cattle to teach me? It's brainwashing, that's what it is! And I refuse to have my brain washed by a bullock!"

"You be surprised what you could learn from a cow," replied the Jersey. "Especially if you insist on being as stubborn as a mule!"

"Fiddlesticks!" retorted Helgayarn, snapping her fingers under the beast's nose. "You've nothing to teach me, old sod! I was stampeding your kind when they were still roaming around in encounter groups!" Having got the last word in she left the cow smiling sadly to itself and grabbing ahold of Brunnhilde, made for the inn proper in order to confront the innkeeper. She'd demand of him a decent room, away from such pedestrian confines and the uppity cud-chewers who chose to live in them!

They pounded on the front door, rousing a bleary-eyed maid with tousled hair who was just getting ready to fetch the morning water from the neighboring well.

"We insist upon seeing the innkeeper!" demanded Helgayarn. "Our lodgings are totally unsatisfactory. They won't do at all and we insist of him that he evict some person of lesser stature in order to make room for us. In fact, we demand it!"

"I'm sorry, ma'am," the maid replied tentatively. "But my master is abed yet and has not risen."

"Well then, wake him, girl. Wake him!"

"I dare not," replied the maiden. "He's of a generally sour disposition and even the more so when awoken needlessly in the middle of the night!"

"Middle of the night? It's dawn, you dolt! The roosters are crowing and the world is waking! Now go see to it that he does likewise!"

The maid, a young woman named Miriam, insisted upon refusal. "My master," she said, "will have nothing to say to you! There are no rooms to be let! Even room 13 is occupied and we rarely book that! We're full to overflowing!"

Helgayarn was about to continue her tirade which, the maid Miriam knew, would surely arouse her master, to the detriment of the entire household as well as the guests. Thinking quickly, she came up with a plan to defuse the situation. "Would you two care to have a seat in the common room and there await my master's pleasure?" she asked. "I've started a warm fire, and if you give me a moment to fetch water, I can put on a hot cup of tea for you while offering you breakfast."

The big witch allowed herself to be pacified by the maiden's offer, eyeing her sternly nevertheless. "Very well," she replied roughly. See us in and seat us at the fire. And see to that tea and do so quickly! My sister and I are very important people where we come from and are not accustomed to the primitive accommodations we've been made to endure!"

"Yes, ma'am." The maid fled just as fast as her sandaled feet would carry her only to realize once she escaped that a fast flight meant a hasty return. She had chores in the common room, she'd promised them tea, and there would be no avoiding those two old crones. She walked to the well while hoping that she'd break her leg along the way. When that didn't happen and she arrived safely, she sent out a silent prayer to the God of Israel, pleading with him to cast her in. When that didn't occur either, she contemplated tossing herself down the well on her own. Anything was better than facing those two again. But she knew that if she didn't serve them their tea and do so quickly, then not only would she have to face their acrimonious rancor but the wrath of her master too, for surely the vocal abuses they were bound to hurl her way would wake her master, who at his best was less than pleasant, especially when awoken early on a Saturday. He was a man who took his Sabbaths seriously—not that he went out of his way to go to temple—but he liked the idea of a day off with pay, especially if there was someone else around to do the work. As a result he could be counted upon to sleep in

THE CHRISTMAS RABBIT

most Sabbaths until at least nine, unless of course, a problem arose with a guest that the household staff were incapable of addressing or unwilling to see to. Then, as if his senses were attuned to such matters and he dreamt of them while sleeping, he would bound out of bed like an angry bear charging from its den, having been unduly and prematurely deprived of its hibernation. When that happened the bear was prone to do more than just growl. He roared and lashed out with his fists. Miriam, having been on the receiving end of many of those blows, knew from bitter experience what she could expect if her inattention led to the master's premature arousal. She didn't know what would be worse, to be caught between the two old hags in the common room or between her master's two fists. She suspected the former but was wary of the latter nevertheless.

Hurrying back from the well, Miriam ran through the inn's front door and into the kitchen where she put the kettle on the fire.

Helgayarn heard her come through the door and hissed at her. "Is my tea ready yet?" she demanded. "Hurry it along, will you? And bring us some breadsticks too!"

Miriam returned to the common room in a jiffy, carrying a tray with two teacups upon it and a small plate of matzo.

"It's about time!" Helgayarn snapped. "Did you go to China for that damned tea or did you have to dig a new well to find water? C'mon, girl! Set the cotton pickin' tray down and then be about your business!"

Brunnhilde nodded while assessing the maid callously. Good domestic help was so hard to find! She'd be sure to add a notation in their guide—*Miserable Meals and the Chefs Who Serve Them*, about the substandard quality of service to be found at this third-rate fleabag!

A tearful Miriam set the tray gently down between them. "The bread is fresh, my ladies," she said. "I was up before the sun in order to bake it."

"You damned well ought to be, you lazy good-for-nothing!" remarked Brunnhilde. "Probably idled away your evening hours nestled in a feather bed while we were made to sleep with the cows! How dare your master be so inconsiderate! Cows and the cattle craps that go with 'em are for serving wenches such as you—not ladies like us!"

"Yes, ma'am," she replied meekly. "I'll be sure to relate your concerns to my master."

"See that you do!" replied Brunnhilde. "Now run along!"

Miriam began to back away, about to make a grateful exit to the relative safety of the kitchen, when Helgayarn stopped her.

"What is this?" asked the big witch in disbelief as she held up a piece of matzo for examination. "You don't expect me to eat this, do you?"

"It's bread, ma'am," replied Miriam, staring down at the floor.

"Bread? It feels like cardboard!"

"It's unleavened, ma'am," replied the maid in an attempt to offer a reasonable explanation. "My master allows only unleavened bread in the house on the Sabbath. We may serve the guests neither yeast nor wine."

Helgayarn looked scandalized. "No yeast? No lard or greasy fat either?"

"No, ma'am," replied a timid Miriam. "Just hard bread and well water."

"You mean, I can't even get an egg and a sausage patty?"

The maid meekly shook her head.

"Or a rasher of bacon either?"

Again the maid offered a negative reply.

"But we're not Jewish!" snapped Brunnhilde. "We're nondenominational!"

The maid shrugged sheepishly, as if to say, "that's your tough luck, not mine."

This was absolutely the last straw. Since their arrival in Jerusalem, in an effort to remain incognito and to move among the populace unnoticed as they sought out the rabbi, they'd been forced to swallow more than their fair share of humble pie at the hands of contemptible camel jockeys, ignominious innkeepers, and now smart-assed serving wenches who hid behind masks of seeming servility whilst denying to them the proper respect and attention they deserved. She would take no more of it! She began to yell, lathering the poor maiden with the

THE CHRISTMAS RABBIT

unwholesome saliva of her misbegotten temper tantrum. Spittle flew from her mouth in ropey stringers, which stuck to the maid's cheeks and clothing like spiderwebs. But Miriam, powerless to do anything else, merely stood there while heeding to the Rabbi's admonishment to turn her other cheek. How she wished him here now! Surely this old hag wouldn't carry on so if the rabbi were present! She tried to pacify the old witch. "Please, my lady," she pleaded. "You'll awaken my master, and sheol will surely follow after him!"

"I'll see him in hell myself," Helgayarn screeched, "if we don't get us some proper service and a decent bite to eat! He'll get more than his fair share of purgatory, pandemonium, and perdition if this Mickey Mouse public house of his doesn't start putting out. I'm not called Helgayarn for nothing, girl!"

Such was the volume of Helgayarn's ranting that the walls of the inn trembled to the throbbing of her discordant whining. Guests could be heard to stir about in their rooms while wondering to themselves if the inn were caught up in the throes of a minor earthquake. Above them and to the left, a door slammed loudly followed by a heavy tread which could be heard coming down the hall. "What in the name of jumpin' Jehosophat is going on around here?" a rumbling voice asked. "Can't a decent Jew get himself a Sabbath slumber anymore? Miriam! Where are you, wench? Answer me when I call for you!"

The maid ran up the stairs and down the hall in order to relate to her master the morning's events. Confronting him, she bowed her head meekly and whispered to him, her tale.

Down in the common room, with smug smiles upon their faces, the Witches took delight in the landlord's discomfort as he bellowed out his displeasure. "You let them in?" he demanded loudly. "Gentiles under my roof, and on the Sabbath at that? What am I, an Arab that I should have to endure such uninvited guests? You know better than to open my door on the Sabbath!"

"But, my lord," pleaded Miriam, "they were knocking so loudly and at such an early hour I feared for your slumber lest it be unnecessarily disturbed—"

The innkeeper cut her off with the wave of his arm as his backhand connected with the side of her head. "Enough out of you!" he fumed. "My slumber has been disturbed nevertheless!"

Helgayarn and Brunnhilde delighted in the maiden's abuse. Serves her right, they thought, for offering us stale bread and tepid tea!

Above them they could hear the landlord continuing his tirade. "I suppose that I'll have to go deal with 'em," he complained. "And the other guests too, who've no doubt been awakened by your incompetence and lack of discretion. They should never have been allowed admission! Oh, how you'd better pray the Pharisees and the Sadducees don't hear about this! You know what traditionalists they are! They'll be citing the Torah from now till next Tuesday, while demanding of me extra sacrifices at temple in order to be forgiven this oversight! But not a word of rebuke will they have for you, will they? No! They won't deign to even look at a pretty slip like yourself—never mind actually speaking to her or burdening her with unwanted scriptural recitals! They'll save all of that for me! God of my fathers why was I ever born a Jew? The life of a simple pagan would be simply idyllic!"

Helgayarn and Brunnhilde were the pictures of innocence as they observed the innkeeper descending the stairs. When he reached the bottom he spread his arms wide in an all-encompassing and sympathetic gesture of commiseration.

"My ladies," he pleaded. "Forgive my maid, a dullard from the boonies of Berea, a simple country wench, witless and lacking in social graces, for her missteps in both mistreating you and allowing you entrance in the first place."

The Witches regarded him with leaden stares. "For you see," he continued, "it is against our law to allow gentiles to seek shelter under the same roof as ourselves. 'Keep ye separate,' so says the Torah. 'Eat no manner of unclean food.'"

"We're anything but 'Gentile,'" replied Helgayarn dryly. "In fact, we take pride in being rough around the edges—in other words, don't get on our bad side, bub! We want a decent room and we want it yesterday!"

THE CHRISTMAS RABBIT

"But my ladies," pleaded the landlord, "You're not descendants of Abraham! You're not of the twelve tribes! You can't just come waltzing in here like a pair of happy-go-lucky Philistines and expect me to put you up! What would my neighbors say?"

Helgayarn yawned in boredom. "I don't give a cattle crap what your neighbors say. Neighbors will always talk and spread gossip—it's the only thing they're good for! Just give us a room!"

The innkeeper sailed off on another tack. "But as I told you last night," he replied, "we've no vacancies!"

Helgayarn wandered over to the front desk and began flipping through the registry.

"Hey!" said the innkeeper, beginning to bridle. "You can't do that! My guests trust me to guard their privacy!" He stomped over to the counter with the intention of forcibly removing the ledger, but one look from the big witch caused him to halt in midstride. He shuffled his feet nervously while wilting under her contemptuous glare. His mouth opened to give utterance to further objections but she silenced him with a wave of her hand. "Let's see, shall we," she said, "just who's been allowed to register here and who has not! Hmm, in room 12 we have one Augustus Agrippa, as *gentile* as Gentle Ben, surely a Roman and obviously here for Herod's big hoe down while being unable to book a decent room in Jerusalem proper. Why else would he overnight here? And upstairs in room 17, we have Sheik Ali Ben Ali. A sheik! He's certainly no Jew! Do your Pharisees and Sadducees know you're entertaining camel jockeys? I'm sure they don't."

"He pays me in gold drachmas," came the innkeeper's humble reply. "And he delivers to me the best spices from Damascus and Baghdad, plus all the news and latest gossip!"

"Doesn't that Torah of yours admonish you not to participate in gossip?"

"It forbids me from spreading it," the innkeeper replied defiantly. "Not listening to it!"

"One cannot spread manure," replied Helgayarn matter-of-factly, "if one does not have a fertile field upon which to scatter it! And you're wrong, my good man, with regard to your interpretation of the Torah. I may not be Jewish, but I've read the book, and I know for myself what it says!"

The innkeeper managed to look contrite while promising himself once he was rid of these two old crones, that he'd take his embarrassment out in full upon that muttonhead, Miriam. "It seems to me," remarked Helgayarn, "that you're housing many a non-Jew within the inn this evening. Do the Pharisees and Sadducees know that?"

"They know!" replied the landlord. "I kick 'em back 10 percent of the gross for every Gentile, Samaritan, and pagan I put up with, and they turn a blind eye. It never ceases to amaze me how money has a way of making you right with the church!"

"Ain't it the truth?" commiserated Helgayarn.

"Damn straight!" replied the innkeeper. "But that still doesn't change the fact that we're booked to capacity. It's not as though I can build you an annex!" Helgayarn continued flipping through the journal's pages. She paused on the last page and looked up at the landlord. "Well, my, my!" said she, "what have we here?" It seems that Augustus Agrippa and party checked out unexpectedly in the middle of the night!"

"Eh?"

"You betcha! Miriam made a notation in your ledger here—and who would've thought that simpleton was lettered? Seems Agrippa and friends were called back suddenly, all the way to Rome itself. They must've done something to needle Tiberius! I pity poor Agrippa. The emperor isn't one to have on your bad side. A nasty bugger he is! But that can be of no concern to us. What is pertinent however, is that with his departure Agrippa's rooms remain vacant! You will therefore let them to us immediately."

"Let me see that journal!" demanded the innkeeper.

Helgayarn graciously handed it to him. He scanned the last entry in disbelief. Agrippa, he knew, was so looking forward to Herod's party.

"Miriam!" he called out.

THE CHRISTMAS RABBIT

The maid, covered now in a kerchief to hide the bruise on the side of her face, came running down the stairs. "Yes, my lord?" she inquired.

"Is this true?" asked the landlord, shoving the journal under her nose. "Did Agrippa leave in the middle of the night?"

"Yes, my lord. A centurion came to the inn inquiring after him and demanding his presence. He's been recalled to Rome."

"Why didn't you wake me?" the landlord asked furiously. "You know I like to be on hand to speed the departing guest!"

"Sire, it was the middle of the night, and you'd spent early yesterday afternoon before sundown deep into two bottles of Boones Farm and one of Manischewitz as you prepared for the Sabbath! Joshua trumpeting around the walls of Jericho couldn't wake you from that kind of drunk!"

"Bah!" replied the innkeeper, kicking her squarely in the can for her embarrassing honesty. The maid, teary-eyed once again, fled to the scullery. Turning his attention back to Helgayarn and Brunnhilde, the innkeeper offered them his best diplomatic smile. "Well this changes everything," he said. "I was unaware we had a vacancy available. Of course you can have it—it's a three-bedroom suite, however, with a common sitting room connecting all three. Therefore it's priced to move. You ladies got drachmas?"

"Indeed. Just see to it that your valet removes our luggage from our camels' saddlebags and delivers it to our room."

The innkeeper looked nonplussed. "This is a simple country inn," he replied, "not the Waldorf! We don't have valets here! I've a manservant named John, however, that you could make use of if you tipped him properly."

Both Helgayarn and Brunnhilde cast apprehensive looks at the innkeeper.

"Did you say his name was John?" Helgayarn tentatively asked.

The landlord returned their looks with a curious appraisal of his own. "Yeah, that's right," he replied. "John bar Baptiste. Bar Baptiste is an affectation he's adopted in honor of that river dipper that Herod beheaded a few months ago. Don't rightly know what his last name is, but he's a good lad, both strong and dependable. Gotta do something about his diet however. The boy eats nothing but locusts and wild honey. It's enough to make a fella go bugshit! Have a lamb chop, I'm always saying to him. Or a good mutton roast!"

"But you did say the fellow's name was John bar?"

"Yeah!"

"And John is Hebrew for Jack, correct?"

"I suppose," replied the innkeeper, "if that's the way you see things."

"I do," replied Helgayarn. "Therefore we can safely infer that this John bar Baptiste fellow, whatever his real name might be, is some John's boy or son of Jack, is that correct. The innkeeper could only nod, unsure of where this conversation was heading. "Ergo," she continued, it's only right to assume that he is, in fact, a 'sonofajack?" The crone and her sisters hated SOJ's more than SOB's. Helgayarn looked to Brunnhilde, who merely nodded. "That fellow won't do at all," said Helgayarn. "My sister and I have a deep-seated and long-standing aversion to anyone or anything named Jack or any of its subsequent namesakes, nomens, nudums, appellatives, or appellations—so if he be named Jack, Jacque, John, or Johann—or if he, in fact be a she and being such is named either Jackie, Jacqueline, Joanne, or Johanna, then we want no truck with that person, is this clear? Send us instead that simple maiden, that peasant Miriam. She'll do just fine for carrying our suitcases!"

"Are you two for real?" the innkeeper asked incredulously. "I saw for myself how your camels were laden! Their knees were buckling under the burden of linens, lingerie, lounging pajamas, and various leggings that you've stuffed in their saddlebags! It would take a whole slew of subjects, slaves, and indentured servants to do your unpacking! Surely you can't expect the poor girl to bear up under that?"

"She'll make out just fine," replied Helgayarn dryly. "After all, she puts up with you, doesn't she?" To that observation the innkeeper had nothing to say other than to remind the duo to tip poor Miriam appropriately.

"You may show us to our room now," demanded Brunnhilde, "and have a servant run us a bath."

THE CHRISTMAS RABBIT

"Sure," replied the landlord. "But as you're now staying in the inn proper, I'm going to need you ladies to sign the register."

Helgayarn and Brunnhilde were at a loss. It was all they could do in light of their magic's mysterious suspension, to maintain their disguises. Their false noses tended to fall from their faces if not constantly administered to and reapplied with process gum and rubber cement. Their colored contacts, with which they hoped to disguise their eyes, were constantly graying out and in need of replacement. Their wax ears drooped and melted if exposed too long to the Judean sun. The frogs they'd placed in their throats to disguise their voices were constantly croaking out complaints while choking to death on the grit and dust that hung in the air like dewdrops on flower petals. If they didn't find the rabbi soon, the jig would be up. Their disguises would fall away and they'd be exposed for the witches they were. Certainly not the worst thing that could happen, they supposed, but they were trying to maintain a low profile. And now this Hebrew wanted their autographs! "We'd rather not," replied Helgayarn. "We're of a mind to keep our names to ourselves."

"That's fine by me," replied the landlord. "However, Tiberius's tax collectors base my taxes on the guests I have registered. I've tried cheating him once or twice and have always paid dearly for it when I did. Fines, levies, whippings, and scourges. Got threatened with crucifixion the next time I try dippin' in their well. Dammit, it's my well! Conquering bastards! Someday our Messiah will come, and boy, howdy when he does! Will they get theirs? You betcha! In the meantime, it's sign the register or sleep in the barn. Your choice."

Both witches dreaded the thought of revealing their names, but even more abhorrent to them was the idea of spending the afternoon in the manger trying to relax, enveloped as they would be in the odor of cattle craps as it wafted in the afternoon breeze while at the same time wrestling with that bothersome omnipresence, which pervaded the manger itself. They desperately needed their rest if they were going to crash Herod's party. For surely that rabbi, if he were half the magician Betty'd made him out to be, would be in attendance. One didn't throw a party, they knew, here in the Middle East, without the proper combination of belly dancers, fortune-tellers, and magicians.

That made the evening rock 'n' roll! And when you could afford the best, as Herod surely could, then you booked it. Surely then this rabbi fellow was on the program. Giving in, Helgayarn took the register from the innkeeper and signed it for both her and Brunnhilde. The innkeeper looked over her signature doubtfully. "Mrs. and Mrs. Smith?" he inquired skeptically. "You're lesbians? Better keep that quiet and take separate bedrooms in the suite! No telling what the Pharisees will do if they here about this! Call for my stoning while running the two of you out of town!" Helgayarn offered him a scowl that would peel the skin off new potatoes. "We're not lesbians," she said adamantly. "We're sisters…in-law."

"Oh, well that's different," said the manager relieved. Sister-in-laws are kosher!" He gave them a measured appraisal. "Say, you ladies aren't married to those cough-drop fellows, are you—you know, the Smith Brothers?"

"Never heard of them," Helgayarn lied, while wishing she had a few of their lozenges in order to keep at bay the rebellious frogs residing in her throat. "Now will you please just see us to our suite and ensure that our baths are drawn and our luggage laid out? Ensure as well that we have a proper meal and put us in a wake-up call for seven p.m. Also see to it that our camels are watered and washed, will you? They smell like camels! Anoint them with something—but no frankincense or myrrh. We don't want 'em smelling like wise guys! Better still, after hosing them off, rub 'em down with vinegar!

"You're kinda pushy for two old crones with no place to stay, aren't ya?"

"Brother, you don't know the half of it," warned Brunnhilde. "Now, if you know what's good for you, you'll do as my sister asks and be quick about it!"

"Okay, okay!" the innkeeper grudgingly replied. "I'm just trying to make conversation! But if you're going to be snotty, I'll just see to your wishes… First however, I'm gonna need them drachmas!"

*****

THE CHRISTMAS RABBIT

Helgayarn and Brunnhilde lay luxuriously in their baths while Miriam busied herself washing their hair and filing their nails. She hardly had the strength after hauling all their luggage up the stairs but somehow made it because she'd been told by the innkeeper to expect a good tip—which she should also expect to split with him. "Pour me another glass of wine, dear," demanded Helgayarn. Miriam stopped filing Brunnhilde's nails in order to see to this latest demand. Out in the common room there was laid on the table half a roast pig, clams on the half shell, and any number of nonkosher foodstuffs, as well as carafe upon carafe of wine. The innkeeper's restrictions regarding the sanctity of the Sabbath did not apply to the high rollers who frequented the inn. *And well they shouldn't*, thought Helgayarn. They were paying top drachma to stay here. Jerusalem prices for a Bethlehem boarding house! It was ridiculous. In total, seventy-five talents a night plus a nonrefundable room key deposit! Did the innkeeper think they were going to steal the room? Well, there was no help for it. They desperately needed creature comforts if they were going to get some rest before the evening ahead. Somehow and without causing a scene, they would have to find a way to crash Herod's party.

Miriam brought Helgayarn her glass of wine.

"That'll be all for now," the witch said. "Be about your business and see to our ironing. We'll ring when we need you."

"Yes, ma'am," replied the maid, who stood there nervously dancing on two feet and awkward with anticipation as if awaiting the arrival of a bus which hadn't been invented yet. Looking up from the warmth of her bath, Helgayarn considered the tiresome creature before her. "What is it?" she asked impatiently.

Miriam bowed her head, fidgeting on her feet and nervously twisting her fingers.

"What is it, girl?" asked Brunnhilde. "Out with it!"

"Well, mums," the maid replied nervously, "not to be rude or anything like that—and I certainly don't mean to remind the two of you of proper hotel etiquette—but…it's customary to tip."

The duo looked at her blankly with the glassy eyes of dead herrings. Finally, Brunnhilde responded with a small chuckle. "Oh, is that all?" she merrily asked. "Well, here's a tip for you then—don't park your camel in front of a water trough!" With a long-suffering sigh poor Miriam fled the room to the sound of girlish laughter echoing off the walls of the suite.

As their mirth subsided, doubt reared its ugly head. "Helly, my dear," asked Brunnhilde, "how are we ever going to crash Herod's party? I'm sure there're palace guards about the place and Roman centurions too. And it's not as though we can turn them into toads. This infernal land has muted our magic!"

"All taken care of, my dear," Helly replied confidently. "You did not notice, and neither did the maid, for I snatched them up quickly, that Master Agrippa in his haste to return to Rome foolishly left his invitations to the party on the parlor table! They're generalized, with no names printed upon them. We'll simply hand these over to the doormen and waltz on in as if we owned the palace!"

"Do you think that they'll grant us entrance?"

"I'm certain of it!"

Brunnhilde had her doubts. "Do you mind if I examine one?"

"Certainly not, my dear," replied Helgayarn. She handed Brunnhilde one of the papyrus scrolls. Emblazoned upon it in red ink was written the following:

HEROD'S HOUSE PARTY & GALA FETE!
A REAL JEWISH JAMBOREE
& SURPRISE PARTY FOR PONTIUS PILATE!
THIS INVITATION ENTITLES BEARER ONLY
TO ADMITTANCE!
FOOD, WINE, SPIRITS!
DANCING GIRLS, DIVINERS, FORTUNE TELLERS!
DIRECT FROM AFRICA—ETHIOPIAN EUNUCHS
WHO'LL DANCE THE MERENGUE!
SAVE THE DATE—IT'S GONNA BE GREAT!
DONATIONS REQUESTED
(B.Y.O.W.)

"Well, it certainly looks genuine," Brunnhilde remarked. "What does BYOW mean? Bring your own witch?"

THE CHRISTMAS RABBIT

Helgayarn shook her head impatiently. "*W* is for *wine*, Brunnhilde!"

The revelation only further confused her. "I don't get it," she replied. "Wine your own witch? What does that mean?"

"No! Bring your own wine! It's stating that the invitees must supply their own booze!"

"That seems rather cheap, doesn't it?" replied Brunnhilde. "After all, a king throwing a party—even if he isn't really a king but just a quarter of one or thereabouts and moreover a Roman puppet at that—should be gracious enough to supply the juice! I wonder if the wineries and the liquor stores will be open after the Sabbath? I was looking forward to getting liquored up!"

"Not to worry," Helgayarn replied acidly. "This rabbi, whoever he is, will most certainly perform the wine trick or I'll know the reason why! But remember, Bunny, don't overimbibe and go making a fool of yourself! You know you can't handle your hooch! Like you said, we're here to observe and evaluate only—not draw unnecessary attention to ourselves!"

"I'll be fine!" replied Brunnhilde. "Just because I've let the sauce get away from me once or twice doesn't mean I'll do so tonight. I know well enough what's at stake!"

"Just see to it that you behave yourself!"

After their bath and a meal of pork chops and little necks, the Witches took a quick nap and then spent the afternoon primping in preparation for the party. They tried on dress after dress, mixing and matching and donning the appropriate belts, buckles, shoes, stockings, veils, scarves, berets, and beanies that went with them. They had Miriam and two other maids working in tandem in order to iron out any remaining wrinkles that remained in their luggage. They applied copious amounts of makeup, including eye shadow, eyeliner, lipstick, rouge, wrinkle remover, nail polish, and mascara—none of which helped for after applying all their war paint when they looked in the mirror, they cracked the glass.

"Just as beautiful as ever," remarked Helgayarn proudly! "We'll be the belles of the ball!"

The sundial on the patio read half past seven and although it was good to arrive fashionably late, the party started at eight and they were still across town in the hamlet of Bethlehem. There was bound to be a receiving line at the door and going through it would take time. They might miss that rabbi's performance if they didn't hurry. "Come, Brunnhilde," said Helgayarn. "Gather up your cloak and let us be off. We don't want to arrive with the evening too far gone!" The old crones hobbled down the stairs and out into the courtyard where the innkeeper had their camels washed, watered, and waiting for departure. With the aid of the house jockey, they were mounted on their beasts, seated comfortably between the humps, and soon on their way.

It was Saturday evening. The sun was going down and the Sabbath ending. There would be partying in the streets of Jerusalem tonight, the Witches knew, as the devotees, freed from the restrictions imposed upon them by their weekly holy day, could get back to the normal routine of day-to-day sinning. Even now Helgayarn took note of one fellow who, walking arm and arm with his maiden, was nevertheless coveting his neighbor's wife. Looking the other way, the maiden in escort took note of a woman bearing false witness against her neighbor. Down a Jerusalem back alley someone else was committing murder while many more were simply lying, stealing, cheating, and worshipping idols. Together, these sinners and idolaters sang a chorus that was music to her ears. If any group of folks ever needed a savior, it was this bunch—lost in the desert for forty years, thrown out of town and exiled to faraway lands time and time again. Conquered over and over. It was obvious to Helgayarn that they were worshipping the wrong deity. Just as it was obvious to her that she, Brunnhilde, and Betty had been in seclusion for far too long, hiding out in their cave in Mesopotamia. Blame the fat man and the rabbits for that! Someday they'd get their comeuppance! Until then, the trio would return here after settling with that rabbi and straighten these people out while leading them to the Promised Land!

They arrived at Herod's palace, a gaudy construction of marble and cedar that boasted excessive overindulgence and stood out like an eyesore, surrounded as it was by Jerusalem's slums. They had

THE CHRISTMAS RABBIT

their camels seen to by the palace jockey, a Samaritan of less than noble birth who deemed himself lucky enough nevertheless in that he was given a royal robe and a bath in order to appear more presentable to the night's many revelers. He helped the Witches down from their mounts and then stood there, waiting for his tip. Brunnhilde's response to him was similar to the one she offered Miriam: "Don't park my camel in front of a water trough!"

Leaving the jockey scowling behind them they made their way up the marble staircase to the palace's front door where Jewish Who's Whos were forming up in line while awaiting admittance. As they drew closer to the guards they took note with some consternation that each reveler, upon presenting his or her invitation, was nevertheless frisked before being allowed entrance. Some, with dirks and other small weapons, kept on their persons for self-defense no doubt, looked on helplessly as the guards removed them. No one was being allowed admittance while in possession of such. Herod, a Roman puppet, was not well liked by anyone, rich or poor, and was taking no chances. Perhaps there'd been rumors of an assassination plot or maybe; not being well liked and for good reason, he was merely on the lookout.

Eventually it became their turn to face the guards. Helgayarn handed over their invitations. The sentries, two beefy gentlemen who certainly had more in the way of brawn than they did brain, examined them casually. Looking up from the papyrus, one of the two motioned them to turn around. "Up against the wall, ladies," he demanded, "and spread 'em!"

Helgayarn chose to be indignant. "I'll do no such thing, sir!" she defiantly replied. "I'm a queen in my own country, and I'll not be subject to such manhandling!"

"Lady," replied the guard, "you'll spread those gams and lift your bloomers, or you'll not be permitted entrance!"

Helgayarn put up a fuss but at Brunnhilde's insistence eventually complied. But not without warning the guard that she intended on having words with Herod himself regarding the affair. They were searched and searched thoroughly and none too gently either.

"Pass on!" the guards demanded.

As Brunnhilde passed the door warden who frisked her, she handed him her card with the address on it of the inn they were staying at in Bethlehem.

"Room 12," she whispered slyly while offering up a flirtatious wink. "I'll be there. After the party—come see me!" It had been centuries since she'd last received a good goosing and the guard, with his gooser, had done much to impress her.

The guard took the card while nodding his compliance but was quick to rip it up when she went through the door. He was due to be relieved in an hour, and to ensure himself that such ugliness wouldn't come looking for him after standing her up, planned on heading straight to the sheep's gate where he'd catch the next caravan bound for Egypt.

The party was in full swing by the time Helgayarn and Brunnhilde gained admittance. The main hall was full of revelers, both Roman and Jewish, as well as dignitaries from as far away as Ethiopia and Egypt, all dressed to the nines, with each trying to outdo the next in both manner and comportment as they made small talk with one another while offering their fellow revelers false compliments and gossiping behind each other's backs. It was a good thing, Helgayarn concluded, that the doormen conducted their weapons search, otherwise this room full of backstabbers would've all murdered each other before the midnight toast. At the far end of the hall and seated upon a dais were Herod and Pilate. The Roman looked bored, as if he considered these affairs a tedious waste of his time. It was obvious to both Helgayarn and Brunnhilde that the governor's attendance was a matter of politics and duty only. The fatigued look on his face made it plain to the duo that he wished he were anywhere else than where he was. He was fit and trim, as befitted a Roman governor, and it was obvious to both Helgayarn and Brunnhilde that he went to great lengths to maintain his physique. Herod, on the other hand, was a gregarious suck-up. A fat wad of leavened bread, he constantly fawned over the governor, telling bad jokes, which Pilate pretended to understand. Herod's stepdaughter, Salome was performing a belly dance at the moment and all eyes were upon her. Helgayarn critically eyed the girl while whispering to Brunnhilde, "That's what Herod

THE CHRISTMAS RABBIT

had the head of the Baptist removed over?" she asked. "That's the tart to whom he promised anything, up to and including half of his kingdom? She's nothing but a common trollop! Look—her teeth are crooked, and she's got love handles! Well, I suppose it's true what they say—that beauty is indeed in the eyes of the beholder. But if that's the truth, then this Herod fellow must be a bit shortsighted!" Salome finished her dance to the polite and abruptly offered applause of her audience. For appearance's sake they'd been compelled to offer up an ovation for her efforts, but most gathered were relieved that the ordeal was over. The girl was ungainly on her feet, as graceful as a gooney bird, and couldn't dance worth a damn. Harder for her audience still, she walked the fine line between beauty and blemish; and although not ugly, per se, she managed to flirt with the handicap as she treaded the tightrope between it and beauty without ever falling one way or the other. She was a plain Jane who just happened to be named Salome, and that was all she was ever going to be. Her birthright was the only thing she had going for her and the guests wondered just what it was that Herod saw in her. Certainly she wasn't worth all the brouhaha that erupted in the wake of the Baptist's beheading. Well, they supposed, it was Herod's own house after all, and if he wanted to bring its roof down atop his head for the sake of the inelegant mud hen who prattled about before them then that was the king's own lookout, wasn't it?

As Salome quit the dance floor slaves and servants hustled about the room laden with trays containing various snack foods and aperitifs. Herod excused himself from Pilate's presence to mingle among the invited guests and share with them his questionable humor. He waddled here and there, stopping every so often to be complimented by a Jewish matron on his choice of dress, or to question a well-to-do merchant about the price of camels or the rate of exchange between talents and drachmas. At one point he cornered a retainer in order to inquire of him information regarding the amount of contributions received and the stockpile of wine and liquor on hand. "How's it going?" demanded the king. "Are donations what we hoped for?"

The retainer fidgeted nervously. "My lord Herod," he replied, "perhaps if we'd established some noteworthy charity upon which to donate, such as the Jewish Relief Fund, the Sons of Zion—or even the PLO—then the gifts forthcoming might have been greater. As it is, our coffers are somewhat empty."

"Empty?" replied Herod. "How can that be? Didn't the guests read the disclaimer on my invitation? It clearly states that donations are requested! A king's request is a subject's command! Our treasuries should be overflowing. Do these revelers think top flight entertainment comes cheap?"

"I've no idea, my lord," replied the retainer. "I just do as my lord commands. The guests, it would seem, do as they please." Herod offered the retainer a scowl. "I knew I should've charged a cover," he said. "Two talents at the door or go home!"

"Had you done so, my lord," the retainer reasoned, "then doubtless the hall would be empty. Pilate would not have appreciated a party in his honor with no guests in attendance."

Herod allowed himself a frustrated sigh. "I suppose you're right," he reluctantly replied. "What about the BYOW? Are the guests drinking their own Manischewitz?"

Again the retainer looked uneasy and hesitated before answering. "No, my lord, he reluctantly replied. "They're guzzling yours and your Ripple too."

"My Ripple? I thought we had that hidden away in the wine cellar where no one could see it?"

"Indeed lord, we did. But the wine stewards had to remove it."

"Why?"

The retainer dreaded his reply and tried to avoid the question. "I'm sure their reasons were justified, sire, it just—"

"Why?"

The retainer paled at his master's insistence upon the truth. Herod would find his response neither edifying nor entertaining. Herod had executed previous messengers for bearing news that was less disturbing than this. "M-my l-lord," he stammered, "you will, of c-course, remember that the wine cellar is located in the d-dungeon."

"I know damned well where my wine cellar is," Herod replied impatiently. "What of it?"

THE CHRISTMAS RABBIT

The retainer, trying his best to be both humble and servile, proceeded cautiously. "W-well, m'lord, the d-dungeon is where you had the b-baptist beheaded!"

Herod's face flushed at the mention of the river dipper and his eyes grew flinty. "My lord!" sputtered the retainer. "The servants say that because of the beheading the cellar is haunted now and they refuse to go down there! I had to have the palace guards move the Ripple upstairs and the Manischewitz too! It was either that or have the wine remain untouched in the dungeon until it turned to vinegar, and being Manechevitz and Ripple, I gave that about a week and a half!" He bowed his head while awaiting his sentence.

"Well this is certainly sour grapes," replied Herod. "I behead the baptist and now I'm troubled by his shade lurking in the shadows of my dungeon! Has anyone, for a certainty, seen his ghost?"

"I cannot say," replied the retainer, "as no one will go down there."

"What of the Ripple then?" demanded Herod. "What became of my Ripple and my Boone's Farm?"

"We tried storing it in the gallows," replied the retainer, "but the hangmen kept helping themselves to it by the quart. They'd get sloshed and end up falling through the trap with their heads in the noose! Ghastly business. That's one hangover that many a hangman will have a hard time recuperating from! In the end, we just kept it in the kitchen and stored in the walk-in where folk have been walking out with it ever since."

"Well that's it!" sniffed Herod. "As of right now, we're going to a cash bar. Pass the word amongst the servants that as of this moment wine, be it Manischewitz or Ripple, is two talents a glass. And if they want the good stuff it's four! And no tabs either!"

"My lord," replied the retainer, "we cannot appear to be less than cordial—not in front of Pilate, nor while hosting a party in his honor! Once he gets wind of the fact that we're charging for drinks he'll only raise our taxes."

"Then we'll raise our own taxes!" Herod replied defiantly. "The cattle craps roll downhill sonny, and it's the peasants who're always in the valley."

"True, my lord," agreed the retainer. "But it's the disenfranchised middle class—those you look upon to provide a buffer between you and the rabble, who'll end up paying the increase. They always do and feel overly put upon already. That madman, Barabbas the Zealot, has them ready to revolt. And the baptist's Essenes are stirring up trouble too!"

"What about the Sadducees and the Pharisees?" asked Herod. "Where do they stand?"

"As always," replied the retainer, "they stand on the side of power, which means Rome, although they'll flatly deny that in public!"

"And the rabbi?"

"He stands apart from them all. Goes his own way, does the rabbi and he doesn't put much stock in anyone's posturings or isms."

"I wish he were with us now," Herod replied forlornly. "Not for his mounting sermons, but I'd sure like to see that Cana trick! Then I wouldn't have to worry about an open versus cash bar. The guests could all get sloshed on well water and when they fell down drunk, we could dig deep in their pockets. Our tax problems would be solved!"

"My lord," replied the retainer tentatively, "I don't think the rabbi would be open to such a questionable action. He doesn't strike me as quite that kind of fellow. And he's often been heard to say, 'Render unto Caesar that which is Caesar's and to God that which is God's.' He says nothing about you, sire, so presumably whatever's left, one's supposed to keep for himself."

Herod's brows knitted together in fury as he listened to his retainer. "Questionable?" he demanded. "Nothing I do is questionable! As king, every action I take is above board and beyond question—so keep your trap snapped! What do you know about such matters? Are you king? Do you sit in judgment while deciding which peasant gets a cow and which goes without? I don't think so! You just stick to retaining and let your betters do the thinking and the plotting!" Thoroughly chastened, the retainer meekly submitted to his master's admonitions. "Yes, m'lord," he said with head bowed. Herod sniffed. "That's better," he replied shortly. "By the way, did you send the Rabbi his invitation to our soiree?" Again the retainer

THE CHRISTMAS RABBIT

shuffled nervously. "I did, my lord. It was returned to us unopened. It seems that the rabbi has better things to do." Herod's eyes glazed over in fury. "Better things to do?" he asked in disbelief while stopping a servant girl carrying a tray in order to grab two goblets of Manechevitz. He downed the first in a single gulp before nursing the second. "If everyone else is going to drink my wine, then I might as well have some too."

"Yes, m'lord."

From the dais, Pilate watched the pair of them. As befitted a Roman, he was observing them to see if they were laying plans and hatching plots. *Well, it took a sneak to know one*, thought Herod, and the Italians were among the sneakiest. Only the Germans were better at sneaking. And backstabbing too! One day, Herod knew, they'd serve each other well and if they threw their lot in with the Japs then they'd really be an axis of evil!

"What about the rabbi?" he continued. "Are you sure the invitation got delivered to the right man and not merely to some wandering conjurer doing card tricks on a Nazareth side street?"

"I'm sure, m'lord," replied the retainer. "Our messenger who delivered the invitation says that he was accompanied by his twelve and that woman who always travels with him. He wouldn't even deign to speak to our messenger but instead had one of his twelve politely turn us down while directing the messenger to return the invitation unopened. The messenger did, however, have words with one of his followers, a fellow named Iscariot, who requested a meeting with you the next time they were all in town."

Herod looked curious. "What did this fellow Iscariot want?" he asked.

"I couldn't say, my lord," replied the retainer. "Our messenger's contact with the fellow was brief, and he could get no details from him other than a plea to pass on his request, followed by an assurance that he would make further contact with us through intermediaries when next in Jerusalem."

"Humph!" snorted a disdainful Herod. "We'll see. In the meantime, what to do about the rabbi? I can't believe he had the nerve to turn down our invitation! I should have him crucified or at the very least whipped! It's not wise to refuse a king!"

"Indeed not, m'lord," replied the retainer. "But perhaps you should reconsider punishing this fellow. After all, he has quite a following. Bigger even than the baptist's. And we all remember the turmoil that ensued in the wake of that one's beheading."

Herod bridled. "Are you blaming me for that?" he asked. "That's all Salome's doing!"

The retainer merely stared at him until Herod reluctantly conceded.

"Oh, very well," he snapped. "I'll take your advice under consideration. Perhaps there's a way to get Pilate to do my killing for me. I'll have to mull that one over for a while and in the interim wait upon this Iscariot fellow and see what he wants. Run along now and leave me to my thoughts—and do be causal about it! Pilate's watching us like a hawk eyeing two wounded fish! He's ever suspicious of me and my loyalties! At the least hint of suspected treachery he'll impeach me and put some up and coming camel jockey on my throne! So saunter away, both slowly and casually, as if we'd been having the most routine of conversations, and I shall continue mixing amongst the crowd!"

Each quietly went their separate ways, the retainer to the kitchen in or order to gain for himself some relief from the pomp and hypocrisy which infected the palace hall until it filled it to overflowing; while Herod remained within the confines of the hall itself, basking in that hypocrisy and pretense offered to him by the various revelers and returning each in kind. As he both listened to the lies being told him while offering up his own in response, he tried to gauge the intentions and motivations on the part of those doing the false complimenting. What was it that they valued him for, he wondered? Why were they really here? Was it because of who he was or the influence he had to bestow? Did they really think well of him or were they just here for the Manischewitz? Would they value him for himself if he were just a simple peasant? Some perhaps, but who? As a political creature who gained his ascendancy to the throne and the monastic prerogative that went along with it, not due to any inherent

THE CHRISTMAS RABBIT

skill he possessed nor the self-imposed regimen of a lifetime of study and application needed to acquire such acumen but who rather owed his ascension to the fickle fates of fortune, good luck, and the ability to fawn upon and curry favor from those more powerful than himself as he ascended sovereignty's rickety staircase, Herod often found that he was incapable nevertheless of judging for himself the motivations of others. That he'd attained his lofty position as a matter of mere inheritance did not serve to improve his judgment any. He was forever mistrustful of others and their motives. He plotted constantly and was himself plotted against by his brothers, who'd also inherited their positions and power from their father, Herod the Great, as each tried to capture for himself the other brother's slice of Papa's pie. As a result, although seeming to have the world at his fingertips, King Herod Antipas, who was not actually a king but merely a tetrarch, which is only one-fourth as good as a king—was more often more miserable than not.

There is an old saying that goes back to the times before Herod and to Olden Days itself and continues on down to this very day and that is, 'misery loves company.' It was true back then and it's just as accurate now. But like so many adages its meaning can be two and three fold and multilayered as well. On the surface it is most certainly true. Misery does indeed, love company. Those who are miserable often wish that not only might they share their misery with others but that they might also enjoy the simple pleasures of company itself—companionship sought after for its own sake rather than for any external benefit such association might render, in order that the miserable might be relieved for a while of their troubles and misfortunes. Too often, we think of the poor and disenfranchised as the miserable and there's some truth to that argument. No one, after all, enjoys living under the burden of hardship. But by and large, the poor and disenfranchised have learned to be comfortable with their lot if not necessarily satisfied. After all, what other choice have they? Our systems of governance are such that most of them are trapped in a vicious cycle wherein it seems that such disenfranchisement and poverty is not only their lot in life but their birthright too. As a result they've learned to make friendships and seek after company not for any external benefit that such association might bring them but merely for the joy and support that such company brings while helping them endure the drudgery and seeming hopelessness of their day-to-day existence. Therefore the poor often make the best of company and the best of friends, and in that light may be deemed the least miserable of us all. They don't have to worry why their friends value them—they have no value other than themselves. The rich and powerful on the other hand, and especially those who've attained such riches and power through no means of their own but rather are gifted these assets through seeming good fortune such as an undeserved inheritance, are forever doubtful of their own abilities and unceasingly mistrustful of those with whom they associate. They have a hard time judging the loyalties and motivations of others. They struggle with themselves when evaluating their own self-worth. When they find true love—even if such love is not without its own faults, weaknesses, and imperfections—on the advice of others, usually their peers, who like them covet first and foremost wealth and power and the luxuries that attainment of such desires affords, will cast true love aside in favor of these desires, only to pay out in heartache for the rest of their lives for having done so. This makes them the truly miserable who are forever seeking out company, not only of their own kind to whom they can then pass on some of their misery while attempting to relieve in part, their own burden; but also the company of one selfless individual who will treasure them for who they are and not what they have. Such was the case of Herod Antipas, a fellow both fortunate in power and riches but who was nonetheless poor in his loneliness and self-doubt. Therefore I admonish all of you reading this—and especially the rich—that should you ever attain the friendship and love of a poor man, regardless of his or her faults, do not cast away such treasure lightly. It is of more value to you than all the gold and power you can attain in this lifetime for such a person's loyalties are not to be questioned. Should you end up discarding such treasure, not only are you apt to break the poor man's heart but in doing so, may find that you poison your own soul as well; and although the poor man, valuing you for who you are and not what you have, will always welcome the chance for reconciliation

THE CHRISTMAS RABBIT

and allow you once again the opportunity to settle comfortably and with ease within the seat of his affections, you may find that having poisoned yourself, you lack the humility to take that first crucial step toward reunion.

As the lonely Herod moved throughout the crowd, rendering and receiving false compliments, Helgayarn and Brunnhilde positioned themselves within the gathering in order to meet him and make his acquaintance. If anyone knew when that rabbi would be performing it would surely be the host of the party.

Herod, his posterior undulating to the rhythm of his legs as he made his way through the revelers, unexpectedly collided with Helgayarn and Brunnhilde, who stood ready to receive him. His bouncing buttocks knocked the glasses of Ripple out of their hands, whereupon they fell to the palace floor and shattered, spilling cheap wine upon the oriental carpet. "Hey—watch we're you're going," exclaimed the testy tetrarch. "Your inattentiveness to my movement caused me to spill your wine, which is actually mine although we find you drinking it!"

Helgayarn and Betty merely stared at the fat slug, saying nothing.

Herod eyed them suspiciously. Who were these two dour old bags? He didn't remember putting them on the guest list. Their silent appraisal of his portliness made him uneasy. "Have you nothing to say for yourselves?" he demanded. "Has the Persian plucked your palate?"

"Say again," inquired Helgayarn, unsure of his meaning.

Herod rolled his eyes. "Has the cat got your tongue? It means, 'Are you mute?' Obviously, however, with the answer just given you remain neither deaf nor dumb, just impolite! It's not wise to remain impolite with royalty. To curry my disfavor is to invite disaster!"

Helgayarn smirked while Betty stood there stone-faced. "I know well enough what the saying means," she replied sardonically. "I was just wondering to myself whether or not you were aware of its many connotations—and as to currying royal disfavor and inviting disaster, both my sister and I are royalty ourselves and we flirt with disaster constantly! We're experts at it. I doubt there's very little Herod, the Tetrarch, could teach us with regard to the matter."

"I prefer King Herod," their host replied.

"What you prefer, versus what you are, are two different matters entirely."

Herod gave the two his curious appraisal. Obviously they were dames of great import as they dared to speak with him so plainly and with such effrontery, but who, in fact, were they?

"What are your names?" he demanded. "Where do you hail from and where are your retainers?"

Helgayarn quickly shot Brunnhilde an apprehensive glance. The junior witch returned it with a look in kind. They should've anticipated such a query from this one, ever suspicious as he was, while at the same time realizing their simple explanation of 'Mrs. and Mrs. Smith' would not do. Although no doubt a fool, the man standing before them was not an ignorant innkeeper who could be buffaloed so easily. "We are the Queens of Sheba," Brunnhilde blurted out. "And we've traveled all the way from Ethiopia to attend the party!" Helgayarn eyed her sister venomously. How after all, was she going to explain that?

Herod looked at them doubtfully. The Queen of Sheba had not put in an appearance at Jerusalem since the days of wise King Solomon. And although that had been hundreds of years ago surely no woman was capable of aging so much in so little time! And as far as he knew, the Queen of Sheba sat on her throne alone, not sharing power with anyone. Had she perhaps married since Solomon's time, and another woman at that? Who knew? Customs after all, were strange in foreign lands. He looked from side to side before replying in order to ensure that no one was listening. It appeared that at least for the moment the crowd had drawn away from them and they were in relative solitude.

"Are you lesbians?" he whispered. "Or do you just avoid men on general principles?"

Helgayarn found that she was clenching her fists. This was the second time in as many days that she'd been accused of sexual deviancy and the charge, no matter who conferred it, did not sit well with

THE CHRISTMAS RABBIT

her. What was it about these Jews and their homophobia? Did they think that any two people of the same sex traveling in pairs or seen with each other in a public square were necessarily fairies, pansies, queens, and bull dykes? Couldn't two women just be friends in this culture or did such alliances necessarily imply an ulterior motive? And besides, what was wrong with lesbians anyway? The way most men proved themselves to be such disappointments, constantly underachieving and falling short of their potential while at the same time engaging in their ridiculous philandering, it was a wonder that there were any straight women left, that they had not all gone 'gay,' and as a consequence done away with men entirely.

"We are not lesbians!" she stated emphatically. "We're sisters-in-law."

"Well," replied Herod, "you did refer to yourselves, as 'queens,' did you not?"

"We'd have to be men in order to be crowned with that particular appellative, wouldn't we?" Helgayarn impatiently replied. "After all, only men can be queens. Real queens, being of the sexual orientation to which you seem to be citing, would perhaps be referred to as kings, would they not? It's obvious to anyone looking, that we're queens, not kings, and therefore must be referred to as kings, not queens, if our tendencies lean in the direction you seem to be implying. However, since we're not queens pretending to be kings, nor kings pretending to be queens, we must therefore be referred to as queens, not kings—however, a simple '*Madame*' will do."

"How is one to know for certain," replied Herod, "what anyone should call another? You may very well be kings or queens or something in between. For all I know, you could be transvestites—it's not as though I've either looked under your covers or have for myself, the desire to do so! Maybe you're Amazons—Hippolytans with a hard-on about men, who find that we're of no value to the world other than the provision of that which dangles between our legs!"

"That comes close to our regard," Helgayarn admitted. "But the same could be said of most women as well although what dangles between our legs does not in fact dangle, but merely resides there waiting to be penetrated." Still, we are not gay. We are not lesbians!

We're celibate, sexually abstinent. We're chaste, stoic, nephalisitc, on the wagon, and sworn off sex."

"No one's that pure," remarked Herod.

"Very well then," replied an agitated Helgayarn. "If the truth must be known—we're two old maids whose husbands gave them up them for a certain hooker a long time ago. We hope that they're happy with her and that's she's passed on to them, the clap! It would serve them right for their infidelities. May their dangling dinguses drop to their ankles!"

Herod considered that particular malediction and all it implied. "That sounds more like a blessing to me than a curse," he said. "Most men would give their right arms to be half as gifted!"

"Oh, what would you know about it?" replied Helgayarn. "A carpenter is judged, not by the size of his hammer, but his ability to swing it! And speaking of carpenters, when do you plan on letting that rabbi perform? It's he we've come to see! We've heard interesting tales regarding the fellow and have come all this way to determine for ourselves if there's any merit to the stories! Surely such a skilled conjurer as this one is purported to be will be making an appearance tonight?"

Herod soured at the mention of the rabbi. "He's not coming," the tetrarch replied shortly. "The Nazarene nincompoop had the nerve to decline my invitation, preferring instead to continue his wanderings along the shores of the Galilee. But don't you worry, when the time's right I'll fix his wagon—see if I don't!"

"I'm sure," replied Helgayarn. "But it's the Nazarene that we came to see nevertheless. We arrived in your country, having landed at the port of Megiddo, and are on our way to Nazareth in order to see him for ourselves." Herod looked at them skeptically. "Megiddo has no port," he replied. "It's in the middle of the freakin' desert! What did you do, drop in out of a cloud?"

Helgayarn shot Brunnhilde a swift glance. "In a manner of speaking," she replied. "But how we arrived is not as important as why we came or where we're headed. As I said, we're on our way to Nazareth."

THE CHRISTMAS RABBIT

Herod let out a long chuckle. "Well then," he replied, "you ladies are well off the map!"

"Eh?"

"Damn straight! Megiddo is some fifty-something miles north of here, as the crow flies!"

"We're well aware of that!" Helgayarn replied impatiently, having remembered every bitter mile of their journey.

"What you're obviously not aware of," the tetrarch replied with glee, "is that Nazareth is another twenty miles or so north of that! You're going the wrong way! If you keep heading the way you have been, you'll reach Zambia before you come to Nazareth! And besides, you won't find the rabbi in Nazareth anyway. They hate him in his hometown! His neighbors feel that he makes more of himself than a mere carpenter has any right to! No, these days you'll find him, along with his twelve, wandering about the shores of Galilee, mixing it up with the peasants while performing his tricks and spouting his inanities."

Helgayarn and Brunnhilde's faces both fell. Not only had they'd been wasting their time and going the wrong way but it seemed that Betty's reports on that rabbi and company he preferred to keep were accurate. Just what kind of fellow was he anyway?

"How did you make such a miscalculation as to direction?" asked Herod. "Are your retainers such idiots that they don't know which way to lead you?"

"We left our retainers in Sheba," Helgayarn said. "Preferring to encounter the carpenter on our own, we left them behind."

"You've no retainers?" asked an incredulous Herod. "No jockeys either?"

"Our jockeys," lied Helgayarn, remain with our camels, parked in the garage. They're refueling them as we speak, checking their tires as it were, and readying them for the next stage of our journey—although we had not anticipated that the next stage would be quite as lengthy as it now appears to be. What's the quickest way to this Sea of Galilee that you speak of? We want no more misadventures or detours during our journey there."

Herod considered their question. "Well," he replied, "since you've all but admitted that you can't read a simple map, then the shortest way may not necessarily be the quickest route. The surest way then to arrive at your destination is to head east of here some thirty miles or so until you strike the Jordan River. From there, follow it north while keeping to this side of the river for about seventy five to a hundred miles, as the crow flies that is—with the river's twists and turns, it's more like a buck fifty—until you reach the point where the river forks. Take the left-hand fork and that will lead you to its headwater, which has as its source the southern end of the Sea of Galilee. From there, ask around. Someone will know where the rabbi is."

They thanked him for his directions and made ready to leave. Just as they were turning to go, the tetrarch pulled them aside. "Do Uncle Herod a favor, will you? Should you find the fellow, and I've no doubt that you will—he's not hard to locate—be sure to tell him how angry I am! His refusal to attend my party is an insult to both my person and my position!"

"We'll consider it," replied Helgayarn.

Brunnhilde, who'd overindulged her love of cheap wine, merely burped her consent and then as the duo turned to depart, staggered off in the arms of Helly.

"Your sister-in-law," remarked Herod to their retreating backs, "has something of a drinking problem, hasn't she? I have a couple of counselors on staff. They have a great eleven-step program and are working on a twelfth. I'm sure she could benefit from it!"

Their shoulders drew taught as the sisters paused, turning to give this quarter-king their disdainful regard. As they did, this quarter-king, ever paranoid and suspicious of everyone, but especially of obvious Gentiles who were obviously not gentle at all because in private even he had to admit that the Hebrews had their point; and moreover being mere women it was obvious, even to him, that they were not mere women nor simply old crones invited to the party for no other reason that he appear magnanimous before the rest of his guests. They were too obviously too out of place and feeling too confident in themselves while being there, to be anything other than possessors of dark and terrible secrets and possible intrigues as well. Suddenly he viewed with skepticism, the offer of his twelve step program and wishing he could take it back, voiced in such a way as to leave no doubt in his listener's ears that the impossibility of what he would offer next was a foregone conclusion, making the offer itself mere pretense and uttered only as a parting remark.

"She'll need a sponsor…"

Helgayarn chose to ignore him and turning her back once again, left the palace fuming and promising herself that from now on there'd be no more of this mere intelligence gathering business and that if she wanted to meddle she'd damn well meddle! Barely a fortnight on the road as yet and she decided that she'd taken all she was going to take. It was time to act!

"Really, Brunnhilde!" she said, voicing her disgust after they'd retrieved their camels and mounted them. "Did I not caution you about overindulgence? Did I not warn you that wine loosens lips and that loose lips sink ships?"

"I thought we were shafe on dry land and beshides, our ships are already shunk," Brunnhilde replied drunkenly, as she swayed between her humps. "Let's just go home, Helly. I've had it with Hebrews and camel jockeys. The Shamaritans too. Let's just whip up a wind and fly home to Betty. She's probably still under her shtone and waiting for us."

She paused while swaying haphazardly in her saddle, which was a bad fit for a camel since it was made for a horse in the first place. Damn that Abdullah!

"Ooh," she commented, "I think I'm due for one heck of hangover come sunrise! Do you hear that abominable sloshing? Is that the water in my camel's humps or the wine in my belly? I think I'm a little unshteady. Either the world is spinning or else it's my head!"

"It's both," Helgayarn replied impatiently. "And each is going in the opposite direction! I had it in mind to set out for Galilee this very evening but in your condition we'd better forget that! We'll instead return to the inn at Bethlehem where I'll try to sober you up while seeing to it that good-for-nothing Miriam repacks our luggage. Then we'll put you to bed! But expect to get up early, hangover or no. We've a long journey to make!"

*****

Their trek as they followed the Jordan north was uneventful despite having gotten underway two days later than planned. Poor Brunnhilde was in no condition to travel under the hot Judean sun. Cheap wine like Manischewitz and Ripple, when overindulged in, produces a katzenjammer that one does not just sleep off in the matter of a single night. Days are needed to overcome the dry heaves and sweats that accompany such Dutch courage—the more so if you're not Dutch. Many regurgitations, of both food and water, are required to settle the stomach upset such cheap booze brings about. In the interim you feel as if you're dying while cursing the fact you remain amongst the living. Your head pounds like a jackhammer, your mouth feels as if it's stuffed with dry cotton, and your insides rumble like Mount St. Helen's. Needless to say, you're not good for anything for a minimum of forty-eight hours. So it was with Brunnhilde. Herod's party began at the close of Sabbath on Saturday evening. Helgayarn and Brunnhilde partied there until well after one o'clock that morning before making their abrupt exit. So it was well into the following Tuesday afternoon before they got underway, and still Brunnhilde did not feel fully restored or rejuvenated.

"I'm never going to drink again," she stated contritely as they were leaving Bethlehem and heading east toward the Jordan. "I'm swearing off cheap wine from this moment onward. From now on it's only the good stuff! I'll not suffer from another hangover like this!"

Helgayarn thought to point out that one could just as easily suffer the pangs of a walloping katzenjammer by overindulging in the 'good stuff,' as Brunnhilde so naively put it, but in the end thought better of it. First, she knew when drunks like Brunnhilde made such promises, they were more often than not farting through their own fannies, offering up words that had no more substance to them than the copious amounts of methane they expended while in the throes of the willy wags. Such addicts had to hop on the wagon

THE CHRISTMAS RABBIT

completely if they were going to avoid repeated misfortunes. Trying board the wagon as it sped ever onward by simply switching to the good stuff availed very little in the way of preventatives when it came to avoiding mornings after. Such ills were just as available at the bottom of a bottle of *good stuff* and therefore were easily encountered by those who nevertheless professed a desire to avoid them. Second, although all this was true enough and as such should've been plain to Brunnhilde, Helgayarn knew that regardless of cold facts Brunnhilde would nonetheless choose to deny truths. Her denials would lead to arguments, and although she knew she'd win, Helgayarn wanted no part of such disagreements and squabbles at the moment, wanting instead to use the opportunity that travel presented to focus her energies on planning for their encounter with the rabbi. Despite her constant bravado and her apparent eagerness to pick a fight, Helgayarn knew they would need all their skills at that meeting—especially in light of their apparent inability to marshal the forces and incite the incantations that allowed them to produce their particular brand of mumbo jumbo. But something happened as they traveled northward. For some reason, which they were at a loss to explain and which was just as strange to them as their mumbo jumbo's initial impotency when arriving in this strange land, their ability to do magic returned to them as they traveled northward. Nor did their powers reappear all at once. But slowly, as they traveled north, they could feel within themselves, their abilities returning. And it wasn't as if they sensed that the omnipresence which hovered about the land grew any less potent the further north their camels took them—in fact as they got closer to the purported whereabouts of the carpenter, it seemed to increase—but rather it seemed to the two of them that for reasons of its own, the mysterious force that they could feel hovering about them as if it were part of the very air itself, was giving them a respite from its unwholesome influence while allowing them, for its own reasons, to recapture their lost vitality. It was eerie—both to Helgayarn and Brunnhilde, but they gratefully accepted the recess, having learned through many past misadventures to never look a gift horse in the mouth.

They made the fork in the river some five days after they'd initially set out from Bethlehem and choosing the left-hand fork, spent another day en route to the Galilean Sea itself. From there they inquired after the rabbi only to discover that he could be found traveling at the north end of the lake, intent on preaching to the Gennesarenes. Sensing that the time for decisive action was quickly passing them by, Helly decided to travel the rest of the way northward on the breath of a wind she would conjure up, since she'd somehow regained the ability. To this end, they sold their camels for much less than they'd initially paid, and most of their wardrobe too, keeping only those necessaries they deemed essential for a visit of an overnight or two. For a bargain price they unloaded all of their bandoliers, baldrics and bellybands. They sold off their snowshoes, ski boots, platforms and pumps, keeping only their sandals as befitted the peasant appearance they were trying to maintain. Their bowlers, bonnets, shakos, and shovel hats, along with their porkpies, pillboxes, beanies, berets, and ball caps, they grudgingly gave away to the poor as no else seemed to be interested in them and the peasantry to whom they'd been gifted had no money to expend on such frippery anyway. Their gloves, muffs, and mittens they got rid of as well but kept their brass knuckles just in case. Added to these and their sandals, they kept only a meager housecoat or two and of course their long underwear, having learned the hard way that one could never be too careful. Finally, having lightened their load by several hundred pounds, it was a matter of mere ease to whip up a small tail wind to carry them across the lake.

They arrived in Gennesaret to discover that they'd beaten the carpenter there by a day or two. This was all to Helgayarn's satisfaction. It allowed her time to survey the field of contention and decide best where to confront him. But after looking the country over carefully and well, they determined that it provided no place from which to confront while taking advantage of good cover. Wherever they went they'd be sure to stick out like sore thumbs. "This won't do," remarked Helgayarn. "How are we going to remain incognito while conducting our reconnoiter?"

Brunnhilde gave their dilemma some thought. The problem as she saw it was their inability to pass for anything but the foreigners they were. And as foreigners they were certain to fall under the rabbi's attention, which they wanted to avoid at all costs while taking their evaluation of him. No simple disguise would serve to detract from their alien status. Finally, Brunnhilde hit upon what she thought was a workable solution. "I have an idea," she said. "Let's leave our bodies behind and stowed behind a rock somewhere. We'll discorporate our spirits from their shells while inhabiting the body of some local in order to better make our observation. It'll be a nifty trick that uppity carpenter is sure to miss!"

Helgayarn looked at her doubtfully. "I don't know," she replied. "Discorporation's a dicey gambit! We know the forces to marshal and the incantations to incite to pull off such magic, but even so, we've never tried it before. Suppose we pull it off only to find that we can't undo the damned thing once it's done? What then? Do you want to spend eternity trapped in the body of some pathetic Semite?"

Brunnhilde conceded the point but continued with her argument. "Yes, there's that risk," she replied. "The safest course would be to just get out of here, although I know that you'll never agree to that! But it's just as risky, and perhaps even more so, to confront this rabbi without knowing the full extent of his abilities. If he's half what those three wise guys claimed or even a third of what Betty reported, then discorporation followed by entrapment within a host body seems to me to be the lesser of two evils. Unless, of course, you have another idea."

Helgayarn reluctantly admitted that she didn't. "Very well," she grudgingly replied. "We'll do it since we can't seem to come up with a better plan—but I'm warning you here and now that if this backfires, I'm holding you personally responsible!"

Brunnhilde scoffed at her sister's implied threat. "Don't you always?" she sarcastically replied. "You've been blaming me for tides, seasons, and Ice Ages for millennia! You also claim that the eastwardly rising sun is might fault too—although I had nothing to do with it! Blame me all you want. If this plan backfires and goes belly-up, I'll have more to worry about than you!"

Helgayarn offered her a scowl. "So be it," she replied. "Let us go find a host body and settle comfortably within it so that we're better able to observe this Johnny-Come-Lately!" They searched high and low, far and wide, for a suitable host. The best candidate, they knew, would be someone who had a low opinion of themselves. A lonely soul who would not be adverse to company and who wouldn't mind temporarily housing both the spirits and personalities of his betters. They first considered the mayor but being a big fish in a small pond, he was too prominent and therefore taken too much notice of to be put to any practical use. Being a minor politician, he was also a power-hungry moneygrubber who, if infected by their presence, might very well try to trap them within his person in order to claim their Manifest Destiny for himself. They next considered a local prostitute, who due to her chosen profession, would be ignored by the crowd, therefore remaining essentially invisible among the mob as it gathered to hear the sermonizing of the Nazarene. They discarded the choice, however, when it became apparent to them that their selection reminded them too much of the Shoe Lady. In the end they chose a gravedigger who lived among the tombs at the local cemetery. No one likes a gravedigger, who with his shovel and his pickaxe provides the last service that any of us are likely to receive in our short sojourns here on Mungo. They're dirty and smell of stale soil and earthworms. Being dirty and smelling of stale soil and earthworms, the gravedigger was shunned already, many considering him unclean, and folk around those parts conferred with him only when their loved ones reached their final need. Corpses were considered unclean and he was regarded as dirty and defiled for being in the business of handling them. He was disliked, unloved, and unwanted already, living a solitary existence amongst the headstones and the crypts. This made him, in the eyes of the Witches, the perfect candidate. His solitary existence would provide for them the privacy they needed in order to perform the possession, while his low opinion of himself would ensure, they felt, his overall willingness to accept their presence as their temporary host. They snuck up upon him when he wasn't looking and inciting the incantations, marshaled the forces and made the mumbo jumbo which allowed them to invade his body like a couple of Nazi storm troopers descending upon a Jewish delicatessen. They fouled his kosher meats with the mere essence of their presence, and unleavened his bread in the bargain. They discovered

THE CHRISTMAS RABBIT

quickly however that there wasn't enough room within his puny body for them to both fit comfortably and much to their consternation, found themselves continually rubbing up against one another while banging their knees and bumping their heads. This caused the poor fellow, whom we'll call Max, much unnecessary pain and discomfort as he rolled upon the ground, writhing in agony at the torment occurring within. Those who came upon him tried to chain him down and bind him for his own safety's sake, but such was his agony that he tore the chains and fetters apart as if made from paper. Night and day he ran among the tombs and over the graves, screaming in agony and beating himself with stones in an effort to dislodge from within him their unwholesome presence.

Finally the day arrived when the Rabbi came to Gennesaret by boat. Max ran down to the shoreline in order to be saved. "Help me, Rabbi," he managed to cry out. The rabbi, who knew Max well, knew also that despite appearances, this was not Max who now stood before him but rather someone else who lay hidden within. "Who are you?" the rabbi demanded, although it was plain to both Helgayarn and Brunnhilde from within their host that the rabbi saw right through Max and already knew.

Never before had they encountered such power and purity. The sun itself seemed to shine from within him, casting a wholesome radiance upon all whom it touched. It hinted at something beyond the rabbi while seeming to be part of the rabbi himself, as if such hidden power were incorporated within his very being. Never before had either Helgayarn or Brunnhilde encountered such an irresistible force. It was a power that could move mountains if it chose to; it could set fire to the very seas itself if it had a mind to. Against it, all other forces, including themselves, were powerless and subservient. Having such power at his command, the rabbi intimidated both Helgayarn and Brunnhilde into an uneasy and frightened silence, which nevertheless had to be overcome as the rabbi's inquiry demanded from them, an answer which couldn't be denied.

In an effort to both inflate their numbers and maintain their anonymity, Helgayarn voiced a bold-faced lie. "We are Legion!" she cried!

"Yah!" agreed Brunnhilde, who in her fright was unable to give voice to anything other than her absent sister's monosyllabic response.

From within Max, Helgayarn offered Brunnhilde the severest of scowls while at the same time kicking her in the shins. This only caused Max further discomfort and he writhed upon the ground in agony. "A lot of good you're doing," Helgayarn whispered. "If that's the best you're capable of, then have the decency to remain quiet!"

Gazing out at the rabbi through the gravedigger's eyes, Helgayarn took note of the Nazarene's mounting fury at their possession of an innocent soul. It was obvious to Helgayarn looking out that he was about to do something the two sisters would come to regret. Perform a discorporation of his own perhaps, scattering their spirits to the four winds and preventing them from ever finding their way back to their own bodies. "Have mercy," she cried, "and send us not from without of the country!" Helgayarn feared being scattered upon those winds only to wind up at the very ends of the earth itself. Above them and to their left on a steep incline that overlooked the sea, there happened to be a herd of pigs feeding upon the hill. "Send us into the swine instead!" pleaded Helgayarn as a last resort. "Let us enter them!"

The rabbi gave them leave and cast them into the pigs.

Helgayarn and Brunnhilde invaded the swine like a herd of stampeding buffalo, with a small part of themselves going into each and every pig. The swine weren't happy about it either. Although always considered unclean and foul, they'd never before been made to feel this dirty. Deciding therefore that death was preferable to the disgrace of having these two trapped within, the head honcho of the herd let out a shout to his fellows. "Follow me, lads!" he cried. "I've the answer to these two old hags!" And then with a snort, led the herd over the side of the cliff and into the sea, where they were mercifully drowned and relieved of their torment.

*****

How Helgayarn and Betty found their way back to their own bodies after the death of the pigs, I do not know. I'm sure that it

THE CHRISTMAS RABBIT

wasn't easy for them, nor was their return trip to Mesopotamia, as they were somewhat rattled by their previous misadventure. But they did make it back only to go crashing at Betty's feet, whereupon, grabbing her, they hid under a rock themselves, fearing the rabbi might track them down. "I told you so," scribbled Betty upon her notepad. "Didn't I warn you not to go messing with the rabbi? But did you listen? Oh no! What does dumb Betty have to say, with her one-word articulation, which could be of any value to the likes of us? Well now you know, don't you?"

The trio hid under their rock for almost two years until they heard from their lurkers in the leaves that the rabbi had been put to death on a Roman cross. Feeling confident, they crawled out of their holes only to learn three days later from those very same leaf lurkers that the rabbi had apparently risen from the grave and was alive and well. It seemed that you couldn't keep a good man down. The trio crawled back under their rock.

After a few years, when the rabbi had not put in a further appearance, they ventured out again, but such was the impression he made upon them that for prudence's sake, they decided to tread lightly and in an effort to align themselves with him should he suddenly appear once again, directed both Santos and Jack Rabbit's descendants to confine their gift giving to only those deserving recipients on the roles who professed a belief in him. *Let the Jews, the Muslims, and the Buddhists blow*, thought the trio. They were going to align themselves with a winner! Their plan proved untenable however, in that the rabbi's followers, led by eleven of his original twelve and the addition of some zealot named Saul, multiplied faster than mad jackrabbits themselves; until the number of followers reached such unlooked for proportions as to make deliveries on the part of both the farmer and the rabbits, virtually impossible. Once again the plotters and whiners, the common complainers, and the agitators who agitated just because they were irritated at everyone else found fault with The Powers That Be, criticizing their administration and, with such criticism, implying that they and they alone were responsible for the mismanagement of available resources. However, this time, they did more than complain. This time those "leaf lurkers" and their like, along with anyone else who happened to lean their way, dared to start lobbing stones and hurling rocks. The witches were capable of dodging a stone or two or even a good-sized boulder while giving back as good as they got, even dozens of stones, I suppose, if anyone had done anything up until then other than grumble and only if the grumbling "leaf lurkers" and their leaners were blind as bats and incapable of seeing three feet in front of themselves. However, when there are hundreds of lurkers along with those who lean likewise who all have in mind to have at hurling, perhaps even thousands—for who, back then, besides the trio themselves, could count past one hundred other than Junior, presumed to be missing and who's around now that plodded upon Mungo back then, besides the Witches, who can say one way or the other—the point is that it doesn't matter. They could be hurling water balloons and Eskimo Pies. Some of those projectiles are going to hit and some of them are even going to hurt. Stones only make the wounds worse and the recoveries harder, and when balloons, Eskimo Pies, and even the stones are passed over in favor of hurtling cattle craps, such projectiles inevitably stick to their target. The witches knew this, so in an effort to preserve their skins the trio packed up the trailer, and in their Winnebago covered wagon, fully insured by Repressive Insurance of Mesozoic Mesopotamia, complete with its V-8 engine of Clydesdale horses harnessed both in tandem and triangulation, and its AC hook-ups and microwave ovens, fled to the as yet untouched lands of southwestern North America, which is where we find them today, drinking the dregs of their own bitterness while blaming all of their troubles at the feet of the that silly farmer and those damned rabbits who in their opinions, lay at the heart of all their woes and miseries.

Now it was the day before Christmas and this evening, that silly farmer, old Santos himself, would overfly their desert in an effort to bestow his gift upon a certain young lass named Lauren Tea Dawe, who even the Witches had to admit, was high upon the role of do-gooders—as well as being, although unknown to the farmer himself, one of his descendants. They'd wait for him therefore, just outside the confines of Lawrence Torrance Dawe, aka Sand Toes of the Apaches; and when Santos landed, they'd settle with the bunch of them, once and for all.

CHAPTER 11

A Lunatic Looks Out

"C'mon, Jackie lad," yelled Sand Toes. "Ye not be getting' w' the program! Ye need t' dig deeper and much faster 'n' ye hae been if we're t' finish this trap by nightfall! It be Christmas Eve soon and we dinna want t' miss our chance t' be capturin' our prey!"

Jack Rabbit, dirty, dusty, and covered in grime, looked across the pit to where Sand Toes was shoveling furiously. It was beyond logic—especially his own—to understand how he'd let himself be talked into going along with this wacky scheme. True, he was an enemy of long-standing when it came to that silly farmer who now presumed to go under the pseudonym of 'Santa Claus.'

As a *nom de guerre*, it did nothing to hide the Tortoise's identity from those who knew him for who he was and many was the past rabbit, both Easter Bunny and no, who relished the opportunity of squaring up with Old Slomoe in order to avenge the indignities he'd help foster upon their ancestor, Jack Rabbit, the First. But was this the way to go about it? Jack wasn't so sure. To begin with, they were miles away from Larry's home and Slomoe, if he could find his way in this barren wasteland at all—a presumption upon which Jack placed serious doubts having become lost in this desert himself—was more likely than not to deliver his gifts to Larry's mine rather than deposit them way out here in the middle of nowhere. There was a certain unwholesomeness about this place that cried out for avoidance. The land that lay about was desolation piled upon desolation, save for the rare sagebrush and mesquite plant hardy enough to put down roots in the sand, and the occasional barrel cactus, both stunted and irregular that took root haphazardly about the landscape, rising up in twisted and tortured shapes, and making the rest of the desert seem lush by comparison. Scorpions and horny toads prowled the sands ceaselessly, while high overhead in the noonday sun, ugly buzzards, their greedy eyes bulging and their wings stretched out like black ribbons of bubonic plague, rode the thermals, circling the skies endlessly while looking to feed upon the flesh and blood of the lost and forlorn. From time to time their raucous screeching rent the hot desert air like clarion bells of doom. It was an altogether inhospitable place, making the few other parts of this desert that Jack had the misfortune to traverse look like the Garden of Eden. Off to the right and away from their diggings, stood an abandoned mineshaft where supposedly, Sand Toes's wife, Larraine, had come to her untimely end, buried in an unanticipated collapse. The wind howling through the adit seemed to scream in her voice, adding to the overall eeriness of the landscape. His daughter Lauren, who was on holiday vacation from school, accompanied them on this dig but refused to help, choosing instead to stand off to the side with an angry frown displayed upon her face. Her Da saw fit to ignore it. Why he brought her along with them to this hellhole was beyond Jack's ability to fathom. The two of them had hardly said a word to each other in the preceding days and Jack, who admittedly did not know them well and who hoped never to get the chance to do so, found their silence puzzling. After all, alone in the desert, one could not be too picky when it came to choosing conversationalists.

"I'm doing the best I can!" he replied to Sand Toes's criticism. "There's something about this place that takes the sap out of a fella!"

"Dinna I know it!" replied the madman. "We be only a furlong or so into Witch Valley and the unwholesome presence o' the waste permeates this entire area! It's here, laddie, that ye be wantin' t' steer clear o'! Even I'm reluctant to visit! Me Apache friends warned me o' this place long ago. Cursed, they said it is, and I'm o' a mind t' be believin' their tales!"

"It seems cursed enough to me," the rabbit forlornly replied.

THE CHRISTMAS RABBIT

Sand Toes paused for a moment in his digging to look over at Jack who stood panting on the far side of their pit. "And so 'tis," replied the lunatic. "It be, after all, right here where me dearly departed Larraine met her untimely end."

"Then what in the name of Cheese and Crackers are we doing here?" asked Jack. "Surely, of all the possible places in which to set a trap, this one must be the most unlikely of locales in which to do it! Wouldn't we be better off constructing our snares in a slightly more hospitable area? After all, no one in his right mind is going to venture out here!"

"We did," argued Sand Toes.

"Point proven," countered Jack.

Sand Toes lazily shoveled out another spadeful of sand while considering his reply. "From what ye told me about our quarry," he said while tossing dirt out of the hole, "he nae be in his right mind anyway! Surely an idiot like that is bound t' come waltzing in here as naive and as careless as may be!"

"I don't know about naiveté and carelessness," replied Jack. "But I wouldn't count upon him waltzing. "The dumb clod is none too light on his feet. He's liable to come tumbling down and rolling in end over end."

"That suits me just fine," Sand Toes replied gleefully. "We be much more likely t' trap 'im if he dinna look where he be plantin' his feet!"

"How do you know that he'll even be able to find this place?" the rabbit inquired while sniffing the air and looking north to an approaching storm that seemed to be heading straight for them. It was some hours away yet, but even at that distance its odor, which Jack could sense with his sensitive smeller, presaged its impending arrival as the metallic smell of ozone, which hinted at lightning and thunder and the seemingly impossible advent of snow, ran before it. "It looks like we're in the line of a real williwaw," the rabbit continued. "If Old Slomoe is caught up in it, he'll never see us down here!"

"I've the answer t' that, lad!" replied the self-assured, adopted son of the Apaches. "I've rented me a generator and a couple o' spotlights from town. We'll turn 'em on when the sun goes down, placin' em at the far end o' our trap and on either side o' the sign I've painted, in order t' lure him in!"

"What sign," asked Jack, "and what are spotlights?"

Sand Toes chuckled. "See there, Jackie lad," he replied. "Ye dinna know everything, di' ye? Take a break for a moment, me hardy hare, and come on over to my side o' our hole, and then together, we'll climb yon ladder and I'll show ye the *coup de grace* o' me trap!"

"The what?"

"The *coup de grace!*"

The rabbit looked at him uncertainly. "Do you mean *coup de grâce?*" he asked.

"Dinna I say that?" replied Sand Toes.

"It's hard to tell," Jack replied sardonically, "when you speak French with an Irish accent!"

"Ye should hear me," the sand man replied, "when I try'n render it in me adopted Apache! A bigger bastardization of either language yer not likely t' be listenin' to—even wi' ears like those!" They climbed up the ladder and out of the hole, proceeding to a pile of equipment that was covered by a tarp. "I was kinda wondering what this gear was all about," said Jack, observing the pile.

"Yer about t' find out!" Sand Toes replied. He pulled away the tarp to reveal two industrial-grade spotlights set upon pivoting transoms and an easel that was further covered with a smaller tarp of its own.

"What are those?" Jack asked, pointing at the kliegs.

"Those are 'lectric lights!" Sand Toes replied in a self-satisfied manner. "Top-grade spotlights to be exact. Ye aim 'em up in the skies and turn 'em on. They revolves on their pivots, spininn' round and round! Car salesmen use 'em to hypnotize an unsuspectin' public! They flash 'em at night and those in the market for an auto get hoodwinked into thinkin' there's a sale goin' on! It's like fishin' without bait! The dumb herrings swim upstream to 'em every time! So will this Santos Fella—once he sees the sign they highlight!"

THE CHRISTMAS RABBIT

"Oh," Jack remarked skeptically, "and what sign is that?" Sand Toes pulled away the smaller tarp with relish to reveal a hand-painted clapboard, which read:

THE OUT-OF-THE-WAY INN
BY LAWRENCE TORRANCE DAWE (aka SAND TOES OF THE APACHES)
LAST STOP THIS SIDE OF THE GREAT WASTELAND!
FINE DINING—SPECIALIZING IN ESKIMO
PIES AND TOADHOUSE COOKIES!
BREAKFAST SERVED 'ROUND THE CLOCK!
REINDEER WELCOME UPON A LEASH—
KIDS AND CARIBOU EAT FREE!
CLEAN SHOWERS & TOWELS!
SENIOR CITIZEN'S DISCOUNTS!
AAA-RATED AND APPROVED!
PROUD TO SERVE OUR APACHE, ELVISH, & IRISH FRIENDS!
YOUR MASTERCARD, DINER'S CLUB, &
AMERICAN EXPRESS WELCOME HERE!
KID-FUN, FAMILY-FRIENDLY!
MERRY CHRISTMAS!
HAPPY HANUKKAH!
KWANZA!
NO SHIRT, NO SHOES—NO SERVICE!
ABSOLUTELY NO HIPPIES!

Jack scrutinized the advertisement critically.

"It might work," he admitted. "Farm Boy's foolish enough to be taken in by it, and from the tales passed down about his wife's cooking, Toadhouse Cookies would be to him, a real treat!"

"They be finger-lickin' good, that's fer sure!" replied Sand Toes enthusiastically. "O' course, no one could bake a Toadhouse like me dearly departed Larraine, and since Little La will hae no part o' this adventure, I had to bake 'em meself! But they'll serve, no doubt, to entice our quarry!"

"I wouldn't bake them," Lauren shouted from the fringes of their dig, "because even if this silly scheme of yours has its basis in fact—and I suppose that I must credit such since Jack here, seems to know of this fellow himself—it's wrong to waylay people and trap them in the desert!"

"But trapping rabbits is okay, is it?" Jack shot back. "Hooking hares and sniggling them in your snares is just fine and dandy, is that it?"

"Well, no," Little La replied guiltily, "of course not. But two wrongs do not a right make! And besides, my Da and I have already apologized for that misunderstanding!"

"You've apologized!" Jack replied. "Your Da, however, hasn't offered up to me so much as the merest 'mea culpa' for having maneuvered me into one of his traps!"

"And such an apology on me part will na' be forthcomin'," replied Sand Toes. "I didn'a go a dancin' before ye like the Pied Piper o' Hamlein and lead ye into me snare. Ye did that on yer own! And I dinna speak such foreign languages as Latin anyway—only French and me native Apache with an Irish accent!"

"And you don't speak those well either," Jack said. "But you did bait your trap with water knowing full well that by doing so you were presenting an irresistible enticement to any thirsty creature who happened by."

Sand Toes rolled his eyes. "What did you expect me to do, Jackie lad," he asked, "bait it with M&Ms? Ye dinna strike me as one who succumbs to the lure o' a sweet tooth! And besides, ye be well now, nae? And fortune and circumstance has placed ye in a position to exact revenge upon yer enemy. Surely, 'tis true what they say then, isn't it, that all things work out for the best?"

"That's the only reason I've chosen to overlook your attack on my person," Jack replied. "Even enemies can be friends if they find they've common adversaries."

"Bet yer arse," the sand dweller replied. "But can they be trusted—that's what I be wonderin'!"

"I'm here, ain't I?" asked the hare. "What more do you want? I'm digging your holes and I'm helping you catch a tortoise!" Further debate was cut short by Lauren who spied in the distance a vehicle coming toward them. "Da!" she exclaimed. "There's a Land Rover heading our way. I think it's Uncles Jim and Slim! There are other vehicles behind them too!" She strained her eyes in an effort to make them out. "I can't see too clearly because of the dust," she continued, "but I believe the entire Society is trailing in their wake!"

"Begorrah!" exclaimed Sand Toes. "What can that mangy mob be wantin' with me, and why now, o' all times?"

"Gold, Da." Lauren replied. "What else do they want?"

"There be nae gold out here!" he replied. "When are the damned fools ever going to accept that and move back to New York? Their mania about that metal is what cost us yer Ma! Obsessions ain't healthy lass. They do strange things to a person!"

"You mean like your obsession with Santa Claus—that kind of strange?"

"'Tis not the same thing!" Lawrence vehemently replied. "I'm not obsessed—I'm fixated! And besides, I have legitimate grievances with the sod! He abandoned me out here! Left me all alone in the desert, he did, and without any footwear!"

Lauren tried to reason with the madman one more time. "But doesn't what you just said to Jack also apply to you?" she asked. "If such had not been the case, you would never have met and married mother and had that not happened, then you would never have had me! Aren't I worth any past trials and heartaches you may have had to endure in order to have fathered me?"

"'Tis the principle o' it." Sand Toes replied shortly. "No one should be disappointin' wee bairns like that! If he did it to me then sure n' begorrrah he'll disappoint some other laddie if I give him the chance! Well I ain't givin it t' him!"

"Da," said Lauren in the most reasonable voice she could manage, "you've been trying every Christmas Eve for as long as I can remember to catch this fellow, and he's never shown up. What makes you think that this yule will be any different?"

"Well, we do hae with us the Easter Bunny—even if he be way too late or way too early, dependin' upon which side o' the calendar ye be standin'—and he's never shown up before either! Therefore I be figurin' if we got us the one then we stand a good chance o' catchin' us the other!" There was a certain insane logic to that argument that Lauren, in possession of all her faculties, found hard to refute. She looked over at Jack who stood watching them both.

"Why haven't you ever shown up before now?" she asked. "Why this time, of all times?"

Jack merely shrugged. "It's not as though we haven't tried," he replied. "To begin with, it's been a long time since either Slomoe or my ancestors have been able to make the deliveries to everyone on our lists. Even separating the deserving from the undeserving leaves us both with an impossible chore. Also, it probably never occurred to either one of you how hard it is to find your mine shaft. Me and mine have been searching for it for years! We gave up hope of ever finding it! I made the attempt this time without any real hope of succeeding. I only stumbled across you by accident!"

"Surely," replied Lauren, "you could have asked about us in town when you made your deliveries there."

"By town, do you mean that collection of huts and general stores that your Secret Society regards as its municipal center? That one-horse, jerkwater jump-off point isn't even on the map! And even if it were we rabbits always avoid it. There's no one in that pissant little burg as deserves one of my eggs! Maybe they get a present or two from Old Slomoe come this time of year, but me and mine are a mite more particular!"

"But I know plenty of kids," Lauren replied, "who've gotten their eggs—and at the right time of the year too! To tell the truth, up until now I've always been a bit jealous of them, thinking that there must be some fault within me that prevented you from making your delivery."

Jack laughed. "Don't give it another thought, little sister," he replied. "You're square in my book! As to those other kids—it wasn't me or mine that delivered their eggs. More likely it was their parents, falsely planting them and giving us the credit. Happens to us, Santos, and the Tooth Fairy all the time—although he operates under a different set of marching orders than Farm Boy and myself."

"Wait a minute," said Lauren, unable to believe what she'd just heard. "Are you telling me that the Tooth Fairy is a he?"

"Of course," replied Jack, in a manner that indicated such information was common knowledge and should've been obvious. "It's just that the little bugger is somewhat effeminate, flitting about as he

THE CHRISTMAS RABBIT

does with his pansy-ass wings humming while waving his cute little wand with that gay star on the end and sporting that silly tutu. He's always being mistaken for a girl. Thus the appellative, 'fairy.' Kind of a sick bugger too—collects all those teeth and makes necklaces and earrings out of them, which he sells to cannibals worldwide who covet his jewelry!"

"What?"

"Honest Injun," the rabbit replied in a matter-of-fact manner. "Where do you think he gets the money to put under your pillow? It has to come from somewhere, honey, and it don't grow on trees!"

"I don't believe any of this," replied a disillusioned Lauren. "It's all a pack of lies!"

"Believe what you want, sweetheart," said Jack. "But I kid you not. And it's true what I said about parents. They can't seem to admit to themselves or to each other that their own children are anything more than ordinary. So rather than own up to the fact that they and theirs are merely mediocre at best and usually worse more often than not, they invent and perpetuate packs of lies like, 'Look what Santa brought!' and 'What did the Tooth Fairy leave?' and, in so doing, teach their children to follow in their footsteps. Someday there'll be an accounting—don't you worry!"

"What gives you the right to make such value judgments?" Lauren asked, shocked at the revelations just revealed. "Who's to say who's deserving and who's not?"

"I am!" Jack replied smugly. "And as to the right—I don't know whether or not I have the right, but I've certainly been handed the sentence!"

Lauren wanted to further express disillusion but was denied the opportunity as Jim and Slim, arriving in their Land Rover and leading the caravan, pulled up to the dig site. Doors opened and closed one after the other as various members of the Secret Society of Lost Gold Miners came to a halt behind them. Out of their Volkswagen Microbus stepped Shamus and Sorcha Sweeney, two sand-shovelers of some note, along with Sean and Ráicheál Dawe, two closely related kin of Lawrence and Lauren. Walking behind them, having just disembarked from their Hummer, were Padraig and Tara Maguire. Both were Dawes from a generation or so back whose parents had somehow found the good sense to marry outside the family. Such good sense, however, proved to be of little benefit as each of their offspring bore the mark, as did their children. Liam and Fiona O'Farrell, their grandchildren, who took the name O'Farrell because they couldn't spell Maguire, were perpetually babysat by their grandparents, and thus could be counted upon to always go along for the ride. There were others as well, too numerous to mention, but bringing up the rear were Richard and Sinead O'Connor. Ms. O'Toole (perpetual schoolmarm, Irish knitter, and seemingly eternal spinster) had found love since last we looked in on her, and she and Richard (Irish linguist and translator of lost languages) had celebrated their nuptials early that spring. They would however produce no descendants and the O'Connor branch of the Dawe family tree would end with them—not that Sinead lacked either the ability or desire to bear children of her own. In fact she was as fertile as the Nile Delta after the rainy season and, had she engaged in the act of procreation, would have produced litters of little Irish lads and lassies. But Sinead, being a schoolmarm, viewed sex and the engagement in thereof as the original sin her parents taught her it was and therefore deemed biting into that particular apple as a bad example to be setting for the wee bairns attending her schoolhouse. In Sinead's view the safest sex was no sex at all and as a consequence Richard was fast falling in love with his right hand.

The throng of mad Irishmen and women approached the pit cautiously like a platoon on dawn patrol with both Slim and Jim in the lead, acting as point and issuing hand signals to proceed or halt as they deemed appropriate.

"What the hell be ye up t'?" asked Sand Toes. "And why ye be tryin' t' sneak up on us in plain daylight? Didn't me' lessons in desert dwellin' leave any impreshun upon ye?"

"Ye can see us?" asked Jim in disbelief.

"O' course we can see ye—ye be standin' there as plain as day!"

"But we hae our camos on!"

Lawrence Torrance Dawe stared at them, dumbfounded. Were there anyone as thick as the Irish? he wondered. Maybe, he reasoned, they weren't all dead above the neck or between the ears. Maybe it was just this particular pedigree. He found it hard to believe that he and they were kin. But there was no denying the mark nor the assurances of his dearly departed Larraine that they were all second and third cousins three and four times removed, whatever that meant. Perhaps he could divorce or disown them. Maybe because he'd been adopted by the Apaches it was now possible to ignore or disregard his blood ties altogether. He'd do it too—march right into town, present himself at the courthouse, and file the necessary papers that addressed such matters, except the shade of Larraine and her uncanny mirage would have a lot to say about it during subsequent visitations and Little La would not much care for the enforced schism either. The two of them were barely talking as it was. Rejecting the family en masse might well create a chasm between them that he'd be unable to bridge. Therefore, like 'em or not, he was stuck with the lunatics. "Yer desert camos, aye?" he asked scornfully. "And what makes the lot o' ye think that ye can be hidin' from us by donnin' that kilgarth and foolishnus?"

Jim looked to Slim to provide the answer. Slim didn't have one. He turned to Padraig, who turned to Seamus, who in turn turned to someone else to supply an adequate response. When the buck had been completely passed back down the line to Richard and Sinead, who still had no reasonable reply, the lot of them answered with a community-wide shrug.

"So that be it then, aye? Not one o' ye has a sensible explanation for what ye be wearin' or why ye be wearin' it—and ye deem me crazy?" Sand Toes looked over the crowd until his eyes came to rest on Sinead O'Connor. "Hae not even ye got a reasonable explanation?"

Sinead meekly shook her head.

Sand Toes sported a frown. "And ye be a schoolteacher?" he asked incredulously. "If only the wee bairns could see ye now! What would they think, I wonder?" He returned his gaze to Jim. "And what be that follishnus that ye be wearin' on yer noggins? Be they miner's helmets?"

Jim looked at him defiantly. "That they be!" he replied. "I canna' see 'im, but I know that gangrel beastie we had the tussle with a while back is hereabouts somewhere."

Jack, by way of acknowledgment, threw a stone at the Society member, which bounced off his helmet.

"There!" Jim said self-righteously, pointing a finger at the rabbit. "Little fella is so small one misses 'im in a crowd. But there he be! A rabbit he is and rabbits be good fer only two things—eatin' and diggin! Since ye ain't ate 'im yet and since like ye he be covered in sand 'n' dirt—then he must be diggin! Fer what, I wonder? There be nae carrots nor taters growin' this far out!"

The crowd behind him murmured their agreement.

"There be nae rutabagas or parsnips either!" he continued. "Therefore, ye must be making use o' his abilities in order t' be diggin' ye some gold!" The crowd again voiced their congruence of opinion, but not this time with mere murmurs. This time they were both loud and vocal.

"Damn straight!" cried one.

"Sure n' begorrah!" cried another.

"Right as rain!" yelled a third.

"*C'est ça!*" bellowed yet a fourth. But since that didn't translate very well overlaid as it was with an Irish brogue, that petitioner went ignored. The crowd gathered about the pit ominously. They were prepared both to take action and to have action taken against them. On the one hand there was suspected gold to be had and as Society members each felt they'd earned the right to it. On the other hand they were about to confront both the enigmatic rabbit and Sand Toes of the Apaches. Many there were members of the original scouting party who'd first fallen afoul of the desert man and his crafty trap. They remembered well the bruises and broken bones they'd acquired as the result of his falling rocks and sly waterspouts. They remembered too his incredible strength and agility, borne of the desert and fueled by his madness. And of course everyone by now had heard of Slim and Jim's encounter with the hardy hare before them whose very presence lent itself to mysterious and inexplicable forces. Therefore, though they proceeded with determination, they advanced with due caution as well. Sand Toes laid hold of his pickaxe. Jack assumed the crane stance and got ready to hurl his harea. All hell would surely have broken loose if someone in the crowd had not at that moment

THE CHRISTMAS RABBIT

chanced to look away westward to the ridge lying yonder and seen the forces amassing there.

"Saints preserve us!" cried the unknown sentry. "It's the Apaches!"

*****

For many years now, Horse's Head had led the people through the deserts, plains, mountains, and foothills of the Southwestern United States that made up the lands of the Apache before they'd been stolen by the white man. 'The people,' as it were, were the social outcasts, undesirables, pariahs, and persona non grata of the three major tribes of the Apache and consisted largely of apostates, lepers, grifters of various and sundry sorts, adulterers, deviants, and demagogues—all of whom were made to feel unwelcome, unwanted, and undesirable by the decent bands of self-respecting Apaches from whom they'd been ostracized. This band of outlaws and reprobates roamed the southwestern territories at will, never having surrendered to the United States government nor been signatories to any of the broken treaties that their 'respectable brethren' had been hoodwinked or horse-collared into signing. Therefore, they were free rangers, roaming at will and going where the winds led them. They were the castaways and misbegotten of the three tribes who preferred that their ostracized ones be forgotten altogether. If necessity demanded that they be made reference to, respectable Apaches simply referred to them as that shiftless band of wandering red trash. Horse's Head himself was a direct descendant of Horse Feathers, aka Geromino, the original Apache reprobate. Horse's Head's own father, Horsin' Around, had found Horse Feathers dead out back of the general store without Geronimo's map and minus the thousand dollars he'd told Horsin' Around he'd be likely get if he got lucky enough to pawn the forgery off on some silly white man. Horsin' Around was furious upon finding his father dead—not that he gave a damn about that rascally recidivist who drank like there was no tomorrow and who spit tobacco juice all over his mother's clean tepee, but a thousand dollars was a thousand dollars and he knew that was no horsin' around, despite his name. Being a good tracker as most

Apaches are whether they're reprobates or not, Horsin' Around followed the footprints left in the sand by Great-granddaddy Dawe as he made his way back east in order to confer upon his brethren, the ill-gotten map. To aid him in this quest, Horsin' Around took with him his brother, Horseplay, and two other braves, Horse Sense and Horseshoe. In order to purchase liquor and cigarettes during their travels, for they were minors at the time as well as minorities, they took along their only white friend, Coolcorron Mill Pearle—whose nickname was Hoss and who was not only twenty-one years of age but who, as coincidence would have it, was of Irish descent. The five of them tracked Great-Granddaddy Dawe through the desert sands as he headed back east until the sands gave out and the elder Dawe hit the hard tarmac. Apache skills fall short when it comes to tracking on asphalt but in this instance they needn't have worried. Rumor of Great-Granddaddy Dawe and his eccentricities went on before them like the majorette in a drum and bugle corps and lingered long after they'd left like an unwanted stain upon a clean linen sheet. Thus it was they were able to follow clues and intimations of his preceding passage all the way back to New York, where they found the situation untenable. To the many Irish immigrants who lived there they looked, being Native American, like simple greasers and wetbacks, which only caused them more trouble than they were willing to put up with for a measly thousand bucks. Needless to say, being vastly outnumbered and with no hope of retrieving their money, they left New York almost as soon as they arrived, but not before planting Hoss amongst the Secret Society as their spy and mole, instructing him to present himself as a long-lost Dawe come home. They'd even gone to a tattoo parlor and had him emblazoned with the mark in order to provide proof of his pedigree. The Secret Society of Lost Gold Miners took him in like a long-sundered relative and whenever the opportunity presented itself and the winds were from the east and blowing westwardly, Hoss snuck up to the roof of the tenement building where the Society lived and lighting a small fire, sent smoke signals back to his confederates, informing them of the Society's status. Thus Horsin' Around was well prepared for the Society's eventual return to his homeland. But when they came they did so in great numbers, more than could hope to

THE CHRISTMAS RABBIT

be coped with by Horsin' Around and his small band of reprobates. Therefore they engaged in a waiting game that played itself out over the course of years. Horsin' Around witnessed from afar the fracture of the Dawe family after the government conducted its first nuclear test in the desert, and as an old man was the fellow who adopted Lawrence Torrance Dawe into the Apache family, giving him the name Sand Toes. By that time the red men had long given up their horses, trading them in for motorcycles—Indians, of course—but they still went where they would providing they could either swindle, steal, or otherwise scarf up, an adequate supply of gasoline to get them there. Too old now to mount an Indian himself, Horsin' Around rode in a sidecar attached to his son, Horse's Head's, bike. He led his castoffs wherever he would, always being careful to avoid the ever increasing amount of white folk that seemed to be littering the landscape like flies on carrion, and the US cavalry, now referred to as simply the Army, and who like the unwanted settlers themselves seemed to multiply at an ever increasing rate while building fortresses and secret bases all over his beloved desert. But wherever they went, Horsin Around ensured that someone was left behind to keep an eye on Sand Toes. He was a Dawe, after all, and eventually, Horsin' Around knew, the others would come looking for him. As with all things mortal, Horsin' Around at long last fell out of the saddle and was buried with great ceremony out in the wastelands. Attending the ceremony was Sand Toes of the Apaches, who'd felt as though he'd lost the only father he'd ever known. Horse's Head took over as chief of the tribe, and Horseplay became its medicine man. Neither, like Horsin' Around before them, was particularly fond of Lawrence, and each resented the Apache name of Sand Toes that had been gifted to him by the old man, but they knew the reasons for it and kept up the pretense.

    Now it appeared that the pretense and the need for maintaining it were drawing to a close. Off to the east Horse's Head and his band of degenerates, tattooed themselves and liquored up on cheap booze, could see that the Secret Society of Lost Gold Miners had gathered together around a great hole, as if for a conference. Obviously, thought Horse's Head—and much to the surprise of both himself and his tribe—the stolen map, finally having been deciphered, had unaccountably and inexplicably led the Irishmen to gold. Why else would they gather so? There were no bars or taverns this far out, no pubs or public houses brewing beer or serving rye to keep them preoccupied. Therefore Geronimo's lost gold provided Horse's Head with the only explanation that seemed the least bit credible. And if he were wrong, well that many bog trotters and shilaeli swingers gathered in one place must certainly have a thousand bucks between 'em. It was time to collect upon an old debt.

    The Apaches kick-started their Harleys—they'd long since ridden their Indians into the ground—and motored down the ridge, heading east toward the destiny that awaited them. Thundering in overhead from the North and soon to pass over Witch Valley was a storm heading right toward them, but Horse's Head could not afford to worry about that on the eve of this white man's holiday. There were debts to be settled. There were overdue notes to be collected on—and as the Native American banker about to call in the IOU, he'd see to it that the debt on those notes was paid in full. "Geromino's revenge!" he cried out in a war whoop. His fellow Apaches took up the mantra, crying out time and again, "Geromino's revenge! Geromino's revenge!" It was D-day in the desert, a virtual Pearl Harbor in the wastelands, as the Apaches, mounted on motorcycles, descended upon the Society like a swarm of zeros dive-bombing a lone destroyer. The rumbling and percussive echoes of the engines as they backfired and belched out spumes of gray smoke, competed with the reverberating resonance of the faraway thunder as it rebounded off the desert floor and the sides of distant mountains.

    The Secret Society of Lost Gold Miners, realizing that they, the hunters, had now become them the hunted, beat a hasty return to their vehicles and turning them over, engaged their four-wheel drives in an effort to circle their wagons while at the same time the Apaches circled their circle, drawing ever closer as they did and firing their deadly arrows from their bows. But if I must tell the truth then I'm forced to admit that the arrows were not all that deadly. Having by and large avoided the white man and his incursions into their territory, this particular band of Apaches missed out as well on all the wonderful advances in weaponry that the white man had employed

THE CHRISTMAS RABBIT

so successfully in their campaign to subjugate and eradicate their less fortunate relations. So the bows they used were not compound bows fashioned from high-tension, space-aged plastic but merely bows carved from petrified wood. Their arrows, not constructed of any alloy or space age metal, were fashioned out of wood as well and their arrowheads made of stone. Certainly they were deadly under normal circumstances, and many were the pioneers who, having circled their wagons in ages past, succumbed nevertheless to the onslaught of such slings and darts. But the days of covered wagons were long gone. Now the settlers were safely ensconced behind the protective barriers of AAA-rated, crash-reinforced side panels, and safety glass. Most of the Apache arrows skipped harmlessly off the hoods, trunks, doors, and windows of the various Hummers, Land Rovers, Escalades, Wagoneers, Scouts, Explorers, and Expeditions they sought in vain to penetrate while scratching only the paint and starring the glass. But the Apaches had come too far, having waited too long, to simply fail now and continued in their efforts, both whooping and hollering as they shot their arrows and threw their spears decorated with war bonnets. Their painted faces looked like dark pagan idols summoning up the very powers of hell as they chanted over and over, "Geromino's revenge! Geromino's revenge!" to the timing of their spear casts and spent arrows.

Sand Toes looked on in admiration at his adopted family, mounted upon their horseless horses, with wheels for hooves and neighing like the very thunders themselves. He spied his adopted brother leading a charge and shouted out to him in Apache, laced with his Irish brogue. "Horse's Head," he cried. "Laddie—what brings ye out here n' these parts?"

Horse's Head took note of his adopted brother and sighting on him, cast his spear.

Trained in the ways of the desert, Sand Toes caught it in midair with ease. "What be ye about, lad?" he asked.

But before he could receive a reply another spear, cast by yet another Apache, caught little La' in the shoulder, whereupon she fell to the ground screaming.

Lawrence Torrance Dawe, despite being a mad man tied to a very short string, was nevertheless a reasonable fellow. He avoided trouble when he could and as a rule only did harm to others when such harm became unavoidable whilst in pursuit of his vocation which was the desert way of life. Thus it was that he set his snares for the various reptiles and snakes which occasionally became entrapped within them. It was for those same reasons that he'd caught, captured, and in some cases injured, the vanguard of the Secret Society so long ago. The desert and the impositions it placed upon a dweller's survival, demanded such acts of cruelty. And although with soles on his feet tougher than elephant hide he didn't really need shoes, he coveted them anyway. Thus he did what he did. But he did it only when he had to. He was willing to live and let live—at least as far as his predispositions and eating habits would allow him the luxury of doing so. All things considered, he was a peaceable fellow willing to get along with anyone other than a Society member, just so long as they stayed out of his way and out of his desert. Now however, looking down at little Lauren writhing in agony on the ground, his attitude toward such matters underwent a drastic sea change. His eyes, taking note of the blood pouring from her shoulder, saw red. His brow knotted in fury, and his eyes blazed fire. Hefting the spear he'd snatched from the air, he gave a mighty cast.

Jack looked upon the erupting carnage surrounding him and knowing that the pellets had at last hit the wind, hurled his harea, knocking a couple of braves off their bikes.

The Society members, trapped in their vehicles but concerned for Little La nevertheless, began to sound their horns in unison. Their braying, coupled with the rumble of the motorcycle engines and the booming of the distant thunder, caused the ground beneath them to tremble. The pit which Sand Toes and Jack had been digging, situated as it was just above one of the shafts which ran out deep into the desert directly from the nearby mine in which Larraine had fallen, suddenly collapsed, dragging down with it a slew of overpriced gas guzzling sport utility vehicles and their occupants, a dozen or so motorcycles and their riders, and one bewildered rabbit, who for the life of him wanted nothing more than to be done with this day.

CHAPTER III

A Fat Man Looks Down

The thunder boomed. The lightning flashed. The crisp scent of ozone permeated the cumuli like the smell of sizzling bacon on a sunny Sunday morning. However it wasn't sunny and it wasn't Sunday either. It was Thursday night, Christmas Eve, and Santos rode in the midst of the maelstrom, strapped to the front seat of his sleigh by means of an ingenious safety belt fashioned for him by Hephaestus, the elf. Grateful in this storm for the assurance of added security, Santos appreciated the lengths the old elf went to in order to design and construct his harness. Hephaestus, an elf of the Old School, had built his reputation on his ability to work with and mold various basic ores such as iron, tin, and lead. The harness, however, was constructed of none of these, and Hephaestus was forced to apply his energies to learning a whole new set of skills in order to complete its construction. Such knowledge was hard to come by up at the Pole, where Santos and the Elves now resided. It wasn't as though ITT tech maintained a campus that far North. The best they could do was Seattle, Washington—which still put their campus almost three thousand miles from home. In an effort to provide his employee the chance to participate in ongoing education while at the same time afford him the opportunity to enhance his work skills, the farmer tried enrolling Hephaestus at ITT's Seattle campus, but their tuition costs were prohibitive and they had no onsite dormitories. A six-thousand-mile, round-trip daily commute in the magic sleigh was possible, Santos supposed, but not very practical. To begin with, he'd have to drop Hephaestus of at eight thirty in the morning and in broad daylight for all to see. Santos was a night rider, having built his reputation on his ability to housebreak in the wee hours of the morning while folk were still fast asleep, although he did very little breaking and entering—in fact he did none. Access to the various homes where his reverse burglary was practiced, leaving items behind rather than taking them with him when he left, was usually obtained by going down the chimney so that nothing was actually broken in the rare home entered. But over the last century or so he'd put on so much weight that chimney-sliding, either up or down—and despite copious applications of magic dust, elbow grease, and KY Jelly—had become for him, an impossibility. These days it was Pixie and Dixie who performed the reverse burglary. Still night flying gave him the ability to remain undetected and to work semianonymously, his burgles being discovered only after the fact. It was a good system, had worked fairly well up until now, and he saw no reason to modify or amend it. Dropping Hephaestus off during the morning commute and at the height of the a.m. rush hour to boot, would change all that. Then there were the caribou. They rested and fattened up all year in preparation for their one evening's excursion. Their round-the-world journey, done in a single night, took a lot of the starch out of them. The average caribou dropped a hundred or so pounds in sweat and exertion before the evening was through, only to arrive back home at the Pole, thoroughly spent and exhausted. They'd spend the following year resting and fattening up in order to prepare themselves for next year's journey. There was a song, Santos knew, which children sang and which over the long course of years had somehow managed to bastardize by shortening and rearranging the lyrics—that told of his old friend Rudolph, and how his buddies wouldn't let him join in reindeer games. Santos didn't know where the unknown lyricist came up with such malarkey but it simply wasn't true. Upon returning to their home at the advent of sunup on December 25, the caribou, now thin as rails, panting madly, foaming at the mouth, and looking as though they were rabid and ravaged, collapsed in exhaustion at the door of the workshop where they did nothing but sleep for the next two weeks. Sometime in mid-January after completing their mini hibernation they would painfully rouse themselves only to begin the slow process of restoring the pounds lost to them in the expenditure of last year's effort. So from mid-January to December 24th they did nothing but loll around, eating, drinking, and sleeping as they went about the business of restoration. Their food had to be shipped in as caribou by nature are wanderers, feeding off the land as they go. These reindeer weren't going anywhere. They were too damned tired. Unable to even scavenge for themselves their daily bread, they certainly weren't going to expend a lot of excess energy by burning up precious body fat, which they could ill afford at this point, in the engagement of 'reindeer games.' Let the deer and the antelope play at those. The caribou were too tired to bother. Making the daily excursion both to and from Seattle and moreover having to do so twice each day, once in the morning when they dropped Hephaestus off and again in the evening when they returned to pick him up, would inhibit their recuperation. Therefore an off-campus apartment would have to be found. Santos bore the expense of having Hephaestus take out an ad in the personals section of the Seattle Times in order to inquire after a roommate. But having described himself, Hephaestus found that he generated very little interest in would be roomies. Santos then tried funding an ad in the Stranger: Seattle's Alternative Arts & Culture Rag, which billed itself as the city's 'Only Newspaper.' Santos was led to this rag on the presumption that those who read such trash were leading alternative lifestyles already and would welcome the chance of bunking up with someone as unique as Hephaestus. Who, after all, was more alternative than an honest-to-God, down-and-dirty, genuine and with-the-papers-to-prove-it, elf? The Moonies perhaps, or the Hara Krishna's, but discounting them you couldn't get much more unique than old Hephaestus. And my how the responses came rolling in! Santos had to detail a whole squadron of elves, normally assigned to reading his fan mail and poring over wish lists, to wade through the thousands of inquiries that the ad produced. Out of those thousands they narrowed the list down to three. The first ended up rejecting the elf because of his questionable appearance. His hunched back, his twisted right arm, his open sores, and his missing front teeth were apparently too unique for the prospective roommate to be seen bunking with. This prospect, of course, cited none of these reasons as his excuse for rejection, stating instead in a follow-up letter that although he welcomed the opportunity to meet and associate with such an exceptional fellow as Hephaestus appeared to be, he would nonetheless have to decline with regret the opportunity of rooming with him due to a prior obligation which had heretofore gone unmentioned or discussed. As an excuse, it was a vague and cheesy and offered only after the prospective roommate had the chance to review the elf's photo. The second potential roommate, although willing with some reservations, to be seen about campus in the company of one so ugly, nevertheless declined the tendered offer when she learned that Hephaestus was not a strict vegetarian like herself. Santos wrote a letter to the prospect personally, in which he offered his assurances that his ward would eat out at McDonald's and Burger King while never bringing back to their flat so much as the merest morsel of meat, but the respondent promptly wrote the sleigh master back, telling him McDonald's and Burger King, being the shrines to butchery that they were, were engaging in the mass slaughter of innocent cows for the sake of mere convenience and the availability of fast food. Santos wrote the respondent yet again to say that those establishments were not engaged in the aforementioned endeavors merely for the sake of convenience and fast food but were simply in them for the money. The respondent replied a final time with a letter that was both hurried and nasty in its overall tone, in which she stated that regardless of their reasons, McDonald's and Burger King were the symbols of all that was wrong with society and that those who maintained commerce with such institutions were nothing more than cankers on the canopy of creation—a blight, a disease, and an infection in desperate need of holistic healing and restoration. The respondent admonished the two of them to submit themselves to a treatment of wheat germ therapy and to undergo a detoxifying colonic in order to cleanse their bodies and reinvigorate their souls. Then promptly ended the letter by warning them to respond no further and to put a point to it, buzz off! Santos and Hephaestus tried to puzzle out the reasons for her apparent anger while polishing off a pair of pork chops.

THE CHRISTMAS RABBIT

The third response came from a pair of lads who were more than eager to room up with the elf. They didn't care what the elf looked like, had no concerns for what he ate, and weren't at all curious as to where Hephaestus would come up with the money needed to cover his share of the obligation. Glad to have at last found correspondents with such apparently lax standards, Hephaestus began a chain of letters, which only led to disappointment. It turned out that they were not only uglier than Hephaestus, however unlikely that seemed, but moreover, were Hara Krishnas and Moonies too and through the course of their correspondence made a concentrated effort to induct Hephaestus into the ranks of their cults while swearing eternal allegiance to the Reverend Sun Myung Moon and the Unification Church. Hephaestus was considered strange—even his elven brethren thought him so—but not that strange. He'd already made the mistake of swearing eternal allegiance to The Powers That Be and had been paying for it ever since. And as fallible as those three were they were nothing compared to the whack jobs whose representatives now tried to recruit him. Hephaestus had all further communication 'returned to sender' unopened and marked as undeliverable.

The elf grew despondent when it became apparent that further training in his professed trade might be forever beyond his reach. It was Pixie and Dixie, two elves ever resourceful and on the ball, who hit upon a seeming solution. They suggested to Santos that Hephaestus further his education by taking his courses online. Logging on to ITT's website however, proved fruitless to the old elf as none of their campuses offered even the most basic of courses in metallurgy. Everything these days was high tech. The boss had nearly fallen out of his sleigh previously and on more than one occasion at that. Cast Iron bands bolted to the sides that snapped in place while at the same time securing him to his seat would only weigh the damned sled down, which when fully laden was already operating at well over rated capacity. The reindeer weren't happy having to lug that across the heavens, Hephaestus knew, and there was talk amongst them despite The Powers That Be, of a generalized strike if working conditions didn't improve. The sleigh itself was constructed of solid oak. Its runners were cast iron. When topped off with presents it weighed well over two and a half ton and that didn't include the extra poundage of the sleigh master! The reindeer weren't getting any younger and hauling around such a load was beginning to tell on them. A modern day solution had to be found. Working together, Hephaestus knew, he and the other elves would surely find it. But the other elves were too busy making gifts and wrapping presents and resented the fact that after putting in a long day on the assembly line, were being asked to log overtime as well on extracurricular projects.

Desperate for a solution—as the boss was riding his back about the problem—Hephaestus began an Internet search for metallurgists whose skills perhaps, exceeded his own. This was not as easy as it might appear at first glance. You or I, living in the modern world would certainly have approached the search in an entirely different manner. Hephaestus, on the other hand, took the long way around the problem. It had been centuries since he'd learned the art of metallurgy. At that time *state of the art* meant turning lead into gold, and Hephaestus was one of the few who could do it. Such skills, however, would not serve his needs now. Lead or gold—either metamict substance would prove itself to be far too heavy for the application he had in mind, making both relatively valueless in this instance. But those and other similar substances were his only frame of referent and as a result he prosecuted his search with such keywords as iron, brass, lead, copper, and silver. The only alloy he'd ever heard tell of was bronze, a combination of copper and brass and like iron and gold, was much too heavy to be of any practical use. He came across aluminum by accident when a pop-up ad for Alcoa displayed itself upon the screen during one of his searches.

Here was an amazing metal, thought Hephaestus. Not only was it lightweight, but sturdy and durable too. And unlike iron it didn't oxidize or rust! He set about learning how to make the metal but soon became overwhelmed by the technical jargon that assaulted him from the pages of the website. To begin with, it was a multi-step process requiring complicated machinery and chemicals, which Hephaestus could not even begin to fathom. Terms like bauxite and sodium hydroxide were meaningless to him. Flash and settling tanks were to him an enigma. Precipitators and calcination kilns would remain forever an indecipherable mystery. Whatever happened to the good old days when all an elf needed were a forge, a bellows, and a decent supply of raw ore? And if all that weren't enough, it appeared to Hephaestus that one had to pass a high voltage electrical charge through the byproducts of the precipitators and calcination kilns in order to derive the finished project. How the hell was a poor elf, living at the top of the world, supposed to pull that off? They barely had enough juice up here to keep the lights running and a good storm could knock the power out for days! In the end he decided to subcontract the job to Alcoa after talking it over with one of their sales reps, paying the bill with gold, which he'd converted from lead. "I don't know about this magical bottomless hole," objected the salesman. "I'll run it by my design guys out at the plant and get their feedback, but no promises. We're scientists down here after all, not magicians!"

Hephaestus told the rep not to worry about the details. "Just leave me a big empty space in back," he replied, "and don't worry about holes, magical or otherwise. I'll retrofit the sled with what I need once you make delivery. And put seat belts on both the front and back seats, okay?"

"Sure thing," replied the rep. "But you modify the design and you invalidate the warranty, understand? Alcoa won't be responsible for design flaws that we had nothing to do with—and we'll need you to sign a rider to that effect protecting our legal standing!"

"Whatever," replied Hephaestus. "Listen, I'm faxing you the design specs now. Look 'em over and get back to me." The sales rep promised to do just that and in an hour or two returned the call. "Yeah, we can do this," said the rep. "But it's gonna cost ya!"

"How much?" replied the wary elf. The salesman quoted his price. "Are you kidding?" the elf cried. "Even a Roll's Royce doesn't cost that much!"

"Hey," the salesman replied defensively, "this ride will be custom-made and state-of-the-art, okay? Ain't no one else out there gonna be driving around in a sleigh like this! And as agreed, once we make the mold we break it! You pay for that kind of service, buddy, and with no existing mold and no patent either, you've got the only ride like it in town!"

The elf could not but agree, however reluctantly, that what the salesman said was true. You got what you paid for.

"By the way," the salesman asked jokingly, "this is quite the fancy rig—who're you building it for anyway, Santa Claus?" The salesman laughed at his own good humor while being treated to uneasy silence as it poured out from the other end of the line. "Hey, buddy—you still there?"

"I'm here," replied Hephaestus nervously. "Of course I'm not building it for Santa Claus! Everyone knows that jolly old fellow is just a fake, that he doesn't exist and that he's just a figment of someone's overactive imagination! Santa Claus? Jeesh! Nah, I've just a mind to be pulled around by eight flying reindeer plus one. The bottomless hole with magical properties is for show."

"Oh," replied the salesman. "Well, that's different."

"So when can I expect delivery?" asked Hephaestus.

"Not until sometime mid-January," replied the rep. "First we have to make the mold, then we have to pour the molten metal. Then there's cooling and polishing, not to mention the zinc coating to further guard against rust. We'll have to test drive it too before we can let it go to ya. Yeah, I figure mid-January at the earliest—probably a bit later if we encounter design flaws."

"No can do," replied the adamant elf. "I have to take delivery by December 20th at the latest or the deal's off!"

"December 20th?" replied the salesman. "Are you out of your elvish mind? It'll take at least that long just to make the mold, never mind cast the metal! I might be able to make delivery by the first week in January, but that's the best I can do!"

"No good," replied the elf. "It's December 20th, or you're stuck with it—and I'll write that into a rider of my own! I still have the bottomless hole to install, you know, and that's going to take me a couple of days. Truth be told, I need it yesterday, but I'll settle for the twentieth."

"What's the big hurry?" asked the salesman.

"I need to load it up for my company picnic," replied the elf. "It's a big company, and we're going to need every inch of that hole."

THE CHRISTMAS RABBIT

"Company picnic? At the North Pole? What's on the menu, snow cones?"

"Yep," replied the elf. "Them and Eskimo pies. So have we got a deal? I'll throw in a substantial bonus for you upon delivery."

The sales rep hated to commit but the enticement of that substantial bonus on top of his already fat commission was too much for him to resist. If necessary he'd ride herd on the design people day and night to ensure they delivered.

"Yeah," he replied, "it's a deal."

*****

Now in the midst of the maelstrom, Santos was glad that the deal was done. The sleigh's lightweight frame made good headway against the wind and the caribou weren't carping any longer about the onerous weight. The seat belts, woven of high-tensile nylon, held him securely in his seat and moreover kept Pixie and Dixie who were sitting in back and tending to the bottomless hole, in their place as well and out of elvish mischief. Hephaestus too came along for the ride as this was the sleigh's maiden voyage and he wanted to be on hand for its shakedown cruise. Sandwiched between Pixie and Dixie, he kept his silence while keeping his own council as well, intent as he was on jotting down notes in an effort to evaluate the sleigh's performance. Throughout their many years of association Santos had come to learn, with the exception of Hephaestus, as there was always *one* of *something* to prove a stated axiom, you couldn't trust elves. They were sneaky little fellows, always engaging in shenanigans and playing practical jokes. They were liars too. Thoroughly disreputable, they had to constantly be watched. Rabble-rousers each and every one, they'd even tried to unionize one year early on in their sentence, demanding vacations, profit sharing, insurance, and a whole slew of other benefits that they neither deserved nor knew what to do with. Take profit sharing for instance. How could you share in the profits of a not-for-profit concern? Insurance was useless to them as well since elves never got sick. And as to vacations—where was there to go up at the North Pole? What was there to see? Santos would testify in Constitutional Cosmic Court if he had to, that one iceberg looked pretty much like the next and that once you've seen one polar bear, you've pretty much seen them all. The Powers That Be put the kibosh on the union drive centuries ago. Still, the elves tried to revisit the issue every year on December 26th, after their annual task had been completed. So in an effort to pacify a crowd The Powers That Be reluctantly let them take the rest of the year off, before returning to their duties on January 1st, to begin the process of preparing for next year's deliveries. And nowadays most of those riding herd on the assembly line rarely had to put it in more than a fifteen hour work week, so they had plenty of time off anyway as the typical recipient worthy enough to make the list didn't want elvish toys with magical springs inside that had been carved out of mere wood. They didn't want puppets, red wagons, or pull trains either. The typical recipient nowadays wanted a Nintendo and an iPod! Their gimme lists were replete with requests for Gameboys, Xboxes, cell phones and DVD players. Not the standard ones either—kids nowadays were demanding Blu-rays! His elves didn't know chalk from cheese when it came to such things. As a result, Santos purchased most of his gifts wholesale from places like Toys Я Us and Wal-Mart. For those who demanded the latest in both hardware and software to run these devices, Santos acquired such items directly online through the websites of Apple and Microsoft. Even buying wholesale he accounted for well over half of Bill Gates's annual gross. Hephaestus was never so busy turning lead into gold. In an effort to keep up with the expense of having to wholesale purchase the items needed to supply an ever-increasing demand, the elves were flooding the market with the metamict substance to the point where someday the shiny yellow metal might prove itself worthless. Then Santos would have to redirect the old elf to turn lead into platinum instead. Heph was still trying to work the kinks out of that bit of alchemy and not having very much luck with it either. Santos longed for the good old days, now barely remembered, when all he had to worry about was standing idly by while watching his carrots and taters grow. Nothing grew up at the North Pole. Nothing but icicles.

THE CHRISTMAS RABBIT

When he'd first been sentenced to this unpleasant task, oh, so long ago, he was of a mind to view his penal servitude as something of a left-handed gift from the fates. After all, traveling the world over in a magical sleigh pulled by eight flying caribou plus one would surely afford him the opportunity of finding his long-lost children. But years of fruitless searching, both on the road as it were, while making his deliveries, and at home as well while peering into his crystal ball, had not turned up so much as a hair on their missing heads. So many fruitless years of searching had passed that he'd all but forgotten what they'd once looked like. Junior and Laddie—surely his offspring had sprung off themselves by now and had long since passed away. How many years had elapsed since Olden Days and the advent of Hurricane Junior? Too many for him to count, of that much he was certain. Still the recollection of their barely remembered visages ate a hole in his aching heart like the memories a discarded lover will foster in a man who foolishly let's slip away the only treasure he's ever had worth holding. In his later years, memories of his lost love come back to haunt him like uneasy ghosts flitting restlessly through the twisted and tortured corridors of his misbegotten and miserable soul. He wrestles with those memories at night as in his mind's eye he sees her cavorting through past experience. Her voice rings constantly in his head. She dances within his nightly reverie just out of reach, and he wakes up in the middle of the night after dreaming of her only to find that he can't recapture sleep for fear of encountering her yet again while trapped within his evening's woolgathering. So he lies there prone in bed, and against both his will and better judgment, envisions her in the arms of someone else and the ache such imaginings cause, both in body and soul, are agonies so severe they would make heaven's own angels weep horrific rivers of sorrow. These musings cause his stomach to roll over upon itself and his insides to wrench with such violence that he feels as if one kidney is abrading against the other. During the day, as he tries to ponder how it was that he'd ever been so foolish as to let her get away from him in the first place, he stares unceasingly at the phone while hoping for a call that in all likelihood will never come. He collides with reminders of her in every woman he meets, but since they're not her and never can be, these encounters only serve to further attenuate the horrible emptiness he bears within his tortured and troubled heart. He tries to lose himself in his work because for him, it's the only thing this life has left. Through sheer stubbornness and a little bit of luck, he may take the one thing left to him, his work, and turn it into a seeming triumph. But of what use are such outward displays of success to him? His success only serves to further bring into relief his prior loss and his ultimate failure. All the wealth and recognition in the world is of no value to him for the one treasure he desires most is forever lost to him while the only display of recognition that he truly longs for lies in the hands of a woman who wouldn't give him the time of day if she accidentally bumped into him on the street. So of what use are such badges to him? For as the rabbi so succinctly put it when delivering his sermon on the mount, "What does a man benefit by gaining the world if in so doing, he loses his soul?" For him his lost lover *is* both his world and his soul, and if not, then surely the God-given gift, which allowed his soul to spring to life and the casting aside of that gift by his own hand, becomes to him in later years a torment that eats away at his very insides like a cancer devouring his heart. Although still possessed of love for his fellow man, he nonetheless has trouble displaying it because the damage he's done each of them has caused him to so hate himself that he can barely stand the scrutiny of his own reflection in the mirror. He's unable to express remorse over the loss of loved ones for his heart is too full with the ache of losing her to contain any other sorrow. He plods through one weary day after another as he struggles to put one foot in front of the next in an effort to just keep going, journeying as he does with misery and regret, his only companions. Through the course of the intervening years, he tries over and over to put her behind him by sampling yet again love's sweet nectar, but invariably each sip from every chalice freely offered turns sour in his mouth—as if such sweet love were but mere vinegar on his tongue, until at last he gives the fruitless search up, resigning himself to the bitter fate that his heart and soul will remain forever thirsty. His glass is never half full but remains perpetually empty, screaming in silence as it stands guard, an uneasy and sorrowful sentinel maintaining an intolerable watch

THE CHRISTMAS RABBIT

over the collection of his woebegone might-have-been's. He wrestles with the spiritual conflict occurring within, knowing full well that he would sell his soul to the devil himself and trade all of his tomorrows for a single yesterday, while at the same time praying to God above every night that he be granted his one chance at redemption and reconciliation. Food for him has lost all its taste and wine, its sweetness. He smothers himself within his own tortured soul, forgetting friends and ignoring family as he eagerly awaits the onset of oblivion. For him, death has no sting and is instead a much sought after release—an advent that he'd hurry along, taking matters into his own hands were it not for the realization that doing so would remove irrevocably any last chance that he still desperately grasps at with regard to such an improbable reunion. So it was with Santos. Junior and Laddie were the only treasures he'd ever possessed that were worth safeguarding. All the letters from would be recipients, all the children in his lap while on his seasonal visitations to the various shopping malls, Kiwanis Clubs, fire stations, and police departments, that he'd been compelled by The Powers That Be to attend at the onset of the silly season in order to double-check his lists, only served to remind him of his own missing children, who no doubt were gone from his life forever. "Why, oh why," he asked himself for the gazillionth time, "did I ever let them walk away, leaving just a trail of radishes and breadcrumbs for me to follow in my useless effort to reunite with them?"

The winds of misfortune blew such meager landmarks off the trail, and what few it missed scavengers greedily ate up so that even if they would, his children were incapable of ever finding their way back to him, just as he'd become powerless to find them. Unsure of himself and of where he stood those long years ago and thinking that he took the only reasonable course of action available to him, he'd foolishly cast them aside, compelling them to make their own way in the world. Well, no doubt they'd done so and had long since given their hearts over to someone else. He should've held on to them. He should have fought for them much harder than he did! He should've grabbed ahold of them! He should have told them he loved them and proved it by facing up to The Powers That Be like a man! Instead, he'd allowed himself to fold under the weight of his own poor decisions, misbegotten circumstances, and an attitude of self-pity that made him unequal to the task laid before him. Those were decisions, he knew, that he'd regret for the rest of his long and miserable life, and if reconciliation and reunion had now become impossible, then he wished fervently nevertheless to be given one chance, just one chance, to tell them how very sorry he was for having let them down by failing to fulfill the promise and potential to which they'd been entitled.

He felt a whack on the back of his head. "Hey, what are you doing up there?" cried Pixie.

"Just woolgathering," Santos replied. "I was thinking about past mistakes. About Junior and Laddie."

"Mistakes?" cried Pixie. "Farm Boy, they were the only two things you ever got right!"

"True," replied the sleigh master. "But it was a colossal error on my part, nevertheless, to have let them go."

"No doubt," yelled Dixie in his southern drawl. "But y'all gonna cause our deaths, drowning yourself as you are, in spilt milk! We're being buffeted all about in this bothersome blow. Pay attention to the reins, will you?"

"The horse knows the way," Santos replied, "to carry the sleigh, o'er the ice and snow."

"Yeah right," replied Pixie. "Except we don't have draft horses pulling us along. We're saddled with caribou! And we're not riding oe'r the ice and snow—we're flying through it!"

The thunder clapped around them as a bolt of lightning flashed directly ahead. Its momentary iridescence paled the phosphorous glow that emanated from the nose of the caribou harnessed at the head of the herd.

"Thank our lucky stars," cried Pixie in Santos's ear, "that we've got this fella now and not the other one!"

"Oh, he wasn't so bad," Santos replied. "A bit of a loudmouth, to be sure. And a deer that liked his magic dust a wee too much. But other than that he was a passable fellow. I miss him, or at least I would were it not for the ache in my heart over my lost children."

THE CHRISTMAS RABBIT

They were referring to Rudolph, of course, who years ago had succumbed to his desire for Helgayarn, Brunnhilde, and Betty's white powder. Magic dust it was and as stated before being magical, was not in and of itself, necessarily addictive. But like all powders and prescriptions of that sort be they addictive or not, they're the stuff of fanciful dreams that can easily turn into nightmarish hells if misused or overly indulged in. So it was with Rudolph. Feeding upon his dreams while never being satisfied with the repast set before him, against the admonitions of not only Santos but the elves and The Powers That Be too, as well as the good advice of his fellow reindeer, snorted one too many lines of magic dust than was good for him. He ended flying aloft like a kite caught up in a kamikaze, soaring higher and higher, unable to come down, until as far as anyone could tell, ended up circling the moons of Jupiter, lost to all who knew him. That had happened years ago, and no one had heard from him since. His fellow reindeer still sing of him this song, the words of which are rarely heard outside the herd, and which are instead substituted by the children's rhyme that we've become so familiar with today:

>Rudolph, the red-nosed reindeer
>Really liked his magic dust
>And so formed a real bad habit—
>The desserts he got, they say, were just
>All of the other reindeer
>Told him not to play that game
>But Rudolph, he wouldn't listen—
>Thus his nose became inflamed
>Then one foggy Christmas night
>Santos came and said:
>Rudolph, with your nose so red—
>Ain't no way you'll steer my sled!
>Then how the reindeer mourned him
>For 'twas plain for all to see
>Rudolph, the red-nosed reindeer
>Would fly away in infamy…

But before he did that, however, and prior to taking wing, he produced an heir whom he'd sired upon a young doe. A chip off the old block with a shiny nose just like his sire, his Da named him Valentino 'ere sailing away into oblivion. Thus it was that these days Rudolph Valentino rode herd at the head of the harness, just like his dearly departed Da, leading the sleigh on the night before Christmas. But whereas old Rudolph sported a schnozzola whose radiance was a mere incandescent glow, Rudolph Valentino did the old stag one better, having been born with a honker housing a halogen lamp. Talk about a nose that glowed! The beams from that klieg could cut through all but the inkiest of nights, turning dark into day and dusk into dawn. It was quite a feat for a fawn, and the deer looking on, knew from then and thereon, and forever and yon, that from dusk until dawn, Valentino the fawn, who had a cousin named Sean, would be thus called upon, as the favorite odds-on, and a trademark icon, to be leading them on. And it wouldn't matter, the herd knew, whether they overflew the Argonne, the Amazon, the Aswan, the Pentagon, Oregon, or Saskatchewan—Valentino was now the see-to-stag. The deer that could get it done when it needed doing. And it certainly needed doing now as the williwaw they were wrapped in challenged even his nose's abilities. As they flew through the storm, snow and hail blew in blustering billows throughout the tempest and about them as well, icing their antlers and freezing their traces. As their harness took on ice, it became more difficult to steer the sleigh. A pull by Santos on the left-hand rein was apt to necessitate a right-hand turn and vice versa. Going up required pulling down; descent dictated the need to draw up and pull back while unstable pockets of violent air caused the sleigh to lurch first one way and then the other. It was the Nantucket sleigh ride from hell and they were caught up within the williwaw of the whale as they rode the tailwinds of turbulence brought about by the flashing of its flukes. No one, not Santos or even Rudolph Valentino himself, knew where they were. The blizzard had blown them so far of course that they could be well over Warsaw for all they knew.

"Let's take her down some," said Santos, pulling slightly upon the reins, "and see if we can figure out just where in the world we are."

"Are you nuts?" cried Dixie. "In this williwaw, we could well hit the ground which for all we can see, could be three feet below!"

"I know," replied the farmer, distress written plainly upon his face, "but it's the only way we have of determining where we are. Caught in the midst of this whiteout we can't see the stars and therefore can't navigate by them either. Perhaps Valentino, or one of the other lads, with their sensitive smellers, can tell where we are by scent! After all nothing smells quite like Passaic, New Jersey, nor the Okefenokee Swamp—each has a distinctive scent as do many other places or so say the Reindeer. Let the caribou cast for clues with their conks, maybe then we'll know where the heck we are. We've only an evening to do this job, you know, and we're already hours behind and miles off course. Remind me when we get home to have Hephaestus look into installing a GPS in this damned thing, will you? He can mount it right here on the console where we can all see it!"

Hephaestus, oblivious to all occurring around him as he busied himself with his notes, barely looked up from his laptop in order to acknowledge his mention. "A Garmin," Santos continued, or a Tom Tom, or even a Sanyo Easy Street, what do I care—they're probably all made in Japan anyway. And unlike an American product, being of oriental manufacture means that they'll probably work! The Powers That Be will break us into little bits if we don't get our jobs done!"

"Helgayarn, Brunnhilde, and Betty can go blow for all I care!" replied Dixie as he hung on for dear life. Even his newly fashioned harness did not provide him with a reasonable assurance of safety while in the midst of this squall. Suppose they took a nosedive, what then? Would he be able to unstrap his seat belt in time, releasing its lever and bail out before they crashed, or would he become caught within its traces unable to free himself, thus ending up as part of the tangled wreckage upon impact? He remembered well that first crash in the old Winnebago covered wagon that occurred during the Great Race of long ago. They'd barely walked away from that while nursing wrenches and sprains and limping upon twisted limbs. And at that time they'd been nowhere near this high or going this fast! To crash now would leave an impact crater in which you could hide a herd of wounded water buffalo. The storm intensified even further. Its winds, increasing in both violence and velocity, whipped through the well of the magic hole blowing out from within it various Nintendos, GameBoys, Xboxes, and the like, as well as a few meager hand-made puppets and push toys that the rare recipient still requested, and catching them in its breath, whipped them furiously into the sky overhead where they became forever lost to those for whom they'd been intended. As the presents went skyrocketing off, both Pixie and Dixie struggled to secure the lid over the magic hole by fastening its Velcro straps to the adhesive strips mounted on the deck of the sleigh while Hephaestus looking on, merely logged their difficulties in the C drive of his laptop. Here was a design flaw that would need addressing upon their return. The wind however laughed at such an inefficacious attempt to safeguard their treasures and howling like a banshee, tore the cover completely from their grasp and sent it sailing into the air as well.

"That's the last straw!" cried the sleigh master pulling up on the reins, "I'm taking her down!"

From the head of the harness Valentino looked back over his shoulder at the madman behind the reins in an effort to ensure himself that he wasn't getting his signals crossed. Descents were dicey enough under the best of conditions and leading the herd to pinpoint landings and doing so quietly while balancing upon the eaves of rooftops was a skill that took many a year to master. Valentino had become adept at such skill, learning the ropes and tackling the trickeries of errant traces when the reins were held in the hands of those who had no business holding them, but even so, such skill as his was hardly equal to the task set before him. Yet like it or not, according to legally standing decree, Old Slomoe was the master and as such had final say on where went the sleigh and how it arrived. Reluctantly, the caribou began his descent, gently applying the brakes while using his sensitive smeller not only as a landing beacon but as an altimeter as well as he tried to gauge their height by capturing some scent of the hidden ground below. At fifteen hundred feet the sleigh and those who pulled it suddenly broke free of the cloud cover although they were still wrapped within a whirling of wind and snow which hid most of the finer details of the ground beneath them. It appeared to Valentino's nose that they were somewhere over the desert. The Sahara perhaps, but perhaps not. It did not quite have that Egyptian smell to it or that altogether sterile scent which only that vast sand land could produce. Still it was a desert that presented itself beneath them and that meant they were at least overflying one of the five inhabited continents and had not been blown off course all the way to Antarctica. Thank the fates for small favors, he supposed, as he brought them in even lower in order to obtain a closer look.

Suddenly a pair of lights almost as bright as the one in Valentino's nose leapt up from the ground about two miles ahead of them and began to trace circular arcs in the sky. Beneath those was a set of strobe lights flashing on and off, as if to highlight what appeared to be the billboard upon which they'd been placed. Blue, red, and gold, they flashed one after the other in sequence and around the edges of the signage like a cheesy Las Vegas strip club in an effort to draw attention to it and the advertisement written upon it. Admittedly, his own eyes weren't that good, so Valentino called for assistance from one of the elves seated in the back seat of the sleigh.

Pixie, with eyes like a hawk, took up the mantle, peering into the darkness ahead in order to decipher the sign.

"It's kind of hard to tell," he yelled out. "All those cheap lights are more of a nuisance than anything else." He strained his eyes even harder. "Okay, wait—I've got it now," he said gleefully. "Ahead of us is an all-night truck stop called the Out-Of-The-Way Inn, run by one Lawrence Torrance Dawe, also known as Sand Toes of the Apaches, whoever that may be! It bills itself as the last stop this side of the great wasteland! They specialize in fine dining and Toadhouse Cookies, whatever they are, with breakfast served round the clock, and you guys," he said, meaning the caribou, "eat for free! But they're happy to serve us too! They're rated and approved. They'll accept Slomoe Diner's Club, and they don't cotton to hippies! Thank the fates—I hate those longhairs!" He paused in his recital to confer with his boss. "Whaddya think," he asked, "should we give it a try?"

Santos looked back at him doubtfully while keeping half an eye upon the glide path ahead. "I could certainly go for a Toadhouse Cookie," he replied, "after all the seal blubber and krill I've eaten over the years—not to say that dear Mrs. Santos can't do wonders with blubber and krill, turning them into a hash that's both hearty and healthy. But since I've lost my children, no meal has any appeal whatsoever and I merely eat now what she serves, as a matter of habit. Even her haggis, when she can dig up an old hag in which to bake it, has lost for me all its *agacerie*. Still, a Toadhouse sounds like a rare treat or would if we weren't so behind in our schedule. I think we'd better skip it."

He began to pull down on the reins in an effort to pull up but the caribou, caught in their icy traces, were slow to respond.

Despite the delay, Pixie pled with him. "C'mon, old man," he whined. "We're all cold, tired, and covered in ice. Besides, we need to rearrange the bottomless hole and repack the presents left to us before continuing onward, and you know that can only be done when we're at a standstill." He looked pleadingly into the sleigh master's eyes. "Have a heart, won't you?" he cried. "A cup of Java or a slug of joy juice—assuming they've a cocktail lounge will go a long way to restoring our spirits. And as to that 'round the clock breakfast'—I don't know about you, but riding within this maelstrom has me so famished that I feel as if I could eat a herd of horses and still have room left over for a plateful of Toadhouses as dessert."

"So be it," replied the farmer with a sigh. "We'll take her in for a landing in order to see for ourselves just what kind of hash this house is slinging. But we're going to have to be quick about it! I know where we are now, and we've a delivery to make in these parts before moving on."

The elf looked at him incredulously. "Out here?" he asked. "In this wasteland? Who in this forbidding sea of sand and rock could possibly earn their place on the list or, having earned it, won for themselves the recognition needed to be noticed?"

Santos chuckled. "Yeah, it's certainly a forbidding tract," replied the sleigh master, "and the demands it places on simple survival surely tax the goodwill of those unfortunate enough to live within

THE CHRISTMAS RABBIT

it, making it harder for them to excel in those acts of kindness and good deeds that win for them a place on my role. But this wasteland boasts of one such little lady. I stumbled across her a few years ago while peering through my glass. I've been keeping half an eye on her ever since. Until this year she'd always come close to securing a place on my role but had never achieved the final cut. This year she did. Therefore she'll be getting her present, come hell or high water! You know that I always go the extra yard to ensure delivery to a first time recipient. It sets a good precedent, the reception of which encourages good behavior that I hope they'll endeavor hard in the future to repeat. Of course, most don't. Such acts of kindness coupled with wholesomeness of character are hard for people to maintain. Being kind and doing good deeds requires one to focus their energies on the task at hand. Most children, having learned bad lessons from their parents, lack that kind of resiliency. In this particular case however, being saddled with such a detriment seems to have aided this child's development rather than retarded it.

"What did she do," asked the elf, "that was so noble as to earn herself a place on your role?"

"She survived."

Pixie looked at him curiously. "You've come a long way," he remarked, "since those days in the old forest. Listening to you, one would even think that you'd gained a modicum of wisdom somewhere along the way!"

The sleigh master regarded him with a smile. "Even an Old Slomoe like me," he said, "is bound to mature a bit after the passage of so much time. Those allusions and misconceptions, which I held so dear to heart while budding within the flower of youth no longer hold for me, much value. It's true what the psalmist says in his proverbs, that sorrows and loss mature a man. They help refine him, building within both character and a sense of purpose that a lifetime of gaiety, frivolity, and self-centered ambition can never hope to instill."

As Pixie looked upon the old man, the sleigh master's eyes took on a faraway look. "Punishment helps refine a man," he continued. "And loneliness brought about by one's own missteps and mistakes, however imposed or by whom, causes him to reevaluate past actions as he judges through hindsight not only those actions but his own motivations for having engaged in them. Good tannings, even inadvertently rendered by one's own hands, if properly administered and applied in the appropriate amounts, can be detoxifying tonics to the soul, providing it a spiritual cleansing that no amount of joyfulness or jubilation can hope to administer. Within the confines of our sorrows, we learn to forgive those who may or may not have had some small part to play in the perpetuation of our hardships."

"You really have come a long way," remarked the elf. "Are you saying that you now forgive the rabbits and their thieving in your garden so long ago?" Santos sighed. "Not entirely," he admitted. "I remain after all, what I am, a farmer whose vegetables were stolen from him. But if I had to do it all over again, before the rabbits could steal so much as a turnip, I'd offer to them the bumper crop of my entire garden. They were, after all, only obeying the dictates of their own proclivities. The weaknesses to which they succumbed were fostered by my own selfishness so that in the end, I suppose I got what I deserved."

Dixie looked at him in disbelief, hardly able to believe his ears. "Are you saying that The Powers That Be were justified in their sentences and their reasons for handing them out?"

Again Santos chuckled. "Not in the least," he replied. "And certainly they gave no thought to the overall improvement of my character when they passed sentence. And remember, although I cannot speak to the sentence handed down to Jack and his rabbits, Helgayarn, Brunnhilde, and Betty did punish him first and foremost while sparing me in the first trial."

"No doubt," replied Dixie. "But certainly you must see that they did so for their own selfish reasons!"

"Of course. But even an action that has as its root motivation, selfish desire, can produce unlooked for good. Fate and circumstance, although both fickle by nature, are repeatedly so kind nevertheless that events frequently play out that way. Not always to be sure, but more often than not or so it seems to me."

THE CHRISTMAS RABBIT

Dixie was, in a word, waylaid. How could the farmer think such inanities? "Surely you don't forgive The Powers That Be?"

"Forgive them?" replied the farmer. "I do more than that. I pity them."

"Pity them? But they're witches!"

"Please do not refer to them that way while in my presence," replied the sleigh master, a hint of impatience lacing his voice. "They are to be pitied rather than reviled."

Dixie shook his head, not wanting to agree.

"Understand," Santos continued, "that I neither condone nor approve of their actions, nor do I hold out any hope for their eventual rehabilitation, but can't you see, that being of such sour dispositions with regard to past injuries perpetuated upon them, whether real or merely perceived, has robbed them of their ability to place their trust in anyone but themselves? And that by themselves I don't mean each other. I mean *themselves!* Helgayarn, Brunnhilde, and Betty would not trust each other as far as the first one could throw the next. Not trusting in anyone but their own selves has led to a self-centeredness within their souls, which manifests itself as simple selfishness. This selfishness and misguided self-reliance excretes from within the ego a poisonous layer of psychic substance not unlike a noisome and noxious fluid, forming around the soul, calcifying and hardening it until it can no longer breathe properly. Then choking on the unwholesome old bones of bitterness upon which their souls have been feeding, they continue worrying those bones, gnawing at them ceaselessly while refusing to give them up and let them go. This diet of bitterness only adds to their mistrust of everyone else. Greedy in their self-reliance and therefore unable to avail themselves of the trust which their own acrimony has denied them, they become incapable of putting their faith in anything other than themselves. Believing only in themselves they cannot see that perhaps beyond their limited perceptions there exists, in fact, a presence greater than they to whom both respect and allegiance are owed. Unable to believe and put trust in such a presence eventually causes them to lose faith in themselves. Their perceptions about where they stand, whom they can trust, and why they were put here, become forever obscured. Their friends, if they have any, are not acknowledged as such. Judging the motivations of others becomes for them an exercise in futility. In their bitterness and refusal to forgive others everything they subsequently touch and come in contact with fades away and returns to the dust; and the emotion of love, both the ability to receive and bestow it, is forever denied them. Their lives, even if short, are nevertheless overlong and weary, filled with the drudgery of failed expectations, both in themselves and in others."

"So you forgive them?"

"I pity them."

"Yet you continue to do their work?"

"It's been my destiny," the sleigh master sadly replied, "to come under their purview while denying that greater power to whom we all owe allegiance."

"Are you talking about God?" the elf asked incredulously.

Santos thought it over. "I suppose I am," he admitted. "Although I've never met the fellow personally. Still, having given much thought to the matter of late while not withholding my pity for those three who have so enslaved me, I've determined nevertheless that it's time to foment rebellion within the ranks."

"Rise up against The Powers That Be? To what purpose? And for whom?"

"For me, that's whom. For me and my own freedom. As to purpose, why to serve that higher power to whom I referred earlier. For you see, Dixie, my good elf, of late I've come to think that the rendering of my gifts to those upon my role, while seemingly a noble endeavor, has nevertheless put me in direct conflict with that higher presence of whom I spoke earlier by focusing his children's attention upon me and my gifts rather than himself and the gift he's given all of us."

"What gift?"

"He walked the earth many ages ago. Now he strides amongst the stars!"

"You mean the rabbi?"

Santos smiled down at the elf. "To quote a phrase," he replied, "That Jew Boy's some fella!"

THE CHRISTMAS RABBIT

"And yourself? Do you forgive yourself?"

Santos looked at the elf with eyes that saw through the disquieting lens of distant memory. "Never!"

They were less than a mile away now and coming in for a landing. "Let me take the reins," cried Pixie, interrupting the sleigh master's uneasy reverie, "you know that I love to drive!"

Santos knew that relinquishing the reins was a mistake he might not live to brag about. Despite his previous revelations about trust and love he found nevertheless that he still had little confidence in the reliability of the elf seated behind him. Like himself, The Powers That Be, Jack Rabbit of Old, or anyone else who'd ever come down the line, elves were what they were. Very few of us ever find the strength within ourselves to change the natures we're born with, especially if such change is to our benefit and to those whom we profess to hold in our hearts. Self-improvement has never been our forte. We may take up a new exercise regimen, adhering to it religiously, or we may break a bad habit such as giving up smoking or swearing off the bottle. We may bring to an end an unwholesome compulsion, such as stealing sneak peeks at dirty magazines while shopping at the 7-Eleven or swiping a pack of gum from the counter while the clerk behind it has his back turned. We may even turn over a whole new leaf. In fact, most of us remain leaf turners from way back, first turning our leaves one way then flipping them back when the change within us that we've tried to compel doesn't take. No. The change I'm talking about is a conversion in thought so powerful and overriding that it alters our very perceptions about the nature of our existence. It redefines our *entire* way of thinking, of how we see not only ourselves but also the world in which we live. It profoundly impacts upon all aspects of our relationships with others. In effect we become entirely different people than who we were before the change in attitude overcame us. Such changes and the revelations upon whose wings they ride, are called epiphanies. Not many of us have 'em. They're rare in this world, being both few and far between—not that each of us couldn't benefit from a good shaking or two, mind you, but most of us are too stubborn to be open to such suggestion. Therefore, epiphanies are like benevolent predators. They lie hidden in the shadows or lurking in the trees, invisible to most passersby whom they'd eagerly gobble up and devour if only those passing beneath or alongside them would pause long enough whilst in the midst of their day-to-day doldrums to give 'em the chance to do so. They cry out like hunters sitting in a blind bugling their duck calls, enticing us and luring us in. But like the wary deer who refuses to acknowledge the hunter's lure, we avoid them, too caught up in our own worldview to risk its rupture by putting it in the path of oncoming revelation. We drop our mud hooks of pride and prejudice and set them deep within the seabed of those harbors sheltering our self-righteous worldviews and around those harbors we erect the jetties and seawalls of bias and doubt, which we hope will protect us from the onslaught of an ocean of conflicting opinions which we feel are forever trying to drown us and whose tides seem bent upon dragging under, the leaky scows holding our preconceived notions, and ill-formed opinions. We hoist ourselves upon our own petards and we'd rather hang from them dangling, as if we all had nooses around our necks and were choking to death on our own misguided perceptions, than to remove ourselves from them by accepting the gangways that epiphanies hold out in their effort to free us from our self-imposed gallows. So it was with both Pixie and Dixie. Pranksters by nature, genetically predisposed toward mischief, malarkey, and mayhem, these little leprechauns, Santos knew, were not likely to change their fur unless an entire pack of epiphanies banded together in a mob and like a herd of caribou fleeing from a starving wolf pack, recklessly ran the two elves down when they got in the way. Only in a similarly described manner would the revelation of epiphany descend upon such as they and perhaps not even then. Their lives were a long investment in the elvish way and neither Pixie nor Dixie were likely to entertain career changes now, and despite all his professions of newly discovered wisdom, neither was Santos. Desipience and dimwittedness were ever his calling card, his hallmark, and perhaps even, his reason for being. Thus he in effect handed the wheel over to Pixie, by relinquishing to him the reins. After all, there appeared to be nothing to crash into out here in the middle of these wastes.

THE CHRISTMAS RABBIT

The elf took control of the traces with glee, whooping it up as he did. "Take it easy, Pixie, my lad," the sleigh master admonished. "Bring her in slowly and don't try anything fancy!"

The elf looked up at him with impish eyes. "Balls on that!" he yelled gleefully. "Yippee-Ti-Yai-Yo! Ride 'em, cowboy! Yahoo!" He lashed the reins like he was a stagecoach driver in an old western movie who being chased by Indians, was hell-bent upon escape.

How could he know rather than being pursued by such Apaches that they were in fact, lying in wait? The sleigh rocketed over the sign and it was only then that Santos took note that although the sign displayed itself with prominence, the Out-Of-The-Way Inn remained mysteriously missing or hidden. Something was fishy. Something was downright dirty within the ducts and dykes of downtown Denmark, and Santos, in one of his rare instances of clarity, determined such.

"Draw down!" he frantically yelled at the elf in an effort to get him to direct the caribou upward. "Draw down, I tell you!"

But the gleeful sprite, caught up in the thrill of mischief, was having none of it. He wanted his breakfast and that shot of joy juice too. Overflying the sign, he heaved upon the reins, bringing the caribou and the sleigh they pulled, around in a tight circle. When they were over the sign he pulled hard again on the reins despite Santos's warning to avoid the humongous hole that suddenly revealed itself below them. This caused Valentino to jam on the breaks, bringing his fellow caribou to a sudden standstill as they hovered in midair. The sleigh, however, had no breaks. It operated at the mercies and whims of those who hauled it. Thus, with the reindeer's sudden stoppage kinetic energy took over and the sleigh flipped end over end, dragging a chain of caribou behind it as it went while spilling piles of presents from out of the hole in the wake of its violent passage. It was a repeat of the crash that occurred during the Great Race but this time enacted upon a much grander scale. Reindeer toppled, one over the other, as caught up in their traces their positions became juxtaposed with those of their fellows. The sleigh itself tumbling end over end while spilling to the ground the rest of the Game Boys, Nintendos, and Xboxes that the storm passing above them had failed to acquire, came crashing into the sand at the far end of the forlorn trap, pulling behind it the line of helpless reindeer who could only hold on for dear life while offering up bovine prayers in an effort to both protect and preserve their behinds. Their entreaties, however, were of little avail as they came crashing down nevertheless, caught up in the wreckage of tangled traces, twisted limbs, and cloven hoofs. The violence of the impact hurled clods of dirt and clumps of snow hundreds of feet into the air where the winds of the passing storm picked them up and carried them away. The sound of tortured and twisted aluminum as it collided with the desert floor, rang throughout the wastelands like the squealing of screeching breaks in a metropolitan subway. It ground itself out in the ears, causing those hidden in the sand to squint and shudder as they looked on in awe at the scene unfolding before them.

As the dust began to settle Hephaestus hauled himself out of the impact crater and with the use of his massive arms helped extricate both his fellow passengers and the reindeer who with their twisted and tortured limbs were nevertheless none the worse for wear. Some were removed to stand trembling upon their own forelegs while others were laid aside to be triaged later in an effort to help them recuperate. Valentino, in addition to his many aches and sprains, found that the halogen lamp housed in his nose had busted its bulb and therefore could offer up no light to aid Hephaestus in his efforts. Gathered there in the dark, cold, miserable, and shivering, the forlorn group of travelers were nonetheless thankful that in their misery they were at least left alive. It was at that very moment that hell itself seemed to descend upon them as a fearful war cry sprang up from those hidden around them.

CHAPTER IV
Larraine Looks On in Wonder

When Jack Rabbit fell through the collapsed hole he seemed to descend forever, the depths of the abandoned mine shaft racing by him as he plunged. Hurtling downward into the hellish deep, he caromed from time to time off stalactites and outcroppings of rock that hung suspended from the sides of the shaft like ancient branches growing from the bole of a mighty sequoia. In an effort to avoid further collisions he tried hurling his harea before him in a forlorn attempt to direct his descent. But his haggard harea was not equal to the task of penetrating the inky blackness of the stygian gloom enveloping him. Only Valentino, with his nose so bright, could have aided him in the depths of such darkness. But while Jack fell, Valentino was busy elsewhere, hurling through the howling winds of a wintry hurricane, completely caught up in problems of his own.

As he plummeted deeper and deeper, diving into the earth's bowels, Jack encountered fewer and fewer outcroppings for the walls surrounding him drew back and the shaft in which he descended opened up into a mighty chasm until it seemed to the rabbit that although falling freely he nevertheless hung suspended in midair, motionless and at rest. Time came to a standstill and the sensation of weight disappeared. Other than the realization that he knew himself to be falling Jack could tell neither the direction he was heading nor his overall orientation, being unable to say for certain which way lie up or which down. The only vague clue he had regarding these matters was the wind whistling by him as the speed of his descent rent a path in the stale air before him creating a vacuum that followed in his wake. Beyond this slight sensation of wind and the low whistle accompanying it, all about him there remained nothing but the oppressive presence of utter silence. He might have been lost in space for all he could tell. How far he fell or for how long would remain forever beyond his ability to articulate for during his descent time had virtually come to a halt. Eventually, how long he knew not, he began to take note of a sound occurring ahead of him in a direction he could only presume was downward. At first it manifested itself in his ear as a quiet hiss, like the near-silent sibilance of a sly snake as it slithered along in serpentine fashion to sneak up from behind while coiling for the strike. As his descent deepened, the hissing grew louder, resonating within his ear like the thrum of a drum, as if some malignant nether-god were beating out an insane tattoo upon a gigantic snare fashioned from the skins of the uneasy dead. His heart beat in erratic palpitations and his breath came to him in uneven and spasmodic gasps, herky-jerky aspirations and inhalations as he tried in vain to draw lungfuls of air that the vacuum enveloping him seemed intent on denying. Descending even further the thrum became to him a mighty roar as if he were treading water within the trough of a colossal tidal wave whose crest threatened to engulf the entire world. Abruptly and all at once, he became aware of the sensation of moisture as the air about him dampened with mist, until at last and all of a sudden he found that he'd plummeted into an underground river whose torrents and turbulent raging threatened to sweep him away to the furthest corner of the subterranean hell into which he'd fallen. Jack was a good swimmer—as far as rabbits were concerned. His curriculum and training, overseen by the Mad Rabbits and administered at the paws of those might-have-been's, while preparing him to face the many different environmental challenges which he could expect to encounter and which he was further expected to defeat in order to complete his journey, demanded that swimming be part of his studies. There were oceans to traverse in the course of his travels and it was expected by his tutors that he should be able to cross 'em; if not by swimming their entire lengths and breadths, then certainly by sailing the span of such vastness in a raft he would have to fashion from whatever handy materials he was able to scavenge upon arriving at the shoreline. Such transverses were wrought with certain probabilities that included among them, sinking. And should the raft he built for himself do so then it was the admonishment of both the Mad Rabbits and the might-have-been's that he'd better be damn well be ready to swim the rest of the way on his own or at least be able to tread water until such time elapsed that a ship passing by could affect a rescue at sea. His tutors wanted no reports returned to them of drowned rabbits who through lack of proper training and preparation, had become derelict in their duty. So as a candidate chosen to continue the quest he was a swimmer who swam beyond all but the best. But even the best of furry frogmen was no Mark Spitz and Jack, caught in the currents of the raging river was no Olympian either. He surely would've been carried off to the far ends of the earth or to wherever the torrent terminated—and with his luck that could well prove itself to be somewhere deep under the Gulf of Mexico—had not Fickle Fate and its partner, Fugacious Fortuity, chose at that very moment to step in and lend him an unexpected hand. They kept a benign but benevolent eye upon him as they'd had all his ancestors. Under enslavement to The Powers That Be, the hapless rabbits were indeed helpless in their circumstances. Thus Fate and Fortuity looking down upon them with pity, felt that they had little choice in the matter. To leave them to their own devices while bearing such an unwanted burden would be beyond merely criminal. It would be derelict. Therefore they stepped in and took an active hand in saving his life.

    As he roiled and rolled within the raging torrent Jack tried desperately to cling to the canyon walls through which the underground river flowed while pulling him helplessly along its course. The walls of the canyon however had been worn too smooth by both the passage of time and raging river water to enable him to gain any purchase or grab hold of any outcrop. Trying desperately to catch a breath while being helplessly carried along, he inadvertently sucked in lungfuls of metallic tasting water that were wrought with minerals and other metamict substances. Choking on these inadvertent draughts, he hacked them back out only to suffer the agonies of continued deluge when he tried to draw breath yet again. He was drowning and as a wet-behind-the-ears rabbit who foolishly allowed himself to become entangled within such tumultuous circumstances, was now paying the price for both his arrogance and foolishness. He felt his life ebbing from him while being caught within the confines of the cataract. Tumbling and rolling, gurgling and gargling, he began mewling and screaming on the rare instances that his head broke through to the raging surface, until at last he was swept around an unseen bend that had upon it a low-lying shelf which served as an embankment where it met the river's edge. It was this instant that Fate and Fortuity determined for themselves as the most precipitous moment in which to butt their noses into his business and as a result Jack suddenly found that the turbulent waters had cast him upon the shelf where they left him to himself as they sped along their raging way. Too weak to move he nevertheless dragged himself up the stone embankment, retching and regurgitating mineral water as he did. When he could go no further and had assured himself that he was far enough away from the river to prevent him from rolling back in, then cold and tired, demoralized and drenched through his fur and down to his dermis, he rolled over and collapsed into an uneasy doze.

*****

How long he lay there cold and shivering while wrestling with fitful sleep, Jack had no way of knowing. But it seemed to him upon waking that while asleep he'd managed to lose himself within the subconscious land of enigmatic reverie for although his dreams were not exactly frightful they were nonetheless odd and unusual. In them he was lying on a shelf of rock much as he was now, beside an underground river much as the one he could hear just below him. All around him lay a frightening shroud of absolute darkness just like the gloom that presently engulfed him, and he was both cold and wet, just as he found himself upon waking. As he lay in his dream apparently asleep, he heard the singsong voice of a mysterious presence calling out to him in an Irish brogue, as much to his surprise he was hearing even now. I must still be asleep, he thought to himself, and being asleep, am having a dream within a dream. The notion was not unheard of in his kind. The concept was deeply explored, both in Thor Rowe's volume '*Zen and the Art of Primitive Tool Repair*' and the collected sayings of Harehito Rabbakami, each of which had a distinctly Japanese flair and both of which in their original printings, were kept safely tucked away in a hermetically sealed hole deep within Jack's home warren under the care and protection of the Mad Rabbits who not only referred to them often when either modifying or amending the current course of studies but who also expounded upon their themes and premises while adding to them as well. Thus in addition to the adages and homilies incorporated within their original pages, each over the years had become thoroughly annotated and now boasted additional bibliographies citing various and key commentators throughout the ages who's insights and criticisms had been appended to the original works. To Jack and his kind they were the *Tao Tê Ching*, the *Lotus of the True Law*, and the *Analects of Confucius*, all rolled into one. Not treated with quite the same degree of reverence that we give the Bible, the Torah, or the Koran, they were nevertheless for those rabbits who read them, their guideposts to a better way of life and 'dreams within dreams' were mentioned more often than not within their pages in addition to being exhaustively commented upon in the bibliopolism that followed. The commentary which comprised these references included many comparisons and contrasts such as this one, attributed to Harehito Rabbakami:

> "*A dream with in a dream is like the sound of one hand clapping—unless it happens within the forest of one's mind where trees fall silently, one cannot hear it*"

Or this one, attributed to Thor Rowe:

> "*A dream within a dream is like a stone axe at the bottom of a cistern, unless one drinks from the well, one cannot grasp it.*"

Or this one, attributed to the Original Jack Rabbit himself:

> "*A dream within a dream is like The Powers That Be, often three-faced it cannot relied upon, either as a guide to righteous living or as a signpost to a better way of life.*"

As the slow passage of years progressed these axioms were added to, often using modern day analogies in order to make their point while attempting to sketch for the reader such insight as the commentator hoped to illustrate. With each addition to the bibliographies the commentaries which made them up became more arcane and bizarre, to the point where one wonders today whether or not such commentators really believed they had a profound insight about those works which they felt needed notation, or were merely trying to make a name for themselves by getting their commentaries logged in and preserved for antiquity. An example of such self-indulgence is as follows:

> "*A dream within a dream is like a Frisbee— tossed into the wind it returns from whence it came.*"

Or this one:

> "*A dream with in a dream is like a Tootise Pop, one never knows how many licks it will take to arrive at its center.*"

The Mad Rabbits dreamt their own dreams within dreams although more often than not such musings and reveries played themselves out within their tortured minds as nightmares.

Jack wasn't sure if he was within the clutches of a nightmare or not nor could he say with a certainty whether he was now awake or still sleeping the uneasy sleep of the drenched and nearly drowned, but either way that sing-song voice with the Irish brogue continued to call out to him. In fact, it seemed to be coming from right next to where he lay!

THE CHRISTMAS RABBIT

"Laddie," the voice said softly, "laddie, be ye all right? What business hae ye t' come a ganglin' on down this 'ere 'ole? Di' ye come all this way just t' take ye a dip in yon river, or are ye here for another purpose altogether, and moreover di' ye know ye the way out?"

Jack remained silent, resisting the urge to answer the question for he knew that there was no point in talking to the inhabitants of one's dreams as you never received from them either the reply you wanted or the answer you expected. Dreams are often the subconscious manifestations of conscious desires that we dare not explore too closely or give too much credence to when awake. As such, the characters who inhabit them, being the avatars of our own subconscious thought processes, often speak to those of us who dream from deep within the wells of our own common sense, but since we dreamers often deny such common sense when awake, our subconscious minds are compelled through the characters who populate them, to render unto we dreamers a repetition and restating of those precepts and axioms, delivering them in a nonsensical manner with the hope that having done so our conscious minds will finally accept them, acknowledge them, and ultimately adhere to them while putting them to good use. Our subconscious minds, however, hold out little hope that such will actually be the case for they know us too well and knowing us, realize that our conscious minds are often as thick as a bricks, accepting and believing only those maxims which neither dispute our assumptions about life in general nor demand of us that we reprioritize and realign our thought processes in order to accommodate legitimate challenges to those perceptions. This is why the interpretation of a dream has always been an arduous undertaking for the average and casual dreamer. To try and diagnose a dream within a dream only doubled the difficulty. Therefore Jack set aside for the moment any notions he held with regard to administering self-prescribed psychiatry and dream analysis, refusing to play Sigmund Freud to his subconscious, in order to better concentrate upon the task at hand. I can't hear you, he thought to himself. I'm not listening. But his dream refused to acknowledge his denial.

"Laddie," it persisted, "can ye nae hear me?" Jack cast his eyes about uselessly in the dark in an effort to pinpoint from where exactly within his dream the unseen voice was emanating. The effort did him no good. Between the echo inherent in the cavern itself and the roar of the river below him it was impossible to determine the voice's exact location although it seemed to him that the invisible avatar attempted communication from somewhere just off to his left. In his dream he watched himself sit up and turning his head, attempt to discover who or what comprised this mysterious presence that called out to him. It was odd, his dream-self thought, that his dream within a dream had no face. Was that because he dreamt in the dark or because the message that his dream within a dream hoped to impart lay hidden from him? What he needed, he knew, was a little light on the subject.

As if in answer to his thought, a beam of light suddenly appeared out of the darkness to cast its effervescent glow upon him. Dreams were like that, he knew. You dreamt a thought and within that dream it became a reality. If such was the case with dreams then he supposed that dreams within dreams probably operated under the same strictures. The light continued to bathe him in its radiance while the unseen voice behind it spoke yet again.

"Why, ye be a rabbit!" It said in surprise and as if to itself. "Sure n' begorrah I took ye t' be one o' me own kind by the nature o' yer screams and yer pitiful cries fer help!"

Now Jack was even more confused. If he were dreaming as he still supposed he was, or caught up even further in a dream within a dream then didn't it stand to reason that the phantoms and manifestations inhabiting them, since they were occurring within his own mind, would know that he was a rabbit and not be surprised by what was so patently obvious? His convoluted logic told him his reasoning was sound. Furthermore, knowing him for what he was, did it not also follow that such manifestations would know *who* he was and therefore address him by name? Again his logic aligned with his reasoning, telling him, "Right on!"

Ergo, if such were the case and yet the unseen manifestation before him remained nevertheless astonished by his unanticipated genus and particular classification and moreover in addition to such bewilderment could not place him by name either, then it stood to

THE CHRISTMAS RABBIT

reason that he was actually awake and not dreaming at all, didn't it? His logic, being the convoluted collection of thought processes that it was, would not go out of its way to say one way or the other as to whether it agreed or disagreed with this bit of circular reasoning and therefore remained silent on the subject. So Jack decided to test his theory by replying. If he were awake he'd get an answer that he would either understand or agree with; if not, then he was apt to get a reply that was either unintelligible or which he had no desire to hear in the first place.

"Of course, I'm a rabbit," he replied with disdain. "What did you take me for, a rock squirrel?"

The light fell to the cavern floor, as if dropped from an invisible hand. It quickly rose again, as if hastily snatched up. "I canna' believe it," replied the mysterious voice. "A talking rabbit! I must be dreaming!"

Now here was a strange twist, thought Jack. A dream within a dream that claimed to be caught up within a dream itself. Was it possible to have a dream within a dream within a dream, or in effect a three-way, threefold, subconscious, self-actualized slice of serendipity? The notion was unprecedented! Not only was it unprecedented but neither was it covered or made mention of in either Thor Rowe's or the great Rabbakami's writings! Had he stumbled upon a hidden truth whose very existence had heretofore gone undiscovered and therefore unmentioned? Was this one of the great truisms of life that sages on down through history had sought forever for in vain? Or was it even, beyond all reasonable objections to the contrary an, honest-to-God, above and beyond, goodness-to-gracious epiphany? Was he so blessed as to have been thrown in its path and moreover if such were the case and it brought to him life changing revelations, would the unfolding of such present him the opportunity of preserving these insights, gaining for himself by virtue of his discovery the right to record such revelations into the bibliographies should he ever be able to return and present his patefaction to the council? And having presented it might not the council itself therefore determine that rather than add to an existing bibliography, his insights and discoveries were of such importance and magnitude as to merit a whole new set of bibliographies in and of themselves? It had been generations, Jack knew, since any returnee had been deemed wise enough to add his thoughts regarding the quest, which was the ultimate dream within a dream, to the bibliographies. Such a revelation as this could well lead to his elevation as head hare of the council. He could in effect and upon his return, become the Mad Rabbit! Oh, for the wonder and glory of that! He began at once, to form within his thoughts, the comparisons and contrasts to be noted down, which would form the essence of his revelation and become his written legacy to all who would follow after.

> *A dream, within a dream, within a dream, is like a rooster within a cage within a henhouse—it crows loudly and with pride amongst company in the morning, but sleeps silently and alone with prejudice at night.*

Or better yet:

> *A dream, within a dream, within a dream, is like a canary within a coalmine within a mountain—we hear its radiant song but the darkness we carry within the quarries of our hearts prevents us from seeing the light.*

Or even better:

> *A dream, within a dream, within a dream, is like a weakfish within a walleye within a whale—the first is consumed by the last.*

Or even better still:

> *A dream, within a dream, with a dream, is like a lurker in the leaf, in the wildwood—it sees us when we're sleeping and knows when we're awake.*

THE CHRISTMAS RABBIT

Or perhaps best and most poignant of all:

A dream, within a dream, within a dream, is like rabbit within its warren within the forest—it cannot see the flowers for the trees!

Jack knew then and there that he was capable of rattling off a million of 'em. *But before I get ahead of myself,* he thought, *I'd better test further the presumed incontrovertibility of my proposed epiphany.*

"You can't be dreaming," he replied, "since I'm the one who's dreaming and the reverie which you inhabit is mine!"

The unseen phantom offered up a tired sigh. "Alas, that it were so," came the lilting reply, "and that I was but a dream within yer dream. But too long hae' I wandered through the depths and the darkness o' this ghastly and gruesome grotto prior t' ye dreamin' me up t' be anythin' other than real meself. Therefore ye be the dream that I be dreamin' or I just be plain crazy! For what Irish lass, right in her own mind, hae ever heard o' or spake to, a talking rabbit?"

"I know of one," replied Jack. "She lies on the surface, perhaps dead now for all I know."

An uneasy silence emanated from the unseen figure standing before him while the light in her trembling hand emitted erratic beams whose stroboscopic flashes cast eerie shadows of himself that cavorted madly like stark raving phantoms on the obsidian wall behind him. His capering shadow reflecting and refracting off the veneer in back of him seemed animated with a life of its own as it danced capriciously on the surface upon which it was displayed. Finally the enigma holding the light offered her hesitant reply. "Who be this Irish lass," she asked in a quivering voice, "that speaks to rabbits?"

"Her name," Jack replied, "is Lauren. And her father is Sand Toes of the Apaches."

A wail broke out from the darkness. "*Imeacht gan teacht ort & Titim gan éirí ort!*" the phantom cried out a Gaelic curse, which when translated into the language of this tale means, 'May you leave without returning and may you fall without rising.' "Alas, I knew that me

Little La was in danger o' going mad like the rest o' me kin! 'Tis the stigmata, I tell ye! 'Tis the curse o' the mark! Oh why in the name o' all saints did I ever venture into this hole on that drear and dreadful day? Who'll watch o'er me sweet little lassie and see t' it that she's brought up proper, now that I be forever trapped 'ere? Dark was the day—dark I tell ye, that I came ganglin' into this grotto! Who'll do battle wi' the mark on me wee bairn's behalf by offering t' her sage councils and parental wisdoms so that she will 'nae fall prey to the vicissitudes o' Fickle Fate which seeks to entrap her, aye? Who alas, but I?"

"Well, she has her father," said the rabbit in a half-hearted attempt at consolation.

"That daffy bastard? I love him dearly, but Lawrence Torrance Dawe and the eccentricities he wears upon his breast like they be badges o' honor are not what me Little La needs t' be assured o' growin' into a true and proper Irish lady!"

All of a sudden, it dawned upon Jack just who this phantom was as well as the realization that before him was no spectre at all but rather a real Irish lady, presumed lost in a cave-in of long ago.

"Larraine," he asked hesitantly, "is that you?"

"I be none other!" she replied defiantly. "And who might ye be, that talks in the language o' men?"

"My name," replied the hare, "is Jack Rabbit."

The as-yet-unseen enigma who stood before him regarded the rabbit in protracted silence while Jack, unable to gauge for himself the tenor of her thought by evaluating the look on her face, was clueless as to her overall appraisal of him and so stood there nervous and fidgeting while awaiting her reply. He had never enjoyed being cross-examined, either by Mad Rabbits and their might-have-been's or by mad Irishmen and their daughters. To undergo such treatment at the hand of a mad Irishman's long-lost wife, who sounded as though she'd taken a slide off the rocker herself, was more, he felt, than one rabbit should be made to put up with. Who, after all, could possibly bear up under such scrutiny?

Finally Larraine consented to speak again, but not with a reply to his name but with another question from far out in left field.

THE CHRISTMAS RABBIT

"How is it, if ye be not a figment o' my misguided imagination nor a phantom inhabitin' one o' me own dreams, that ye've come t' know me Little La and have had conversation with her, aye?"

The rabbit shuffled nervously. "That's a tale long in telling," he replied evasively.

"Look around ye at the darkness which surrounds us, me little leporide," she replied. "We nae be ganglin' off anywhere in any great hurry."

Jack debated the pros and cons of revealing to her both his true identity and nature of his quest. Although under no official decree by Mad Rabbits or might-have-been's to the contrary it was nevertheless recommended by both that such subjects be avoided wherever and whenever possible. For instance, it was their advice that should he ever find himself at sea, either swimming along or merely treading water as a result of attempting a transverse in a leaky scow that subsequently sank and further, should then find that he was rescued by a ship whose captain and crew demanded of him an accounting of his unlikely presence out there in the briny blue, and who even further than that subsequently found himself to be the victim of undo coercion and perhaps even torture while being forced to undergo a round of questioning whose aim it was to wring such information from him, and who found even further still that having undergone hours or perhaps even days of such mistreatment no longer possessed the willpower and inner fortitude necessary to maintain ongoing silence in the face of such continued instances of 'enhanced interrogation,' should then feel free if he felt so inclined, to spill the beans about the whats, whens, and wheres of how he came to be there and why. But first it was recommended to him that he try his hand at mendacity and prevarication; that he concoct and cook up a slice of warm fudge; that he fib, falsify, and speak with a forked tongue; and that he misrepresent, misstate, and misquote himself in an effort to both stretch the truth and bend the longbow. A probable falsehood, they argued, was easier to believe than an unlikely truth. You could say you were the Easter Bunny, but having lost all your ova to Davy Jones and his locker what proof had you for such a bold-faced statement other than your given word and having given it were the seamen then likely to believe such an outrageous claim? Most likely not was the opinion of the Mad Rabbits and the might-have-been's who served under them. And not believing it, they were then likely to inflict upon you even further punishments and harassments. It was a no-win situation and when in a no-win situation the Mad Rabbits felt that one had nothing to lose; and if one had nothing to lose then the Mad Rabbits further deemed that one had nothing to gain either by giving away something to one's interrogator which was apt to be regarded as most likely nothing at all in the first place. Turn a no-win situation into a can't-lose contingency, and you were bound to come out a winner every time—even if you failed to survive the day or lived to tell about it. There was a certain protracted and schizophrenic logic in this bit of circular reasoning that Jack could identify with and therefore decided to try his hand at the suggested mendacity.

"Since you find me in this hole," he replied, "isn't it obvious? I'm the March Hare from *Alice's Adventures in Wonderland*!"

The unseen stranger before the rabbit regarded him skeptically. "If ye indeed be the March Hare, then where be yer timepiece?" she asked.

"Say again?"

"Yer timepiece! The March hare was forever lookin' at his timepiece and blatherin' on abou' bein' late fer an important date! So where be ye timepiece?"

"I must have lost it somewhere along the way," Jack meekly replied.

"Balderdash!" said Larraine. "That little leporide was too concerned o'er time's passage t' ever let the damned thing out o' his sight fer even a moment!"

Jack had no answer to her insight other than to try his hand at another prevarication. "You caught me," he replied. "The truth is that I'm the rabbit that Lenny, the Feeb, killed through neglect in Steinbeck's *Of Mice and Men*, and having died, I now find that I'm in hell."

"Ye nae be cute enough, as Lenny describes him, to be that rabbit!"

"Beauty is in the eye of the beholder," Jack replied.

THE CHRISTMAS RABBIT

"Sure n' begorrah!" Larraine said. "And though feeble minded with nary but bats in his belfry, one thing Lenny did hae was an eye for beauty! Ye nae be Lenny's rabbit no matter how loudly ye proclaim otherwise!"

"Okay then! The truth of it is, I'm Bugs Bunny!"

"Are not."

"Roger Rabbit?"

"Nope, nor Ricochet Rabbit, the Cartoon Cowboy—so don't ye even be goin' there!"

Jack was out of mendacities, prevarications, fibs, and falsehoods and being so, found his forked tongue cloven to the roof of his mouth. If he ever got back to tell the Mad Rabbits of this strange encounter with the lady from down under he would declare as well that their isms regarding the benefits of prevarication when in such situations weren't worth the parchment they'd been inscribed upon when entered into the bibliographies. "My name is Jack Rabbit," he said again, "and since you persist upon knowing, then I say with all candor that I am the Easter Bunny."

Larraine gave voice to a disdainful harrumph, which echoed throughout the cavern's darkness. "That's an even bigger lie than all the others!" she said. "I'd sooner believe ye t' be Bugs, Bunny, Ricochet Rabbit, and the March Hare all rolled into one as be fooled into thinkin' ye the Easter Bunny! What kind o' posh n' nonsense be that?"

"It's the truth," replied Jack. "The only reason I'm here is that I happened to be out this way in an attempt to deliver to your daughter Lauren, her Easter egg. A misadventure while in the company of your husband now finds me in this hole with you."

"If ye be who ye claim," asked Larraine, "then how is it that ye've never delivered to me Little La before now? Surely she's a good enough sort to have gotten her egg sooner rather than later?"

Jack rolled his eyes. Was he going to have to go through all that again? He tried a shorter version of the tale. "You folk's do live a bit on the fringe," he replied, "and finding you ain't exactly been easy."

There was some truth to that, Larraine knew. Living in the middle of the desert did indeed place them upon the outer fringes of civilization and Larry, she knew, only further added to their isolation by his insistence that they live within the confines of the abandoned shaft where he'd grown up rather than moving into the relative comforts of town along with the rest of the Society as any reasonable family would have. But he'd been her man and she'd owed him her life and therefore bowed to his wishes. And as stated before, given that he gave her no choice in the matter she struggled long and hard within the mine itself, cleaning and vacuuming, dusting and turning it out, until she made of it a cave that any miner forty-niner otherwise, would have been proud to call home. Still that had been oh, so long ago. Now, trapped in a cavern with this enigma before her she had to nevertheless and against her better judgment, credit the veracity of his tale. The honesty she saw registered in his eyes spoke to the truth of his yarn or at least his own belief in it. "How is it that ye talks?" asked Larraine. "For certainly, with the exception o' fairy tales and the like, no one, that I know o' at least, has ever heard tell o' a talkin' rabbit!"

Jack offered a tired sigh. After suffering the horrors of near drowning only to come face-to-face with the disappointment that his dream within a dream within a dream was merely a factual delusion after all and as such denied him his chance to be remembered within the bibliographies, he subsequently found that he was tired of answering pointless questions as the one placed before him who's answer lie so far back within the depths of arcane myth and barely remembered legend as to be less than actual lore and more in line with fiction and fairy tales than anything else. "I don't know," he reluctantly replied, "other than to ask you the same question—how is it that you speak my language? For who's to say that it's yours and not mine or which of us has the right to lay claim to having spoken it first? Honestly, I do not know and therefore have no answer to give. But this much I do know, that once, a long, long, time ago, way back in Olden Days, before you or I, or our parents and grandparents, or even our great-grandparents were born, when the seas were bluer and the grass greener, when the lands about the earth lay differently than they do now and the stars splayed across the heavens were hung in different positions than those which they presently occupy—when in fact, The Powers That Be had more influence in the world than they do at present, men and rabbits and all the other living things in the Old Forest spoke among themselves, one language and with very little variation.' It's said by my people that when your kind—if you take my meaning—began to drift away from my kind as well as every other kind too, that those kinds, including most of my kind, were granted the kindness of receiving a language like unto their own kind, if they'd only be so kind as to give your kind and the lingo they termed language, the boot. Most every kind, with the exception of a few of my kind, in an effort to put as much distance between themselves and your kind as possible, jumped at the chance when they'd been given the opportunity to do so. Even my kind, or so the legend goes, were eager to separate themselves, both in language and manner, from the farmer of old and those who resembled him. But The Powers That Be denied us that blessing when they imposed upon us, our sentence." He paused for a moment, sensing even in this darkness that his tale had produced a profound effect within her. "What is it?" he asked. "What is it I've said that has you trembling so? For the light that you hold, quivering in your hand as it does, gives evidence to the palsy that my words have wrought."

Larraine was a moment or two in replying. "Your tale," she said in a voice filled with awe and completely devoid of Irish brogue, "begins with the very same words used in the Dawe family encyclopedia, which describes our mark! We do not know exactly from whence or where the stigmata first appeared amongst our people—our book does not say other than allude to the notion that the mark is indeed from ancient times! But our book begins with the very same words you just cited, 'Once, a long, long time ago, way back in Olden Days, etc.' How can this be, for surely being man and rabbit, we cannot share the same ancestry!"

"That much is certain," replied Jack. "But perhaps, though our ancestries are different our histories are nevertheless the same, or at least in linkage? Might that not be possible?"

"Perhaps," replied Larraine. "But if so, then you're arrival here seems to me to be more than mere coincidence! It bears the hallmark of being a turning point in our mutual destinies! So tell me if you will all you can about Little La and my husband, La T. Da. How is it that you've become involved with them, for they each bear the mark, as do I. Why is it that you think of her as possibly expired and moreover what was the exact nature of this 'misadventure' between you and my husband of which you spoke earlier?"

"I'll tell you all I can," replied the rabbit. "But that too is a tale long in telling and if what you say about mutual destinies and turning points is true then we may not have time for such a saga—for it seems to me that if I'm in agreement with you with regard to this—which, by the way, I find myself being, then the time needed to spin such a yarn may well be a luxury that neither of us can afford. We need to somehow make our way back to the surface and together confront the collision of our karmas!"

Your words ring true in my ears, little friend," she replied. "But even if such an ascent is possible, and I've found no way out as yet—I will not consent to attempting such till I know full well the williwaw into which I'll be walking!"

Jack allowed himself a shrug and a sigh. "I suppose that's reasonable," he reluctantly replied. "But before I begin, I've a question or two to ask about you.

"Just one or two?" she asked with a laugh. "I would've thought you'd have an entire logbook of them in your head ready to be fired at me!"

Jack laughed in return. "So I do," he replied. "But I understand as well as you that we're under a bit of a time constraint and will therefore try to amend them!"

"Fire when ready, Gridley!"

Jack did not recognize the reference but took the meaning nevertheless. "First off," he asked, "what happened to your Irish accent? Why did your brogue suddenly disappear?"

"I can't say for certain," replied Larraine. "As a fifth-generation Irish American, I was never overly fond of the brogue to begin with. Refraining from its usage, I looked upon with mild contempt those within my family who'd adopted it as an affectation to further enhance their overall *'Irishness.'* But having been brought up around it the brogue became a part of me with which I had to contend con-

THE CHRISTMAS RABBIT

stantly in an effort to avoid its usage, falling into it only when I became extremely upset or agitated. Of all the members of my family, Lawrence, or Sand Toes as you call him, a name given to him by his so-called 'Apache friends,' and one I might add that I despise, is the only person whose brogue is not an affectation but the genuine article, as it was in all my family as little as a couple of generations ago. But as wacky as we are and we are indeed wacky, we've nevertheless come so far as to fully assimilate into the American Culture so that the brogue we give voice to is by and large a conceit on our parts as well as a denial of our American Heritage. For though we come from Irish stock we are no longer Irish—we are American! So as said, my usage of such only occurs when I'm upset or angry. Being down here for as long as I have must've driven me slightly mad and in that insanity I fell back upon its use. The recent revelation you imparted to me by your recitation of ancient words common to us both, that our destinies were not only linked but were perhaps coming to a turning point and moreover reaching a watershed moment wherein they would each come into collision with the forces which moved them, drove such insanity from me. It rid me of it. Dueling with destiny allows one no room in his or her mental closet for the storage of such handicaps as insanity and madness. One must be bold and above all be sane in one's mind if one is to confront such foreordination and fortune!"

"Well then, I'd better hurry my questions along," replied Jack, "because Sand Toes, although mighty, is mighty mad nevertheless, being as you say, 'a daffy bastard!' But one thing needs answering for me and that is, how have you survived for so long down here? To hear Lawrence tell it you've been lost in this hellhole for well near two years now!"

"Is that how long it's been?" Larraine asked in disbelief. "I've often wondered how many days had passed since I'd become trapped. I gave up trying to keep track of them long ago as I saw no hope of ever escaping, nor to be truthful, do I see any now. At times it seems so long and at other times even longer than that! "Twas the separation indeed, from me own kith an' kin, that ate away at me so, drivin' me mad."

"Your Irish is showing, love," Jack interjected.

"So it is," Larraine remarked with a bitter smile. "I'll try to refrain from it. Let me think now. It was sometime about two and a half years ago, I would guess, just about six months prior to the cave-in, that the Secret Society of Lost Gold Miners discovered this abandoned shaft. From what we could decipher from Great-Granddaddy Dawe's map it appeared to each of us that we'd at last found what our family had so long sought after—Geronimo's Lost Gold Mine! We began exploring the shaft, digging a little here, probing a little there, all the while reinforcing the walls and ceilings of the various side tunnels and quarries and the main shaft as well with newly cut timber we'd had shipped in from the coast in an effort to refortify the underground passageways so that we could safely prosecute our search for the mother lode!"

"Did you ever find it?" asked Jack.

"Not at that time," replied Larraine. "But after two years of stumbling around here in the dark, armed only with my flashlight, I finally hit upon it—for all the good it will do either me or my Society! Even if you and I were to somehow magically find our way out of here, the vein itself lies so far beneath the earth and away from the tunnels as to make extraction impossible. The big operators like Homestake Mining, NovaGold Resources, and US Gold, with their fancy earth-moving machines and such, could no doubt find a way to get at it, but for small timers like us, armed only as we are with pickaxes and pushcarts, such an undertaking is unlikely."

"Why not sell the map then?" asked Jack. "If there's as much gold as you claim, then surely one of those firms would be willing to buy from you the secret of its location!"

"Never in million years!" Larraine replied vehemently. "Always in the past, they sent their hatchet men and bully boys to try and coerce from us either the mine's location or the map itself. When simple coercion didn'a obtain for them that which they sought, they turned to intimidation and harassment instead! Filin' false charges o' claim jumpin' and pursuin' our womenfolk about town, makin' threats and castin' disparagin' remarks our way abou' our pedigrees! Callin' our women daughters o' micks and our menfolk shilaeli

THE CHRISTMAS RABBIT

swingers and the like, while tryin' t' mix it up with 'em by startin' brawls in our taverns an all that kilgarth—"

"Your Irish, dear," Jack interrupted. "Your Irish."

"Well, what o' it?" she replied angrily. "The only reason that their harassing o' us stopped is that me kin finally decided to entrust the map into me husband's keeping!" She paused for a moment to allow herself a small chuckle before continuing. "So along comes these bully boys one day, armed with their knives and clubs and whatnot with a mind t' be intimidatin' Lawrence Torrance Dawe! But they could'na see the trees fer the forest could they? Nor the sand fer the cactus—and soon learned that you don't mess with Sand Toes of the Apaches! Like Tarzan of the Apes is Lord o' the jungle, so is Sand Toes of the Apaches ruler of the wastelands! A daffy bastard he may be but here in the desert my man hae nae master! So they lies in wait fer him with the intention o' makin' 'im give 'em our map, not knowin' that he in turn lies waitin' fer them! He leads 'em, on a merry chase he does, until at last when he has 'em alone, has his way with 'em. And nae one o' those cladhaires is heard from since. Nae one!"

"What happened to them?" Jack asked. "What did he do to them?"

"I dinna know," Larraine replied softly. "He never told me or any member o' the Society what became o' them, other than t' tell me one night, that they '*Tiéigh I dtigh diahal*'..."

"Say what?" asked the puzzled rabbit. "I didn't get that."

"Nae reason that ye should," replied Larraine. "It be an old Irish curse and translated means roughly that 'he sent 'em to the devil's own house'!"

"You mean, he killed them."

"Well, he sartainly did'na kiss their arses, darlin'," replied Larraine, "but sent 'em to the 'ell they deserved!"

"You're letting your Irish get away from you again."

Larraine's eyes flashed at his mention of the trait that she fought so hard to repress but then she sighed and taking a deep breath, brought her emotions back into good order. "You're right, of course," she went on to say. "Getting angry does no good, especially here and especially now. But given their treatment of us even you must agree that they had it coming."

Jack merely offered her a shrug. Who was he to say? Her complaint surely sounded legitimate to his ears—he had after all an enemy upon whom he hoped to enact a similar fate, but viewing her tale dispassionately he had to ask himself if any wrong inflicted upon one by another was deserving of such harsh retribution and if not, then what did that say about his own grievances and his need to settle a certain account in order to resolve them? Were his claims to injury any more valid or any more worthy of a great vengeance enacted upon the perpetrator in an effort to seek redress? Jack buried such doubts beneath the acrimony and pent-up ill will that had been amassing in him and his kind over the course of the long years regarding his bitter feud with Santos. Surely, the Tortoise had it coming for all the trouble he'd caused. The Powers That Be too! But there was no way that mere rabbits were going to exact a revenge upon three such as they, even if in this day and age they were to be found—for no one to his knowledge had heard from the trio in a long count of years. Therefore Slomoe should he be captured and trapped by those above, assuming the Apaches left any of 'em alive, that is, would have to bear the full penalty for the malfeasance in which he'd been both a key and integral player. *Too bad*, Jack thought, *I can't be up there to participate in the grand vengeance!*

"Well," Larraine continued, "regardless of how you feel about such matters, the fact nevertheless remains that they're no doubt dead and buried and that what's done is done and cannot be undone."

Jack nodded his head as he could at least agree with that much. "But we're getting off track," he replied. How is it that you came to survive down here?

"Having completed our shoring," Larraine said, "and reinforced all the passageways, we determined that the best way of exploring such a vastness as the one confronting us was to detail a group of twenty armed with all the necessary provisions to last them three months, who would remain in the mine, mapping it out, and discovering its secrets. It was my job to see to it that the supplies for such an expedition were delivered to the staging area, which we determined

THE CHRISTMAS RABBIT

to be the fourth level down in the shaft. I spent a week hauling down to that level-assorted pickaxes, mining helmets, rechargeable flashlights, and foodstuffs in order to prepare and provide for the chosen twenty who'd be selected to perform the incursion. In addition to all that I hauled down two crank generators and a couple of chemical toilets! Getting them down there wasn't easy my friend! On my final descent, while stowing away some canned peaches, there occurred an earthquake somewhere out in the desert that sent the upper three levels crashing down upon the fourth. There was no way, with mere pickaxes and shovels, that my family were ever going to dig me out. I've no doubt that they tried and are trying even still, not only t' find me but to reopen the shaft in an effort to continue their exploration. But after two years, I doubt they'll succeed."

Jack merely nodded his head in agreement, not having the heart to tell her that the Society, and even Sand Toes himself, long despaired of such efforts and had given them up.

"It's a wonder," Larraine continued, "that I survived the initial quake, let alone managed to eke out an existence for two years buried beneath this rubble while living on canned peaches, potatoes, and pork rinds—all of which, I must tell you, I've grown damned sick of—as will you before too much time passes. But now to your tale. Tell me of Lauren and Lawrence. How goes it with them and what of the misadventure to which you made reference to earlier?"

Jack laced his paws, cracking what for rabbits passed as knuckles, while stretching his neck and rotating it upon his shoulders in an effort to relax himself before taking up the tale.

"Where to begin?" he asked the darkness. "It would help," he said, "if I had a bit more light so as to be able to see you while relating, my saga."

"That's easily enough accomplished," said Larraine, tossing him another flashlight. "I charged these up before coming down to the river to get my daily ration of water." Jack tried to catch the light but missed, his paws not being built that way. "All thumbs, are you?" asked Larraine.

"Actually," Jack replied, "just the opposite. Unlike you, I lack opposable thumbs, which makes catching things like tossed flashlights—to say nothing about gathering eggs—nearly impossible. Instead of criticisms, I'm entitled to commendations."

"Sorry," replied Larraine. "Your speeches and mannerisms are so akin to my own that my first inclination, even though I can see plainly enough that you're not human, is to endow you with such attributes nevertheless."

Jack shrugged. "Don't think twice about it," he replied. "The same thing happens to me all the time. Knowing that you're not rabbits and never will be, I nevertheless sometimes find in the occasional person with whom I have contact, such qualities as wisdom, love, and the ability to discern a parsnip from a carrot or a leek from a lettuce leaf, that I end up imagining they possess the same qualities I see in myself."

From out of the darkness, Larraine looked upon the hare with skepticism. "Are you saying that my kind lack wisdom and the ability to love?"

"It would sure seem that way, wouldn't it?" replied the rabbit.

"How so?"

"Well, for one thing," Jack replied, "you won't find rabbits engaging in the wholesale slaughter of their own kind for things so transitory and meaningless as territory and money. As warrens, we don't fight wars with neighboring warrens over such silly things nor do we, as individuals, engage in the murder of our fellows in order to obtain them. Can your kind say as much?"

Larraine shook her head.

"I thought not," Jack replied. "And not thinking so, I would further argue that your species, engaging in such insane activities, has lost its ability to love. Oh you play the game well enough, I suppose, occupying yourselves in the pursuit of its mimicry by fostering sentiments upon those with whom you feel closest and with whom you've formed seeming bonds of love, such as your dearest friends and immediate families, but beyond that limited scope your ability to display genuine affection and concern towards your fellow creatures lies dormant within hardened hearts which have little enough room inside them for those who live outside your immediate purview. Thus you teach your children, often by taking them to your churches, mosques, and synagogues, on a Friday, Saturday, or Sunday, to 'love their neighbor, and to do unto them, as they would have done.' Then you spend the rest of the week from Monday through Thursday instilling fear and hatred within them by spouting off against those damned Jews and Muslims, Buddhists and Christians, referring to them as Kikies or Christ-Killers, Camel Jockeys, Towel Heads, Slant Eyes, Rice Merchants, Jesus freaks, or Holy Rollers. Do you think that the Higher Power, which governs us all, looks down with delight upon your kind when you engage in such slander and moreover, teach your children to do so? Do you think that the perpetuation of such folly is an act of love on your parts? It's a sickness! It's schizophrenic to teach your children to love their neighbor one day and then hate and mistrust them the rest of the week. Moreover, it's dangerous and ultimately suicidal. Mark my words—these hatreds you foster and divisions you sow will bring about your own destruction. Do you not realize that your own government, in its paranoia and mistrust of those living beyond its borders, has buried within these very desert sands upon bases which they keep hidden, weapons of such absolute horror that their release would cause not only the destruction of your fellow man but of yourselves as well? And we're not talking about just the atomic bomb here but whole bases dedicated to the housing of various plagues, pestilences, murrains, and epizootics of such virulence that once released they'd devour the whole world, infecting it beyond curing! And this is supposed to be an enlightened country! A land where the noble ideal of brotherhood and love of fellow man is routinely referred to by leaders and politicians who stump across the country every election cycle to tell you how wonderful you all are! Nor is this the only country where such hypocrisies take place. They happen everywhere to one degree or another. You all say, no matter in what language you speak such lies, that you act out of concern and love, as you strive to be part of a 'community of nations,' but what really motivates your actions is fear and mistrust, which compel your participation in that community not with the intention of building bridges of harmony between yourselves but merely as a means of keeping an eye on the other guy. What bridges you do build, you erect in order to more quickly move your tanks and halftracks onto the other fellow's ground should he get in your way! Such actions are not motivated by love, but rather fear and mistrust, both of which have their roots in hate. You'll be the death of not only yourselves, I tell you, but moreover the death of the rest of us too."

Larraine adjusted the light he'd let fall in order to better allow him to see the look of derision written upon her face. "If you're done preaching," she replied sardonically, "then feel free to step down from your pulpit before continuing your tale."

"Sorry," the rabbit replied. "But having been forced into this occupation long ago, an undeserved sentence I might add, and furthermore, carrying out the terms of such sentence by the only method available to us, the wholesale theft of eggs which I might add even further, and the redistribution of same to children whose innocence could be arguably called into question while observing through the long count of years, despite an ever increasing population, that such children of even questionable character become increasingly more difficult to find as the ages advance, we EBs and the might-have-been's behind us and most certainly the Mad Rabbits behind them, have developed a somewhat jaded outlook—not only about our quest, but also about those whom our sentence compels us to serve."

"You make our children sound like used cars," Larraine snapped, offended and feeling naked in the face of his unspoken implications, "when you speak of 'servicing them' as if they lived under the dictates of some sort of mystical and magical maintenance schedule that only you have a copy of, and that you were 'under their hoods' as it were, performing some perverse inspection of one kind or another. It sounds dirty!"

"Being a grease monkey always is!" Jack laughed. "But I like your analogy, so I'll use it! You may consider my annual droppings as the stickers on your children's windshields, certifying them 'safe for the road' while attesting to their overall soundness of character and disposition."

"It still sounds dirty!" Larraine replied. "What kind of chap anyway, be he Easter Bunny or nae, goes around handing out candy to little children? We've a word for that now, you know? It's not a nice one."

THE CHRISTMAS RABBIT

"Hey, that candy rap is just bad public relations, okay? That's all the Tooth Fairy's doing! He's got a gang of gay little henchmen, all as wee as himself and all dressed in tutu's, flitting their wings and waving their gay little wands with the stars on 'em, that slave away night and day in an effort to get your kids to eat that garbage! Cavities are what drive his business. He's got a vested interest in 'em! Me? I'm all against that sort of thing and encourage kids when they can to avoid M&Ms, Gummi Bears and the like, while encouraging them to floss daily! As to the rep, yeah, I've heard it," Jack replied. "More than once. So what? Everybody's a critic and everybody thinks they can do my job better—well don't judge either me or my performance until you've hopped a mile in my feet!"

"That's a rather cynical view for the Easter Bunny, isn't it?"

"What do you mean?"

"To be critical, not only of the children to whom you deliver, but to their parents as well, who as role models have not measured up to your standards of morality by the examples they've set, while at the same time delivering to their children eggs whose procurement it could be argued was derived at through less than moral means, seems to me to be overly hypocritical."

"Let the birds blow," Jack replied angrily while emitting a few noxious pheromones. "They're just lurkers in the leaves—every one of 'em! Spying upon innocent rabbits as they do and taking the information they've gathered while hiding in the trees, back to their mistresses. They deserve to have their eggs stolen—every damned one of them!"

By the continued look on her face, it was evident to Jack that Larraine still harbored doubts about not only the height of his moral high ground, but his reasons for holding it. "You may not have heard of them," he continued, but Helgayarn, Brunnhilde, and Betty, The Powers That Be, although uncharacteristically silent now for ages, remain what they are, the Witches! And being such, you can rest assured that they have in their employ various birds of a feather who, flocking together, spy upon the rest of us in order to bring back to the trio, tales of our peccadilloes and perfidies which they exaggerate in the telling! No—the birds get what they deserve! As does Old

Slomoe and his elvish henchmen! Only rabbits stand innocent of the crimes we're accused of committing!"

"Slomoe and his elvish henchman," asked Larraine, not knowing that she'd put forward the sixty-four dollar question, "who are they?"

"Enemies of long-standing," Jack replied shortly. "Our feud with Old Slomoe goes back through the long years of time and into the very annals of antiquity. It was he, who through no effort of his own, grew such wholesome and luscious vegetables and in such vast amounts that come harvest time he could not hire enough immigrants and day laborers to pick 'em! Rich in his overabundance, he nevertheless denied us a reasonable tater or two—it wasn't as if we were going to lay waste to his entire garden! Anyway, rather than starve, we retaliated! The brouhaha that ensued provided the opportunity for The Powers That Be to stick their noses into what had, up until then, been a private affair. Their subsequent involvement and the public trials that followed, only served to exacerbate the situation by compounding and adding to those grievances. At the first trial they sentenced we jackrabbits to the servitude in which you find us today. When our ancestor, Father Jack, performed such service far better than expected, and in doing so earned for himself a reputation that those who'd imposed such sentence soon grew jealous of, they gave to Slomoe an army of elves, directing him to lead their divisions in a campaign of sabotage and harassment against Father Jack and his warren in an effort to disrupt the successful implementation of their sentence."

"It all sounds rather protracted and confusing to me," replied Larraine. "Just who is this Slomoe anyway?"

"The Tortoise!" Jack replied. "Pithecanthropus Wideass! Slomoe! The idiot farmer named Santos, who now travels the earth once a year, under the alias of Santa Claus and who, like us, has been sentenced to forever distribute unearned gifts and goodies into the hands of the undeserving!"

Larraine blanched while her tongue momentarily slid back into broguish inflection. "Ye dinna mean him!" she cried out in distress. "Sand Toes, much t' me own admonishments t' the contrary, hae

THE CHRISTMAS RABBIT

been forever tryin' t' catch that fella! I, fer one, didn'a believe the blighter even existed as he never put in an appearance at me own home, and spent most o' me marriage, beyond those parts which occur outside o' the boudoir o' course, tryin' t' talk him out o' such a foolish endeavor. Not believin' in the fellow, I saw nae hope o' Larry's quest reachin' fulfillment, nor did I agree at all with the reasons that motivated him t' pursue it! Now ye be tellin' me that such a feller actually exists? Does he indeed travel the world in a magic sleigh pulled by eight tiny reindeer?"

Jack spit out his reply, his voice laced with disgust and jealousy. "He does at that," the rabbit answered. "But they're not tiny. They're caribou and being such are amongst the largest of hoofers out there. Not as massive as moose mind you, they're pretty hefty even so—and there's not eight of 'em there's nine, mind you, if you count the young buck with the searchlight in his snout!"

"And they fly around as if by magic, while pulling the sleigh?"

Jack waved a paw in disdain. "There's no magic to it," he replied matter-of-factly. "Although the hoofers would appear to have gained such skills through both mystical and magical means, their abilities are in fact, drug induced, having been derived by the snorting and subsequent inhalation of a white powder supplied to them by the witches, which has been euphemistically termed 'magic dust.' The only thing magical about such powder that I can see is the seemingly unending supply of it which they have, that keeps them afloat. But one of these days their supply will run out. Their dealers and suppliers, The Powers That Be, will be revealed to the world for what they truly are and when that happens the reindeer will be cut off! They'll come down crashing and burning to impact with the solid and unforgiving ground of sober reality. All the twelve-step programs in the world won't help them then! They'll have to make their own way through the tortured and twisted pathways of enforced sobriety without the aid of sponsors and benevolent patrons to support them as they try to wrestle with and overcome the throes of their dependencies! What a glorious day that'll be! Santos, left on his own as he tries to complete his rounds in a single night, without the aid of his herd in harness!"

Larraine decided to pass over and thereby not comment upon, what she perceived to be a petty display of wishful thinking on Jack's part, focusing instead on a question which Jack's descriptions of the fellow whom they were currently discussing caused to rise to the forefront of her troubled thoughts. "This Santos fella," she asked, "is he likewise emblazoned with the stigmata? For as ye describe him, he certainly sounds like poor blighter who'd be so tattooed."

"You keep referring to this mark," Jack replied, "or this stigmata. What on earth are you talking about?"

"Well, I canna' shew ye' mine," Larraine replied, turning red with embarrassment, "as it be located within the confines o' me private person! But the stigmata be a birthmark, in the shape o' an eagle's talon and those who bear it bear as well the burden o' Fickle Fate that forever embroils 'em in a sea o' outrageous fortune, against whose tide they must constantly swim!"

"The talon!" Jack replied. "Indeed he does! Our histories state that he bears such a mark beneath the beard that encompasses his face! It was revealed once to my ancestors of long ago, according to our bibliographies, when Old Slomoe suffered under the effects of massive depilation at the directive of The Powers That Be! In fact, not too long ago, I encountered two men, relatives of yours I believe, named Slim and Jim, who bore as well, such a device upon their faces."

"I bear it too," Larraine replied. "As do Larry and Lauren and most o' me kinfolk."

"A look of horror displayed itself upon Jack's features. "Oh no," he said with a grimace, "that can only mean one thing."

"What be that?" asked Larraine.

"That you and your Society, Larry and Lauren included, must be bloodline descendants of Old Slomoe himself! That's why I chose to attack those fools, Slim and Jim! Recognizing in the talon a clue as to their pedigree, I perceived them to be descendants of my enemy of old and therefore enemies themselves. Had I known that Lawrence and Lauren were similarly tattooed, I would never have ventured into this horrible desert. I would've left you all to your fate and good riddance!" He expelled a frustrated sigh. "Now what's to be done?"

he asked rhetorically. "I've aligned myself with a descendant of my enemy who claims to be his enemy as well! There are more twists to this plot than a sidewinder slithering over the sands of the Sahara! How can my friend in fact be my enemy? And how can my enemy be as well an enemy to my enemy, when he be, in fact, a long-lost son? Would that not in fact make him a son of a gun in rebellion against his father and therefore my friend? How does one untangle such protracted and intersecting alliances in order to tell friend from foe?"

Frustrated by the dilemma confronting him, Jack rested his paw on his chin as he tried to seek a solution to the enigma. Suddenly another thought occurred to him even more horrible than the one he'd just had, turning his fur an even chalkier shade of gray. The thought had to do with Santos and one of the reasons implied within the bibliographies that he'd been handed his individual sentence. "We've got to get out of here," the rabbit said, springing suddenly up as he gave vent to his fear and frustration. "We're all in terrible danger—you, me, Lawrence, Lauren, the Apaches, the Society, and even Old Slomoe himself if he should put in an appearance!"

"What have the Apaches to do with this?" cried Larraine. "How in the name o' Saint Paddy did they become involved?"

"They were attacking the Society at the time I fell through the hole," he replied in an offhand manner. "Lauren herself appeared to have taken a spear in her shoulder."

"Those heathen have hurt me Little La?"

"Relax," replied Jack. "Even from where I stood before my fall, it looked as though she'd recover. And your man, Sand Toes, was fully revenged upon them for their attack, having cast a spear of his own through at least three of them!"

"But Lauren," Larraine replied, "she lies wounded?"

"Yeah," said Jack. "But that's the least of her worries right now. We've got to get moving, get outta here, and get to them quick before all hell breaks loose!"

Larraine shook her head, confused. "Certainly I want t' be with me own daughter in her time o' tribulation," she replied, "and I can see the need for haste as she lies wounded and in harm's way. But ye seem t' be referrin' to even greater danger than that! What could be worse than my little bairn lying on her back with a spear in her shoulder?" Jack looked up at her with eyes full of worry. "The Powers That Be, that's what! It's written in our histories and bibliographies that one of the reasons Santos received the sentence he did was the hope on the part of the Witches that being sentenced to deliver presents to children worldwide, he would inevitably discover the whereabouts of his own missing rug rats and thereby lead the trio to them. They've longed for the chance to take their revenge out upon him and his eldest for Hurricane Junior. However being the clodhopper that he is and despite the aid of elves, magical sleighs, and drug dependent deer, Old Slomoe has never been able to locate them—and a good thing for us all that such has been the case for our bibliographies go on to further state that should such an unlikely eventuality occur then The Powers That Be, who for so long have remained silent and seemingly withdrawn from the day-to-day occurrences which form the tapestry of our lives, will awake from their slumber and suddenly rise up to take their vengeance upon not only Santos and his children but the rest of us as too. No doubt, after the passage of so many years and being denied the aid of such mundunuguism as The Powers That Be saw fit to bestow upon their father, the original children of Santos, being Junior and Laddie, have long since passed away and are therefore safe from any retribution the trio might have planned. But believe me when I tell you that having been denied, both by Fate and the passage of time, their opportunity to enact such a revenge, Helgayarn, Brunnhilde, and Betty are not above taking such vengeance out upon lost sons, once discovered, no matter by how many generations they be removed. It must be his youngest, Laddie, by whom you're related, for legend tells us that Junior was, in fact, an unknown adoptee who did not bear the mark and was thus incapable of passing along such a problematic and perturbing pedigree."

"You do go on so," Larraine remarked, "for a fellow who has to be somewhere in a hurry! But, Jack, I've searched for two years and have found no way to get out."

"No way for you to get out," the rabbit replied. "But I'm not you! Among my many other talents, I'm a tunneler extraordinaire! If there's a way out of here, I'll find it!" He paused, rising up on his hind legs to sniff the air, then lowered himself to the floor and did likewise. "Tell me," he continued, "have you explored every side shaft and tunnel throughout this cavern?"

"There've been far too many of 'em for that," Larraine replied, "perhaps by the time I run out of food, I'll have explored them all but I doubt it. Why do you ask?"

"Because there's a draft of fresh air running along the floor of the cave that must be coming from above. Maybe I can trace it back and find us a way out!"

CHAPTER V
Fate and Fortune Put Forward an Armistice

A bad situation about to get worse came to an abrupt and thankful halt soon after Lauren fell victim to the carelessly tossed spear. When the lance impacted her all those milling about, the Irish, the Apaches, and Sand Toes himself looked on in horror as she fell. Jack, too, was filled with dread ere falling through the hole. Without much hope for it, he hurled his harea before plummeting and then because he did not witness the onset of sudden stillness and doubt which fast filled the hearts of the various warring parties doing battle on the desert floor, assumed the worst.

Sand Toes hurled his spear as Jack hurled his harea. The harea hit the spear, deflecting it, but then had nowhere to go. Harea hurled can go anywhere, especially if the hare hurling the harea happens to fall down a hole and can't see where he's hurling, and as Jack disappeared through the rift his harea hurled but out of control, hit Sand Toes, pinning his arms helplessly to his sides as it passed. From there it hurled itself at the Apaches, knocking many of their horseless horses and sending riders and their mounts headlong into the sand. Still caught in the hurled harea, Sand Toes looked on dumbfounded, seeing nothing but *feeling everything* as the harea hurling onward, passed him by while the spear, hit by hurled harea and deep into deflection, passed through the Apaches without hitting anyone. The only thing it pierced were the flaps of two rawhide buckskins, blown off their owner's backs just as the owners were blown off their bikes.

THE CHRISTMAS RABBIT

The two Apaches, who'll remain nameless because they only appear in this paragraph, were on opposite sides of the war charge and with brother bikers, Apaches all, between them when both spear and harea were hurled, made hitting them highly improbable. A hit that hit only their jackets while leaving both untouched and unharmed, was deemed impossible and if not impossible then was of such improbable occurrence as to be taken for the only thing it could be, a sign. A portent, an omen, a warning from someone beyond them much smarter than they, that this silliness must stop. That when children got hurt it was time for adults to stop playing their stupid games. The few Apaches still horsed, circling furiously and whooping war cries, came to a halt, having had the harea kicked out of them and having seen for themselves what they couldn't see at all but felt nevertheless and therefore could not entirely believe. But being Apaches and therefore superstitious, such improbable circumstances were to them big medicine, and some began to look to Horse's Head, their chief, for an explanation.

"What am I," he replied to the confusion of queries, "a medicine man?"

But they all knew he wasn't just as they knew Horseplay, his son riding right alongside him, was. And all thought that as leader, Horse's Head should have at least known that! So they turned to their medicine man, who was really a medicine lad, being merely thirteen and barely trained in the rites. A journeyman at best and still more of a medicine man wannabe than a licensed practitioner, he tried, with his father's permission, to interpret the miraculous omen, for his tribe. "Look, guys," he said, "I don't know what the heck's going on either, but I do know it involves that guy!" He pointed at Sand Toes who, having been released from the hurled harea's unwholesome influence, had rushed to his daughter and now knelt at her side gently holding her in his arms while finally understanding the meaning of the word *panic*. Like most everyone else he knew, Horseplay didn't much care for the make believe Indian before him and could never understand what the Old Man saw in him but see it he did and that made Sand Toes family whether the Apaches liked it or not. The girl, he knew, was daughter to the woman lost in the mine who visited their adopted brother through means of desert mirages and manifestations that only he could see and hear. This made him big medicine even if they looked upon him as castor oil, but it made even bigger medicine of his dearly departed Larraine, and when you wound the child of big medicine, that's bad juju, and all Apaches, even the shunned ones, know that.

Trapped within their SUVs and blaring their horns, the Society's membership looked out their windows at the forlorn figure of fallen Little La and as one, ceased their efforts to sound the alarm. Stretched out on the ground lay the little lass who had in one way or another won the hearts of each and every member and who was therefore regarded by all as a pearl beyond price, being even more valuable to them than lost gold itself. What good did it do then to trumpet the horn of warning when the enemy had already overcome their defenses and taken their one treasure of value?

Above them, the sky rumbled with the oppressive presence of the oncoming storm. Beneath them the ground trembled uneasily, caught up in one of the earthquakes that so frequently happen out in the deep desert. Amongst the warring factions there hovered an uneasy silence, a sense of foreboding as everyone, Irishman and Apache alike, interpreted these manifestations as divine warnings from their gods to engage in no further hostilities.

They stood there staring one at the other with dull looks of helpless befuddlement displayed upon their faces until at last Lauren's pitiful cries brought them out of their uneasy reverie. Peter O'Toole, Sinead's brother and paramedic at large to the Society he served, came forward with his medical bag to offer assistance, while a word from his chief brought Horseplay, the current medicine man of the Apache, to her aid as well.

As fortune would have it although pierced by a spear, Lauren's injury turned out to be not much more than a flesh wound, uglier than it looked and by no means untreatable. To effect such treatment, however, would take the efforts of the medicine men from each faction working both together and in concert; for each brought to the operating table a unique set of skills that he alone possessed and which the other would need, in order to facilitate healing.

THE CHRISTMAS RABBIT

Rummaging through his bag, Peter let out a desperate wail. "I canna' do too much fer the lassie. Though her wound nae be deep, it's a bleeder! I'm in need o' something' to staunch the flow o' blood before I can stitch her up. Me coagulators and blood clotters I left behind at the clinic and wi' a wound such as this a pressure bandage will nae do!" He looked about at those gathered around him, knowing that the likelihood of receiving aid from anyone in the crowd rested somewhere just to the left of zero. Thus he was more than surprised when zero multiplied itself into one.

"Here," said Horseplay, reaching into his medicine pouch, "use this. It will stop the bleeding." Not understanding Apache, the Irish paramedic looked up at the Indian in puzzlement. Sand Toes, however, quickly rendered a translation while holding his wounded daughter in his helpless arms. Peter reached out and taking hold of the offered canister cautiously unscrewed the cap. The content within revealed itself to be a vile and greenish substance, waxy in texture and smelling of fermented cacti and mesquite. What in the name o' Saint Paddy be this," he asked doubtfully, "and moreover, what do I do with it?"

"It's Apache medicine," replied Sand Toes. "A salve, which applied directly to a wound, stops the blood flow."

"Does it sting?" asked a doubtful Peter.

"What de ye care?" replied an impatient Sand Toes. "Ye'll nae be wearin' it! Just administer the bloody thing and be done with it!"

"I was thinking o' the lass," Peter replied. "I dinna want t' cause her any more discomfort than she's presently suffering."

"Let me do the thinkin' fer me Little La," Sand Toes snapped, "while you and this 'ere fella beside ye do the healin'!" He looked down into his daughter's eyes. "La, my love," he said reassuringly. "This 'ere balm, made from the bark o' the cacti, is goin' t' bite somewhat. Just ye be a brave little lass and bear up under it."

La blinked her tear-stained eyes while summoning up from deep within her the strength needed to answer. "I will," she whispered. "I'll be as brave and silent as Sand Toes of the Apaches!"

Her Da, smiling down at her, gave her an encouraging nod, then motioned for Peter to proceed.

"But I dinna know the proper dosage nor prescribed amount t' be administered," the paramedic complained. "Nor am I familiar with the technique used to apply it."

Horseplay shook his head in frustration. Leave it to city-slicker doctors, he thought, who were generally white, to make more out of frontier medicine than such a simple notion called for. Mumbling an Apache epithet under his breath, Horseplay snatched back the can he'd handed to Peter and bending down, prepared to administer the palliative. "You just rub it in there, kemosabe," he said to Peter while looking up. "Just rub it in there and work it within the entire length of the wound. It sure as shootin' smarts like a son of a gun, but it does the trick!" He proceeded to apply the balm while gesturing to Peter that he should look on as he did and so learn a thing or two. As the Indian worked the salve into the wound its astringent properties attacked the stricken blood vessels, chemically cauterizing them and staunching their flow. Lauren ground her teeth. The smell alone was enough to make anyone, hurting or healthy, grind their choppers in discomfort. When added to an open wound the burning it caused only increased its overall unpleasantness. But Little La took it like the Irish lass she was and moreover, like a patrisib of Sand Toes should—silently and with quiet dignity.

When her wound had ceased its bleeding, Peter prepared to stitch her up. He figured the gash in her shoulder would need at least twenty over-and-under stitches in order to effectively suture. Again he rummaged through his med kit but found no suture within. It seemed he'd left that item back at the clinic too. Horseplay offered Sand Toes a frown. "Where did you get these guys," he whispered, "and moreover, why do you put up with 'em?"

Lawrence Torrance Dawe merely shrugged his shoulders in resigned acceptance of his fate. How could one explain to another that destiny forced one to play the cards he was dealt and that if in his relations he'd been dealt a bum hand as the Indian seemed to imply, then it was Sand Toe's recent revelation that the Apaches were no bargain either. "He be what he be," replied the sandman, "as ye be what ye be and I be what I be. T' expect more o' less than that which providence provides ye is t' spit into the wind. Ye play the cards yer dealt, and that's the beginnin' and end o' it!"

"You can always turn in your cards," replied the medicine man, "and draw three more. A pair of deuces, after all, is worth more than a high king!"

Lawrence was unfamiliar with poker and didn't understand the analogy. He could have gone into greater detail, Horseplay supposed, but before him lay the wounded daughter of Big Medicine and so determined that the time for lengthy and detailed explanations had not yet arrived and that such analogies therefore had to be put to the side in order to better focus on the crisis at hand. Too many, both Irishman and Indian, had lost their lives this day by falling into the collapsed pit. He would not add to that number by becoming embroiled in useless conversation aimed at exposing the relative merits of analogizing or not if doing so prevented him from rendering needed aid to the stricken child who lay before him. Reaching once again into his medicine bag, he pulled out a length of dried deer tendon and smashing it between two rocks, broke it down into individual collagen fibers thin enough to be used as suture.

"Here," he said to Peter, handing them over, "use these."

"How?"

Horseplay couldn't believe his ears. Now was not the time to be offering up greetings and salutations! He let loose a torrent of frustrated Apache, filled with curses and epithets regarding the stupid white man before him who had the nerve to call himself a medicine man. No doubt the paleface was incapable of removing even cacti thorns, let alone sewing up an injury like this! Snow, rare for that part of the world, began to accumulate in drifts nevertheless as the eye of the storm moved ever closer. Couldn't this white fool see for himself that now was not the time to be exchanging pleasantries? "Just thread the damned needle and sew!" Sand Toes supplied the translation and Peter, doubt written upon his face, performed the task. In the end it took twenty-two over and under stitches plus a couple of butterflies to close the wound. Having accomplished that they wrapped Lauren up in a buffalo skin and set her with her back to a rock and out of the oncoming wind.

Sand Toes knew that snow in those parts, even at the height of December, was a rarity and usually fell only atop the mountains. No one could remember an instance where such precipitation reached the floor of the desert itself. To be confronted with it now and on this day of all days, spoke volumes to the madman about the convergence of destinies and the fulfillment of his quest.

"We canna' linger here flappin' our jaws and offerin' up how do ye do's! My enemy fast approaches riding upon the wings of yonder storm. I must see t' his capture and the removal o' his boots! Me Little La must be ganglin on home and since she canna' do so on her own, then one o' ye must take her!"

Horse's Head and Horseplay pulled Slim and Jim to the side and with the aid of Richard, the linguist, questioned them regarding Sand Toes's enigmatic statement. "What's this idiot talking about?" asked Horse's Head. "Who is the enemy to whom he refers?"

Jim offered up a shrug. "I dinna know," he replied. "Sand Toes has always been somethin' o' a strange duck! Goes about the wastelands on his own, he does, mutterin' t' himself and diggin' his holes. We thought he was makin' use o' the rabbit to uncover our gold."

"It's not your gold," replied Horse's Head. "It's Geronimo's and as such, belongs to the Apache."

"Look here, Tonto," Jim replied, "That gold, if it be under there, is ours! We have a map that our Great-Granddaddy Dawe purchased from a fella named Geromino, which gives us rights t' it!"

"Your great-grandfather," said Horseplay, "never paid for the map. When Geromino fell dead, he simply took it and fled back east. We Apache are owed a thousand dollars, plus interest! No more will the white man break his promises to our people! The gold, if it's there, is ours!"

In an effort to table the matter, at least for the present, Horse's Head reinserted himself into the ongoing debate. "The gold and who owns it are worries for another day," he said. "We have many moons to decide. But who is this enemy of whom Sand Toes speaks? We Apache thought you were his enemy!"

Slim's ample gut shook with laughter. "Us?" he replied. "We're worse than enemies—we're family! Ye can pick 'n' choose yer enemies as ye can yer friends, but yer family yer stuck with, like 'em or nae! We always assumed ye t' be the enemy of whom he spoke, and certainly the way ye came tearin' in here, whoopin' and hollerin' and castin' yer spears, would seem t' lend credence to that assumption!"

"All white men are our enemies," replied Horse's Head. "We never signed the treaties! But perhaps it is not too late for us to smoke the pipe of peace. We came to avenge, yes, and to set matters right, but the little one, whom you call La, was not to be harmed. She's Big Medicine to the Apache, as is the fallen squaw who gave birth to her. To do harm to either is to invite a curse upon our people. Sand Toes is their guardian and therefore is under the same protection. He came to the aid of my father, Horsin' Around, who repaid him, much to our bitter regret, by adopting him into our tribe and conferring upon him, his Apache name. We'd just as soon disown the paleface but as the old saying goes, 'Once an Apache, always an Apache,' so like you, we're stuck with him. His enemies are our enemies. We thought you were his enemies and that, along with your lust for our gold, compelled us to attack. But you claim the tie of kinship to our brother who states that his enemy is approaching upon wings of thunder. How's a simple desert dwelling Apache supposed to unravel such riddles? Who is this enemy of whom Sand Toes speaks and is this adversary your enemy too? For if so, then working together along with our brother—although it breaks our Apache hearts to do so, we can capture this enemy and make the peace between us. The gold however, stays in the ground unless you white trash fork over the thousand plus interest!"

Jim gave the Native American a cagey appraisal. Dressed in his war bonnet festooned with the feathers of many eagles and painted on both his face and chest with Apache runes and symbols, he looked to the casual observer to be just what he was—an Apache war chief atop his mount, who held within his hand the power of life and death. But the Irish had faced down far worse in their time than one renegade war chief. They'd struggled through the potato famine and endured the incursions of the English. They put up with the invasions of both Normans and Vikings, and fought bitterly in this century, suffering through Society-wrenching divisions in both politics and religion while doing so, to win their independence from the English dogs who overran not only their people but their country as well. Those seeking asylum from such ills fled here in the late eighteen and early nineteen hundreds, packed like sardines into dirty and dank ridden cargo holds of creaky and dilapidated sailing vessels where disease flourished and took root, as if the vessels themselves were huge Petri dishes floating upon a sterile sea and the Irishmen cramped inside, the culture upon which such disease fed. Many died. Those lucky enough to survive the crossing soon found themselves rounded up like a herd of cattle to be corralled within the confines of Ellis Island where they awaited with nagging uncertainty an arbitrary decision from the desk of a faceless bureaucrat who would determine the legality their citizenship. They'd been beaten, spit upon, and kicked around by almost every European Country that deemed itself civilized. Jim and Slim, along with the rest of the Secret Society of Lost Gold Miners, were the end result of such international abuse fostered upon an innocent people inhabiting a quaint little island while in the hands of greater nations who should've known better. Their ancestors had seen their share of struggles, passing down to each generation the hard lessons learned from such travails, until at last in the desert there stood a hardy band of people who no matter how foolish in thought or insane in pedigree, were not about to let themselves be bullied or buffaloed by some rampaging redskin and his meager band of twenty to thirty, whom they easily outnumbered three to one. If the Indian wanted to pick a fight over gold then they'd damned well give him more than he bargained for…but not today. Today was for smoking the pipe of peace and for puzzling out between them the mysterious party whom Sand Toes saw fit to paint as "The Enemy."

"If ye nae be his adversary," said Jim, "and we nae be either, then perhaps we'd better just gangle on over to 'im and put the question directly!"

It seemed like a sensible plan regardless of who'd put it forward and so Horse's Head, in the company of the Irishman, made his way to where Sand Toes stood over his daughter. Despite her injuries and his obvious concern regarding them, he kept his eyes peeled on the

THE CHRISTMAS RABBIT

skies above. Noticing the direction of his gaze Jim thought to inquire about it. "Yer lass is at yer feet! What are ye looking up fer, ye daffy blighter? "If I didn'a know any better, this bein' the twenty-fourth o' December, I'd say ye was scanning the skies for St. Nick himself!"

"That be exactly who I seek," replied Sand Toes. "He left me alone in the desert when me Da and Ma passed onward. Orphaned and wi' nae shoes on me feet! Now be the time fer me revenge! He's coming in yonder storm. I can almost smell 'im! The hole that collapsed was t' be the snare I hoped to catch 'im in. It was a trap that the rabbit and I were diggin' not an excavation to find gold. Now however, me plans be in shambles. I nae have me trap ready in time to snare the blighter."

Resting at his feet, Lauren looked up at her father. "Let it go, Da," she pleaded. "Let the fellow pass—if he comes this way at all! Forgive and let live as all of you gathered here are trying to do with each other. Don't let old animosity, which draws its strength from a wound you refuse to let heal, rule the day." She mumbled a little more, incoherent, and then passed out in a fitful doze.

In the meantime both Horse's Head and Jim returned to their own people in order to confer. Both knew that such a plan was doomed to failure as each of them knew that the subject of Sand Toes's predation was no more than a myth. A fairy tale told to children by their parents in an effort to coerce good behavior. There was no one, they knew, who could travel the whole world over in a single night delivering toys to girls and boys and even if there were, it was certain that he'd never put in an appearance here. The entire notion was wacky. But wacky is as wacky does, and both Jim and Horse's Head were of the opinion, despite the plan's obvious inanities made apparent in its manifested impossibilities, that if anyone could pull off such an outrageous scheme, then Sand Toes of the Apaches was just the fellow to do it. Both leaders reasoned that since they and their people were here already, they might as well stick around and help out. What harm could come of it? Little La, although uncomfortable, was in no danger of dying so long as she was kept warm, and if the impossible fiction that Sand Toes paraded before them turned out to be an improbable reality then there might be some benefit to be had in being part of this fellow's capture. Jim thought about Santa's and his elven assistants who supposedly aided him in his annual quest. If the former turned out to be a reality then likely so would the latter. And as everyone knew, elves, like leprechauns, possessed untold amounts of gold to be had for the taking. Their pockets, or so it was said, literally overflowed with the metamict substance and all one had to do to get it was catch 'em, and then taking 'em by their little elvish feet, turn 'em upside down and shake the treasure from them. No panning, no digging—just a shimmy and a shake and a fellow could be set for life!

Horse's Head saw no gain in being part of this misadventure for surely the object of his adopted son's attention did not exist. *But suppose it were true*, wondered the Indian, *what then?* He knew full well that many other tribes across the nation were getting rich off the white man by running casinos and gaming parlors where they fleeced their conquerors for every nickel they could squeeze. All those tribes however, had signed treaties, both past and present, which gave them permission to do so. Horse's Head and his band of renegades refused to add their names to such documents, knowing that doing so would cause their eventual assimilation into a hated culture that would demand the relinquishing of their heritage. Not right away and certainly not all at once. But it would happen. Horse's Head had witnessed it many times in the past. First you got a brave to give up his ancestral home and then you tied him to the reservation. Soon after, he was made to cut his hair, attend white man's school, and vote the democratic ticket, until the proud red man who once stood defiantly before his oppressors became just another meek white man despite the color of his skin, believing everything he saw on television or read in the newspapers and who, for the life of him, forgot the ancestry from which he'd sprung, paying it mere lip service while performing by rote the rites of his fathers which he no longer understood and dancing to the beat of a war drum he could no longer keep time with. Such a fate was not for Horse's Head or his people. They'd rather be red and dead than rich and well fed. Although much could be said for rich and well fed—especially if such wealth could be gotten in a way that did not compromise the values of their heri-

THE CHRISTMAS RABBIT

tage while allowing them to stick it to the white man in the bargain. Therefore as unlikely as the advent of this fellow's capture appeared, Horse's Head decided to humor Sand Toes nevertheless in case the unlikely proved to be the undeniable however unfreakinbelievable and far out. If such indeed became the case then he and his tribe would take possession of the fat man and his caribou too, and hold them out for ransom to all the white folk to whom he delivered. They'd pay and arm and a leg, Horse's Head knew, for the chance to redeem their yuletide reveler.

Horse's Head and Jim returned to where Sand Toes was standing to offer him their assistance in the completion of his unlikely endeavor.

"But who be takin' me Little La home?" he asked. "She canna' stay 'ere, exposed t' the elements! She'll catch a desert draft, she will, and get sick in 'er lungs!"

From the ground Lauren looked up at her Da and heard his distress. But sick as she was she determined to stay put while trying to talk some sense into the old man and get him to give up this foolishness. Forcing herself to sit upright, she defiantly spoke out. "I'm not going anywhere," she said, "unless you come with me!"

Lawrence looked down fretfully at his brave little daughter, determined nevertheless to be firm with her. There were some things a man had to do if he were to continue being a man! Just as there were some injuries and insults that a man, being a man, could not let pass. The little lady lying before him would just have to understand that. "La," he began, but was immediately cut off by the severe appraisal of those violet eyes which she'd inherited from her mother. Lawrence knew that look well, having seen it displayed many times on the features of his dearly departed Larraine. Through the course of its many repetitions he'd come to learn to bow in defeat before it. But not this time! He was the Da! Moreover he was Sand Toes of the Apaches, the will-o'-the-wisp who ruled wastelands and neither Geronimo nor St. Paddy himself, should either suddenly put in an appearance, was going to gainsay him on his own ground!

"Listen 'ere, lassie," he started to say, but was interrupted by Jim, who, looking northward toward the approaching storm, saw within it a light so bright but not lightning nevertheless and seeing such a sparkle, gave the alarm. "A star descends midst the maelstrom!" he cried. "A star descends!"

Larry looked off in the direction that his third cousin, twice removed, indicated with the pointing of a palsied finger. "That be nae star!" he cried out triumphantly. "That be the head o' the herd, haulin' the sleigh! I knew it! I knew this be the year o' my revenge! Ah, if only me dearly departed could be 'ere t' see me now! What would she say, I wonder?"

From down in her blanket Lauren looked up to supply the answer. "Posh 'n' nonsense!"

Sand Toes considered a smarmy reply but decided he couldn't afford the luxury of a wasted moment. The light was cutting a path through the cumuli and would soon break through the cloud cover to reveal itself.

"Quickly!" he yelled to Jim. "Start yon generator and turn on the lights while I get me billboard in place! Perhaps we can entice the sod t' land whether the trap be ready or nae!" Looking about, he took note of the Irishmen and the Apaches, staring up at the clouds in wonder. "Scatter ye daffy bastards!" he said. "Hide yerselves amongst the rocks and sand and when the blighter lands, fall upon him with all ye number and tie 'im up!"

CHAPTER VI
A Dawe Sees Daylight

Jack and Larraine made their slow and protracted way as they tried to hurry along through the unexplored tunnels and shafts of the abandoned mine, following Jack's nose as he tracked the current of fresh air flowing intermittent and impotent along the base of the cavern floor. From time to time they made a wrong turn, veering right when they should've veered left or going up when they should've gone down while occasionally erring in their choice of conduit, opting for misleading apertures or accesses that led unexpectedly but inevitably to dead ends which they'd hoped would lead to the surface. But they made headway nevertheless, crawling under fallen beams and around huge blocks of gray granite that lie lurking in the shadows, torn loose from their lodgings in the previous quake. All about them they were aware of the sweet whisper of gurgling water running in little rivulets and streams, chuckling as it fell to feed the raging river that could be heard below. At first they were inclined to try and scale the shaft through which Jack plummeted but the banks of the underground torrent did not wend their way back far enough to lead them to that frightful chasm and both knew that any attempt on their part to pit themselves against the river would only result in their being swept away by the raging current. Another means of escape would have to be found. So they journeyed on through the dark, advancing in fits and starts, aided only by the miner's light which Larraine wore at the front of her helmet. Neither wanted to stop and rest. Jack's description of her daughter's plight hung heavily on Larraine and her first impulse was to panic and charge off blindly. But even with her headlight she was near blind in the dark and so determined to move forward both as quickly and efficiently as possible by suppressing such thoughts and the mad throes of panic they wrought, keeping them at bay by concentrating on the situation at hand. She could do Little La little good whatsoever by giving into even the least bit of trepidation. The rabbit guiding her, with his sensitive smeller and his harea hurled ahead of him—whatever the heck that was, while en route to the high road, provided her with the only chance of escape that Fickle Fate was likely toss her way. She therefore determined to make the best use of it by remaining calm and keeping herself under control. The time to give vent to her emotions would make itself known when she escaped, and if that eventuality occurred then Horse's Head and his band of irascibles were apt to see hell break loose.

As they made their ascent they discussed amongst themselves the conditions they might find and the situation they could expect to encounter should they successfully gain the surface. They talked of Apaches and arrows, and Irish horns uselessly blaring in the waning of the afternoon as the storm swept dark and angry cloud cover across a helplessly timid sky, robbing it of light and depriving it of warmth. As the rabbit answered her questions regarding the circumstances which led to their improbable meeting it occurred to Larraine that other than his obvious concern for Lauren, he had no reason to display such nervousness and need for haste when speaking of such matters. Sand Toes, she knew, could well look after himself, the Apaches Jack didn't know, and from what she could gather, the Secret Society he did not much care for. So why, beyond his concern for Lauren, did he display such worry? For display it he did, his agitation written plainly upon a face whose lips spoke in hurried tones, of the need for speed as they related to her, his tale. Surely he had plenty of time yet, to make his way to the surface and reclaim his seat at the site of his enemy's waterloo. After all, it was only April or thereabouts, as evidenced by his own presence. Still Jack displayed an inordinate amount of haste, to the point where he began taking chances not only with his own fur, but with hers as well.

THE CHRISTMAS RABBIT

"Why the hurry, little friend?" she asked. "You and dear Larry have nearly three full seasons ahead of you to prepare your trap. Yet you make it sound as if your quarry were arriving tomorrow."

"Today actually," Jack replied. "It's December 24."

Larraine looked on in puzzlement at his receding back. "How can that be?" she asked. "Isn't it Easter?"

"No," he replied. "It's a little before that."

"Then it canna' be December!"

"Okay," Jack reluctantly admitted, "it's a lot before that! Actually your husband had it right when he said that I was either very late or altogether too early—depending upon what side of the calendar you're standing. From where I stand, it's early. I wasn't even supposed to get on the road till the beginning of next March, but I graduated ahead of my class and since we'd always had a hard time finding your daughter I thought to myself, what the heck, I'll set out early, making her the last stop on my list and thereby get a hop ahead of the season!" He gazed over his shoulder back toward her, a look of wistfulness displayed in his ironic eyes. "I should've stayed home until well into spring!"

"You're saying then that Santa's capture, should he put in an appearance, which by the way I'm still finding hard to swallow despite my own eccentric pedigree and the word of a talking rabbit standing before my very eyes, is therefore imminent?"

"Yes, Ma'am," replied the rabbit.

"And that being imminent, should it prove to be true, could possibly presage an appearance by those *Cailleaches,* those three old *Bitseaches* of whom you spoke earlier—Helgayarn, Brunnhilde, and Betty?"

"None other," Jack replied. "And it would be just like them to put in an unwated appearance at an inappropriate time."

"And ye wasted all this time speakin' o' dreams within dreams and pontificatin' from yer moral high ground? I should hae ye own guts fer me garter belt!"

"Your Irish, dear," he replied. "Your Irish. Save it for The Powers That Be."

"Well, all I can say," replied Larraine, "is that those *Smúrlógs* and *Soachàns* best look t' their pettiskirts if they think t' be tanglin' with Larraine Dawe!" Picking up the pace, she began pushing him from behind. "Hurry now, laddie," she urged. "We dinna want t' be late in coming to the aid o' my Lawrence and Lauren!"

*****

Eventually they found their way to a hidden side shaft more timbered than any other, as if some special care had been paid to its construction in order to better assure its ability to withstand a cave in, at which it had apparently succeeded if one judged such matters by the lack of detritus to be discovered throughout its confines. The only trash lying around came from the only animal who littered. Most tunnels and passageways had been girded and timbered every twenty feet or so. This one had supports and braces every ten feet. The shaft began as a slight grade, tending steadily upward for maybe a mile until reaching just below the surface where it ran parallel to it for many thousands of yards. It was wide enough for two and tall enough for Larraine to pass without having to bow her head although occasionally she did hit her noggin on an overhanging timber truss wedged imperfectly within the ceiling above and supported on either side by two thick planks of differing heights the size of railroad ties, which seemingly had been pounded into place and made to fit tightly by means of a sledgehammer and the application of Indian elbow grease, for as Larraine took note of the passageway as revealed in her headlight, she saw carvings which decorated the timber supports that could only be Apache. Thunder gods, buffalo, the Great Spirit—even a carving of old Geronimo himself. Those certainly weren't Irish and that meant the timber predated the Society's discovery and that the carvings were probably done by the venerated war chief himself, further authenticating their map and the discovery to which it led. Not that such discoveries were of much import now. But in the back of her mind, which was the only place where she had room at the moment for such thoughts, she began to wonder why the old man had his braves back then, reinforce this one section of

THE CHRISTMAS RABBIT

tunnel, because she knew for a certainty that prior to the cave-in no other usage of timber as a means of reinforcement had been discovered other than their own planks, which they installed as they went. It was a mystery, she supposed, which would remain unresolved, in their need to make haste from this place.

The tunnel revealed itself to be an apparent dead end with a solid granite wall that rose up forbiddingly to the cave's ceiling.

"What happens now?" asked Larraine. "We canna' afford to backtrack nor can we gangle on any further!" She allowed herself to sink to the floor, frustrated.

"Wait a minute," Jack replied, "I can smell the fresh air, I'm telling you! Let me, with my smeller, cast around a bit in an effort to determine from whence it comes!"

He began to crawl about the immediate area, along the floor and the base of the walls, snuffing and sniffling and making use of his sensitive smeller as he went. At the base of the wall blocking their passage he took note of the slightest downdraft, which ran from the ceiling down the face of the wall until it met the floor, whereupon following its twisted passage backward, made its way into the lower depths of the mine below.

"Cast your light up at the ceiling," he said, "I see the faint tracings of a door, outlined in the shadows." Larraine tilted her head and the light from her lamp revealed a door hidden within the ceiling itself, its outline the thin gaps in its seam that had developed over time, allowing the telltale air current entry into the tunnel's access. Jack looked up at the door to ponder in puzzlement the strange markings that were carved upon its face. "What are those?" he asked. "It looks like some sort of writing to me."

"It is," replied Larraine. "It's Apache. Larry taught me to read it years ago. It's the directions for getting out."

"What does it say?" asked the curious rabbit.

"It says, 'Geronimo's Bolt Hole.' In case of cowboys or cavalry, pull pin and release lever.' I wonder what that means?"

"Well obviously," Jack said looking up, "you pull that piece of bone there in the left hand corner, away from the leather strap securing it and in doing so, release the lever."

"It sounds too simple to me," Larraine said. "There's got t' be more t' it than that! Ye dinna know these Apaches like I do, Jack. The de'il's own tribe they be—full o' tricks and Indian mischief!"

"Your Irish, Larraine. Your Irish!"

"I dinna care!" she replied testily. "I know these Apache fellers well, coming occasionally as they do, t' visit Sand Toes in his hole—and even before the spear which you say pierced me daughter, I ain't niver been one t' trust 'em too far!"

"This door reveals itself to be what it is," replied Jack. "Obviously Geronimo's one means of flight should he ever find himself trapped in here by those from whom he wished to keep this place hidden. If they surrounded him or had all the adits covered, then this must have been set up as his secret passageway to escape and as such, holds no danger for us now."

"I wouldn'a be t' certain," Larraine said. "Just ye be careful when ye pull the pin!"

"Me?" cried Jack. "I'm too short to reach that high! You do it!"

"Are ye sure, Jackie lad?"

"Yes, damn it! Pull it!" Larraine looked down at him, eyes full of reservation. "On yer own head be it," she replied. She pulled the pin and that's just what happened. A secret spring attached to a hidden counterweight behind the wall let go and the falling counterweight caused the door to collapse upon a carefully disguised hinge, only to come descending down upon Jack's head, revealing a primitive step ladder. The bottom rung impacted squarely with the crown of Jack's noggin, catching him right between the ears and driving him to his knees. "That one hurt," he remarked to no one in particular. "That one hurt a lot." Kneeling there, he tried to shake the cobwebs out of his head and the stars out of his eyes. But the more he shook the thicker they came, causing a slight case of vertigo and an eerie feeling of disorientation that caused him to tumble over with a hollow thud.

"Yeah," he said still speaking to no one in particular, "that one hurt a lot."

Larraine knelt down to gently cradle him. "Easy there, lad," she said. "Just take a moment to breathe and while you're doing so take a gander up yon step ladder and see for yourself the clouds racing

THE CHRISTMAS RABBIT

overhead in the sky above us! You did it, Jack! By following your nose you found the way out! Well I never, even with all o' the flamboyant history captured within me peculiar pedigree, heard o' the like!" She looked down at him, both with pride and warmth. "You're my hero, little leporide," she said with a laugh. "Are ye ready now t' go on?"

Jack indicated that he was. Raising him to her breast, Larraine picked him up and ascended the stepladder to climb out of the hole.

*****

In the waning of the wintry afternoon and even as the storm approached, there remained still enough light in the sky despite the clouds gathering overhead, to prove itself distressful to Larraine, whose eyes had not been subject to such a largess in lumens for quite some time. Gaining the surface, she tumbled to her knees, dropping Jack as she did. Her hands flew to her sockets in an attempt to cover her eyes and provide them some relief.

"Blinded by the light, are ya?" asked Jack while picking himself up off the ground.

Larraine offered him a frown, squinting and blinking as she did. "That's what stumblin' abou' in the dark fer two years, does t' ye!" she replied.

She knelt there, her teary eyes weeping rivers as they tried unsuccessfully to adjust to a stranger who although by now familiar, was temporarily forgotten. Having ascended from the hell which held her helpless, and hell-bent upon achieving the victory which would win her the surface, and after stumbling about in the dark for two years afraid to travel too far or too often from either her food source or her hand crank generator, had finally done so only to find when she reached for the light that darkness descended anyway. She almost gave up. "I'm blind, Jackie lad," she whispered as she wiped away water. Recognizing both the need and the inevitable, she found her resolve and in a voice somewhat firmer continued, "my eyes, staring into the darkness for so long, have finally seen the glory and been blinded by it. They will nae work, at least nae fer now, so ye'll have t' be leadin' me by the hand to wherever we're goin'."

Jack looked about him in the twilight while suffering the indignities of his own squint. They could be anywhere in this waste, and the waning light which even now fled the skies in the face of the oncoming storm, provided them little aid in determining their location. Jack's eyes finally adjusted as he'd only been down in the hole a few hours and being the sneaks they are, rabbits see much better in the dark anyway. Awakening in birth within the depths of their warrens, they're born into it. But barren was barren both before and behind and to either side as well, leaving nothing but blind options from which to choose, when suddenly off in the distance Jack took note of Larry's spotlight as it leapt unexpectedly into the stormy cloud cover descending upon it.

"Look," he cried "it's Sand Toes's lamp! He's turned on the signal!"

Larraine cast about uselessly, her eyes dead to her as she tried to determine for herself in which direction lie her man.

"Sorry," Jack said, taking note of her puzzled features, "I guess you can't look anywhere at the moment. It's a few miles south of us and it seems from its location in relation to our own, that we've surfaced further north than where we both were when we first descended. Yonder lies the ruined entrance to the abandoned mine which you deem as having once belonged to Geronimo. It's not too far from that where Sand Toes and I were digging our pit before we were overrun, first by the Irish and then by the Apaches. I would have thought he'd given up his quest in the face of all that occurred after! I wonder what in the world could be going on out there."

"How far away, Jack?" asked Larraine. "How far away?"

"Perhaps three miles, maybe more. The terrain's pretty flat. It's hard to tell."

Larraine tentatively put forward her hand. "Take hold of me Jack," she demanded, her resolve evident in the tenor of her voice, "and lead me to them."

"Are you sure?" he replied. "We've three miles to run and straight into a williwaw at that! That's one heck of a storm blowing!" He paused to look up at the sky.

THE CHRISTMAS RABBIT

Suddenly breaking through the cloud cover, there came to his eye the sight of a light oh so bright, and to his ears, the tinkling of sleigh bells passing above him and heading south.

"The game's up!" he cried. "That was Old Slomoe in his sled passing just overhead! Leave it to him to arrive with all that flash, puffed up with pride and boldly announcing his presence while at the same time carrying out a sentence that's supposed to be performed in the dark and in secret!"

Larraine looked up needlessly. "Which way is he headed?" she cried.

"South, toward the abandoned mine and the light!"

"Take me there!" she demanded.

He took her hand in an effort to guide her across the hardscrabble but soon found that her newly discovered handicap, coupled with his own inability to proceed at anything close to a good pace while walking upright and leading her along by touch, only added to the challenge of the undertaking they were attempting. When running a race Jack was much better on all four feet. At this pace they'd never arrive in time. He needed to do some thinking—quick and preferably 'out of the box' as it were, if he were going to come up with a plan that brought them safely where they needed to be and do so in a timely fashion.

"You'll need to carry me," he said, "heading into the wind as you feel it upon your face, while I, hurling my harea before us, will attempt to guide you and your pace."

"Your what?" asked a bewildered Larraine. "Certainly I can carry you as surely as I can feel the wind upon my face, but what's this harea you're talking of hurling, and how's hurlin' it gonna help me find my way?"

"It's one's center," replied Jack. "One's inner strength and awareness of oneself. Japanese folk, both two- and four-legged, call it *hara*, although we rabbits call it *harea* 'cause we found it first, and it's centered just below your navel... Recent revelations however, by returnees and other mad rabbits, argue for its location as being somewhere within the left ankle, but no matter. Harea-gei is the art of hurling your harea wherever it's harnessed, before you with the view that it's not so much a Zen koan occurring within, as a tool to be taken advantage of without!"

"What?"

"A Harea-gei master can take his inner strength and channel it beyond the confines of his body until it manifests itself as an unseen force which when hurled can be made to do almost anything! It is said that a Hara-gei master has eyes in the back of his head but a Harea-gei master has eyes in the back of those eyes as well! He can hurl his harea before him and knock enemies out of his path. With it he can walk on water or if not, at least walk across the fabled rice paper and not leave a mark. When he sits in the lotus position while contemplating his navel his harea enables a master to float free from the ground. In one of its more esoteric applications, he can for a time at least, hurl it upon someone else less fortunate than himself and with it, guide them in the dark."

"If it's so handy," argued Larraine, "then why weren't you using it back in the mine?"

"Lady," replied the rabbit, "I had all I could do back there to find fresh air, and just so you know, it was my harea that led me to the trapdoor. But don't go looking for miracles."

"And you're one of these 'Harea-gei' masters, are you?" asked Larraine.

"The truth is, I never made it much past green belt," Jack replied, "but I try."

"Very well," Larraine reluctantly replied, not at all comforted by the prospect of running blindly across the desert while holding on to a hare who hurled his harea ahead of them. But did she have any choice? "What do I do?"

"You do nothing!" Jack urged. "To not do a thing is to do it completely! Just stand there and let it happen. Don't fight either me or my harea when I hurl it. Simply let it soak in like it were life-giving water and you the thirsty sponge in need of a drink—but beware of the dark side!"

"The dark side? Are we talking harea or the Force? Are you a Harea-gei master or a Jedi master?"

THE CHRISTMAS RABBIT

"Jedi masters," replied the rabbit, "are just harea-gei masters with fancy flashlights for swords who show themselves off on the big screen while searching for the next sequel. Any rabbit worth his salt who could hurl even the slightest of hareas could easily handle Yoda or Vader in a tussle. We'd kick their butts while hurling our hareas down their throats! We'd sit 'em on their own swords which being light sabers, would smart 'em plenty! They'd know they'd been forced into doing a thing or two by the time we got done! We'd rattle their ribcages! Scramble their eggs! Fry their bacon! Beat 'em like unwanted stepchildren! Why, we'd—"

"That all be well and good, Jack," interrupted Larraine, "if you be challenging the Dark Lord o' the Sith to a duel to the death. But yer just trying to lead me across the desert!"

"It doesn't matter," replied the rabbit. "It's the same skill, applied in a slightly different manner, and remember, we go not to confront the 'Dark Lord o' the Sith,' as you so quaintly put it, but to perhaps challenge Three Dark Maids o' the Myth—any one of whom could take old Vader and stand him on his head! We'll need all the Harea-gei and help we can get. So hang in there and hold on!" He recited a silent mantra while bringing his harea into focus, then hurling it outward, soon had it hovering around Larraine and himself.

"It feels as though we're caught up in goo," Larraine remarked. "Everything's clammy to the touch and damp, as if I were enveloped in a fog which I can surprisingly see through. Or see around which might be a better way o' putting it."

The soupy mists of his hurled harea hovered around Larraine like a paranoid ghost, making her see things she was sure weren't there while looking upon them through eyes she was sure weren't her own. The pictures she saw formed in the back of her eye rather than the front, appearing to her as if they were negative cutouts in black superimposed upon a stark canvass of white, empty of everything else save potential. It was a blank page upon which anything might be written. It was light without shadow, form without figure, *without* without *within*. It was knowing all things without knowing any of them while knowing as well that in knowing them least lie the greatest knowledge of all. It was like a dream within a dream, and she said as much. "You know, Jack," she remarked, "this Harea-gei business is like a dream within a dream. Sometimes it is and sometimes it ain't!"

Jack looked gazed up at her in wonder. "Say," he remarked, "should we make it through this misadventure and live, do you mind if I use that line some day? I know the back of a great book in which to notate it."

"I'll bet ye do! But what about now, Jack?"

The tired rabbit uttered a weary sigh. It had been a long day already and only looked to get longer; a day whose needs and demands would drag on and drag out until well after the required twenty-four hours had been attained and surpassed. A day measured in the depths of one's eyes the following morning and the wrinkles added to them the previous night. A day that would live in infamy. An exaggeration perhaps, but certainly a day not to be forgotten in quite a long while nevertheless. "Pick me up," he said, "and set me upon your shoulder with my hind legs dangling over either side of your neck."

"Like ye was me own child and I was paradin' ye about the county fair? Nae bloody likey! I'm the one as can't see, or couldn't until a moment ago when you hurled all that harea at me—even now I dinna know what it is exactly, that I'm seeing. You should be carrying me!"

The rabbit looking up at her from two feet below regarded her frankly. "We both know that ain't happening here with this hare," he replied. "So pick me up and let's be on our way."

Voicing another objection, Larraine reluctantly complied and reaching out tentatively, grasped at his shadow, which she could see plainly, superimposed as it was upon the whiteout of empty yet pregnant possibility parading itself before her. With a little effort and a chain of thought that both drew tight and traveled in a direction she wanted it to go, she could make the images upon such a canvass move! She didn't know how and in not knowing knew only that such was the case nevertheless. She was a koan come to life, a haiku in the midst of happening! A Hara Krishna with a Vishna who could see things others couldn't while dancing to the beat of a different drum.

Well, rock, baby, and roll on, she thought. What happens next?

THE CHRISTMAS RABBIT

As if in answer to her unspoken question Jack replied, almost it seemed, from the very wells of her own deepest thoughts. "You just start running," he said, "with the wind in your face while I, holding on to one of your ears with each paw, will pull right or left as necessary in an effort to steer you clear of oncoming obstacles."

"Are we the blind leading the blind?"

"If we are," replied Jack, "then let us hope that Harea-gei keeps us from falling headlong into the pit!"

They took off, proceeding in fits and starts and with intermittent pauses spaced in between for Larraine to stop and get her bearing while catching her breath. With Jack holding on for dear life and pulling upon one ear or the other as needed, they avoided most of the boulders and occasional cacti that sprang up before them while en route and so made their way in a generally safe and southerly direction. That's not to say they didn't arrive at their destination without a few scrapes and a couple of burrs in their saddles, for their journey was a saga in and of itself which could fill the pages of another book entirely and as such, is much too lengthy to be related in full here. Needless to say despite many a misadventure, they made it. Hurtling along and caught up within the harea that Jack hurled just ahead of them, they advanced to the sight of their presumed confrontation. As they drew nearer, coming closer to the edge of a desert butte overlooking the pit itself, there began to play upon their ears the strange sounds of varied voices propounding opposing arguments in multiple languages and dialects. A virtual Sodom and Gomorrah wrapped within a Tower of Babel whose strident echoes came wafting up to them waxing and waning, as they were carried aloft by the remaining winds of the storm passing overhead. In the breeze blowing by Larraine distinctly heard the beloved voice of her darling La. She was alive then and Larraine's first impulse was to rush out and greet her. She held herself in check however, not knowing fully what lay ahead nor trusting entirely in the tenor of those voices carried to her upon the wind. There was trouble brewing in such woeful tones, carried as they were, upon ill winds. There was hurt, fright and confusion. And there was vindictiveness as well, and the frightful rumbling that arises out of the need to blame others for one's own mistakes. In the jumble of conflicting opinions she could hear not only her beloved La but her beloved Larry as well, emoting in a brogue that was too Irish to be anything other than genuine, and Horse's Head and Horseplay, two voices she'd just as soon forget. She heard Slim and Jim too as well as Richard and Sinead and a host of others. Some were familiar and some were not. Some sounded more antagonistic and some less so. And one seemed louder than the rest but three voices seemed absolutely horrid in their nature altogether. The two crept up to the edge of the butte and peering over, looked down to see Larry alongside the Irish and the Apaches and protecting Little La while facing off against three old crones. Between them and tied to a stake driven deep into the ground stood the largest man Larraine had ever seen, alongside which even Slim would seem small. Not overly tall it was nevertheless not much of an exaggeration to describe his can as being larger than Canada.

That can't be Santa, thought Larraine, who, looking down upon him while assessing his size, doubted his ability to get in and out of his own sleigh unaided, let alone slide up and down chimneys with apparent ease while loaded down with packages. Milling about him uneasily and as if under duress were three little fellows who were reluctantly gathering up what little sagebrush and scrub there was to be found in the immediate area and casting it at his feet.

Helgayarn, Brunnhilde, and Betty had arrived to take their revenge.

"What'll we do now?" Jack whispered in frustration. "It's not as if we can go waltzing in there and demand of the Witches that they let everyone go!"

"Give me a minute to think," Larraine replied, looking down upon the scene unfolding below her. "What we need is a plan…"

CHAPTER VII
Fate Finds That an Enemy Is Often a Friend When Facing a Mutual Foe

As the sleigh crashed, and to the sounds of war cries both elvish and Irish, Sand Toes sprang up from the sand to attack Hephaestus, but elves being elvish, Heph easily sidestepped the charge and sprang out of harm's way. The desert man rocketed past him to go careening into the wreckage of the downed sleigh, becoming entangled in its traces and intertwined with the injured reindeer still outfitted in harness. As he struggled within the melee, hoofs and antlers of differing girths and sizes continually assaulted him with a barrage of various bangs, bumps, and secondary scrapes, as each individual caribou caught up in the carnage sought frantically after a means of escape, until suddenly amidst fractured forelocks and wrenched forelegs Sand Toes came face-to-face with his enemy. They lay there tangled in limbs and torn traces, each confronting the other with neither having anything to say. Sand Toes stared at Santos who uncertainly returned his gaze with an incredulous regard of his own. It had been many a year and many a sleigh ride behind him but surely the face he beheld lying next to his was none other than that of his long-lost Laddie now grown to manhood! Sand Toes, who was not Laddie but who'd once been called that anyway by parents who were into cliff-jumping, returned his regard and found he beheld the nearly forgotten image of his long-lost sire. He looked a bit older to be sure and of a certainty his hair had grayed and my, how the old sod had put on the pounds! A sudden thought chilled him right down to the very digits for which he was named. Was his barely remembered Da, who was recognizable to him only because he from time to time haunted the tortured and twisted reverie of his infrequent and uneasy sleep, in fact Santa Claus? What might that mean? Had his Da and Ma, along with Beatnik Bob, faked their own deaths, leaving him behind while they took their trip? They must've all bought one-way tickets because his sire's unlikely return was a long time in coming. But if improbably late then who lay buried at the foot of that faraway butte? Lawrence strained his eyes but even for him the cliff was a good ways off. Of a certainty he could say he saw Beatnik Bob's petrified legs sticking up out the ground like two pieces of deadwood but beyond that wouldn't commit to saying he saw too much one way or the other as he was having trouble believing his own eyes and the unlikelihood of the possibility confronting him. If this were his Da then where were the promised shoes? Long ago his Da had promised that Santa was bringing him boots and *if* his Da was indeed the Santa who'd been promised but who was just getting round to making his deliveries this late in the day, then he had a lot of explaining to do.

"Would you mind explaining to me," asked the sleigh master lying beside him, "just what it is you think you're doing, Laddie, lying in wait for me like this? What's your gimmick, eh, and where did you pick up all these noisy friends?"

Sand Toes said nothing, his mere regard a picture that spoke thousands of words. You could speak a million of 'em however, and if the person looking on didn't understand the language then your face was pretty much tongue-tied. That left the tongue itself and fortunately for each, they both spoke in the same one, although neither did so in quite the same fashion.

"Ye be wantin' explanations o' me, do ye? Well, I'll be wantin' a few o' me own—like, where are me shoes!"

"Your shoes?" asked Santos. "Aren't they on your feet?"

Somehow Larry managed to push a foot up through the tangle of limbs and wave it before the sleigh master's face.

"Do ye see any booties on these, mate?" he asked. "Do ye see so much as a stocking?"

THE CHRISTMAS RABBIT

Santos admitted that he didn't while hiding not in the least his admiration for the dog displayed before him. If the other foot still buried in the wreckage, was anything like the one flapping in front of him, then this fellow had a pair of feet that a body could feel proud of! Large but not overly so, rugged with no-nonsense toenails clipped neat and even, its five digits displayed proudly and capped off by a sizeable thumb all callused and corned, which led the other four members in a wiggle waltz as they hung suspended from their foot. "That's one fabulous fetlock!" the sleigh master remarked. "Why would you want to cover up a pair of feet like that?" A horrible thought occurred to him and he struggled to find exactly the right words to say that would lead him through this potential faux pas into which he'd just blundered. "That is, assuming, of course, that you have two? I mean, you're not handicapped, are you?"

Sand Toes regarded his potential prey with utter disbelief. Although the enmity which lay between them had at its heart a pair of missing shoes certainly long since lost, still he could hardly believe his ears as they took note of the conversation and the way it was proceeding. He'd envisioned his enemy's capture many a time while digging and training and preparing for this great day but never in any of his most bizarre imaginings had the conversation between them gone quite like this. Of course he hadn't pictured a face quite like the one before him either and to be staring across at it while caught up in these most unlikely of circumstances served only to bring further into relief the ironies of his life, which he realized now were not ironies at all but simply circumstances that unfolding, were being brought into karmic alignment. The seeming irony lie in the notion that the broken pieces of one's life, if put on display, could somehow be pieced together again and made to fit.

"O' course I got two feet, ya *plab*!" he replied. "Think ye that I made this charge on one leg?"

"You could've hopped," replied Santos. "I know. I've seen it done. It's crazy to be sure, but no worse for having been tried before... What's a *plab*?"

"An idiot!" replied Sand Toes. "And ye be *a plab amadáin, a plab óinsighe, and ableitheach boimbealóir!*"

"Meaning?"

"Ye be a fat one too! *A biatach, and builtéir! A claiséir and a Cráiceachán! A práiblín and a púdarlach!*"

Santos considered his girth. It was true. He was quite hefty and growing larger as the years grew shorter. On planet Earth, or Mungo, as Santos still liked to refer to it, there's an annual decrease in the length of each year. Every annum as it comes to a close is of slightly less duration than the one preceding it, and its decreasing duration of orbit can be measured in practically nanoseconds as it passes. Hardly to be counted unless you added up all of the nanoseconds and compounded them by the innumerable years such decreases had been occurring. Then those meaningless nanoseconds took on a whole new significance entirely. Especially when you considered the end sum of their product, fiery death and annihilation, for planet Mungo is constantly falling toward the sun at the rate of a few micrometers every year, and this accounts for the loss in nanoseconds as Mungo completes its circuit around Sol. *Sol* what, you might ask? Well we've lost close to a year and a half off our calendars already, that's what, and it's only getting worse as these nanoseconds add up and compound. A side effect of seasons, this decline in dateage stemmed from the misguided efforts of The Powers That Be to push the world in a direction it had no desire to go. It was perfectly content to hang there motionless in space but for spinning on its axis, which brought about both day and night. Then The Powers got that silly notion about seasons and set it upon its elliptical orbit. *We're paying for that already*, thought Santos, as he reviewed the logistical demands of migration both literally and laterally while the planet magically fell up. Every other object in the universe had a tendency to fall down. Mungo however, fell up toward the sun which warmed it. Only if left in the hands of The Powers That Be could something so wacky and ultimately so suicidal occur. Because of seasons, Santos knew, one day in the not too distant future the whole planet would find itself in the biggest boxcar of cattle craps ever to be contended with when the express train of its existence crashed like a fireball into disregarded depot of its own destruction. Fun with the sun! Most of the poor plebes living here and now would be mercifully spared the ignominy. But would he? He'd been languishing on this rock for so many years, caught up in the day-to-day doldrums of his undeserved discipline and chastisement as he tried to fulfill the harsh demands of his sentence, that he despaired of ever being free of such matters and therefore foresaw with eagerness the day when forced to greet the final dawn, he'd rise harnessed behind his caribou one last time and with a smile on his face, confront the monster who for eons hung suspended and in plain sight while anticipating his approach and contemplating his consumption. But was that any reason to suffer under the barrage of insults and less than complimentary descriptions of his person being hurled his way by his captor? Santos didn't think so—especially if that captor turned out to be a long-lost son! "You've a lot of words for *fat*, laddie!" he replied. "With most of 'em being thicker than my middle! Where did you pick up such limberness in language anyway? On what mean and tawdry street corners have you been spending your nights and with what foulmouthed trash have you been associating?"

"There be nae streets out here nae corners t' go with 'em," replied Sand Toes. "And as t' foulmouthed trash, I learned them adjectives under the careful tutelage o' me dearly departed Larraine. So dinna ye be castin disparagin' remarks about 'em!"

The groans and complaints ushering up from beneath them as the caribou fought gamely to escape the confines of their crash brought to a close any further debate regarding the proper application of Irish appellatives used to describe obesity. The 'fat chat' would have to undergo its conclusion on another day as the immediate situation presented more pressing concerns.

Above them and with the aid of elvish magic, Hephaestus gamely stood his ground, holding off platoons of Irishmen and Indians from completing their advance upon the crash site and those still trapped within.

"What about them?" Santos shouted out while pointing to the angry crowd, "What are they up to?"

"Ye bleedin' well think I know?" cried the Irishman. "I did nae invite 'em! Mad Irishmen lookin' fer gold and mad Apaches—who know's what they be lookin' fer! Revenge o' one kind o' another, I suppose. Maybe ye invited 'em fer all o' me! Me Little La lyin' hurt whilst bein' set upon by those what wounded her!" Helplessly bound up in tangles and traces, he frowned fiercely at his antagonist. "I see it all now," he continued. "A counter plot o' ye own devisin' as ye be bringin' along all o' those to whom ye've given shoes already!"

"Whoa! Hold on there, fella!" Santos interrupted. "I don't know any of these people! Never saw 'em before in my life…although looking around, well over half of them appear strangely familiar. Isn't it odd, the notions that pass through your head when you're at the mercy of a hostile audience? But be that as it may, did you say that your Little La lie hurt?"

Lawrence looked at him warily. "I did," replied the desertman. "What o' it?"

"Would that be Lauren Tea Dawe?"

Larry's frown deepened. "Why di' ye ask?" he replied.

"I have a gift here," Santos replied, "for a 'La T. Da'—names get kinda fuzzy in my ball, and I'm assuming that's her although truth to tell I never hoped to find her this far out and especially in this storm. We thought we were someplace else entirely…as you know, we most often are."

Sand Toes was indeed sanguine of that although sour nevertheless, and why shouldn't he be? The truth buried in that last statement added significantly, if only circumstantially, to the charges he would lay at his betrayer's feet. And now came such a one, too many years too late and bearing supposedly, gifts for his daughter with which he hoped to bribe a bit of goodwill. It was the opinion of Sand Toes of the Apaches that the desert could well go to dung before that would happen.

"La T. Da is me own name too," he replied. "As well as me dearly departed's. Hae ye come t' bring gifts to the dead?"

So that's what happened to her, thought Santos who'd often caught glimpses of Larraine in his crystal ball while making his early observations on Lauren. He'd frequently spied Larry too but the ball itself focused only upon those worthy enough to be seen and taken note of, causing their images to become plastered in reverse as if painted backward on the outer rim of the ball itself. The images and the events surrounding the chosen appeared stretched like taffy or like the reflections of cheap funhouse mirrors, so as a discerner of do-gooders, the crystal ball with its fuzzy background and disregard for detail, left much to supposition. He could see Lauren as plain as day within—proof of her own virtue, but the events surrounding her and those who peopled them were a blur as they were with all whom the ball revealed. Therefore Santos could know that Lauren was good but could not know why while being aware of such rectitude as a process of elimination only, and presumably supposition as well, and not as actual fact. The crystal ball revealed only the virtuous and none of the mischievous and was haphazard in its revelations at best, as apt to catch a potential enrollee asleep and doing nothing as reveal them in the broad light of day where their actions might cast disparaging reflections upon their overall evaluations. So don't believe any of that malarkey, especially those of you upon his roles, about his ability to see you when sleeping or awake or when good or bad. The truth of it is he catches us when he can which isn't often, and therefore most of the good deeds we do in a life frequently misspent go largely ignored and disregarded. So you kids out there reading this, don't take it too personally if you never get a gift from the real Santa and have to be satisfied instead with a cheap forgery propounded and put forward by your parents. It only means that you, like they, were in the wrong place at the wrong time.

A head appeared at the rim of the hole which formed the crash site. It was Peter the Paramedic shouting down to Sand Toes whom he could barely make out in the tangle of twisted limbs that presented itself. "Lawrence!" he cried. "Ye best be on up here man—yer lassie's taken a turn fer the worse—dinna ask me how!"

Freeing himself from the traces that held him trapped, Sand Toes sprang from the pit to confront Hephaestus who knew well enough to keep out of his way when it came to matters regarding the little lass. The elf stepped to the side and let him pass. Then reaching down while taking note of the ambivalent crowd surrounding them, began the slow process of extricating the sleigh master and those buried beneath him from the tangle of wreckage.

Those looking on who remembered their own misadventure when trying to extract Slim from one of Lawrence's pits so long ago could well commiserate with Hephaestus and the task which now presented itself. Were it not for his mighty arms made strong by centuries of application and effort at manning the bellows, then a crane might've been needed in order to remove the sleigh master from the current predicament in which he found himself. As it was the old elf tore a tendon and herniated a disc in his lower back before completing the extraction, with Santos having yet to be accounted for, being the last one out of the hole.

Having been given a hand up by Hephaestus, Pixie and Dixie stood at the edge of the crash site dusting themselves off while warily taking note of the hundreds of greedy eyes regarding them. Being keepers of secret treasure and lost gold since before Olden Days and beyond, elves have learned to recognize the look of avarice displayed upon the faces of men when contemplating such prizes. That look was in the eyes of both the Irish and Apaches surrounding them. The elves were completely ringed in and no matter how fleet of foot, knew there'd be no escaping with their treasure without a fight. "It looks as though the cattle craps are about to hit the fan," whispered Pixie. He looked about him uneasily. "And the pellets, the wind," replied Dixie. "Y'all have any of that magic dust in your pockets? Jumpin' Jefferson Davis—I think we're gonna need it!" Pixie searched his right pocket, finding a shamrock, his seven-league boots and his wishing well, but no magic dust. In his left he encountered his wishbone, his magic belt, his lucky bean, and his scarabee, but none of the white powder. A frantic perusal of his remaining pockets produced one lucky charm after another including a bowlful of the famous cereal but nary a grain of dust was to be found. "Maybe you should ask Valentino," he whispered slyly. "That caribou is always thinking that things go better with coke, just like his old man! I'll bet ya he's got a line or two squirreled away on him somewhere!" Dixie thought it an excellent idea and proceeded to do just that, making his way over to where Valentino resting on his forelocks, lie licking his wounds. "Sorry pal," the caribou replied. "I did my last line just before liftoff at the Pole—and I'm tweakin' now!" Dixie offered Valentino a look

THE CHRISTMAS RABBIT

that would curdle milk. A caribou, or any other deer for that matter, had no business dancing with dust. Let them stick to Heinekens or well-rolled reefers but the hard stuff should be left well enough alone—and available only to those who knew how use it! And they could use it now, he knew, but instead it lie compacted within the sinuses of the caribou before him where magical or not, it availed them little.

Sand Toes bent over the blanket in which Lauren lay wrapped. She was unconscious and in a fitful doze, with sweat pouring off her in rivers and her hair damp and stringy with perspiration. Her eyes moved frantically back and forth within their sockets and she mumbled incoherently about her mother and Jack. As Sand Toes listened he heard her plainly say that Larraine and Jack were just over the next rise and coming hither, that they would be here shortly and that they'd save the day. Save it from who? Save it from what? The poor dear was delirious, even Lawrence could see that. But how had she taken such a drastic turn so quickly? He looked over to Peter and Horseplay for the answer.

"Dinna be inquirin' o' me," replied Peter. "I be just a glorified x-ray tech—maybe if I had a picture o' the lass from the inside out I could tell ye somehin'. As it is, I be unable t' offer ye a diagnosis." He turned to Horseplay with the hope that his familiarity with frontier medicine and the cures that went with it would provide Sand Toes an answer.

But Horseplay just shook his head. "No can help, kemosabe," he replied. "White girl not like Apache medicine. Not FDA-approved. White girl burn with fire. Bad medicine. Horseplay think white man in the red suit to blame. Girl was fine before he showed up."

"Fine?" asked Sand Toes. "How in the name o' Jumpin' Geronimo can ye be sayin' she was fine? Me Little La had a hole in her shoulder!"

"Other than hole, medicine, and stitches," replied Horseplay diffidently, "young squaw was just fine and dandy and on the road to recovery and wellness! If she's had setback all of a sudden, then Horseplay says its due to outside influences, and that fella there is about as outside an influence as an inbred Irishman is likely to get!"

There was no denying that their captive was from out of town, yet that did not necessarily mean that he was either Irish or responsible for Little La's condition. But Larry was taking no chances. "Bring the fat sod up here," he said to Peter, "and his little henchmen too!"

Under guard, Santos, Pixie, and Dixie were brought before Sand Toes and made to stand in front of Little La.

"What have ye t' say fer yerselves?" Larry demanded. "Are ye responsible fer me Little La takin' on so?"

Pixie and Dixie looked up at the sleigh master. "Is this guy for real?" asked Pixie. "We were just passing through when all this went down! All we wanted was a shot of joy juice and a cookie and then to be on our way! We certainly weren't looking to foment this kind of trouble!"

Larry cautioned the sprite with a warning hand. "I be talkin' t yer master," he replied. "When I be wantin any o' yer lip, I'll bend down t' git it!"

Pixie was about to offer the sand man a gesture universally known amongst rabbits when Santos cut the little squirt off with a warning hand of his own. "I don't know how we can be held responsible," he replied, while keeping the little elf at bay. "we were just passing overhead and certainly were hurling no spears from the sleigh as we did. Still, we might be able to help."

"How's that?" Larry asked, torn between distrust and desperation. "And why should ye want to?"

"Well," the sleigh master replied, as if unsure he should say anything more and unable to believe the self-evident truth which he saw standing before him, "I can't see your mark, to be sure, but you do have the family look about you—if you take my meaning and if I do say so myself."

"Mark?" replied Sand Toes. "Di' ye mean the eagle's talon? O' course I got it! Most o' us Dawes do! What o' it?"

"The talon!" cried Santos. "I knew you were family the moment I laid eyes on you! Laddie, it's been years! Where's Junior? How did you get away in the flood, and did the Witches ever find you? I'm sure they didn't or else they would have told me. Still I don't wonder that—"

THE CHRISTMAS RABBIT

"Whoa there, neighbor!" It was Jim, who along with Slim and Richard were hovering in the immediate area and who'd overheard the conversation between Sand Toes and Santos. "What be all this guff about marks? Are ye sayin' ye have the Dawe birthmark?"

"No," replied Santos. "I'm saying I have the Santos birthmark, and it's shaped like an eagle's talon. Most folk in my family have it, and if he has it, then he must be family. You have something of the look about you too!"

"Balderdash!" replied Jim. "I be a Dawe, tried and true. I be no *Sand Toes*!"

"You do bear the mark," replied the sleigh master.

"I bear *a* mark," countered the Irishman. "I'm nae sayin' it be yers!"

"Since it's as plain as the nose on your face," replied Santos, "I'm saying that it is, and believe me, I had it first!"

"Prove it!" demanded Jim. "Show me yers!"

Santos gave his long white whiskers a thoughtful tug. "That's gonna be kind of hard," he replied. "My beard covers it."

"How convenient!" Jim replied.

"It does!" said Santos. "Not all of us are as lucky as you, bearing our badge so proudly or so prominently on our protuberances—at least those you can see!" He paused for a moment to look about, as if seeking after someone. "Hey, Rudolph," he cried out to Valentino, searching for him in the dark, "Get a load of this guy! He's got a snout on him that'd give yours a run for its money, even if you had a replacement bulb handy!"

From where he lay next to the crash site while nursing his injuries, Valentino looked up forlornly as he attempted a reply but found in the effort that he just didn't give a damn. He'd had it out any number of times with the sleigh master regarding traces and tricksters but still the old man, from time to time, let the elves take the reins and always with the same result! If he'd just kept those damned elves strapped in back they'd well be over Wake Island by now and halfway home! Even now Hephaestus was going over the sleigh's frame, which despite its space age metals and high tech manufacture, was probably bent like a noodle, and *if* they could get it airborne at all—which itself was highly suspect, would shimmy and shake like a cocktail mixer if taken over anything above two hundred. At best that meant hours of overtime and working straight through Sunday. Valentino laid his head on his weary paws.

When young master Rudolph deigned not to answer, the sleigh master returned to the matter at hand. "So what do you want me to do," he asked Jim, "shave? I'm kinda proud of my locks and beard, especially after once losing both ages ago. I haven't cut either since and I don't intend to now! Besides, along with my famous chartreuse suit, my beard has become something of a trademark of which I've grown rather fond."

"Chartreuse?" Jim asked. "I'm an Irishman, fella, and believe ye me that as one, I know green when I sees it and that suit of yers ain't! It's red!"

Santos looked embarrassed. "It's red," he said, "as is the cap on my head. But they were green once! It seems my coveralls caught the frostbite when we moved north, and bled red. Been that way ever since no matter how many times the old lady washes 'em. She even tried dying 'em once or twice. No good. The green just wouldn't take. It—"

Sand Toes interrupted the sleigh master. He was sure the old man's story was interesting but now wasn't the time. "There be nae 'Juniors' around here," he said. "Everyone one o' us has seniority! But what has that t' do with the price o' beer and moreover, what has it t' do with me Little La?"

"Why, it has everything to do with her!"

"How so?"

"Because you're family," replied Santos, "For family I'll do anything within my power to make things right even though I had little to do with making them wrong."

"Little t' do?" asked Sand Toes. "Why, ye bleedin' sod! We would'na be out here in the first place if it nae be fer ye!"

"That's awfully nice of you, friend," Santos replied, "to stand outside in the cold, exposing yourself to both elements and Indians in order to wave and send me on my way!"

THE CHRISTMAS RABBIT

If there were any doubt in Larry's mind that the two of them were related, such skepticism got squashed in Santos's reply. The fat man standing before him was dumber than a pile of rocks, which put him, as far as Larry was concerned, on the same intellectual plateau that the Irish standing around him were proud to occupy. Proof enough, he supposed, of their familial ties! "We dinna come out here t' cheer ye on, ye plab! I'm here t' put a stop t' ye and yer broken promises!"

"But I promise to make her better," replied Santos. "Surely you're not going to put a stop to that, are you?"

Larry looked longingly down at his daughter who lie there mumbling incoherently. No, he could not very well put a stop to that, could he? Still he'd been burned by this fellow once before and so was slow to trust him now.

"How are you going to make her better?" he asked.

"With the first aid kit I have packed in my sleigh—assuming, of course, that the storm didn't make off with it."

Setting his biases aside, it sounded reasonable to Lawrence. Larraine, when she'd been around to do it, had insisted upon having a first aid kit handy in the mine shaft and many was the time she availed herself of its contents in order to treat a cut or a sprain that she or Lauren may have acquired in a life lived underground. Lawrence seemed impervious to such things. Still, he was familiar with the first aid kit's efficiency when it came to treating ills, but had enough presence of mind nevertheless to know that a large part of its effectiveness was due to the medicine man who wielded it.

"Go and get yer kit," he reluctantly replied. "But mind ye—I'll be watchin' yer every move!"

Santos sent the two elves back to the wreckage of the sleigh in order to retrieve the box. They returned carrying a monstrosity of a container, which opened up in three tiers like a tackle box and was filled with an assortment of nostrums, pill boxes, swabs, Band-Aids, and alcohol swatches. There was a box of rubber gloves in the bottom tray as well as tongue depressors, syringes, surgical suture and needles, cough drops, ace bandages, splints, eyewash, dental floss, and breath mints. The middle tray housed an aspirator, a bedpan, and an artificial heart as well as a number of items Larry could only guess at. It was littered with Aspirin, Excedrin, Tylenol, and Motrin. There was a blue bottle of calamine lotion and a bottle of Carter's little pills too. In a can with a pull-tab there were eight ounces of prune juice sandwiched between a bottle of Pepto Bismal and one of Milk of Magnesia. The top tray housed wart remover, acne scrub, suntan lotion and even a snake bite kit, although what one needed with that up in the North Pole Larry couldn't even begin to guess. And there was hair tonic, foot powder, and corn remover, which Larry eyed greedily.

"You see something in there you want?" asked the sleigh master. "Then go ahead and take it. Ain't never had the damned thing open before and this is the wrong box anyhow!"

"The wrong box? That canna' be," he replied. "Ye hae a bleedin' frontier clinic in ye briefcase there!" The sleigh master offered a chuckle. "More than that!" he replied. "Look at this baby!" From the middle tray he removed one of the objects foreign to Lawrence and proudly held it up for display. It was about four inches long and it looked like a saltshaker with a glass top. On its face was engraved an inverted *V* that looked more like a boomerang than anything else.

The desert with its many lessons to impart extolling the value of parsimony as one went about the arduous and often grueling chore of obtaining from it the necessaries needed to survive, taught a lifelong curriculum in conservatism as you parceled out while stretching to the limit, the meager bounty the land had to offer. And when you got right down to it, conservatism was the big brother of caution. A little bolder because he was a little older, he was careful nevertheless and as a rule evoked little enthusiasm for innovation and 'new-fangled' ideas. So it was with Larry although his actions seemed to belie a conservative bent entirely. Still he saw anything new as potentially dangerous. He'd first approached the rabbit bearing that in mind and he'd do so now with regard to the gizmo that his captive displayed in his hands.

"What be that?" he asked, eyeing it curiously.

"That's a doctor dispenser," Santos replied matter-of-factly. "I don't know what its right name is—in fact, I don't even think they've

THE CHRISTMAS RABBIT

named it yet, but I've got this deal with my sales rep at Best Buy, who has his own deal with his sales rep at Sony, who told him they too have a deal running with the people from Paramount and Star Trek, to wheel out the next generation in franchise merchandizing. That makes us wheelers and dealers, where no wheeler's dealt before!"

Sand Toes looked at him skeptically. "What's a *Star Trek*, aye?" he asked. "And who's it paramount t' and what be franchise merchandisin'?"

"Don't you watch TV?" Santos asked incredulously.

"Dinna own one," Larry stated flatly. "The rabbit ears give me the creeps!"

"Perfectly understandable," replied the sleigh master, "if a bit silly. They have cable now, you know. And satellite too!"

Sand Toes looked at him derisively. "Di ye know how much the cable guy wants to run a wire from town this far out? And he be family! Nae, I'll be stickin' t' me radio."

Santos couldn't see how Sand Toes survived out here in the middle of nowhere without TV. Up at the pole and assuming they didn't lose power and were forced on generator, the TV was a constant presence twenty four-seven. Santos made sure there was one in every room with all of them broadcasting round the clock. With the polar climate being somewhat on the windward side it paid to have the Weather Channel airing in every other room.

"Star Trek," he replied, "is a show on television that takes place in the future—"

"How can that be," Larry interrupted, "when we all be here in the present?"

"It's an imagined future," Santos replied, "taking place in the mind."

"Then why dinna ye say that?" asked Sand Toes. "So this *Star Trek* then, be a television show that takes place in the mind?"

"You could look at it that way," he replied, "but—"

"If ye be imaginin' it in the first place then what in the name o' Jumpin' James Joyce di' ye be needin' a TV fer anyway?"

"Never mind that!" the farmer replied. "The point is that along with the original show there've been a number of spin-offs, many of which have had a doctor as a central character. This device, due out in 2026, is a medical library housing the three top reference manuals most generally referred to by physicians worldwide. The library itself is stored on a computer chip, voice actuated, and programmed to offer up both diagnosis and treatment regimens for any number of ailments or injuries, using its three source guides as a referent. But here's the best part—this lenslike thing at the top is actually a mini holographic projector and the guys at Sony got together with the guys at Paramount, and editing for content all of the original and spin-off episodes, put together programs that mimic the three most popular doctors, using them as the face and voice that offer to the patient at home the much sought after analysis of whatever it is that ails them. This here model is the McCoy 1000, and there's also one called the EMH 2000. Both of these when they hit the market, will retail for somewhere around five grand. But the kicker and the one they're still working on to get perfect before the release date is the Crusher 5000! It comes complete with a holographic image of Gates McFadden in a nurse's uniform and doing the tango! And baby, let me tell you—there's gonna be a lot of sick time called in at the jobsite come 2027!"

Lawrence looked impressed but then remembered all of the horses that were supposedly under the hood of Jim's Range Rover and his skepticism returned. "If it be that smart," he replied, "why nae turn the bleedin' contraption on and let it tell us what be the matter with me Little La?"

"Bad idea," replied Santos. "All three models speak only in medicalese, which is hard for folks like us to understand. Suppose we turned McCoy on, pointing him at her while describing her condition? Suppose then he offered up not only a diagnosis but a treatment as well, for gallstones? Would you, even with his hands on guidance be willing and moreover be able, to perform the necessary surgery in order to remove 'em?" Sand Toes shook his head. "I thought not," replied the sleigh master. In order to be effectively led, one has to see where one is going and such is not the case here!"

"Let Peter then," Larry said pointing to him, "listen t' the bloody thing! He be a paramedic, after all!" Santos shook his head, continuing his disagreement. "Any doctor," he replied, who forgets his clotters and coagulators in addition to his suture, is surely not expert enough in his field to follow in the footsteps of Starfleet's greatest surgeon! "Besides, as I told you before, the cure to Lauren's troubles doesn't lie in this box but in another entirely." He offered the two elves standing beside him a decidedly sour look. "Did I not tell you," he asked, "to bring up the medical kit and only if it hadn't been sucked out of the sleigh by the storm overhead prior to our crash?" The elves nodded their agreement. "And wasn't this particular kit, which I'm now holding, bolted down and strapped in so securely as to make it all but impossible to be lost in the wind?" Again the elves nodded. "Then obviously," said the sleigh master, "I must've been talking about another kit entirely, and one that might have blown out of the magic hole!" The elves, allowing the possibility without understanding in the least what he was talking about, merely shrugged. "The presents, you idiots!" the farmer said. "Don't you even remember who's who or who gets what?"

"You keep the list pal, not us," Pixie replied.

"That's right!" agreed Dixie. "Y'all are the one who keeps the list and checks it twice! Our job is just to hump packages!"

"Whatever!" replied the sleigh master. "Go back to the wreck and, searching through the rubble, see if you can locate the present marked 'La T. Da.' If you find it then hump it on back here!"

"But what will—"

"Just do it!" replied the sleigh master, "and save your questions for our flight home!"

Grumbling, Pixie and Dixie stalked off to carry out their assigned task. In the long passage of time since the great race and their subsequent sentence, whilst being exiled for all but one day of the year to the cold lands in the north, Santos had over the slow elapse of ages become something of an autocrat, issuing orders as if expecting them to be carried out and obeyed. True, the Witches did leave him nominally in charge while ordering them and their kind to provide him with any and every assistance they were capable of, but did he have to be so pushy? There was such a thing as consensus and after a long life such as his, the elves deemed that he should've learned something of it.

Turning to the girl, the sleigh master looked down at her thoughtfully. "We need to wake her up," he told Larry, "and get her coherent if this cure of mine is going to work."

"What cure?" replied the Sandman. "Even yer two wee henchmen haven't a clue as to what yer up to! What kind o' medicine hae ye, that be more effective or vigorous than Irish and Apache remedies? What kind o' medicine be that, aye?'

"It not be medicine at all," replied Santos, "but magic!"

Those gathered about, including Sand Toes, looked at the sleigh master warily. All were prone to superstitious beliefs. The Apaches, parading about the desert on their motorcycles while clinging nevertheless to their ancestry and primitive roots, saw superstitious portents in even the most prosaic of circumstances. A sudden and unanticipated gust of wind, an early morning desert fog—rare certainly but not entirely unheard of, a turkey buzzard high overhead and circling counter-clockwise, or a sandstorm springing up out of nowhere to move seemingly against the wind which drove it—all of these occurrences and many more were viewed by the Apaches in their superstition as portents, signs, and mostly bad omens, probably magical and most certainly under the control of supernatural forces. The Society being themselves descended from him in whom superstition and magical forces seemed to hold sway, were as a pedigree inordinately sensitive to anything that smacked of supernatural or superstitious influence. Fickle Fate and Fugacious Fortuity, they knew, often proved themselves to be magical, in both their means and their ends and the family stigmata was a magnet for both. But there was black magic just as there was white and when invoking either you could never be sure of just which one you were going to get. "Why di' we need t' wake the lass?" Sand Toes asked. "She be restin' as comfortably as may be. Why disturb her?"

Santos looked at his long-lost descendant lovingly. There was a lot of Laddie in the man standing before him but very little of Junior as far as he could tell. Still, a son was a son, even if only a grandson many times removed.

THE CHRISTMAS RABBIT

"The magic," Santos replied, "is in the opening of the present. Therefore in order to be effective, it must be unwrapped by individual to whom it's gifted. If we open it then it becomes just another box and the contents within merely toys to be played with or not. But if she opens it—well it's Christmas Eve, a magical night in and of itself. Anything could happen!"

Sand Toes sported a frown as he considered his elder statesman's last remark. *Anything* covered quite a lot of territory—a virtually endless panoply of varying vistas and circumstances in which to become lost and entangled. His family had a history of such excursions and he saw no reason with Little La's overall well-being at stake to start down the trail of another one.

Santos bent over the young lass, gently tickling her under the chin. Lauren's eyes fluttered as she fought for consciousness. They darted back and forth, trapped within their sockets, finally focusing and coming to rest on the enigmatic stranger before her.

"You're real," she whispered weakly, more to herself than anyone else. "I never really believed in you and thought you were just a figment of my Da's imagination. But you're real! And now we've gone and brought down your sleigh. I'm sorry for the inconvenience that me and mine have caused you."

The sleigh master chided her gently. "Think nothing of it," he said. "The fault, if it belongs to anyone, is mine for letting that damned elf take the reins in the first place. But a long life often filled with mistakes has taught me that everything happens for a reason even if we're unable to see that reason for what it is. I'd planned on sneaking into your mine tonight, sending either Pixie or Dixie inside with your gift while you slept, but see—an errant wind, coupled with elven mischief, has led me directly to you and to where I'm needed most. But it's you now, who must grasp hold of the magic and perform a miracle."

Lauren struggled to sit up, fighting off a wave of nausea as she did. "But what can I do?" she asked. "I'm just a little girl who loves her Da and who lies wounded and helpless. I thought I was getting better, but I seem to be suffering a setback."

Santos examined her injury. "Indeed," he replied, taking note of the uneven sutures sewn haphazardly into her flesh, around which a red inflammation appeared. "Your wound has grown septic," he said, "becoming inflamed and swollen. It's the infection that's driving up your fever and making you ill. At home, wrapped within your blanket and lying before a warm fire, you could fight it. Out here however, lying on the cold desert floor as a storm passes overhead, you haven't a chance and will surely succumb unless unlooked for aid arrives in a timely fashion. I'm that aid but you must play an active role in helping me to bestow the benefits of the magic I bring."

"How?" asked the troubled girl, nervously clutching her Da's hand. "What can a little Irish lass do in a situation like this?"

"Simply believe," replied the sleigh master. "Believe in me, believe in yourself, and believe in the magic of the gift I bear."

"I've been wishing for a new Nintendo and a television upon which to play it!" Lauren replied. "How's 'Hot Shot's Golf' going to help me now?"

"Is that what you wanted for Christmas?" Santos asked with a laugh. "I never got a letter from you nor had you in my lap when I was in Vegas two weeks ago. My crystal ball doesn't provide me with that much clarity so I had to make a guess and brought you this!" He reached behind him to where Pixie and Dixie stood, having returned from the sleigh where they prosecuted their search.

"We found it," Dixie replied. "'Twas one of the few gifts left in the well that the wind didn't seize!" He held it out to the fat man, who took it and subsequently handed it to Lauren.

"This is the watershed moment," remarked the sleigh master, "the time for you to set aside doubt and surrender to belief. Simply trust in me, open your present, and soon things will be better."

Lauren looked at him doubtfully. Lying on her bed of pain, injured and surrounded by mad Irishmen and savage Apaches, how could any of it be made to be better? Still with little choice before her other than the one offered, Lauren let go of doubt, casting it upon the winds of the passing storm where it was blown to tatters and eventually away. Grasping hold of the box wrapped daintily in red paper with little pictures of reindeer cavorting on its face, she gently

THE CHRISTMAS RABBIT

tugged at the gay ribbon which bound it. Tied in a slipknot, when pulled it unknotted and came away easily, resting comfortably in her hand. She cautiously slipped a fingernail under one of the wrapping's folds, intending to loosen the flap by breaking the tape that bound it rather than tearing the paper itself. This was a gift and from the real Santa, and as such, even the paper it came wrapped in had value. She carefully undid the wrapping's folds, revealing a little plastic box with a Red Cross prominently displayed upon it.

"That be a toy!" Sand Toes objected. "It be nothin' more than a child's version o' the kit you just showed me! What could possibly be inside that could be o' any benefit to me Little La?" She undid the clasp and tentatively opened the lid, revealing the toy bandages and medical supplies within. "There be nothing here of any value!" said Sand Toes. "All within be nothin' but a fake and a sham!"

"Not so," replied the sleigh master as he pushed a few bandages aside to reveal a tiny vial filled with white powder. Holding it up he presented it to those gathered for inspection. "This is magic dust," he said confidently, "and if used properly, in the appropriate amounts and for the right reasons, it can affect many a cure and heal many an ill."

Pixie and Dixie eyed the little vial greedily. Valentino, they knew, would lead his herd in a stampede of selfish desire if he knew that there was even a meager line of the powder to be found in the immediate area.

"Do you think this wise?" Pixie whispered into the sleigh master's ear. "After all, we may be needing a little of the powder ourselves before this evening's done! A quick snort would enable us to float away and escape."

Santos offered the elf a rare smile. "That's exactly what I'm doing," he replied, "sowing the seeds of our release and parole."

He uncapped the vial and taking the powder, shook the magic dust all over the little one's wound. As individual flakes of the thaumaturgic substance fell gently upon her lesion they ate away at the unsanitary stitching while binding the wound and closing the skin until all that was left was a little scar, hardly to be noticed. The redness and inflammation disappeared entirely and the swelling surrounding her shoulder abated. Taking what was left in the vial, the sleigh master asked for a cup of water. Peter, a paramedic who'd seen many a miraculous recovery in his day, stood flabbergasted while handing Santos a canteen. How was this possible, he wondered? Surely the AMA, should they ever get wind of a miracle cure like this, would put the quash on it for good. Why avail oneself of doctors and the outrageous bills that went with them when one could cure anything from hangovers to a heart attacks with a little white powder! Taking the canteen, Santos poured the remaining substance within, stirring it with his finger as he had no coke spoon handy.

"Drink this now," he said to Lauren. "The powder is affecting a cure from the outside but must work from within as well to be truly effective."

Lauren took the offered cup and drained it. "It's rather bitter," she replied, "and numbing to the tongue."

Santos offered her a chuckle while gently stroking her hair. "That means it's working, darling," he said. "Never trust medicine that tastes good. Those who make such nostrums generally imbue them with sweet tastes and pleasant smells because they're worthless! When it comes to taking one's medicine, if the cure you ingest caresses your palette, then chances are it will be of very little utility and probably has more sugar in it than anything else!"

The magically charged beverage coursed through her body, bringing with it new health and vitality as it did. Lauren felt its affects from the top of her head to the tips of her toes as the decoction coursed through the veins and capillaries that carried it. She felt her strength return and her stamina increase to a level greater than it was prior to her injury. Her copper hair, so beautiful even in this dim light, stood out on end and the tips of her fingers seemed to be thrumming. Her eyes saw with greater clarity and her hearing became sharper. Her sense of smell grew more acute and she became light-headed, feeling as though she were hovering in midair.

"Grab her!" cried Santos, "and hold her down! She's beginning to float!"

It was true. Before the startled eyes of those gathered the young Irish lass hovered four inches off the ground and was gaining altitude even as the unbelieving looked on.

THE CHRISTMAS RABBIT

"What in the name o' Saint Paddy is happenin' now?" demanded Sand Toes. "What hae ye done t' me Little La?"

"Relax," replied the sleigh master. "It's a common side effect of the treatment, that's all. It's what enables my caribou to cruise the airways! It helps keep 'em up when all the world wants to bring 'em down. She's just getting a little high, is all. It'll wear off in a while. In the meantime fill her pockets with rocks to help weigh her down and if that doesn't work, tie her to a tree!"

There were no trees as far as Larry could see, just a couple of faraway barrel cacti, and he was not going to secure La to one of those and have her get prickled and pierced by its oversized thorns—she had enough holes in her already! He turned his attention to the sleigh master who'd just saved his daughter's life. What to do now? It had been his intention to steal the sleigh master's boots and to set free his caribou as partial payment for the childhood betrayal he'd been made to suffer. But the sleigh master had just saved the only person of any import in his life and moreover it seemed that he was family too. One didn't rob family, even Sand Toes knew that. Especially if they'd just saved your daughter. But could he simply let the old man go? Wouldn't the sleigh master's release nullify a lifetime of effort and planning? Wouldn't the sleigh master's parole point to an overall criticism regarding the quest itself and a life spent trying to achieve it? Had he put in all this effort only to find that he'd ultimately wasted his time?

As Sand Toes pondered these conundrums, Slim and Jim gathered the Society members around them in order to confer about present circumstances. When they'd first learned the identity of Larry's quarry, they were of a mind to go along with his fantasy on the unlikely possibility that the potential target was in fact a reality. If such proved to be the case then their victim would be more valuable to them than any lode of gold that they as yet had been incapable of unearthing. He could be ransomed or perhaps even sold to the highest bidder. National Geographic alone would pay millions for film footage that detailed the events of his capture. The Smithsonian would reward them handsomely for his carcass before stuffing him and putting him on display. There'd be the talk show circuit and perhaps even a Hollywood movie tie-in. They'd be set for life while never having to pick up another pickax or gold pan for the rest of their days! They could even move back to New York and with their new found wealth purchase from that cheapskate of a landlord, their tenement building and fixing it up, turn it into an apartment complex that rivaled the Dakota. Maybe they could even get Yoko, who must be tired of living in that lonely apartment on her own, to move in! Now having proven himself a reality, the sleigh master claimed as well paternal status within the Society while saving Little La's life as he did so. Most members felt therefore, with Jim objecting, of course, that such callous treatment offered up as a reward, both for good deeds recently displayed and in the face of a paternity yet to be proven, was in remarkably poor taste. "But he hae nae shown us his mark!" Jim objected.

"His existence alone," said Slim, "and the circumstances surrounding his presence here today are proof enough for me, of his family crest!"

The others concurred, nodding quietly and voicing their agreement. Most were still skeptical of the old man's claim but cautious enough nevertheless not to regard his statement lightly. If he was bearer of the badge and grandsire to them all then he was no one to cross or to get in the way of. An idiot wind blew a gale all about the ship upon which he sailed, tossing to and fro those who tried to chart a course in his wake.

With the healing of Lauren the Apaches found that their attitudes toward the enigmatic stranger had undergone a drastic sea change as well. It was bad medicine all around that the Sand Man's daughter had taken a spear and Horse's Head was going to personally see to it that the brave who chucked it got his can handed to him when they got back to their teepees. In the meantime, in order to appease the Irish woman's shade and avoid bad medicine, he'd immediately assigned Horseplay to assist in her care and treatment. When such treatment proved itself to be of little utility, whether the fault of the Irishman or Indian—and in this instance, Horse's Head was apt to blame the latter as he'd known Horseplay to be ineffectual in treating a head cold, Horse's Head along with the rest of his tribe, grew ever more nervous and increasingly on edge as he read in the portents and omens occurring around him the bad medicine they'd brewed by staging the assault in the first place. Surely Lauren, should she pass, would prompt Larraine's shade to shadow them so that even beneath the noonday sun, she would dog them from one end of the desert to the other, haunting and harassing them and making their nomadic existence next to impossible. It could get so bad, Horse's Head knew, that he might have to take up his tribe and move to another desert entirely where the shade of Larraine couldn't see 'em. In most instances, another desert meant camels and although the Apache were well balanced while upon their bikes, retaining the bare vestiges of the horsemanship they'd once proudly displayed when atop their wild ponies, there were in this present day no jockeys among them. Thus he along with the rest of the tribe uttered a great sigh of relief when the sleigh master's treatment provided a seeming cure. When it caused the little squaw to float the superstitious tribesmen along with the biker chicks who rode bitch at their backs, were buffaloed and bowled over by the bold display of such powerful medicine and being so, would not contend against it. Let the old one go, they reasoned. There were still the Irish, and they could always be settled with on another day. The caribou looked tasty but Horse's Head decided to pass on them as well.

They were all staring, one at the other. Sand Toes at Santos, Jim at Slim, Peter at Pradaig, and Horse's Head at Horseplay, wondering what to do next when the storm overhead which had all but passed them by, suddenly shifted, coming completely about, and descended upon them once again. The skies grew evermore dark. The wind quickened and moaned, blowing tumbleweeds across their path and bouncing them upon the desert floor before their feet. Hail started to fall in fist-sized stones and a cover was quickly erected over Lauren to protect her while she lay huddled in her blanket. Horse's Head watched helplessly as most of the eagle's feathers proudly displayed in his war bonnet were torn from their stitches and carried away on the wind. A lightning bolt descending like a fallen angel, stuck a solitary boulder just off to their left, shattering it with the violence of its strike and scattering small stone-sized chunks of rock like munitions in a cluster bomb. They flew every which way, striking both Irishman and Apache with indifference and many would be the onlooker who would walk away unbowed but bloody by the end of the day. Jim had a piece of an earlobe clipped off. Slim caught a chunk of rock in his left bicep which buried itself painfully in his flesh. Horseplay dodged a missile aimed directly at his head and in doing so walked into another that caught him squarely in the keister. They were caught between both hail and slingstone and getting hammered. Despite all his years in the desert and his familiarity with its temperamental changes in weather which could descend upon a traveler both quickly and in the extreme, Larry had never seen a storm so suddenly reverse itself to come tearing back with such violence, as above him he took note of the funnel cloud beginning to form and about to descend upon them.

"What in the name o' shiverin' shamrocks be happenin' now?" he asked no one in particular while gazing uneasily up at the sky. Knowing full well from memory what the advent of such a sign displayed so prominently in the sky most likely portended, Santos chose to answer him anyway while dreading his response nevertheless. "It's them," the erstwhile farmer replied with a resigned whimper. "After all the ages passed, they've finally decided to put in an appearance."

"Who?" asked a bewildered Sand Toes.

"The Powers That Be, that's who," replied Santos. "Helgayarn, Brunnhilde, and Betty—the Witches!"

Still staring at the sky, Sand Toes took note of the funnel descending. "Be they family," he asked, "and di' we hae to feed 'em?"

"No," replied Santos with a sigh. "But remind me that I have a bowl of the missus's shark fin soup in the thermos of my lunch bucket in case we need it!"

CHAPTER VIII
Fate Favors the Furies

Dressed in battle fatigues, Helgayarn looked about her immediate area in a self-satisfied manner. Farm Boy was trapped like the sacrificial lamb he'd soon become. The elves were reluctantly, although obediently, seeing to his immediate and final needs while behind them both stood an overabundance of his long-lost relatives and relatively innocent bystanders upon whom to take out their latent revenge, chief amongst whom was that wild-eyed fella over there who looked so much like Laddie and who was someone they'd been keeping an eye upon for quite some time now. In fact, ever since the first Dawe had stumbled within a stone's throw of their desolate valley they'd been keeping tabs upon the entire family and on both branches at that—many of whom displayed the mark upon their visible persons and were therefore recognizable. That most of them had at one time resided in New York did little to deter the trio in their trifold effort to maintain their vigilance. There were 'Lurkers In The Leafs' everywhere who could be bought for the price of a song and although the journey was indeed a long one there were nevertheless many carrier and homing pigeon scrounging around the tenements of New York that were willing to speed a tale westward. The trio looked in on as well, Old Hoss and his smoke signals, taking note of his erratic reports regarding the Society's status. The trio had also overheard Slim and Jim's ardent conversation a few weeks back as they drove away from the mine, concerning their encounter with the mysterious rabbit who got trapped in one of the mad Irishman's snares. From the description given by the two men the trio knew well enough that the hare hereabouts must be none other than a descendant of the infamous Jack Rabbit, although what he was doing out in the desert in the middle of December was anyone's guess. Certainly Helgayarn, Brunnhilde, and Betty hadn't a clue. Still, the trio held it fortuitous that such should be so for it seemed to them that all of the pigeons were coming home to roost. For years they'd laughingly looked on as each December saw Sand Toes, long-lost descendant of Santos, engaged in a futile effort to capture his great-grandsire so many times removed, for an insignificant slight that the old sod had little to do with and which the trio helped put forward in the first place. It was they who sent Pixie and Dixie while Sand Toes was taking his afternoon nap, out into the desert deep those many years ago to confront Daddy and Lulu Dawe and their guest, Beatnik Bob, after they'd popped their peyote buttons. The elves were just beginning the process of gearing up for the following year and thinking it was an over-eager supplier calling them regarding an early purchase order for the upcoming season's hottest gadget, Pixie nonchalantly answered his cell phone without checking the number first. It was Helgayarn, calling him from one of the rare pay phones still in existence. With the advent of the cell phone most call boxes that ate change for a living had gone the way of the dinosaur, being dismantled, disconnected, and disposed of, due to the inevitable decrease in the number of dimes dropped in 'em. This one owed its continued existence to its remote location. Set upon the fringes of the desert on a hardscrabble road not noted on any map and situated at the rear of the parking lot behind an abandoned building that had once housed "Kappy's Kape Kod Kohogs" and whose marquee still proudly boasted of semifresh clams served nearly every other day, it's not surprising that it got overlooked. Actually the phone company did send a repairman out to see to the matter of disconnection while Kappy's was still a going concern, but the repairman arrived just in time for lunch. Being from the desert, he'd never had clams and therefore didn't know that semifresh served nearly every other day was not necessarily something you wanted sitting in your stomach. But he'd heard so much about the quality of New England Seafood that he decided to give them a try since there wasn't a 7-Eleven handy enough to give him

THE CHRISTMAS RABBIT

any other choice. A part-time cowboy with a small herd of his own which he worked on the weekends and held as a hobby, the repairman was a "steak and potatoes" kind of dude, knowing little about bass and bluefish, clams, or quahogs. The prices on the menu looked a bit steep but that was to be expected, he supposed, since the fare had to be shipped in. He ordered a dozen cherrystones, and as the waiter served them, they looked to the repairman like lungas lying on the half shell. Mrs. Santos would've been impressed. The repairman however was not and ran from the place screaming. He never returned and the phone company never sent him back, leaving the phone in both good repair and working order.

Pixie knew it was Helgayarn on the other end of the line the minute he heard the operator ask him if he'd accept the charges for the call. Very few had his number and there were only three who would dare call collect. When Helgayarn told him what she wanted of both himself and Dixie he tried to object, claiming that they were already behind schedule with regard to next Christmas, but the big Witch would hear none of it. This was important. Part of the karmic wheel turning as it brought the events and the folk inhabiting them, into alignment—and the two elves had better damned well remember, despite the signatures on their paychecks, just who it was they were really working for... So Pixie and Dixie caught an errant tail wind that the Witches sent north and riding it south, got off in the desert to perform the bit of mischief the trio had set for them, taking the rainbow home when they were finished.

Having successfully set up the animosity between father and son or the modern day equivalent thereof, the trio had simply to sit out the long passage of years while allowing the karmic wheel to roll onward toward its inevitable conclusion. So when Santos finally passed over their valley on his way to the mine, the Witches hitched a ride on the tailwind of the storm in which he'd become embroiled. They'd follow him to the others and then settle with the lot of 'em once and for all!

The funnel touched down to reveal the trio to the Irish and Indians gathered there. They arrived in the latest version of their custom-made Winnebago—a prototype not available to the public and on loan to them for a test drive from the manufacturer, who long ago hired them as its official spokespersons for their product. It still had AC hook-ups, slept eight, and had all the microwaves and wet bars a body could build into it, but gone were the Clydesdales harnessed in V-8 and the wagon wheels which rolled it. Instead it thrummed to the roar of an unseen engine while it went about like a tank upon tracks—which is what it essentially was. Painted in overlapping shades of two-toned green with intermittent shadings of dust and beige, it sported antenna and radar dishes upon various nodes of its exterior and had a turret on the roof upon which was mounted a 120 mm gun with a smoothbore barrel. It sent out clouds of diesel exhaust, choking those who looked with surprise, upon it. A hatch, built into the top of the turret, rose up and Helgayarn's head popped out. She had a tank driver's leather cap pulled tightly down over her head with the flaps hanging loose upon either side of her face and her eyes were hidden behind desert goggles, but even in such outrageous attire and while in command of so unlikely a vehicle she remained nevertheless recognizable to the one person in the crowd who could point her out.

"My lady fair!" cried Santos as he performed an exaggerated bow. "Whatever brings you here, and what in the world are you driving?"

"It's our Winnebago, you fool," Brunnhilde replied from somewhere deep within its bowels. "You know that we never travel in anything but our Winnebago!"

"Yah!"

Santos eyed the monstrosity incredulously. "I've overflown many a park," replied the sleigh master, "both national and trailer and seen many a Winnebago in each, but never have I seen one quite like this! Are you sure you didn't switch dealerships in the last century?"

From the top of the turret Helgayarn offered up a sour frown as she considered her soon-to-be victim. Still as dull-pated and dunderheaded as ever, full of dimwittedness and desipience to the ninth degree! "It's a Winnebago indeed, you fool!" she replied. "Government-Issue. Or will be a few years down the road. With the economy tanking, Chrysler and GM filing for chapter 11, Fanny

THE CHRISTMAS RABBIT

Mae and Freddy Mac both with their thumbs up their fannies, and unemployment figures flying through the roof, folk in these parts will soon lose their fondness for four-wheeled monstrosities such as the Winnebago, being unable to afford either the outright purchase or the fuel required to motor it. It'll drive Winnebago into chapter 11, and like GM, the government will soon come to own it. Reluctantly, they'll partner up with GM itself and in a year or so award it a military contract to design and manufacture the next line of battle tank! We simply whisked ourselves ahead a few years and brought one back with us! Pretty nifty, eh?"

Santos had to admit that it was a pretty neat trick. But it didn't make sense to him that the government would try and rescue a company by bailing it out and then steer it toward the manufacture of hardware of which it had no previous knowledge or experience, and he told her so.

"Since when has the government ever made sense?" asked Helgayarn.

"Not since the three of you got involved," Santos mumbled under his breath.

"What was that?"

"Oh, nothing, nothing at all." Taking note of the fast fading funnel as it flung itself northward, it occurred to the sleigh master that even the mightiest of storms would have difficulty lifting the monstrosity before him. It was ten times the size of his sled, fully armored, and a herd of caribou coked up and higher than wet in a waterspout wouldn't get it off the ground. A tornado might tumble it. A twister might tear off an antennae or two. Even the worst williwaw to ever come whistling out of the west would do little to it other than scratch the paint. Santos took note of the long barrel protruding out of the turret, which incidentally was pointed directly at him. He was familiar with it, having given away too many toy replicas of the damned things on yuletides past. They looked scary enough scaled down to pint-size. At full size, the oily barrel with its metallic sheen seemed to him, the be all and end all of obscenity and capering horror—an abominable phallus whose seed when spewed brought about death rather than life. It hung from the turret, erect and full and standing at attention, its one eye staring balefully down upon him as he returned the regard while gazing timidly upward into a hole straight from hell. The Winnebago backfired, causing both the turret and its target to quiver imperceptibly. The diesel regurgitation was so loud that the sleigh master was certain the damned cannon had been discharged.

"Is that thing real?" he asked Helly, meaning the barrel.

"Of course it's real, you fool!" Helgayarn replied. "It can shoot a shell over two miles or more! This close it could vaporize you!"

Again Santos reviewed the monstrosity before him, not only the obscenity of the oily barrel itself, but the entire malignant hunk of scrap metal to which it was attached. "How'd you ever get it off the ground?"

"We fed some magic dust into the engine's air intake," replied Helgayarn. "She took off like a rocket!"

Santos offered up an appreciative whistle as he regarded the monstrosity while thinking back to ages past and the great battle with Rabakami. "We could've used it back in the day!" he said matter-of-factly. "Had I one of these babies back when I had my garden then we might not be standing here today!" He paused for a moment, a puzzled frown displayed upon his face. "If it was such an easy matter to take a step or two forward into time in order to retrieve this then why did you wait so long and moreover, why show up with it now?"

Helgayarn eyed him darkly. Who had this old sod grown into that he now had the temerity to question the what's and how's of why they did anything?

"It's a few simple steps from here, dimwitted one," she replied, "as it's only a few years down the road. But from those mad days in Mesozoic Mesopotamia it's much more than a simple step or two—it's a marathon of century upon century both there and back, and at the time was hardly worth our while. Besides, given the primitive conditions back then, we thought such an indulgence to be a bit excessive. Even for us!"

"Has it got a magic well?" as Santos.

"A what?"

THE CHRISTMAS RABBIT

"A magic well. You know, unlimited storage capacity for stowing packages, bundles, and the like!"

"We're not pizza deliverymen," replied Helgayarn. "And we don't work for Dominoes!"

"Too bad," replied the sleigh master wistfully. "It's been ages since I had a cheese pizza! The best the Mrs. can do is krill cakes in tomato sauce with a bit of melted provolone. What I wouldn't give for a slice of pepperoni—"

"Be quiet, you dolt!" Helgayarn snapped. "We didn't come here to feed you, but to feed upon you! Every dog has his day and today's yours sonny! Yours and the rabbit's—speaking of which, where is the little fur ball?"

Santos looked up at the turret innocently. "There are no hares here," he replied. "Never have been."

"Liar!" screeched Helgayarn. "We heard those two," she said, pointing to Slim and Jim, "say that one," pointing at Sand Toes, "was currently housing a hare and that moreover the hare being hosted was a little hellion! If that doesn't describe Jack Rabbit or one of his descendants then you tell me, what does?"

"It sure sounds like him," Santos admitted, "but as you can see," he continued, indicating the immediate area about him, "the hare's not here!"

Helgayarn looked about her. If the hare was hereabouts then he was certainly well hidden. She'd deal with him later. "So what's it to be, then?" she asked. "I'm feeling magnanimous! Would you prefer death by dismemberment or disembowelment?"

Santos uttered a weak laugh. "G-good joke, my ladies," he stammered. "But who'll deliver the presents?"

"Don't worry about that, slick," said Brunnhilde, sticking her head out of the hatch. "No one pays much attention to that stuff anymore and for those who do—we've a million imposters all dressed in red suits and waiting in shopping malls, to service 'em! No one really believes it's you anyway—even when it is! So they'll keep buying their kiddies presents, all the while claiming that they're from you and in doing so, continue to drive up the profits of those companies engaged in the manufacturing! We have stock in a lot of 'em you know, and maybe this year at long last, we'll finally recoup our losses from the Great Race! So you see, you've outlived your usefulness. You and all of your children!" Betty popped her head out of the hatch, and together The Powers That Be eyed the crowd menacingly. Revenge long anticipated, was often the sweetest.

"But these aren't my children," Santos replied. "Sure, the wild-eyed one looks like Laddie as do many of 'em, but Junior and Laddie were lost long ago and ain't never been found."

"They have the family look," Helgayarn replied sardonically, "they'll do. Your genes are pretty recessive, and the pool don't look like it's spread much!"

"We Santoses were never ones to go mixing it up much with outsiders," the sleigh master proudly replied. "We stick together—through thick and thin!"

"Dawes," someone in the crowd shouted. "We all be Dawes!" The sleigh master offered the interloper a sour stare. Now was not the time for young children to be putting themselves forward. "What about them?" the sleigh master asked, pointing to the Apaches. "Surely one look at them is enough to convince you that we're not related."

"Eyewitnesses," Helgayarn replied. "Can't have any."

"We're Apache!" cried Horse's Head. "Nobody'd believe us!"

Horse's Head knew well enough who these three were despite never having had the misfortune of actually meeting them. Everyone in his little band, from Geromino, aka Horse Feathers, on down to his uncle Horsin' Around and himself, had on their tepees, which they carried folded up on the floors of their sidecars when they traveled, rough paintings and silhouettes done in gray charcoals and dull earth tones, depicting The Powers That Be. All of them smudged and sooty, each representation, described as they were upon the tent flaps of every tepee, were purposely vague, as Apache legend held the trio to be too ugly to actually depict. Now seeing them face-to-face, Horse's Head was forced to admit that his Apache holdings weren't the half of it and that pictures weren't necessarily worth a thousand words or even one or two, while at the same time hypothesizing to himself that should their outward appearances and the looks displayed upon their

THE CHRISTMAS RABBIT

faces in any way portend or presage the trio's apparent demeanor and deportment with regard to those gathered before them, then he and his, as well as the Irish and everyone else, caribou included, were up to their breadbaskets in Buffalo BMs, which were about to leak through the tent flap of the tepee door. Every Apache, whether cast out or not, learned early on in life who these three were, where Witch Valley was, and why they should stay away from it. Apache legends spoke of a paradise in these lands before the arrival of those three and all Apache present knew that it was they who ratted out Geronimo to their ancestor, Horse Feathers, encouraging him to steal the map while cursing him at the same time with the promise that it would cause him to die a rich man. And it did. It was only after he dropped dead while wealthy that Great-Granddaddy Dawe robbed the corpse. So none of the Apache were predisposed toward trusting in the goodwill of The Powers That Be and all of them, from the bravest of braves to the most skittish of squaws both nervous and jumpy, out of desperation and an overwhelming desire to be rid once and for all of unwanted squatters who were nevertheless there first, would have tried ganging up on them and forcing the issue but for the hope held out that on some far flung day the white man in his foolishness, would stumble upon the trio and thereby get repaid in full for all his sins committed against their people. But it hadn't happened until now and as luck would have it sin like misery, loved company. Horses' Head sought furiously after a logical argument that would spare their skins.

"Apache speak with forked tongue," he added as a last resort. "Everyone will say so!"

"Not if there's no one to say it to," replied Helgayarn with a self-satisfied smug. "And there'll be no one to say it to if there's no one to say so in the first place!"

"Hold yer guff!" cried Jim. "I dinna ken who ye are nae what ye want but I'll be assurin' ye we be nae kin o' that fat feller there!" He pointed at the sleigh master in order to be sure that his words were understood. "Though I'll admit t' a certain resemblance t' the chap, 'tis unlikely he's family as he's never made any o' the reunions nor Society meetin's! Still, the sod saved Lauren, he did, and we all be obliged t' him."

"Well Lahteedah!" Helgayarn screeched from the turret.

"Yes?" asked Larry and Lauren in unison.

From the top of the tank Helgayarn turned her regard until it came to rest upon father and daughter. Here were the two in whom all this unlikely history converged. It was as plain as her proboscis that the father was certainly a son of Santos who, over the long passage of years had gone gray through and through and in addition to his silver locks now sported as well a crisscross grid of broken veins and capillaries displayed prominently upon his nose and across his cheeks. The results of both wind and weather—and a good bottle of Scotch, no doubt tucked away in the folds of one of his many pockets. But it was in the eyes and in the look of befuddlement displayed proudly upon his features that Sand Toes most readily resembled his erstwhile sire. The girl, on the other hand, was the spitting image of a long-lost cousin still caught up in the innocence of youth and the vigor of childhood, where the repetition of each day, one after the other as they plodded ever onward toward eternity, brought with them their own novelties nevertheless, and a sense of wonder as one experienced the new and unique. The trio were jealous of her and somewhat leery as well for there was power in the sense of awe which emanated from her. It was the foundation upon which faith was built, and even they knew that with faith the size of a mustard seed, one could move mountains! They wanted no Everests dropped upon them when they weren't looking and so maintained close watch on her. Of course it went without saying that her Da, being the madman he was, bore intense scrutiny anyway. It was a certainty that the fruit didn't fall too far from the bole of this familial tree and the daughter, although seemingly unprepossessing, was a Dawe nevertheless and a Santos all the more and therefore was unconventional and almost certainly unpredictable. Helgayarn remained unconvinced as to her relative harmlessness despite being wrapped tight in a blanket and under her thumb. Taking all of these matters under consideration while evaluating a threat was thirsty work.

THE CHRISTMAS RABBIT

"Bunny," she said offhandedly, "go below will you, and pull me a soda out of the fridge."

Bunny offered her sister a sour glance. "Do you want a Coke or Pepsi?" she asked derisively.

"I'll have an Un-Cola," Helly replied, "on the rocks with a twist of lime!"

Brunnhilde disappeared to do as she was told.

"So where's the rabbit?" Helgayarn demanded of the two.

Father and daughter looked to each other before replying.

"Jack's been lost in the bottom of yon pit," replied Sand Toes. "He was helpin' me dig a trap for this this fella here," he continued, pointing at Santos, "when the desert floor gave way, cavin' in and sendin' him to his doom and down in the depths!"

"Jack, you say?" inquired an incredulous Helgayarn. "You claim his name was Jack?"

"I didn'a claim anythin'," replied Sand Toes. "'Twas him did all the claimin'! Truth be told, I believed less than half o' what he said."

Helgayarn gave an uneasy appraisal of the immediate area, as if expecting the rabbit to pop up from behind a rock.

"What are the odds, do you suppose," she asked no one in particular, "that after all these years and all this waiting, the receptacle upon whom we wish to pour out our vengeance should, like his ancestor of old, be named Jack? How fitting. Too bad the little leporide isn't here to settle up with! I call his one-way plummet into the bottomless pit a last ditch attempt to get off cheaply!" She looked about her again in a self-satisfied manner. "There'll always be more of his kind where he came from," she continued. "And more than enough opportunity for us to settle the 'rabbit issue' at a later date. That says nothing, however, for the rest of you!" She gathered the forces, incited the mumbo jumbo and invoked the charms of making while her two sisters, including Brunnhilde with 7 Up in hand, joined in her chanting. They were casting a lethargic spell upon those standing before them, a bit of voodoo for their would-be victims, designed to make 'em more manageable prior to sacrifice by simply putting them to sleep. A siren song sung high and sweet—which was no mean feat as Helgayarn and Brunnhilde still had those frogs stuck in their throats from those bad old days back in Judea.

Snow White's Apple, they collectively called the curse, having used it once long ago to poison a piece of fruit they'd rendered unto a certain princess…a charming gambit on their parts to grab more power which was ultimately foiled by a pain-in-the-ass prince, who with a kiss, ruined all their plans. Apache and Irishman alike, heavy lidded and nodding where they stood, began dropping like flies as the siren song held sway, causing them to swoon and fall away into a dead faint upon the desert floor. Only Lauren, too done up on dust to be done in by anything else, managed to retain consciousness, and being injured, the continued awareness of her current predicament availed her little.

After the *Snow White's Apple* was finally sung and the last note sounded, Irishman and Apache alike began to awake only to discover that they'd all been moved to one side by Hephaestus, Pixie, and Dixie. They saw as well that the sleigh master had been tied to a stake before them and that all their feet were currently glued to the desert floor.

CHAPTER IX
The Luck O' the Irish and Everyone Else

Jack didn't like it, not one bit, this marching into the lion's den unarmed, unaided, and leading the blind. They were as helpless as fish impaled upon hooks, resigned to the inevitable and offering no resistance as they were invariably reeled in. Walking toward what could well be their execution ground, Jack was reminded of death row inmates in high-security prisons as they trod meekly upon that last mile which led to the chamber or the chair. He saw displayed upon Larraine's countenance a haggard look of resigned acceptance that he imagined must paint the faces of those who made such journeys and was confident that such ambivalence clearly paraded itself upon his own features too.

Helgayarn, Brunnhilde, and Betty, about to exact their revenge upon those whom they'd captured, took note of the couple as they approached slowly from across the wasteland. Their vision, failing them somewhat in their later years, revealed to the trio what appeared to be a maiden, much in form and likeness to their lost cousin, the Shoe Lady, carrying on her shoulders an enemy of long-standing, as she approached.

"Well!" cried Helly gleefully, who thought they'd been robbed of the full measure of their revenge. "Fancy the two of you showing up!"

The gathering turned toward the direction in which she spoke, and Irishmen and Apache alike could not believe what their incredulous eyes revealed. Like a mirage rising majestically up from the desert floor, Larraine T. Dawe, a blank look in her eyes, appeared to the crowd as if conjured up from the very dust devils themselves.

Sand Toes knew himself to be less than sane. Nevertheless he stood stunned and stupefied as he watched the approach of his dearly departed. There was a wildness displayed upon her features as she stumbled forward which Larry, as he viewed her, deemed delightful. Other than that, she hadn't changed a day, had Larraine—despite being gone for nearly 730 of 'em. An uneasy thought suddenly occurred to him as he watched her approach. Was she just another mirage? A phantom with no substance, who would as likely fade from view as quickly as she'd materialized? Or even worse—suppose this Larraine was, in fact, the real deal, miraculously brought back from the dead only to find herself walking headlong into its clutches once again? Was it fair that fate and fortune should play her so fickle? Larry thought not and as Sand Toes of the Apaches, determined then and there to do something about it. He leaped to her defense and fell face down on the desert floor, forgetting that his feet were still glued to it.

As she looked with derision upon his fallen form any lingering doubts Helly still held regarding Larry's lineage vanished. The Great Sand Toes of the Apaches! Look at him lying there, forlorn and helpless!

Lauren, who from time to time had trouble bringing into clarity the hazy recollections of her dearly departed Ma, looked upon the approaching form of Larraine with wonder. Suddenly those recollections took shape and she saw approaching toward them a beloved face, which through grief and despair, she'd relegated to the cluttered closets of uneasy and bittersweet memory. Perusing such closets while stumbling across remembrances that memory haphazardly hung on its hangers often brought smiles to one's lips as one sorted through the closet in order to determine which memories would be saved, only to be recalled later and savored in the lonely seasons ahead, and which would ultimately be stored away in the disposal bin of one's subconscious where they were given up to goodwill like clothing that no longer fit. But such perusals brought with them pain as well, as one struggled with personal loss and failure. As a result such closets

THE CHRISTMAS RABBIT

were rarely ransacked, especially with the intention of cleaning them out, and often contained piles of jumbled and discarded recollections and retrospections, lying helter-skelter, one atop of the other and in a tangle, which needed to be sorted and sifted through in order to be made sense of. The memories blended, one with the other, as the details of each became fuzzy and unclear. Now however, Larraine's approaching form brought Lauren's memories into stark relief and the young girl cried a tear of joy, all her moisture disciplined body would allow.

Horse's Head, along with Horsin' Around and a whole host of Apaches, were agog with wonder at the vision displayed before them. They'd heard Lawrence prattle on, both often and loudly, about the miraculous visitations of his Irish *isdzán* lost in a landslide. To the Apaches those suffering under insanity, whether well regarded or otherwise, were nevertheless treated with respect, however grudgingly conferred, as that intrepid band of indigenous people held that such folk were touched by the Great Spirit. The touched saw things others couldn't and didn't want to and in that respect were much like the Mad Rabbits. To be sane nevertheless and seeing them regardless, was the biggest medicine of all, as those desert wayfarers who deemed such improbable visitations from so strange an apparition as a supposedly dead woman brought back to life, to be messengers sent from the Great Spirit himself.

The Irish, viewing their cousin with a rabbit upon her shoulders, merely determined that they'd drunk far too heavily the evening before from an apparently bottomless bottle of unblended rye and were now suffering under the delusions and DT's brought about by overimbibing in cheap liquor. After all, James Stewart, who was also Irish, often saw and spoke to his little leporide friend Harvey after diving deep in the bottle, or so said Turner Classic Movies.

Pixie and Dixie, two elves noted for their pragmatism and practicality, along with Hephaestus who was not noted for much of anything since turning lead into gold was such a carefully guarded secret, viewed the scene unfolding before them as the foregone conclusion to a tawdry four-act play, which ran overlong but whose ending had finally been staged and blocked, while Rudolph Valentino and the injured caribou lying alongside him interpreted the unlooked for appearance of Larraine as the omen it rightly was...a sure sign that the pellets were about to hit the wind.

Helgayarn chose to address the rabbit first. "We're glad you could make it," she said. "And I'm elated that not only are you named after that infamous rabbit of old but moreover, look like him too!"

"That so?" Jack asked casually, pretending indifference. There was no point in hiding the full range of his abilities any longer from either the Irishmen or the Apaches. And as to look-alikes, he hadn't a clue as to what the original Jack looked like. There were no pictures nor illustrations in the bibliographies and Our Rabbit of Later Days had always assumed that to the two-legged, one rabbit looked pretty much like another.

"That's so," agreed Helgayarn, "and the woman you're riding is our cousin, the Shoe Lady, sure'n begorrah—or our eyes ain't what they used to be!"

"Yah!"

"What have you to say for yourself woman, and where have you been hiding?"

Larraine wasn't sure of her response. It would aid her in forming a reply, she knew, if she were able to see the whites of her accuser's eyes and thereby judge for herself Helgayarn's demeanor. But being blind, her peepers were superfluous and what little she was able to perceive by employing Jack's Hareagei, appeared in her mind's eye as vague and fuzzy shadows superimposed upon a field of white. Therefore any clue regarding the mood of the three antagonists before her and this one in particular, would have to be gleaned through aural means, which meant making use of her ears. How she wished at that moment, for a pair like Jack's so she might turn her handicap into an advantage! "I'm sure we've never met before," replied Larraine, "as I've been living in a hole for the past two years. And I'm willing to forego introductions even now if you'll just let me leave with my family!"

"Leave?" asked Helgayarn with a cruel laugh. "Why the party's just getting started, my dear, and has been a long time in the planning! Surely you remember those days back in the Old Forest and the

THE CHRISTMAS RABBIT

Great Race, when you placed that sneaky wager and robbed us of our rightful winnings? You've much to answer for, darling."

Larraine had no idea of what the old hag was so on about but clearly heard the menace in the voice before her and prayed that the plan she'd been forced to concoct upon the spur of the moment had its merits and would therefore be capable of being enacted. In her nervousness she fell back on her much-despised brogue. "I dinna gamble," she replied. "And sartainly nae when the odds seem so stacked agin' me!"

"You're aversion to wagering," Helgayarn shot back, "certainly didn't deter you on Race Day!"

"Ye hae me confused wi' another," replied Larraine. "I dinna go in fer races and those who run 'em! I'm a homebody am I, or was, up until two years ago. And that's all I be lookin' fer in this here short life—t' return home and be tendin' to me beloved bodies whom fate has seen fit t' be keepin' me apart from these last two years. Let me and me family go. Let me take me husband, me wee bairn, all me weird family, and I suppose the Apaches too, and go home. I promise we will na' trouble ye further. Ye hae me word upon it!"

"Nae bloody likely!" replied Helgayarn shrewishly. "Here is where you are and here is where you'll stay!"

"Yah!"

Larraine shrugged her shoulders and had Jack steer her over toward her husband and daughter. She could see Lauren's shadow wrapped in a blanket as plain as if it were daylight, but for her own life couldn't see her daughter's face. It was likewise with Larry who having picked himself up, stood rooted to the ground beside her.

"Me love," he whispered hesitantly, "be ye really me long-lost Larraine or be ye just another phantom sprung up and sprouted from the desert floor?"

Larraine offered her pet madman a reassuring smile. "It's really me," she replied, "although sure n' begorrah after two years o' crawlin' through caves and tunnels, I must indeed look a sight!"

Sand Toes eyed his wife lovingly, not caring really what she looked like but happy nevertheless to be simply reunited, however brief that reunion might prove itself to be. Still she'd implied a question and Larraine had always been one for having her questions answered.

"Ye could use a bath," he said with a laugh, "and yer hair need's combin'. A little 'Secret,' strong enough fer a man but made fer a woman, wouldn'a hurt either!"

Larraine offered up a chuckle of her own. She must indeed look a sight! Would she ever be able to see so for herself?

Larry could sense the doubt residing deep within her. "Yer eyes," he said, "are as beautiful as ever, but appear a bit dim. Are ye all right?"

"I'm blind, my love," she replied. "As blind as the bats which once inhabited our belfry before I swept 'em out! I be makin' use o' Jack's eyes now in a manner o' speakin' and they be leadin' me where I need t' be goin'."

Larry eyed the rabbit on her shoulders doubtfully. The little leporide's eyes appeared to be in their own sockets and not hers so how she was making use of them was beyond him. Still if Larraine said it was so, then so it must be, but Sand Toes still had his reservations. "That all be well and good," he whispered in reply, "but dinna be trustin' the wee beastie too far. I nae be too sure whether he be a chicken or a rabbit despite his claims!"

Larraine offered up another small chuckle. "Relax, love," she replied. "Our friend here is true blue! 'Twas he what led me out o' the mine, and were it not fer him, I wouldn'a be standin' here today!"

"That be somethin', I suppose," Larry replied. "But I ask ye, what hae he done fer Sand Toes lately?"

"Am I not enough?" asked Larraine incredulously.

Larry looked about him cautiously. "Given our circumstances," he replied, "'tis barely scratchin' the surface! Ye may nae see it too well, Larraine dear, but we be up t' our necks in a sea o' cattle craps and the tide be fast movin' in! Bein' desert bred, I dinna swim too well!"

"Fret not," Larraine replied. "Jack and I have a plan."

"A plan? Fer this?"

"Well, more o' a spur-o'-the-moment improvisation than anythin' else—but we're sartain it'll work!"

THE CHRISTMAS RABBIT

Larry looked upon his dearly departed wife so recently returned, with utter disbelief. "Surely," said he, "ye will na' be puttin' our fate in the paws o' that little leporide?"

From atop her shoulders and seated behind her head, Jack offered the madman a scowl of his own. "Good to see you again too, bub," he replied, his voice dripping sarcasm, "and your daughter!" He looked about him, surveying the situation as it stood.

"Hey, Slomoe," he yelled out to the sleigh master, observing him tied to the stake. "Hey, Wideass! We rabbits always held that eventually you'd get your comeuppance! Hoist upon your own petard, are you? Looks to me as though you've chosen the wrong friends!"

From his stake, the erstwhile farmer offered up a tired reply. "I did not choose them," he said. "As I remember, they were chosen for me, and I was brought into this alliance against both my will and better judgment."

"You've never possessed much of either," replied Jack. "So don't be laying the blame upon anyone but yourself!"

"I don't," replied Santos. "And if I had it all to do over again, I'd let your ancestor walk away with his measly carrot and as many rutabagas as he could carry!"

"Is that an apology?" asked an incredulous Jack.

"It's merely an admission!" Santos replied shortly, his dander rising. "But it's as close to an apology as you're likely to get! Those were my vegetables and your ancestors should've offered up a trade!"

"Which brings us back to where all this foolishness started!" interjected Helgayarn. "For the price of a few lousy vegetables we find that the world has gone to hell in its own hand basket and that the two of you are largely to blame. The time has come to carry out judgment!"

"Yah!"

The trio lowered a Jacob's ladder attached to the top of the turret and climbed down the tank to confront their victims directly.

"Us?" replied the incredulous sleigh master. "What about you three?"

Helgayarn looked to both Brunnhilde and Betty who returned her gaze with equal puzzlement. Whatever in the world could Old

Slomoe be talking about? "We weren't the ones who elected to be so stingy with our carrots," Helgayarn replied, "nor were we the ones who confronted that stinginess with out-and-out theft of that which didn't belong to us."

"Yah!" cried Betty.

"Furthermore," continued Brunnhilde with her two sisters' approval, "we weren't the ones who engaged in interspecies warfare and moreover lost it! Your manhandling at the furry paws of those four-footed ruffians only served to turn an embarrassing situation into an untenable one! How were we supposed to rule over creation when those created have no clue regarding their proper place? You should've skinned the little leporide way back when. Had you done that, we'd all most likely be living out pleasant retirements by now!"

Lying upon the desert floor, weighted down by rocks and wrapped in her blanket of pain, Lauren chose that moment to let herself be heard.

"Who says you have the right to rule over anyone?" she asked. "Isn't that the sole province of the being to whom we all owe our existence?"

Helgayarn eyed the young lass dangerously. "It is written," she replied, "in many ancient books of wisdom, that children should be seen and not heard!"

"It is also written," countered Lauren, "in the greatest book of wisdom ever, that out of the mouths of babes—"

Helgayarn cut her off before she could finish. "Don't go throwing quotations at me, missy," she replied, "or I'll make you eat 'em while your parents watch!"

Up until this point, Helgayarn had been peeved but pleasant. Now she was furious. How dare that little imp throw quotations at her, and especially those of that long gone rabbi who's influence could still be felt throughout the world, turning many a would be sycophant away from them and toward himself. It seemed that after two thousand years, they were not done with the rabbi yet nor his inane teachings either.

THE CHRISTMAS RABBIT

"We made the world in our own image," Helgayarn lied. "We formed it out of the dust and clay and set it spinning upon its axis and in its orbit!"

"Yeah," muttered the sleigh master, "and we've all been paying for it ever since."

"What was that?"

"Nothing," replied Santos innocently. "Just clearing my throat."

Helgayarn, who still had a frog stuck in hers, offered him an evil frown. "Well see to it that you do so quietly," she replied, "and don't lend your voice, which lacks both wit and wisdom, to conversations that are beyond your ken. Just stand there silently, do as you're told, and accept your punishment!"

An uneasy silence spun out as everyone gave thought to what would come next. Everyone that is, but Lauren. She he hadn't finished making her point.

"What about the dust and the clay? Did you make that too?"

Brunnhilde looked at Helgayarn and shrugged. "We found it lying on the ground," she half-heartedly replied, "and then shaped it as we saw fit."

"So you had help," said Lauren, "and a source beyond yourselves who provided the raw materials."

"Eh?"

"You say you formed the world out of the dust and clay you found lying on the ground," Lauren continued, "but that implies the ground was already here and the ground itself is nothing more than dust and clay in one form or another—so the dust that you found was lying atop of more of the same when you found it. Is that right?"

Brunnhilde could barely nod.

"Therefore the bulk of it was here already by the time you three came waltzing on by. Is that also true?"

Helgayarn gave thought to saying otherwise but then reconsidered. What was the point? Bunny had already let the cat out of the bag by admitting that they'd actually stumbled upon this ball of wax rather than whipping it up from a whole lot of willpower alone coupled with a few *Let There Be Lights*. Thank the fates that they were way out here in the middle of nowhere and out of range of eavesdropping ears, which listening in might have overheard such a foolish slip of the tongue.

"You say for yourself that you found it—which means you clearly didn't make it and therefore cannot claim ownership over it or the right to rule it either!"

"Might makes right, little daughter," the big witch replied darkly. "Be careful in your criticisms, or you just might find that out!"

"I'm just a little girl," Lauren replied. "You wouldn't dare!"

Helgayarn pointed at the young lady's shoulder. "Obviously someone dared," she said. "If they can sling a dart or two, then who's to say we can't do likewise? And I assure you," she furthered while looking pointedly at the sleigh master, "that our darts come dipped in a poison more corrosive than any alkali or infusion that any of you are likely to whip up—be you Apache or Irish!"

"Oh." Lauren was at a loss. *You could lead a horse to water, but you couldn't make it drink. You could lead three crones through logic, but you couldn't make 'em think. You could play upon their conscience, but such consciences don't blink. When they're out to do you dirty, they'll drop you in the drink.* Where had that silly rhyme come from? she wondered. It sounded almost like an incantation. Lace it with a couple of Irish epithets, and you'd have a sure n' begorrah curse to cast! "I still don't believe that might makes right," she defiantly replied. "Wisdom—which is the one thing we seem to be lacking around here, is the only quality which bestows right, both in privilege and example."

"That's a bit wordy," replied Helgayarn. "Even for someone like you."

"She be a very bright lass," Sinead shouted out from the crowd, "and at the head o' her class!"

"Reviewing the gene pool," Helgayarn replied, "I find that nothing to brag about."

"That may be," Larraine spoke out. "But even so, such things are nae fer the likes o' ye three t' be castin dispersions at!" Just because ye be three Bitseachs and Cailleachs, dinna give ye the right t' be throwin' stones! I wanna take me man home now and me Little La too. Release 'em!"

"After it took us all these centuries to bring the lot of you together? Have you gotten into our magic dust, or what? You must be higher than Keith Richards on a five-day bender if you think that's gonna happen!"

"Is that why he's always so fuzzy in my glass?" asked Santos. "All this time I thought it was the London fog!"

Helgayarn rolled her eyes. "See what we've had to put up with throughout the long count of years? Is it any wonder that we want to expunge this fellow and his entire bloodline too? The world would be better off without him, presents or not—and that goes double for any descendant of Jack Rabbit!"

"Well, you can certainly kill us," replied Larraine. "Any bully with a burr in their behind is capable o' that! With the exception o' Jack and meself, and me Little La, lying here wounded, the three o' ye hae the rest o' us hogtied and glued to the floor! So a simple killin' be easy! But are the three o' ye woman enough, I wonder, t' be challengin' me to a duel?" Seated upon her shoulders, Jack whispered into Larraine's ear his uncertainties. "Are you sure about this?" he asked. "There's got to be another way of preserving our pelts."

"I be open t' suggestions," Larraine whispered back. "And furthermore, I'll be takin' 'em too—that is, if ye hae any."

Jack didn't and wasn't ashamed to admit it. *What would Jack Rabbit of old have done?* he wondered. Or his mate, Nutmeg? They'd squared off against these three before, Jack knew, and at least fought them to a draw, even though it cost the first Jack his very life to do so. Was that called for now? A sacrifice? Although he was beginning to warm to them, especially Larraine and surprisingly Old Slomoe too, still Jack didn't feel that he cared enough about them one way or the other to be laying his life down in their hour of need. He just might get through this ordeal yet, he reasoned, and in doing so, escape to make his rounds until he delivered his last egg. Then it would be a simple journey home to claim his seat on the council as The Mad Rabbit. He wouldn't need a koan contrasting one thing against another to claim his place in the bibliographies now. Simple survival in the face of these three was enough to earn him his spot. Then would come his life of luxury as he was referred to and made mention of by the might-have-been's who hadn't the juice to do what he'd done. They'd tell the trainees of his exploits while parading them before him to be handpicked and chosen or simply passed over in favor of some other rabbit who he deemed more worthy to carry on in his footsteps. All the while there'd be breeders by the bunch brought to his boudoir every evening and on Saturday afternoons too! As a rare returnee, the warren would make every effort to preserve his bloodline and in so doing, provide the necessary fodder for the continued fulfillment of the quest. Hares from here, there, and everywhere would seek him out, sitting at his feet and listening attentively as he imparted to them the wisdom he'd gathered while on his hellish road trip. Fathers would send their sons to him to be trained and mothers, their daughters. Whether or not he would actually train 'em or simply break 'em in, Jack had no idea as yet. But he was looking forward to dealing with the conundrum. None of that would happen however if he foolishly lost his life. Gone, and soon-to-be-forgotten is all he'd ever amount to if he died now. The rabbi of old might well be remembered for his self-sacrifice but Jack was smart enough to realize that the last thing he was, was the rabbi. Jack wasn't even Jewish and held himself, in the face of these three, to be more of an agnostic than anything else. It wasn't that he was an out-an-out atheist but in the trio before him he saw only that which served to further his doubts. What god, if any, would allow these three to go on as long as they had while causing as much misery as they did? Maybe there was no god. Maybe they were all placed here by blind luck and a cosmic roll of the dice, which had they turned up threes instead of sevens, would have changed matters entirely.

"Don't you believe it, Jack," said Lauren from her blanket. "The very fact that you're here and talking tells me that there must be a god somewhere." Jack looked down at her in surprise. "Are you reading my thoughts?" he asked.

"No," she replied. Just scenting your pheromones, which are as plain as the nose on your face. That magic dust must've heightened my senses! I swear that I could taste light or see music if they were paraded before me. The dust seems to have endowed me with knowing a thing or two without actually being aware of 'em."

Jack offered her a keen appraisal. "To not know a thing," he replied, "is to know it completely."

"Really," replied Lauren. "Such reasoning sounds rather convoluted and circular, if you ask me." No one did.

On the far side of Santos, Helgayarn, Brunnhilde, and Betty were triangulated in another of their infamous huddles as they considered Larraine and her challenge. What kind of contest could a blind Irishwoman hope to win? Was this a trick or merely an act of last minute desperation? Helgayarn looked up from their huddle to confront Larraine. "Why should we agree to your challenge," she asked. "What have we to gain by answering it, eh? And what trick do you have up your sleeve, another rabbit?"

"I nae be wearin' sleeves," Larraine replied while displaying her bare arms for all to see. And the only rabbit I be sportin' 'tis the one on me shoulder. As t' why ye should accept me challenge, well, the reasons should be obvious. If ye simply kill us then ye prove yerselves t' be nae but bullies. If however, ye accept me challenge and defeat me on me own terms, then ye be regarded as fair champions by all and can do with us as ye please!"

"We can do with you as we please already," assured Helgayarn. "And we don't need your approval to do it."

"True enough," replied Larraine. "But if ye be afraid t' meet me challenge, then I say yer be nothin' but a flock o' chickens!"

Helgayarn's demeanor darkened even further as she gave thought to her antagonist's challenge. No one had dared call her a chicken since a long-ago rooster had last the temerity to do so. That had been ages past and the clucker had been strutting around as a turkey ever since, gobbling up what little sympathy he could find in a world that had an underabundance of it. Now along comes this woman with the same kind of attitude and giving them guff! They'd accept her challenge then and show her a thing or two. They might be old and decrepit but they had ages of experience to bring to bear. Larraine was the Shoe Lady's lookalike but not the Shoe Lady herself. They had nothing to fear from her!

"We accept your challenge," replied Helgayarn. "State your contest, and name your terms!"

Brunnhilde pulled the senior witch aside. "Do you think that wise," she asked, "to be accepting blindly, terms and conditions which we know nothing about?"

Helgayarn laughed. "C'mon, Bunny," she condescendingly replied, "this is a mere mortal standing before us! How much of a threat can she be?"

Brunnhilde thought back to days of old. "Rabbakami was mortal," she replied, "and being so, nearly proved our undoing!"

"Oh, you do go on about that Rabbakami, don't you?" Helgayarn retorted. "We had a bad day, that's all. Even we're allowed to have one every millennium or so! Trust me, if that little leporide were here today we'd make him eat his own pellets—and this one before us is no Rabbakami!"

"And the rabbi?" Brunnhilde insisted. "What about him? He almost got our goat as well, and could've had it if he'd really wanted it. There was never any doubt about who held the upper hand in that encounter! What about him?"

"I refuse to talk about the rabbi," replied Helgayarn, "and what, if anything, might have happened that day!"

"Very well then," replied Brunnhilde, "but if we find ourselves up a creek once again and with our necks in a sling, don't say I didn't give you fair warning!"

Helgayarn offered her sister a tired sigh. "Bunny," she replied, "the Irish woman is just that—an Irish woman. She's no threat to us."

"Then why accept her challenge," asked Brunnhilde. "Why not just kill her and the rest of 'em and be done with it?"

"Because it pleases me to do so," Helgayarn replied. "It's been a centuries since we've had a good laugh at someone else's expense! I'm tired of taking life so seriously! Let's have some fun!" It was true, living as they did out here in the wastelands, there'd been very little fun to be had of late, whether at their own expense or somebody else's. Surely a little skylarking on their part, which could only end in death for one and all whether the trio won or not, wouldn't amount to anything more than a bit of harmless fun at the expense of others.

THE CHRISTMAS RABBIT

"Okay," replied Brunnhilde, "let's hear the lady's terms!"

"Yah!"

They broke from their huddle to confront their would-be challenger. "How can you duel," asked Helgayarn, "when you can't see three feet in front of your face?"

"Leave me t' worry about that," replied Larraine. "You'd do well to look out for yourselves!"

"Which of us was it that you had in mind to challenge?" asked Helgayarn. "And what are the rules of the joust?"

"You misunderstand me," replied Larraine. "I dinna challenge just any one o' ye! I wanna piece o' all three o' yer bloomin' arses! As to rules, why they be simple enough. Last one standing wins. Should that be one o' you three, then do with us as ye will. But should I defeat ye, then ye have t' let us all go, and moreover, release the rabbit and the fat man from the sentence ye've imposed upon 'em and let the wee folk go too!"

"It seems," Helgayarn replied, "that should you win then you get everything. But should we win, why we only end up with what we already have. Sorry love, but you'll have to do better than that!" Larraine was at a loss. It wasn't likely that she'd win this contest anyway but she'd certainly lose everything she had if she couldn't get the trio to pony up. The sticking point however, had been succinctly stated. Other than themselves the captives had no further enticement with which to persuade them.

"What is it that ye want?" asked Larraine. "What could we possibly hae that would be o' any use to the likes o' you three?"

Helgayarn made a big show of considering her reply. There wasn't much these people had other than their own lives, which would be of any value to her. Their youth she could never hope to recapture no matter how many spells and charms of making she invoked in order to do so. Their ties of friendship and family held no value for her while their ancestries and particular pedigrees, should she decide to absorb them, could well prove themselves a burden that she'd come to regret being saddled with. What then was there to entice her into accepting this challenge? She considered the crowd before her. Who they were and what drove them to be here. Irish and Apache alike, they had one thing in common.

"Wager your gold against your lives," she replied, "and we'll accept your challenge!"

Larraine was taken aback. "We have nae gold," she replied. "Though we've searched it out for years, we've nary a nugget t' show fer our efforts."

"Then this conversation is pointless," replied Helgayarn, "and we should just be about our business by killing you and having done with it. We've other folk to barge in on and befuddle, you know. We can't be wasting precious time on the likes of you without some surety of recompense!"

She began to incite the incantations, mumble the mumbo jumbo, and gather the forces, with her sisters joining the effort. The skies, already dark with the passing storm, grew inky black, blotting out the few stars whose beams were capable of penetrating the cumuli passing overhead. The wind picked up, howling furiously. It tore at the clothing of the captives, causing all to shiver and many to catch cold. Lightning flashed in the skies overhead. Thunder boomed and the earth beneath their feet quivered in uneasy anticipation of the horror to come.

Hephaestus gathered Pixie and Dixie to him. For too long now they and all their brethren had been pressed and coerced into serving both a master and three mistresses whom they'd just as well be rid of as not. If the trio had their way, exterminating both the Irish and the Indians, then surely in an effort to quell and silence any witnesses they'd come gunning for them once they'd completed their dirty work. Having slaughtered Santos and then themselves, Helgayarn, Brunnhilde, and Betty would soon come to see that there remained no use for the other elves either and would head directly to the North Pole where they'd conclude their slaughter by wiping out the rest of their elvish family. Hephaestus couldn't allow that. Although powerless to confront the trio directly it was nevertheless obvious to him that the Irishwoman, be she insane in her challenge or not, had some sort of plan by which she hoped to defeat The Powers That Be. But the trio weren't biting as she had no reasonable wager to place upon the table with which to entice them. Perhaps then, here was where he could help. In aiding her should she win, he'd be rescuing his own who laboring away in the Northlands, were blissfully unaware of the danger that would inevitably descend upon them.

"I'll put up the gold," he replied. "Although I'll need me a forge and some lead in order to do so."

"You?" replied Helgayarn. "What gold have you got, and where is it hidden?"

"In here," replied Hephaestus, pointing to his head. "And here," he said again, this time pointing to his heart. "I know the secret of turning lead into gold. It's an old elvish trick and one, by the way, in which I excel!"

The queen bee eyed him savagely, the muscles in her throat convulsing and constricting as she gave thought to the implications of the elf's last statement. A Power That Be, although a prestigious position, does not pay well, there being no one above you from whom to expect a paycheck. You have to eke out a living on tribute and taxes while your subjects continually look for ways to cheat you. There are no 401(k) plans and no health benefits other than those you pay for yourself and through the long count of years Repressive's premiums hadn't gotten any cheaper. Turning lead into gold was a bit of wanga worth its own weight in the substance it purported to perpetuate! Had she known about such power, she'd have traded all her other magic for it ages ago! "All these years," she stammered, barely keeping the frog in her throat from croaking insanely, "we've had you hidden away, working for and spying upon Old Slomoe here, and you could do that? Why didn't you tell us and more importantly, who gave you such skill?"

Hephaestus looked dumfounded. "I didn't tell you," he replied, "because I thought you already knew."

"Knew? You speak as though we'd endowed you with such gifts!"

Again Hephaestus looked nonplussed. "Didn't you?"

"I'm most certain," Helgayarn replied, "that we in fact did not!" She looked to her companions for confirmation and both Brunnhilde and Betty nodded their support.

"Well then," the old elf reasoned, "it must be another of your infamous unanticipated results like tides and seasons!"

The look of fury painted upon Helgayarn's features deepened even further till the thunderclouds upon her brow rivaled those of the passing storm.

"Our interventions," she replied in a voice that rained ice, "never produce unexpected consequences. The outcomes are always foregone conclusions, immune from fallout and impervious to the domino effect!"

Hephaestus was immediately reminded of migraines—both in latitude and longitude as well as Ice Ages and the whole host of other ecological and social miscues, backfires, blunders, and bungles that had been fostered upon all folk, both two- and four-footed, which could be laid at the feet of The Powers That Be. The list was vast beyond determining even without the inclusion of rabbits and farmers, and Hephaestus thought to point that out to the trio but wisely decided to keep his criticisms to himself. What was the use of such analytical observation anyway? It would only add fuel to a fire, which in the elf's opinion, was burning dangerously out of control already. He offered the trio a half-hearted shrug. "What can I say then?" he asked. "I've had the ability to do so ever since you transformed me, so either the credit for such skill gets laid at your feet or we agree that someone more powerful than you slipped a mickey into one of your spells when you weren't looking!"

"Well, no one certainly did that," Brunnhilde interjected diffidently.

"Whatever you ladies say," the elf replied contritely. "But whether from you or from some other, I stand ready now to put my skills to use in order to accommodate your demand. Are you willing that I should do so?"

Again the trio triangulated in order to hash the offer out. Brunnhilde was of a mind to forego the whole thing with Betty nodding her support while "yahing" out her agreement. Things were already getting out of hand and they'd only arrived less than an hour ago. Who knew the elf had such skill? Having missed or overlooked something so potentially significant, did it not stand to reason that they'd misjudged or failed to grasp other pertinent aspects of their plan too? Although she was loathe to admit it, bitter experience had taught Brunnhilde that such omissions on their parts were to be regarded as more than mere probabilities and treated instead as near certainties. Far better, she knew, to just pass final judgment as originally planned and then have the elf whip 'em up a whole mountain of gold afterward. They could settle down on top of it to a pleasant and peaceful retirement. The world really didn't want them anymore and in fact barely remembered them, relegating their memories whether individually or collectively, to the confines of poorly related children's tales and nursery rhymes, which were often misquoted and almost certainly told from a prejudiced point of view wherein alone or together, the trio were invariably cast as villains. It seemed that no good deed went unpunished. Take the whole Snow White fiasco and that of Sleeping Beauty too—there were two high-hatted and heavy-handed debutantes, both patronizing and condescending, who were snooty, snotty, and snobbish in their day-to-day dealings with others, especially the servants, who tried their best to please them. And that Cinderella—what a bitch she'd been! Snowy and Sleepy got no more than they deserved when Helgayarn poisoned first the one and then Brunnhilde the other; and less than they earned when both were respectively awakened by their Prince Charming's who, though children's stories tended to whitewash such things, were nothing more than over sexed teenage delinquents giving vent to their hormones. Where were their parents to enforce a little discipline and put a halt to such behavior? Same thing for Cinderella wherein this instance, she and Betty were cast as the evil stepsisters and Helgayarn as the diabolical stepmom. Again, a totally unfair portrayal. Cindy had been a lazy good-for-nothing peasant. A worse homemaker than even Mrs. Santos herself, The Powers That Be thought to be gracious and try her out as their domestic nevertheless. Another of their infamous mistakes. Cinderella could neither cook nor clean worth a fig, had her hand constantly in the household cookie jar, was forever mixing opposing potions and elixirs such as *Filet Of Drought* and *Tidal Wave Tea*, and was a general all around good-for-nothing who just happened to look good when she got gussied up. So what happens? Along comes some interfereing busybody claiming to be a Power That Be's of one kind or another, supposedly enthroned on the far side of creation wherever that was, and who happened to be passing through their neck of the woods while on vacation, or so she told Cindy when she heard the scullery maid whining to herself in the kitchen. So the interfering old biddy, with the nerve to call herself "Fairy Godmother" no less, stuck her nose in where it didn't belong, falling for the spew of cattle craps issuing forth from the forked tongue of the prevaricating Cinderella, as she told lie after lie, heaping exaggeration atop exaggeration, while describing the pitiful conditions of her predicament and plight. So Helgayarn, Betty, and herself, knowing she was getting too big for her own britches, sought to knock Cindy down a peg or two by reversing the spells of that interfering busybody and turning her coachmen back into mice and her carriage into a pumpkin as Cindy returned from the royal dance. Things would have gone on fine from there but being too dumb to tie her own shoelaces, Cindy managed to lose one of her glass slippers at the ball in the confusion of her hurried departure and her prince, who was not as charming as subsequent retellings of the tale made him out to be, used the footwear to track her down. She ended up living out the remainder of her days as a princess and finally a queen, haughtily issuing orders from the seat of power where she spent her days eating chocolate covered cherries and other dainties until she put on so much weight that it became impossible for her to get off the throne. From her first chocolate cherry on down to the day of her much desired demise, her subjects, when speaking of her behind her back, dropped the sobriquet of Cinderella and took to calling her Boxcar Bertha instead as her can grew to the size of a caboose and the gas produced from an overindulgence in fatty foods caused her to backfire like a runaway locomotive. So it was best, Brunnhilde knew, to settle this whole issue quietly and without a lot of fanfare as such contentious encounters, when related down through the ages, were always told from the wrong point of view. But Helly would never go for it. She'd as much as said so already, demanding of the Irishwoman that she state her terms. Brunnhilde checked her pockets in order to assure that she had in her possession,

THE CHRISTMAS RABBIT

her collapsible paddle and her pair of water wings, should they once again, through Helgayarn's obstinacy, find themselves up that fabled river and caught in a cross-current.

"Heat up your forge and make with the Mumbo," demanded Helgayarn. "Ten tons of gold against an eternity of terror and torture that will last ten times their own lifetimes—and only if they're lucky!" Hephaestus tried to puzzle out that bit of hoodoo for himself but was having very little luck doing so. How did one measure out an individual lifetime, which was different for everyone, and then times it by ten in order to arrive at a uniform figure that would fit the overall parameters of those upon whom it was fostered? It sounded like fiddlesticks but he busied himself with his task nevertheless, all the while hoping that the Irishwoman had a lucky rabbit's foot hidden in her bra, as she'd already pointed out her short sleeves.

It took freeing up the Irishmen and ungluing their feet from the floor while still holding their loved ones captive, to get the job done. Leading his brethren who followed behind him in their various Land Rovers, after having a quick word in private with Larraine, Jim guided the men of the Society back to the desert outpost which served as their town to gather up all of the lead pipe and sheeting they could lay hands to and loading it into their Land Rovers, beat a hasty return to where their siblings were being held prisoner.

During their brief absence the Witches deigned to release the sleigh master from the stake, allowing him to join his descendants and the Apaches, as they stood glued to the floor and against the wall of the overhanging butte. The captives complained of hunger and Helgayarn graciously allowed them enough freedom of movement to go to their saddlebags and other transportable storage devices in order to obtain what food they could. Even Helgayarn believed that the condemned were entitled to a last meal. Both Santos and Sand Toes were allowed to retrieve their dinner pails, each of which was enormous and both of which held a singular item peculiar to each. Great-grandfather and long-lost great-grandson so many times removed ended up sharing out of each other's bucket, as one provided the other a delicacy that only he, with the eating habits already cultivated, would ever think to pack for lunch. For Santos, the much sought after taste of Toadhouse Cookies was everything he'd dreamt it to be and determined to himself that as a last meal Toadhouses were certainly worthy of being the main course. Sand Toes found that seal blubber and krill tasted pretty much like old toad and leapin' lizard and having expected much more if not better, was thoroughly disappointed in the fare being offered to him under the guise of what Santos so euphemistically termed a "fair trade agreement."

"So what's the plan, darlin'?" he asked his wife as he stood chewing his seal blubber. "I dinna think I can be o' much help t' ye this time. It'll be ye, like it as nae, who'll be savin' me."

Larraine stood there, her daughter now cradled protectively in her arms, reunited with her family, surrounded by long-standing enemies and family relations while confronting the reality of not only two legendary figures out of fable and myth, but apparently three cailleachs as well, who'd set the two against each other and in doing so, made celebrities out of the pair while fading into obscurity themselves. The Irishwoman viewed these unlikely circumstances through the eyes of a rabbit who clearly held his own orbs in their sockets while at the same time clinging to her daughter in an effort to prevent her from floating away and did all of this without the slightest bit of incredulousness or amazement. It didn't strike her as odd that after two years of separation her husband appeared to regard her sudden return as a matter of course, to be treated cavalierly and as an item of secondary importance. Although he appeared as a cut-out before the blank page of her mind's eye, Larraine was aware nevertheless of the surprise and ecstatic elation confined within that wanted only to burst forth in joyful song. She sensed them because she could feel such emotions residing in her as well while threatening to erupt, and knew that Lawrence kept such passions sublimated in order to better focus his attentions, which were always on the verge of distraction, upon the precarious predicament in which they found themselves; while Lauren, poor dear, had put in a heck of an afternoon already, having been forced by circumstance to endure far more this day then most children had to put up with in a lifetime and so had justifiably fallen asleep and could therefore be excused her lack of exuberance. It didn't strike her as odd that any of this should be so. Despite her con-

THE CHRISTMAS RABBIT

cern regarding their immediate futures should they be determined by the three before her, Larraine viewed the unfolding circumstances as merely an ordinary aspect of an unusual life that was subject to the fickle whim of a peculiar pedigree whose stamp of strangeness almost guaranteed that those bearing it would find themselves so caught up. "Dinna worry," she replied. "The blind, following the blind, will lead themselves into the pit!"

It was a bit cryptic—even for Sand Toes. But the marvelous appearance of his long-lost wife only further served to cement his faith in the magical and miraculous so he decided to wait upon circumstance and see if it would reveal to him the answer to Larraine's perplexing puzzle.

The hours played themselves out uneasily and in near silence as both predators and victims awaited the return of Jim and the others. "I hope they won't be too much longer," Santos remarked to no one in particular, "otherwise we may have to call off Christmas entirely! We've lost almost the whole evening already and it looks as though we'll lose another, if not our lives too! But even if we should somehow be spared, I have a reputation to uphold as the guy who can get it done in a single night. I will not sully my good name by being so crass as to slide down someone's chimney on December 26th, a day late and dollars short!" He looked to his herd of wounded caribou. "As it is," he continued, "half the fleet is bruised and banged up and may be aerodynamically unable to attempt proper flight anyway. We might achieve airlift only to find once we do that we're incapable of landing while perpetually circling Mungo and chasing the sun until my caribou, dropping dead from exhaustion, fall from the sky, crashing and burning and dragging me and my sleigh down with them."

"I wouldn't worry too much about that fat man," replied Brunnhilde. "Once this farce of duels is over, your worries about late deliveries and crashing and burning will be permanently put to rest!"

Santos morosely munched on another of Larry's Toadhouses. Larraine, who hadn't eaten anything for the last two years that hadn't come out of a can, joined him in his lackluster repast. She carelessly took a cookie from Larry's bucket and without thought, popped it into her mouth. She grew as green as the reptiles from which it was made before spitting it back out in her hand. "Ugh," she said with disgust. "What are these, and who baked 'em?"

"Why they be yer famous Toadhouse Cookies," replied Sand Toes in an injured tone. "Since ye have nae been around to make 'em yerself, employin' yer secret recipie t' do so, I've had t' make 'em on me own, improvisin' here and there in order t' compensate fer unknown ingredients!

"They're Tollhouse cookies, not Toadhouse," Larraine long sufferingly replied, "and the unknown ingredient is chocolate chips, not diced frog!" She continued to stare at the ungainly lump resting uneasily in her hand. "Sorry, love," she continued, "but these are most certainly not my Tollhouses!

"But delicious nevertheless," replied the sleigh master. Larraine looked at him skeptically, unable to believe her ears or his taste buds. "What?" asked the sleigh master, noticing her regard. "Are they too pungent for you? You should try my wife's cooking! Her Haggis or Shark fin Soup. Now there's gamey eating for you! And gassy too!"

Larraine rolled her eyes. Jack took the break in conversation as an opportunity to question Brunnhilde. "If you kill us," he said to the junior sister regarding him from the other side of the now empty stake, "then you're left with the problem you've always had—no one to carry out your sentences and do your dirty work!"

Brunnhilde waved her hand in dismissal. "Don't worry about that," she replied nonchalantly. "There's always another over eager fat farmer to be had, whose willing to try his hand at sleigh mastery—and as to hares apparent, well there are plenty handy who would be willing to be heir to your great work. Let us hope we find one a little less rambunctious and more willing to be a team player! But no matter, folk don't go in much, for such things anymore, preferring to buy their own presents and paint their own eggs in order to avoid the unsavory truth about their children's mediocrity! You'll not be missed much or needed either!"

"You're wrong on both accounts," replied Jack. "And whatever rabbit you wrangle into doing this job, he will not be Jack Rabbit. What kind of qualifications will he have? Will he be able to guarantee deliveries? It takes preparation and the ability to lead! It takes

THE CHRISTMAS RABBIT

knowing your charges first hand by looking in on their day-to-day activities and evaluating them impartially. It takes experience and accountability—just like Jack Rabbit of Old!"

Helgayarn looked at the rabbit derisively. "I knew the original Jack Rabbit," she replied. "He was my friend," she lied, "serving under us willingly, and alongside us bravely, and you, sir, are no Jack Rabbit!"

"I come by the moniker honestly," the hare replied.

"You're a thief," Helgayarn replied icily, "from a long line of thieves! Therefore everything about you is tainted with dishonesty!"

Jacked offered her a sour appraisal. "Well," he replied, "I've known the three of you for just a little over an hour now and I'm sick of you already. You can't get more honest than that!"

Jack's remark infuriated the head honchette, but Helgayarn, knowing how this day would end, was willing to credit the humor contained in his last statement. "You're right," she laughed. "But don't worry—any lingering concerns that arise as a result of today's encounter and challenge will be addressed before sunup, I assure you."

"From what the bibliographies report," replied the rabbit, "nothing regarding the three of you can be assured other than the certainty that treating with you surely leads a poor soul from the frying pan into the fire!"

The Irishmen and Apaches looked on and listened in, with both greed and amazement. All knew the rabbit to be an enigma of some significance but never in their wildest dreams did they imagine him to be the Easter Bunny and moreover, gifted with ability to speak. Too bad, each thought, that they were reluctantly on the same side now and in the same boat, because such a creature would surely fetch a commanding price if sold down the river to some exotic animal trainer or traveling circus. But one could hardly do that to a comrade, especially if they stood with you toe-to-toe, in the face of certain death. Doing that, they realized, meant that certain considerations would have to be conceded to. Perhaps, thought many, instead of selling him down the river they could rent him out instead, from time to time and on a limited basis—guest appearances, birthday parties, and things of that nature. Surely that was a more proper and much fairer way of treating an erstwhile ally.

All gathered gave thought to these matters as the hours of waiting spun out, each in his or her own way, with no one agreeing entirely one way or the other with the opinion of the person next to them whether that individual made known his or her sentiments or not. Just after one am a line of headlights could be seen cresting the horizon and making its way toward them. It was Jim in his Land Rover, returning and leading the troops, now leaden with lead with which they hoped to purchase the succor of their loved ones and Apache acquaintances. The squadron of SUVs formed a serpentine line as they snaked across the desert floor, headlights flashing erratically in the night as the sports utilities jostled and bounced along the hardpack.

"Well," exclaimed Helgayarn, the surprise evident in her voice, "it would seem that your friends have come back for you! I had them pegged to turn tail and run. I thought that surely we'd have to track 'em all down later. How nice of them to join you in your just desserts and so save us the bother!"

"I wouldn't count my chickens before they're hatched," replied Jack. "It ain't over till the fat lady sings!"

Helgayarn offered the rabbit a smug smile. "Slomoe's wife," she laughingly replied, "has been detained at the Pole. There'll be no fat ladies singing here nor any skinny and underfed nuns under the influence of bad habits, humming Gregorian Chants either! Your ducks are in a row and you're about to be sauce for the goose—or so says the gander!"

Jack couldn't help but notice the Freudian slip and, since his behind was about to be handed to him anyway, could not resist the urge to comment upon it.

"Gander?" he asked, referring to gender. "Aren't ganders male?"

"What of it?" Helgayarn asked dangerously. "What are you implying?"

"You're three females of note, aren't you?"

Helgayarn nodded silently.

THE CHRISTMAS RABBIT

"And yet you just referred to yourself and by inference the two hags with you as ganders. Does that mean that you secretly wish you were men? Are you, in fact, lesbians?"

Helgayarn had all she could do to keep herself from fricasseeing the rabbit right on the spot. She thought she'd put rest to that misunderstanding way back in old Jerusalem! To have it rearing its ugly head now after having been squelched and buried these past two millennia, and to do so, rising up in the face of their greatest triumph like the mold ridden corpse of the uneasy dead, was an insult, whether intentionally implied or otherwise, to the majesty of their positions and the authority of their titles and as such, deserved a response which in other circumstances might be deemed as 'a little over the top' but which as a reaction to the aforementioned insult was certainly no more than the little leporide had coming. She'd tie its ears around its throat before the evening was done!

The vehicles arrived upon the scene of confrontation and came to an uneasy halt. Those within began to exit, dragging behind them yards of lead pipe, boxes of old ammunition, x-ray shields, gallons of old paint, cans of insecticide, and ten thousand number 2 pencils which Sinead O'Connor had stored away in the basement of the Society's little red schoolhouse in preparation for next year's mandatory SATs. All told and not counting the weight of the by-products in which they'd become embedded, the Society returned with better than two tons of the metamict substance. Helgayarn eyed the pile greedily. Two tons of gold would go a long way in purchasing for them, the retirement they so richly deserved. She immediately set Hephaestus to the task of implementing the transition, admonishing him to "get the lead out."

"How's he gonna do that?" someone asked.

"I'll simply burn away the unwanted detritus," replied the elf, taking note of the pile laid at his feet.

During the wait, Heph had constructed his forge and with the application of a little elven magic, had a minor conflagration burning within. There were however, no materials handy with which to construct a bellows. He therefore had the fat sleigh master, who was the biggest windbag around with the exception of the three who held them captive, down on his knees and blowing for all he was worth upon the base of the fire in order to fan the flames and raise the temperature.

"Well, if this don't beat all!" replied the sleigh master. "In all my wildest imaginings, never did I see myself adding fuel to a fire which could well end up being my own funeral pyre! The stigmata comes laden with ironies for those who bear it!"

"Oh, do be quiet, you old ass," replied Brunnhilde, "and just keep blowing! You've been adding fuel to that fire ever since your miscue in the garden and it's only by our good graces that its flames have not consumed you already. You've been living on borrowed time!"

"Then I must've accrued a ton of interest," replied Santos, "and therefore should be given a little more of it!"

"It's interest owed, not interest due, you idiot!"

"Exactly!" replied the sleigh master. "Interest due to your ridiculous ruling—therefore, I'm owed!"

"And you will be repaid in full," replied Helgayarn. "Rest assured of that!"

Between huffs and puffs, the sleigh master made it known that he did not feel assured of anything and that resting was quite beyond him at the moment.

"Then keep blowing and be quiet," replied Helgayarn.

"Yah!"

By now Hephaestus had a small inferno hot enough to serve his purposes. At his direction Irish and Apache alike began dumping pencils, insecticides, paints, and lengths of old pipe onto the fire. Sand Toes dropped the ammunition into the small hell blazing at his feet. Those looking on, including The Powers That Be, saw him do it and immediately hit the dirt, covering their heads while seeking what little cover there was to be had, in anticipation of what was to come. And come it did. The fire ate away at the wooden crate, at first charring it and blackening the Smith & Wesson logo stamped on the box. Tasting the wood, the flames found that they liked it and so began to consume more. The contents within heated up as did the contents within the contents, until the gunpowder stored at the base of the shells and used as a propellant to discharge the bullets, attained critical temperature and exploded. Shots flew off in every direction, whistling as they did while ricocheting off rocks and boulders as they went screaming errantly into the night. It was a wonder that no one was injured. It was a seven days' wonder that Sand Toes himself, who'd been standing in front of the fire when the ammo exploded, wasn't out-and-out killed and cut in half by the hail of bullets that went miraculously tearing past him. But not so much as a scratch did the mad man receive. To Brunnhilde, this augured nothing but trouble and she told Helly so. No one should have that much luck and if they did, they were best left alone and not interfered with. Looking on as well, Helgayarn secretly agreed with her sister, suddenly doubting her own abilities and power when placed in direct confrontation with such fate and seemingly good fortune. But what was there to be done? They couldn't back off now, could they? Granted, their reputations weren't what they used to be but what little notoriety they had left she was determined to keep, refusing to give it up by conceding to erstwhile farmers and smart-assed rabbits. A few leftover bullets, somehow spared in the initial explosion, suddenly went off with the rattle of precision machinery, causing everyone but Sand Toes and Santos to duck again. One errant missile passed through the confines of Helgayarn's bluish perm, leaving a scorching line of black down the middle of her scalp as evidence of its passage.

"That's it!" she snapped. "Enough of this malarkey! Hephaestus make with the mojo and turn this pile of burning cattle craps into the gold you promised!"

"Please, mistress," pleaded the elf, "the contents within have to cook a bit till they attain a certain magmatic consistency, which is determined more by feel than thought. We're almost there, but if we go now we're apt to end up with anything from tin to titanium. We're sure to Ti one on and end up with nothing but a FeSS."

Helgayarn offered him a puzzled glare that was both impatient and uncertain. "Come again?"

Hephaestus returned her look until suddenly, he perceived her confusion. "Pardon me, mistress," he replied with a slight bow, "but

I was speaking in periodicalese, a private language into which master alchemists will often digress when discoursing upon the elements."

Helgayarn eyed him critically. She was pretty sure she knew all about the four elements—earth, air, fire, and water, and what spells went into constituting each, but knew of no passages in any of them that made references to such things as Tis and FeSSes and was quick to say so.

Knowing that she demanded of him a clearer explanation of Tis and FeSSes and too timid in the face of the trio to tactfully deflect such inquiry or simply out-and-out lie, Hephaestus realized that answering her inquiry would place him in the path of *Hurricane Helgayarn* which, as any elf who'd been there previously could tell you, was no place from which you wanted to observe the weather, so he bowed his head even lower in an effort to appear ever more contrite as he formulated his reply. "Mistress," he said in a voice barely above a whisper, "I'm afraid you're a bit behind the times, and if you'll pardon me for saying it, were so even way back when."

A muscle began to quiver and twitch erratically at the base of Helgayarn's neck. The quiver spilled slowly but inexorably over her shoulders and down the length of her spine, twitching along the way as it did, until it poured into both arms and legs as she tried to contain her mounting fury while giving thought to the temerity of the servant standing before her who presumed to lecture and offer criticism. Even Brunnhilde, she saw, could barely contain her rage at his effrontery, while Betty, she could see, was reaching behind her head and into her blue-tinted bun to retrieve her poisoned pin. Helgayarn admonished them both to patience with a wave of her hand. Let the elf blow his trumpet if he would. It would be his last hurrah!

"Explain yourself."

"Ma'am," he hesitantly continued, "it's been common knowledge for quite some time now that what abounds around us is made up of more than merely the four 'archaical' elements."

"Do tell!" Helgayarn responded derisively while her cohorts supported her with sour sneers of their own.

THE CHRISTMAS RABBIT

"Yes, ma'am," Hephaestus respectfully replied. "There's ninety different elements in all as men count 'em. One hundred and eighteen if you count the lanthanoids and actinoids as well."

"And just what in the good gravy are those?"

"Any of the periodicals," he replied, that inhabit the numbers 57 through 70 and 89 through 102 respectively."

"What?"

"Yes, ma'am. There got to be so many of 'em that we had to number 'em just to keep track of how many there were."

"You did this?"

"Oh, not me, ma'am," the elf replied. "I'm a simple alchemist after all, not a highfalutin scientist! But even us alchemists have known for a long time that there was more out there than earth, air, fire, and water! There's the big five—from which almost everything else is derived."

"The big five? What in tarnation are you talking about?"

"Carbon, nitrogen, oxygen, and helium," he replied. "They're what almost everything else is made of. And hydrogen, from which the previous four are derived"

"Nonsense!" replied Helly. "Everyone knows that nature is comprised of the four basic elements, earth air, fire, and water, combined and apportioned by incantation and charms of making into constituting all that we see and touch."

"Yeah right," replied the elf. "And evolution is a myth and the sun circles the earth."

"Well it is and it does!" replied Helgayarn diffidently.

"Yah!" exclaimed Betty in a show of support.

Hephaestus shrugged. "Have it your way," he replied. "But those of us living in the twenty-first century know better. Be that as it may, the first attempt to codify and catalogue these elements was done by a master alchemist named Johan Dobreiner, who in 1817, developed the law of triads, which grouped certain elements, such as chlorine, bromine, and iodine, together in groups of threes, based on atomic weight, with the middle element being exactly halfway in weight between the other two opposed on either side."

Helgayarn attempted to shake the cobwebs out of her head. "What in the heck is atomic weight?" she asked.

Hephaestus shrugged. "Be darned if I know," he replied.

"And chlorine, bromine, and iodine," Helgayarn asked, "what are those, eh?"

"Don't know," replied the elf. "We alchemists, following the old ways, don't use 'em! I assume they're elements of one sort or another since they're listed on the table as it now stands, which by the way is not only numbered but lettered as well."

"What?"

"Yeah! Can you believe it? Men went and assigned each element a letter designation, which in most cases, at least as far as I can tell, has nothing to do with the element itself. Take tin for example—do you know it?"

Helgayarn nodded.

"Men call it Sn," the elf continued, although why they do so is beyond me—as is most of the foolishness in which they engage."

At least on that point, Helgayarn was willing to concede that they were in agreement. Yet she still didn't have her answers. "What are Ti and FeSS?" she demanded again.

"Ti," the old elf replied, "is periodialese for titanium. FeSS is periodicalese for iron pyrite, or fool's gold—which is what we might end up with if we try to hurry things along. Actually, FeSS works out, in proper periodicalese, to FeS_2."

"Isn't that wonderful?" Helgayarn commented dryly. "But have they given such silly monikers to everything?"

"Everything on the periodic table," the elf replied, "and any alloy derived at by combining the listed elements."

"Well it sounds like an absurd tongue-twister to me," Helgayarn replied, "and a big waste of time too!"

"You don't know the half of it," replied the elf. "Try calling Alcoa sometime and ordering a gross ton of an alloy called $CuAgAuFeNiPb$ and see what kind of response you get—and they're metal guys! Periodicalese makes Mandarin look like a grade school spelling bee!"

"I don't care how you spell it," replied Helgayarn, "or say it. Just make with the gold!"

"Your pardon, madam, but it'll be a couple of hours yet," replied the elf. "When the pickin's are ripe, I guarantee not only their delivery but the quality of their carats too—in fact, all twenty-four of 'em! But in the meantime there's nothing to do but watch and wait and a watched pot, well you know what that never does!" He stood waiting for an acknowledgment but never got one. So do yourselves a favor," he continued, "and begin the contest. It'll kill time. After you've finished with the woman and her friends, I'm sure that your gold will be ready."

Helgayarn was of a mind to chastise him properly for having the cheek to offer up unwanted advice but at the last moment decided to forego her response as in this instance, the elf was most certainly correct. She hated standing around and doing nothing while waiting for her own spells to take effect. To be waiting upon the incantations and invocations of others was much like being seated at a restaurant while reluctantly sipping coffee in anticipation of a meal that had been ordered twenty minutes ago—another thing she detested and much of the reason she tipped so poorly. Helgayarn was all about instant gratification and in truth, had she not been so old and ugly, would have made the perfect poster child for ADD.

"Very well," she replied. "To the challenge then! What are your terms, woman, and your preferred weapons?"

Larraine eyed her intently. It was time then to force the showdown, which she saw as the only hope of saving her family. Turning to Jim, who'd just deposited the last number 2 pencil into the fire, she asked him if he brought in addition to the lead, the items she'd requested just prior to his departure. The Irishman nodded. Indeed, the items were stacked high in the rear of the last SUV.

"Good," she replied. "Set up the table then with shot glasses and tankards, and the folding chairs too. Let's get on with it!"

From their triangle the trio looked on as Jim, with the help of Slim and a few others, carried out Larraine's wishes. "Set it up in the overhang of the mine shaft," Larraine replied, "where we'll be out o' the wind, and rig us a few o' those kliegs," she said, "along the overhang as well so we hae us some light on the subject!" Her directives carried out, Larraine then turned her attention to the three matrons of old.

"Follow me, ladies, and take yer seats if ye will, while I explain t' ye, the rules o' me contest. Lawrence, love, grab Little La, will ye, and bring her into the mouth o' the shaft where ye can keep yer eye on her whilst we four ladies joust!"

Finding his feet suddenly freed from the glue that bound them, Sand Toes took a cautious step or two and reached out to take his daughter from his wife.

"Follow Jack and I," Larraine said, both to him and Santos too. "The rest o' ye, if the ladies will allow it, follow as well and be witnesses."

The trio released the others, allowing them a little freedom of movement but placing limits on that freedom to ensure their victims didn't turn tail and run whilst they were in the midst of challenge with the woman before them.

As they entered the opening of the mine shaft Helgayarn eyed the table and the accoutrements placed upon it with criticism and disdain.

"What kind of challenge do you envision anyway," she asked, "musical chairs?"

"Nae," replied Larraine. "Ye takes the seat o' yer choice and ye pretty much keeps it throughout the challenge, although to be sure, as the early mornin' wanes, there'll be plenty o' opportunity fer music!"

Helgayarn eyed her suspiciously, intrigued nevertheless by the woman's implications and her own inferences, while quietly admitting to her own doubts now for if music were indeed called for, she knew herself and her sisters to be sirens who sang in a somewhat sour and out-of-key scale, unable to carry a tune and for all practical purposes, tone deaf. Betty could barely talk—was she going to be required to offer up an aria as well? Perhaps Brunnhilde had been right. Maybe they would've been wise to seek further clarification as to the challenge's particulars before agreeing to its terms.

Well, thought she, little matter as those before her were all the walking dead anyway; and if the trio, through loss, were forced

THE CHRISTMAS RABBIT

to renege on the terms of the challenge, then the dead rarely got a chance to tell anyone about it.

The trio cautiously took their seats, feeling strangely suffocated by the crowd gathered around them and milling about the mouth of the cave. Ill at ease with the unfamiliar sensation of claustrophobia which seemed to be mounting inexorably around her and secretly a bit apprehensive about the particulars of what was to happen next, although she'd go to her grave denying such, it suddenly occurred to Helgayarn, with the glassware set before her, that they were being invited to dinner and that could only mean one thing… They'd miscalculated once again and mistook the whereabouts of the redoubtable Mrs. Santos who it seemed, had been obviously hiding in the bottomless hole of the magical sleigh and who'd escaped to cook dinner while they'd been otherwise distracted. Helgayarn shot Brunnhilde a worried glance. Brunnhilde read it, agreed with it, and likewise paled an even ghastlier shade of white while Betty, equally ashen, nervously took notes. So that was to be it then, a face-off with the farmer's wife, and after the passage of these many years, it was to be a family affair to boot, as those gathered before them, with the exception of the Apaches, were all family of a sort and most bore the stamp of strangeness to prove it. As to the Apaches, it wasn't unheard of for anyone, be they descended from prodigal farmers, first-person Celts, or an unlikely and unusual union of each, to have guests over for dinner. It was socially accepted almost everywhere except in their own house, where it was wholeheartedly despised, the owners having undergone a prior meal at the hands of a previous guest, who for all intelligence to the contrary appeared ready to materialize on the spot in an effort to attempt a repeat performance. The trio strove in vain to peer around the crowd and into the dark and dim corners of the mine shaft's depths, attempting to discern for themselves where Le Chef of Death might lie hidden. As they did they again made ready to triangulate, should such a defensive posture be called for, by joining hands under the card table in order to flip it up and out of their way, thus clearing the space between them while better enabling each to guard the other's back should the redoubtable Mrs. show up bearing so much as an olive tray. Sitting there tense and expectant, they took note of Larraine as she claimed the last seat at the table before them, apparently at ease and unconcerned. Had she eaten earlier, they wondered, and if so, did that offer her a legitimate reason for excusing herself from the meal, and if it did, would doing that negate the challenge altogether? After all, by definition, one had to participate in a challenge in order to refer to it as such, didn't one? You couldn't claim victory if you didn't contest; otherwise it was just a dare, wasn't it? And anyone who dared to could do that! It was a potential loophole, should she choose to employ it, and who wouldn't in the face of this? As such, the Irishwoman was keeping the ploy hidden and saving the stratagem until the last moment. It was an old lawyer's trick and the sly shyster before them, reveling in the bloody chum of grueling cross-examination like the shark she now revealed herself to be, swam smoothly through such sordid waters as she continually manipulated them, employing carefully couched opinions and pointed statements, into increasingly smaller corners from which it became perpetually more difficult to maneuver, lowering the boom while hoisting them upon the petards of their own contradictions and inconsistencies, with Mrs. Santos being both the surprise and star witness with which the young lawyer hoped to close her case! So be it! They had much to teach this one about the power of the law and if they had to eat a little crow as well as a helping or two of whatever the Mrs. served, then bring on the Maalox! The trio were ready to rock!

"Bring forth the farmer's wife," cried Helly as Brunnhilde and Betty looked about nervously, "and let us see for ourselves what culinary disaster that dame has deemed we dine upon tonight!"

Larraine, however, was not into rocking but rolling instead, and Rolling Rock at that and only if at some point in the remainder of the evening, they ran out of pints of Guinness. But Jim had taken pains to assure her when he could get a word with her unobserved, that they'd returned well stocked and that the Rolling Rock which still remained iced in Styrofoam coolers which sat unemptied in the backs of the rearmost SUVs was brought along for emergency purposes only and not really expected to be made use of. There was plenty of Guinness to be had for that, she'd been told, as well as

THE CHRISTMAS RABBIT

a seemingly unending supply of Connemara Cask Strength Peated Single Malt Whiskey, unquestionably the heavyweight champion of the Irish Whiskey world and an occasional indulgence which she'd come to miss during her time getting the shaft. Of an evening she would often enjoy its wood-fired aroma as well as its unexpectedly light and perfumed body, partaking of it undiluted, sip after contemplative sip, whilst sitting before the fire with a dram or two in a snifter and awaiting the return of her wayfaring wanderer. This was the good stuff, being 60 percent alcohol by volume, which was 120 proof and considerably stronger than the well brand you got served at your typical bar if you weren't too careful and as such, was meant to be parceled out slowly and enjoyed within reasonable limits. Larraine reasoned they had no time for limits, however, and determined alcohol, in the largest volumes she could get, was the only proof available she could present before this particular court that had any hope of acquitting not only herself but the body of peers surrounding her. Thus Helgayarn's arcane references to a certain chef who will remain nameless remained unintelligible to Larraine, who'd not gone out of her way to ask Jim to return with any food in addition to the booze and who was now only serving up the good hooch as a matter of necessity. Let these *Caillteacháns* bring their own breadsticks! "You misunderstand me," she replied. "I didn'a invite ye t' a banquet but t' a drinkin' contest and one I'm sartain t' be winnin' as I be the only one o' us that's Irish! The odds therefore, are in me favor and the fates smile upon me! Here then are the rules, madams, if ye will: Each o' us in turn will put forward a small song or a shanty as a toast t' one another's good health. Then we drinks a shot o' whisky and follows it with a pint o' beer while our audience looking on, offer up applause, not only fer the verse offered but as an encouragement fer the next. Ye can o' course, drop yer shot glasses into yer empty tankards and once filled with Guinness, enjoy a boilermaker fer yer efforts, but either way, straight or mixed, enjoy 'em we will till there's only one o' us left standing. I'll go first." She cleared her throat once or twice as she rose to sing. "Jimmy lad," she asked, before launching into song, pour us a pint o' the Guinness, will ye, and a shot o' Connemara's too. It looks t' be a long night." Her voice, when she let loose her verse, rose up softly like an Irish harp, lilting at first, and then slowly rising in both volume and crescendo as if played by a mystical druidess offering a chant to the forces of nature, until it rang out like a bell, echoing off the walls of the cave which it filled, and this is what she sang:

> Ye can lead a horse to moisture but ye canna' make it drink,
> Ye can lead three crones through logic but ye canna' make 'em think,
> Ye can play upon their conscience but their conscience dinna blink—
> When they're out t' do ye dirty, why they'll drop ye in the drink!

"Here's lookin' at ye, ladies, and may *Go dtacha an diabhal thú 'n' Go stróice diabhal thú!*" She quaffed her shot and upended her beer, pulling it down her and chasing the whiskey in three quick chugs. "Aye," she remarked, "that was right 'n' proper, that was—Uughh!" She offered up a hearty burp as a testament to the truth of her observation while looking down at Lauren who returned her regard with one of amazement, having had her own words sung back to her in the unlikely voice of her unanticipated mother, who like good women in many a fairy tale, always seemed to turn up at a dime and in the nick of time too!

Larraine, unable to see the look of wonder displayed upon her daughter's face was aware of it nevertheless and secretly offered her a sly wink as an assurance to her that things would ultimately be all right and that Jack's haregi, which she now held in her possession, was good for more things than merely seeing the light.

Brunnhilde had been apprehensive about this whole ordeal from the moment Larraine gave voice to it. Now however she found herself itchy with anticipation. She hadn't had a drop since Jerusalem and the old days, whereupon Helly had made her swear off the stuff, and she relished the chance of breaking her vow. Wine of one sort or another and mulled more often than not, was what she'd been most

THE CHRISTMAS RABBIT

used to imbibing and although beer was not completely unknown to her, whiskey was something new altogether. Still, if it was drinkable then Brunnhilde would try anything once. And usually twice just to be certain. It didn't do, she knew, to prejudge a particular brew or vintage. One often had to sample it any number of times before one could decide for oneself the quality of the grapes or hops being passed over the palette; and in the interest of being fair and judging such matters impartially, Brunnhilde had always been eager to do so and now found her desire rekindled. But she had to sing for her supper, as it were, even though the meal being offered was liquid only. That was fine with her, who never let carelessly regarded eating get in the way of seriously contemplated drinking and who'd always been eager to push the one aside in order to make room for the other. As the applause died down she gathered her wits about her in order to compose her verse. "Must the verse be a tribute or a salute per se, and to one of us sitting at the table in particular, or can it be composed around more general themes?"

"The challenge allows fer some latitude," Larraine remarked dryly. "Just sing us yer song and raise yer glass!"

Brunnhilde shrugged and gave it a go. "When Irish eyes are smiling," she began, but was abruptly brought to a halt by the severe looks of disapproval displayed upon the faces of those gathered around her. Larraine uncomfortably coughed into the back of her hand, as if clearing her throat.

"We dinna sing in mixed company," she replied, "songs, nor recite verse, which could be deemed overly patriotic or particularly ethnic, even if such stanzas be true and therefore complimentary t' the Irish way o' life and t' ourselves in particular. Fer sure enough, once we did and with all this booze bein' passed around, like it as nae some Italian in the crowd or some wanderin' Jew will then feel it incumbent upon himself to sing out with a bit o' verse extolling the particulars o' his own pedigree and then where would we be? Headin' toward disaster, I tell ye, as rounds are quaffed and songs sung, until finally after many a raised glass t' loosen 'im up and get the cattle prod removed from his own arse, some English prig is bound to stand up and sing us a lay about the virtues o' bein overly pale while being a citizen of an empire upon which the sun never sets! It's conceited, inflammatory, and in this day and age maudlin, as it's no longer true. Nae, 'tis better to stick to less controversial subjects than Irish eyes, nae matter how beautiful, and whether they be smilin' or nae, while lending voice instead t' less controversial subjects, such as the weather."

"The weather?" asked an incredulous Brunnhilde. "Whoever sings about the weather?"

"We do all the time!" replied Horse's head from somewhere deep in the crowd. "We sing for the rain and dance for it too! Wanna hula baby, or you want we should have a seat at the table?"

"Never mind either!" Brunnhilde, who didn't want to miss her chance for a drink, sharply replied. "It's my turn to sing and so I shall!" She thought for a moment then rose to begin once again.

>It's been a coon's age since I drank—
>Or poured this tiger in my tank
>What happens next I dare not think,
>And so I'll raise my glass and drink!

The crowd erupted in applause, not so much for the quality of her effort, which sounded rather like a wounded wildebeest caught up in the throes of a kidney stone's passage, but rather for the sentiment of her lyric, which kidney stone or nae, the crowd could wholeheartedly agree with. She downed her shot in imitation of Larraine, nearly choking upon it as she did. The Irishwoman smiled slightly at her discomfort. "Is it nae t' yer likin'?" she asked. Between gasps for air and a conscious effort to keep herself from retching, the witch uttered her reply. "No," she sputtered hoarsely. "It's smooth, real smooth!" She followed this with a much-needed draught of Guinness. "Ahh, that's better," she replied after the beer, working its way down her gullet, eased the burning in her throat. "That's some powerful sauce, missy, that you pour," she replied. "It explodes in your stomach like an infamous soup I once had the misfortune of sampling, but chased by a beer—my it does the heart a world of good!"

THE CHRISTMAS RABBIT

Larraine laughed heartily. "Wait till yer next," she replied with good humor, "and the one after that! Soon such gay song and strong spirit will hae ye soul singing!"

Through eyes that still watered and a throat still raw despite the beer poured down it, Brunnhilde offered Larraine her reply of assurance. "I can well believe that," said she, "and can hardly wait to find out for myself!" The two then looked to Helgayarn and Betty to see who would be next to follow suit. Helgayarn offered them nothing but a blank faced scowl while Betty rose to take her turn. The most junior of the trio knew one song only and only partially at that. What little of the lyrics she could remember, she suddenly gave voice to.

"Yah! Yah! Yah!" she cried. "Yah! Yah! Yah!"

The Beatles, being English, were not well regarded by the Irish and to the Apaches, were virtually unknown, so Betty's rendition, when completed, garnished only polite applause, offered up half-heartedly and only as a means to make room for the next contestant. It was Helgayarn's turn now although she tried to pretend otherwise.

"I drank when no one was looking," she said, "and I sang to myself!"

"Ye must sing t' the crowd," replied Larraine, "and drain yer glass in front o' all t' see!"

Helgayarn eyed her evilly. She'd never been one to hold out much, for the pleasures of drinking, having often counseled Brunnhilde any number of times in ages past regarding her overindulgences. Helgayarn was willing to allow as how there was nothing wrong with an occasional glass of wine with dinner or even two or three if the meal was overly heavy and the table conversation particularly boring, but the lure of strong drink never held its appeal for her and she preferred of an evening, a hot cup of tea instead, or a warm mug of cocoa. Strong drink and the irresponsibility it engendered in those who imbibed it, held no charm for her. She'd seen many a drunk on down through the ages, from old Rome to nearby Reno, which lie beyond yonder hills, go stumbling through life, sauced as a goose, and weaving like they were three sheets to the wind as they swayed from side to side in a failed effort to maintain their balance and keep themselves erect. The good life passed those by in favor of the high life and Helgayarn had always determined not to allow herself to get caught between the two. Now, after centuries of apparent success, stuck in the middle was right where she'd allowed herself to become trapped. Even if they won this contest, Helgayarn knew, there'd be hell to pay tomorrow morning when the three of them awoke to giant katzenjammers upon which to hang their heads. Such hangovers and sour stomachs were apt to last them days, and Brunnhilde, who'd had much experience with such matters, ought to have considered that before raising her glass and setting their ship on a course of drunken overindulgence. John Barleycorn did not lend himself to sober thought or rational planning. John Barleycorn was a laissez faire kind of guy who let the drinks fall where they drained while giving little thought to the consequences that might occur afterward. Not the proper attitude for a Power That Be who had responsibilities, not only to herself but those around her, to remain sober while seeing to it that planet Mungo turned true in its orbit while spinning steadily upon its axis. A drunk could hardly be called upon to oversee a task such as that. You didn't trust a sot with a copper sou let alone the value of a whole planet, even if said planet's value were questionable. She'd hold true to her own then, denying to play this foolish game and refusing to drink while her sisters, apparently none too eager to do either, could carry on in her stead.

"Your turn," Larraine said innocently while batting an eye. "Sing us your song now, madam, if ye will, and tell us yer tale!"

Helgayarn cast a baleful eye upon the contestants seated at the table and the onlookers surrounding them. "I'm not playing," she snidely replied. "This challenge of yours is silly! What kind of duel is this, I ask, and what is the likelihood of the outcome? Where are the weapons, I wonder, and who's wielding them?"

Larraine offered the witch sitting opposite her a motherly smile, one full of patience and understanding. "There, there, my dear," she commiserated. "I knows exactly how ye feels about such things but it takes patience, my lady, and years o' being Irish to see their value, for the Irish know that the words of a bard, as sweet as the first shamrock in spring, can often be as sharp as a sword nevertheless, and when

THE CHRISTMAS RABBIT

used as a weapon, can flense the skin off the ears o' those listenin' and in some cases, lop off their heads! And as to the occasional pull on the bottle, we Irish are familiar enough with the pastime to know that both the 'ruddy cup' and the little brown jug have laid many a maid low before now. So ye'll just hae t' be trustin' me when I tell ye that singin' and drinkin' be serious business!" She paused for a moment, as any good bard will whether or not they be singing or simply telling a tale, in order to let her words do their work for her. "Of course, ye can pass yer turn," she finally continued, "but that be a forfeit and since me challenge was issued to all three o' ye *Cailleaches*, if even one o' ye dinna sing nae drink either, then the lot o' ye must be declared the loser and be on yer way!"

"I dinna think so!" Helgayarn replied shrewishly while haughtily aping Larraine's Irish brogue and making a mockery of it. "Here is where I be and here is where I'll stay! I'll drown in the lowest river of hell before I leave this place!"

Larraine had just that in mind and looked at her smugly. "Then ye must sing fer yer supper lassie, like the rest o' us!"

The big witch looked to Brunnhilde and Betty who were eagerly awaiting her acquiescence. "C'mon, Helly," Bunny urged, "let your curlers down for once and loosen up a bit! The three of us know how this ends one way or the other, so unstrap your girdle and take a drink!"

Betty nodded her agreement while offering an enthusiastic, "Yah!"

Helgayarn offered her sisters a sour stare as her initial reply. "All right," she finally said with a tired sigh. "I'll play along and sing you a tune, but only because I know how this all comes out. But I warn the lot of you—I sing like a frog, both off-key and out of pitch, and therefore my tune, when sung, is likely to shatter a tankard or two."

She looked about to make sure that everyone gathered understood what they were in for. The crowd indicated their acknowledgment by offering her nods of approval and encouragement.

"And as to the two of you," she said while pointedly looking at her sisters, "no matter how this comes out or in what conditions our heads are hung come high morning, we've a full day of work ahead of us and I simply will not entertain any notions on either of your parts of taking the day off and calling in sick in order to recuperate! The three of us are going to damned well work through our hangovers, and there's to be no upping or chucking either! We've had more than our fill of that in ages past, and I simply will not tolerate an encore performance! Is that clear?"

The two gleefully nodded their understanding, eager for the game to continue and a chance to get drunk.

"So be it," said Helly. Rising to her feet, she cleared her throat once or twice in an attempt to dislodge the frog that had been stuck there since Jerusalem. The effort did little good and the toad barely turned over. Her tune, when she gave voice to it, grated on the ears like a San Francisco trolley car in dire need of a break job. She screeched more than sang, her tune abrading the ears of those who listened like number 1 sandpaper as it attacked the various lobes and drums upon which it fell. Tankards shattered and shot glasses cracked, while the noses and ears of many bled red under the vocal assault. This is the musical poem that pealed forth from Helgayarn's pallid lips:

> "I'm a big witch, proud and true
> You dinna like me and I dinna like you!
> You're all gonna end up in my stew
> Have a drink, you say—don't mind if I do!"

She quaffed her shot with authority while brazenly chasing it down with suds. Brunnhilde and Betty applauded avidly, giving her a standing ovation, to which the big witch offered a slight bow. But the response from the crowd was uncommitted at best. There were a few slight handclaps being offered up erratically and barely to be heard at that. Tradition demanded, however poor her effort and regardless of how grating her tune proved to be to those ears upon whom it fell, that her endeavor be acknowledged nevertheless. It would be considered the epitome of rude behavior to simply ignore her undertaking; although standing there, many with bleeding ears and noses, it was no wonder that the crowd offered her the barest minimum of politeness and acknowledgment that tradition and good manners allowed.

THE CHRISTMAS RABBIT

Larraine called for another shot and an additional mug as she prepared herself for round two. Standing to her feet, she gave voice to her sweet Irish tilt.

> "My grandda was an Irish lad, a corker lad, was he!
> In Dublin town he boarded ship to sail across the sea!
> He left his lands, he fled the Brits
> Their tyrannies and woe, and heading west he sailed his ship t' seek a land o' gold!
> Oh come ye one, and come ye all, and sing this Irish song
> We'll sing and dance and drink all night then mine our gold come morn!

This verse received the loudest applause yet, and Larraine was encouraged to add another.

> My grandma was an Irish lass
> She left with her old man, to sail on ship across the sea in search of a new land.
> Her Irish hearth, her Irish home
> She left 'em far behind, to sail the seas with Granda Dawe, the family gold to find.
> Oh, come ye one and come ye all, and sing this Irish song
> We'll sing and dance and drink all night then mine our gold come morn!"

The crowd called for yet another verse, but she good-naturedly waved them off, downing her shot instead and drinking her beer while explaining to those still demanding an encore that this was a community effort and that more than two verses by any one bard at any one time was merely showing off. If she kept on singing, after all, how were they going to continue drinking? The crowd laughingly saw it her way while upending their steins and calling for the next reveler. Brunnhilde eagerly arose from her chair. The crowd looking on could swig from their steins anytime they wanted but as a contestant she had to limit her drinking to those times when she offered up song as payment. It hardly seemed equitable to her to be forced to whistle while she worked while those around her drank for free! Still, drinking was drinking and her next dram was calling out to her invitingly. She rose to the occasion and in her off-tenor soprano offered up this verse:

> A witch am I, a witch I'll be—a bitseache till I die.
> So raise your glass and drink your toast and pour
>   another rye!

Short and sweet but able to be toasted, she was joined by the others as she quaffed her potables. Betty followed suit, doing her Beatles impression again but this time sounding as if John and Paul were seated at the table and harmonizing with her.

"Yah, Yah, Yah!" She sang her song and drank her drink.

It was Helgayarn's turn once again but before she'd condescend to another round of this foolishness, the Irishwoman had just committed a breach in the stated rules, forfeiting the contest and losing the challenge, at least as far as Helly was concerned, and the witch was quick to point it out.

"I thought," said she, "that tunes and tales of an overly ethnic flavor were disallowed in mixed company! That last lilt of yours," she said to Larraine, "certainly sounded as though it had an Irish flavor to it, sure 'n' begorrah!"

"Aye, indeed it did!" replied Larraine. "Fer after the first round be over and the shot glasses and their accompanyin' schooners be emptied, "then everyone at the table, be they Celtic or nae, are deemed nevertheless t' be Irish at heart! Now sing us another song, madam, and let not the words o' yer tune fall upon deaf ears!"

Helgayarn chose to frown at the poor excuse being offered up. But the crowd looking on seemed to agree wholeheartedly with Larraine and her reasoning, and when you were in another's house and even if you were a Power That Be and ensconced within one so

THE CHRISTMAS RABBIT

metaphorically strange and unusual as this, you still played by that house's rules, at least until it was time to break them. To do so was only polite. Still, the Irishwoman had done a good job of ensnaring them so far, much as her lookalike had done so often so long ago, that Helgayarn offered up this little heard ditty from way back when, as a partial tribute to their hostess.

> "This one's for you, honey," She said with a smirk
> and then began:
> There was an old harlot who lived in a boot
> With too many young'uns and too little loot
> She had nae social skills by which to keep 'em all fed
> So She lay upon her back and sold booty instead!
> When fear of our arrival kept her men-folk at home
> She laced up her boot and She took to the road
> Selling off her booty as She went door-to-door
> There goes the Shoe Lady—one hell of a whore!"

Again her offer was greeted with perfunctory applause even though this time she carried the tune well enough. For it wasn't that she was off- key or that her tune marched to a beat that couldn't be danced to. It was snappy enough, the listeners supposed, and the wordplay had a certain attraction to it; it was just a bit too bawdy this early in the evening—even for a drunken Irish sing-along and would have been received better much later after a few more rounds had been quaffed. Also, there was a child present if the trio hadn't forgotten that, now awake and partaking of all that occurred within the adit. Young lasses between seven and ten are at an impressionable age. Every Irish mother knew that and took great pains to sift through and edit for content, any song or tale that might be picked up by the listening ears of little lasses looking in on irresponsible adults.

"That was quite a tale," Larraine replied, "that ye sang t' us! Nae quite the one I would've chosen whilst midst the company o' young and tender ears like me Little La's, but I did nae forbid such when first statin' the rules so I'll let it be. However, ye'd do well t' consider me daughter lyin' there in her bed o' pain before ye offer up her next verse!"

"Say what you will," replied Helgayarn. "It's your funeral!"

"Indeed!" cried Jim. "This sing-along be getting' more 'n' more like an Irish wake—rowdy, festive, and full o' drunken debauchery! Let us therefore, since it indeed be our own, return to our vehicles to gather up fiddles and harps and make a real shindig out o' the affair!"

This suggestion was greeted with enthusiasm by all but Helly, who saw no point in participating in such things as music, gaiety, and frivolity, until well after the job at hand was done and their duty completed. There'd be time enough for song and dance later, once these Irishmen and Indians, caribou and other critters, were laid to rest. However, her reservations regarding such matters held no sway whatsoever. Instead Irishmen and women alike flocked to their vehicles in order to retrieve their various instruments while the Apaches, one and all, retired to their horseless horses to fetch war drums of various sizes and tones, that they might join the festivities and participate in the fun. Soon the crowd returned, fife and drum in hand, and after a general tuning up, were ready to get down to the business of making music to beat the brass band. Before that however, they toasted one another's health and then did so again, all the while admonishing Helgayarn to join in the good cheer. After all, it was still Christmas Eve, or so said the sun who hadn't risen yet to greet December 25. Helgayarn wanted as little mention made of the date, and by inference, the rabbi as well. How she'd ever let Brunnhilde and Betty embroil her in this unpleasant situation wherein at least by association, they'd become not only tied to this fellow whom through egotism and selfishness, they'd just as soon deny, but moreover, down through the course of ages had become dependent upon for a living, having invested highly in the various commercial enterprises that by and large earned their profit margins around his holidays and which in two quick months provided the bulk of the annual income that The Powers That Be needed to get by on. Again, the job of Power That Be, however you get it, be you elected, appointed, or a usurper of the throne, does not pay well and moreover provides no social security payments when you get older since what little salary

THE CHRISTMAS RABBIT

you earn is never taxed. Therefore she wanted no reminders of their untenable situation. Besides, who knew really, whether this was the rabbi's birthday or not? Certainly Helly, who'd even had the unfortunate occasion to meet the fellow, couldn't say for sure and was certain that there were no actual eyewitness to the event left standing who could clarify the matter one way or the other. December 25 was just an effort on her part to enact some sort of crowd control over those who even long ago, were expecting his return and saw both Santos and Jack as heralders of that unlikely event. Well it was her own fault as the date was chosen and implemented at the Nicene Council when Helly disguised as a nun, proposed out of habit, by whispering into Constantine's ear one night as he slept, the date as fact to be taken on faith and as a solution to one of the more contentious divisions that still separated the council's participants. Even in his sleep Constantine knew it to be a capital idea, and the Nicene Council, merely mad rabbits of another sort, accepted it wholeheartedly. So she acquiesced with regard to the music, reluctantly but quickly nevertheless and for the moment, at least, the rabbi had been laid to rest. She'd have to be careful, however, in agreeing to anything more for resurrection was this rabbi fellow's specialty and she wanted no further encounters with, or made of, him for the rest of the evening.

"So who's turn is it," cried out Jim with delight, "t' offer us up a song or sing us a verse or two?"

Many there offered to do so but by and large the requests went up for Jim himself to lead them in a lay or two.

"Me?" replied the Irishman with false modesty. Jim loved to sing, especially an Irish tune and moreover loved being the center of attention. "I canna' sing," he humbly objected, "at least nae near as well as some o' those seated at the table." This was only half true. He could sing, after a fashion, not great but adequately anyway, and could carry a tune well enough so long as you weren't looking forward to being overly impressed. And although no Larraine, could certainly hold his own against the vocalizations of the three dour dames seated before him. "Oh, all right already," he finally consented, although it had been his intention to sing since he'd first been requested. "Follow me lead then, laddies," he cried and burst out in the following song:

> An Irish lad is what I am, you'll find me with me
>   drink in hand.
> All saints preserve me mother land—an Irish lad
>   I am!

It was a familiar song to many gathered there and as he began the second verse, those bearing musical instruments began to *wield* them, and as narrator I use that word willingly and in place of *play*. If you've ever had the good fortune to attend an Irish wake after the corpse has been toasted into the wee hours o' the morn, then you'll know what I'm talking about. With their lively rhythms and tightly arranged melodies that lend themselves both to methodology and carefully arranged scales while remaining at the same time open to both interpretation and improvisation, your typical Celtic dirge at your average Irish wake demands of its musicians that they not merely play their instruments in order to facilitate the incorporated notes but rather, wield them like weapons so that the sound of highly strung fiddles sliced through the air while flute and pipe danced merrily upon their edges. It's a lively form of music and in this instance was made more so by the addition of Native American drums whose rhythms, although not complimentary to the particular tunes being performed, somehow seemed to fit the beat anyway. Jim began the second verse and those who knew the tune and who were not wielding woodwinds or any other type of reed, joined in the singing.

> An Irish lad is all I be—'tis taters and an ale fer me
> Just look around, what do ye see—an Irish lad,
>   that's me!

It was an old drinking song and a pub favorite from way back in the auld country where many a reveler, having sung and drank to its innumerable stanzas while adding one or two of their own, crawled home cockeyed drunk, befuddled, boozy, and overtaken,

THE CHRISTMAS RABBIT

both by national pride and a goodly blend, served alongside a mug o' Guinness. They played through the tune three more times with Jim leading them in vocalization while admonishing them between versus to raise their glasses in good cheer. Everyone did so, including Helly who despite her initial resistance was now beginning to feel the effects of not only the alcohol but the comradely joining of voices in song, as they blended one with the other, to tell an Irish tale in general of a peculiar family in particular. Nor was the history of Clan Dawe, or the Santos line of the family the only two tales related. The crowd regaled each other with toasts, all the while offering up songs and stories from out of both legend and imagination. The elves, with Hephaestus taking the solo while taking a break from the forge as well, sang a song of lead and gold and the turning of one into the other. The apaches performed a rain dance to the tune of an Irish jig. The reindeer turned in their rendition of Ghost Riders in the Sky and Sand Toes and Santos, turned in a remarkable rendition of Father and Son as they toasted each other in between musical dissentions.

Another person not entirely enthused with the idea was Lauren who sat up comfortably now, but still nestled within her blanket while laden with rocks as the last of the magic dust coursed its way through her, reinvigorating body and soul, while adding to her, awareness of not only her immediate surroundings but gifting her as well with a seemingly prescient insight into the immediate situation wherein she could assess a possibility's potential to become probable fact. And the fact of the matter was that despite her Ma's miraculous return and notwithstanding the love and wisdom she'd bestowed upon the young lass after the advent of such, Lauren had little faith in the utility of her mother's plan as she perceived it. Her Ma was Irish, and as such, Little La knew she could drink most souls under the table but Lauren was doubtful that the three seated before her even had souls and if they did those souls had certainly been around a lot longer than her Ma had been drinking and therefore probably had a lot more practice at it. This insight, as well as the stories she'd heard, told both in verse and song and by those who'd been there, mentioned often in their lyrics the mythical confrontation between The Powers That Be and the redoubtable Mrs. Santos, and Lauren with her newfound awareness perceived that having withstood Mrs. Santos's shark fin soup, no mere potable poured out of a bottle and into a glass, however many proof it contained, was likely to lay the trio low and in doing, win for her Ma, the challenge she'd set. Wasn't likely and plainly, wasn't happening. Irishman and Apache alike were getting tanked to the gills while the trio before her had barely started swaying in their seats. She got up and out of her blanket to approach her Ma.

Using Jack's Haregei and the eyes it placed in the back of her head, Larraine was well aware of her daughter's approach even though the young lass came upon her from behind. "What is it, La?" she asked as she got ready to down another round. "Little lassies such as yerself may not be able t' see it for themselves but sometimes, even after a lengthy absence and as much as they might want to, an Irish Ma can be too busy t' give a lassie her full attention!"

"What abou' me?" asked Larry, who stood just behind her, "Ain't I deservin' o' some attention too?"

"You'll get yours tonight," she replied while casting a glance at Helgayarn. "Assumin' that is, we hae a tonight left t' us!"

Mellowed by the booze, Helgayarn offered up a slight smile and a shrug of her shoulders. "Who knows?" she laughingly remarked. "Anything's possible! But I wouldn't count on it!" Feeling their tea, the trio broke out in raucous laughter.

The early morning wore on with both shot glasses and tankards being refilled liberally. Having a predisposed weakness to drink of this sort, the Apaches began to get rowdy, dancing around, whooping it up with war cries, and beating out rhythms on their drums that were in no way synchronized or in time with the music being offered up by the other musicians at the party. The Apaches, being the motorcycle toughs that they were, began to resent the fact that the Irish music couldn't be made to dance to a Native American beat and so started picking fights with the Irish musicians in order to get them to play straight. The one thing a drunken Irishman enjoys more than another shot and its subsequent tankard is a good tavern brawl, and the Society, well into their cups, were more than willing to give the Indians exactly what they wanted. However, as far as

THE CHRISTMAS RABBIT

Helgayarn was concerned, there would be no injuries offered up or lives taken unless she was the one to do it and therefore recast the spell that bound them to the floor.

Even Jack, who had little use for man-things like whiskey and Guinness, found himself with a shot glass in one paw and a tankard in the other. Nor was it the first time this evening that he'd discovered his mitts so occupied. As far as he could tell this was his third shot, along with its subsequent beer, and although that may not sound like much to you and I, both of whom can put away a six-pack or two along with their attendant shots before we start thinking our silly notions are in any way connected with sober and logical thought processes, it was nevertheless a hefty amount of suds and hard liquor for a four pound rabbit to imbibe while hoping to remain sober. He found his ears drooping and his sense of smell diminished. As he swayed on his feet he tried, as an experiment, to cast a caustic pheromone or two at the senior Power That Be but Helgayarn merely shrugged off his attack with another chuckle. Even Larraine managed to remark to him on the sly that the reverse sight imparted to her by his harea-gei was becoming dull and fuzzy and just a bit blurred. Jack offered up a shrug of his own as well as a hearty belch and then rose on his hind legs to render the following tune.

> "Tend ye now my story 'bout a rabbit brave and bold…
> With trouble from the You-Know-Whos he came in from the cold
> He came unto our rescue, having traveled from the east
> A hard case and a bullyboy was Rabbakami, the beast!"

This offering earned itself a hearty applause from everyone listening, including Helgayarn, Brunnhilde, and Betty, who although they'd almost had their cans handed to them by that little leporide on that long-ago afternoon, had won the day regardless and who now, after the passage of centuries, felt that enough time had elapsed for them to view their near demise with a little more objectivity and in doing, offer up praise for him who despite his ego and effrontery had proven himself to be a worthy adversary nevertheless.

    The drinking continued hard and heavy, as did the songs and the stories. Somewhere in the last hour or so the liquor had loosened up Betty's cloven tongue, and she now held forth unceasingly about the mean-spirited attitudes of her sisters while spouting off line after line of ancient Greek and Mesopotamian poetry in between tirades. Helgayarn and Brunnhilde laughed at her efforts while the captives merely looked on in puzzlement, as only Richard was familiar with the ancient languages. Finally, in an effort to both ignore her sisters and appease her captive audience, she recited a few lines from "The Raven" by Poe. It was her personal favorite but for the whimsical Irishmen and carefree Apaches, the symbolism and allegory contained within its stanzas were far too dark for their lighthearted spirits. She tried a verse or two from Lord Byron, but being English, his verses went over with the Irish about as well as they did with the French. She then recited a sonnet of her own but the themes were so dark even Poe's Raven wanted nothing to do with 'em. It wasn't until she stumbled upon the dimly remembered poem of "Leda and the Swan" by William Butler Yeats, reciting a tentative line or two for her audience's ears, that she received any form of recognition whatsoever. Emboldened by the scattered clapping which accompanied her bow, she then launched with even more bravado and determination into a rendition of "The Ancient Elf" by James Stephens. This earned her a full round of applause from both Irishman and Apache, as well as a standing ovation from Pixie, Dixie. Santos was noncommital. It was his turn to drink and recite. Santos knew only one song. As a rule, music didn't make its way up north, where notes were apt to freeze solid in the Arctic air, falling to the icy tundra like frozen popsicles, only to lie still till the spring thaw and in that short season of slightly milder weather, melt away in the runoff, washing out to the Arctic Ocean before anyone had a chance to hear them. The song he knew, although sung to what you and I would call a whimsical melody, was nevertheless a dirge and sure to upset Valentino, who'd already

THE CHRISTMAS RABBIT

lost his light, sprained a foreleg, and was therefore in a foul mood to begin with. Still he gave it a go.

"Rudolph, the red-nosed reindeer
Really liked his magic dust…"

He sang it through twice, encouraging his listeners to join him in the chorus. When he finished, Larraine saw a drunken tear or two in the eyes of all three witches and knew that it was time for step two in her plan. She spoke to the thoughtful silence that had descended upon them as they gave regard to poor Rudolph.

"We been poundin' down fer quite some time now, ladies," she ventured, "and even a hardy lass like meself, who can stand toe t' tow with any sod who be deep in his cups, needs t' let a little o' the liquid drain off, if 'n' ye takes me meaning."

"We do indeed," replied Helgayarn, with a slight slur, "but since we do not drain ourselves, if you take *my* meaning, I see no good reason fer granting your wish!"

"Come now, dearie," Larraine replied in her sweetest Irish tilt. "Hae nae we shared songs and drink together, and win or lose, dinna that make us sisters o' a sort?"

"More like cousins," replied Helgayarn, "and third cousins twice removed at that!"

"But even ye," said Larraine, "canna' take any satisfaction out o' seein' a distant cousin pee their pants, can ye?"

"Why not?" replied Helgayarn. "We once saw that one," she said, while pointing at Santos, "standing hip deep in his own manure!"

"And did ye enjoy it?" asked Larraine.

The trio recollected that they, in fact, did not.

"Then let a poor lass relieve herself, and any other also that feels the urge!"

Helgayarn was about to reiterate her refusal when Brunnhilde, who clung to her chair in an effort to keep from sliding off, spoke up. "Aw, t' hell wish it, Shelly," she drunkenly said, "let the poor shouls go if they haf ta! After all, can it hurt after all these years, t' be a good shport for once?" she asked, teetering in her chair.

Betty called a halt to her poetry reading in order to support her middle sister. "Yah!" she replied. "Most assuredly and most vociferously, Yah!"

Helgayarn arched her eyebrow in disbelief. Betty had spoken more in the last hour than she had in the last century while hardly jotting down a note in her journal! Reluctantly and against her better judgment, she acquiesced. "But there's no restroom at this locale," she replied. "Where will you be going?"

"Behind a mesquite bush be restroom enough for this lass," replied Larraine, "and a bit o' privacy under the nighttime stars is all I be askin'. Let loose on yer spell a bit, why don't ye, and give us freedom o' movement fer about a hundred yards or so. This'll allow those what need it the privacy to be about their own business, while allowin' me at the same time, to check on that elf o' yours and see how he's makin' out with the gold!"

Helgayarn thought it over. It would be good to check on Hephaestus, who after his song, returned to his chores. She no longer trusted his motives or his allegiances after his recent revelation concerning his abilities. The damned fool should've spoken up about that long before now! And her captives, she knew, could not run too far if they were tethered to a hundred yard leash.

"Very well," she finally said. "Whoever feels the need or the urge may exit the mine to go potty where they will—and no fidgeting! Only two at a time, mind you, and the next doesn't leave till one of the first returns!"

"That be only fair," cried Larraine, "sure n' begorrah! Larry, me foine husband, lend an arm t' yer woman and escort her out into the night, and La, love," she said looking sweetly down at Lauren, "be a foine young Irish lass and take me other arm, will ye? Yer Ma be a bit tipsy!"

Larry offered her his arm while Helgayarn eyed the trio suspiciously.

"Hold there!" she demanded in an intoxicated slur, "I said two at a time, not three!"

Larraine gazed back at her innocently. "But we be Ma, Da, and Little La," she replied, "a family under one roof, so t' speak and as such, should be counted as one. Besides, I'm sure me Little La hae to go as well and someone hae t' hold her hand in the dark! She be too much o' a young lady now, fer her Da t' be standin' in fer that duty so who does it leave, I ask ye, other than her dear ole Ma?"

"Who," Helgayarn went to great pains to point out, "up until a few hours ago, had been 'dearly departed' which had she remained so, would have necesshitated that someone else lend a hand in her shtead. So you shee, there always is another hand, handy!"

Larraine regarded her jailer. Her slurred speech was evidence enough that the miserable old harridan was well into her cups. *So much the better*, she thought. "But I be afraid o' her floatin' off," Larraine replied, "while under the influence o' yer dust as she is! As her dearly departed but recently returned Ma, I will nae be trustin' any other hand than me own, exceptin' me husband's o' course, t' the task o' seein' that she remains tethered! Ye hae me word on it that the three o' us will nae try ganglin' off together while ye be keepin' an eye on everyone else! After all, a good many o' them be family too and besides, me and my man are still tied t' yer hundred yard leash! Nor will we try lettin' the rocks out o' Little La's trousers in an effort t' aid her escape by allowin' her t' just float away on the clouds as it were, t' be tossed about by a fickle wind blown by fortuitous fate! She, like her Ma and Da, bears the badge after all; and the mark, in combination with this fancy flyin' ability with which yer dust hae endowed her, may prove too much, even with the luck o' the Irish, fer the little lassie t' get hold o' so young as she is! Nae, she be far safer here with us where we can keep our eyes—or at least my husband's anyway, upon her and out o' trouble! After all, I still aim t' win this binge!" The big witch eyed her adversary doubtfully but adjusted her spell to allow them leeway nevertheless. If they tried to take advantage of her good nature by running beyond the limits she'd set then they'd only suffer the worse because of it.

"Very good o' ye!" said Larraine with a hearty laugh. "Come along now," she said to her husband and daughter, "take me hands then and follow me, oh and Larry dear, bring a shovel."

What, wondered Helgayarn, was he going to do with that? "Why does the Sand Man need a tool to take a leak?" she queried.

"He'll be needin' it to dig us a latrine,' replied Larraine, "and then t' fill it in when we passes our water!"

"It sheems a bit excshessive to me," replied The Power That Be, "and overly modest at that! Request denied!"

"But what will me friends and family say," the Irishwoman replied, "all o' whom will be needin' a toilet too, when they see our stains lyin' plain on the desert floor?" She implored them with pleading eyes, which lie dead and blank in their sockets, to see a bit of reason. "There's such a thing as decorum, ladies," she furthered, "and a proper Irish lass, be she mother or daughter, need t' be constantly aware o' it. We dinna fart in public nae do we leave a trail o' our droppin's behind us to show others where we been!"

"Oh, all right!" replied Helgayarn, exasperated with the woman's eccentricities. Let him take the shovel! But do you mean to say that he'll be digging latrines and trenches for the lot of you?"

Larraine offered her antagonist a blank-faced stare. "But o' course," she replied. "This duel ain't near done yet and we'll all be in need o' a latrine soon enough, says I. Therefore someone hae t' be in the business o' diggin' 'em!" She looked around to survey the crowd. "Me husband be the best digger in these parts," she furthered, "unless, o' course, ye be countin' yonder rabbit, who nae look like he's up to achievin' much more than a scrape or two in the sand!"

Helgayarn considered Jack, who sitting on a nearby crate, swayed unceasingly in his seat while his ears drooped into his tankard as he sat with a drunkard's idiotic smile painted squarely upon his features, contemplating another shot of Connemara's Cask Strength. The woman had a point. Let the sand man dig some holes then. In the meantime she'd have another drink.

"Barkeep," she yelled, "pour us all another round!"

Pixie, who was tending bar at the moment, readily complied as Larraine and Larry staggered out into the evening while Helgayarn eyed the foamy head of the proffered tankard. "It's a little frothier than I prefer," she remarked to the elf, blowing the foam off the rim of the stein and into his face. "Be careful next time," she chided, "when you pour, and make sure to tilt the tankard properly!"

"Yes, ma'am," came the elf's contrite reply.

THE CHRISTMAS RABBIT

Five minutes or so passed and Helgayarn began to fret about the whereabouts of her charges. *What were they up to?* she wondered. For certainly it didn't take this long to pass water! And what was that elf up to? She staggered to her feet, intending to march out into the desert night and see to these concerns but found upon rising that her head spun wildly, forcing her abruptly down into her chair. She was just about to ask Brunnhilde, who had more experience with this sort of thing and who therefore should be able to ambulate with some degree of efficiency, to check on their charges in her stead when, with Lauren in hand, Larraine came lurching back through the mine's entrance.

"Next in line!" she yelled bawdily. "Men t' the right, and ladies t' the left!"

"Where's that silly husband of yours?" asked Helgayarn as she carefully regarded the Irishwoman through bloodshot eyes. "I hope he's not fool or chicken enough to leave you here while he tries to make good his own escape!"

"Foolish be as foolish do," replied Larraine, "and though me husband may indeed be so, he nae be a chicken. O' that ye can be sure!"

"Then where is he?" asked Helgayarn.

"He be tendin' t' his business," replied Larraine.

"It does not take this long to go number 1," Helgayarn countered matter-of-factly. "You could fill Crater Lake in the time it's taking him to go!"

"Actually," Larraine replied red-faced, "me man be in the throes o' workin' on number 2, in between diggin' trenches. It's all those Toadhouse cookies o' his, lubricated by liquid and workin' their way through his innards that accounts fer his tardiness! He hae a serious case o' the cramps, sure n' begorrah! He'll be a few minutes more rightin' himself and then he'll need t' dig a toilet or two! But Hephaestus now, there be a lad working right and proper! Two thirds o' a ton he hae already and still he be meltin' and smeltin'!" She turned to the sleigh master. "That's a foine lad ye hae in yer employ there, Mr. Santos," she said. "A foine lad indeed!"

Santos was about to thank her for the compliment when Betty cut him off, "The old elf doshen't work fer Shlomoe," she mumbled. "He works for ush!"

"He be a corker anyway," said Larraine. "And an elf what knows his trade! She looked about her yet again. "Jimmy lad!" she cried to her cousin, "Ye look as though yer dancin' to the compulsion fidget! Why nae pass a little water through the willy and make it easier on yerself?"

"I dinna hae the urge one way or t' other," he replied, "and can hold it or nae as I choose!"

Larraine eyed him darkly. "Come now," she said, "her voice made grim by her urging, "surely after all o' the barleycorn, ye need's t' be relievin' yerself? Remember, ye be a bed wetter from long ago! We dinna need any accidents in front o' the ladies!"

Jim flinched with embarrassment, his cheeks coloring slightly as he did. It was true, he had been a bed-wetter from way back, but who wasn't? It was also true that he hadn't committed such an embarrassing faux pas, even when stone dead drunk, since diapers, and Larraine knew that as well as any. How dare she embarrass him so? He began to bridle and was about to call her on her bad manners when Larraine, being leader, cut him off.

"Dinna be embarrassed," she said. "Just do as yer ordered fer the sake o' decency, "and go relieve yerself, taking Slim and one or two o' the Apaches with ya!"

"Jusht hold your horshes," Helgayarn slurred. "He's not going anywhere with anyone. I said no more than two at a time and your man is still out there! If the Irishman wants to go then he can just do so himself. The next can follow when either he or Shand Toes returns!"

Jim was about to reiterate his position when he took note of the pleading glance Larraine flashed in his general direction. Even blind, Larraine's gaze clearly communicated her desire that he not to defy her in this. The lass was up to something beyond his ken, of that much he was certain, but regardless of that insight he could not say one way or the other what her plan might be but had a sneaky suspicion nevertheless that because he was still absent, it somehow involved his

THE CHRISTMAS RABBIT

long-standing rival Sand Toes. The Irishman rolled his eyes. It would be a cruel fate, almost worse than that which awaited them all, if present circumstances were to force him into a temporary alliance with his perennial adversary. Still, both the situation at hand and the mistress who'd handed it to him, would not be gainsaid, so he reluctantly made his exit in order to relieve himself and find his cousin.

He returned ever and anon with just a glimmer or hope displayed upon his features which he tried his best to keep hidden. Having found Larry he reluctantly approached him and was made fully aware of Larraine's plan in the privacy of the desert night. After hearing the details of her scheme, he hurried back to the mouth of the cave in order to defer any further suspicions on the part of The Powers That Be as to Larraine and her intentions. It was a wacky plan to be sure, even for this family, and only had a prayer of working if every one of them had a hand in buying Larry a little more time while coming to his aid under the guise of bathroom breaks.

Lauren, too, had been appraised of her Ma's machination and her own role within it while relieving herself in the night and although she now better understood her Ma's intentions while seeing for herself the increased probabilities of her success in the drunken countenances of those whom they faced, was nevertheless not entirely happy with the plan as it now stood, despite her confidence that she could hold up her own end. The stamp of strangeness which emblazoned most of them while affecting them all regardless, was often a burden to bear to those thus tattooed. It too often landed them, as well as the unfortunates within their influence, in untenable situations full of trial and heavy burden. Therefore those who bore it, she felt, were often to be pitied and looked upon with sympathy. These harridans, she knew, who carried themselves like miserable old aunties, bore a stamp of strangeness too that was all their own and despite their mean spiritedness and overall nastiness and notwithstanding their stated desire to do away with the lot of 'em en masse, the little lass was still moved to pity them nevertheless. The trio must have had long and lonely lives, she thought, saddled as they were with only each other for company. Who wouldn't grow sour, she reasoned, in the face of that misery. She determined then, to try to defuse the situation by offering up a song or two of her own, more in tune with the holiday spirit, in the hope that doing so would help to quell the tide threatening to rise by reminding everyone there of whose birthday drew nigh and the lessons of brotherly love and forgiveness that he'd endeavored to impart prior to being hanged on a tree for his chutzpah.

"Silent night," she began. "Holy night. All is calm, all is—"

"Enough of that," Helgyarn interrupted, cutting her off in midsong. "We'll have no verse that alludes to that fellow! Try another one instead. Something a little more secular if you don't mind."

Lauren did not appreciate at all, being interrupted nor did she enjoy having to switch songs in midverse, but she was trying her best to salvage an untenable situation and knew that doing so would call for patience. "Oh, little town of Bethlehem…" she ventured, but was cut off yet again.

"We'll have no verse either," furthered Helgayarn, "that refers to or makes mention of, his place of birth! Just leave the fellow well enough out of it when engaging in your vocalizations!"

"But it's his birthday," replied Lauren, looking upon the pale pink of the faraway eastern horizon, "or soon will be. The least we can do is sing him a verse or two!"

"Who says it's his birthday?" replied the witch. "Were you there? Even I wasn't around to witness that! It could've been any day or any time of the year, for that matter! It was I, by and large, who had a big hand in referring to this day as his day and I did it for reasons of my own that had little to do with him. Therefore I want no part of him now—especially as we near the culmination of our great revenge and the subsequent victory party we'll throw once it's attained." She looked down at the lass smugly, having effectively enforced her will upon the young lady and silencing her effort. "Sing us instead," she said, "a composition of your own making. And be sure that it's poignant, timely, and has some direct bearing upon the situation in which we find ourselves!"

That was it then, Lauren knew. There would be no turning these ladies from their chosen path or derailing them from riding their trains to a foregone conclusion, which could only end in their own destruction or that of their captives. Well, she'd tried, she reasoned. And she'd try one last time, to both forewarn and forestall, by singing to them this familiar holiday tune instead and replacing its lyrics with a verse or two of her own:

> "You better watch out—you better not try—to
>   mess with the mark, I'm tellin' ye why
> My dear Ma's rose up from, her grave! She need
>   ye nae list, nae checkin' it twice
> T' see if yerselves be ye naughty or nice
> My dear Ma's rose up from, her grave! Da saw her
>   in his sleepin's and daydreamed when awake
> Now she's standin' 'fore his very eyes—won't ye
>   see fer goodness sake!
> Oh, ye better watch out—ye better not try t'
>   mess with the mark, I'm tellin' ye why
> My dear Ma's returned from, her grave!"

This earned applause from everyone, including the trio, who admired the little lady's spunk, appreciating her effort to tough it out while putting on a brave face till the very end. For her own part, Little La had done all she could, she reasoned, to be as poignant and timely as possible, forewarning the trio while effectively covering up her Ma's intentions at the same time. As a warning, it should have served to all familiar with the mark, but Lauren knew that her words of caution fell upon deaf ears. She therefore launched into a repeat rendition of a song, which her Ma had sung earlier. She sang:

> "Ye can lead a horse t' water
> But ye canna' make it drink
> Ye can lead three crones through logic but ye
>   canna' make 'em think.
> Ye can play upon their conscience but their conscience dinna blink—
> When they're out t' do ye dirty, why they'll drop
>   ye in the drink!"

She sang it with feeling and with gusto, her repeat performance earning for her a standing ovation from Irishman and Indian alike, including Larraine, who rose eagerly from her chair in order to applaud her efforts. The sudden change of posture in one who'd so imbibed brought upon Larraine an overwhelming sense of vertigo, causing her head to spin errantly as she fought to maintain balance. She was a tough Irish lady and not unused to drinking matches of this sort even though prior circumstance had forced her to remain somewhat out of practice. But even the hardiest of lads and lassies had their own individual limits when it came to the barleycorn, and Larraine, out of desperation, had long exceeded hers. She fell over, much to the consternation of the Irish and Indians looking on, with a dull thud, her keister impacting squarely with the desert floor. An uneasy silence gathered itself around those in attendance who looked in on her plight, as they gave thought to her failure and its probable implications. The rules of the challenge stated that the last one at the table who remained standing would be declared the winner. Since Larraine had challenged all three to a duel simultaneously, the three could therefore be deemed as one and furthermore with Larraine on her can could be counted as the only ones standing.

The Powers That Be took the same view, declaring themselves the winners and demanding that the loser, along with all her relations and guests, submit themselves to the trio's long anticipated sentence.

In barely a blink of an eye, all within the mine suddenly found that they'd been magically transported to just outside the mouth of the cave, where once again, standing with their feet glued to the floor, they nervously awaited their fates. Lawrence, who suddenly found himself amongst them and next to his wife as well, whispered in her ear, that all was ready. Larraine, offering up a silent prayer to the Good Lord in heaven, nodded her reply.

The trio exited the cave, arm-in-arm and stumbling themselves but happier nevertheless, than they'd been in ages. They were about to exact their final revenge of the farmer and the rabbit by doing away with them once and for all and wiping out Farm Boy's descendants too. Though not Junior and Laddie, per se, there were enough "Junior's" and "Laddie's" gathered together to more than make up

THE CHRISTMAS RABBIT

for the absence of the originals! It was a revenge long in the planning, whose enactment had been anticipated for countless ages and whose culmination, now that the day had finally arrived, was to be savored and made the most of. To that end the trio cast another of their spells. Those looking on suddenly found that the scaffolding and materials used to construct Lawrence's billboard had suddenly transformed themselves into a gallows, complete with a trap and a rope tied conveniently in a noose.

Helgayarn, now dressed in her robes of state, as were Brunnhilde and Betty, raised her hand in a call for silence. The air about them grew still, becoming heavy and thick with anticipation and dread as those looking on, saw for themselves, the petard upon which they were about to be hung.

"Hear ye, Hear ye," cried Helgayarn. "This duly constituted Cosmic Court is now in session, having gathered over the ages, evidence against the defendants present, and will now impose sentence. The defendants will please take one step forward."

Santos and Jack, as well as all of the sleigh master's Irish descendants, found their feet moving against their will, in the direction Helgayarn commanded. Still rooted to the ground, the Apaches let out a collective sigh of relief, whistling past the graveyard as it were, as they considered the status of their stasis, while determining incorrectly that the trio had elected to show them mercy.

"Do not read too much into your lack of movement," Helgayarn replied to them. "It's just that we're a bit busy at the moment!" She looked them all over, taking delight in having shattered their allusions of safety. "Rest assured," she continued, "that we'll get around to you in a minute or two, once we've seen to the business at hand!" She cast her glance about the entire crowd as she determined for herself, how best to begin and with whom to start in order to ensure the most misery to all gathered.

Why, the little one, of course. That much was obvious. She cast her gaze, which did little to hide her intent, upon the helpless form of Lauren, as she stood beside her mother. "Come forward, little one," she demanded. "It's time to duel with destiny!" Brunnhilde nodded her heartfelt agreement while Betty offered an enthusiastic "Yah!" In her excitement regarding the proceedings to come, the junior witch had reverted to her monosyllabic response.

Lauren refused to concede to Helly's demands and began to back away instead, crossing the desert floor as she fled the gallows upon which hung her fate.

"Spare the little one!" cried Larraine. "Dinna take yer revenge out upon Little La! Have yer way with me instead and let the girl go, fer the love o' all that be holy!"

"We love nothing of that sort whatsoever," replied Helgayarn, "and do not worry that you're being overlooked in favor of your daughter! We'll get around to you soon enough!"

"Ye *drochruds* and *fia chailleaches!*" cried Sand Toes despairingly, as helpless he watched Little La bravely face the doom awaiting her. "I curse the very ground ye trod upon! May it swallow ye whole and may ye *Téigh i dtigh diabhail.*" He wept openly before continuing, "Please, Lord," he cried to the heavens, "I niver been one t' put much stock in thee, relyin' as I hae, on me own abilities and skills t' see me through the needs o' the day. But I'm askin' ye now, please! Dwell among us fer the moment if ye would, and save us from the clutches o' these three *Fuaids* who will nae show the innocent mercy by deigning t' turn their other cheeks as ye've so often instructed! Protect yer lost sheep by scatterin' these three wolves!"

Helgayarn offered up a chuckle. "It seems the old man is busy elsewhere," she replied, "and being so, cannot afford to waste the time necessary to look in on the likes of you. The three of us are all of God that you're likely to see, at least in this life! As to the next, why you can spend an eternity of it complaining to him about his absence here today, if you have the mind. It makes no difference to me!"

Along with Brunnhilde and Betty, she began her slow advance on Lauren, step by step, as she made ready to carry out her threat. The poor girl, helpless despite her mark and her own portion of Irish luck, could take no action in her own defense other than to back away, one pace at a time with each step the trio took toward her. With her back to the gallows, she reluctantly lead them across the desert floor while those looking on, did so with a mixture of anticipation and dread. The situation was working itself out just as Larraine had envisioned but had yet to reach its culmination as yet and between now and then anything might happen.

    The girl continued to lead the trio slowly across the desert floor while the crowd looking on, fell into an uneasy hush as they awaited the outcome with baited breath.

    Brunnhilde, walking drunkenly between her two sisters, felt the ground beneath her feet give way slightly but thought nothing of it. No doubt she merely stumbled in her inebriation, and thus her momentary loss of footing. She quickly righted herself in order to maintain pace with her sisters, continuing the slow but deliberate stalking of the helpless victim before them.

    Larraine, who prayed to heaven above that the magic dust coursing within her daughter still had the power to enable her to float, knew that the four of them, as they made their slow way from the gallows, would soon reach that critical point in the desert floor which she'd had Larry prepare beforehand under the guise of latrine digging. The floor beneath the trio took a strain as it bore up under their combined weight, creaking and groaning as it did. Suddenly with a loud crack, the petrified timber and mesquite lashings, which lie hidden beneath the carefully disguised tarp below their feet, let go and the earth swallowed the four of them whole.

    All the while he'd been supposedly going number 2 and digging latrines, Sand Toes, with the help of those coming out to relieve themselves, had instead, at his wife's direction, made hasty repairs to the trap in which he'd originally planned to capture his progenitor and which Jack had partially sprung when first falling through it. Using the hands that were handy, the desert man reset the cover, reinforcing that part which had collapsed in Jack's fall and placing the entirety once again, over the pit that he and Jack had dug. He covered it again with sand and local flora until anyone looking on would have seen only the desert floor beneath and nothing more.

    When the trap sprang, shouldering upon itself the weight of three dames and one little girl, it did so fully and the foursome plummeted into the depths to which Jack had previously fallen. Lauren, however, had been well prepared for this contingency by her mother and knew therefore exactly what to do. As she plummeted downward she began emptying her pockets of the rocks weighing her down. One after another she cast the stones from her until at last, free from their weight, her descent came to a halt and she slowly began to rise. The trio, however, dead weight that they were, plummeted like the stones cast from Lauren's pockets. As she rose above the entrance to the hole, Larry, who still had his feet planted to the floor, managed to snag a piece of nearby rope and using it as a lasso, threw it around her rising form, capturing her and reeling her in. The trio however, kept falling, screaming, and cursing both at those above and at each other. Their descent, like Jack's, seemed to go on forever with no end in sight, and like he, they unexpectedly plummeted into the raging river miles below, which annoyed at their unanticipated arrival, did its best to tumble and twist them in its currents while churning in its course, and eventually carrying them far underground and out into the gulf of Mexico where they were immediately set upon by three great whites, each of whom swallowed a single witch whole. Sharks will eat almost anything, including tin cans, tires, and any haplessly disregarded trash that gets cast away or dumped over the side by careless boaters who should know better. They bit into the Witches, much like those baby white sharks of long ago, without giving much thought to the matter. They didn't stop to consider that such reeking flesh was bound to sour stomachs—even such hardy ones as sharks possessed. They were about to regurgitate for their own good, the meal they'd so hastily devoured when along came a pod of killer whales who in turn, feasted upon the sharks, chomping them and those who resided within into a thousand bite-sized pieces before swallowing them and moving on. But such fare sat sour in the stomach of the Orca as well. They were used to shark, which they dined on whenever they couldn't get seal or walrus but tough old witches with hides like shoe leather were an entirely new assault upon their digestive tracts and one which the whales were quite unprepared for. They regurgitated as well, only to feed the thousands of plankton gathered round them who broke down the sharks and the meal they contained into even further miniscule portions, thus discorporating the trio even further from their flesh while separating to an even greater degree their rancid bodies from their sour souls. No spell on their part or mojo to be made was equal to the task of reknitting body to soul when said body was so thoroughly made minced meat of, and it's hoped by this author that being so completely disposed of, The Powers That Be were, in fact, rendered entirely powerless and so can never cause misery to the Dawes, or to any of us, ever again.

EPILOGUE

With the demise of the dour dames from deep within Witch Valley, the spell which held those bound to the desert floor dissipated as well, leaving loved ones to rush into the arms of one another as they gave voice to their good luck and to the Good Lord's providence in watching over them through troubled times.

Sand Toes crushed his wife to him fiercely and those looking on, including Jim, applauded his efforts while wishing the couple a long and happy life.

The Apaches danced the dance of victory as they gave thought to the Witches demise, realizing that with their absence Witch Valley might one day become inhabitable and in so doing, open up lands to them which they'd previously been denied, while providing additional acreage in which to remain well hidden and out of the white man's way.

At the time of the collapse Hephaestus had smelted nearly two tons of gold, so there was more than enough of the metamict substance to be had by anyone who felt the desire to take it without having the need to resort to greedy behavior in order to obtain it. They were all, to a man and woman as well, rich beyond the wildest dreams, and Irish and Apache alike shared in their good fortune.

"So what happens now?" asked the rabbit while looking upon a group of friends who for all practical purposes had once been indifferent enemies at best. "Are we, like them, to forget past injuries and agree to live and let live?'

"Well, in light of all that's happened," replied the farmer, "it seems the most logical of choices, does it not?" Jack Rabbit readily agreed with the sleigh master's insight, promising to answer for his brethren as well. "But what about eggs and presents," he asked, "what's to be done with them?"

"I don't rightly know," replied the sleigh master, "other than to say that I'm sure two smart fellows such as we can figure it out. But before we do, the both us, being somewhat magical, if no longer exactly needed—at least here and now that is, must be on our way, leaving these people to their lives and to themselves."

"Agreed!" replied Jack wholeheartedly who since his arrival in this hellhole wanted nothing more than to make good his escape.

"But poor Sand Toes," he said to the sleigh master, "after all these years of dealing with disappointment, surely you will not just up and leave him without trying to make amends?"

"Of course not," replied Santos, making his way over to Larry to have a final word. "Listen, lad," he said to the desert man. "I know we did not get off on exactly the right foot, so to speak, and that you have an issue or two of long-standing regarding an undelivered pair of footwear, but I swear to you that I did not know you were stranded here those many years ago and it was by ignorance and oversight only that I passed you by."

Larry, who had his life back as well as those of his wife and daughter now found that he cared little for past injuries or misplaced boots and was of a mind to forget the whole matter, suggesting to Santos that he think nothing of it. The fat man, however, would not be gainsaid and to the wonder and smiles of those looking on, bent down to remove his black galoshes and, handing them to Larry, presented them to him as a long-belated Christmas present.

"Sorry," he said as he handed them over, "but there wasn't enough time to wrap 'em!"

Those looking on applauded while offering up hearty cheers, both in Irish and Apache.

Jack approached Lauren, who although happy with the day's outcome, was nevertheless saddened as she gave thought to her charge and his imminent departure.

"I want to thank you," said Jack, "for providing me with the succor you did. I'd probably be dead by now if it weren't for you. As it is, I now find myself with a warren to return to and a kingship of

THE CHRISTMAS RABBIT

sorts to claim as I make my bid to become the Mad Rabbit. Should I do so, there'll be some changes instituted, no doubt, which would never have been set in motion were it not for your kindness." He gazed passively upward into her beautiful violet eyes.

"You're an example to be followed by rabbits and all other folk everywhere," he said and then bowed. Turning to Larraine, he offered her a friendly laugh. "Do you mind, dear lady," he asked, "if I return my haregei to myself? My eyes, I think, serve us both better when working out of their own sockets!"

"I couldn'a agree more," Larraine said with a laugh as Jack's Haregei returned to him. With its departure Larraine found that her own eyes had regained their sight and with a whoop of joy told her news to Larry, proving it to him by counting correctly the number of fingers he held up in front of her. The mark and the fates which ruled over it had treated her and hers fairly in the end.

With the sleigh fully restored and the caribou traced and harnessed, the sleigh master and the elves, along with Jack Rabbit, who managed to hitch himself a lift while riding atop of Valentino and wearing a miner's helmet in place of the caribou's lost light, prepared to speak their final words of departure.

"Goodbye, good friends," said the erstwhile farmer. "It's been an adventure indeed and an unusual undertaking on down through the ages!"

"Here hare!" said the rabbit wholeheartedly and with that, the sleigh master gave the command to the tethered caribou, and they were lifted off into the skies beyond.

Thus enslaved for so many years to the fickle whims of The Powers That Be, the two former enemies were at last freed, as were we all, to decide for ourselves, the true meaning of the holidays and the sacrifice of him for whom they'd been instituted.

Gilman Jeffers
August 22, 2020

ABOUT THE AUTHOR

Gilman Jeffers is a fifty-year resident of Martha's Vineyard. Currently single—despite his best efforts to the contrary—he's always on the lookout for the next ex-Mrs. Jeffers! His interests include singing, songwriting, and acting. He has performed before live audiences in many productions—including *The King and I*, *Gypsy*, and *Domestic Violence*—in which he had the principal role. Gilman loves to fish and bow-hunt and is avid about golf…although truth to tell, he's not very good at it and is forever trying to attain par!